A MODERN COMEDY

John Galsworthy, the son of a solicitor, was born in 1867 and educated at Harrow and the New College, Oxford. He was called to the Bar in 1890, but a chance meeting with Joseph Conrad, and the strong influence of his future wife, turned him to writing. A collection of short stories, *From the Four Winds* (1897), was followed by a novel entitled *Jocelyn* (1898), *The Man of Property* appeared in 1906 and, together with *In Chancery* and *To Let*, completed the first volume of the Forsyte trilogy. *The Forsyte Saga*, published in 1922. His playwriting career began in 1906 with *The Silver Box*, the first of a long line of plays with social and moral themes. The second Forsyte trilogy, which included *The White Monkey*, *The Silver Spoon* and *Swan Song*, was published as *A Modern Comedy* in 1929. In 1931 Galsworthy followed the immense success of the Forsyte books with a further collection of stories, *On Forsyte Change*. The final Forsyte trilogy, containing *Maid in Waiting*, *Flowering Wilderness* and *Over the River*, was published posthumously as *The End of the Chapter* in 1934. The nine novels in his three Forsyte trilogies are published in Penguins. A television serial of the Forsyte chronicles, presented by the BBC in 1967, received great critical acclaim in Great Britain and over the world.

The first President of the PEN Club, John Galsworthy was the recipient of several honorary degrees and other literary honours. He was made an OM in 1929 and received the Nobel Peace Prize in 1932. He lived on Dartmoor for many years and afterwards at Bury on the Sussex Downs. He died in 1933.

D0183227

John Galsworthy

A MODERN COMEDY

THE WHITE MONKEY
THE SILVER SPOON
SWAN SONG

PENGUIN BOOKS

PENGUIN BOOKS

Published by the Penguin Group
Penguin Books Ltd, 27 Wrights Lane, London w8 5tz, England
Viking Penguin, a division of Penguin Books USA Inc.
375 Hudson Street, New York, New York 10014, USA
Penguin Books Australia Ltd, Ringwood, Victoria, Australia
Penguin Books Canada Ltd, 2801 John Street, Markham, Ontario, Canada l3r 1b4
Penguin Books (NZ) Ltd, 182–190 Wairau Road, Auckland 10, New Zealand

Penguin Books Ltd, Registered Offices: Harmondsworth, Middlesex, England

The White Monkey first published by William Heinemann Ltd 1944
Published in Penguin Books 1967

The Silver Spoon first published by William Heinemann Ltd 1926
Published in Penguin Books 1967

Swan Song first published by William Heinemann Ltd 1928
Published in Penguin Books 1967

These three books (the fourth, fifth and sixth parts of the nine-
volume *Forsyte Chronicles*) published together in Penguin
Books 1980
5 7 9 10 8 6 4

Printed in England by Clays Ltd, St Ives plc
Set in Linotype Granjon

THE WHITE MONKEY

Contents

TO

Max Beerbohm

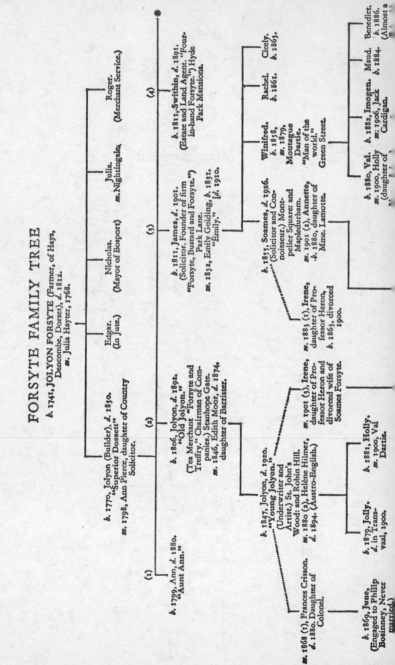

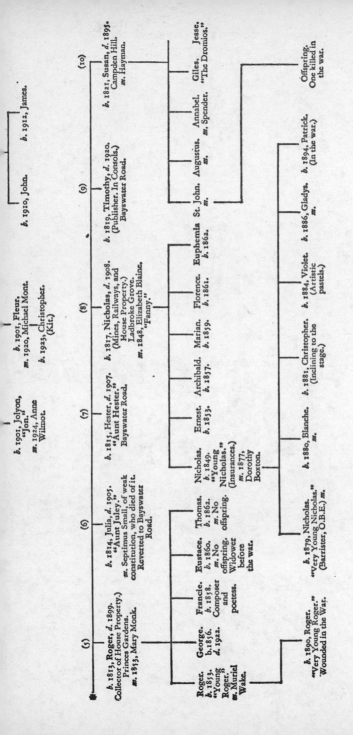

PREFACE

❧

In naming this second part of The Forsyte Chronicles 'A Modern Comedy' the word comedy is stretched, perhaps, as far as the word Saga was stretched to cover the first part. And yet, what but a comedic view can be taken, what but comedic significance gleaned, of so restive a period as that in which we have lived since the war? An Age which knows not what it wants, yet is intensely preoccupied with getting it, must evoke a smile, if rather a sad one.

To render the forms and colours of an epoch is beyond the powers of any novelist, and very far beyond the powers of this novelist; but to try and express a little of its spirit was undoubtedly at the back of his mind in penning this trilogy. Like the Irishman's chicken, our Present runs about so fast that it cannot be summed up; it can at most be snapshotted while it hurries looking for its Future without notion where, what, or when that Future will be.

The England of 1886, when the Forsyte Saga began, also had no Future, for England then expected its Present to endure, and rode its bicycle in a sort of dream, disturbed only by two bogles – Mr Gladstone and the Irish Members.

The England of 1926 – when the Modern Comedy closes – with one foot in the air and the other in a Morris Oxford, is going round and round like a kitten after its tail, muttering: 'If one could only see where one wants to stop!'

Everything being now relative, there is no longer absolute dependence to be placed on God, Free Trade, Marriage, Consols, Coal, or Caste.

Everywhere being now overcrowded, there is no place where

anyone can stay for long, except the mere depopulated country-side, admittedly too dull, and certainly too unprofitable to dwell in.

Everyone, having been in an earthquake which lasted four years, has lost the habit of standing still.

And yet, the English character has changed very little, if at all. The General Strike of 1926, with which the last part of this trilogy begins, supplied proof of that. We are still a people that cannot be rushed, distrustful of extremes, saved by the grace of our defensive humour, well-tempered, resentful of interference, improvident and wasteful, but endowed with a certain genius for recovery. If we believe in nothing much else, we still believe in ourselves. That salient characteristic of the English will bear thinking about. Why, for instance, do we continually run ourselves down? Simply because we have not got the inferiority complex and are indifferent to what other people think of us. No people in the world seems openly less sure of itself; no people is secretly more sure. Incidentally, it might be worth the while of those who own certain public mouths inclined to blow the British trumpet to remember, that the blowing of one's own trumpet is the insidious beginning of the inferiority complex. Only those strong enough to keep silent about self are strong enough to be sure of self. The epoch we are passing through is one which favours misjudgement of the English character, and of the position of England. There never was a country where real deterioration of human fibre had less chance than in this island, because there is no other country whose climate is so changeable, so tempering to character, so formative of grit, and so basically healthy. What follows in this preface should be read in the light of that remark.

In the present epoch, no Early Victorianism survives. By Early Victorianism is meant that of the old Forsytes, already on the wane in 1886; what has survived, and potently, is the Victorianism of Soames and his generation, more self-conscious, but not sufficiently self-conscious to be either self-destructive or self-forgetful. It is against the background of this more or less fixed quantity that we can best see the shape and colour of the present intensely self-conscious and all-questioning generation. The old Forsytes – Old Jolyon, Swithin and James, Roger, Nicholas and Timothy – lived their lives without ever asking whether life was worth living. They found it interesting, very absorbing from day to day, and even if they had no very intimate belief in a future life, they had very great faith in the progress of their own positions, and in laying up treasure for their children. Then came Young Jolyon and Soames and their contemporaries, who, although they had imbibed, with Darwinism and the 'Varsities, definite doubts about a future life, and sufficient introspection to wonder whether they themselves were progressing, retained their sense of property and their desire to provide for, and to live on in their progeny. The generation which came in when Queen Victoria went out, through new ideas about the treatment of children, because of new modes of locomotion, and owing to the Great War, has decided that everything requires re-valuation. And, since there is, seemingly, very little future before property, and less before life, is determined to live now or never, without bothering about the fate of such offspring as it may chance to have. Not that the present generation is less fond of its children than were past generations – human nature does not change on points so elementary – but when everything is keyed to such a pitch of uncertainty, to secure the future at the expense of the present no longer seems worth while.

This is really the fundamental difference between the present and the past generations. People will not provide against that which they cannot see ahead.

All this, of course, refers only to that tenth or so of the population whose eyes are above the property line; below that line there are no Forsytes, and therefore no need for this preface to dip. What average Englishman, moreover, with less than three hundred a year ever took thought for the future, even in Early Victorian days?

This Modern Comedy, then, is staged against a background of that more or less fixed quantity, Soames, and his co-father-in-law, light weight and ninth baronet, Sir Lawrence Mont, with such subsidiary neo-Victorians as the self-righteous Mr Danby,

Elderson, Mr Blythe, Sir James Foskisson, Wilfred Bentworth, and Hilary Charwell. Pooling their idiosyncrasies, qualities, and mental attitudes, one gets a fairly comprehensive and steady past against which to limn the features of the present – Fleur and Michael, Wilfrid Desert, Aubrey Greene, Marjorie Ferrar, Norah Curfew, Jon, the Rafaelite, and other minor characters. The multiple types and activities of today – even above the Plimsoll line of property – would escape the confines of twenty novels, so that this Modern Comedy is bound to be a gross understatement of the present generation, but not perhaps a libel on it. Symbolism is boring, so let us hope that a certain resemblance between the case of Fleur and that of her generation chasing the serenity of which it has been defrauded may escape notice. The fact remains that for the moment, at least, youth is balancing, twirling on the tiptoes of uncertainty. What is to come? Will contentment yet be caught? How will it all settle down? Will things ever again settle down – who knows? Are there to come fresh wars, and fresh inventions hot-foot on those not yet mastered and digested? Or will Fate decree another pause, like that of Victorian times, during which revaluated life will crystallize, and give property and its brood of definite beliefs a further innings?

But, however much or little 'A Modern Comedy' may be deemed to reflect the spirit of an Age, it continues in the main to relate the tale of life which sprang from the meeting of Soames and Irene in a Bournemouth drawing-room in 1881, a tale which could but end when its spine snapped, and Soames 'took the ferry' forty-five years later.

The chronicler, catechized (as he often is) concerning Soames, knows not precisely what he stands for. Taking him for all in all he was honest, anyway. He lived and moved and had his peculiar being, and now he sleeps. His creator may be pardoned for thinking there was something fitting about his end, for, however far we have travelled from Greek culture and philosophy, there is still truth in the old Greek proverb: 'That which a man most loves shall in the end destroy him.'

JOHN GALSWORTHY

'No retreat, no retreat
They must conquer or die
Who have no retreat!'

Mr Gay

PART ONE

Chapter One

PROMENADE

-◄-►-

COMING down the steps of 'Snooks' Club, so nicknamed by
George Forsyte in the late eighties, on that momentous mid-
October afternoon of 1922, Sir Lawrence Mont, ninth baronet,
set his fine nose towards the east wind, and moved his thin legs
with speed. Political by birth rather than by nature, he reviewed the revolution which had restored his Party to power
with a detachment not devoid of humour. Passing the Remove
Club, he thought: 'Some sweating into shoes, there! No more
confectioned dishes. A woodcock – without trimmings, for a
change!'

The captains and the kings had departed from 'Snooks' before he entered it, for he was not of 'that catch-penny crew,
now paid off, no sir; fellows who turned their tails on the land
the moment the war was over. Pah!' But for an hour he had
listened to echoes, and his lively twisting mind, embedded in
deposits of the past, sceptical of the present and of all political
protestations and pronouncements, had recorded with amusement the confusion of patriotism and personalities left behind by
the fateful gathering. Like most landowners, he distrusted doctrine. If he had a political belief, it was a tax on wheat; and so
far as he could see, he was now alone in it – but then he was not
seeking election; in other words, his principle was not in danger
of extinction from the votes of those who had to pay for bread.
Principles – he mused – *au fond* were pocket; and he wished
the deuce people wouldn't pretend they weren't! Pocket, in the
deep sense of that word, of course, self-interest as member of a
definite community. And how the devil was this definite community, the English nation, to exist, when all its land was going
out of cultivation, and all its ships and docks in danger of

destruction by aeroplanes? He had listened that hour past for a single mention of the land. Not one! It was not practical politics! Confound the fellows! They had to wear their breeches out – keeping seats or getting them. No connexion between posteriors and posterity! No, by George! Thus reminded of posterity, it occurred to him rather suddenly that his son's wife showed no signs as yet. Two years! Time they were thinking about children. It was dangerous to get into the habit of not having them, when a title and estate depended. A smile twisted his lips and eyebrows which resembled spinneys of dark pothooks. A pretty young creature, most taking; and knew it, too! Whom was she not getting to know? Lions and tigers, monkeys and cats – her house was becoming quite a menagerie of more or less celebrities. There was a certain unreality about that sort of thing! And opposite a British lion in Trafalgar Square Sir Lawrence thought: 'She'll be getting these to her house next! She's got the collecting habit. Michael must look out – in a collector's house there's always a lumber-room for old junk, and husbands are liable to get into it. That reminds me: I promised her a Chinese Minister. Well, she must wait now till after the General Election.'

Down Whitehall, under the grey easterly sky, the towers of Westminster came for a second into view. 'A certain unreality in that, too,' he thought. 'Michael and his fads! Well, it's the fashion – Socialistic principles and a rich wife. Sacrifice with safety! Peace with plenty! Nostrums – ten a penny!'

Passing the newspaper hubbub of Charing Cross, frenzied by the political crisis, he turned up to the left towards Danby and Winter, publishers, where his son was junior partner. A new theme for a book had just begun to bend a mind which had already produced a *Life of Montrose, Far Cathay*, that work of Eastern travel, and a fanciful conversation between the shades of Gladstone, and Disraeli – entitled *A Duet*. With every step taken, from ʹSnooksʹ eastward, his erect thin figure in Astrakhan-collared coat, his thin grey-moustached face, and tortoiseshell rimmed monocle under the lively dark eyebrow, had seemed more rare. It became almost a phenomenon in this dingy back street, where carts stuck like winter flies, and persons went by with books under their arms, as if educated.

He had nearly reached the door of Danby's when he encountered two young men. One of them was clearly his son, better dressed since his marriage, and smoking a cigar – thank goodness – instead of those eternal cigarettes; the other – ah! yes – Michael's sucking poet and best man, head in air, rather a sleek head under a velour hat! He said:

'Ha, Michael!'

'*Hallo*, Bart! You know my governor, Wilfrid? Wilfrid Desert. *Copper Coin* – some poet, Bart, I tell you. You must read him. We're going home. Come along!'

Sir Lawrence went along.

'What happened at "Snooks"?'

'*Le roi est mort.* Labour can start lying, Michael – election next month.'

'Bart was brought up, Wilfrid, in days that knew not Demos.'

'Well, Mr Desert, do *you* find reality in politics now?'

'Do you find reality in anything, sir?'

'In income tax, perhaps.'

Michael grinned.

'Above knighthood,' he said, 'there's no such thing as simple faith.'

'Suppose your friends came into power, Michael – in some ways not a bad thing, help 'em to grow up – what could they do, eh? Could they raise national taste? Abolish the cinema? Teach English people to cook? Prevent other countries from threatening war? Make us grow our own food? Stop the increase of town life? Would they hang dabblers in poison gas? Could they prevent flying in war-time? Could they weaken the possessive instinct – anywhere? Or do anything, in fact, but alter the incidence of possession a little? All party politics are top dressing. We're ruled by the inventors, and human nature; and we live in Queer Street, Mr Desert.'

'Much my sentiments, sir.'

Michael flourished his cigar.

'Bad old men, you two!'

And removing their hats, they passed the Cenotaph.

'Curiously symptomatic – that thing,' said Sir Lawrence; 'monument to the dread of swank – most characteristic. And the dread of swank –'

'Go on, Bart,' said Michael.

'The fine, the large, the florid – all off! No far-sighted views, no big schemes, no great principles, no great religion, or great art – aestheticism in cliques and backwaters, small men in small hats.'

'As panteth the heart after Byron, Wilberforce, and the Nelson Monument. My poor old Bart! What about it, Wilfrid?'

'Yes, Mr Desert – what about it?'

Desert's dark face contracted.

'It's an age of paradox,' he said. 'We all kick up for freedom, and the only institutions gaining strength are Socialism and the Roman Catholic Church. We're frightfully self-conscious about art – and the only art development is the cinema. We're nuts on peace – and all we're doing about it is to perfect poison gas.'

Sir Lawrence glanced sideways at a young man so bitter.

'And how's publishing, Michael?'

'Well, *Copper Coin* is selling like hot cakes; and there's quite a movement in *A Duet*. What about this for a new ad.: "A Duet, by Sir Lawrence Mont, Bart. The most distinguished Conversation ever held between the Dead." That ought to get the psychic. Wilfrid suggested "G.O.M. and Dizzy – broadcasted from Hell." Which do you like best?'

They had come, however, to a policeman holding up his hand against the nose of a van horse, so that everything marked time. The engines of the cars whirred idly, their drivers' faces set towards the space withheld from them; a girl on a bicycle looked vacantly about her, grasping the back of the van, where a youth sat sideways with his legs stretched out towards her. Sir Lawrence glanced again at young Desert. A thin, pale-dark face, good-looking, but a hitch in it, as if not properly timed; nothing *outré* in dress or manner, and yet socially at large; less vivacious than that lively rascal, his own son, but as anchorless, and more

sceptical – might feel things pretty deeply, though! The policeman lowered his arm.

'You were in the war, Mr Desert?'

'Oh, yes.'

'Air service?'

'And line. Bit of both.'

'Hard on a poet.'

'Not at all. Poetry's only possible when you may be blown up
at any moment, or when you live in Putney.'

Sir Lawrence's eyebrow rose. 'Yes?'

'Tennyson, Browning, Wordsworth, Swinburne – they could
turn it out; *ils vivaient, mais si peu.*'

'Is there not a third condition favourable?'

'And that, sir?'

'How shall I express it – a certain cerebral agitation in connexion with women?'

Desert's face twitched, and seemed to darken.

Michael put his latchkey into the lock of his front door.

Chapter Two

HOME

━◄┽►━

THE house in South Square, Westminster, to which the young
Monts had come after their Spanish honeymoon two years before, might have been called 'emancipated'. It was the work of
an architect whose dream was a new house perfectly old, and
an old house perfectly new. It followed therefore, no recognized
style or tradition, and was devoid of structural prejudice; but it
soaked up the smuts of the metropolis with such special rapidity
that its stone already respectably resembled that of Wren. Its
windows and doors had gently rounded tops. The high-sloping
roof, of a fine sooty pink, was almost Danish, and two 'ducky
little windows' looked out of it, giving an impression that very

tall servants lived up there. There were rooms on each side of
the front door, which was wide and set off by bay trees in black
and gold bindings. The house was thick through, and the staircase, of a broad chastity, began at the far end of a hall which
had room for quite a number of hats and coats and cards. There
were four bathrooms; and not even a cellar underneath. The
Forsyte instinct for a house had co-operated in its acquisition.
Soames had picked it up for his daughter, undecorated, at that
psychological moment when the bubble of inflation was pricked,
and the air escaping from the balloon of the world's trade.
Fleur, however, had established immediate contact with the
architect – an element which Soames himself had never quite
got over – and decided not to have more than three styles in
her house: Chinese, Spanish, and her own. The room to the
left of the front door, running the breadth of the house, was
Chinese, with ivory panels, a copper floor, central heating, and
cut-glass lustres. It contained four pictures – all Chinese – the
only school in which her father had not yet dabbled. The fireplace, wide and open, had Chinese dogs with Chinese tiles for
them to stand on. The silk was chiefly of jade green. There were
two wonderful old black tea-chests, picked up with Soames's
money at Jobson's – not a bargain. There was no piano, partly
because pianos were too uncompromisingly occidental, and
partly because it would have taken up much room. Fleur aimed
at space – collecting people rather than furniture or *bibelots*.
The light, admitted by windows at both ends, was unfortunately
not Chinese. She would stand sometimes in the centre of this
room, thinking – how to 'bunch' her guests, how to make her
room more Chinese without making it uncomfortable; how to
seem to know all about literature and politics; how to accept
everything her father gave her, without making him aware
that his taste had no sense of the future; how to keep hold of
Sibley Swan, the new literary star, and to get hold of Gurdon
Minho, the old; or how Wilfrid Desert was getting too fond of
her; of what was really her style in dress; of why Michael had
such funny ears; and sometimes she stood not thinking at all –
just aching a little.

When those three came in she was sitting before a red lacquer tea-table, finishing a very good tea. She always had tea brought in rather early, so that she could have a good quiet preliminary 'tuck-in' all by herself, because she was not quite twenty-one, and this was her hour for remembering her youth. By her side Ting-a-ling was standing on his hind feet, his tawny forepaws on a Chinese foot-stool, his snubbed black and tawny muzzle turned up towards the fruits of his philosophy.

'That'll do, Ting. No more, ducky I *No more!*'

The expression of Ting-a-ling answered:

'Well, then, stop, too I Don't subject me to torture I'

A year and three months old, he had been bought by Michael out of a Bond Street shop window on Fleur's twentieth birthday, eleven months ago.

Two years of married life had not lengthened her short dark chestnut hair; had added a little more decision to her quick lips, a little more allurement to her white-lidded, dark-lashed hazel eyes, a little more poise and swing to her carriage, a little more chest and hip measurement; had taken a little from waist and calf measurement, a little colour from cheeks a little less round, and a little sweetness from a voice a little more caressing.

She stood up behind the tray, holding out her white round arms without a word. She avoided unnecessary greetings or farewells. She would have had to say them so often, and their purpose was better served by look, pressure, and slight inclination of head to one side.

With a circular movement of her squeezed hand, she said:

'Draw up. Cream, sir? Sugar, Wilfrid? Ting has had too much — don't feed him I Hand things, Michael. I've heard all about the meeting at "Snooks". You're not going to canvass for Labour, Michael — canvassing's so silly. If anyone canvassed me, I should vote the other way at once.'

'Yes, darling; but you're not the average elector.'

Fleur looked at him. Very sweetly put I Conscious of Wilfrid biting his lips, of Sir Lawrence taking that in, of the amount of silk leg she was showing, of her black and cream teacups, she adjusted these matters. A flutter of her white lids – Desert ceased to bite his lips; a movement of her silk legs – Sir Lawrence ceased to look at him. Holding out her cups, she said:

'I suppose I'm not modern enough?'

Desert, moving a bright little spoon round in his magpie cup, said without looking up:

'As much more modern than the moderns, as you are more ancient.'

' 'Ware poetry!' said Michael.

But when he had taken his father to see the new cartoons by Aubrey Greene, she said:

'Kindly tell me what you meant, Wilfrid.'

Desert's voice seemed to leap from restraint.

'What does it matter? I don't want to waste time with that.'

'But I want to know. It sounded like a sneer.'

'A sneer? From me? Fleur!'

'Then tell me.'

'I meant that you have all their restlessness and practical gettheress; but you have what they haven't, Fleur – power to turn one's head. And mine is turned. You know it.'

'How would Michael like that – from *you*, his best man?'

Desert moved quickly to the windows.

Fleur took Ting-a-ling on her lap. Such things had been said to her before; but from Wilfrid it was serious. Nice to think she had his heart, of course! Only, where on earth could she put it, where it wouldn't be seen except by her? He was incalculable – did strange things! She was a little afraid – not of him, but of that quality in him. He came back to the hearth, and said:

'Ugly, isn't it? Put that damn' dog down, Fleur; I can't see your face. If you were really fond of Michael – I swear I wouldn't; but you're not, you know.'

Fleur said coldly:

'You know very little; I *am* fond of Michael.'

Desert gave his little jerky laugh.

'Oh yes; not the sort that counts.'

Fleur looked up.

'It counts quite enough to make one safe.'

'A flower that I can't pick.'

Fleur nodded.

'Quite sure, Fleur? Quite, quite sure?'

Fleur stared; her eyes softened a little, her eyelids, so excessively white, drooped over them; she nodded. Desert said slowly:

'The moment I believe that, I shall go East.'

'East?'

'Not so stale as going West, but much the same – you don't come back.'

Fleur thought: 'The East? I should love to know the East! Pity one can't manage that, too. Pity!'

'You won't keep me in your Zoo, my dear. I shan't hang around and feed on crumbs. You know what I feel – it means a smash of some sort.'

'It hasn't been my fault, has it?'

'Yes; you've collected me, as you collect everybody that comes near you.'

'I don't know what you mean.'

Desert bent down, and dragged her hand to his lips.

'Don't be riled with me; I'm too unhappy.'

Fleur let her hand stay against his hot lips.

'Sorry, Wilfrid.'

'All right, dear. I'll go.'

'But you're coming to dinner tomorrow?'

Desert said violently:

'*Tomorrow?* Good God – no! What d'you think I'm made of?'

He flung her hand away.

'I don't like violence, Wilfrid.'

'Well, good-bye; I'd better go.'

The words 'And you'd better not come again' trembled up to her lips, but were not spoken. Part from Wilfrid – life would lose a little warmth! She waved her hand. He was gone. She heard the door closing. Poor Wilfrid? – nice to think of a flame at which to warm her hands! Nice but rather dreadful! And suddenly, dropping Ting-a-ling, she got up and began to walk about the room. Tomorrow! Second anniversary of her wedding-day! Still an ache when she thought of what it had not been. But there was little time to think – and she made less. What good in thinking? Only one life, full of people, of things to do and have, of things wanted – a life only void of – one thing, and that – well, if people had it, they never had it long! On her lids two tears, which had gathered, dried without falling. Sentimentalism! No! The last thing in the world – the unforgivable offence! Whom should she put next whom tomorrow? And whom should she get in place of Wilfrid, if Wilfrid wouldn't come – silly boy! One day – one night – what difference? Who should sit on her right, and who on her left? Was Aubrey Greene more distinguished, or Sibley Swan? Were they either as distinguished as Walter Nazing or Charles Upshire? Dinner of twelve, exclusively literary and artistic, except for Michael and Alison Charwell. Ah! Could Alison get her Gurdon Minho – just one writer of the old school, one glass of old wine to mellow effervescence? He didn't publish with Danby and Winter; but he fed out of Alison's hand. She went quickly to one of the old tea-chests, and opened it. Inside was a telephone.

'Can I speak to Lady Alison – Mrs Michael Mont ... Yes ... That you, Alison? ... Fleur speaking. Wilfrid has fallen through tomorrow night ... Is there any chance of your bringing Gurdon Minho? I don't know him, of course; but he might be interested. You'll try? ... That'll be ever so delightful. Isn't the "Snooks" Club meeting rather exciting? Bart says they'll eat each other now they've split ... About Mr Minho. Could you let me know tonight? Thanks – thanks awfully! ... Good-bye!'

Failing Minho, whom? Her mind hovered over the names in her address book. At so late a minute it must be someone who didn't stand on ceremony; but except Alison, none of Michael's relations would be safe from Sibley Swan or Nesta Gorse, and their subversive shafts; as to the Forsytes – out of the question; they had their own sub-acid humour (some of them), but they were not modern, not really modern. Besides, she saw as little of them as she could – they dated, belonged to the dramatic period, had no sense of life without beginning or end. No! If Gurdon Minho was a frost, it would have to be a musician, whose works were hieroglyphical with a dash of surgery; or, better, perhaps, a psychoanalyst. Her fingers turned the pages till she came to those two categories. Hugo Solstis? A possibility; but suppose he wanted to play them something recent? There was only Michael's upright Grand, and that would mean going to his study. Better Gerald Hanks – he and Nesta Gorse would get off together on dreams; still, if they did, there would be no actual loss of life. Yes, failing Gurdon Minho, Gerald Hanks; he would be free – and put him between Alison and Nesta. She closed the book, and, going back to her jade-green settee, sat gazing at Ting-a-ling. The little dog's prominent round eyes gazed back; bright, black, very old. Fleur thought: 'I *don't* want Wilfrid to drop off.' Among all the crowd who came and went, here, there and everywhere, she cared for nobody. Keep up with them, keep up with everything, of course! It was all frightfully amusing, frightfully necessary! Only – only – what?

Voices! Michael and Bart coming back. Bart had noticed Wilfrid. He *was* a noticing old Bart. She was never very comfortable when he was about – living and twisting, but with something settled and ancestral in him; a little like Ting-a-ling – something judgematic, ever telling her that she was fluttering and new. He was anchored, could only move to the length of his old-fashioned cord, but he could drop on to things disconcertingly. Still, he admired her, she felt – oh! yes.

Well! What had he thought of the cartoons? Ought Michael to publish them, and with letterpress or without? Didn't he think that the cubic called 'Still Life' – of the Government, too frightfully funny – especially the 'old bean' representing the Prime? For answer she was conscious of a twisting, rapid noise; Sir Lawrence was telling her of his father's collection of electioneering cartoons. She did wish Bart would not tell her about his father; he had been so distinguished, and he must have been so dull, paying all his calls on horseback, with

trousers strapped under his boots. He and Lord Charles Cariboo
and the Marquis of Forfar had been the last three 'callers' of
that sort. If only they hadn't, they'd have been clean forgot.
She had that dress to try, and fourteen things to see to, and
Hugo's concert began at eight-fifteen! Why did people of the
last generation always have so much time? And, suddenly, she
looked down. Ting-a-ling was licking the copper floor. She took
him up: 'Not that, darling; nasty!' Ah! the spell was broken!
Bart was going, reminiscent to the last. She waited at the foot of
the stairs till Michael shut the door on him, then flew. Reaching
her room, she turned on all the lights. Here was her own style –
a bed which did not look like one, and many mirrors. The
couch of Ting-a-ling occupied a corner, whence he could see
himself in three. She put him down, and said: 'Keep quiet,
now!' His attitude to the other dogs in the room had long become indifferent; though of his own breed and precisely his
colouring, they had no smell and no licking power in their
tongues – nothing to be done with them, imitative creatures,
incredibly unresponsive.

Stripping off her dress, Fleur held the new frock under her
chin.

'May I kiss you?' said a voice, and there was Michael's image
behind her own reflection in the glass.

'My dear boy, there isn't time! Help me with this.' She
slipped the frock over her head. 'Do those three top hooks. How
do you like it? Oh! and – Michael! Gurdon Minho may be
coming to dinner tomorrow – Wilfrid can't. Have you read his
things? Sit down and tell me something about them. All novels,
aren't they? What sort?'

'Well, he's always had something to say. And his cats are
good. He's a bit romantic, of course.'

'Oh! Have I made a gaff?'

'Not a bit; jolly good shot. The vice of our lot is, they say it
pretty well, but they've nothing to say. They won't last.'

'But that's just why they will last. They won't date.'

'Won't they? My gum!'

'Wilfrid will last.'

'Ah! Wilfrid has emotions, hates, pities, wants; at least sometimes; when he has, his stuff is jolly good. Otherwise, he just
makes a song about nothing – like the rest.'

Fleur tucked in the top of her undergarment.

'But, Michael, if that's so, we – I've got the wrong lot.'

Michael grinned.

'My dear child! The lot of the hour is always right; only
you've got to watch it, and change it quick enough.'

'But d'you mean to say that Sibley isn't going to live?'

'Sib? Lord, no!'

'But he's so perfectly sure that almost everybody else is dead
or dying. Surely he has critical genius!'

'If I hadn't more judgement than Sib, I'd go out of publishing
tomorrow.'

'You – more than Sibley Swan?'

'Of course, I've more judgement than Sib. Why! Sib's judgement is just his opinion of Sib – common or garden impatience
of anyone else. He doesn't even read them. He'll read one
specimen of every author and say: "Oh! that fellow! He's
dull, or he's moral, or he's sentimental, or he dates, or he
drivels" – I've heard him dozens of times. That's if they're
alive. Of course, if they're dead, it's different. He's always digging up and canonizing the dead; that's how he's got his name.
There's always a Sib in literature. He's a standing example of
how people can get taken at their own valuation. But as to
lasting – of course he won't; he's never creative, even by mistake.'

Fleur had lost the thread. Yes! It suited her – quite a nice
line! Off with it! Must write those three notes before she
dressed.

Michael had begun again.

'Take my tip, Fleur. The really big people don't talk – and
don't bunch – they paddle their own canoes in what seem backwaters. But it's the backwaters that make the main stream. By
Jove, that's a *mot*, or is it a bull; and are bulls *mots* or *mots*
bulls?'

'Michael, if you were me, would you tell Frederic Wilmer

31

that he'll be meeting Hubert Marsland at lunch next week?
Would it bring him or would it put him off?'

'Marsland's rather an old duck, Wilmer's rather an old
goose – I don't know.'

'Oh I do be serious, Michael – you never give me any help in
arranging – No I Don't maul my shoulders please.'

'Well, darling, I *don't* know. I've no genius for such things,
like you. Marsland paints windmills, cliffs and things – I doubt
if he's heard of the future. He's almost a Mathew Maris for
keeping out of the swim. If you think he'd like to meet a Vertiginist –'

'I didn't ask you if he'd like to meet Wilmer; I asked you if
Wilmer would like to meet him.'

'Wilmer will just say: "I like little Mrs Mont, she gives
deuced good grub" – and so you do, ducky. A Vertiginist wants
nourishing, you know, or it wouldn't go to his head.'

Fleur's pen resumed its swift strokes, already become slightly
illegible. She murmured:

'I think Wilfrid would help – you won't be there; one – two
– three. What women?'

'Four painters – pretty and plump; no intellect.'

Fleur said crossly:

'I can't get them plump; they don't go about now.' And her
pen flowed on:

DEAR WILFRID – Wednesday – lunch; Wilmer, Hubert Marsland, two other women. Do help me live it down.

Yours ever,
FLEUR

'Michael, your chin is like a bootbrush.'

'Sorry, old thing; your shoulders shouldn't be so smooth.
Bart gave Wilfrid a tip as we were coming along.'

Fleur stopped writing. 'Oh I'

'Reminded him that the state of love was a good stunt for
poets.'

'*A propos* of what?'

'Wilfrid was complaining that he couldn't turn it out now.'

'Nonsense! His last things are his best.'

'Well, that's what I think. Perhaps he's forestalled the tip. Has he, d'you know?'

Fleur turned her eyes towards the face behind her shoulder. No, it had its native look – frank, irresponsible, slightly faun-like, with its pointed ears, quick lips, and nostrils.

She said slowly,

'If *you* don't know, nobody does.'

A snuffle interrupted Michael's answer. Ting-a-ling, long, low, slightly higher at both ends, was standing between them, with black muzzle upturned. 'My pedigree is long,' he seemed to say : 'but my legs are short – what about it?'

Chapter Three

MUSICAL

ACCORDING to a great and guiding principle, Fleur and Michael Mont attended the Hugo Solstis concert, not because they anticipated pleasure, but because they knew Hugo. They felt, besides, that Solstis, an Englishman of Russo-Dutch extraction, was one of those who were restoring English music, giving to it a wide and spacious freedom from melody and rhythm, while investing it with literary and mathematical charms. And one never could go to a concert given by any of this school without using the word 'interesting' as one was coming away. To sleep to this restored English music, too, was impossible. Fleur, a sound sleeper, had never even tried. Michael had, and complained afterwards that it had been like a nap in Liège railway station. On this occasion they occupied those gangway seats in the front row of the dress circle of which Fleur had a sort of natural monopoly. There Hugo and the rest could see her taking her place in the English restoration movement. It was easy, too, to escape into the corridor and exchange the word 'interesting' with side-whiskered cognoscenti; or, slipping out a cigarette from the little gold case, wedding present of Cousin Imogen Cardigan, get a whiff or two's repose. To speak quite honestly, Fleur had a natural sense of rhythm which caused her discomfort during those long and 'interesting' passages which evidenced, as it were, the composer's rise and fall from his bed of thorns. She secretly loved a tune, and the impossibility of ever confessing this without losing hold of Solstis, Baff, Birdigal, MacLewis, Clorane, and other English restoration composers, sometimes taxed to its limits a nature which had its Spartan side. Even to Michael she would not 'confess'; and it was additionally trying when, with his native disrespect of persons, accentuated by life in the trenches and a publisher's office, he would mutter: 'Gad! Get on with it!' or: 'Cripes! Ain't he took bad!' especially as she knew that Michael was really putting up with it better than herself, having a more literary disposition, and a less dancing itch in his toes.

The first movement of the new Solstis composition – 'Phantasmagoria Piémontesque' – to which they had come especially to listen, began with some drawn-out chords.

'What oh!' said Michael's voice in her ear: 'Three pieces of furniture moved simultaneously on a parquet floor!'

In Fleur's involuntary smile was the whole secret of why her marriage had not been intolerable. After all, Michael was a dear! Devotion and mercury – jesting and loyalty – combined, they piqued and touched even a heart given away before it was bestowed on him. 'Touch' without 'pique' would have bored; 'pique' without 'touch' would have irritated. At this moment he was at peculiar advantage! Holding on to his knees, with his ears standing up, eyes glassy from loyalty to Hugo, and tongue in cheek, he was listening to that opening in a way which evoked Fleur's admiration. The piece would be 'interesting' – she fell into the state of outer observation and inner calculation very usual with her nowadays. Over there was L.S.D., the greater dramatist; she didn't know him – yet. He looked rather frightening, his hair stood up so straight. And her eye began picturing him on her copper floor against a Chinese picture. And there – yes! Gurdon Minho! Imagine *his* coming to anything so modern! His profile *was* rather Roman – of the Aurelian period! Passing on from that antique, with the pleased thought that by this time tomorrow she might have collected it, she quartered the assembly face by face – she did not want to miss anyone important.

'The furniture' had come to a sudden standstill.

'Interesting!' said a voice over her shoulder. Aubrey Greene! Illusive, rather moonlit, with his silky fair hair brushed straight back, and his greenish eyes – his smile always made her feel that he was 'getting' at her. But, after all, he was a cartoonist!

'Yes, isn't it?'

He curled away. He might have stayed a little longer – there wouldn't be time for anyone else before those songs of Birdigal's! Here came the singer Charles Powls! How stout and efficient he looked, dragging little Birdigal to the piano.

Charming accompaniment – rippling, melodious!

The stout, efficient man began to sing. How different from the accompaniment! The song hit every note just off the solar plexus, it mathematically prevented her from feeling pleasure. Birdigal must have written it in horror of someone calling it 'vocal'. Vocal! Fleur knew how catching the word was; it would run like a measle round the ring, and Birdigal would be no more! Poor Birdigal! But this was 'interesting'. Only, as Michael was saying: 'O, my Gawd!'

Three songs! Powls was wonderful – so loyal! Never one note hit so that it rang out like music! Her mind fluttered off to Wilfrid. To him, of all the younger poets, people accorded the right to say something; it gave him such a position – made him seem to come out of life, instead of literature. Besides, he had done things in the war, was a son of Lord Mullyon, would get the Mercer Prize probably for *Copper Coin*. If Wilfrid abandoned her, a star would fall from the firmament above her copper floor. He had no right to leave her in the lurch. He must learn not to be violent – not to think physically. No! she couldn't let Wilfrid slip away; nor could she have any more sob-stuff in her life, searing passions, *cul de sacs*, aftermaths. She had tasted of that; a dulled ache still warned her.

Birdigal was bowing, Michael saying: 'Come out for a whiff! The next thing's a dud!' Oh! ah! Beethoven. Poor old Beethoven! So out of date – one did *rather* enjoy him!

The corridor, and refectory beyond, were swarming with the restoration movement. Young men and women with faces and heads of lively and distorted character, were exchanging the word 'interesting'. Men of more massive type, resembling sedentary matadors, blocked all circulation. Fleur and Michael passed a little way along, stood against the wall, and lighted cigarettes. Fleur smoked hers delicately – a very little one in a tiny amber holder. She had the air of admiring blue smoke rather than of making it; there were spheres to consider beyond this sort of crowd – one never knew who might be about! – the sphere, for instance, in which Alison Charwell moved, politico-literary, catholic in taste, but, as Michael always put it: 'Convinced, like a sanitary system, that it's the only sphere in the world; look at the way they all write books of reminiscence about each other!' They might, she always felt, disapprove of women smoking in public halls. Consorting delicately with iconoclasm, Fleur never forgot that her feet were in two worlds at least. Standing there, observant of all to left and right, she noted against the wall one whose face was screened by his programme. 'Wilfrid!' she thought, 'and doesn't mean to see me!' Mortified, as a child from whom a sixpence is filched, she said:

'There's Wilfrid! Fetch him, Michael!'

Michael crossed, and touched his best man's sleeve; Desert's face emerged, frowning. She saw him shrug his shoulders, turn and walk into the throng. Michael came back.

'Wilfrid's got the hump tonight; says he's not fit for human society – queer old son!'

How obtuse men were! Because Wilfrid was his pal, Michael did not see; and that was lucky! So Wilfrid really meant to avoid her! Well, she would see! And she said:

'I'm tired, Michael; let's go home.'

His hand slid round her arm.

'Sorry, old thing; come along!'

They stood a moment in a neglected doorway, watching Woomans, the conductor, launched towards his orchestra.

'Look at him,' said Michael; 'guy hung out of an Italian window, legs and arms all stuffed and flying! And look at the Frapka and her piano – that's a turbulent union!'

There was a strange sound.

'Melody, by George!' said Michael.

An attendant muttered in their ears: 'Now, sir, I'm going to shut the door.' Fleur had a fleeting view of L.S.D. sitting upright as his hair, with closed eyes. The door was shut – they were outside in the hall.

'Wait here, darling; I'll nick a rickshaw.'

Fleur huddled her chin in her fur. It was easterly and cold.

A voice behind her said:

'Well, Fleur, am I going East?'

Wilfrid! His collar up to his ears, a cigarette between his lips, hands in pockets, eyes devouring.

'You're very silly, Wilfrid!'

'Anything you like; am I going East?'

'No; Sunday morning – eleven o'clock at the Tate. We'll talk it out.'

'*Convenu!*' And he was gone.

Alone suddenly, like that, Fleur felt the first shock of reality. Was Wilfrid truly going to be unmanageable? A taxi-cab ground up; Michael beckoned; Fleur stepped in.

Passing a passionately lighted oasis of young ladies displaying to the interested Londoner the acme of Parisian undress, she felt Michael incline towards her. If she were going to keep Wilfrid, she must be nice to Michael. Only:

'You needn't kiss me in Piccadilly Circus, Michael!'

'Sorry, duckie! It's a little previous – I meant to get you opposite the Partheneum.'

Fleur remembered how he had slept on a Spanish sofa for the first fortnight of their honeymoon; how he always insisted that she must not spend anything on him, but must always let him

give her what he liked, though she had three thousand a year
and he twelve hundred; how jumpy he was when she had a
cold – and how he always came home to tea. Yes, he was a dear!
But would she break her heart if he went East or West tomorrow?

Snuggled against him, she was surprised at her own cynicism.

A telephone message written out, in the hall, ran: 'Please
tell Mrs Mont I've got Mr Gurding Minner. Lady Alisson.'

It was restful. A real antique! She turned on the lights in her
room, and stood for a moment admiring it. Truly pretty! A
slight snuffle from the corner – Ting-a-ling, tan on a black
cushion, lay like a Chinese lion in miniature; pure, remote,
fresh from evening communion with the Square railings.

'I see you,' said Fleur.

Ting-a-ling did not stir; his round black eyes watched his
mistress undress. When she returned from the bathroom he was
curled into a ball. Fleur thought: 'Queer! How does he know
Michael won't be coming?' And slipping into her well-warmed
bed, she too curled herself up and slept.

But in the night, contrary to her custom, she awoke. A cry –
long, weird, trailing, from somewhere – the river – the slums at
the back – rousing memory – poignant, aching – of her honeymoon – Granada, its roofs below, jet, ivory, gold; the watchman's cry, the lines in Jon's letter:

> Voice in the night crying, down in the old sleeping
> Spanish City darkened under her white stars.
> What says the voice – its clear, lingering anguish?
> Just the watchman, telling his dateless tale of safety?
> Just a road-man, flinging to the moon his song?
>> No! 'Tis one deprived, whose lover's heart is weeping,
>> Just his cry: 'How long?'

A cry, or had she dreamed it? Jon, Wilfrid, Michael! No use
to have a heart!

Chapter Four

DINING

<<-->>

LADY Alison Charwell, born Heathfield, daughter of the first
Earl of Campden, and wife to Lionel Charwell, K.C., Michael's
somewhat young uncle, was a delightful Englishwoman brought
up in a set accepted as the soul of society. Full of brains, energy,
taste, money, and tinctured in its politico-legal ancestry by blue
blood, this set was linked to, but apart from 'Snooks' and the
duller haunts of birth and privilege. It was gay, charming, free-
and-easy, and, according to Michael, 'Snobbish, old thing,
aesthetically and intellectually, but they'll never see it. They think
they're the top notch – quick, healthy, up-to-date, well-bred,
intelligent; they simply can't imagine their equals. But you see
their imagination is deficient. Their really creative energy would
go into a pint pot. Look at their books – they're always *on*
something – philosophy, spiritualism, poetry, fishing, themselves; why, even their sonnets dry up before they're twenty-
five. They know everything – except mankind outside their
own set. Oh! they work – they run the show – they have to;
there's no one else with their brains, and energy, and taste.
But they run it round and round in their own blooming
circle. It's the world to them – and it might be worse. They've
patented their own golden age; but it's a trifle fly-blown since
the war.'

Alison Charwell – in and of this world, so spryly soulful,
debonaire, free, and cosy – lived within a stone's throw of
Fleur, in a house pleasant, architecturally, as any in London.
Forty years old, she had three children and considerable beauty,
wearing a little fine from mental and bodily activity. Something of an enthusiast, she was fond of Michael, in spite of his
strange criticisms, so that his matrimonial venture had piqued

39

her from the start. Fleur was dainty, had quick natural intelligence – this new niece was worth cultivation. But, though adaptable and assimilative, Fleur had remained curiously unassimilated; she continued to whet the curiosity of Lady Alison, accustomed to the close borough of choice spirits, and finding a certain poignancy in contact with the New Age on Fleur's copper floor. She met with an irreverence there, which, not taken too seriously, flipped her mind. On that floor she almost felt a back number. It was stimulating.

Receiving Fleur's telephonic inquiry about Gurdon Minho, she had rung up the novelist. She knew him, if not well. Nobody seemed to know him well; amiable, polite, silent, rather dull and austere; but with a disconcerting smile, sometimes ironical, sometimes friendly. His books were now caustic, now sentimental. On both counts it was rather the fashion to run him down, though he still seemed to exist.

She rang him up. Would he come to a dinner tomorrow at her young nephew, Michael Mont's, and meet the younger generation? His answer came, rather high-pitched:

'Rather! Full fig, or dinner jacket?'

'How awfully nice of you! they'll be ever so pleased. Full fig, I believe. It's the second anniversary of their wedding.' She hung up the receiver with the thought: 'He must be writing a book about them!'

Conscious of responsibility, she arrived early.

It was a grand night at her husband's Inn, so that she brought nothing with her but the feeling of adventure, pleasant after a day spent in fluttering over the decision at 'Snooks'. She was received only by Ting-a-ling, who had his back to the fire, and took no notice beyond a stare. Sitting down on the jade green settee, she said:

'Well, you funny little creature, don't you know me after all this time?'

Ting-a-ling's black shiny gaze seemed saying: 'You recur here, I know; most things recur. There is nothing new about the future.'

Lady Alison fell into a train of thought: The new generation! Did she want her own girls to be of it! She would like to talk to Mr Minho about that — they had had a very nice talk down at Beechgroves before the war. Nine years ago — Sybil only six, Joan only four then! Time went, things changed! A new generation! And what was the difference! 'I think we had more tradition!' she said to herself softly.

A slight sound drew her eyes up from contemplation of her feet. Ting-a-ling was moving his tail from side to side on the hearth-rug, as if applauding. Fleur's voice, behind her, said:

'Well, darling, I'm awfully late. It *was* good of you to get me Mr Minho. I do hope they'll all behave. He'll be between you and me, anyway; I'm sticking him at the top, and Michael at the bottom, between Pauline Upshire and Amabel Nazing. You'll have Sibley on your left, and I'll have Aubrey on my right, then Nesta Gorse and Walter Nazing; opposite them Linda Frewe and Charles Upshire. Twelve. You know them all. Oh! and you mustn't mind if the Nazings and Nesta smoke between the courses. Amabel will do it. She comes from Virginia — it's the reaction. I do hope she'll have some clothes on; Michael always says it's a mistake when she has; but having Mr Minho makes one a little nervous. Did you see Nesta's skit in *The Bouquet*? Oh, too frightfully amusing — clearly meant for L.S.D.! Ting, my Ting, are you going to stay and see all these people? Well, then, get up here or you'll be trodden on. Isn't he Chinese? He does so round off the room.'

Ting-a-ling laid his nose on his paws, in the centre of a jade green cushion.

'Mr Gurding Minner!'

The well-known novelist looked pale and composed. Shaking the two extended hands, he gazed at Ting-a-ling, and said:

'How nice! How are *you*, my little man?'

Ting-a-ling did not stir. 'You take me for a common English dog, sir!' his silence seemed to say.

'Mr and Mrs Walter Nazon, Miss Lenda Frow.'

Amabel Nazing came first, clear alabaster from her fair

hair down to the six inches of gleaming back above her waist-line, shrouded alabaster from four inches below the knee to the gleaming toes of her shoes; the eminent novelist mechanically ceased to commune with Ting-a-ling.

Walter Nazing, who followed a long way up above his wife, had a tiny line of collar emergent from swathes of black, and a face, cut a hundred years ago, that slightly resembled Shelley's. His literary productions were sometimes felt to be like the poetry of that bard, and sometimes like the prose of Marcel Proust. 'What oh!' as Michael said.

Linda Frewe, whom Fleur at once introduced to Gurdon Minho, was one about whose work no two people in her draw-ing-room ever agreed. Her works *Trifles* and *The Furious Don* had quite divided all opinion. Genius according to some, drivel according to others, those books always roused an interest-ing debate whether a slight madness enhanced or diminished the value of art. She herself paid little attention to criticism — she produced.

'*The* Mr Minho? How interesting! I've never read anything of yours.'

Fleur gave a little gasp.

'What — don't you know Mr Minho's cats? But they're won-derful. Mr Minho, I do want Mrs Walter Nazing to know you. Amabel — Mr Gurdon Minho.'

'Oh! Mr Minho — how perfectly lovely! I've wanted to know you ever since my cradle.'

Fleur heard the novelist say quietly:

'I could wish it had been longer;' and passed on in doubt to greet Nesta Gorse and Sibley Swan, who came in, as if they lived together, quarrelling over L.S.D., Nesta upholding him because of his 'panache', Sibley maintaining that wit had died with the Restoration; this fellow was alive!

Michael followed with the Upshires and Aubrey Greene, whom he had encountered in the hall. The party was complete.

Fleur loved perfection, and that evening was something of a nightmare. Was it a success? Minho was so clearly the least brilliant person there; even Alison talked better. And yet he had such a fine skull. She did hope he would not go away early. Someone would be almost sure to say 'Dug up!' or 'Thick and bald!' before the door closed behind him. He was pathetically agreeable, as if trying to be liked, or, at least, not despised too much. And there must, of course, be more in him than met the sense of hearing. After the crab soufflé he did seem to be talking to Alison, and all about youth. Fleur listened with one ear.

'Youth feels ... main stream of life ... not giving it what it wants. Past and future getting haloes ... Quite! Contemporary life no earthly just now ... No ... Only comfort for us – we'll be antiquated, some day, like Congreve, Sterne, Defoe ... have our chance again ... *Why?* What *is* driving them out of the main current? Oh! Probably surfeit ... newspapers ... photographs. Don't see life itself, only reports ... reproductions of it; all seems shoddy, lurid, commercial ... Youth says: "Away with it, let's have the past or the future!"'

He took some salted almonds, and Fleur saw his eyes stray to the upper part of Amabel Nazing. Down there the conversation was like Association football – no one kept the ball for more than one kick. It shot from head to head. And after every set of passes someone would reach out and take a cigarette, and blow a blue cloud across the unclothed refectory table. Fleur enjoyed the glow of her Spanish room – its tiled floor, richly coloured fruits in porcelain, its tooled leather, copper articles, and Soames's Goya above a Moorish divan. She headed the ball promptly when it came her way, but initiated nothing. Her gift was to be aware of everything at once. 'Mrs Michael Mont presented' the brilliant irrelevances of Linda Frewe, the pricks and stimulations of Nesta Gorse, the moonlit sliding innuendoes of Aubrey Greene, the upturning strokes of Sibley Swan, Amabel Nazing's little cool American audacities, Charles Upshire's curious bits of lore, Walter Nazing's subversive contradictions, the critical intricacies of Pauline Upshire; Michael's happy-go-lucky slings and arrows, even Alison's knowledgeable quickness, and Gurdon Minho's silences – she presented them all, showed them off, keeping her eyes and ears on the ball of talk lest it should touch earth and rest. Brilliant evening; but – a success?

On the jade green settee, when the last of them had gone and Michael was seeing Alison home, she thought of Minho's 'Youth – not getting what it wants.' No! Things didn't fit. 'They don't fit, do they, Ting!' But Ting-a-ling was tired, only the tip of one ear quivered. Fleur leaned back and sighed. Ting-a-ling uncurled himself, and putting his forepaws on her thigh, looked up in her face. 'Look at me,' he seemed to say, 'I'm all right. I get what I want, and I want what I get. At present I want to go to bed.'

'But I don't,' said Fleur, without moving.

'Just take me up!' said Ting-a-ling.

'Well,' said Fleur, 'I suppose – It's a nice person, but not the right person, Ting.'

Ting-a-ling settled himself on her bare arms.

'It's all right,' he seemed to say. 'There's a great deal too much sentiment and all that, out of China. Come on!'

Chapter Five

EVE

◄-◄-►-►

T H E Honourable Wilfrid Desert's rooms were opposite a picture gallery off Cork Street. The only male member of the aristocracy writing verse that anyone would print, he had chosen them for seclusion rather than for comfort. His 'junk', however, was not devoid of the taste and luxury which overflows from the greater houses of England. Furniture from the Hampshire seat of the Cornish nobleman, Lord Mullyon, had oozed into two vans, when Wilfrid settled in. He was seldom to be found, however, in his nest, and was felt to be a rare bird, owing his rather unique position among the younger writers partly to his migratory reputation. He himself hardly, perhaps, knew where he spent his time, or did his work, having a sort of mental claustro-phobia, a dread of being hemmed in by people. When the war broke out he had just left Eton; when the war was over he was twenty-three, as old a young man as ever turned a stave. His friendship with Michael, begun in hospital, had languished and renewed itself suddenly, when in 1920 Michael joined Danby and Winter, publishers, of Blake Street, Covent Garden. The scattery enthusiasm of the sucking publisher had been roused by Wilfrid's verse. Hob-nobbing lunches over the poems of one in need of literary anchorage, had been capped by the firm's surrender to Michael's insistence. The mutual intoxication of the first book Wilfrid had written and the first book Michael had sponsored was crowned at Michael's wedding. Best man! Since then, so far as Desert could be tied to anything, he had been tied to those two; nor, to do him justice, had he realized till a month ago that the attraction was not Michael, but Fleur. Desert never spoke of the war, it was not possible to learn from his own mouth an effect which he might have summed up thus: 'I lived so long with horror and death; I saw men so in the raw; I put hope of anything out of my mind so utterly, that I can never more have the faintest respect for theories, promises, conven-tions, moralities, and principles. I have hated too much the men who wallowed in them while I was wallowing in mud and blood. Illusion is off. No religion and no philosophy will satisfy me – words, all words. I have still my senses – no thanks to them; am still capable – I find – of passion; can still grit my teeth and grin; have still some feeling of trench loyalty, but whether real or just a complex, I don't yet know. I am dangerous, but not so dangerous as those who trade in words, principles, theories, and all manner of fanatical idiocy to be worked out in the blood and sweat of other men. The war's done one thing for me – converted life to comedy. Laugh at it – there's nothing else to do!'

Leaving the concert hall on the Friday night, he had walked straight home to his rooms. And lying down full length on a monk's seat of the fifteenth century, restored with down cushions and silk of the twentieth, he crossed his hands behind his head and delivered himself to these thoughts: 'I am not going on like this. She has bewitched me. It doesn't mean anything to her. But it means hell to me. I'll finish with it on Sunday – Persia's a good place. Arabia's a good place – plenty of blood and sand! She's incapable of giving anything up. How has she hooked herself into me! By trick of eyes, and hair, by her walk, by the sound of her voice – by trick of warmth, scent, colour. Fling her cap over the windmill – not she! What then? Am I to hang about her Chinese fireside and her little Chinese dog; and have this ache and this fever because I can't be kissing her? I'd rather be flying again in the middle of Boche whiz-bangs! Sunday! How women like to drag out agonies! It'll be just this afternoon all over again. "How unkind of you to go, when your friendship is so precious to me! Stay, and be my tame cat, Wilfrid!" No, my dear, for once you're up against it! And – so am I, by the Lord! ...'

When in that gallery which extends asylum to British art, those two young people met so accidentally on Sunday morning in front of Eve smelling at the flowers of the Garden of Eden, there were present also six mechanics in various stages of decom-position, a custodian and a couple from the provinces, none of whom seemed capable of observing anything whatever. And, indeed, that meeting was inexpressive. Two young people, of the disillusioned class, exchanging condemnations of the past. Desert with his off-hand speech, his smile, his well-tailored in-formality, suggested no aching heart. Of the two Fleur was the paler and more interesting. Desert kept saying to himself: 'No melodrama – that's all it would be!' And Fleur was thinking: 'If I can keep him ordinary like this, I shan't lose him, because he'll never go away without a proper outburst.'

It was not until they found themselves a second time before the Eve, that he said:

'I don't know why you asked me to come, Fleur. It's playing the goat for no earthly reason. I quite understand your feeling. I'm a bit of "Ming" that you don't want to lose. But it's not good enough, my dear; and that's all about it.'

'How horrible of you, Wilfrid!'

'Well! Here we part! Give us your flipper.'

His eyes – rather beautiful – looked dark and tragic above the smile on his lips, and she said stammering:

'Wilfrid – I – I don't know. I want time. I can't bear you to be unhappy. Don't go away! Perhaps I – I shall be unhappy, too; I – I don't know.'

Through Desert passed the bitter thought: 'She *can't* let go – she doesn't know how.' But he said quite softly: 'Cheer up, my child; you'll be over all that in a fortnight. I'll send you something to make up. Why shouldn't I make it China – one place is as good as another? I'll send you a bit of real "Ming", of a better period than this.'

Fleur said passionately:

'You're insulting! Don't!'

'I beg your pardon. I don't want to leave you angry.'

'What is it you want of me?'

'Oh! no – come! This is going over it twice. Besides, since Friday I've been thinking. I want nothing, Fleur, except a blessing and your hand. Give it me! Come on!'

Fleur put her hand behind her back. It was too mortifying! He took her for a cold-blooded, collecting little cat – clutching and playing with mice that she didn't want to eat!

'You think I'm made of ice,' she said, and her teeth caught her upper lip: 'Well, I'm not!'

Desert looked at her; his eyes were very wretched. 'I didn't mean to play up your pride,' he said. 'Let's drop it, Fleur. It isn't any good.'

Fleur turned and fixed her eyes on the Eve – rumbustious-looking female, care-free, avid, taking her fill of flower perfume! Why not be care-free, take anything that came along? Not so much love in the world that one could afford to pass, leaving it unsmelled, unplucked. Run away! Go to the East! Of course, she couldn't do anything extravagant like that! But, perhaps – What did it matter? one man or another, when neither did you really love!

From under her drooped, white, dark-lashed eyelids she saw the expression on his face, and that he was standing stiller than the statues. And suddenly she said: 'You will be a fool to go. Wait!' And without another word or look, she walked away, leaving Desert breathless before the avid Eve.

Chapter Six

'OLD FORSYTE' AND 'OLD MONT'

◄◄─►►

MOVING away, in the confusion of her mood, Fleur almost trod on the toes of a too-familiar figure standing before an Alma Tadema with a sort of grey anxiety, as if lost in the mutability of market values.

'Father! *You* up in town? Come along to lunch, I have to get home quick.'

Hooking his arm and keeping between him and Eve, she guided him away, thinking: 'Did he see us? Could he have seen us?'

'Have you got enough on?' muttered Soames.

'Heaps!'

'That's what you women always say. East wind, and your neck like that! Well, I don't know.'

'No, dear, but I do.'

The grey eyes appraised her from head to foot.

'What are you doing here?' he said. And Fleur thought: 'Thank God he didn't see. He'd never have asked if he had.' And she answered:

'I take an interest in art, darling, as well as you.'

'Well, I'm staying with your aunt in Green Street. This east wind has touched my liver. How's your – how's Michael?'

'Oh, he's all right – a little cheap. We had a dinner last night.'

Anniversary! The realism of a Forsyte stirred in him, and he looked under her eyes. Thrusting his hand into his overcoat pocket, he said:

'I was bringing you this.'

Fleur saw a flat substance wrapped in pink tissue paper.

'Darling, what is it?'

Soames put it back into his pocket.

'We'll see later. Anybody to lunch?'

'Only Bart.'

'Old Mont! Oh, Lord!'

'Don't you like Bart, dear?'

'Like him? He and I have nothing in common.'

'I thought you fraternized rather over the state of things.'

'He's a reactionary,' said Soames.

'And what are you, ducky?'

'I? What should *I* be?' With these words he affirmed that policy of non-commitment which, the older he grew, the more he perceived to be the only attitude for a sensible man.

'How is Mother?'

'Looks well. I see nothing of her – she's got her own mother down – they go gadding about.'

He never alluded to Madame Lamotte as Fleur's grand-mother – the less his daughter had to do with her French side, the better.

'Oh!' said Fleur. 'There's Ting and a cat!' Ting-a-ling, out for a breath of air, and tethered by a lead in the hands of a maid, was snuffling horribly and trying to climb a railing whereon was perched a black cat, all hunch and eyes.

'Give him to me, Ellen. Come with Mother, darling!'

Ting-a-ling came, indeed, but only because he couldn't go, bristling and snuffling and turning his head back.

'I like to see him natural,' said Fleur.

'Waste of money, a dog like that,' Soames commented. 'You should have had a bull-dog and let him sleep in the hall. No end of burglaries. Your aunt had her knocker stolen.'

'I wouldn't part with Ting for a hundred knockers.'

'One of these days you'll be having *him* stolen – fashionable breed.'

Fleur opened her front door. 'Oh!' she said, 'Bart's here, already!'

49

A shiny hat was reposing on a marble coffer, present from Soames, intended to hold coats and discourage moth. Placing his hat alongside the other, Soames looked at them. They were too similar for words, tall, high, shiny, and with the same name inside. He had resumed the 'tall hat' habit after the failure of the general and coal strikes in 1921, his instinct having told him that revolution would be at a discount for some considerable period.

'About this thing,' he said, taking out the pink parcel, 'I don't know what you'll do with it, but here it is.'

It was a curiously carved and coloured bit of opal in a ring of tiny brilliants.

'Oh !' Fleur cried : 'What a delicious thing !'

'Venus floating on the waves or something,' murmured Soames. 'Uncommon. You want a strong light on it.'

'But it's lovely. I shall put it on at once.'

Venus ! If Dad had known ! She put her arms round his neck to disguise her sense of *à propos*. Soames received the rub of her cheek against his own well-shaved face with his usual stillness. Why demonstrate when they were both aware that his affection was double hers?

'Put it on then,' he said, 'and let's see.'

Fleur pinned it at her neck before an old lacquered mirror. 'It's a jewel. Thank you, darling ! Yes, your tie is straight. I like that white piping. You ought always to wear it with black. Now, come along !' And she drew him into her Chinese room. It was empty.

'Bart must be up with Michael, talking about his new book.'

'Writing at his age?' said Soames.

'Well, ducky, he's a year younger than you.'

'I don't write. Not such a fool. Got any more new-fangled friends?'

'Just one – Gurdon Minho, the novelist.'

'Another of the new school?'

'Oh, no, dear ! Surely you've heard of Gurdon Minho; he's older than the hills.'

'They're all alike to me,' muttered Soames. 'Is he well thought of?'

'I should think his income is larger than yours. He's almost a classic – only waiting to die.'

'I'll get one of his books and read it. What name did you say?'

'Get *Big and Little Fishes*, by Gurdon Minho. You can remember that, can't you? Oh! here they are! Michael, look at what Father's given me.'

Taking his hand, she put it up to the opal at her neck. 'Let them both see,' she thought, 'what good terms we're on.' Though her father had not seen her with Wilfrid in the gallery, her conscience still said: 'Strengthen your respectability, you don't quite know how much support you'll need for it in future.'

And out of the corner of her eye she watched those two. The meetings between 'Old Mont' and 'Old Forsyte' – as she knew Bart called her father when speaking of him to Michael – always made her want to laugh, but she never quite knew why. Bart knew everything, but his knowledge was beautifully bound, strictly edited by a mind tethered to the 'eighteenth century'. Her father only knew what was of advantage to him, but the knowledge was unbound, and subject to no editorship. If he *was* late Victorian, he was not above profiting if necessary by even later periods. 'Old Mont' had faith in tradition; 'Old Forsyte' none. Fleur's acuteness had long perceived a difference which favoured her father. Yet 'Old Mont's' talk was so much more up-to-date, rapid, glancing, garrulous, redolent of precise information; and 'Old Forsyte's' was constricted, matter-of-fact. Really impossible to tell which of the two was the better museum specimen; and both so well-preserved!

They did not precisely shake hands; but Soames mentioned the weather. And almost at once they all four sought that Sunday food which by a sustained effort of will Fleur had at last deprived of reference to the British character. They partook, in fact, of lobster cocktails, and a mere risotto of chickens' livers, an omelette *au rhum*, and dessert trying to look as Spanish as it could.

'I've been in the Tate,' Fleur said; 'I do think it's touching.'

'Touching?' queried Soames with a sniff.

'Fleur means, sir, that to see so much old English art together is like looking at a baby show.'

'I don't follow,' said Soames stiffly. 'There's some very good work there.'

'But not grown-up, sir.'

'Ah! You young people mistake all this crazy cleverness for maturity.'

'That's not what Michael means, Father. It's quite true that English painting has no wisdom teeth. You can see the difference in a moment, between it and any Continental painting.'

'And thank God for it!' broke in Sir Lawrence. 'The beauty of this country's art is its innocence. We're the oldest country in the world politically, and the youngest aesthetically. What do you say, Forsyte?'

'Turner is old and wise enough for me,' said Soames curtly 'Are you coming to the P.P.R.S. Board on Tuesday?'

'Tuesday? We were going to shoot the spinneys, weren't we, Michael?'

Soames grunted. 'I should let them wait,' he said. 'We settle the report.'

It was through 'Old Mont's' influence that he had received a seat on the Board of that flourishing concern, the Providential Premium Reassurance Society, and, truth to tell, he was not sitting very easily in it. Though the law of averages was, perhaps, the most reliable thing in the world, there were circumstances which had begun to cause him disquietude. He looked round his nose. Light weight, this narrow-headed, twisting-eyebrowed baronet of a chap – like his son before him! And he added suddenly: 'I'm not easy. If I'd realized how that chap Elderson ruled the roost, I doubt if I should have come on to that Board.'

One side of 'Old Mont's' face seemed to try to leave the other.

'Elderson!' he said. 'His grandfather was my grandfather's parliamentary agent at the time of the Reform Bill; he put him through the most corrupt election ever fought – bought every vote — used to kiss all the farmer's wives. Great days, Forsyte, great days!'

'And over,' said Soames. 'I don't believe in trusting a man's judgement as far as we trust Elderson's; I don't like this foreign insurance.'

'My dear Forsyte — first-rate head, Elderson; I've known him all my life, we were at Winchester together.'

Soames uttered a deep sound. In that answer of 'Old Mont's' lay much of the reason for his disquietude. On the Board they had all, as it were, been at Winchester together! It was the very deuce! They were all so honourable that they dared not scrutinize each other, or even their own collective policy. Worse than their dread of mistake or fraud was their dread of seeming to distrust each other. And this was natural, for to distrust each other was an immediate evil. And, as Soames knew, immediate evils are those which one avoids. Indeed, only that tendency, inherited from his father, James, to lie awake between the hours of two and four, when the chrysalis of faint misgiving becomes so readily the butterfly of panic, had developed his uneasiness. The P.P.R.S. was so imposing a concern, and he had been connected with it so short a time, that it seemed presumptuous to smell a rat; especially as he would have to leave the Board and the thousand a year he earned on it if he raised smell of rat without rat or reason. But what if there were a rat? That was the trouble! And here sat 'Old Mont' talking of his spinneys and his grandfather. The fellow's head was too small! And visited by the cheerless thought: 'There's nobody here, not even my own daughter, capable of taking a thing seriously,' he kept silence. A sound at his elbow roused him. That marmoset of a dog, on a chair between him and his daughter, was sitting up! Did it expect him to give it something? Its eyes would drop out one of these days. And he said: 'Well, what do *you* want?' The way the little beast stared with those boot-buttons! 'Here,' he said, offering it a salted almond. 'You don't eat these.'

Ting-a-ling did.

'He has a passion for them, Dad. Haven't you, darling?'

Ting-a-ling turned his eyes up at Soames, through whom a

queer sensation passed. 'Believe the little brute likes me,' he thought, 'he's always looking at me.' He touched the dog's nose with the tip of his finger. Ting-a-ling gave it a slight lick with his curly blackish tongue.

'Poor fellow!' muttered Soames involuntarily, and turned to 'Old Mont'.

'Don't mention what I said.'

'My dear Forsyte, what was that?'

Good Heavens! And he was on a Board with a man like this! What had made him come on, when he didn't want the money, or any more worries – goodness knew. As soon as he had become a director, Winifred and others of his family had begun to acquire shares to neutralize their income tax – seven per cent preference – nine per cent ordinary – instead of the steady five they ought to be content with. There it was, he couldn't move without people following him. He had always been so safe, so perfect a guide in the money maze! To be worried at his time of life! His eyes sought comfort from the opal at his daughter's neck – pretty thing, pretty neck! Well! She seemed happy enough – had forgotten her infatuation of two years ago! That was something to be thankful for. What she wanted now was a child to steady her in all this modern scrimmage of twopenny-ha'penny writers and painters and musicians. A loose lot, but she had a good little head on her. If she had a child, he would put another twenty thousand into her settlement. That was one thing about her mother – steady in money matters, good French method. And Fleur – so far as he knew – cut her coat according to her cloth. What was that? The word 'Goya' had caught his ear. New life of him coming out? H'm! That confirmed his slowly growing conviction that Goya had reached top point again.

'Think I shall part with that,' he said, pointing to the picture. 'There's an Argentine over here.'

'Sell your Goya, sir?' It was Michael speaking. 'Think of the envy with which you're now regarded!'

'One can't have everything,' said Soames.

'That reproduction we've got for *The New Life* has turned

out first-rate. "Property of Soames Forsyte, Esquire." Let's get the book out first, sir, anyway.'

'Shadow or substance, eh, Forsyte?'

Narrow-headed baronet chap — was he mocking?

'*I've* no family place,' he said.

'No, but we have, sir,' murmured Michael; 'you could leave it to Fleur, you know.'

'Well,' said Soames, 'we shall see if that's worth while.' And he looked at his daughter.

Fleur seldom blushed, but she picked up Ting-a-ling and rose from the Spanish table. Michael followed suit. 'Coffee in the other room,' he said. 'Old Forsyte' and 'Old Mont' stood up, wiping their moustaches.

Chapter Seven

'OLD MONT' AND 'OLD FORSYTE'

◄-◄-►-►

THE offices of the P.P.R.S. were not far from the College of Arms. Soames, who knew that 'three dexter buckles on a sable ground gules' and a 'pheasant proper' had been obtained there at some expense by his Uncle Swithin in the sixties of the last century, had always pooh-poohed the building, until, about a year ago, he had been struck by the name Golding in a book which he had absently taken up at the Connoisseurs' Club. The affair purported to prove that William Shakespeare was really Edward de Vere, Earl of Oxford. The mother of the earl was a Golding — so was the mother of Soames! The coincidence struck him; and he went on reading. The tome left him with judgement suspended over the main issue, but a distinct curiosity as to whether he was not of the same blood as Shakespeare. Even if the earl were not the bard, he felt that the connexion could only be creditable, though, so far as he could make out, Oxford was a shady fellow. Recently appointed on the Board of the P.P.R.S., so that he passed the college every other Tuesday, he had thought: 'Shan't go spending a lot of money on it, but might look in one day.' Having looked in, it was astonishing how taken he had been by the whole thing. Tracing his mother had been quite like a criminal investigation, nearly as ramified and fully as expensive. Having begun, the tenacity of a Forsyte could hardly bear to leave him short of the mother of Shakespeare de Vere, even though she would be collateral; unfortunately, he could not get past a certain William Gouldyng, Ingerer – whatever that might be, and he was almost afraid to inquire – of the time of Oliver Cromwell. There were still four generations to be unravelled, and he was losing money and the hope of getting anything for it. This it was which caused him to gaze askance at the retired building while passing it on his way to the Board on the Tuesday after the lunch at Fleur's. Two more wakeful early mornings had screwed him to the pitch of bringing his doubts to a head and knowing where he stood in the matter of the P.P.R.S.; and this sudden reminder that he was spending money here, there and everywhere, when there was a possibility, however remote, of financial liability somewhere else, sharpened the edge of a nerve already stropped by misgivings. Neglecting the lift and walking slowly up the two flights of stairs, he 'went over' his fellow-directors for the fifteenth time. Old Lord Fontenoy was there for his name, of course; seldom attended, and was what they called 'a dud' – h'm! – nowadays; the chairman, Sir Luke Sharman, seemed always to be occupied in not being taken for a Jew. His nose was straight, but his eyelids gave cause for doubt. His surname was impeccable, but his Christian dubious; his voice was reassuringly roughened, but his clothes had a suspicious tendency towards gloss. Altogether a man who, though shrewd, could not be trusted – Soames felt – to be giving his whole mind to other business. As for 'Old Mont' – what was the good of a ninth baronet on a Board? Guy Meyricke, King's Counsel, last of the three who had been 'together', was a good man in court, no doubt, but with no time for business and no real sense of it! Remained that converted Quaker, old Cuthbert Mothergill – whose family name had been a by-word for successful integrity throughout the last century, so that people still put Mothergills on to boards almost mechanically – rather deaf, nice clean old chap, and quite bland, but nothing more. A perfectly honest lot, no doubt, but perfunctory. None of them really giving their minds to the thing! In Elderson's pocket, too, except perhaps Sharman, and he on the wobble. And Elderson himself – clever chap, bit of an artist, perhaps; managing director from the start, with everything at his finger-tips! Yes! That was the mischief! Prestige of superior knowledge, and years of success – they all kow-towed to him, and no wonder! Trouble with a man like that was that if he once admitted to having made a mistake he destroyed the legend of his infallibility. Soames had enough infallibility of his own to realize how powerful was its impetus towards admitting nothing. Ten months ago, when he had come on to the Board, everything had seemed in full sail; exchanges had reached bottom, so they all thought – the 're-assurance of foreign contracts' policy, which Elderson had initiated about a year before, had seemed, with rising exchanges, perhaps the brightest feather in the cap of possibility. And now, a twelvemonth later, Soames suspected darkly that they did not know where they were – and the general meeting only six weeks off! Probably not even Elderson knew; or, if he did, he was keeping knowledge which ought to belong to the whole directorate severely to himself.

He entered the board-room without a smile. All there – even Lord Fontenoy and 'Old Mont' – given up his spinneys, had he! Soames took his seat at the end on the fireside. Staring at Elderson, he saw, with sudden clearness, the strength of the fellow's position; and, with equal clearness, the weakness of the P.P.R.S. With this rising and falling currency, they could never know exactly their liability – they were just gambling. Listening to the minutes and other routine business, with his chin clasped in his hand, he let his eyes move from face to face – old Mothergill, Elderson, Mont opposite; Sharman at the head; Fontenoy, Meyricke, back to himself – decisive board of the year. He could not, must not, be placed in any dubious position! At his first general meeting on this concern, he must not face the shareholders

57

without knowing exactly where he stood. He looked again at Elderson — sweetish face, bald head rather like Julius Caesar's, nothing to suggest irregularity or excessive optimism — in fact, somewhat resembling that of old Uncle Nicholas Forsyte, whose affairs had been such an example to the last generation but one. The managing director having completed his exposition, Soames directed his gaze at the pink face of dosey old Mothergill, and said:

'I'm not satisfied that these accounts disclose our true position. I want the Board adjourned to this day week, Mr Chairman, and during the week I want every member of the Board furnished with exact details of the foreign contract commitments which do *not* mature during the present financial year. I notice that those are lumped under a general estimate of liability. I am not satisfied with that. They ought to be separately treated.' Shifting his gaze past Elderson to the face of 'Old Mont', he went on: 'Unless there's a material change for the better on the Continent, which I don't anticipate (quite the contrary), I fully expect those commitments will put us in Queer Street next year.'

The scraping of feet, shifting of legs, clearing of throats which accompany a slight sense of outrage greeted the words 'Queer Street'; and a sort of satisfaction swelled in Soames; he had rattled their complacency, made them feel a touch of the misgiving from which he himself was suffering.

'We have always treated our commitments under one general estimate, Mr Forsyte.'

Plausible chap!

'And to my mind wrongly. This foreign contract business is a new policy. For all I can tell, instead of paying a dividend, we ought to·be setting this year's profits against a certain loss next year.'

Again that scrape and rustle.

'My dear sir, absurd!'

The bulldog in Soames snuffled.

'So you say!' he said. 'Am I to have those details?'

'The Board can have what details it likes, of course. But permit me to remark on the general question that it *can* only be a matter of estimate. A conservative basis has always been adopted.'

'That is a matter of opinion,' said Soames; 'and in my view it should be the Board's opinion after very careful discussion of the actual figures.'

'Old Mont' was speaking.

'My dear Forsyte, to go into every contract would take us a week, and then get us no further; we can but average it out.'

'What we have not got in these accounts,' said Soames, 'is the relative proportion of foreign risk to home risk – in the present state of things a vital matter.'

The Chairman spoke.

'There will be no difficulty about that, I imagine, Elderson! But in any case, Mr Forsyte, we should hardly be justified in penalizing the present year for the sake of eventualities which we hope will not arise.'

'I don't know,' said Soames. 'We are here to decide policy according to our common sense, and we must have the fullest opportunity of exercising it. That is my point. We have not enough information.'

That 'plausible chap' was speaking again:

'Mr Forsyte seems to be indicating a lack of confidence in the management.' Taking the bull by the horns – was he?

'Am I to have that information?'

The voice of old Mothergill rose cosy in the silence.

'The Board could be adjourned, perhaps, Mr Chairman; I could come up myself at a pinch. Possibly we could all attend. The times are very peculiar – we mustn't take any unnecessary risks. The policy of foreign contracts is undoubtedly somewhat new to us. We have no reason so far to complain of the results. And I am sure we have the utmost confidence in the judgement of our managing director. Still, as Mr Forsyte has asked for this information, I think perhaps we ought to have it. What do you say, my lord?'

'I can't come up next week. I agree with the chairman that on these accounts we couldn't burke this year's dividend. No good getting the wind up before we must. When do the accounts go out, Elderson?'

'Normally at the end of this week.'

'These are not normal times,' said Soames. 'To be quite plain, unless I have that information I must tender my resignation.' He saw very well what was passing in their minds. A newcomer making himself a nuisance – they would take his resignation readily – only it would look awkward just before a general meeting unless they could announce 'wife's ill-health' or something satisfactory, which he would take very good care they didn't.

The chairman said coldly:

'Well, we will adjourn the Board to this day week; you will be able to get us those figures, Elderson?'

'Certainly.'

Into Soames's mind flashed the thought: 'Ought to ask for an independent scrutiny.' But he looked round. Going too far – perhaps – if he intended to remain on the Board – and he had no wish to resign – after all, it was a big thing, and a thousand a year! No! Mustn't overdo it!

Walking away, he savoured his triumph doubtfully, by no means sure that he had done any good. His attitude had only closed the 'all together' attitude round Elderson. The weakness of his position was that he had nothing to go on, save an uneasiness, which when examined was found to be simply a feeling that he hadn't enough control himself. And yet, there couldn't be two managers – you must trust your manager!

A voice behind him tittupped: 'Well, Forsyte, you gave us quite a shock with your alternative. First time I remember anything of the sort on that Board.'

'Sleepy hollow,' said Soames.

'Yes, I generally have a nap. It gets very hot in there. Wish I'd stuck to my spinneys. They come high, even as early as this.'

Incurably frivolous, this tittupping baronet!

'By the way, Forsyte, I wanted to say: With all this modern birth control and the rest of it, one gets uneasy. We're not the royal family; but don't you feel with me it's time there was a movement in heirs?'

Soames did, but he was not going to confess to anything so indelicate about his own daughter.

'Plenty of time,' he muttered.

'I don't like that dog, Forsyte.'

Soames stared.

'Dog!' he said. 'What's that to do with it?'

'I like a baby to come before a dog. Dogs and poets distract young women. My grandmother had five babies before she was twenty-seven. She was a Montjoy; wonderful breeders, you remember them – the seven Montjoy sisters – all pretty. Old Montjoy had forty-seven grandchildren. You don't get it nowadays, Forsyte.'

'Country's over-populated,' said Soames grimly.

'By the wrong sort – less of them, more of ourselves. It's almost a matter for legislation.'

'Talk to your son,' said Soames.

'Ah! but they think us fogeys, you know. If we could only point to a reason for existence. But it's difficult, Forsyte, it's difficult.'

'They've got everything they want,' said Soames.

'Not enough, my dear Forsyte, not enough; the condition of the world is on the nerves of the young. England's dished, they say, Europe's dished. Heaven's dished, and so is Hell! No future in anything but the air. You can't breed in the air; at least, I doubt it – the difficulties are considerable.'

Soames sniffed.

'If only the journalists would hold their confounded pens,' he said; for, more and more of late, with the decrescendo of scare in the daily Press, he was regaining the old sound Forsyte feeling of security. 'We've only to keep clear of Europe,' he added.

'Keep clear and keep the ring! Forsyte, I believe you've hit it. Good friendly terms with Scandinavia, Holland, Spain, Italy, Turkey – all the outlying countries that we can get at by sea. And let the others dree their weirds. It's an idea!' How the chap rattled on!

'I'm no politician,' said Soames.

'Keep the ring! The new formula. It's what we've been coming to unconsciously! And as to trade – to say we can't do without trading with this country or with that – bunkum, my dear Forsyte. The world's large – we can.'

'I don't know anything about that,' said Soames. 'I only know we must drop this foreign contract assurance.'

'Why not confine it to the ring countries? Instead of "balance of power", "keep the ring"! Really, it's an inspiration!'

Thus charged with inspiration, Soames said hastily:

'I leave you here, I'm going to my daughter's.'

'Ah! I'm going to my son's. Look at these poor devils!'

Down by the Embankment at Blackfriars a band of unemployed were trailing dismally with money-boxes.

'Revolution in the bud! There's one thing that's always forgotten, Forsyte, it's a great pity.'

'What's that?' said Soames, with gloom. The fellow would tittup all the way to Fleur's!

'Wash the working-class, put them in clean, pleasant-coloured jeans, teach 'em to speak like you and me, and there'd be an end of class feeling. It's all a matter of the senses. Wouldn't you rather share a bedroom with a clean, neat-clothed plumber's assistant who spoke and smelled like you than with a profiteer who dropped his aitches and reeked of opoponax? Of course you would.'

'Never tried,' said Soames, 'so don't know.'

'Pragmatist! But believe me, Forsyte – if the working class would concentrate on baths and accent instead of on their political and economic tosh, equality would be here in no time.'

'I don't want equality,' said Soames, taking his ticket to Westminster.

The 'tittupping' voice pursued him entering the tube lift.

'Aesthetic equality, Forsyte, if we had it, would remove the wish for any other. Did you ever catch an impecunious professor wishing he was the King?'

'No,' said Soames, opening his paper.

Chapter Eight

BICKET

◄◄‹›►

BENEATH its veneer of cheerful irresponsibility, the character
of Michael Mont had deepened during two years of anchorage
and continuity. He had been obliged to think of others; and his
time was occupied. Conscious, from the fall of the flag, that he
was on sufferance with Fleur, admitting as whole the half-truth:
'Il y a toujours un qui baise, et l'autre qui tend la joue,' he had
developed real powers of domestic consideration; and yet he did
not seem to redress the balance in his public or publishing
existence. He found the human side of his business too strong
for the monetary. Danby and Winter, however, were bearing up
against him, and showed, so far, no signs of the bankruptcy
prophesied for them by Soames on being told of the principles
which his son-in-law intended to introduce. No more in publishing than in any other walk of life was Michael finding it possible to work too much on principle. The field of action was so
strewn with facts – human, vegetable and mineral.

On this same Tuesday afternoon, having long tussled with
the price of those vegetable facts, paper and linen, he was
listening with his pointed ears to the plaint of a packer discovered with five copies of *Copper Coin* in his overcoat pocket,
and the too obvious intention of converting them to his own use.

Mr Danby had 'given him the sack' – he didn't deny that he
was going to sell them, but what would Mr Mont have done?
He owed rent – and his wife wanted nourishing after pneumonia – wanted it bad. 'Dash it!' thought Michael, 'I'd snoop
an edition to nourish Fleur after pneumonia!'

'And I can't live on my wages with prices what they are. I
can't, Mr Mont, so help me!'

Michael swivelled. 'But look here, Bicket, if we let you snoop

63

copies, all the packers will snoop copies; and if they do, where are Danby and Winter? In the cart. And, if they're in the cart, where are all of you? In the street. It's better that one of you should be in the street than that all of you should, isn't it?'

'Yes, sir, I quite see your point – it's reason; but I can't live on reason, the least thing knocks you out, when you're on the bread line. Ask Mr Danby to give me another chance.'

'Mr Danby always says that a packer's work is particularly confidential, because it's almost impossible to keep a check on it.'

'Yes, sir, I should feel that in future; but with all this unemployment and no reference, I'll never get another job. What about my wife?'

To Michael it was as if he had said: 'What about Fleur?' He began to pace the room; and the young man Bicket looked at him with large dolorous eyes. Presently he came to a standstill, with his hands deep plunged into his pockets and his shoulders hunched.

'I'll ask him,' he said; 'but I don't believe he will; he'll say it isn't fair on the others. You had five copies; it's pretty stiff, you know – means you've had 'em before, doesn't it? What?'

'Well, Mr Mont, anything that'll give me a chance, I don't mind confessin'. I have 'ad a few previous, and it's just about kept my wife alive. You've no idea what that pneumonia's like for poor people.'

Michael pushed his fingers through his hair.

'How old's your wife?'

'Only a girl – twenty.'

Twenty! Just Fleur's age!

'I'll tell you what I'll do, Bicket; I'll put it up to Mr Desert; if he speaks for you, perhaps it may move Mr Danby.'

'Well, Mr Mont, thank you – you're a gentleman, we all sy that.'

'Oh! hang it! But look here, Bicket, you were reckoning on those five copies. Take this to make up, and get your wife what's necessary. Only for goodness' sake don't tell Mr Danby.'

'Mr Mont, I wouldn't deceive you for the world – I won't sy a word, sir. And my wife – well!'

A sniff, a shuffle – Michael was alone, with his hands plunged deeper, his shoulders hunched higher. And suddenly he laughed. Pity! Pity was pop! It was all dam' funny. Here he was rewarding Bicket for snooping *Copper Coin*. A sudden longing possessed him to follow the little packer and see what he did with the two pounds – see whether 'the pneumonia' was real or a figment of the brain behind those dolorous eyes. Impossible, though! Instead he must ring up Wilfrid and ask him to put in a word with old Danby. His own word was no earthly. He had put it in too often! Bicket! Little one knew of anybody, life was deep and dark, and upside down! What was honesty? Pressure of life *versus* power of resistance – the result of that fight, when the latter won, was honesty! But why resist? Love thy neighbour as thyself – but not more! And wasn't it a darned sight harder for Bicket on two pounds a week to love him, than for him on twenty-four pounds a week to love Bicket? ...

'Hallo! ... That you, Wilfrid? ... Michael speaking. ... One of our packers has been sneaking copies of *Copper Coin*. He's "got the sack" – poor devil! I wondered if you'd mind putting in a word for him – old Dan won't listen to me ... yes, got a wife – Fleur's age; pneumonia, so he says. Won't do it again with yours anyway, insurance by common gratitude – what! ... Thanks, old man, awfully good of you – will you bob in, then? We can go round home together ... Oh! Well! You'll bob in anyway. Aurev!'

Good chap, old Wilfrid! Real good chap – underneath! Underneath – what?

Replacing the receiver, Michael saw a sudden great cloud of sights and scents and sounds, so foreign to the principles of his firm that he was in the habit of rejecting instantaneously every manuscript which dealt with them. The war might be 'off'; but it was still 'on' within Wilfrid, and himself. Taking up a tube, he spoke:

'Mr Danby in his room? Right! If he shows any signs of flitting, let me know at once. ...'

Between Michael and his senior partner a gulf was fixed, not less deep than that between two epochs, though partially filled in by Winter's middle-age and accommodating temperament. Michael had almost nothing against Mr Danby except that he was always right – Philip Norman Danby, of Sky House, Campden Hill, a man of sixty and some family, with a tall forehead, a preponderance of body to leg, and an expression both steady and reflective. His eyes were perhaps rather close together, and his nose rather thin, but he looked a handsome piece in his well-proportioned room. He glanced up from the formation of a correct judgement on a matter of advertisement when Wilfrid Desert came in.

'Well, Mr Desert, what can I do for you? Sit down!'

Desert did not sit down, but looked at the engravings, at his fingers, at Mr Danby, and said:

'Fact is, I want you to let that packer chap off, Mr Danby.'

'Packer chap. Oh! Ah! Bicket. Mont told you, I suppose?'

'Yes; he's got a young wife down with pneumonia.'

'They all go to our friend Mont with some tale or other, Mr Desert – he has a very soft heart. But I'm afraid I can't keep this man. It's a most insidious thing. We've been trying to trace a leak for some time.'

Desert leaned against the mantelpiece and stared into the fire.

'Well, Mr Danby,' he said, 'your generation may like the soft in literature, but you're precious hard in life. Ours won't look at softness in literature, but we're a deuced sight less hard in life.'

'I don't think it's hard,' said Mr Danby, 'only just.'

'Are you a judge of justice?'

'I hope so.'

'Try four years' hell, and have another go.'

'I really don't see the connexion. The experience you've been through, Mr Desert, was bound to be warping.'

Wilfrid turned and stared at him.

'Forgive my saying so, but sitting here and being just is much more warping. Life is pretty good purgatory, to all except about thirty per cent of grown-up people.'

Mr Danby smiled.

'We simply couldn't conduct our business, my dear young

man, without scrupulous honesty in everybody. To make no distinction between honesty and dishonesty would be quite unfair. You know that perfectly well.'

'I don't know anything perfectly well, Mr Danby; and I mistrust those who say they do.'

'Well, let us put it that there are rules of the game which must be observed, if society is to function at all.'

Desert smiled, too: 'Oh! hang rules! Do it as a favour to me. I wrote the rotten book.'

No trace of struggle showed in Mr Danby's face; but his deepset, close-together eyes shone a little.

'I should be only too glad, but it's a matter — well, of conscience, if you like. I'm not prosecuting the man. He must leave — that's all.'

Desert shrugged his shoulders.

'Well, good-bye!' and he went out.

On the mat was Michael in two minds.

'Well?'

'No go. The old blighter's too just.'

Michael stivered his hair.

'Wait in my room five minutes while I let the poor beggar know, then I'll come along.'

'No,' said Desert, 'I'm going the other way.'

Not the fact that Wilfrid was going the other way — he almost always was — but something in the tone of his voice and the look on his face obsessed Michael's imagination while he went downstairs to seek Bicket. Wilfrid was a rum chap — he went 'dark' so suddenly!

In the nether regions he asked:

'Bicket gone?'

'No, sir, there he is.'

There he was, in his shabby overcoat, with his pale narrow face, and his disproportionately large eyes, and his sloping shoulders.

'Sorry, Bicket, Mr Desert has been in, but it's no go.'

'No, sir?'

'Keep your pecker up, you'll get something.'

'I'm afryde not, sir. Well, I thank you very 'eartily; and I thank Mr Desert. Good night, sir; and good-bye!'

Michael watched him down the corridor, saw him waver into the dusky street.

'Jolly!' he said, and laughed. ...

The natural suspicions of Michael and his senior partner that a tale was being pitched were not in fact justified. Neither the wife nor the pneumonia had been exaggerated; and wavering away in the direction of Blackfriars Bridge, Bicket thought not of his turpitude nor of how just Mr Danby had been, but of what he should say to her. He should not, of course, tell her that he had been detected in stealing; he must say he had 'got the sack for cheeking the foreman'; but what would she think of him for doing that, when everything as it were depended on his not cheeking the foreman? This was one of those melancholy cases of such affection that he had been coming to his work day after day feeling as if he had 'left half his guts' behind him in the room where she lay, and when at last the doctor said to him:

'She'll get on now, but it's left her very run down – you must feed her up,' his anxiety had hardened into a resolution to have no more. In the next three weeks he had 'pinched' eighteen *Copper Coins*, including the five found in his overcoat. He had only 'pitched on' Mr Desert's book because it was 'easy sold', and he was sorry now that he hadn't pitched on someone else's. Mr Desert had been very decent. He stopped at the corner of the Strand, and went over his money. With the two pounds given him by Michael and his wages he had seventy-five shillings in the world, and going into the Stores he bought a meat jelly and a tin of Benger's food that could be made with water. With pockets bulging he took a bus, which dropped him at the corner of his little street on the Surrey side. His wife and he occupied the two ground floor rooms, at eight shillings a week, and he owed for three weeks. 'Py that!' he thought, 'and have a roof until she's well.' It would help him over the news, too, to show her a receipt for the rent and some good food. How lucky they had been careful to have no baby! He sought the basement. His landlady was doing the week's washing. She paused, in sheer surprise at such full and voluntary payment, and inquired after his wife.

'Doing nicely, thank you.'

'Well, I'm glad of that, it must be a relief to your mind.'

'It is,' said Bicket.

The landlady thought: 'He's a thread-paper – reminds me of a shrimp before you bile it, with those eyes.'

'Here's your receipt, and thank you. Sorry to 'ave seemed nervous about it, but times are 'ard.'

'They are,' said Bicket. 'So long!'

With the receipt and the meat jelly in his left hand, he opened the door of his front room.

His wife was sitting before a very little fire. Her bobbed black hair, crinkly towards the ends, had grown during her illness; it shook when she turned her head and smiled. To Bicket – not for the first time – that smile seemed queer, 'pathetic-like', mysterious – as if she saw things that one didn't see oneself. Her name was Victorine, and he said: 'Well, Vic? This jelly's a bit of all right, and I've pyde the rent.' He sat on the arm of the chair and she put her hand on his knee – her thin arm emerging blue-white from the dark dressing-gown.

'Well, Tony?'

Her face – thin and pale with those large dark eyes and beautifully formed eyebrows – was one that 'looked at you from somewhere; and when it looked at you – well! it got you right inside!'

It got him now and he said: 'How've you been breathin'?'

'All right – much better. I'll soon be out now.'

Bicket twisted himself round and joined his lips to hers. The kiss lasted some time, because all the feelings which he had not been able to express during the past three weeks to her or to anybody, got into it. He sat up again, 'sort of exhausted', staring at the fire, and said: 'News isn't bright – lost my job, Vic.'

'Oh! Tony! Why?'

Bicket swallowed.

'Fact is, things are slack, and they're reducin'.'

There had surged into his mind the certainty that sooner than tell her the truth he would put his head under the gas!

'Oh! dear! What shall we do, then?'

Bicket's voice hardened.

'Don't you worry – I'll get something;' and he whistled.

'But you liked that job.'

'Did I? I liked some o' the fellers; but as for the job – why, what was it? Wrappin' books up in a bysement all dy long. Let's have something to eat and get to bed early – I feel as if I could sleep for a week, now I'm shut of it.'

Getting their supper ready with her help, he carefully did not look at her face for fear it might 'get him agyne inside!' They had only been married a year, having made acquaintance on a tram, and Bicket often wondered what had made her take to him, eight years her senior and C3 during the war! And yet she must be fond of him, or she'd never look at him as she did.

'Sit down and try this jelly.'

He himself ate bread and margarine and drank cocoa, he seldom had any particular appetite.

'Shall I tell you what I'd like?' he said; 'I'd like Central Austrylia. We had a book in there about it; they sy there's quite a movement. I'd like some sun. I believe if we 'ad sun we'd both be twice the size we are. I'd like to see colour in your cheeks, Vic.'

'How much does it cost to get out there?'

'A lot more than we can ly hands on, that's the trouble. But I've been thinkin'. England's about done. There's too many like me.'

'No,' said Victorine: 'There aren't enough.'

Bicket looked at her face, then quickly at his plate.

'What myde you take a fancy to me?'

'Because you don't think first of yourself, that's why.'

'Used to before I knew you. But I'd do anything for you, Vic.'

'Have some of this jelly, then, it's awful good.'

Bicket shook his head.

70

'If we could wyke up in Central Austrylia,' he said. 'But there's only one thing certain, we'll wyke up in this blighted little room. Never mind, I'll get a job and earn the money yet.'

'Could we win it on a race?'

'Well, I've only got forty-seven bob all told, and if we lose it, where'll you be? You've got to feed up, you know. No, I must get a job.'

'They'll give you a good recommend, won't they?'

Bicket rose and stacked his plate and cup.

'They would, but that job's off – overstocked.'

Tell her the truth? Never! So help him!

In their bed, one of those just too wide for one and just not wide enough for two, he lay, with her hair almost in his mouth, thinking what to say to his Union, and how to go to work to get a job. And in his thoughts as the hours drew on he burned his boats. To draw his unemployment money he would have to tell his Union what the trouble was. Blow the Union! He wasn't going to be accountable to them! *He* knew why he'd pinched the books; but it was nobody else's business, nobody else could understand his feelings, watching her so breathless, pale and thin. Strike out for himself! And a million and a half out o' work! Well, he had a fortnight's keep, and something would turn up – and he might risk a bob or two and win some money, you never knew. She turned in her sleep. 'Yes,' he thought, 'I'd do it agyne ...'

Next day, after some hours on foot, he stood under the grey easterly sky in the grey street, before a plate-glass window protecting an assortment of fruits and sheaves of corn, lumps of metal, and brilliant blue butterflies, in the carefully golden light of advertised Australia. To Bicket, who had never been out of England, not often out of London, it was like standing outside Paradise. The atmosphere within the office itself was not so golden, and the money required considerable; but it brought Paradise nearer to take away pamphlets which almost burned his hands, they were so warm.

Later, he and she, sitting in the one armchair – advantage of being thin – pored over these alchemized pages and inhaled their glamour.

'D'you think it's true, Tony?'

'If it's thirty per cent true it's good enough for me. We just must get there somehow. Kiss me.'

From around the corner in the main road the rumbling of the trams and carts, and the rattling of their window-pane in the draughty dry easterly wind increased their feeling of escape into a gas-lit Paradise.

Chapter Nine

CONFUSION

◄◄-►►

T w o hours behind Bicket, Michael wavered towards home. Old Danby was right as usual – if you couldn't trust your packers, you might shut up shop! Away from Bicket's eyes, he doubted. Perhaps the chap hadn't a wife at all! Then Wilfrid's manner usurped the place of Bicket's morals. Old Wilfrid had been abrupt and queer the last three times of meeting. Was he boiling-up for verse?

He found Ting-a-ling at the foot of the stairs in a conservative attitude. 'I am not going up,' he seemed saying, 'until someone carries me – at the same time it is later than usual!'

'Where's your mistress, you heraldic little beast?'

Ting-a-ling snuffled. 'I could put up with it,' he implied, 'if *you* carried me – these stairs are laborious!'

Michael took him up. 'Let's go and find her.'

Squeezed under an arm harder than his mistress', Ting-a-ling stared as if with black-glass eyes; and the plume of his emergent tail quivered.

In the bedroom Michael dropped him so absent-mindedly that he went to his corner plume pendent, and crouched there in dudgeon.

Nearly dinner time and Fleur not in! Michael went over his sketchy recollection of her plans. Today she had been having Hubert Marsland and that Vertiginist – what was his name? – to lunch. There would have been fumes to clear off. Vertiginists – like milk – made carbonic acid gas in the lungs! Still! Half-past seven! What was happening tonight? Weren't they going to that play of L.S.D.'s? No – that was tomorrow! Was there conceivably nothing? If so, of course she would shorten her unoccupied time as much as possible. He made that reflection humbly. Michael had no illusions, he knew himself to be commonplace, with only a certain redeeming liveliness, and, of course, his affection for her. He even recognized that his affection was a weakness, tempting him to fussy anxieties, which on principle he restrained. To inquire, for instance, of Coaker or Philips – their man and their maid – when she had gone out, would be thoroughly against that principle. The condition of the world was such that Michael constantly wondered if his own affairs were worth paying attention to; but then the condition of the world was also such that sometimes one's own affairs seemed all that were worth paying attention to. And yet his affairs were, practically speaking, Fleur; and if he paid too much attention to them, he was afraid of annoying her.

He went into his dressing-room and undid his waistcoat.

'But no!' he thought; 'if she finds me "dressed" already, it'll put too much point on it.' So he did up his waistcoat and went downstairs again. Coaker was in the hall.

'Mr Forsyte and Sir Lawrence looked in about six, sir. Mrs Mont was out. What time shall I serve dinner?'

'Oh! about a quarter-past eight. I don't think we're going out.'

He went into the drawing-room and passing down its Chinese emptiness, drew aside the curtain. The square looked cold and dark and draughty; and he thought: 'Bicket – pneumonia – I hope she's got her fur coat.' He took out a cigarette and put it back. If she saw him at the window she would think him fussy; and he went up again to see if she had put on her fur!

Ting-a-ling, still couchant, greeted him plume dansetti arrested as at disappointment. Michael opened a wardrobe. She had! Good! He was taking a sniff round, when Ting-a-ling passed him trottant, and her voice said: 'Well, my darling!' Wishing that he was, Michael emerged from behind the wardrobe door. Heaven! She looked pretty, coloured by the wind! He stood rather wistfully silent.

'Hallo, Michael! I'm rather late. Been to the Club and walked home.'

Michael had a quite unaccountable feeling that there was suppression in that statement. He also suppressed, and said: 'I was just looking to see that you'd got your fur, it's beastly cold. Your dad and Bart have been and went away fasting.'

Fleur shed her coat and dropped into a chair. 'I'm tired. Your ears are sticking up so nicely tonight, Michael.'

Michael went on his knees and joined his hands behind her waist. Her eyes had a strange look, a scrutiny which held him in suspense, a little startled.

'If *you* got pneumonia,' he said, 'I should go clean out of curl.'

'Why on earth should I?'

'You don't know the connexion – never mind, it wouldn't interest you. We're not going out, are we?'

'Of course we are. It's Alison's monthly.'

'Oh! Lord! If you're tired we could cut that.'

'My dear! Impos.! She's got all sorts of people coming.'

Stifling a disparagement, he sighed out: 'Right-o! War-paint?'

'Yes, white waistcoat. I like you in white waistcoats.'

Cunning little wretch? He squeezed her waist and rose. Fleur laid a light stroke on his hand, and he went into his dressing-room comforted. ...

But Fleur sat still for at least five minutes – not precisely 'a prey to conflicting emotions', but the victim of very considerable confusion. *Two* men within the last hour had done this thing – knelt at her knees and joined their fingers behind her waist. Undoubtedly she had been rash to go to Wilfrid's rooms. The moment she got there she had perceived how entirely unprepared she really was to commit herself to what was physical. True he had done no more than Michael. But – Goodness! – she had seen the fire she was playing with, realized what torment he was in. She had strictly forbidden him to say a word to Michael, but intuitively she knew that in his struggle between loyalties she could rely on nothing. Confused, startled, touched, she could not help a pleasant warmth in being so much loved by two men at once, nor an itch of curiosity about the upshot. And she sighed. She had added to her collection of experiences – but how to add further without breaking up the collection, and even perhaps the collector, she could not see.

After her words to Wilfrid before the Eve: 'You will be a fool to go – wait!' she had known he would expect something before long. Often he had asked her to come and pass judgement on his 'junk'. A month, even a week, ago she would have gone without thinking more than twice about it, and discussed his 'junk' with Michael afterwards! But now she thought it over many times, and but for the fumes of lunch, and the feeling, engendered by the society of the 'Vertiginist', of Amabel Nazing, of Linda Frewe, that scruples of any kind were 'stuffy', sensations of all sorts 'the thing', she would probably still have been thinking it over now. When they departed, she had taken a deep breath and her telephone receiver from the Chinese tea-chest.

If Wilfrid were going to be in at half-past five, she would come and see his 'junk'.

His answer: 'My God! Will you?' almost gave her pause. But dismissing hesitation with the thought: 'I will be Parisian – Proust!' she had started for her Club. Three-quarters of an hour, with no more stimulant than three cups of China tea, three back numbers of the *Glass of Fashion*, three back views of country members 'dead in chairs', had sent her forth a careful quarter of an hour behind her time.

On the top floor Wilfrid was standing in his open doorway, pale as a soul in purgatory. He took her hand gently, and drew her in. Fleur thought with a little thrill: 'Is this what it's like?

75

Du côté de chez Swann!' Freeing her hand, she began at once to flutter round the 'junk', clinging to it piece by piece.

Old English 'junk' rather manorial, with here and there an Eastern or First Empire bit, collected by some bygone Desert, nomadic, or attached to the French court. She was afraid to sit down, for fear that he might begin to follow the authorities; nor did she want to resume the intense talk of the Tate Gallery. 'Junk' was safe, and she only looked at him in those brief intervals when he was not looking at her. She knew she was not playing the game according to 'La Garçonne' and Amabel Nazing; that, indeed, she was in danger of going away without having added to her sensations. And she couldn't help being sorry for Wilfrid; his eyes yearned after her, his lips were bitter to look at. When at last from sheer exhaustion of 'junk' she sat down, he had flung himself at her feet. Half hypnotized, with her knees against his chest, as safe as she could hope for, she really felt the tragedy of it – his horror of himself, his passion for herself. It was painful, deep; it did not fit in with what she had been led to expect; it was not in the period, and how – how was she to get away without more pain to him and to herself? When she *had* got away, with one kiss received but not answered, she realized that she had passed through a quarter of an hour of real life, and was not at all sure that she liked it. ... But now, safe in her own room, undressing for Alison's monthly, she felt curious as to what she would have been feeling if things had gone as far as was proper according to the authorities. Surely she had not experienced one-tenth of the thoughts or sensations that would have been assigned to her in any advanced piece of literature! It had been disillusioning, or else she was deficient, and Fleur could not bear to feel deficient. And, lightly powdering her shoulders, she bent her thoughts towards Alison's monthly.

Though Lady Alison enjoyed an occasional encounter with the younger generation, the Aubrey Greenes and Linda Frewes of this life were not conspicuous by their presence at her gatherings. Nesta Gorse, indeed, had once attended, but one legal and two literary politicos who had been in contact with her, had complained of it afterwards. She had, it seemed, rent little spiked holes in the garments of their self-esteem. Sibley Swan would have been welcome, for his championship of the past, but he seemed, so far, to have turned up his nose and looked down it. So it was not the intelligentsia, but just intellectual society, which was gathered there when Fleur and Michael entered, and the conversation had all the sparkle and all the '*savoir faire*' incidental to talk about art and letters by those who – as Michael put it – 'fortunately had not to *faire*.'

'All the same, these are the guys,' he muttered in Fleur's ear, 'who make the names of artists and writers. What's the stunt, tonight?'

It appeared to be the London *début* of a lady who sang Balkan folk songs. But in a refuge to the right were four tables set out for bridge. They were already filled. Among those who still stood listening, were, here and there, a Gurdon Minho, a society painter and his wife, a sculptor looking for a job. Fleur, wedged between Lady Feynte, the painter's wife, and Gurdon Minho himself, began planning an evasion. There – yes, there was Mr Chalfont! At Lady Alison's, Fleur, an excellent judge of '*milieu*', never wasted her time on artists and writers – she could meet *them* anywhere. Here she intuitively picked out the biggest 'bug', politico-literary, and waited to pin him. Absorbed in the idea of pinning Mr Chalfont, she overlooked a piece of drama passing without.

Michael had clung to the top of the stairway, in no mood for talk and skirmish; and, leaning against the balustrade, wasp-thin in his long white waistcoat, with hands deep thrust into his trousers' pockets, he watched the turns and twists of Fleur's white neck, and listened to the Balkan songs, with a sort of blankness in his brain. The word: 'Mont!' startled him. Wilfrid was standing just below. Mont? He had not been that to Wilfrid for two years!

'Come down here.'

On that half-landing was a bust of Lionel Charwell, K.C., by

Boris Strumolowski, in the genre he had cynically adopted when June Forsyte gave up supporting his authentic but unrewarded genius. It had been almost indistinguishable from any of the other busts in that year's Academy, and was used by the young Charwells to chalk moustaches on.

Beside this object Desert leaned against the wall with his eyes closed. His face was a study to Michael.

'What's wrong, Wilfrid?'

Desert did not move. 'You've got to know – I'm in love with Fleur.'

'What!'

'I'm not going to play the snake. You're up against me. Sorry, but there it is! You can let fly!' His face was death-pale, and its muscles twitched. In Michael, it was the mind, the heart that twitched. What a very horrible, strange, 'too beastly' moment! His best friend – his best man! Instinctively he dived for his cigarette-case – instinctively handed it to Desert. Instinctively they both took cigarettes, and lighted each other's. Then Michael said:

'Fleur – knows?'

Desert nodded: 'She doesn't know I'm telling you – wouldn't have let me. You've nothing against her – yet.' And, still with closed eyes, he added: 'I couldn't help it.'

It was Michael's own subconscious thought! Natural! Natural! Fool not to see how natural! Then something shut-to within him, and he said: 'Decent of you to tell me; but – aren't you going to clear out?'

Desert's shoulders writhed against the wall.

'I thought so; but it seems not.'

'Seems? I don't understand.'

'If I knew for certain I'd no chance – but I don't,' and he suddenly looked at Michael: 'Look here, it's no good keeping gloves on. I'm desperate, and I'll take her from you if I can.'

'Good God!' said Michael. 'It's the limit!'

'Yes! Rub it in! But, I tell you, when I think of you going home with her, and of myself,' he gave a dreadful little laugh, 'I advise you *not* to rub it in.'

'Well,' said Michael, 'as this isn't a Dostoievsky novel, I suppose there's no more to be said.'

Desert moved from the wall and laid his hand on the bust of Lionel Charwell.

'You realize, at least, that I've gone out of my way – perhaps dished myself – by telling you. I've not bombed without declaring war.'

'No,' said Michael dully.

'You can chuck my books over to some other publisher.' Michael shrugged.

'Good night, then,' said Desert. 'Sorry for being so primitive.'

Michael looked straight into his 'best man's' face. There was no mistaking its expression of bitter despair. He made a half-movement with his hand, uttered half the word 'Wilfrid,' and, as Desert went down, he went upstairs.

Back in his place against the balustrade, he tried to realize that life was a laughing matter, and couldn't. His position required a serpent's cunning, a lion's courage, a dove's gentleness: he was not conscious of possessing such proverbial qualities. If Fleur had loved him as he loved her, he would have had for Wilfrid a real compassion. It was so natural to fall in love with Fleur! But she didn't – oh! no, she didn't! Michael had one virtue – if virtue it be – a moderate opinion of himself, a disposition to think highly of his friends. He had thought highly of Desert; and – odd! – he still did not think lowly of him. Here was his friend trying to do him mortal injury, to alienate the affection – more honestly, the toleration – of his wife; and yet he did not think him a cad. Such leniency, he knew, was hopeless; but the doctrines of free-will, and free contract, were not to him mere literary conceptions, they were part of his nature. To apply duress, however desirable, would not be on his cards. And something like despair ravaged the heart of him, watching Fleur's ingratiating little tricks with the great Gerald Chalfont. If she left him for Wilfrid! But surely – no – her father, her house, her dog, her friends, her – her collection of – of – she would not – could not give *them* up? But suppose she kept everything, Wilfrid included! No, no!

She wouldn't! Only for a second did that possibility blur the natural loyalty of his mind.

Well, what to do? Tell her – talk the thing out? Or wait and watch? For what? Without deliberate spying, he could not watch. Desert would come to their house no more. No! Either complete frankness; or complete ignoring – and that meant living with the sword of Damocles above his head! No! Complete frankness! And not do anything that seemed like laying a trap! He passed his hand across a forehead that was wet. If only they were at home, away from that squalling and these cultivated jackanapes! Could he go in and hook her out? Impossible without some reason! Only his brain-storm for a reason! He must just bite on it. The singing ceased. Fleur was looking round. Now she would beckon! On the contrary, she came towards him. He could not help the cynical thought: 'She's hooked old Chalfont!' He loved her, but he knew her little weaknesses. She came up and took hold of his sleeve.

'I've had enough, Michael, let's slip off; d'you mind?'

'Quick!' he said, 'before they spot us!'

In the cold air outside he thought: 'Now? Or in her room?'

'I think,' said Fleur, 'that Mr Chalfont is overrated – he's nothing but a mental yawn. He's coming to lunch tomorrow week.'

Not now – in her room!

'Whom do you think to meet him, besides Alison?'

'Nothing jazzy.'

'Of course not; but it must be somebody intriguing, Michael. Bother! sometimes I think it isn't worth it.'

Michael's heart stood still. Was that a portent – sign of 'the primitive' rising within his adored practitioner of social arts? An hour ago he would have said:

'You're right, my child; it jolly well isn't!' But now – any sign of change was ominous! He slipped his arm in hers.

'Don't worry, we'll snare the just-right cuckoos, somehow.'

'A Chinese Minister would be perfect,' mused Fleur, 'with Minho and Bart – four men – two women – cosy. I'll talk to Bart.'

Michael had opened their front door. She passed him; he lingered to see the stars, the plane trees, a man's figure motionless, collared to the eyes, hatted down to them. 'Wilfrid!' he thought: 'Spain! Why Spain? And all poor devils who are in distress – the heart – oh! darn the heart!' He closed the door.

But soon he had another to open, and never with less enthusiasm. Fleur was sitting on the arm of a chair, in the dim lavender pyjamas she sometimes wore just to keep in with things, staring at the fire. Michael stood, looking at her and at his own reflection beyond in one of the five mirrors – white and black, the pierrot pyjamas she had bought him. 'Figures in a play,' he thought, 'figures in a play! Is it real?' He moved forward and sat on the chair's other arm.

'Hang it!' he muttered. 'Wish I were Antinous!' And he slipped from the arm into the chair, to be behind her face, if she wanted to hide it from him.

'Wilfrid's been telling me,' he said quietly.

Off his chest! What now? He saw the blood come flushing into her neck and check.

'Oh! What business – how do you mean "telling you"?'

'Just that he's in love with you – nothing more – there's nothing more to tell, is there?' And drawing his feet up on to the chair, he clasped his hands hard round his knees. Already – already he had asked a question! Bite on it! Bite on it! And he shut his eyes.

'Of course,' said Fleur, very slowly, 'there's nothing more. If Wilfrid chooses to be so silly.'

Chooses! The word seemed unjust to one whose own 'silliness' was so recent – so enduring! And – curious! his heart wouldn't bound. Surely it ought to have bounded at her words!

'Is that the end of Wilfrid, then?'

'The end? I don't know.'

Ah! Who knew anything – when passion was about?

'Well,' he said, holding himself hard together, 'don't forget I love you awfully!'

He saw her eyelids flicker, her shoulders shrugging.

'Am I likely to?'

Bitter, cordial, simple – which? Suddenly her hands came round and took him by the ears. Holding them fast she looked down at him, and laughed. And again his heart *would* not bound. If she did not lead him by the nose, she – ! But he clutched her to him in the chair. Lavender and white and black confused – she returned his kiss. But from the heart? Who knew? Not Michael.

Chapter Ten

PASSING OF A SPORTSMAN

◄‹·›►

S o a m e s, disappointed of his daughter, said: 'I'll wait,' and took his seat in the centre of the jade green settee, oblivious of Ting-a-ling before the fire, sleeping off the attentions of Amabel Nazing, who had found him 'just too cunning'. Grey and composed, with one knee over the other, and a line between his eyes, he thought of Elderson and the condition of the world, and of how there was always something. And the more he thought, the more he wondered why he had ever been such a flat as to go on to a Board which had anything to do with foreign contracts. All the old wisdom that in the nineteenth century had consolidated British wealth, all the Forsyte philosophy of attending to one's own business, and taking no risks, the close-fibred national individualism which refused to commit the country to chasing this wild goose or that, held within him silent demonstration. Britain was on the wrong tack politically to try and influence the Continent, and the P.P.R.S. on the wrong tack monetarily to insure business outside Britain. The special instinct of his breed yearned for resumption of the straight and private path. Never meddle with what you couldn't control! 'Old Mont' had said: 'Keep the ring!' Nothing of the sort: Mind one's own business! That was the real 'formula'. He became conscious of his calf – Ting-a-ling was sniffing at his trousers.

'Oh!' said Soames. 'It's you!'

Placing his forepaws against the settee, Ting-a-ling licked the air.

'Pick you up?' said Soames. 'You're too long.' And again he felt that faint warmth of being liked.

'There's something about me that appeals to him,' he thought, taking him by the scruff and lifting him on to a cushion. 'You and I,' the little dog seemed saying with his stare – Chinese little object! The Chinese knew what they were about, they had minded their own business for five thousand years!

'I shall resign,' thought Soames. But what about Winifred, and Imogen, and some of the Rogers and Nicholases who had been putting money into this thing because he was a director? He wished they wouldn't follow him like a lot of sheep! He rose from the settee. It was no good waiting, he would walk on to Green Street and talk to Winifred at once. She would have to sell again, though the shares had dropped a bit. And without taking leave of Ting-a-ling, he went out.

All this last year he had almost enjoyed life. Having somewhere to come and sit and receive a certain sympathy once at least a week, as in old days at Timothy's, was of incalculable advantage to his spirit. In going from home Fleur had taken most of his heart with her; but Soames had found it almost an advantage to visit his heart once a week rather than to have it always about. There were other reasons conducing to light-heartedness. That diabolical foreign chap, Prosper Profond, had long been gone he didn't know where, and his wife had been decidedly less restive and sarcastic ever since. She had taken up a thing they called Coué, and grown stouter. She used the car a great deal. Altogether she was more domestic. Then, too, he had become reconciled to Gauguin – a little slump in that painter had convinced him that he was still worth attention, and he had bought three more. Gauguin would rise again! Soames almost regretted his intuition of that second coming, for he had quite taken to the chap. His colour, once you got used to it, was very attractive. One picture, especially, which meant nothing so far as he could see, had a way of making you keep your eyes on it. He even felt uneasy when he thought of having to part with the thing at an enhanced price. But, most of all, he had been feeling so well, enjoying a recrudescence of youth in regard to Annette, taking more pleasure in what he ate, while his mind dwelt almost complacently on the state of money. The pound going up in value; Labour quiet! And now they had got rid of that Jack-o'-lantern, they might look for some years of solid Conservative administration. And to think, as he did, stepping across St James's Park towards Green Street, that he had gone and put his foot into a concern which he could not control, made him feel – well, as if the devil had been in it!

In Piccadilly he moused along on the Park side, taking his customary look up at the 'Iseeum' Club. The curtains were drawn, and chinks of light glowed, long and cosy. And that reminded him – someone had said George Forsyte was ill. Certainly he had not seen him in the bay window for months past. Well, George had always eaten and drunk too much. He crossed over and passed beneath the Club; and a sudden feeling – he didn't know what – a longing for his own past, a sort of nostalgia – made him stop and mount the steps.

'Mr George Forsyte in the Club?'

The janitor stared, a grey-haired, long-faced chap, whom he had known from away back in the eighties.

'Mr Forsyte, sir,' he said, 'is very ill indeed. They say he won't recover, sir.'

'What?' said Soames. 'Nobody told me that.'

'He's very bad – *very* bad indeed. It's the heart.'

'The heart! Where is he?'

'At his rooms, sir; just round the corner. They say the doctors have given him up. He *will* be missed here. Forty years I've known him. One of the old school, and a wonderful judge of wine and horses. We none of us last for ever, they say, but I never thought to see him out. Bit too full-blooded, sir, and that's a fact.'

With a slight shock Soames realized that he had never known where George lived, so utterly anchored had he seemed to that bay window above.

'Just give me the number of his rooms,' he said.

'Belville Row – No. 11, sir; I'm sure I hope you'll find him better. I shall miss his jokes – I shall, indeed.'

Turning the corner into Belville Row, Soames made a rapid calculation. George was sixty-six, only one year younger than himself! If George was really *in extremis* it would be quite unnatural! 'Comes of not leading a careful life,' he thought; 'always rackety – George! When was it I made his will?' So far as he remembered, George had left his money to his brothers and sisters – no one else to leave it to. The feeling of kinship stirred in Soames, the instinct of family adjustment. George and he had never got on – opposite poles of temperament – still he would have to be buried, and who would see to it if not Soames, who had seen to so many Forsyte burials in his time? He recalled the nickname George had once given him, 'the undertaker'! H'm! Here was poetical justice! Belville Row! Ah! No. 11 – regular bachelor-looking place! And putting his hand up to the bell, he thought: 'Women!' What had George done about women all his life?

His ring was answered by a man in a black cut-away coat with a certain speechless reticence.

'My cousin, Mr George Forsyte? How is he?'

The man compressed his lips.

'Not expected to last the night, sir.'

Soames felt a little clutch beneath his Jaeger vest.

'Conscious?'

'Yes, sir.'

'Could you show him my card? He might possibly like to see me.'

'Will you wait in here, sir?' Soames passed into a low room panelled up to the level of a man's chest, and above that line decorated with prints. George – a collector! Soames had never supposed he had it in him! On those walls, wherever the eye roved, were prints coloured and uncoloured, old and new, depicting the sports of racing and prize-fighting! Hardly an inch of the red wall space visible! About to examine them for marks of value, Soames saw that he was not alone. A woman – age uncertain in the shaded light – was sitting in a very high-backed chair before the fire with her elbow on the arm of it, and a handkerchief held to her face. Soames looked at her, and his nostrils moved in a stealthy sniff. 'Not a lady,' he thought. 'Ten to one but there'll be complications.' The muffled voice of the cut-away man said:

'I'm to take you in, sir.' Soames passed his hand over his face and followed.

The bedroom he now entered was in curious contrast. The whole of one wall was occupied by an immense piece of furniture, all cupboards and drawers. Otherwise there was nothing in the room but a dressing-table with silver accoutrements, an electric radiator alight in the fireplace, and a bed opposite. Over the fireplace was a single picture, at which Soames glanced mechanically. What! Chinese! A large whitish sidelong monkey, holding the rind of a squeezed fruit in its outstretched paw. Its whiskered face looked back at him with brown, almost human eyes. What on earth had made his inartistic cousin buy a thing like that and put it up to face his bed? He turned and looked at the bed's occupant. 'The only sportsman of the lot', as Montague Dartie in his prime had called him, lay with his swollen form outlined beneath a thin quilt. It gave Soames quite a turn to see that familiar beef-coloured face pale and puffy as a moon, with dark corrugated circles round eyes which still had their japing stare. A voice, hoarse and subdued, but with the old Forsyte timbre, said:

'Hallo, Soames! Come to measure me for my coffin?'

Soames put the suggestion away with a movement of his hand; he felt queer looking at that travesty of George. They had never got on, but – !

And in his flat, unemotional voice he said:

'Well, George! You'll pick up yet. You're no age. Is there anything I can do for you?'

A grin twitched George's pallid lips.

'Make me a codicil. You'll find paper in the dressing-table drawer.'

Soames took out a sheet of 'Iseeum' Club notepaper. Standing at the table, he inscribed the opening words of a codicil with his stylographic pen, and looked round at George. The words came with a hoarse relish.

'My three screws to young Val Dartie, because he's the only Forsyte that knows a horse from a donkey.' A throaty chuckle sounded ghastly in the ears of Soames. 'What have you said?'

Soames read: 'I hereby leave my three racehorses to my kinsman, Valerius Dartie, of Wansdon, Sussex, because he has special knowledge of horses.'

Again the throaty chuckle. 'You're a dry, file, Soames. Go on. To Milly Moyle, of 12, Claremont Grove, twelve thousand pounds, free of legacy duty.'

Soames paused on the verge of a whistle.

The woman in the next room!

The japing in George's eyes had turned to brooding gloom.

'It's a lot of money,' Soames could not help saying.

George made a faint choleric sound.

'Write it down, or I'll leave her the lot.'

Soames wrote. 'Is that all?'

'Yes. Read it!'

Soames read. Again he heard that throaty chuckle.

'That's a pill. You won't let *that* into the papers. Get that chap in, and you and he can witness.'

Before Soames reached the door, it was opened and the man himself came in.

'The – er – vicar, sir,' he said in a deprecating voice, 'has called. He wants to know if you would like to see him.'

George turned his face, his fleshy grey eyes rolled.

'Give him my compliments,' he said, 'and say I'll see him at the funeral.'

With a bow the man went out, and there was silence.

'Now,' said George, 'get him in again. I don't know when the flag'll fall.'

Soames beckoned the man in. When the codicil was signed and the man gone, George spoke :

'Take it, and see she gets it. I can trust you, that's one thing about you, Soames.'

Soames pocketed the codicil with a very queer sensation.

'Would you like to see her again?' he said.

George stared up at him a long time before he answered.

'No. What's the good? Give me a cigar from that drawer.'

Soames opened the drawer.

'Ought you?' he said.

George grinned. 'Never in my life done what I ought; not going to begin now. Cut it for me.'

Soames nipped the end of the cigar. 'Shan't give him a match,' he thought. 'Can't take the responsibility.' But George did not ask for a match. He lay quite still, the unlighted cigar between his pale lips, the curved lids down over his eyes.

'Good-bye,' he said, 'I'm going to have a snooze.'

'Good-bye,' said Soames. 'I – I hope – you – you'll soon –'

George reopened his eyes – fixed, sad, jesting, they seemed to quench the shams of hope and consolation. Soames turned hastily and went out. He felt bad, and almost unconsciously turned again into the sitting-room. The woman was still in the same attitude; the same florid scent was in the air. Soames took up the umbrella he had left there, and went out.

'This is my telephone number,' he said to the servant waiting in the corridor; 'let me know.'

The man bowed.

Soames turned out of Belville Row. Never had he left George's presence without the sense of being laughed at. Had he been laughed at now? Was that codicil George's last joke? If he had not gone in this afternoon, would George ever have made it, leaving a third of his property away from his family to that florid woman in the high-backed chair? Soames was beset by a sense of mystery. How could a man joke at death's door? It was, in a way, heroic. Where would he be buried? Somebody would know – Francie or Eustace. And what would they think when they came to know about that woman in the chair — twelve thousand pounds! 'If I can get hold of that white monkey, I will,' he thought suddenly. 'It's a good thing.' The monkey's eyes, the squeezed-out fruit — was life all a bitter jest and George deeper than himself? He rang the Green Street bell.

Mrs Dartie was very sorry, but Mrs Cardigan had called for her to dine and make a fourth at the play.

Soames went in to dinner alone. At the polished board below which Montague Dartie had now and again slipped, if not quite slept, he dined and brooded. 'I can trust you, that's one thing about you, Soames.' The words flattered and yet stung him. The depths of that sardonic joke! To give him a family shock and trust him to carry the shock out! George had never cared twelve thousand pounds for a woman who smelled of patchouli. No! It was a final gibe at his family, the Forsytes, at Soames himself! Well! one by one those who had injured or gibed at him — Irene, Bosinney, old and young Jolyon, and now George, had met their fates. Dead, dying, or in British Columbia! He saw again his cousin's eyes above that unlighted cigar, fixed, sad, jesting — poor devil! He got up from the table, and nervously drew aside the curtains. The night was fine and cold. What happened to one — after? George used to say that he had been Charles the Second's cook in a former existence! But reincarnation was all nonsense, weak-minded theorizing! Still, one would be glad to hold on if one could, after one was gone. Hold on, and be near Fleur! What noise was that? Gramophone going in the kitchen! When the cat was away, the mice —! People were all alike — take what they could get, and give as little as they could for it. Well! he would smoke a cigarette. Lighting it at a candle — Winifred dined by candlelight, it was the 'mode' again — he thought: 'Has he still got that cigar between his teeth?' A funny fellow, George — all his days a funny fellow! He watched a ring of smoke he had made without intending to — very blue, he never inhaled! Yes! George had lived too fast, or he would not have been dying twenty years before his time — too fast! Well, there it was, and he wished he had a cat to talk to! He took a little monster off the mantelboard. Picked up by his nephew Benedict in an Eastern bazaar the year after the War, it had green eyes – 'Not emeralds,' thought Soames, 'some cheap stone!'

'The telephone for you, sir.'

He went into the hall and took up the receiver.

'Yes?'

'Mr Forsyte has passed away, sir – in his sleep, the doctor says.'

'Oh!' said Soames: 'Had he a cig –? Many thanks.' He hung up the receiver.

Passed away! And, with a nervous movement, he felt for the codicil in his breast pocket.

Chapter Eleven

VENTURE

◄◄-►►

FOR a week Bicket had seen 'the job', slippery as an eel, evasive as a swallow, for ever passing out of reach. A pound for keep, and three shillings invested on a horse, and he was down to twenty-four bob. The weather had turned sou'-westerly and Victorine had gone out for the first time. That was something off his mind, but the cramp of the unemployed sensation, that fearful craving for the means of mere existence, a protesting, agonizing anxiety, was biting into the very flesh of his spirit. If he didn't get a job within a week or two, there would be nothing for it but the work-house, or the gas. 'The gas,' thought Bicket, 'if she will, I will. I'm fed up. After all, what is it? In her arms I wouldn't mind.' Instinct, however, that it was not so easy as all that to put one's head under the gas, gave him a brain-wave that Monday night. Balloons – that chap in Oxford Street to-day! Why not? He still had the capital for a flutter in them, and no hawker's licence needed. His brain, working like a squirrel in the small hours, grasped the great, the incalculable advantage of coloured balloons over all other forms of commerce. You couldn't miss the man who sold them – there he was for every eye to see, with his many radiant circumferences dangling in front of him! Not much profit in them, he had gathered – a penny on a sixpenny globe of coloured air, a penny on every three small twopenny globes; still their salesman was alive, and probably had pitched him a poor tale for fear of making his profession seem too attractive. Over the Bridge, just where the traffic – no, up by St Paul's! He knew a passage where he could stand back a yard or two, like that chap in Oxford Street! But to the girl sleeping beside him he said nothing. No word to her till he had thrown the die. It meant gambling with his last penny. For a bare living he would have to sell – why, three dozen big and four dozen small balloons a day would only be twenty-six shillings a week profit, unless that chap was kidding. Not much towards 'Austrylia' out of that! And not a career – Victorine would have a shock! But it was neck or nothing now – he must try it, and in off hours go on looking for a job.

Our thin capitalist, then, with four dozen big and seven dozen small on a tray, two shillings in his pocket, and little in his stomach, took his stand off St Paul's at two o'clock next day. Slowly he blew up and tied the necks of two large and three small, magenta, green and blue, till they dangled before him. Then with the smell of rubber in his nostrils, and protruding eyes, he stood back on the kerb and watched the stream go by. It gratified him to see that most people turned to look at him. But the first person to address him was a policeman, with:

'I'm not sure you can stand there.'

Bicket did not answer, his throat felt too dry. He had heard of the police. Had he gone the wrong way to work? Suddenly he gulped, and said: 'Give us a chance, constable; I'm right on my bones. If I'm in the way, I'll stand anywhere you like. This is new to me, and two bob's all I've got left in the world besides a wife.'

The constable, a big man, looked him up and down. 'Well, we'll see. I shan't make trouble for you if no one objects.'

Bicket's gaze deepened thankfully.

'I'm much obliged,' he said; 'tyke one for your little girl – to please me.'

'I'll buy one,' said the policeman, 'and give you a start. I go off duty in an hour, you 'ave it ready – a big one, magenta.'

He moved away. Bicket could see him watching. Edging into the gutter, he stood quite still; his large eyes clung to every face that passed; and, now and then, his thin fingers nervously touched his wares. If Victorine could see him! All the spirit within him mounted. By Golly! he would get out of this somehow into the sun, into a life that was a life!

He had been standing there nearly two hours, shifting from foot to unaccustomed foot, and had sold four big and five small – sixpenny worth of profit – when Soames, who had changed his route to spite those fellows who couldn't get past William Gouldyng, Ingerer, came by on his way to the P.P.R.S. board. Startled by a timid murmur: 'Balloon, sir, best quality,' he looked round from that contemplation of St Paul's which had been his lifelong habit, and stopped in sheer surprise.

'Balloon!' he said. 'What should I want with a balloon?'

Bicket smiled. Between those green and blue and orange globes and Soames's grey self-containment there was incongruity which even he could appreciate.

'Children like 'em – no weight, sir, waistcoat pocket.'

'I dare say,' said Soames, 'but I've no children.'

'Grandchildren, sir.'

'Nor any grandchildren.'

'Thank you, sir.'

Soames gave him one of those rapid glances with which he was accustomed to gauge the character of the impecunious. 'A poor, harmless little rat!' he thought. 'Here, give me two – how much?'

'A shilling, sir, and much obliged.'

'You can keep the change,' said Soames hurriedly, and passed on, astonished. Why on earth he had bought the things, and for more than double their price, he could not conceive. He did not recollect such a thing having happened to him before. Extremely peculiar ! And suddenly he realized why. The fellow had been humble, mild – to be encouraged, in these days of Communistic bravura. After all, the little chap was – was on the side of Capital, had invested in those balloons ! Trade ! And, raising his eyes towards St Paul's again, he stuffed the nasty-feeling things down into his overcoat pocket. Somebody would be taking them out, and wondering what was the matter with him ! Well, he had other things to think of ! ...

Bicket, however, stared after him, elated. Two hundred and fifty odd per cent profit on those two – that was something like. The feeling, that not enough women were passing him here, became less poignant – after all, women knew the value of money, no extra shillings out of them ! If only some more of these shiny-hatted old millionaires would come along !

At six o'clock, with a profit of three and eightpence, to which Soames had contributed just half, he began to add the sighs of deflating balloons to his own; untying them with passionate care he watched his coloured hopes one by one collapse, and stored them in the drawer of his tray. Taking it under his arm, he moved his tired legs in the direction of the Bridge. In a full day he might make four to five shillings – Well, it would just keep them alive, and something might turn up ! He was his own master, anyway, accountable neither to employer nor to union. That knowledge gave him a curious lightness inside, together with the fact that he had eaten nothing since breakfast.

'Wonder if he was an alderman,' he thought; 'they say those aldermen live on turtle soup.' Nearing home, he considered nervously what to do with the tray? How prevent Victorine from knowing that he had joined the ranks of Capital, and spent his day in the gutter? Ill luck ! She was at the window ! He must put a good face on it. And he went in whistling.

'What's that, Tony?' she said, pointing to the tray.

'Ah ! ha ! Great stunt – this ! Look 'ere !'

Taking a balloon out from the tray, he blew. He blew with a desperation he had not yet put into the process. They said the things would swell to five feet in circumference. He felt somehow that if he could get it to attain those proportions, it would soften everything. Under his breath the thing blotted out Victorine, and the room, till there was just the globe of coloured air. Nipping its neck between thumb and finger, he held it up, and said:

'There you are; not bad value for sixpence, old girl!' and he peered round it. Lord, she was crying! He let the 'blymed' thing go; it floated down, the air slowly evaporating till a little crinkled wreck rested on the dingy carpet. Clasping her heaving shoulders, he said desperately:

'Cheerio, my dear, don't quarrel with bread and butter. I shall get a job, this is just to tide us over. I'd do a lot worse than that for you. Come on, and get my tea, I'm hungry, blowin' up those things.'

She stopped crying, looked up, said nothing – mysterious with those big eyes! You'd say she had thoughts! But what they were Bicket could not tell. Under the stimulus of tea, he achieved a certain bravado about his new profession. To be your own master! Go out when you liked, come home when you liked – lie in bed with Vic if he jolly well pleased. A lot in that! And there rose in Bicket something truly national, something free and happy-go-lucky, resenting regular work, enjoying a spurt, and a laze-off, craving independence – something that accounted for the national life, the crowds of little shops, of middlemen, casual workers, tramps, owning their own souls in their own good time, and damning the consequences – something inherent in the land, the race, before the Saxons and their conscience and their industry came in – something that believed in swelling and collapsing coloured air, demanded pickles and high flavours without nourishment – yes, all that something exulted above Bicket's kipper and his tea, good and strong. He would rather sell balloons than be a packer any day, and don't let Vic forget it! And when she was able to take a job, they would get on fine, and not be long before they'd saved enough to get out of it to where those blue butterflies came from. And he spoke of Soames. A few more aldermen without children –

say two a day, fifteen bob a week outside legitimate trade. Why, in under a year they'd have the money! And once away, Vic would blow out like one of those balloons; she'd be twice the size, and a colour in her cheeks to lay over that orange and magenta. Bicket became full of air. And the girl, his wife, watched with her large eyes and spoke little; but she did not cry again, or, indeed, throw any water, warm or cold, on him who sold balloons.

Chapter Twelve

FIGURES AND FACTS

◀◀▶▶

WITH the exception of old Fontenoy – in absence as in presence ornamental – the Board was again full; Soames, conscious of special ingratiation in the manner of 'that chap' Elderson, prepared himself for the worst. The figures were before them; a somewhat colourless show, appearing to disclose a state of things which would pass muster, if within the next six months there were further violent disturbances of currency exchange. The proportion of foreign business to home business was duly expressed in terms of two to seven; German business, which constituted the bulk of the foreign, had been lumped – Soames noted – in the middle section, of countries only half bankrupt, and taken at what might be called a conservative estimate.

During the silence which reigned while each member of the Board digested the figures, Soames perceived more clearly than ever the quandary he was in. Certainly, these figures would hardly justify the forgoing of the dividend earned on the past year's business. But suppose there were another Continental crash and they became liable on the great bulk of their foreign business, it might swamp all profits on home business next year, and more besides. And then his uneasiness about Elderson himself – founded he could not tell on what, intuitive, perhaps silly.

'Well, Mr Forsyte,' the chairman was speaking; 'there are the figures. Are you satisfied?'

Soames looked up; he had taken a resolution.

'I will agree to this year's dividend on condition that we drop this foreign business in future, lock, stock and barrel.' The manager's eyes, hard and bright, met his, then turned towards the chairman.

'That appears to savour of the panicky,' he said; 'the foreign business is responsible for a good third of our profit this year.'

The chairman seemed to garner the expressions of his fellow-directors, before he said:

'There is nothing in the foreign situation at the moment, Mr Forsyte, which gives particular cause for alarm. I admit that we should watch it closely –'

'You can't,' interjected Soames. 'Here we are four years from the Armistice, and we know no more where we stand than we did then. If I'd realized our commitment to this policy, I should never have come on the Board. We must drop it.'

'Rather an extreme view. And hardly a matter we can decide in a moment.'

The murmur of assent, the expression, faintly ironical, of 'that chap's' lips, jolted the tenacity in Soames.

'Very well! Unless you're prepared to tell the shareholders in the report that we are dropping foreign business, you drop me. I must be free to raise the question myself at the general meeting.' He did not miss the shift and blink in the manager's eyes. That shot had gone home!

The chairman said:

'You put a pistol to our heads.'

'I am responsible to the shareholders,' said Soames, 'and I shall do my duty by them.'

'So we all are, Mr Forsyte; and I hope we shall all do our duty.'

'Why not confine the foreign business to the small countries – their currency is safe enough?'

'Old Mont,' and his precious 'ring' !

'No,' said Soames, 'we must go back to safety.'

'Splendid isolation, Forsyte?'

'Meddling was all very well in the war, but in peace – politics or business – this half-and-half interference is no good. We can't control the foreign situation.'

He looked around him, and was instantly conscious that with those words he had struck a chord. 'I'm going through with this !' he thought.

'I should be glad, Mr Chairman' – the manager was speaking – 'if I might say a word. The policy was of my initiation, and I think I may claim that it has been of substantial benefit to the Society so far. When, however, a member of the Board takes so strong a view against its continuance, I certainly don't press the Board to continue it. The times *are* uncertain, and a risk, of course, is involved, however conservative our estimates.'

'Now why?' thought Soames: 'What's he ratting for?'

'That's very handsome of you, Elderson; Mr Chairman, I think we may say that is very handsome of our manager.'

Old Dosey Cosey ! Handsome ! The old woman !

The chairman's rather harsh voice broke a silence.

'This is a very serious point of policy. I should have been glad to have Lord Fontenoy present.'

'If I am to endorse the report,' said Soames shortly, 'it must be decided today. I have made up my mind. But please yourselves.'

He threw in those last three words from a sort of fellow feeling – it was unpleasant to be dragooned ! A moment's silence, and then discussion assumed that random volubility which softens a decision already forced on one. A quarter of an hour thus passed before the chairman said :

'We are agreed then, gentlemen, that the report shall contain the announcement that, in view of Continental uncertainty, we are abandoning foreign risks for the present.'

Soames had won. Relieved and puzzled, he walked away alone.

He had shown character; their respect for him had gone up,

he could see; their liking for him down, if they'd ever had any –
he didn't know I But why had Elderson veered round? He recalled the shift and blink of the fellow's steely eyes at the idea
of the question being raised at the general meeting.

That had done it I But why? Were the figures faked? Surely
not I That would be too difficult, in the face of the accountants.
If Soames had faith, it was in chartered accountants. Sandis
and Jevon were tip-top people. It couldn't be that I He glanced
up from the pavement. The dome of St Paul's was dim already
in evening sky – nothing to be had out of it I He felt badly in
need of someone to talk to; but there was nobody; and he
quickened his pace among the hurrying crowd. His hand, driven
deep into his overcoat pocket, came into sudden contact with
some foreign sticky substance. 'Gracious I' he thought: 'those
things I' Should he drop them in the gutter? If only there were
a child he could take them home to I He must get Annette to
speak to Fleur. He knew what came of bad habits from his
own experience of long ago. Why shouldn't he speak to her
himself? He was staying the night there I But there came on
him a helpless sense of ignorance. These young people I What
did they really think and feel? Was old Mont right? Had they
given up interest in everything except the moment, abandoned
all belief in continuity, and progress? True enough that
Europe was in Queer Street. But look at the state of things
after the Napoleonic Wars. He couldn't remember his grandfather 'Superior Dosset', the old chap had died five years before
he was born, but he perfectly remembered how Aunt Ann,
born in 1799, used to talk about 'that dreadful Bonaparte – we
used to call him Boney, my dear'; of how her father could get
eight or ten per cent for his money; and of what an impression
'those Chartists' had made on Aunts Juley and Hester, and that
was long afterwards. Yet, in spite of all that, look at the Victorian era – a golden age, things worth collecting, children
worth having I Why not again I Consols had risen almost con-
tinuously since Timothy died. Even if Heaven and Hell had
gone, they couldn't be the reason; none of his uncles had
believed in either, and yet had all made fortunes, and all had

families, except Timothy and Swithin. No! It couldn't be the want of Heaven and Hell! What, then, was the reason of the change — if change there really were? And suddenly it was revealed to Soames. They talked too much — too much and too fast! They got to the end of interest in this and that and the other. They ate life and threw away the rind, and — and —. By the way, he must buy that picture of George's! ... Had these young folk more mind than his own generation? And if so — why? Was it diet? That lobster cocktail Fleur had given him the Sunday before last. He had eaten the thing — very nasty! But it hadn't made him want to talk. No! He didn't think it could be diet. Besides — Mind! Where were the minds now that equalled the Victorians — Darwin, Huxley, Dickens, Disraeli, even old Gladstone? Why, he remembered judges and advocates who seemed giants compared with those of the present day, just as he remembered that the judges of James his father's youth had seemed giants to James compared with those of Soames's prime. According to that, mind was steadily declining. It must be something else. There was a thing they called psycho-analysis, which so far as he could understand attributed people's action not to what they ate at breakfast, or the leg they got out of bed with, as in the good old days, but to some shock they had received in the remote past and entirely forgotten. The sub-conscious mind! Fads! Fads and microbes! The fact was this generation had no digestion. His father and his uncles had all complained of liver, but they had never had anything the matter with them — no need of any of these vitamins, false teeth, mental healing, newspapers, psycho-analysis, spiritualism, birth control, osteopathy, broadcasting, and what not. 'Machines!' thought Soames. 'That's it — I shouldn't wonder!' How could you believe in anything when everything was going round so fast? When you couldn't count your chickens — they ran about so? But Fleur had got a good little head on her! 'Yes,' he mused, 'and French teeth, she can digest anything. Two years! I'll speak to her before she gets the habit confirmed. Her mother was quick enough about it!' And perceiving the Connoisseurs' Club in front of him, he went in.

The hall porter came out of his box. A gentleman was waiting.

'What gentleman?' said Soames, sidelong.

'I think he's your nephew, sir, Mr Dartie.'

'Val Dartie! H'm! Where?'

'In the little room, sir.'

The little room – all the accommodation considered worthy of such as were not Connoisseurs – was at the end of a passage, and in no taste at all, as if the Club were saying: 'See what it is not to be one of us!' Soames entered it, and saw Val Dartie smoking a cigarette and gazing with absorption at the only object of interest, his own reflection in the glass above the fire.

He never saw his nephew without wondering when he would say: 'Look here, Uncle Soames, I'm up a stump.' Breeding racehorses! There could only be one end to that!

'Well?' he said, 'how are *you*?'

The face in the glass turned round, and became the back of a clipped sandyish head.

'Oh! bobbish, thanks! *You* look all right, Uncle Soames. I just wanted to ask you: Must I take these screws of old George Forsyte's? They're dashed bad.'

'Gift horse in the mouth?' said Soames.

'Well,' said Val, 'but they're *so* dashed bad; by the time I've paid legacy duty, boxed them to a sale, and sold them, there won't be a sixpence. One of them falls down when you look at it. And the other two are broken-winded. The poor old boy kept them, because he couldn't get rid of them. They're about five hundred years old.'

'Thought you were fond of horses,' said Soames. 'Can't you turn them out?'

'Yes,' said Val, drily; 'but I've got my living to make. I haven't told my wife, for fear she should suggest that. I'm afraid I might see them in my dreams if I sold them. They're only fit for the kennels. Can I write to the executors and say I'm not rich enough to take them?'

'You can,' said Soames, and the words: 'How's your wife?'

died unspoken on his lips. She was the daughter of his enemy, young Jolyon. That fellow was dead, but the fact remained.

'I will, then,' said Val. 'How did his funeral go off?'

'Very simple affair – I had nothing to do with it.' The days of funerals were over. No flowers, no horses, no plumes – a motor hearse, a couple of cars or so, was all the attention paid nowadays to the dead. Another sign of the times!

'I'm staying the night at Green Street,' said Val. 'I suppose you're not there, are you?'

'No,' said Soames, and did not miss the relief in his nephew's countenance.

'Oh! by the way, Uncle Soames – do you advise me to buy P.P.R.S. shares?'

'On the contrary. I'm going to advise your mother to sell. Tell her I'm coming in tomorrow.'

'Why? I thought –'

'Never mind my reasons!' said Soames shortly.

'So long, then!'

Exchanging a chilly hand-shake, he watched his nephew withdraw.

So long! An expression, old as the Boer war, that he had never got used to – meant nothing so far as he could see! He entered the reading-room. A number of Connoisseurs were sitting and standing about, and Soames, least clubbable of men, sought the solitude of an embrasured window. He sat there polishing the nail of one forefinger against the back of the other, and chewing the cud of life. After all, what was the point of anything. There was George! He had had an easy life – never done any work! And here was himself, who had done a lot of work! And sooner or later they would bury him too, with a motor hearse probably! And there was his son-in-law, young Mont, full of talk about goodness knew what – and that thin-cheeked chap who had sold him the balloons this afternoon. And old Fontenoy, and that waiter over there; and the out-of-works and the in-works; and those chaps in Parliament, and the parsons in their pulpits – what were they all for? There was the old gardener down at Mapledurham pushing his roller over and over the lawn, week after week, and if he didn't, what would the lawn be like? That was life – gardener rolling lawn! Put it that there was another life – he didn't believe it, but for the sake of argument – that life must be just the same. Rolling lawn – to keep it lawn! What point in lawn? Conscious of pessimism, he rose. He had better be getting back to Fleur's – they dressed for dinner! He supposed there was something in dressing for dinner, but it was like lawn – you came un-rolled – undressed again, and so it went on! Over and over and over to keep up to a pitch, that was – ah! what *was* the pitch for?

Turning into South Square, he cannoned into a young man, whose head was craned back as if looking after someone he had parted from. Uncertain whether to apologize or to wait for an apology, Soames stood still.

The young man said abruptly: 'Sorry, sir,' and moved on; dark, neat-looking chap with a hungry look obviously uncon-nected with his stomach. Murmuring: 'Not at all!' Soames moved forward and rang his daughter's bell. She opened to him herself. She was in hat and furs – just in. The young man re-curred to Soames. Had he left her there? What a pretty face it was! He should certainly speak to her. If she once took to gad-ding about!

He put it off, however, till he was about to say 'Good night' – Michael having gone to the political meeting of a Labour can-didate, as if he couldn't find something better to do!

'Now you've been married two years, my child, I suppose you'll be looking towards the future. There's a great deal of non-sense talked about children. The whole thing's much simpler. I hope you feel that.'

Fleur was leaning back among the cushions of the settee, swinging her foot. Her eyes became a little restless, but her colour did not change.

'Of course!' she said; 'only there's no hurry, Dad.'

'Well, I don't know,' Soames murmured. 'The French and the royal family have a very sound habit of getting it over early. There's many a slip and it keeps them out of mischief. You're very attractive, my child – I don't want to see you take too much to gad-about ways. You've got all sorts of friends.'

'Yes,' said Fleur.

'You get on well with Michael, don't you?'

'Oh! yes.'

'Well, then, why not? You must remember that your son will be a what-you-call-it.'

In those words he compromised with his instinctive dislike of titles and flummery of that nature.

'It mightn't be a son,' said Fleur.

'At your age that's easily remedied.'

'Oh, I don't want a lot, Dad. One, perhaps, or two.'

'Well,' said Soames, 'I should almost prefer a daughter, something like – well, something like you.'

Her softened eyes flew, restive, from his face to her foot, to the dog, all over the room.

'I don't know, it's a tie – like digging your own grave in a way.'

'I shouldn't put it as high as that,' murmured Soames, persuasively.

'No man would, Dad.'

'Your mother wouldn't have got on at all without you,' and recollection of how near her mother had been to not getting on at all with her – of how, but for him, she would have made a mess of it, reduced him to silent contemplation of the restive foot.

'Well,' he said, at last, 'I thought I'd mention it. I – I've got your happiness at heart.'

Fleur rose and kissed his forehead.

'I know, Dad,' she said, 'I'm a selfish pig. I'll think about it. In fact, I – I have thought about it.'

'That's right,' said Soames; 'that's right! You've a good head on you – it's a great consolation to me. Good night, my dear!'

And he went up to his bed. If there was point in anything, it was in perpetuation of oneself, though, of course, that begged the question. 'Wonder,' he thought, 'if I ought to have asked her whether that young man –!' But young people were best left alone. The fact was, he didn't understand them. His eye lighted on the paper bag containing those – those things he had bought. He had brought them up from his overcoat to get rid of them. – but how? Put into the fire, they would make a smell. He stood at his dressing-table, took one up and looked at it. Good Lord! And, suddenly, rubbing the mouthpiece with his handkerchief, he began to blow the thing up. He blew until his cheeks were tired, and then, nipping the aperture, took a bit of the dental cotton he used on his teeth every night and tied it up. There the thing was! With a pettish gesture he batted the balloon. Off it flew – purple and extravagant, alighting on his bed. H'm! He took up the other, and did the same to it. Purple and green! The deuce! If anyone came in and saw! He threw up the window, batted them, balloon after balloon, into the night, and shut the window down. There they'd be in the dark, floating about. His lips contracted in a nervous grin. People would see them in the morning. Well! What else could you do with things like that?

Chapter Thirteen

TENTERHOOKS

<del>-<->-</del>

MICHAEL had gone to the Labour candidate's meeting partly because he wanted to, and partly out of fellow feeling for 'old Forsyte', whom he was always conscious of having robbed. His father-in-law had been very decent about Fleur, and he liked the 'old man' to have her to himself when he could.

In a constituency which had much casual and no trades-union labour to speak of, the meeting would be one of those which enabled the intellectuals of the Party to get it 'off their chests'. Sentiment being 'slop', and championship mere condescension, one might look for sound economic speeches which left out discredited factors, such as human nature. Michael was accustomed to hearing people disparaged for deprecating change because human nature was constant; he was accustomed to hearing people despised for feeling compassion; he knew that one ought to be purely economic. And anyway that kind of speech was preferable to the tub-thumpings of the North or of the Park, which provoked a nasty underlying class spirit in himself.

The meeting was in full swing when he arrived, the candidate pitilessly exposing the fallacies of a capitalism which, in his view, had brought on the war. For fear that it should bring on another, it must be changed for a system which would ensure that nations should not want anything too much. The individual – said the candidate – was in every respect superior to the nation of which he formed a part; and the problem before them was to secure an economic condition which would enable the individual to function freely in his native superiority. In that way alone, he said, would they lose those mass movements and emotions which imperilled the sanity of the world. He spoke well. Michael listened, purring almost audibly, till he found that he was thinking of himself, Wilfrid and Fleur. Would he ever function so freely in a native superiority that he did not want Fleur too much? And did he wish to? He did not. That seemed to introduce human nature into the speaker's argument. Didn't everybody want something too much? Wasn't it natural? And if so, wouldn't there always be a collective wanting too much – pooling of primary desire, such as the desire of keeping your own head above water? The candidate's argument seemed to him suddenly to leave out heat, to omit friction, to be that of a man in an armchair after a poor lunch. He looked attentively at the speaker's shrewd, dry, doubting face. 'No juice!' he thought. And when 'the chap' sat down, he got up and left the hall.

This Wilfrid business had upset him horribly. Try as he had to put it out of his mind, try as he would to laugh it off, it continued to eat into his sense of security and happiness. Wife and best friend! A hundred times a day he assured himself that he trusted Fleur. Only, Wilfrid was so much more attractive than himself, and Fleur deserved the best of everything. Besides,

Wilfrid was going through torture, and it was not a pleasant thought! How end the thing, restore peace of mind to himself, to him, to her? She had told him nothing; and it simply was impossible to ask. No way even of showing his anxiety! The whole thing was just 'dark', and, so far as he could see, would have to stay so; nothing to be done but screw the lid on tighter, be as nice as he could to her, try not to feel bitter about him. Hades!

He turned down Chelsea Embankment. Here the sky was dark and wide and streaming with stars. The river wide, dark and gleaming with oily rays from the Embankment lamps. The width of it all gave him relief. Dash the dumps! A jolly, queer, muddled, sweet and bitter world; an immensely intriguing game of chance, no matter how the cards were falling at the moment! In the trenches he had thought: 'Get out of this, and I'll never mind anything again!' How seldom now he remembered thinking that! The human body renewed itself – they said – in seven years. In three years' time his body would not be the body of the trenches, but a whole-time peace body with a fading complex. If only Fleur would tell him quite openly what she felt, what she was doing about Wilfrid, for she must be doing something! And Wilfrid's verse? Would his confounded passion – as Bart suggested – flow in poetry? And if so, who would publish it? A miserable business! Well the night was beautiful, and the great thing not to be a pig. Beauty and not being a pig! Nothing much else to it – except laughter – the comic side! Keep one's sense of humour, anyway! And Michael searched, while he strode beneath plane trees half-stripped of leaves and plume-like in the dark, for the fun in his position. He failed to find it. There seemed absolutely nothing funny about love. Possibly he might fall out of love again some day, but not so long as she kept him on her tenterhooks. Did she do it on purpose? Never! Fleur simply could not be like those women who kept their husbands hungry and fed them when they wanted dresses, furs, jewels. Revolting!

He came in sight of Westminster. Only half-past ten! Suppose he took a cab to Wilfrid's rooms, and tried to have it out with him. It would be like trying to make the hands of a clock move backwards to its ticking. What use in saying: 'You love Fleur – well, don't!' or in Wilfrid saying it to him. 'After all, I was first with Fleur,' he thought. Pure chance, perhaps, but fact! Ah! And wasn't that just the danger? He was no longer a novelty to her – nothing unexpected about him now! And he and she had agreed times without number that novelty was the salt of life, the essence of interest and drama. Novelty now lay with Wilfrid! Lord! Lord! Possession appeared far from being nine points of the law! He rounded-in from the Embankment towards home – jolly part of London, jolly Square; everything jolly except just this infernal complication. Something, soft as a large leaf, tapped twice against his ear. He turned, astonished; he was in empty space, no tree near. Floating in the darkness, a round thing – he grabbed, it bobbed. What? A child's balloon! He secured it between his hands, took it beneath a lamp-post – green, he judged. Queer! He looked up. Two windows lighted, one of them Fleur's! Was this the bubble of his own happiness expelled? Morbid! Silly ass! Some gust of wind – a child's plaything lodged and loosened! He held the balloon gingerly. He would take it in and show it to her. He put his latchkey in the door. Dark in the hall – gone up! He mounted, swinging the balloon on his finger. Fleur was standing before a mirror.

'What on earth's that?' she said.

The blood returned to Michael's heart. Curious how he had dreaded its having anything to do with her!

'Don't know, darling; fell on my hat – must belong to heaven.' And he batted it.

The balloon floated, dropped, bounded twice, wobbled and came to rest.

'You *are* a baby, Michael. I believe you bought it.'

Michael came closer, and stood quite still.

'My hat! What a misfortune to be in love!'

'You think so!'

'*Il y a toujours un qui baise, et l'autre qui ne tend pas la joue.*'

'But I do.'

'Fleur !'

Fleur smiled.

'*Baise* away.'

Embracing her, Michael thought: 'She holds me – does with me what she likes; I know nothing of her !'

And there arose a small sound – from Ting-a-ling smelling the balloon.

PART TWO

Chapter One

THE MARK FALLS

◄◄─►►

THE state of the world had been getting more and more on Soames's nerves ever since the general meeting of the P.P.R.S. It had gone off with that fatuity long associated by him with such gatherings – a watertight rigmarole from the chairman; butter from two reliable shareholders; vinegar from shareholders not so reliable; and the usual 'gup' over the dividend. He had gone there glum, come away glummer. From a notion once taken into his head Soames parted more slowly than a cheese parts from its mites. Two-sevenths of foreign business, nearly all German! And the mark falling! It had begun to fall from the moment that he decided to support the dividend. And why? What was in the wind? Contrary to his custom, he had taken to sniffing closely the political columns of his paper. The French – he had always mistrusted them, especially since his second marriage – the French were going to play old Harry, if he was not greatly mistaken! Their papers, he noticed, never lost a chance of having a dab at English policy; seemed to think they could always call the tune for England to pipe to! And the mark and the franc, and every other sort of money, falling. And, though in Soames was that which rejoiced in the thought that one of his country's bits of paper could buy a great quantity of other countries' bits of paper, there was also that which felt the whole thing silly and unreal, with an ever-growing consciousness that the P.P.R.S. would pay no dividend next year. The P.P.R.S. was a big concern; no dividend would be a sign, no small one, of bad management. Assurance was one of the few things on God's earth which could and should be conducted without real risk. But for that he would never have gone on the Board. And to find assurance had not been so conducted and that by himself, was – well! He had caused Winifred to sell.

anyway, though the shares had already fallen slightly. 'I thought it was such a good thing, Soames,' she had said plaintively: 'it's rather a bore, losin' money on these shares.' He had answered without mercy: 'If you don't sell, you'll lose more.' And she had done it. If the Rogers and Nicholases who had followed him into it hadn't sold too – well, it was their look out! He had made Winifred warn them. As for himself, he had nothing but his qualifying shares, and the missing of a dividend or two would not hurt one whose director's fees more than compensated. It was not, therefore, private uneasiness so much as resentment at a state of things connected with foreigners and the slur on his infallibility.

Christmas had gone off quietly at Mapledurham. He abominated Christmas, and only observed it because his wife was French, and her national festival New Year's Day. One could not go so far as to observe that, encouraging a foreign notion. But Christmas with no child about – he still remembered the holly and snapdragons of Park Lane in his own childhood – the family parties; and how disgusted he had been if he got anything symbolic – the thimble, or the ring – instead of the shilling. They had never gone in for Santa Claus at Park Lane, partly because they could see through the old gentleman, and partly because he was not at all a late thing. Emily, his mother, had seen to that. Yes; and, by the way, that William Gouldyng, Ingerer, had so stumped those fellows at the Heralds' College, that Soames had dropped the inquiry – it was just encouraging them to spend his money for a sentimental satisfaction which did not materialize. That narrow-headed chap, 'Old Mont', peacocked about his ancestry; all the more reason for having no ancestry to peacock about. The Forsytes and the Goldings were good English country stock – that was what mattered. And if Fleur and her child, if one came, had French blood in them – well, he couldn't help it now.

In regard to the coming of a grandchild, Soames knew no more than in October. Fleur had spent Christmas with the Monts; she was promised to him, however, before long, and her mother must ask her a question or two!

The weather was extremely mild; Soames had even been out in a punt fishing. In a heavy coat he trailed a line for perch and dace, and caught now and then a roach – precious little good, the servants wouldn't eat them, nowadays! His grey eyes would brood over the grey water under the grey sky; and in his mind the mark would fall. It fell with a bump on that eleventh of January when the French went and occupied the Ruhr. He said to Annette at breakfast: 'Your country's cracked! Look at the mark now!'

'What do I care about the mark?' she had answered over her coffee. 'I care that they shall not come again into my country. I hope they will suffer a little what we have suffered.'

'You,' said Soames; 'you never suffered anything.'

Annette put her hand where Soames sometimes doubted the existence of a heart.

'I have suffered here,' she said.

'I didn't notice it. You never went without butter. What do you suppose Europe's going to be like now for the next thirty years! How about British trade?'

'We French see before our noses,' said Annette with warmth. 'We see that the beaten must be kept the beaten, or he will take revenge. You English are so sloppy.'

'Sloppy, are we?' said Soames. 'You're talking like a child. Could a sloppy people ever have reached our position in the world?'

'That is your selfishness. You are cold and selfish.'

'Cold, selfish and sloppy – they don't go together. Try again.'

'Your slop is in your thought and your talk; it is your instinct that gives you your success, and your English instinct is cold and selfish, Soames. You are a mixture, all of you, of hypocrisy, stupidity and egoism.'

Soames took some marmalade.

'Well,' he said, 'and what are the French? – cynical, avaricious and revengeful. And the Germans are sentimental, heady and brutal. We can all abuse each other. There's nothing for it but to keep clear. And that's what you French won't do.'

Annette's handsome person stiffened.

'When you are tied to a person, as I am tied to you, Soames, or as we French are tied to the Germans, it is necessary to be top dog, or to be bottom dog.'

Soames stayed his toast.

'Do you suppose yourself top dog in this house?'

'Yes, Soames.'

'Oh! Then you can go back to France tomorrow.'

Annette's eyebrows rose quizzically.

'I would wait a little longer, my friend; you are still too young.'

But Soames had already regretted his remark; he did not wish any disturbance at his time of life, and he said more calmly:

'Compromise is the essence of any reasonable existence between individuals or nations. We can't have the fat thrown into the fire every few years.'

'That is so English,' murmured Annette. 'We others never know what you English will do. You always wait to see which way the cat jumps.'

However deeply sympathetic with such a reasonable characteristic, Soames would have denied it at any ordinary moment — to confess to temporizing was not, as it were, done. But, with the mark falling like a cartload of bricks, he was heated to the point of standing by his nature.

'And why shouldn't we? Rushing into things that you'll have to rush out of! I don't want to argue. French and English never did get on, and never will.'

Annette rose. 'You speak the truth, my friend. *Entente, mais pas cordiale.* What are you doing today?'

'Going up to town,' said Soames glumly. 'Your precious Government has put business into Queer Street with a vengeance.'

'Do you stay the night?'

'I don't know.'

'*Adieu*, then, *jusqu'au revoir!*' And she got up.

Soames remained brooding above his marmalade — with the mark falling in his mind — glad to see the last of her handsome figure, having no patience at the moment for French tantrums. An irritable longing to say to somebody 'I told you so' pos-

sessed him. He would have to wait, however, till he found somebody to say it to.

A beautiful day, quite warm; and, taking his umbrella as an
assurance against change, he set out for the station.

In the carriage going up they were talking about the Ruhr.
Averse from discussion in public, Soames listened from behind
his paper. The general sentiment was surprisingly like his own.
In so far as it was unpleasant for the Huns – all right; in so far
as it was unpleasant for British trade – all wrong; in so far as
love of British trade was active and hate of Huns now passive –
more wrong than right. A Francophil remark that the French
were justified in making themselves safe at all cost, was coldly
received. At Maidenhead a man got in whom Soames connected
automatically with disturbance. He had much grey hair, a san-
guine face, lively eyes, twisting eyebrows, and within five minutes had asked in a breezy voice whether anyone had heard of
the League of Nations. Confirmed in his estimate, Soames
looked round the corner of his paper. Yes, that chap would get
off on some hobby-horse or other! And there he went! The question – said the newcomer – was not whether the Germans
should get one in the eye, the British one in the pocket, or the
French one in the heart, but whether the world should get peace
and goodwill. Soames lowered his paper. If – this fellow said –
they wanted peace, they must sink their individual interests, and
think in terms of collective interest. The good of all was the
good of one! Soames saw the flaw at once; that might be, but
the good of one was not the good of all. He felt that if he did
not take care he would be pointing this out. The man was a perfect stranger to him, and no good ever came of argument. Unfortunately his silence amid the general opinion that the League
of Nations was 'no earthly', seemed to cause the newcomer to
regard him as a sympathizer; the fellow kept on throwing his
eyebrows at him! To put up his paper again seemed too pointed,
and his position was getting more and more false when the train
ran in at Paddington. He hastened to a cab. A voice behind
him said:

'Hopeless lot, sir, eh! Glad to see *you* saw my point.'

'Quite!' said Soames. 'Taxi!'

'Unless the League of Nations functions, we're all for Gehenna.'

Soames turned the handle of the cab door.

'Quite!' he said again. 'Poultry!' and got in. He was not going to be drawn. The fellow was clearly a firebrand!

In the cab the measure of his disturbance was revealed. He had said 'Poultry', an address that 'Forsyte, Bustard and Forsyte' had abandoned two-and-twenty years ago when, merged with 'Cuthcott, Holliday and Kingson,' they became 'Cuthcott, Kingson and Forsyte'. Rectifying the error, he sat forward, brooding. Fall of the mark! The country was sound about it, yes – but when they failed to pay the next dividend, could they rely on resentment against the French instead of against the directors? Doubtful! The directors ought to have seen it coming! That might be said of the other directors, but not of himself – here was a policy that he personally never would have touched. If only he could discuss the whole thing with someone – but old Gradman would be out of his depth in a matter of this sort. And, on arrival at his office, he gazed with a certain impatience at that changeless old fellow, sitting in his swivel chair.

'Ah! Mr Soames, I was hopin' you might come in this morning. There's a young man been round to see you from the P.P.R.S. Wouldn't give his business, said he wanted to see you privately. Left his number on the phone.'

'Oh!' said Soames.

'Quite a young feller – in the office.'

'What did he look like?'

'Nice, clean young man. I was quite favourably impressed – name of Butterfield.'

'Well, ring him up, and let him know I'm here.' And going over to the window, he stood looking out on to a perfectly blank wall.

Suited to a sleeping partner, his room was at the back, free from disturbance. Young man! The call was somewhat singular! And he said over his shoulder: 'Don't go when he comes, Gradman, I know nothing of him.'

The world changed, people died off, the mark fell, but Gradman was there – embodiment, faithful and grey, of service and integrity – an anchor.

Gradman's voice, grating, ingratiating, rose.

'This French news – it's not nice, Mr Soames. They're a hasty lot. I remember your father, Mr James, coming into the office the morning the Franco-Prussian war was declared – quite in his prime then, hardly more than sixty, I should say. Why, I recall his very words: "There," he said, "I told them so." And here they are – at it still. The fact is, they're cat and dog.'

Soames, who had half turned, resumed his contemplation of a void. Poor old Gradman dated! What would he say when he heard that they had been insuring foreign business? Stimulated by the old-time quality of Gradman's presence, his mind ranged with sudden freedom. He himself had another twenty years, perhaps. What would he see in that time? Where would old England be at the end of it? 'In spite of the papers, we're not such fools as we look,' he thought. 'If only we can steer clear of flibberty-gibbering, and pay our way!'

'Mr Butterfield, sir.' H'm! The young man had been very spry. Covered by Gradman's bluff and greasy greeting, he 'took a lunar', as his Uncle Roger used to call it. The young fellow in a neat suit, a turndown collar, with his hat in his hand, was a medium modest-looking chap. Soames nodded.

'You want to see me?'

'Alone, if I might, sir.'

'Mr Gradman here is my right-hand man.'

Gradman's voice purred gratingly; 'You can state your business. Nothing goes outside these walls, young man.'

'I'm in the office of the P.P.R S., sir. The fact is, accident has just put some information in my hands, and I'm not easy in my mind. Knowing you to be a solicitor, sir, I preferred to come to you, rather than go to the chairman. As a lawyer, would you tell me: Is my first duty to the Society, being in their employ?'

'Certainly,' said Soames.

'I don't like this job, sir, and I hope you'll understand that

I'm not here for any personal motive — it's just because I feel I ought to.'

Soames regarded him steadily. Though large and rather swimming, the young man's eyes impressed him by their resemblance to a dog's. 'What's it all about?' he said.

The young man moistened his lips.

'The insurance of our German business, sir.'

Soames pricked his ears, already slightly pointed by Nature.

'It's a very serious matter,' the young man went on, 'and I don't know how it'll affect me, but the fact is, this morning I overheard a private conversation.'

'Oh!' said Soames.

'Yes, sir. I quite understand your tone, but the very first words did it. I simply couldn't make myself known after hearing them. I think you'll agree, sir.'

'Who were the speakers?'

'The manager, and a man called Smith — I fancy by his accent his name's a bit more foreign — who's done most of the agenting for the German business.'

'What were the words?' said Soames.

'Well, sir, the manager was speaking, and then this Smith said: "Quite so, Mr Elderson, but we haven't paid you a commission on all this business for nothing; if the mark goes absolutely phut, you will have to see that your Society makes it good for us!" '

The intense longing, which at that moment came on Soames to emit a whistle, was checked by sight of Gradman's face. The old fellow's mouth had opened in the nest of his grizzly short beard; his eyes stared puglike, he uttered a prolonged: 'A-ow!'

'Yes,' said the young man, 'it was a knock-out!'

'Where were you?' asked Soames, sharply.

'In the lobby between the manager's room and the board-room. I'd just come from sorting some papers in the board-room, and the manager's door was open an inch or so. Of course I know the voices well.'

'What after?'

'I heard Mr Elderson say: "H'ssh! Don't talk like that!" and

I slipped back into the board-room. I'd had more than enough, sir, I assure you.'

Suspicion and surmise clogged Soames's thinking apparatus. Was this young fellow speaking the truth? A man like Elderson – the risk was monstrous! And, if true, what was the directors' responsibility? But proof – proof? He stared at the young man, who looked upset and pale enough, but whose eyes did not waver. Shake him if he could! And he said sharply:

'Now mind what you're saying! This is most serious!'

'I know that, sir. If I'd consulted my own interest, I'd never have come here. I'm not a sneak.'

The words rang true, but Soames did not drop his caution.

'Ever had any trouble in the office?'

'No, sir, you can make inquiry. I've nothing against Mr Elderson, and he's nothing against me.'

Soames thought suddenly: 'Good heavens! He's shifted it on to me, and in the presence of a witness. And I supplied the witness!'

'Have you any reason to suppose,' he said, 'that they became aware of your being there?'

'They couldn't have, I think.'

The implications of this news seemed every second more alarming. It was as if Fate, kept at bay all his life by clever wrist-work, had suddenly slipped a thrust under his guard. No good to get rattled, however – must think it out at leisure!

'Are you prepared, if necessary, to repeat this to the Board?'

The young man pressed his hands together.

'Well, sir, I'd much rather have held my tongue; but if you decide it's got to be taken up, I suppose I must go through with it now. I'm sure I hope you'll decide to leave it alone; perhaps it isn't true – only why didn't Mr Elderson say: "You ruddy liar!"?'

Exactly! Why didn't he? Soames gave a grunt of intense discomfort.

'Anything more?' he said.

'No, sir.'

'Very well. You've not told anyone?'

'No, sir.'

'Then don't, and leave it to me.'

'I'll be only too happy to, sir. Good morning!'

'Good morning!'

No – very bad morning! No satisfaction whatever in this sudden fulfilment of his prophetic feeling about Elderson. None!

'What d'you think of that young fellow, Gradman? Is he lying?'

Thus summoned, as it were, from stupor, Gradman thoughtfully rubbed a nose both thick and shining.

'It's one word against another, Mr Soames, unless you get more evidence. But I can't see what the young man has to gain by it.'

'Nor I; but you never know. The trouble will be to get more evidence. Can I act without it?'

'It's delicate,' said Gradman. And Soames knew that he was thrown back on himself. When Gradman said a thing was delicate, it meant that it was the sort of matter on which he was accustomed to wait for orders – presumptuous even to hold opinion! But had he got one? Well, one would never know! The old chap would sit and rub his nose over it till Kingdom Come.

'I shan't act in a hurry,' he said, almost angrily: 'I can't see to the end of this.'

Every hour confirmed that statement. At lunch the tape of his city club showed the mark still falling – to unheard-of depths! How they could talk of golf, with this business on his mind, he could not imagine!

'I must go and see that fellow,' he said to himself. 'I shall be guarded. He may throw some light.' He waited until three o'clock and repaired to the P.P.R.S.

Reaching the office, he sought the board-room. The chairman was there in conference with the manager. Soames sat down quietly to listen; and while he listened he watched that fellow's face. It told him nothing. What nonsense people talked when they said you could tell character from faces! Only a perfect idiot's face could be read like that. And here was a man of experience and culture, one who knew every rope of business life and polite society. The hairless, neat features exhibited no more concern than the natural mortification of one whose policy had met with such a nasty knock. The drop of the mark had already wiped out any possible profit on the next half-year. Unless the wretched thing recovered, they would be carrying a practically dead load of German insurance. Really it was criminal that no limit of liability had been fixed! How on earth could he ever have overlooked that when he came on the Board? But he had only known of it afterwards. And who could have foreseen anything so mad as this Ruhr business, or realized the slack confidence of his colleagues in this confounded fellow? The words 'gross negligence' appeared 'close up' before his eyes. What if an action lay against the Board! Gross negligence! At his age and with his reputation! Why! The thing was plain as a pikestaff; for omitting a limit of liability this chap had got his commission! Ten per cent probably, on all that business – he must have netted thousands! A man must be in Queer Street indeed to take a risk like that! But conscious that his fancy was running on, Soames rose, and turned his back. The action suggested another. Simulate anger, draw some sign from that fellow's self-control! He turned again, and said pettishly: 'What on earth were you about, Mr Manager, when you allowed these contracts to go through without limit of liability? A man of your experience! What was your motive?'

A slight narrowing of the eyes, a slight compression of the lips. He had relied on the word 'motive', but the fellow passed it by.

'For such high premiums as we have been getting, Mr Forsyte, a limited liability was not possible. This is a most outrageous development, and I'm afraid it must be considered just bad luck.'

'Unfortunately,' said Soames, 'there's no such thing as luck in properly regulated assurance, as we shall find, or I'm much mistaken. I shouldn't be surprised if an action lay against the Board for gross negligence!'

That had got the chairman's goat! – Got his goat? What

expressions they used nowadays! Or did it mean the opposite? One never knew! But as for Elderson – he seemed to Soames to be merely counterfeiting a certain flusteration. Futile to attempt to spring anything out of a chap like that. If the thing were true, the fellow must be entirely desperate, prepared for anything and everything. And since from Soames the desperate side of life – the real holes, the impossible positions which demand a gambler's throw – had always been carefully barred by the habits of a prudent nature, he found it now impossible to imagine Elderson's state of mind, or his line of conduct if he were guilty. For all he could tell, the chap might be carrying poison about with him; might be sitting on a revolver like a fellow on the film. The whole thing was too unpleasant, too worrying for words. And without saying any more he went away, taking nothing with him but the knowledge that their total liability on this German business, with the mark valueless, was over two hundred thousand pounds. He hastily reviewed the fortunes of his co-directors. Old Fontenoy was always in low water; the chairman a dark horse; Mont was in land, land right down in value, and mortgaged at that; old Cosey Mothergill had nothing but his name and his director's fees; Meyricke must have a large income, but light come, light go, like most of those big counsel with irons in many fires and the certainty of a judgeship. Not a really substantial man among the lot, except himself! He ploughed his way along, head down. Public companies! Preposterous system! You had to trust somebody, and there you were! It was appalling!

'Balloons, sir – beautiful colours, five feet circumference. Take one, gentleman!'

'Good gad!' said Soames. As if the pricked bubble of German business were not enough!

Chapter Two

VICTORINE

⤙⤙⤚⤚

ALL through December balloons had been slack – hardly any movement about them, even in Christmas week, and from the Bickets Central Australia was as far ever. The girl Victorine, restored to comparative health, had not regained her position in the blouse department of Messrs Boney Blayds & Co. They had given her some odd sewing, but not of late, and she had spent much time trying to get work less uncertain. Her trouble was – had always been – her face. It was unusual. People did not know what to make of a girl who looked like that. Why employ one who without qualification of wealth, rank, fashion, or ability (so far as they knew) made them feel ordinary? For – however essential to such as Fleur and Michael – dramatic interest was not primary in the manufacture or sale of blouses, in the fitting-on of shoes, the addressing of envelopes, making-up of funeral wreaths, or the other ambitions of Victorine. Behind those large dark eyes and silent lips, what went on? It worried Boney Blayds & Co., and the more wholesale firms of commerce. The lurid professions – film-super, or mannequin – did not occur to one, of self-deprecating nature, born in Putney.

When Bicket had gone out of a morning with his tray and his balloons not yet blown up, she would stand biting her finger, as though to gnaw her way to some escape from this hand-to-mouth existence which kept her husband thin as a rail, tired as a rook, shabby as a tailless sparrow, and, at the expense of all caste feeling, brought them in no more than just enough to keep them living under a roof. It had long been clear to them both that there was no future in balloons, just a cadging present. And there smouldered in the silent, passive Victorine a fierce resentment. She wanted better things for herself, for him, chiefly for him.

121

On the morning when the mark was bumping down, she was putting on her velveteen jacket and toque (best remaining items of her wardrobe), having taken a resolve. Bicket never mentioned his old job, and his wife had subtly divined some cause beyond the ordinary for his loss of it. Why not see if she could get him taken back? He had often said: 'Mr Mont's a gent and a sort o' socialist; been through the war, too; no high-and-mighty about *him*.' If she could 'get at' this phenomenon! With the flush of hope and daring in her sallow cheeks, she took stock of her appearance from the window-glasses of the Strand. Her velveteen of jade-green always pleased one who had an eye for colour, but her black skirt – well, perhaps the wear and tear of it wouldn't show if she kept behind the counter. Had she brass enough to say that she came about a manuscript? And she rehearsed with silent lips, pinching her accent: 'Would you ask Mr Mont, please, if I could see him; it's about a manuscript.' Yes! and then would come the question: 'What name, please?' 'Mrs Bicket?' Never! 'Miss Victorine Collins?' All authoresses had maiden names. Victorine – yes! But Collins! It didn't sound like. And no one would know what her maiden name had been. Why not choose one? They often chose. And she searched. Something Italian, like – like – Hadn't their landlady said to them when they came in: 'Is your wife Eyetalian?' Ah! Manuelli! That was certainly Italian – the ice-cream man in Little Ditch Street had it! She walked on practising beneath her breath. If only she could get to see this Mr Mont!

She entered, trembling. All went exactly as foreseen, even to the pinching of her accent, till she stood waiting for them to bring an answer from the speaking-tube, concealing her hands in their very old gloves. Had Miss Manuelli an appointment? There was no manuscript.

'No,' said Victorine, 'I haven't sent it yet. I wanted to see him first.' The young man at the counter was looking at her hard. He went again to the tube, then spoke.

'Will you wait a minute, please – Mr Mont's lady secretary is coming down.'

Victorine inclined her head towards her sinking heart. A lady secretary! She would never get there now! And there came on her the sudden dread of false pretences. But the thought of Tony standing at his corner, ballooned up to the eyes, as she had spied out more than once, fortified her desperation.

A girl's voice said: 'Miss Manuelli? Mr Mont's secretary, perhaps you could give me a message.'

A fresh-faced young woman's eyes were travelling up and down her. Pinching her accent hard, she said: 'Oh! I'm afraid I couldn't do that.'

The travelling gaze stopped at her face. 'If you'll come with me, I'll see if he can see you.'

Alone in a small waiting-room, Victorine sat without movement, till she saw a young man's face poked through the doorway, and heard the words:

'Will you come in?'

She took a deep breath, and went. Once in the presence, she looked from Michael to his secretary and back again, subtly daring his youth, his chivalry, his sportsmanship, to refuse her a private interview. Through Michael passed at once the thought: 'Money, I suppose. But what an interesting face!' The secretary drew down the corners of her mouth and left the room.

'Well, Miss – er – Manuelli?'

'Not Manuelli, please – Mrs Bicket; my husband used to be here.'

'What!' The chap that had snooped *Copper Coin!* Phew! Bicket's yarn – his wife – pneumonia! She looked as if she might have had it.

'He often spoke of you, sir. And, please, he hasn't any work. Couldn't you find room for him again, sir?'

Michael stood silent. Did this terribly interesting-looking girl know about the snooping?

'He just sells balloons in the street now; I can't bear to see him. Over by St Paul's he stands, and there's no money in it; and we do so want to get out to Australia. I know he's very nervy, and gets wrong with people. But if you *could* take him back here. ...'

No! she did not know!

'Very sorry, Mrs Bicket. I remember your husband well, but
we haven't a place for him. Are *you* all right again?'

'Oh! yes. Except that I can't get work again either.'

What a face for wrappers! Sort of Mona Lisa-ish! Storbert's
novel! Ha!

'Well, I'll have a talk with your husband. I suppose you
wouldn't like to sit to an artist for a book-wrapper? It might
lead to work in that line if you want it. You're just the type for
a friend of mine. Do you know Aubrey Greene's work?'

'No, sir.'

'It's pretty good – in fact, very good in a decadent way. You
wouldn't mind sitting?'

'I wouldn't mind anything to save some money. But I'd
rather you didn't tell my husband I'd been to see you. He might
take it amiss.'

'All right! I'll see him by accident. Near St Paul's, you said?
But there's no chance here, Mrs Bicket. Besides, he couldn't
make two ends meet on this job, he told me.'

'When I was ill, sir.'

'Of course, that makes a difference.'

'Yes, sir.'

'Well, let me write you a note to Mr Greene. Will you sit
down a minute?'

He stole a look at her while she sat waiting. Really, her sallow, large-eyed face, with its dead-black, bobbed, frizzy-ended
hair, was extraordinarily interesting – a little too refined and
anaemic for the public; but, dash it all! the public couldn't always
have its Reckitt's blue eyes, corn-coloured hair, and poppy
cheeks. 'She's not a peach,' he wrote, 'on the main tree of taste;
but so striking in her way that she really might become a type,
like Beardsley's or Dana's.'

When she had taken the note and gone, he rang for his
secretary.

'No, Miss Perren, she didn't take anything off me. But some
type, eh?'

'I thought you'd like to see her. She wasn't an authoress, was
she?'

'Far from it.'

'Well, I hope she got what she wanted.'

Michael grinned. 'Partly, Miss Perren – partly. You think I'm an awful fool, don't you?'

'I'm sure I don't; but I think you're too soft-hearted.'

Michael ran his fingers through his hair.

'Would it surprise you to hear that I've done a stroke of business?'

'Yes, Mr Mont.'

'Then I won't tell you what it is. When you've done pouting, go on with that letter to my father about *Duet*: "We are sorry to say that in the present state of the trade we should not be justified in reprinting the dialogue between those two old blighters; we have already lost money by it!" You must translate, of course. Now can we say something to cheer the old boy up? How about this? "When the French have recovered their wits, and the birds begin to sing – in short, when spring comes – we hope to reconsider the matter in the light of – of –" – er – what, Miss Perren?'

' "The experience we shall have gained." Shall I leave out about the French and the birds?'

'Excellent! "Yours faithfully, Danby and Winter." Don't you think it was a scandalous piece of nepotism bringing the book here at all, Miss Perren?'

'What is "nepotism"?'

'Taking advantage of your son. He's never made a sixpence by any of his books.'

'He's a very distinguished writer, Mr Mont.'

'And we pay for the distinction. Well, he's a good old Bart. That's all before lunch, and mind you have a good one. That girl's figure wasn't usual either, was it? She's thin, but she stands up straight. There's a question I always want to ask, Miss Perren: Why do modern girls walk in a curve with their heads poked forward? They can't all be built like that.'

The secretary's cheeks brightened.

'There *is* a reason, Mr Mont.'

'Good! What is it?'

The secretary's cheeks continued to brighten. 'I don't really know whether I can –'

'Oh! sorry. I'll ask my wife. Only she's quite straight herself.'

'Well, Mr Mont, it's this, you see: They aren't supposed to have anything be – behind, and, of course, they have, and they can't get the proper effect unless they curve their chests in and poke their heads forward. It's the fashion-plates and manne-quins that do it.'

'I see,' said Michael; 'thank you, Miss Perren; awfully good of you. It's the limit, isn't it?'

'Yes, I don't hold with it, myself.'

'No, quite!'

The secretary lowered her eyelids and withdrew.

Michael sat down and drew a face on his blotting-paper. It was not Victorine's. ...

Armed with the note to Aubrey Greene, Victorine had her usual lunch, a cup of coffee and a bit of heavy cake, and took the tube towards Chelsea. She had not succeeded, but the gentleman had been friendly and she felt cheered.

At the studio door was a young man inserting a key – very elegant in smoke-grey Harris tweeds, a sliding young man with no hat, beautifully brushed-back bright hair, and a soft voice.

'Model?' he said.

'Yes, sir, please. I have a note for you from Mr Mont.'

'Michael? Come in.'

Victorine followed him in. It was 'not half' sea-green in there; a high room with rafters and a top light, and lots of pictures and drawings on the walls, and as if they had slipped off on to the floor. A picture on an easel of two ladies with their clothes sliding down troubled Victorine. She became conscious of the gentleman's eyes, sea-green like the walls, sliding up and down her.

'Will you sit for anything?' he asked.

Victorine answered mechanically: 'Yes, sir.'

'Do you mind taking your hat off?'

Victorine took off the toque, and shook out her hair.

'Ah !' said the gentleman. 'I wonder.'

Victorine wondered what.

'Just sit down on the dais, will you?'

Victorine looked about her, uncertain. A smile seemed to fly up his forehead and over his slippery bright hair.

'This is your first shot, then?'

'Yes, sir.'

'All the better.' And he pointed to a small platform.

Victorine sat down on it in a black oak chair.

'You look cold.'

'Yes, sir.'

He went to a cupboard and returned with two small glasses of a brown fluid.

'Have a Grand Marnier?'

She noticed that he tossed his off in one gulp, and did the same. It was sweet, strong, very nice, and made her gasp.

'Take a cigarette.'

Victorine took one from a case he handed, and put it between her lips. He lit it. And again a smile slid up away over the top of his head.

'You draw it in,' he said. 'Where were you born?'

'In Putney, sir.'

'That's very interesting. Just sit still a minute. It's not as bad as having a tooth out, but it takes longer. The great thing is to keep awake.'

'Yes, sir.'

He took a large piece of paper and a bit of dark stuff, and began to draw.

'Tell me,' he said, 'Miss –'

'Collins, sir – Victorine Collins.' Some instinct made her give her maiden name. It seemed somehow more professional.

'Are you at large?' He paused, and again the smile slid up over his bright hair: 'Or have you any other occupation?'

'Not at present, sir. I'm married, but nothing else.'

For some time after that the gentleman was silent. It was interesting to see him, taking a look, making a stroke on the paper, taking another look. Hundreds of looks, hundreds of

strokes. At last he said: 'All right! Now we'll have a rest.
Heaven sent you here, Miss Collins. Come and get warm.'

Victorine approached the fire.

'Do you know anything about expressionism?'

'No, sir.'

'Well, it means not troubling about the outside except in so
far as it expresses the inside. Does that convey anything to you?'

'No, sir.'

'Quite! I think you said you'd sit for the – er – altogether?'

Victorine regarded the bright and sliding gentleman. She did
not know what he meant, but she felt that he meant something
out of the ordinary.

'Altogether what, sir?'

'Nude.'

'Oh!' She cast her eyes down, then raised them to the sliding
clothes of the two ladies. 'Like that?'

'No, I shouldn't be treating you cubistically.'

A slow flush was burning out the sallow in her cheeks. She
said slowly:

'Does it mean more money?'

'Yes, half as much again – more perhaps. I don't want you to
if you'd rather not. You can think it over and let me know
next time.'

She raised her eyes again, and said: 'Thank you, sir.'

'Righto! Only please don't "sir" me.'

Victorine smiled. It was the first time she had achieved this
functional disturbance, and it seemed to have a strange effect.
He said hurriedly: 'By George! When you smile, Miss Collins,
I see you *im*pressionistically. If you've rested, sit up there
again.'

Victorine went back.

The gentleman took a fresh piece of paper.

'Can you think of anything that will keep you smiling?'

She shook her head. That was a fact.

'Nothing comic at all? I suppose you're not in love with your
husband, for instance?'

'Oh! Yes.'

'Well, try that.'

Victorine tried that, but she could only see Tony selling his balloons.

'That won't do,' said the gentleman. 'Don't think of him! Did you ever see *L'après-midi d'un Faune?*'

'No, sir.'

'Well, I've got an idea. *L'après-midi d'une Dryade.*' About the nude you really needn't mind. It's quite impersonal. Think of art, and fifteen bob a day. Shades of Nijinsky, I see the whole thing!'

All the time that he was talking his eyes were sliding off and on to her, and his pencil off and on to the paper. A sort of infection began to ferment within Victorine. Fifteen shillings a day! Blue butterflies!

There was a profound silence. His eyes and hand slid off and on. A faint smile had come on Victorine's face – she was adding up the money she might earn.

At last his eyes and hand ceased moving, and he stood looking at the paper.

'That's all for today, Miss Collins. I've got to think it out. Will you give me your address?'

Victorine thought rapidly.

'Please, sir, will you write to me at the post office. I don't want my husband to know that I'm – I'm –'

'Affiliated to art? Well! Name of post office?'

Victorine gave it and resumed her hat.

'An hour and a half, five shillings, thank you. And tomorrow, at half-past two, Miss Collins – not "sir".'

'Yes, s–, thank you.'

Waiting for her bus in the cold January air, the altogether appeared to Victorine improbable. To sit in front of a strange gentleman in her skin! If Tony knew! The slow flush again burned up the sallow in her cheeks. She climbed into the bus. But fifteen shillings! Six days a week – why, it would be four pound ten! In four months she could earn their passage out. Judging by the pictures in there, lots must be doing it. Tony must know nothing, not even that she was sitting for her face.

He was all nerves, and that fond of her! He would imagine things; she had heard him say those artists were just like cats. But that gentleman had been very nice, though he did seem as if he were laughing at everything. She wished he had shown her the drawing. Perhaps she would see herself in an exhibition some day. But without – oh! And suddenly she thought: 'If I ate a bit more, I'd look nice like that, too!' And as if to escape from the daring of that thought, she stared up into the face opposite. It had two chins, was calm and smooth and pink, with light eyes staring back at her. People had thoughts, but you couldn't tell what they were! And the smile which Aubrey Greene desired crept out on his model's face.

Chapter Three

MICHAEL WALKS AND TALKS

THE face Michael drew began by being Victorine's, and ended by being Fleur's. If physically Fleur stood up straight, was she morally as erect? This was the speculation for which he continually called himself a cad. He saw no change in her movements, and loyalty refrained from inquiring into the movements he could not see. But his aroused attention made him more and more aware of a certain cynicism, as if she were continually registering the belief that all values were equal and none of much value.

Wilfrid, though still in London, was neither visible nor spoken of. 'Out of sight and hearing, out of mind,' seemed to be the motto. It did not work with Michael – Wilfrid was constantly in his mind. If Wilfrid were not seeing Fleur, how could he bear to stay within such tantalizing reach of her? If Fleur did not want Wilfrid to stay, why had she not sent him away? He was finding it difficult, too, to conceal from others the fact that Desert and he were no longer pals. Often the impetus to go and have it out with him surged up and was beaten back. Either there was nothing beyond what he already knew, or there was something – and Wilfrid would say there wasn't. Michael accepted that without cavil; one did not give a woman away ! But he wanted to hear no lies from a war comrade. Between Fleur and himself no word had passed; for words, he felt, would add no knowledge, merely imperil a hold weak enough already. Christmas at the ancestral manor of the Monts had been passed in covert-shooting. Fleur had come and stood with him at the last drive on the second day, holding Ting-a-ling on a lead. The Chinese dog had been extraordinarily excited, climbing the air every time a bird fell, and quite unaffected by the noise of guns. Michael, waiting to miss his birds – he was a poor shot – had watched her eager face emerging from grey fur, her form braced back against Ting-a-ling. Shooting was new to her; and under the stimulus of novelty she was always at her best. He had loved even her 'Oh, Michaels !' when he missed. She had been the success of the gathering, which meant seeing almost nothing of her except a sleepy head on a pillow; but, at least, down there he had not suffered from lurking uneasiness.

Putting a last touch to the bobbed hair on the blotting-paper, he got up. St Paul's, that girl had said. He might stroll up and have a squint at Bicket. Something might occur to him. Tightening the belt of his blue overcoat round his waist, he sallied forth, thin and sprightly, with a little ache in his heart.

Walking east, on that bright, cheerful day, nothing struck him so much as the fact that he was alive, well, and in work. So very many were dead, ill, or out of a job. He entered Covent Garden. Amazing place ! A human nature which, decade after decade, could put up with Covent Garden was not in danger of extinction from its many ills. A comforting place – one needn't take anything too seriously after walking through it. On this square island were the vegetables of the earth and the fruits of the world, bounded on the west by publishing, on the east by opera, on the north and south by rivers of mankind. Among discharging carts and litter of paper, straw and men out of drawing, Michael walked and sniffed. Smell of its own, Covent Garden,

earthy and just not rotten ! He had never seen – even in the war
– any place that so utterly lacked form. Extraordinarily English !
Nobody looked as if they had anything to do with the soil –
drivers, hangers-on, packers, and the salesmen inside the covered
markets, seemed equally devoid of acquaintanceship with sun,
wind, water, earth or air – town types all ! And – Golly ! – how
their faces jutted, sloped, sagged and swelled, in every kind of
featural disharmony. What was the English type amongst all
this infinite variety of disproportion? There just wasn't one ! He
came on the fruits, glowing piles, still and bright – foreigners
from the land of the sun – globes all the same size and colour.
They made Michael's mouth water. 'Something in the sun,' he
thought; 'there really is.' Look at Italy, at the Arabs, at Australia – the Australians came from England, and see the type now !
Nevertheless – a Cockney for good temper ! The more regular
a person's form and features, the more selfish they were ! Those
grape-fruit looked horribly self-satisfied, compared with the
potatoes !

He emerged still thinking about the English. Well ! They
were now one of the plainest and most distorted races of the
world; and yet was there any race to compare with them for
good temper and for 'guts'? And they needed those in their
smoky towns, and their climate – remarkable instance of adapta-
tion to environment, the modern English character ! 'I could
pick out an Englishman anywhere,' he thought, 'and yet,
physically, there's no general type now !' Astounding people ! So
ugly in the mass, yet growing such flowers of beauty, and such
strange sprigs – like that little Mrs Bicket; so unimaginative in
bulk, yet with such a blooming lot of poets ! How would old
Danby like it, by the way, when Wilfrid took his next volume
to some other firm; or rather what should he – Wilfrid's particular friend ! – say to old Danby? Aha ! He knew what he should
say :

'Yes, sir, but you should have let that poor blighter off who
snooped the *Copper Coin*s. Desert hasn't forgotten your refusal.'
One for old Danby and his eternal in-the-rightness ! *Copper
Coin* had done uncommonly well. Its successor would probably

do uncommonly better. The book was a proof of what he – Michael – was always saying: The 'cockyolly-bird period' was passing. People wanted life again. Sibley, Walter Nazing, Linda – all those who had nothing to say except that they were superior to such as had – were already measured for their coffins. Not that they would know when they were in them; not blooming likely! They would continue to wave their noses and look down them!

'*I'm* fed-up with them,' thought Michael. 'If only Fleur would see that looking down your nose is a sure sign of inferiority!' And, suddenly, it came to him that she probably did. Wilfrid was the only one of the whole lot she had ever been thick with; the others were there because – well, because she was Fleur, and had the latest things about her. When, very soon, they were no longer the latest things, she would drop them. But Wilfrid she would not drop. No, he felt sure that she had not dropped, and would not drop Wilfrid.

He looked up. Ludgate Hill! 'Near St Paul's – sells balloons?' And there – sure enough – the poor beggar was!

Bicket was deflating with a view to going off his stand for a cup of cocoa. Remembering that he had come on him by accident, Michael stood for a moment preparing the tones of surprise. Pity the poor chap couldn't blow himself into one of those coloured shapes and float over St Paul's to Peter. Mournful little cuss he looked, squeezing out the air! Memory tapped sharply on his mind. Balloon – in the square – November the first – joyful night! Special! Fleur! Perhaps they brought luck. He moved and said in an astounded voice: '*You*, Bicket? Is this your stunt now?'

The large eyes of Bicket regarded him over a puce-coloured sixpennyworth.

'Mr Mont! Often thought I'd like to see you again, sir.'

'Same here, Bicket. If you're not doing anything, come and have some lunch.'

Bicket completed the globe's collapse, and, closing his tray-lid, said: 'Reelly, sir?'

'Rather! I was just going into a fish place.'

Bicket detached his tray.

'I'll leave this with the crossing-sweeper.' He did so, and followed at Michael's side.

'Any money in it, Bicket?'

'Bare livin', sir.'

'How about this place? We'll have oysters.'

A little saliva at the corner of Bicket's mouth was removed by a pale tongue.

At a small table decorated with a white oilcloth and a cruet stand, Michael sat down.

'Two dozen oysters, and all that; then two good soles, and a bottle of Chablis. Hurry up, please.'

When the white-aproned fellow had gone about it, Bicket said simply:

'My Gawd!'

'Yes, it's a funny world, Bicket.'

'It *is*, and that's a fact. This lunch'll cost you a pound, I shouldn't wonder. If I take twenty-five bob a week, it's all I do.'

'You touch it there, Bicket. I eat my conscience every day.'

Bicket shook his head.

'No, sir, if you've got money, spend it. I would. Be 'appy if you can – there yn't too many that are.'

The white-aproned fellow began blessing them with oysters. He brought them fresh-opened, three at a time. Michael bearded them; Bicket swallowed them whole. Presently above twelve empty shells, he said:

'That's where the Socialists myke their mistyke, sir. Nothing keeps me going but the sight of other people spendin' money. It's what we might all come to with a bit of luck. Reduce the world to a level of a pound a dy – and it won't even run to that, they sy! It's not good enough, sir. I'd rather 'ave less with the 'ope of more. Take awy the gamble, and life's a frost. Here's luck!'

'Almost thou persuadest me to be a capitalist, Bicket.'

A glow had come up in the thin and large-eyed face behind the greenish Chablis glass.

'I wish to Gawd I had my wife here, sir. I told you about her and the pneumonia. She's all right agyne now, only thin. She's the prize I drew. I don't want a world where you can't draw prizes. If it were all bloomin' conscientious an' accordin' to merit, I'd never have got her. See?'

'Me, too,' thought Michael, mentally drawing that face again.

'We've all got our dreams; mine's blue butterflies – Central Austrylia. The Socialists won't 'elp me to get there. Their ideas of 'eaven don't run beyond Europe.'

'Cripes!' said Michael. 'Melted butter, Bicket?'

'Thank you, sir.'

Silence was not broken for some time, but the soles were.

'What made you think of balloons, Bicket?'

'You don't 'ave to advertise, they do it for you.'

'Saw too much of advertising with us, eh?'

'Well, sir, I did use to read the wrappers. Astonished me, I will sy – the number of gryte books.'

Michael ran his hands through his hair.

'Wrappers! The same young woman being kissed by the same young man with the same clean-cut jaw. But what can you do, Bicket? They *will have it*. I tried to make a break only this morning – I shall see what comes of it.' 'And I hope *you* won't!' he thought: 'Fancy coming on Fleur outside a novel!'

'I did notice a tendency just before I left,' said Bicket, 'to 'ave cliffs or landskips and two sort of dolls sittin' on the sand or in the grass lookin' as if they didn't know what to do with each other.'

'Yes,' murmured Michael, 'we tried that. It was supposed not to be vulgar. But we soon exhausted the public's capacity. What'll you have now – cheese?'

'Thank you, sir; I've had too much already, but I won't say "No".'

'Two Stiltons,' said Michael.

'How's Mr Desert, sir?'

Michael reddened.

'Oh! He's all right.'

Bicket had reddened also.

'I wish – I wish you'd let him know that it was quite a – an accident my pitchin' on his book. I've always regretted it.'

'It's usually an accident, I think,' said Michael slowly, 'when we snoop other people's goods. We never *want* to.'

Bicket looked up.

'No, sir, I don't agree. 'Alf mankind's predytory – only, I'm not that sort, meself.'

In Michael loyalty tried to stammer. 'Nor is he.' He handed his cigarette-case to Bicket.

'Thank you, sir, I'm sure.'

His eyes were swimming, and Michael thought: 'Dash it! This is sentimental. Kiss me good-bye and go!' He beckoned up the white-aproned fellow.

'Give us your address, Bicket. If integuments are any good to you, I might have some spare slops.'

Bicket backed the bill with his address and said, hesitating: 'I suppose, sir, Mrs Mont wouldn't 'ave anything to spare. My wife's about my height.'

'I expect she would. We'll send them along.' He saw the 'little snipe's' lips quivering, and reached for his overcoat. 'If anything blows in, I'll remember you. Good-bye, Bicket, and good luck.'

Going east, because Bicket was going west, he repeated to himself the maxim: 'Pity is tripe – pity is tripe!' Then getting on a bus, he was borne back past St Paul's. Cautiously 'taking a lunar' – as old Forsyte put it – he saw Bicket inflating a balloon; little was visible of his face or figure behind that rosy circumference. Nearing Blake Street, he developed an invincible repugnance to work, and was carried on to Trafalgar Square. Bicket had stirred him up. The world was sometimes almost unbearably jolly. Bicket, Wilfrid, and the Ruhr! 'Feeling is tosh! Pity is tripe!' He descended from his bus, and passed the lions towards Pall Mall. Should he go into 'Snooks' and ask for Bart? No use – he would not find Fleur there. That was what he really wanted – to see Fleur in the daytime. But – where? She was everywhere to be found, and that was nowhere.

She was restless. Was that his fault? If he had been Wilfrid –

would she be restless? 'Yes,' he thought stoutly, 'Wilfrid's restless, too.' They were all restless – all the people he knew. At least all the young ones – in life and in letters. Look at their novels! Hardly one in twenty had any repose, any of that quality which made one turn back to a book as a corner of refuge. They dashed and sputtered and skidded and rushed by like motor-cycles – violent, oh! and clever. How tired he was of cleverness! Sometimes he would take a manuscript home to Fleur for her opinion. He remembered her saying once: 'This is exactly like life, Michael, it just rushes – it doesn't dwell on anything long enough to mean anything anywhere. Of course the author didn't mean it for satire, but if you publish it, I advise you to put: "This awful satire on modern life" outside the cover.' And they had. At least, they had put: 'This wonderful satire on modern life.' Fleur *was* like that! She could see the hurry, but, like the author of the wonderful satire, she didn't know that she herself veered and hurried, or – did she know? Was she conscious of kicking at life, like a flame at air?

He had reached Piccadilly, and suddenly he remembered that he had not called on her aunt for ages. That was a possible draw. He bent his steps towards Green Street.

'Mrs Dartie at home?'

'Yes, sir.'

Michael moved his nostrils. Fleur used – but he could catch no scent, except incense. Winifred burnt joss-sticks when she remembered what a distinguished atmosphere they produced.

'What name?'

'Mr Mont. My wife's not here, I suppose?'

'No, sir. Only Mrs Val Dartie.'

Mrs Val Dartie! Yes, he remembered, nice woman – but not a substitute for Fleur! Committed, however, he followed the maid.

In the drawing-room Michael found three people, one of them his father-in-law, who had a grey and brooding aspect, and, from an Empire chair, was staring at blue Australian butterflies' wings under a glass on a round scarlet table. Winifred had jazzed the Empire foundation of her room with a superstructure more suitable to the age. She greeted Michael with fashionable warmth. It was good of him to come when he was so busy with all these young poets. 'I thought *Copper Coin*,' she said – 'what a *nice* title! – such an intriguing little book. I do think Mr Desert is clever! What is he doing now?'

Michael said: 'I don't know,' and dropped on to a settee beside Mrs Val. Ignorant of the Forsyte family feud, he was unable to appreciate the relief he had brought in with him. Soames said something about the French, got up, and went to the window; Winifred joined him – their voices sounded confidential.

'How is Fleur?' said Michael's neighbour.

'Thanks, awfully well.'

'Do you like your house?'

'Oh, fearfully. Won't you come and see it?'

'I don't know whether Fleur would –?'

'Why not?'

'Oh! Well!'

'She's frightfully accessible.'

She seemed to be looking at him with more interest than he deserved, to be trying to make something out from his face, and he added:

'You're a relation – by blood as well as marriage, aren't you?'

'Yes.'

'Then what's the skeleton?'

'Oh! nothing. I'll certainly come. Only – she has so many friends.'

Michael thought: 'I like this woman!' 'As a matter of fact,' he said, 'I came here this afternoon thinking I might find Fleur. I should like her to know you. With all the jazz there is about, she'd appreciate somebody restful.'

'Thank you.'

'You've never lived in London?'

'Not since I was six.'

'I wish she could get a rest – pity there isn't a d-desert handy.' He had stuttered; the word was not pronounced the same – still! He glanced, disconcerted, at the butterflies. 'I've just been talking to a little Cockney whose S.O.S. is "Central Austrylia". But what do you say – Have we got souls to save?'

'I used to think so, but now I'm not so sure – something's struck me lately.'

'What was that?'

'Well, I notice that anyone at all out of proportion, or whose nose is on one side, or whose eyes jut out, or even have a special shining look, always believes in the soul; people who are in proportion, and have no prominent physical features, don't seem to be really interested.'

Michael's ears moved.

'By Jove!' he said; 'some thought! Fleur's beautifully proportioned – *she* doesn't seem to worry. I'm not – and I certainly do. The people in Covent Garden must have lots of soul. You think "the soul's" the result of loose-gearing in the organism – sort of special consciousness from not working in one piece.'

'Yes, rather like that – what's called psychic power is, I'm almost sure.'

'I say, is your life safe? According to your theory, though, we're in a mighty soulful era. I must think over my family. How about yours?'

'The Forsytes! Oh, they're quite too well-proportioned.'

'I agree, they haven't any special juts so far as I've seen. The French, too, are awfully close-knit. It really is an idea, only, of course, most people see it the other way. They'd say the soul produces the disproportion, makes the eyes shine, bends the nose, and all that; where the soul is small, it's not trying to get out of the body, whence the barber's block. I'll think about it. Thanks for the tip. Well, do come and see us. Good-bye! I don't think I'll disturb them in the window. Would you mind saying I had to scoot?' Squeezing a slim, gloved hand, receiving and returning a smiling look, he slid out, thinking: 'Dash the soul, where's her body?'

Chapter Four

FLEUR'S BODY

————

FLEUR's body, indeed, was at the moment in one of those difficult positions which continually threaten the spirit of compromise. It was in fact in Wilfrid's arms; sufficiently, at least, to make her say:

'No, Wilfrid – you promised to be good.'

It was a really remarkable tribute to her powers of skating on thin ice that the word 'good' should still have significance. For eleven weeks exactly this young man had danced on the edge of fulfilment, and was even now divided from her by two clenched hands pressed firmly against his chest, and the word 'good'; and this after not having seen her for a fortnight.

When she said it, he let her go, with a sort of violence, and sat down on a piece of junk. Only the sense of damnable iteration prevented him from saying: 'It can't go on, Fleur.' She knew that! And yet it did! This was what perpetually amazed him. How a poor brute could hang on week after week saying to her and to himself: 'Now or never!' when it wasn't either? Subconsciousness, that, until the word 'now' had been reached, Fleur would not know her own mind, alone had kept him dancing. His own feelings were so intense that he almost hated her for indecision. And he was unjust. It was not exactly indecision. Fleur wanted the added richness and excitement which Wilfrid's affection gave to life, but without danger and without loss. How natural! His frightful passionateness was making all the trouble. Neither by her wish, nor through her fault, was he passionate! And yet – it was both nice and proper to inspire passion; and, of course, she had the lurking sense that she was not 'in the mode' to cavil at a lover, especially since life owed her one.

Released, she smoothed herself and said: 'Talk of something sensible; what have you been writing?'

'This.'

Fleur read. Flushing and biting her lips, she said:

'It's frightfully bitter.'

'It's frightfully true. Does *he* ever ask you now whether you see me?'

'Never.'

'Why?'

'I don't know.'

'What would you answer if he did?'

Fleur shrugged her shoulders.

Desert said quietly: 'Yes, that's your attitude. It can't last, Fleur.' He was standing by the window. She put the sheets down on his desk and moved towards him. Poor Wilfrid! Now that he was quiet she was sorry.

He said suddenly: 'Stop! Don't move! *He's* down there in the street.'

Recoiling, she gasped: 'Michael! Oh! But how – how could he have known?'

Desert said grimly: 'Do you only know him as little as that? Do you suppose he'd be there if he knew you were here?'

Fleur winced.

'Why *is* he there, then?'

'He probably wants to see me. He looks as if he couldn't make up his mind. Don't get the wind up, he won't be let in.'

Fleur sat down; she felt weak in the legs. The ice seemed suddenly of an appalling thinness – the water appallingly cold.

'Has he seen you?' she said.

'No.'

The thought flashed through him: 'If I were a blackguard, I could force her hand, by moving one step and crooking my finger.' Pity one wasn't a blackguard – at all events, not to that point – things would be so much simpler!

'Where is he now?' asked Fleur.

'Going away.'

In profound relief, she sighed out:

141

'But it's queer, isn't it, Wilfrid?'

'You don't suppose he's easy in his mind, do you?'

Fleur bit her lips. He was jeering, because she didn't or couldn't really love either of them. It was unjust. She *could* have loved – she *had* loved! Wilfrid and Michael – they might go to the deuce!

'I wish I had never come here,' she said suddenly: 'and I'll never come again!'

He went to the door, and held it open.

'You are right.'

Fleur stood quite still, her chin on the collar of her fur, her clear-glancing eyes fixed on his face, her lips set and mutinous.

'You think I'm a heartless beast,' she said slowly. 'So I am – now. Good-bye!'

He neither took her hand nor spoke, he only bowed. His eyes were very tragic. Trembling with mortification, Fleur went out. She heard the door closed, while she was going down the stairs. At the bottom she stood uncertain. Suppose Michael had come back! Almost opposite was that gallery where she had first met him and – Jon. Slip across in there! If he were still hovering round the entrance of the little street, she could tell him with a good conscience where she had been. She peeped. Not in sight! Swiftly she slid across into the doorway opposite. They would be closing in a minute – just on four o'clock! She put down a shilling and slipped in. She must see – in case! She stood revolving – one-man show, the man – Claud Brains! She put down another shilling for a catalogue, and read as she went out. 'No. 7. Woman getting the wind up.' It told her everything; and with a lighter heart she skimmed along, and took a taxi. Get home before Michael! She felt relieved, almost exhilarated. So much for skating on thin ice! It wasn't good enough. Wilfrid must go. Poor Wilfrid! Well, he shouldn't have sneered – what did he know of her? Nobody knew anything of her! She was alone in the world. She slipped her latchkey into the hall door. No Michael. She sat down in the drawing-room before the fire, and took up Walter Nazing's last. She read a page three times. It meant no more with every reading – it meant less; he was the

kind of author who must be read at a gallop, and given away
lest a first impression of wind in the hair be lost in a sensation of
wind lower down; but Wilfrid's eyes came between her and the
words. Pity! Nobody pitied her; why, then, should she pity
them? Besides, pity was 'pop', as Amabel would say. The situation demanded cast-iron sense. But Wilfrid's eyes! Well – she
wouldn't be seeing them again! Beautiful eyes when they smiled
or when – so much more often – they looked at her with longing, as now between her and the sentence: 'Solemnly and with a
delicious egoism he more than awfully desired her who snug
and rosy in the pink shell of her involuted and so petulant social
periphrasis –' Poor Wilfrid! Pity was 'pop', but there was pride!
Did she choose that he should go away thinking that she had
'played him up' just out of vanity, as Walter Nazing said American women did? Did she? Would it not be more in the mode,
really dramatic – if one 'went over the deep end', as they said,
just once? Would that not be something they could both look
back on – he in the East he was always talking of, she in this
West? The proposition had a momentary popularity in that
organism called Fleur too finely proportioned for a soul according to the theory which Michael was thinking over. Like all
popularities, it did not last. First: Would she like it? She did
not think she would; one man, without love, was quite enough.
Then there was the danger of passing into Wilfrid's power. He
was a gentleman, but he was passionate; the cup once sipped,
would he consent to put it down? But more than all was a physical doubt of the last two or three weeks which awaited verifica-
tion, and which made her feel solemn. She stood up and passed
her hands all over her, with a definite recoil from the thought
of Wilfrid's hands doing the same. No! To have his friendship,
his admiration, but not at that price. She viewed him suddenly,
as a bomb set on her copper floor; and in fancy ran and seized
and flung him out into the Square – poor Wilfrid! Pity was
'pop'! But one might be sorry for *oneself*, losing him; losing
too that ideal of modern womanhood expounded to her one
evening by Marjorie Ferrar, pet of the 'panjoys', whose red-
gold hair excited so much admiration: 'My ambition – old thing

– is to be the perfect wife of one man, the perfect mistress of another, and the perfect mother of a third, all at once. It's perfectly possible – they do it in France.'

But was it really so perfectly possible – even if pity *was* posh? How be perfect to Michael, when the slightest slip might reveal to him that she was being perfect to Wilfrid; how be perfect to Wilfrid, when every time she was perfect to Michael would be a dagger in Wilfrid's heart? And if – if her physical doubt should mature into certainty, how be perfect mother to the certainty, when she was either torturing two men, or lying to them like a trooperess? Not so perfectly possible as all that! 'If only I were all French!' thought Fleur. . . .

The clicking door startled her – the reason that she was not all French was coming in. He looked very grey, as if he had been thinking too much. He kissed her, and sat down moodily before the fire.

'Have you come for the night, Dad?'

'If I may,' murmured Soames. 'Business.'

'Anything unpleasant, ducky?'

Soames looked up as if startled.

'Unpleasant? Why should it be unpleasant?'

'I only thought from your face.'

Soames grunted. 'This Ruhr!' he said. 'I've brought you a picture. Chinese!'

'Oh, Dad! How jolly!'

'It isn't,' said Soames; 'it's a monkey eating fruit.'

'But that's perfect! Where is it – in the hall?'

Soames nodded.

Stripping the coverings off the picture, Fleur brought it in, and setting it up on the jade-green settee, stood away and looked at it. The large white monkey with its brown haunting eyes, as if she had suddenly wrested its interest from the orange-like fruit in its crisped paw, the grey background, the empty rinds all round – bright splashes in a general ghostliness of colour, impressed her at once.

'But, Dad, it's a masterpiece – I'm sure it's of a frightfully good period.'

'I don't know,' said Soames. 'I must look up the Chinese.'

'But you oughtn't to give it to me, it must be worth any amount. You ought to have it in your collection.'

'They didn't know its value,' said Soames, and a faint smile illumined his features. 'I gave three hundred for it. It'll be safer here.'

'Of course it'll be safe. Only why safer?'

Soames turned towards the picture.

'I can't tell. Anything may come of this.'

'Of what, dear?'

'Is "old Mont" coming in tonight?'

'No, he's at Lippinghall still.'

'Well, it doesn't matter — he's no good.'

Fleur took his hand and gave it a squeeze.

'Tell me!'

Soames's tickled heart quivered. Fancy her wanting to know what was troubling him! But his sense of the becoming, and his fear of giving away his own alarm, forbade response.

'Nothing you'd understand,' he said. 'Where are you going to hang it?'

'There, I think; but we must wait for Michael.'

Soames grumbled out:

'I saw him just now at your aunt's. Is that the way he attends to business?'

'Perhaps,' thought Fleur, 'he was only on his way back to the office. Cork Street *is* more or less between! If he passed the end of it, he would think of Wilfrid, he might have been wanting to see him about books.'

'Oh, here's Ting! Well, darling!'

The Chinese dog, let in, as it were, by Providence, seeing Soames, sat down suddenly with snub upturned eyes brilliant. 'The expression of your face,' he seemed to say, 'pleases me. We belong to the past and could sing hymns together, old man.'

'Funny little chap,' said Soames: 'he always knows me.'

Fleur lifted him. 'Come and see the new monkey, ducky.'

'Don't let him lick it.'

Held rather firmly by his jade-green collar and confronted by an inexplicable piece of silk smelling of the past, Ting-a-ling raised his head higher and higher to correspond with the action of his nostrils, and his little tongue appeared, tentatively savouring the emanation of his country.

'It's a nice monkey, isn't it, darling?'

'No,' said Ting-a-ling, rather clearly. 'Put me down!'

Restored to the floor, he sought a patch where the copper came through between two rugs, and licked it quietly.

'Mr Aubrey Greene, ma'am!'

'H'm!' said Soames.

The painter came gliding and glowing in; his bright hair slipping back, his green eyes sliding off.

'Ah!' he said, pointing to the floor. 'That's what I've come about.'

Fleur followed his finger in amazement.

'Ting!' she said severely, 'stop it! He will lick the copper, Aubrey.'

'But how perfectly Chinese! They do everything we don't.'

'Dad – Aubrey Greene. My father's just brought me this picture, Aubrey – isn't it a gem?'

The painter stood quite still, his eyes ceased sliding off, his hair ceased slipping back.

'Phew!' he said.

Soames rose. He had waited for the flippant; but he recognized in the tone something reverential, if not aghast.

'By George,' said Aubrey Greene, 'those eyes! Where did you pick it up, sir?'

'It belonged to a cousin of mine – a racing man. It was his only picture.'

'Good for him! He must have had taste.'

Soames stared. The idea that George should have had taste almost appalled him.

'No,' he said, with a flash of inspiration: 'What he liked about it was that it makes you feel uncomfortable.'

'Same thing! I don't know where I've seen a more pungent satire on human life.'

'I don't follow,' said Soames dryly.

'Why, it's a perfect allegory, sir! Eat the fruits of life, scatter the rinds, and get copped doing it. When they're still, a monkey's eyes are the human tragedy incarnate. Look at them! He thinks there's something beyond, and he's sad or angry because he can't get at it. That picture ought to be in the British Museum, sir, with the label: "Civilization, caught out."'

'Well, it won't be,' said Fleur. 'It'll be here, labelled "The White Monkey."'

'Same thing.'

'Cynicism,' said Soames abruptly, 'gets you nowhere. If you'd said "*Modernity* caught out"—'

'I do, sir; but why be narrow? You don't seriously suppose this age is worse than any other?'

'Don't I?' said Soames. 'In my belief the world reached its highest point in the eighties, and will never reach it again.'

The painter stared.

'That's frightfully interesting. I wasn't born, and I suppose you were about my age then, sir. You believed in God and drove in *diligences*.'

Diligences! The word awakened in Soames a memory which somehow seemed appropriate.

'Yes,' he said, 'and I can tell you a story of those days that you can't match in these. When I was a youngster in Switzerland with my people, two of my sisters had some black cherries. When they'd eaten about half a dozen they discovered that they all had little maggots in them. An English climber there saw how upset they were, and ate the whole of the rest of the cherries – about two pounds – maggots, stones and all, just to show them. That was the sort of men they were then.'

'Oh! Father!'

'Gee! He must have been gone on them.'

'No,' said Soames, 'not particularly. His name was Powley; he wore side-whiskers.'

'Talking of God and diligences: I saw a hansom yesterday.'

'More to the point if you'd seen God,' thought Soames, but

he did not say so; indeed, the thought surprised him, it was not the sort of thing he had ever seen himself.

'You mayn't know it, sir, but there's more belief now than there was before the war – they've discovered that we're not all body.'

'Oh!' said Fleur. 'That reminds me, Aubrey. Do you know any mediums? Could I get one to come here? On our floor, with Michael outside the door, one would know there couldn't be any hanky. Do the dark *séance* people ever go out? – they're much more thrilling they say.'

'Spiritualism!' said Soames. 'H'mph!' He could not in half an hour have expressed himself more clearly.

Aubrey Greene's eyes slid off to Ting-a-ling. 'I'll see what I can do, if you'll lend me your Peke for an hour or so tomorrow afternoon. I'd bring him back on a lead, and give him every luxury.'

'What do you want him for?'

'Michael sent me a most topping little model today. But, you see, she can't smile.'

'Michael?'

'Yes. Something quite new; and I've got a scheme. Her smile's like sunlight going off an Italian valley; but when you tell her to, she can't. I thought your Peke could make her, perhaps.'

'May I come and see?' said Fleur.

'Yes, bring him tomorrow; but, if I can persuade her, it'll be in the "altogether".'

'Oh! Will you get me a *séance*, if I lend you Ting?'

'I will.'

'H'mph!' said Soames again. *Séances*, Italian sunlight, the 'altogether'! It was time he got back to Elderson, and what was to be done now, and left this fiddling while Rome burned.

'Good-bye, Mr Greene,' he said; 'I've got no time.'

'Quite, sir,' said Aubrey Greene.

'Quite!' mimicked Soames to himself, going out.

Aubrey Greene took his departure a few minutes later, crossing a lady in the hall who was delivering her name to the man-servant.

Alone with her body, Fleur again passed her hands all over it. The 'altogether' — was a reminder of the dangers of dramatic conduct.

Chapter Five

FLEUR'S SOUL

━<━>━

'MRS VAL DARTIE, ma'am.'

A name which could not be distorted even by Coaker affected her like a finger applied suddenly to the head of the sciatic nerve. Holly! Not seen since the day when she did not marry Jon. Holly! A flood of remembrance — Wansdon, the Downs, the gravel pit, the apple orchard, the river, the copse at Robin Hill! No! It was not a pleasant sensation – to see Holly, and she said: 'How awfully nice of you to come!'

'I met your husband this afternoon at Green Street; he asked me. What a lovely room!'

'Ting! Come and be introduced! This is Ting-a-ling; isn't he perfect? He's a little upset because of the new monkey. How's Val, and dear Wansdon? It was too wonderfully peaceful.'

'It's a nice backwater. I don't get tired of it.'

'And –' said Fleur, with a little laugh, 'Jon?'

'He's growing peaches in North Carolina. British Columbia didn't do.'

'Oh! Is he married?'

'No.'

'I suppose he'll marry an American.'

'He isn't twenty-two, you know.'

'Good Lord!' said Fleur: 'Am I only twenty-one? I feel forty-eight.'

'That's living in the middle of things and seeing so many people –'

'And getting to know none.'

'But don't you?'

'No, it isn't done. I mean we all call each other by our Christian names; but *après* –'

'I like your husband very much.'

'Oh! yes, Michael's a dear. How's June?'

'I saw her yesterday – she's got a new painter, of course – Claud Brains. I believe he's what they call a Vertiginist.'

Fleur bit her lip.

'Yes, they're quite common. I suppose June thinks he's the only one.'

'Well, she thinks he's a genius.'

'She's wonderful.'

'Yes,' said Holly, 'the most loyal creature in the world while it lasts. It's like poultry farming – once they're hatched. You never saw Boris Strumolowski?'

'No.'

'Well, don't.'

'I know his bust of Michael's uncle. It's rather sane.'

'Yes. June thought it a pot-boiler, and he never forgave her. Of course it was. As soon as her swan makes money, she looks round for another. She's a darling.'

'Yes,' murmured Fleur; 'I liked June.'

Another flood of remembrance – from a tea-shop, from the river, from June's little dining-room, from where in Green Street she had changed her wedding dress under the upward gaze of June's blue eyes. She seized the monkey and held it up.

'Isn't it a picture of "life"?' Would she have said that if Aubrey Greene hadn't? Still it seemed very true at the moment.

'Poor monkey!' said Holly. 'I'm always frightfully sorry for monkeys. But it's marvellous, I think.'

'Yes. I'm going to hang it here. If I can get one more I shall have done in this room; only people have so got on to Chinese things. This was luck – somebody died – George Forsyte, you know, the racing one.'

'Oh!' said Holly softly. She saw again her old kinsman's japing eyes in the church when Fleur was being married, heard his throaty whisper: 'Will she stay the course?' And was she staying it, this pretty filly? 'Wish she could get a rest. If only there were a desert handy!' Well, one couldn't ask a question so personal, and Holly took refuge in a general remark.

'What do all you smart young people feel about life, nowadays, Fleur! when one's not of it and has lived twenty years in South Africa, one still feels out of it.'

'Life! Oh! well, we know it's supposed to be a riddle, but we've given it up. We just want to have a good time because we don't believe anything can last. But I don't think we know how to have it. We just fly on, and hope for it. Of course, there's art, but most of us aren't artists; besides, expressionism – Michael says it's got no inside. We gas about it, but I suppose it hasn't. I see a frightful lot of writers and painters, you know; they're supposed to be amusing.'

Holly listened, amazed. Who would have thought that this girl *saw*? She might be seeing wrong, but anyway she saw!

'Surely,' she said, 'you enjoy yourselves?'

'Well, I like getting hold of nice things, and interesting people; I like seeing everything that's new and worth while, or seems so at the moment. But that's just how it is – nothing lasts. You see, I'm not of the "Pan-joys", nor of the "new-faithfuls".'

'The new-faithfuls?'

'Oh! don't you know – it's a sort of faith-healing done on oneself, not exactly the old "God-good, good-God!" sort; but a kind of mixture of will-power, psycho-analysis, and belief that everything will be all right on the night if you say it will. You must have come across them. They're frightfully in earnest.'

'I know,' said Holly; 'their eyes shine.'

'I dare say. I don't believe in them – I don't believe in anyone; or anything – much. How can one?'

'How about simple people, and hard work?'

Fleur sighed. 'I dare say. I will say for Michael – *he's* not spoiled. Let's have tea? Tea, Ting?' and, turning up the lights, she rang the bell.

When her unexpected visitor had gone, she sat very still before the fire. Today, when she had been so very nearly Wilfrid's!

So Jon was not married! Not that it made any odds! Things did not come round as they were expected to in books. And anyway sentiment was swosh! Cut it out! She tossed back her hair; and, getting hammer and nail, proceeded to hang the white monkey. Between the two tea-chests with their coloured pearl-shell figures, he would look his best. Since she couldn't have Jon, what did it matter – Wilfrid or Michael, or both, or neither? Eat the orange in her hand, and throw away the rind! And suddenly she became aware that Michael was in the room. He had come in very quietly and was standing before the fire behind her. She gave him a quick look and said:

'I've had Aubrey Greene here about a model you sent him, and Holly – Mrs Val Dartie – she said she's seen you. Oh! and father's brought us this. Isn't it perfect?'

Michael did not speak.

'Anything the matter, Michael?'

'No, nothing.' He went up to the monkey. From behind him now Fleur searched his profile. Instinct told her of a change. Had he, after all, seen her going to Wilfrid's – coming away?

'Some monkey!' he said. 'By the way, have you any spare clothes you could give the wife of a poor snipe – nothing too swell?'

She answered mechanically: 'Yes, of course!' while her brain worked furiously.

'Would you put them out, then? I'm going to make up a bunch for him myself – they could go together.'

Yes! He was quite unlike himself, as if the spring in him had run down. A sort of *malaise* overcame her. Michael not cheerful! It was like the fire going out on a cold day. And, perhaps for the first time, she was conscious that his cheerfulness was of real importance to her. She watched him pick up Ting-a-ling and sit down. And going up behind him, she bent over till her hair was against his cheek. Instead of rubbing his cheek on hers, he sat quite still, and her heart misgave her.

'What is it?' she said, coaxing.

'Nothing!'

She took hold of his ears.

'But there is. I suppose you know somehow that I went to see Wilfrid.'

He said stonily: 'Why not?'

She let go, and stood up straight.

'It was only to tell him that I couldn't see him again.'

That half-truth seemed to her the whole.

He suddenly looked up, a quiver went over his face; he took her hand.

'It's all right, Fleur. You must do what you like, you know. That's only fair. I had too much lunch.'

Fleur withdrew to the middle of the room.

'You're rather an angel,' she said slowly, and went out.

Upstairs she looked out garments, confused in her soul.

Chapter Six

MICHAEL GETS 'WHAT-FOR'

◄─‹›─►

AFTER his Green Street quest Michael had wavered back down Piccadilly, and, obeying one of those impulses which make people hang around the centres of disturbance, on to Cork Street. He stood for a minute at the mouth of Wilfrid's backwater.

'No,' he thought at last, 'ten to one he isn't in; and if he is, twenty to one that I get any change except bad change!'

He was moving slowly on to Bond Street, when a little light lady, coming from the backwater, and reading as she went, ran into him from behind.

'Why don't you look where you're going! Oh! You? Aren't you the young man who married Fleur Forsyte? I'm her cousin, June. I thought I saw her just now.' She waved a hand which held a catalogue with a gesture like the flirt of a bird's wing. 'Opposite my gallery. She went into a house, or I should have spoken to her – I'd like to have seen her again.'

Into a house! Michael dived for his cigarette-case. Hard-grasping it, he looked up. The little lady's blue eyes were sweeping from side to side of his face with a searching candour.

'Are you happy together?' she said.

A cold sweat broke out on his forehead. A sense of general derangement afflicted him – hers, and his own.

'I beg your pardon?' he gasped.

'I hope you are. She ought to have married my little brother – but I hope you are. She's a pretty child.'

In the midst of a dull sense of stunning blows, it staggered him that she seemed quite unconscious of inflicting them. He heard his teeth gritting, and said dully: 'Your little brother, who was he?'

'What! Jon – didn't you know Jon? He was too young, of course, and so was she. But they were head over – the family feud stopped that. Well! it's all past. I was at your wedding. I hope you're happy. Have you seen the Claud Brains show at my gallery? He's a genius. I was going to have a bun in here; will you join me? You ought to know his work.'

She had paused at the door of a confectioner's. Michael put his hand on his chest.

'Thank you,' he said, 'I have just had a bun – two, in fact. Excuse me!'

The little lady grasped his other hand.

'Well, good-bye, young man! Glad to have met you. You're not a beauty, but I like your face. Remember me to that child. You should go and see Claud Brains. He's a real genius.'

Stock-still before the door, he watched her turn and enter, with a scattered motion, as of flying, and a disturbance among those seated in the pastry-cook's. Then he moved on, the cigarette unlighted in his mouth, dazed, as a boxer from a blow which knocks him sideways, and another which knocks him straight again.

Fleur visiting Wilfrid – at this moment in his rooms up there – in his arms, perhaps! He groaned. A well-fed young man in a new hat skipped at the sound. Never! He could never stick that! He would have to clear out! He had believed Fleur

honest! A double life! The night before last she had smiled on
him. Oh! God! He dashed across into Green Park. Why hadn't
he stood still and let something go over him? And that luna-
tic's little brother — John — family feud? Himself — a *pis aller*,
then — taken without love at all — a makeshift! He remembered
now her saying one night at Mapledurham: 'Come again when
I know I can't get my wish.' So that was the wish she couldn't
get! A makeshift! 'Jolly,' he thought: 'Oh! jolly!' No wonder,
then! What could she care? One man or another! Poor little
devil! She had never let him know — never breathed a word!
Was that decent of her — or was it treachery? 'No,' he thought,
'if she *had* told me, it wouldn't have made any difference — I'd
have taken her at any price. It was decent of her not to tell me.'
But how was it he hadn't heard from someone? Family feud?
The Forsytes! Except 'Old Forsyte', he never saw them; and
'Old Forsyte' was closer than a fish. Well! he had got what-for!
And again he groaned, in the twilight spaces of the Park. Buckingham Palace loomed up unlighted, huge and dreary. Conscious of his cigarette at last, he stopped to strike a match, and
drew the smoke deep into his lungs with the first faint sense of
comfort.

'You couldn't spare us a cigarette, Mister?'

A shadowy figure with a decent sad face stood beside the
statue of Australia, so depressingly abundant!

'Of course!' said Michael; 'take the lot.' He emptied the case
into the man's hand. 'Take the case too — "present from Westminster" — you'll get thirty bob for it. Good luck!' He hurried
on. A faint: 'Hi, Mister!' pursued him unavailingly. Pity was
pulp! Sentiment was bilge! Was he going home to wait till
Fleur had — finished and come back? Not he! He turned towards Chelsea, batting along as hard as he could stride. Lighted
shops, gloomy great Eaton Square, Chester Square, Sloane
Square, the King's Road — along, along! Worse than the trenches — far worse — this whipped and scorpioned sexual jealousy!
Yes, and he would have felt even worse, but for that second
blow. It made it less painful to know that Fleur had been in love
with that cousin, and Wilfrid, too, perhaps, nothing to her. Poor

little wretch! 'Well, what's the game now?' he thought. The game of life – in bad weather, in stress? What was it? In the war – what had a fellow done? Somehow managed to feel himself not so dashed important; reached a condition of acquiescence, fatalism, 'Who dies if England live' sort of sob-stuff state. The game of life? Was it different? 'Bloody but unbowed' might be tripe; still – get up when you were knocked down! The whole was big, oneself was little! Passion, jealousy, ought they properly to destroy one's sportsmanship, as Nazing and Sibley and Linda Frewe would have it? Was the word 'gentleman' a dud? Was it? Did one keep one's form, or get down to squealing and kicking in the stomach?

'I don't know,' he thought, 'I don't know what I shall do when I see her – I simply don't know.' Steel-blue of the fallen evening, bare plane trees, wide river, frosty air! He turned towards home. He opened his front door, trembling, and trembling, went into the drawing-room. . . .

When Fleur had gone upstairs and left him with Ting-a-ling he didn't know whether he believed her or not. If she had kept that other thing from him all this time, she could keep anything! Had she understood his words: 'You must do as you like, that's only fair'? He had said them almost mechanically, but they were reasonable. If she had never loved him, even a little, he had never had any right to expect anything; he had been all the time in the position of one to whom she was giving alms. Nothing compelled a person to go on giving alms. And nothing compelled one to go on taking them – except – the ache of want, the ache, the ache!

'You little Djinn! You lucky little toad! Give me some of your complacency – you Chinese atom!' Ting-a-ling turned up his boot-buttons. 'When you have been civilized as long as I,' they seemed to say: 'In the meantime, scratch my chest.'

And scrattling in that yellow fur Michael thought: 'Pull yourself together! Man at the South Pole with the first blizzard doesn't sing ''Want to go home! Want to go home!'' – he sticks it. Come, get going!' He placed Ting-a-ling on the floor, and made for his study. Here were manuscripts, of which the readers to Danby and Winter had already said: 'No money in this, but a genuine piece of work meriting consideration.' It was Michael's business to give the consideration; Danby's to turn the affair down with the words: 'Write him (or her) a civil letter, say we were greatly interested, regret we do not see our way – hope to have the privilege of considering next effort, and so forth. What!'

He turned up his reading-lamp and pulled out a manuscript he had already begun.

> 'No retreat, no retreat; they must conquer or die who have
>   no retreat;
> No retreat, no retreat; they must conquer or die who have
>   no retreat!'

The black footmen's refrain from *Polly* was all that happened in his mind. Dash it! He must read the thing! Somehow he finished the chapter. He remembered now. The manuscript was all about a man who, when he was a boy, had been so greatly impressed by the sight of a maidservant changing her clothes in a room over the way, that his married life was a continual struggle not to be unfaithful with his wife's maids. They had just discovered his complex, and he was going to have it out. The rest of the manuscript no doubt would show how that was done. It went most conscientiously into all those precise bodily details which it was now so timorous and Victorian to leave out. Genuine piece of work, and waste of time to go on with it! Old Danby – Freud bored him stiff; and for once Michael did not mind old Danby being in the right. He put the thing back into the drawer. Seven o'clock! Tell Fleur what he had been told about that cousin? Why? Nothing could mend *that*! If only she were speaking the truth about Wilfrid! He went to the window – stars above, and stripes below, stripes of courtyard and back garden. 'No retreat, no retreat; they must conquer or die who have no retreat!'

A voice said:

'When will your father be up?'

Old Forsyte! Lord! Lord!

'Tomorrow, I believe, sir. Come in! You don't know my den, I think.'

'No,' said Soames. 'Snug! Caricatures. You go in for them – poor stuff!'

'But not modern, sir – a revived art.'

'Queering your neighbours – I never cared for them. They only flourish when the world's in a mess and people have given up looking straight before them.'

'By Jove!' said Michael; 'that's good. Won't you sit down, sir?'

Soames sat down, crossing his knees in his accustomed manner. Slim, grey, close – a sealed book, neatly bound! What was *his* complex? Whatever it was, he had never had it out. One could not even imagine the operation.

'I shan't take away my Goya,' he said very unexpectedly; 'consider it Fleur's. In fact, if I only knew you were interested in the future, I should make more provision. In my opinion death duties will be prohibitive in a few years' time.'

Michael frowned. 'I'd like you to know, sir, once for all, that what you do for Fleur, you do for Fleur. I can be Epicurus whenever I like – bread, and on feast days a little bit of cheese.'

Soames looked up with shrewdness in his glance. 'I know that,' he said, 'I always knew it.'

Michael bowed.

'With this land depression your father's hard hit, I should think.'

'Well, he talks of being on the look-out for soap or cars; but I shouldn't be surprised if he mortgages again and lingers on.'

'A title without a place,' said Soames, 'is not natural. He'd better wait for me to go, if I leave anything, that is. But listen to me: I've been thinking. Aren't you happy together, you two, that you don't have children?'

Michael hesitated.

'I don't think,' he said slowly, 'that we have ever had a scrap, or anything like it. I have been – I am – terribly fond of her, but you have known better than I that I only picked up the pieces.'

'Who told you that?'

'Today – Miss June Forsyte.'

'*That* woman!' said Soames. 'She can't keep her foot out of anything. A boy and girl affair – over months before you married.'

'But deep, sir,' said Michael gently.

'Deep – who knows at that age? Deep?' Soames paused: 'You're a good fellow – I always knew. Be patient – take a long view.'

'Yes, sir,' said Michael, very still in his chair, 'if I can.'

'She's everything to me,' muttered Soames abruptly.

'And to me – which doesn't make it easier.'

The line between Soames's brows deepened.

'Perhaps not. But hold on! As gently as you like, but hold on! She's young. She'll flutter about; there's nothing in it.'

'Does he know about the other thing?' thought Michael.

'I have my own worries,' went on Soames, 'but they're nothing to what I should feel if anything went wrong with her.'

Michael felt a twinge of sympathy, unusual towards that self-contained grey figure.

'I shall try my best,' he said quietly; 'but I'm not naturally Solomon at six stone seven.'

'I'm not so sure,' said Soames, 'I'm not so sure. Anyway, a child – well, a child would be – a – sort of insur–' He baulked, the word was not precisely – !

Michael froze.

'As to that, I can't say anything.'

Soames got up.

'No,' he said wistfully, 'I suppose not. It's time to dress.'

To dress – to dine, and if to dine, to sleep – to sleep, to dream! And then what dreams might come!

On the way to his dressing-room Michael encountered Coaker; the man's face was long.

'What's up, Coaker?'

'The little dog, sir, has been sick in the drawing-room.'

'The deuce he has!'

'Yes, sir; it appears that someone left him there alone. He

makes himself felt, sir. I always say: He's an important little dog....'

During dinner, as if visited by remorse for having given them advice and two pictures worth some thousands of pounds, Soames pitched a tale like those of James in his palmy days. He spoke of the French — the fall of the mark — the rise in Consols — the obstinacy of Dumetrius, the picture-dealer, over a Constable skyscape which Soames wanted and Dumetrius did not, but to which the fellow held on just for the sake of a price which Soames did not mean to pay. He spoke of the trouble which he foresaw with the United States over their precious Prohibition. They were a headstrong lot. They took up a thing and ran their heads against a stone wall. He himself had never drunk anything to speak of, but he liked to feel that he could. The Americans liked to feel that he couldn't, that was tyranny. They were overbearing. He shouldn't be surprised if everybody took to drinking over there. As to the League of Nations, a man that morning had palavered it up. That cock wouldn't fight — spend money, and arrange things which would have arranged themselves, but as for anything important, such as abolishing Bolshevism, or poison gas, they never would, and to pretend it was all-me-eye-and-Betty-Martin. It was almost a record for one habitually taciturn, and deeply useful to two young people only anxious that he should continue to talk, so that they might think of other things. The conduct of Ting-a-ling was the sole other subject of consideration. Fleur thought it due to the copper floor. Soames that he must have picked up something in the Square — dogs were always picking things up. Michael suggested that it was just Chinese — a protest against there being nobody to watch his self-sufficiency. In China there were four hundred million people to watch each other being self-sufficient. What would one expect of a Chinaman suddenly placed in the Gobi Desert? He would certainly be sick.

'No retreat, no retreat; they must conquer or die who have no retreat!'

When Fleur left them, both felt that they could not so soon again bear each other's company, and Soames said:

'I've got some figures to attend to – I'll go to my room.'

Michael stood up. 'Wouldn't you like my den, sir?'

'No,' said Soames, 'I must concentrate. Say good night to Fleur for me.'

Michael remained smoking above the porcelain effigies of Spanish fruits. That white monkey couldn't eat those and throw away the rinds! Would the fruits of his life be porcelain in future? Live in the same house with Fleur, estranged? Live with Fleur as now, feeling a stranger, even an unwelcome stranger? Clear out, and join the Air Force, or the 'Save the Children' corps? Which of the three courses was least to be deplored? The ash of his cigar grew long, dropped incontinent, and grew again; the porcelain fruits mocked him with their sheen and glow; Coaker put his head in and took it away again. (The Governor had got the hump – good sort, the Governor!) Decision waited for him, somewhere, somewhen – Fleur's, not his own. His mind was too miserable and disconcerted to be known; but she would know hers. She had the information which alone made decision possible about Wilfrid, that cousin, her own actions and feelings. Yes, decision would come, and would it matter in a world where pity was punk and only a Chinese philosophy of any use?

But not be sick in the drawing-room, try and keep one's end up, even if there were no one to see one being important! ...

He had been asleep and it was dark, or all but, in his bed-dressing-room. Something white by his bed. A fragrant faint warmth close to him; a voice saying low: 'It's only me. Let me come in your bed, Michael.' Like a child – like a child! Michael reached out his arms. The whiteness and the warmth came into them. Curls smothered his mouth, the voice in his ear: 'I wouldn't have come, would I, if there'd – if there'd been anything?' Michael's heart, wild, confused, beat against hers.

Chapter Seven

'THE ALTOGETHER'

⤜⟡⟶

TONY BICKET, replete, was in vein that fine afternoon; his balloons left him freely, and he started for home in the mood of a conqueror.

Victorine, too, had colour in her cheeks. She requited the story of his afternoon with the story of hers. A false tale for a true – no word of Danby and Winter, the gentleman with the sliding smile, of the Grand Marnier, or 'the altogether'. She had no compunction. It was her secret, her surprise; if, by sitting in or out of 'the altogether', not yet decided, she could make their passage money – well, she should tell him she had won it on a horse. That night she asked:

'Am I so very thin, Tony?' more than once. 'I do so want to get fat.'

Bicket, still troubled that she had not shared that lunch, patted her tenderly, and said he would soon have her as fat as butter – he did not explain how.

They dreamed together of blue butterflies, and awoke to chilly gaslight and a breakfast of cocoa and bread-and-butter. Fog! Bicket was swallowed up before the eyes of Victorine ten yards from the door. She returned to the bedroom with anger in her heart. Who would buy balloons in a fog? She would do anything rather than let Tony go on standing out there all the choking days! Undressing again, she washed herself intensively, in case – ! She had not long finished when her landlady announced the presence of a messenger boy. He bore an enormous parcel entitled 'Mr Bicket.'

There was a note inside. She read:

DEAR BICKET, – Here are the togs. Hope they'll be useful. –
Yours, MICHAEL MONT

In a voice that trembled she said to the boy:

'Thank you, it's O.K. Here's twopence.'

When his rich whistle was heard writhing into the fog, she flung herself down before the 'togs' in ecstasy. The sexes were divided by tissue paper. A blue suit, a velour hat, some brown shoes, three pairs of socks with two holes in them, four shirts only a little frayed at the cuffs, two black-and-white ties, six collars, not too new, some handkerchiefs, two vests beautifully thick, two pairs of pants, and a brown overcoat with a belt and just two or three nice little stains. She held the blue suit up against her arms and legs, the trousers and sleeves would only need taking-in about two inches. She piled them in a pyramid, and turned with awe to the spoil beneath the tissue paper. A brown knitted frock with little clear yellow buttons – unsoiled, uncreased. How could anybody spare a thing like that! A brown velvet toque with a little tuft of goldeny-brown feathers. She put it on. A pair of pink stays ever so little faded, with only three inches of bone above the waist, and five inches of bone below, pink silk ribbons, and suspenders – a perfect dream. She could not resist putting them on also. Two pairs of brown stockings; brown shoes; two combinations, a knitted camisole. A white silk jumper with a hole in one sleeve, a skirt of lilac linen that had gone a little in the wash; a pair of pallid pink silk pants; and underneath them all an almost black-brown coat, long and warm and cosy, with great jet buttons, and in the pocket six small handkerchiefs. She took a deep breath of sweetness – geranium!

Her mind leaped forward. Clothed, trousseaued, fitted out – blue butterflies – the sun! Only the money for the tickets wanting. And suddenly she saw herself with nothing on standing before the gentleman with sliding eyes. Who cared! The money!

For the rest of the morning she worked feverishly, shortening Tony, mending the holes in his socks, turning the fray of his cuffs. She ate a biscuit, drank another cup of cocoa – it was fattening, and went for the hole in the white silk jumper. One o'clock. In panic she stripped once more, put on a new combination, pair of stockings, and the stays, then paused in superstition. No! Her own dress and hat – like yesterday! Keep the rest until –! She hastened to her bus, overcome alternately by heat and cold. Perhaps he would give her another glass of that lovely stuff. If only she could go swimmy and not care for anything!

She reached the studio as two o'clock was striking, and knocked. It was lovely and warm in there, much warmer than yesterday, and the significance of this struck her suddenly. In front of the fire was a lady with a little dog.

'Miss Collins – Mrs Michael Mont; she's lending us her Peke, Miss Collins.'

The lady – only her own age, and ever so pretty – held out her hand. Geranium! This, then, was she whose clothes –!

She took the hand, but could not speak. If this lady was going to stay, it would be utterly impossible. Before her – so pretty, so beautifully covered – oh! no!

'Now, Ting, be good, and as amusing as you can. Good-bye, Aubrey! Good luck to the picture! Good-bye, Miss Collins; it ought to be wonderful.'

Gone! The scent of geranium fading; the little dog snuffling at the door. The sliding gentleman had two glasses in his hands.

'Ah!' thought Victorine, and drank hers at a gulp.

'Now, Miss Collins, you don't mind, do you! You'll find everything in there. It's really nothing. I shall want you lying on your face just here with your elbows on the ground and your head up a little turned this way; your hair as loose as it can be, and your eyes looking at this bone. You must imagine that it's a faun or some other bit of all right. The dog'll help you when he settles down to it. F-a-u-n, you know, not f-a-w-n.'

'Yes,' said Victorine faintly.

'Have another little tot?'

'Oh! please.'

He brought it.

'I quite understand; but you know, really, it's absurd. You wouldn't mind with a doctor. That's right. Look here, I'll put this little cow-bell on the ground. When you're in position, give it a tinkle, and I'll come out. That'll help you.'

Victorine murmured:

'You *are* kind.'

'Not at all – it's natural. Now will you start in? The light won't last for ever. Fifteen bob a day, we said.'

Victorine saw him slide away behind a screen, and looked at the little cow-bell. Fifteen bob! And fifteen bob! And fifteen bob! Many, many, fifteen bobs before –! But not more times of sitting than of Tony's standing from foot to foot, offering balloons. And as if wound up by that thought, she moved like clockwork off the dais, into the model's room. Cosy in there, too; warm, a green silk garment thrown on a chair. She took off her dress. The beauty of the pink stays struck her afresh. Perhaps the gentleman would like – no, that would be even worse –! A noise reached her – from Ting-a-ling complaining of solitude. If she delayed, she never would –! Stripping hastily, she stood looking at herself in a glass. If only that slim, ivory-white image could move out on to the dais and she could stay here! Oh! It was awful – awful! She couldn't – no! she couldn't. She caught up her final garment again. Fifteen bob! But fifteen bob! Before her eyes, wild and mournful, came a vision: Of a huge dome, and a tiny Tony, with little, little balloons in a hand held out! Something cold and steely formed over her heart as icicles form on a window. If that was all they would do for him, she would do better! She dropped the garment; and, confused, numb, stepped forth in 'the altogether'. Ting-a-ling growled at her above his bone. She reached the cow-bell and lay down on her face as she had been told, with feet in the air, crossed. Resting her chin on one hand, she wagged the bell. It made a sound like no bell she had ever heard; and the little dog barked – he did look funny!

'Perfect, Miss Collins! Hold that!'

Fifteen bob! and fifteen bob!

'Just point those left toes a bit more. That's right! The flesh tone's perfect! My God, why must one walk before one runs! Drawing's a bore, Miss Collins; one ought to draw with a brush only; a sculptor draws with a chisel, at least when he's a Michelangelo. How old are you?'

'Twenty-one,' came from lips that seemed to Victorine quite far away.

'I'm thirty-two. They say our generation was born so old that it can never get any older. Without illusions. Well! I never had any beliefs that I can remember. Had you?'

Victorine's wits and senses were astray, but it did not matter, for he was rattling on:

'We don't even believe in our ancestors. All the same, we're beginning to copy them again. D'you know a book called *The Sobbing Turtle* that's made such a fuss? – sheer Sterne, very well done; but sheer Sterne, and the author's tongue in his cheek. That's it in a nutshell, Miss Collins – our tongues are in our cheeks – bad sign. Never mind; I'm going to out-Piero Cosimo with this. Your head an inch higher, and that curl out of your eye, please. Thanks! Hold that! By the way, have you Italian blood? What was your mother's name, for instance?'

'Brown.'

'Ah! You can never tell with Browns. It may have been Brune – or Bruno – but very likely she was Iberian. Probably all the inhabitants of Britain left alive by the Saxons were called Brown. As a fact, that's all tosh, though. Going back to Edward the Confessor, Miss Collins – a mere thirty generations – we each of us have one thousand and seventy-four million, five hundred and seventy-three thousand, nine hundred and eighty-four ancestors, and the population of this island was then well under a million. We're as inbred as race-horses, but not so nice to look at, are we? I assure you, Miss Collins, you're something to be grateful for. So is Mrs Mont. Isn't she pretty? Look at that dog!'

Ting-a-ling, indeed, with forelegs braced, and wrinkled nose, was glaring, as if under the impression that Victorine was another bone.

'He's funny,' she said, and again her voice sounded far away. Would Mrs Mont lie here if he'd asked her? *She* would look pretty! But *she* didn't need the fifteen bob!

'Comfortable in that position?'

In alarm, she murmured:

'Oh! yes, thank you!'

'Warm enough?'

'Oh! yes, thank you!'

'That's good. Just a little higher with the head.'

Slowly in Victorine the sense of the dreadfully unusual faded. Tony should never know. If he never knew, he couldn't care. She could lie like this all day – fifteen bob, and fifteen bob! It was easy. She watched the quick, slim fingers moving, the blue smoke from the cigarette. She watched the little dog.

'Like a rest? You left your gown; I'll get it for you.'

In that green silk gown, beautifully padded, she sat up, with her feet on the floor over the dais edge.

'Cigarette? I'm going to make some Turkish coffee. You'd better walk about.'

Victorine obeyed.

'You're out of a dream, Miss Collins. I shall have to do a Mathew Maris of you in that gown.'

The coffee, like none she had ever tasted, gave her a sense of well-being. She said:

'It's not like coffee.'

Aubrey Greene threw up his hands.

'You have said it. The British are a great race – nothing will ever do them in. If they could be destroyed, they must long ago have perished of their coffee. Have some more?'

'Please,' said Victorine. There was such a little in the cup.

'Ready, again?'

She lay down, and let the gown drop off.

'That's right! Leave it there – you're lying in long grass, and the green helps me. Pity it's winter; I'd have hired a glade.'

Lying in long grass – flowers, too, perhaps. She did love flowers. As a little girl she used to lie in the grass, and make daisy-chains, in the field at the back of her grandmother's lodge at Norbiton. Her grandmother kept the lodge. Every year, for a fortnight, she had gone down there – she had liked the country ever so. Only she had always had something on. It would be nicer with nothing. Were there flowers in Central Australia? With butterflies there must be! In the sun – she and Tony – like the Garden of Eden! . . .

'Thank you, that's all for today. Half a day – ten bob. Tomorrow morning at eleven. You're a first-rate sitter, Miss Collins.'

Putting on the pink stays, Victorine had a feeling of elation. She had done it! Tony should never know! The thought that he never would gave her pleasure. And once more divested of the 'altogether', she came forth.

Aubrey Greene was standing before his handiwork.

'Not yet, Miss Collins,' he said; 'I don't want to depress you. That hip-bone's too high. We'll put it right tomorrow. Forgive my hand, it's all chalk. *Au revoir!* Eleven o'clock. And we shan't need this chap. No, you don't!'

For Ting-a-ling was showing signs of accompanying the larger bone. Victorine passed out smiling.

Chapter Eight

SOAMES TAKES THE MATTER UP

◄◄─►►

Soames had concentrated, sitting before the fire in his bedroom till Big Ben struck twelve. His reflections sum-totalled in a decision to talk it over with 'old Mont' after all. Though light-brained, the fellow was a gentleman, and the matter delicate. He got into bed and slept, but awoke at half-past two. There it was! '*I won't* think of it,' he thought; and instantly began to. In a long life of dealings with money, he had never had such an experience. Perfectly straightforward conformity with the law – itself so often far from perfectly straightforward – had been the *sine qua non* of his career. Honesty, they said, was the best policy. But was it anything else? A normally honest man couldn't keep out of a perfect penitentiary for a week. But then a perfect penitentiary had no relation to prison, or the Bankruptcy Court. The business of working honesty was to keep out of those two institutions. And so far he had never had any difficulty. What, besides the drawing of fees and the drinking of tea, were the duties of a director? That was the point. And how far, if he failed in them, was he liable? It was a director's duty to be perfectly straightforward. But if a director were perfectly straightforward, he couldn't be a director. That was clear. In the first place, he would have to tell his shareholders that he didn't anything like earn his fees. For what did he do on his Boards? Well, he sat and signed his name and talked a little, and passed that which the general trend of business decided must be passed. Did he initiate? Once in a blue moon. Did he calculate? No, he read calculations. Did he check payments out and in? No, the auditors did that. There was policy! A comforting word, but – to be perfectly straightforward – a director's chief business was to let the existing policy alone. Take his own case! If he had done his duty, he would have stopped this foreign insurance business which he had instinctively distrusted the moment he heard of it – within a month of sitting on the Board, or, having failed in doing so, resigned his seat. But he had not. Things had been looking better! It was not the moment, and so forth! If he had done his duty as a perfectly straightforward director, indeed, he would never have become a director of the P.P.R.S., because he would have looked into the policy of the Society much more closely than he had before accepting a position on the Board. But what with the names, and the prestige, and not looking a gift horse too closely in the mouth – there it had been! To be perfectly straightforward, he ought now to be circularizing the shareholders, saying: 'My *laissez-faire* has cost you two hundred odd thousand pounds. I have lodged this amount in the hands of trustees for your benefit, and am suing the rest of the directors for their quotas of the amount.' But he was not proposing to do so, because – well – because it wasn't done, and the other directors wouldn't like it. In sum: You waited till the shareholders found out the mess, and you hoped they wouldn't. In fact, just like a Government, you confused the issues, and made the best case you could for yourselves. With a sense of comfort Soames thought of Ireland: The late Government had let the country in for all that mess in

Ireland, and at the end taken credit for putting an end to what
need never have been! The Peace, too, and the Air Force, and
Agriculture, and Egypt – the five most important issues they'd
had to deal with – they had put the chestnuts into the fire in
every case! But had they confessed to it? Not they. One didn't
confess. One said: 'The question of policy made it imperative at
the time.' Or, better still, one said nothing; and trusted to the
British character. With his chin resting on the sheet, Soames felt
a momentary relief. The late Government weren't sweating into
their sheets – not they – he was convinced of it! Fixing his
eyes on the dying embers in the grate, he reflected on the in-
equalities and injustices of existence. Look at the chaps in politics and business, whose whole lives were passed in skating on
thin ice, and getting knighted for it. They never turned a
hair. And look at himself, for the first time in forty years on thin
ice, and suffering confoundedly. There was a perfect cult of
hoodwinking the public, a perfect cult of avoiding the consequences of administrative acts; and here was he, a man of the
world, a man of the law, ignorant of those cults, and – and glad
of it. From engrained caution and a certain pride, which had
in it a touch of the fine, Soames shrank from that coarse-grained
standard of honesty which conducted the affairs of the British
public. In anything that touched money he was, he always had
been, stiff-necked, stiff-kneed. Money was money, a pound a
pound, and there was no way of pretending it wasn't and keeping your self-respect. He got up, drank some water, took a number of deep breaths, and stamped his feet. Who was it said the
other day that nothing had ever lost him five minutes' sleep.
The fellow must have the circulation of 'an ox, or the gift of
Baron Munchausen. He took up a book. But his mind would
only turn over and over the realizable value of his resources.
Apart from his pictures, he decided that he could not be worth
less than two hundred and fifty thousand pounds, and there
was only Fleur – and she already provided for more or less. His
wife had her settlement, and could live on it perfectly well in
France. As for himself – what did he care? A room at his club
near Fleur – he would be just as happy, perhaps happier! And

suddenly he found that he had reached a way out of his disturbance and anxiety. By imagining the far-fetched, by facing the loss of his wealth, he had exorcized the demon. The book, *The Sobbing Turtle*, of which he had not read one word, dropped from his hand; he slept. ...

His meeting with 'old Mont' took place at 'Snooks' directly after lunch. The tape in the hall, at which he glanced on going in, recorded a further heavy drop in the mark. Just as he thought: The thing was getting valueless!

Sitting there, sipping coffee, the baronet looked to Soames almost offensively spry. Two to one he had realized nothing! 'Well!' thought Soames, 'as old Uncle Jolyon used to say, I shall astonish his weak nerves!'

And without preamble he began.

'How are you, Mont? This mark's valueless. You realize we've lost the P.P.R.S. about a quarter of a million by that precious foreign policy of Elderson's. I'm not sure an action won't lie against us for taking unjustifiable risk. But what I've come to see you about is this.' He retailed the interview with the clerk, Butterfield, watching the eyebrows of his listener, and finished with the words: 'What do you say?'

Sir Lawrence, whose foot was jerking his whole body, fixed his monocle.

'Hallucination, my dear Forsyte! I've known Elderson all my life. We were at Winchester together.'

Again! Again! Oh! Lord! Soames said slowly:

'You can't tell from that. A man who was at Marlborough with me ran away with his mess fund and his colonel's wife, and made a fortune in Chile out of canned tomatoes. The point is this: If the young man's story's true, we're in the hands of a bad hat. It won't do, Mont. Will you tackle him, and see what he says to it? You wouldn't like a story of that sort about yourself. Shall we both go?'

'Yes,' said Sir Lawrence, suddenly. 'You're right. We'll both go, Forsyte. I don't like it, but we'll both go. He ought to hear it.'

'Now?'

'Now.'

With solemnity they assumed top hats, and issued.

'I think, Forsyte, we'll take a taxi.'

'Yes,' said Soames.

The cab ground its way slowly past the lions, then dashed on down to the Embankment. Side by side its occupants held their noses steadily before them.

'He was shooting with me a month ago,' said Sir Lawrence. 'Do you know the hymn "O God, our help in ages past"? It's very fine, Forsyte.'

Soames did not answer. The fellow was beginning to tittup!

'We had it that Sunday,' went on Sir Lawrence. 'Elderson used to have a fine voice – sang solos. It's a foghorn now, but a good delivery still.' He gave his little whinnying laugh.

'Is it possible,' thought Soames, 'for this chap to be serious?' and he said:

'If we find this is true of Elderson, and conceal it, we could all be put in the dock.'

Sir Lawrence refixed his monocle. 'The deuce!' he said.

'Will you do the talking,' said Soames, 'or shall I?'

'I think you had better, Forsyte; ought we to have the young man in?'

'Wait and see,' said Soames.

They ascended to the offices of the P.P.R.S. and entered the Board Room. There was no fire, the long table was ungarnished; an old clerk, creeping about like a fly on a pane, was filling ink-stands out of a magnum.

Soames addressed him:

'Ask the manager to be so kind as to come and see Sir Lawrence Mont and Mr Forsyte.'

The old clerk blinked, put down the magnum, and went out.

'Now,' said Soames in a low voice, 'we must keep our heads. He'll deny it, of course.'

'I should hope so, Forsyte; I should hope so. Elderson's a gentleman.'

'No liar like a gentleman,' muttered Soames, below his breath.

After that they stood in their overcoats before the empty grate, staring at their top hats placed side by side on the table.

'One minute!' said Soames, suddenly, and crossing the room, he opened a door opposite. There, as the young clerk had said, was a sort of lobby between Board Room and Manager's Room, with a door at the end into the main corridor. He stepped back, closed the door, and, rejoining Sir Lawrence, resumed his contemplation of the hats.

'Geography correct,' he said with gloom.

The entrance of the manager was marked by Sir Lawrence's monocle dropping on to his coat-button with a tinkle. In cutaway black coat, clean-shaven, with grey eyes rather baggy underneath, a pink colour, every hair in place on a rather bald egg-shaped head, and lips alternately pouting, compressed, or smiling, the manager reminded Soames ridiculously of old Uncle Nicholas in his middle period. Uncle Nick was a clever fellow – 'cleverest man in London,' someone had called him – but none had ever impugned his honesty. A pang of doubt and disinclination went through Soames. This seemed a monstrous thing to have to put to a man of his own age and breeding. But young Butterfield's eyes – so honest and dog-like! Invent a thing like that – was it possible? He said abruptly:

'Is that door shut?'

'Yes; do you feel a draught?' said the manager. 'Would you like a fire?'

'No, thank you,' said Soames. 'The fact is, Mr Elderson, a young man in this office came to me yesterday with a very queer story. Mont and I think you should hear it.'

Accustomed to watching people's eyes, Soames had the impression of a film (such as passes over the eyes of parrots) passing over the eyes of the manager. It was gone at once, if, indeed, it had ever been.

'By all means.'

Steadily, with that power he had over his nerves when it came to a point, and almost word for word, Soames repeated a story which he had committed to heart in the watches of the night. He concluded with:

'You'd like him in, no doubt. His name is Butterfield.'

During the recital Sir Lawrence had done nothing but scrutinize his finger nails; he now said:

'You had to be told, Elderson.'

'Naturally.'

The manager was crossing to the bell. The pink in his cheeks looked harder; his teeth showed, they had a pouted look.

'Ask Mr Butterfield to come here.'

There followed a minute of elaborate inattention to each other. Then the young man came in, neat, commonplace, with his eyes on the manager's face. Soames had a moment of compunction. This young fellow held his life in his hands, as it were – one of the great army who made their living out of self-suppression and respectability, with a hundred ready to step into his shoes at his first slip. What was that old tag of the provincial actor's declamation – at which old Uncle Jolyon used to cackle so? 'Like a pale martyr with his shirt on fire.'

'So, Mr Butterfield, you have been good enough to exercise your imagination in my regard.'

'No, sir.'

'You stick to this fantastic story of eavesdropping?'

'Yes, sir.'

'We have no further use for your services then. Good morning!'

The young man's eyes, dog-like, sought the face of Soames; a string twitched in his throat, his lips moved without a sound. He turned and went out.

'So much for that,' said the manager's voice; *'he'll* never get another job.'

The venom in those words affected Soames like the smell of Russian fat. At the same moment he had the feeling: This wants thinking out. Only if innocent, or guilty and utterly resolved, would Elderson have been so drastic. Which was he?

The manager went on:

'I thank you for drawing my attention to the matter, gentlemen. I have had my eye on that young man for some time. A bad hat all round.'

Soames said glumly:

'What do you make out he had to gain?'

'Foresaw dismissal, and thought he would get in first.'

'I see,' said Soames. But he did not. His mind was back in his own office with Gradman rubbing his nose, shaking his grey head, and Butterfield's: 'No, sir, I've nothing against Mr Elderson, and he's nothing against me.'

'I shall require to know more about that young man,' he thought.

The manager's voice again cut through.

'I've been thinking over what you said yesterday, Mr Forsyte, about an action lying against the Board for negligence. There's nothing in that; our policy has been fully disclosed to the shareholders at two general meetings, and has passed without comment. The shareholders are just as responsible as the Board.'

'H'm!' said Soames, and took up his hat. 'Are you coming, Mont?'

As if summoned from a long distance, Sir Lawrence galvanitically refixed his monocle.

'It's been very distasteful,' he said; 'you must forgive us, Elderson. You had to be told. I don't think that young man can be quite all there – he had a peculiar look; but we can't have this sort of thing, of course. Good-bye, Elderson.'

Placing their hats on their heads simultaneously the two walked out. They walked some way without speaking. Then Sir Lawrence said:

'Butterfield? My brother-in-law has a head gardener called Butterfield – quite a good fellow. Ought we to look into that young man, Forsyte?'

'Yes,' said Soames, 'leave him to me.'

'I shall be very glad to. The fact is, when one has been at school with a man, one has a feeling, don't you know.'

Soames gave vent to a sudden outburst.

'You can't trust anyone nowadays, it seems to me,' he said. 'It comes of – well, I don't know what it comes of. But I've not done with this matter yet.'

Chapter Nine

SLEUTH

<<->>

THE Hotch-potch Club went back to the eighteen-sixties. Founded by a posse of young sparks, social and political, as a convenient place in which to smoulder, while qualifying for the hearth of 'Snooks', The Remove, The Wayfarers, Burton's, Ostrich Feather, and other more permanent resorts, the club had, chiefly owing to a remarkable chef in its early days, acquired a stability and distinction of its own. It still, however, retained a certain resemblance to its name, and this was its attraction to Michael – all sorts of people belonged. From Walter Nazing, and young semi-writers and patrons of the stage, who went to Venice, and talked of being amorous in gondolas, or of how so-and-so ought to be made love to; from such to bottle-brushed demi-generals, who had sat on courts-martial and shot men out of hand for the momentary weaknesses of human nature; from Wilfrid Desert (who never came there now) to Maurice Elderson, in the card-room, he could meet them all, and take the temperature of modernity. He was doing this in the Hotchpotch smoking-room, the late afternoon but one after Fleur had come into his bed, when he was informed:

'A Mr Forsyte, sir, in the hall for you. Not the member we had here many years before he died; his cousin, I think.'

Conscious that his associates at the moment would not be his father-in-law's 'dream', nor he theirs, Michael went out, and found Soames on the weighing machine.

'I don't vary,' he said, looking up. 'How's Fleur?'

'Very well, thank you, sir.'

'I'm at Green Street. I stayed up about a young man. Have you any vacancy in your office for a clerk – used to figures. I want a job for him.'

'Come in here, sir,' said Michael, entering a small room.

Soames followed and looked round him.

'What do you call this?' he said.

'Well, we call it "the grave"; it's nice and quiet. Will you have a sherry?'

'Sherry!' repeated Soames. 'You young people think you've invented sherry; when I was a boy no one dreamed of dining without a glass of dry sherry with his soup, and a glass of fine old sherry with his sweet. Sherry!'

'I quite believe you, sir. There really is nothing new. Venice, for instance – wasn't that the fashion, too; and knitting, and royalties? It's all cyclic. Has your young man got the sack?'

Soames stared. 'Yes,' he said, 'he has. His name is Butterfield; he wants a job.'

'That's frightfully rife; we get applications every day. I don't want to be swanky, but ours is a rather specialized business. It has to do with books.'

'He strikes me as capable, orderly, and civil; I don't see what more you want in a clerk. He writes a good hand, and, so far as I can see, he tells the truth.'

'That's important, of course,' said Michael; 'but is he a good liar as well? I mean, there's more likely to be something in the travelling line; selling special editions, and that kind of thing. Could you open up about him a bit? Anything human is to the good – I don't say old Danby would appreciate that, but he needn't know.'

'H'm! Well – he – er – did his duty – quite against his interest – in fact, it's ruination for him. He seems to be married and to have two children.'

'Ho, ho! Jolly! If I got him a place, would he – would he be doing his duty again, do you think?'

'I am serious,' said Soames; 'the young man is on my mind.'

'Yes,' said Michael, ruminative, 'the first thing in such a case is to get him on to someone else's, sharp. Could I see him?'

'I told him to step round and see you tonight after dinner. I thought you'd prefer to look him over in private before considering him for your office.'

'Very thoughtful of you, sir! There's just one thing. Don't you think I ought to know the duty he did – in confidence? I don't see how I can avoid putting my foot into my mouth without, do you?'

Soames stared at his son-in-law's face, where the mouth was wide; for the *n*th time it inspired in him a certain liking and confidence; it looked so honest.

'Well,' he said, going to the door and ascertaining that it was opaque, 'this is matter for a criminal slander action, so for your own sake as well as mine you will keep it strictly to yourself', and in a low voice he retailed the facts.

'As I expected,' he ended, 'the young man came to me again this morning. He is naturally upset. I want to keep my hand on him. Without knowing more, I can't make up my mind whether to go further or not. Besides –' Soames hesitated; to claim a good motive was repulsive to him: 'I – it seems hard on him. He's been getting three hundred and fifty.'

'Dashed hard!' said Michael. 'I say, Elderson's a member here.'

Soames looked with renewed suspicion at the door – it still seemed opaque, and he said: 'the deuce he is! Do you know him?'

'I've played bridge with him,' said Michael; 'he's taken some of the best off me – snorting good player.'

'Ah!' said Soames – he never played cards himself. 'I can't take this young man into my own firm for obvious reasons; but I can trust you.'

Michael touched his forelock.

'Frightfully bucked, sir. Protection of the poor – some sleuth, too. I'll see him tonight, and let you know what I can wangle.'

Soames nodded. 'Good Gad!' he thought; 'what jargon! ...'

The interview served Michael the good turn of taking his thoughts off himself. Temperamentally he sided already with the young man Butterfield; and, lighting a cigarette, he went into the card-room. Sitting on the high fender, he was impressed – the room was square, and within it were three square card-tables, set askew to the walls, with three triangles of card players.

'If only,' thought Michael, 'the fourth player sat under the table, the pattern would be complete. It's having the odd player loose that spoils the cubes.' And with something of a thrill he saw that Elderson was a fourth player! Sharp and impassive, he was engaged in applying a knife to the end of a cigar. Gosh! what sealed books faces were! Each with pages and pages of private thoughts, interests, schemes, fancies, passions, hopes and fears; and down came death – splosh! – and a creature wiped out, like a fly on a wall, and nobody any more could see its little close mechanism working away for its own ends, in its own privacy and its own importance; nobody any more could speculate on whether it was a clean or a dirty little bit of work. Hard to tell! They ran in all shapes! Elderson, for instance – was he a nasty mess, or just a lamb of God who didn't look it? 'Somehow,' thought Michael, 'I feel he's a womanizer. Now why?' He spread his hands out behind him to the fire, rubbing them together like a fly that has been in treacle. If one couldn't tell what was passing in the mind of one's own wife in one's own house, how on earth could one tell anything from the face of a stranger, and he one of the closest bits of mechanism in the world – an English gentleman of business! If only life were like *The Idiot* or *The Brothers Karamazov*, and everybody went about turning out their inmost hearts at the tops of their voices! If only club card-rooms had a dash of epilepsy in their composition! But – nothing! Nothing! The world was full of wonderful secrets which everybody kept to themselves without captions or close-ups to give them away!

A footman came in, looked at the fire, stood a moment expressionless as a stork, waiting for an order to ping out, staccato, through the hum, turned and went away.

Mechanism! Everywhere – mechanism! Devices for getting away from life so complete that there seemed no life to get away from.

'It's all,' he thought, 'awfully like a man sending a registered letter to himself. And perhaps it's just as well. Is "life" a good thing – is it? Do I want to see "life" raw again?'

Elderson was seated now, and Michael had a perfect view of the back of his head. It disclosed nothing.

'I'm no sleuth,' he thought; 'there ought to be something in the way he doesn't part his hair behind.' And, getting off the fender, he went home.

At dinner he caught one of his own looks at Fleur and didn't like it. Sleuth! And yet how not try to know what were the real thoughts and feelings of one who held his heart, like an accordion, and made it squeak and groan at pleasure!

'I saw the model you sent Aubrey yesterday,' she said. 'She didn't say anything about the clothes, but she looked ever so! What a face, Michael! Where did you come across her?'

Through Michael sped the thought: 'Could I make her jealous?' And he was shocked at it. A low-down thought – mean and ornery! 'She blew in,' he said. 'Wife of a little packer we had who took to snooping – er – books. He sells balloons now; they want money badly.'

'I see. Did you know that Aubrey's going to paint her in the nude?'

'Phew! No! I thought she'd look good on a wrapper. I say! Ought I to stop that?'

Fleur smiled. 'It's more money and her look-out. It doesn't matter to you, does it?'

Again that thought; again the recoil from it!

'Only,' he said, 'that her husband is a decent little snipe for a snooper, and I don't want to be more sorry for him.'

'She won't tell him, of course.'

She said it so naturally, so simply, that the words disclosed a whole attitude of mind. One didn't tell one's mate what would tease the poor brute! He saw by the flutter of her white eyelids that she also realized the give-away. Should he follow it up, tell her what June Forsyte had told him – have it all out – all out? But with what purpose – to what end? Would it change things, make her love him? Would it do anything but harass her a little more; and give him the sense that he had lost his wicket trying to drive her to the pavilion? No! Better adopt the principle of secrecy she had unwittingly declared her own, bite on it, and grin. He muttered:

'I'm afraid he'll find her rather thin.'

Her eyes were bright and steady; and again he was worried by that low-down thought: 'Could he make her —?'

'I've only seen her once,' he added, 'and then she was dressed.'

'I'm not jealous, Michael.'

'No,' he thought, 'I wish to heaven you were!'

The words: 'A young man called Butterfill to see you, sir,' were like the turning of a key in a cell door.

In the hall the young man 'called Butterfill' was engaged in staring at Ting-a-ling.

'Judging by his eyes,' thought Michael, 'he's more of a dog than that little Djinn!'

'Come up to my study,' he said, 'it's cold down here. My father-in-law tells me you want a job.'

'Yes, sir,' said the young man, following up the stairs.

'Take a pew,' said Michael; 'and a cigarette. Now then! I know all about the turmoil. From your moustache, you were in the war, I suppose, like me! As between fellow-sufferers: Is your story O.K.?'

'God's truth, sir; I only wish it wasn't. I'd nothing to gain and everything to lose. I'd have done better to hold my tongue. It's his word against mine, and here I am in the street. That was my first job since the war, so I can whistle for a reference.'

'Wife and two children, I think?'

'Yes, and I've put them in the cart for the sake of my conscience! It's the last time I'll do that, I know. What did it matter to me, whether the Society was cheated? My wife's quite right, I was a fool, sir.'

'Probably,' said Michael. 'Do you know anything about books?'

'Yes, sir; I'm a good book-keeper.'

'Holy Moses! *Our* job is getting rid of them. My firm are publishers. We were thinking of putting on an extra traveller. Is your tongue persuasive?'

The young man smiled wanly.

'I don't know, sir.'

'Well, look here,' said Michael, carried away by the look in his eyes, 'it's all a question of a certain patter. But, of course, that's got to be learned. I gather that you're not a reader.'

'Well, sir, not a great reader.'

'That, perhaps, is fortunate. What you would have to do is to impress on the poor brutes who sell books that every one of the books on your list — say about thirty-five — is necessary in large numbers to his business. It's lucky you've just chucked your conscience, because, as a matter of fact, most of them won't be. I'm afraid there's nowhere you could go to to get lessons in persuasion, but you can imagine the sort of thing, and if you like to come here for an hour or two this week, I'll put you wise about our authors, and ready you up to go before Peter.'

'Before Peter, sir?'

'The Johnny with the keys; luckily it's Mr Winter, not Mr Danby; I believe I could get him to let you in for a month's trial.'

'Sir, I'll try my very best. My wife knows about books, she could help me a lot. I can't tell you what I think of your kindness. The fact is, being out of a job has put the wind up me properly. I've not been able to save with two children; it's like the end of the world.'

'Right-o, then! Come here tomorrow evening at nine, and I'll stuff you. I believe you've got the face for the job, if you can get the patter. Only one book in twenty is a necessity really, the rest are luxuries. Your stunt will be to make them believe the nineteen are necessaries, and the twentieth a luxury that they need. It's like food or clothes, or anything else in civilization.'

'Yes, sir, I quite understand.'

'All right, then. Good night, and good luck!'

Michael stood up and held out his hand. The young man took it with a queer reverential little bow. A minute later he was out in the street; and Michael in the hall was thinking: 'Pity is tripe! Clean forgot I was a sleuth!'

Chapter Ten

FACE

◄◄►►►

WHEN Michael rose from the refectory table, Fleur had risen,
too. Two days and more since she left Wilfrid's rooms, and
she had not recovered zest. The rifling of the oyster Life, the
garlanding of London's rarer flowers which kept colour in her
cheeks, seemed stale, unprofitable. Those three hours, when
from shock off Cork Street she came straight to shocks in her
own drawing-room, had dislocated her so that she had settled
to nothing since. The wound re-opened by Holly had nearly
healed again. Dead lion beside live donkey cuts but dim figure.
But she could not get hold again of — what? That was the
trouble: What? For two whole days she had been trying.
Michael was still strange, Wilfrid still lost, Jon still buried alive,
and nothing seemed novel under the sun. The only object that
gave her satisfaction during those two dreary, disillusioned days
was the new white monkey. The more she looked at it, the more
Chinese it seemed. It summed up the satirical truth of which
she was perhaps subconscious, that all her little modern veerings
and flutterings and rushings after the future showed that she
believed in nothing but the past. The age had overdone it and
must go back to ancestry for faith. Like a little bright fish out
of a warm bay, making a splash in chill, strange waters, Fleur
felt a subtle nostalgia.

In her Spanish room, alone with her own feelings, she stared
at the porcelain fruits. They glowed, cold, uneatable! She took
one up. Meant for a passion fruit? Alas! Poor passion! She
dropped it with a dull clink on to the pyramid, and shuddered a
little. Had she blinded Michael with her kisses? Blinded him to
— what? To her incapacity for passion?

'But I'm not incapable,' she thought; 'I'm not. Some day I'll

show him; I'll show them all.' She looked up at 'the Goya'
hanging opposite. What gripping determination in the painting
— what intensity of life in the black eyes of a rather raddled
dame! *She* would know what she wanted, and get it, too! No
compromise and uncertainty there — no capering round life,
wondering what it meant, and whether it was worth while,
nothing but hard living for the sake of living!

Fleur put her hands where her flesh ended, and her dress
began. Wasn't she as warm and firm — yes, and ten times as
pretty, as that fine and evil-looking Spanish dame, with the
black eyes and the wonderful lace? And, turning her back on
the picture, she went into the hall. Michael's voice and another's! They were coming down! She slipped across into the
drawing-room and took up the manuscript of a book of poems,
on which she was to give Michael her opinion. She sat, not reading, wondering if he were coming in. She heard the front door
close. No! He had gone out! A relief, yet chilling! Michael not
warm and cheerful in the house — if it were to go on, it would
be wearing. She curled herself up and tried to read. Dreary
poems — free verse, blank introspective, all about the author's
inside! No lift, no lilt! Duds! She seemed to have read them a
dozen times before. She lay quite still — listening to the click and
flutter of the burning logs! If the light were out she might go
to sleep. She turned it off, and came back to the settee. She could
see herself sitting there, a picture in the firelight; see how lonely
she looked, pretty, pathetic, with everything she wished for, and
— nothing! Her lip curled. She could even see her own spoiled-
child ingratitude. And what was worse, she could see herself
seeing it — a triple-distilled modern, so subtly arranged in life-
tight compartments that she could not be submerged. If only
something would blow in out of the unkempt cold, out of the
waste and wilderness of a London whose flowers she plucked.
The firelight — soft, uncertain — searched out spots and corners
of her Chinese room, as on a stage in one of those scenes, seduc-
tive and mysterious, where one waited, to the sound of tam-
bourines, for the next moment of the plot. She reached out and
took a cigarette. She could see herself lighting it, blowing out

the smoke – her own half-curled fingers, her parted lips, her white rounded arm. She was decorative! Well, and wasn't that all that mattered? To be decorative, and make little decorations; to be pretty in a world that wasn't pretty! In *Copper Coin* there was a poem of a flicker-lit room, and a spoiled Columbine before the fire, and a Harlequin hovering without, like 'the spectre of the rose'. And suddenly, without warning, Fleur's heart ached. It ached definitely, rather horribly, and, slipping down on to the floor before the fire, she snuggled her face against Ting-a-ling. The Chinese dog raised his head – his black eyes lurid in the glow.

He licked her cheek, and turned his nose away. Huf! Powder! But Fleur lay like the dead. And she saw herself lying – the curve of her hip, the chestnut glow in her short hair; she heard the steady beat of her heart. Get up! Go out! Do something! But what – what was worth doing? What had any meaning in it? She saw herself doing – extravagant things; nursing sick women; tending pale babies; making a speech in Parliament; riding a steeplechase; hoeing turnips in knickerbockers – decorative. And she lay perfectly still, bound by the filaments of her self-vision. So long as she saw herself she would do nothing – she knew it – for nothing would be worth doing! And it seemed to her, lying there so still, that not to see herself would be worse than anything. And she felt that to feel this was to acknowledge herself caged for ever.

Ting-a-ling growled, turning his nose towards the windows. 'In here,' he seemed to say, 'we are cosy; we think of the past. We have no use for anything outside. Kindly go away – whoever it is out there!' And again he growled – a low, continuous sound.

'What is it, Ting?'

Ting-a-ling rose on his fore-legs, with muzzle pointed at the window.

'Do you want your walk?'

'No,' said the growl.

Fleur picked him up. 'Don't be so silly!' And she went to the window. The curtains were closely drawn; rich, Chinese lined, they excluded the night. Fleur made a chink with one hand, and started back. Against the pane was a face, the forehead pressed against the glass, the eyes closed, as if it had been there a long time. In the dark it seemed featureless, vaguely pale. She felt the dog's body stiffen under her arm – she felt his silence. Her heart pumped. It was ghastly –face without body.

Suddenly the forehead was withdrawn, the eyes opened. She saw – the face of Wilfrid. Could he see in – see her peering out from the darkened room? Quivering all over, she let the curtains fall to. Beckon? Let him in? Go out to him? Wave him away? Her heart beat furiously. How long had he been out there – like a ghost? What did he want of her? She dropped Ting-a-ling with a flump, and pressed her hands to her forehead, trying to clear confusion from her brain. And suddenly she stepped forward and flung the curtains apart. No face! Nothing! He was gone! The dark, draughty square – not a soul in it! Had he ever been – or was the face her fancy? But Ting-a-ling! Dogs had no fancies. He had gone back to the fire and settled down again.

'It's not my fault,' she thought passionately. 'It's not! I didn't want him to love me. I only wanted his – his –!' Again she sank down before the fire. 'Oh! Ting, have a feeling heart!' But the Chinese dog, mindful of the flump, made no response. ...

Chapter Eleven

COCKED HAT

◄-◄-►-►

AFTER missing his vocation with the young man Butterfield, Michael had hesitated in the hall. At last he had not gone upstairs again, but quietly out. He walked past the Houses of Parliament and up Whitehall. In Trafalgar Square, it occurred to him that he had a father. Bart might be at 'Snooks', The

Coffee House, The Aeroplane; and, with the thought, 'He'd be restful,' he sought the most modern of the three.

'Yes, Sir Lawrence Mont is in the lounge, sir.'

He was sitting with knees crossed, and a cigar between his fingertips, waiting for someone to talk to.

'Ah! Michael! Can you tell me why I come here?'

'To wait for the end of the world, sir?'

Sir Lawrence sniggered. 'An idea,' he said. 'When the skies are wrecking civilization, this will be the best-informed tape in London. The wish to be in at the death is perhaps the strongest of our passions, Michael. I should very much dislike being blown up, especially after dinner; but I should still more dislike missing the next show if it's to be a really good one. The air-raids were great fun, after all.'

Michael sighed.

'Yes,' he said, 'the war got us used to thinking of the millennium, and then it went and stopped, and left the millennium hanging over us. Now we shall never be happy till we get it. Can I take one of your cigars, sir?'

'My dear fellow! I've been reading Frazer again. Extraordinary how remote all superstition seems, now that we've reached the ultimate truth: That enlightenment never can prevail.'

Michael stopped the lighting of his cigar.

'Do you really think that, sir?'

'What else can one think? Who can have any reasonable doubt now that with the aid of mechanics the head-strong part of man must do him in? It's an unavoidable conclusion from all recent facts. "*Per ardua ad astra*," "Through hard knocks we shall see stars." '

'But it's always been like that, sir, and here we are alive?'

'They say so, but I doubt it. I fancy we're really dead, Michael. I fancy we're only living in the past. I don't think – no, I don't think we can be said to expect a future. We talk of it, but I hardly think we hope for one. Underneath our protestations we subconsciously deduce. From the mess we've made of it these last ten years, we can feel the far greater mess we shall

187

make of it in the next thirty. Human nature can argue the hind legs off a donkey, but the donkey will be four-legged at the end of the discussion.'

Michael sat down suddenly and said:

'You're a bad, bold Bart.'

Sir Lawrence smiled.

'I should be glad to think that men really believed in humanity, and all that, but you know they don't – they believe in novelty and getting their own way. With rare exceptions they're still monkeys, especially the scientific variety; and when you put gunpowder and a lighted match into the paws of monkeys, they blow themselves up to see the fun. Monkeys are only safe when deprived of means to be otherwise.'

'Lively, that!' said Michael.

'Not livelier than the occasion warrants, my dear boy. I've been thinking. We've got a member here who knows a trick worth twenty of any played in the war – an extraordinarily valuable fellow. The Government have got their eye on him. He'll help the other valuable fellows in France and Germany and America and Russia to make history. Between them, they'll do something really proud – something that'll knock all the other achievements of man into a cocked hat. By the way, Michael, new device of "*Homo sapiens*" – the cocked hat.'

'Well,' said Michael, 'what are you going to do about it?'

Sir Lawrence's eyebrow sought his hair.

'Do, my dear fellow? What should I do? Can I go out and grab him and the Government by the slack of their breeches; yes, and all the valuable fellows and Governments of the other countries? No! All I can do is to smoke my cigar and say: "God rest you, merry gentlemen, let nothing you dismay!" By hook or crook, they will come into their own, Michael; but in the normal course of things I shall be dead before they do.'

'I shan't,' said Michael.

'No, my dear; but think of the explosions, the sights, the smells. By Jove, you've got something to live for, yet. Sometimes I wish I were your age. And sometimes,' Sir Lawrence relighted his cigar, 'I don't. Sometimes I think I've had enough of our pretences, and that there's nothing left but to die like gentlemen.'

'Some Jeremiad, Dad!'

'Well,' said Sir Lawrence, with a twirl of his little grizzled moustache, 'I hope I'm wrong. But we're driving fast to a condition of things when millions can be killed by the pressing of a few buttons. What reason is there to suppose that our bumps of benevolence will increase in time to stop our using these great new toys of destruction, Michael!'

' "Where you know little, place terrors." '

'Very nice; where did you get that?'

'Out of a life of Christopher Columbus.'

'Old C.C.! I could bring myself to wish sometimes that he hadn't been so deucedly inquisitive. We were snugger in the dark ages. There were something to be said for not discovering the Yanks.'

'Well,' said Michael, '*I* think we shall pedal through, yet. By the way, about this Elderson stunt: I've just seen the clerk – he doesn't look to me the sort that would have made that up.'

'Ah! That! But if Elderson could do such a thing, well – really, anything might happen. It's a complete stumper. He was such a pretty bat, always went in first wicket down. He and I put on fifty-four against Eton. I suppose old Forsyte told you?'

'Yes, he wanted me to find the chap a job.'

'Butterfield. Ask him if he's related to old Butterfield the gardener! It would be something to go on. D'you find old Forsyte rather trying?'

Loyal to Fleur, Michael concealed his lips. 'No, I get on very well with him.'

'He's straight, I admit that.'

'Yes,' said Michael, 'very straight.'

'But somewhat reticent.'

'Yes,' said Michael.

On this conclusion they were silent, as though terrors had been placed beyond it. And soon Michael rose.

'Past ten, I'd better go home.'

Returning the way he came, he could think of nothing but Wilfrid. What wouldn't he give to hear him say: 'It's all right, old man; I've got over it!' — to wring him by the hand again. Why should one catch this fatal disease called love? Why should one be driven half crazy by it? They said love was Nature's provision against Bart's terrors, against the valuable fellows. An insistent urge — lest the race die out. Prosaic, if true! Not that he cared whether Fleur had children. Queer how Nature camouflaged her schemes — leery old bird! But over-reaching herself a bit, wasn't she? Children might yet go clean out of fashion if Bart was right. A very little more would do it; who would have children for the mere pleasure of seeing them blown up, poisoned, starved to death? A few fanatics would hold on, the rest of the world go barren. The cocked hat! Instinctively Michael straightened his own, ready for crossing under Big Ben. He had reached the centre of Parliament Square, when a figure coming towards him swerved suddenly to its left and made in the direction of Victoria. Tall, with a swing in its walk. Wilfrid! Michael stood still. Coming from — South Square! And suddenly he gave chase. He did not run, but he walked his hardest. The blood beat in his temples, and he felt confused to a pitch past bearing. Wilfrid must have seen him, or he wouldn't have swerved, wouldn't be legging it away like a demon. Black! — black! He was not gaining, Wilfrid had the legs of him — to overtake him, he must run! But there rose in Michael a sort of exaltation. His best friend — his wife! There was a limit. One might be too proud to fight that. Let him go his ways! He stood still, watched the swift figure disappear, and slowly, head down under the now cocked hat, turned towards home. He walked quite quietly, and with a sense of finality. No use making a song about it! No fuss, but no retreat! In the few hundred yards before he reached his Square he was chiefly conscious of the tallness of houses, the shortness of men. Such midgets to have made this monstrous pile, lighted it so that it shone in an enormous glittering heap whose glow blurred the colour of the sky! What a vast business this midget activity! Absurd to think that his love for another midget mattered! He turned his key in the lock, took off his cocked hat and went into the drawing-room. Unlighted – empty? No. She and Ting-a-ling were on the floor before the fire! He sat down on the settee, and was abruptly conscious that he was trembling and sweating as if he had smoked a too strong cigar. Fleur had raised herself, cross-legged, and was staring up at him. He waited to get the better of his trembling. Why didn't she speak? Why was she sitting there, in the dark? 'She knows'; he thought: 'we both know this is the end. O God, let me at least be a sport!' He took a cushion, put it behind him, crossed his legs, and leaned back. His voice surprised him suddenly:

'May I ask you something, Fleur? And will you please answer me quite truly?'

'Yes.'

'It's this: I know you didn't love me when you married me. I don't think you love me now. Do you want me to clear out?'

A long time seemed to pass.

'No.'

'Do you mean that?'

'Yes.'

'Why?'

'Because I don't.'

Michael got up.

'Will you answer one thing more?'

'Yes.'

'Was Wilfrid here tonight?'

'Yes – no. That is –'

His hands clutched each other; he saw her eyes fix on them, and kept them still.

'Fleur, don't!'

'I'm not. He came to the window there. I saw his face – that's all. His face – it – Oh! Michael, don't be unkind tonight!'

Unkind! Unkind! Michael's heart swelled at that strange word.

'It's all right,' he stammered: 'So long as you tell me what it is you want.'

Fleur said, without moving :

'I want to be comforted.'

Ah ! She knew exactly what to say, how to say it ! And going
on his knees, he began to comfort her.

Chapter Twelve

GOING EAST

＞＜＞＞

H E had not been on his knees many minutes before they suffered from reaction. To kneel there comforting Fleur brought
him a growing discomfort. He believed her tonight, as he had
not believed her for months past. But what was Wilfrid doing?
Where wandering? The face at the window – face without
voice, without attempt to reach her ! Michael ached in that
illegitimate organ the heart. Withdrawing his arms, he stood
up.

'Would you like me to have a look for him? If it's all over –
he might – I might –'

Fleur, too, stood up. She was calm enough now.

'Yes, I'll go to bed.' With Ting-a-ling in her arms, she went
to the door; her face, between the dog's chestnut fur and her
own, was very pale, very still.

'By the way,' she said, 'this is my second no go, Michael; I
suppose it means –'

Michael gasped. Currents of emotion, welling, ebbing, swirl-
ing, rendered him incapable of speech.

'The night of the balloon,' she said : 'Do you mind?'

'Mind? Good God ! Mind !'

'That's all right, then. *I* don't. Good night !'

She was gone. Without reason, Michael thought : 'In the
beginning was the Word, and the Word was with God, and the
Word was God.' And he stood, as if congealed, overcome by an
uncontrollable sense of solidity. A child coming ! It was as

though the barque of his being, tossed and drifted, suddenly rode tethered – anchor down. He turned and tore at the curtains. Night of stars! Wonderful world! Jolly – jolly! And – Wilfrid! He flattened his face against the glass. Outside there Wilfrid's had been flattened. He could see it if he shut his eyes. Not fair! Dog lost – man lost! S.O.S. He went into the hall, and from the mothless marble coffer rived his thickest coat. He took the first taxi that came by.

'Cork Street! Get along!' Needle in bundle of hay! Quarter-past eleven by Big Ben! The intense relief of his whole being in that jolting cab seemed to him brutal. Salvation! It *was* – he had a strange certainty of that as though he saw Fleur suddenly 'close up' in a very strong light, concrete beneath her graceful veerings. Family! Continuation! He had been unable to anchor her, for he was not of her! But her child could and would! And, perhaps, he would yet come in with the milk. Why did he love her so – it was not done! Wilfrid and he were donkeys – out of touch, out of tune with the times!

'Here you are, sir – what number?'

'All right! Cool your heels and wait for me! Have a cigarette!'

With one between his own lips which felt so dry, he went down the backwater.

A light in Wilfrid's rooms! He rang the bell. The door was opened, the face of Wilfrid's man looked forth.

'Yes, sir?'

'Mr Desert in?'

'No, sir. Mr Desert has just started for the East. His ship sails tomorrow.'

'Oh!' said Michael blankly. 'Where from?'

'Plymouth, sir. His train leaves Paddington at midnight. You might catch him yet.'

'It's very sudden,' said Michael, 'he never –'

'No, sir. Mr Desert is a sudden gentleman.'

'Well, thanks; I'll try and catch him.'

Back in the cab with the words: 'Paddington – flick her along!' he thought: 'A sudden gentleman!' Perfect! He

remembered the utter suddenness of that little interview beside
the bust of Lionel Charwell. Sudden their friendship, sudden
its end – sudden even Wilfrid's poems – offspring of a sudden
soul! Staring from window to window in that jolting, rattling
cab, Michael suffered from St Vitus's dance. Was he a fool?
Could he not let well alone? Pity was posh! And yet! With
Wilfrid would go a bit of his heart, and in spite of all he would
like him to know that. Upper Brook Street, Park Lane! Emptying streets, cold night, stark plane trees painted-up by the lamps
against a bluish dark. And Michael thought: 'We wander!
What's the end – the goal? To do one's bit, and not worry! But
what is my bit? What's Wilfrid's? Where will he end up, now?'

The cab rattled down the station slope and drew up under
cover. Ten minutes to twelve, and a long heavy train on platform one!

'What shall I do?' thought Michael: 'It's so darned crude!
Must I go down – carriage by carriage? "Couldn't let you go,
old man, without" – blurb!'

Bluejackets! If not drunk – as near as made no matter. Eight
minutes still! He began slowly walking along the train. He had
not passed four windows before he saw his quarry. Desert was
sitting back to the engine in the near corner of an empty first.
An unlighted cigarette was in his mouth, his fur collar turned
up to his eyes, and his eyes fixed on an unopened paper on his
lap. He sat without movement; Michael stood looking at him.
His heart beat fast. He struck a match, took two steps, and
said:

'Light, old boy?'

Desert stared up at him.

'Thanks,' he said, and took the match. By its flare his face
was dark, thin, drawn; his eyes dark, deep, tired. Michael leaned
in the window. Neither spoke.

'Take your seat, if you're going, sir.'

'I'm not,' said Michael. His whole inside seemed turning
over.

'Where are you going, old man?' he said suddenly.

'Jericho.'

'God, Wilfrid, I'm sorry!'

Desert smiled.

'Cut it out!'

'Yes, I know! Shake hands?'

Desert held out his hand.

Michael squeezed it hard.

A whistle sounded.

Desert rose suddenly and turned to the rack above him. He took a parcel from a bag. 'Here,' he said, 'these wretched things! Publish them if you like.'

Something clicked in Michael's throat.

'Thanks, old man! That's great! Good-bye!'

A sort of beauty came into Desert's face.

'So long!' he said.

The train moved. Michael withdrew his elbows; quite still, he stared at the motionless figure slowly borne along, away. Carriage after carriage went by him, full of bluejackets leaning out, clamouring, singing, waving handkerchiefs and bottles. Guard's van now – the tail light – all spread – a crimson blur – setting East – going – going – gone!

And that was all – was it? He thrust the parcel into his coat pocket. Back to Fleur, now! Way of the world – one man's meat, another's poison! He passed his hand over his eyes. The dashed things were full of – blurb!

PART THREE

Chapter One

BANK HOLIDAY

⤛⤜

WHITSUNTIDE Bank Holiday was producing its seasonal invasion of Hampstead Heath, and among the ascending swarm were two who meant to make money in the morning and spend it in the afternoon.

Tony Bicket, with balloons and wife, embarked early on the Hampstead Tube.

'You'll see,' he said, 'I'll sell the bloomin' lot by twelve o'clock, and we'll go on the bust.'

Squeezing his arm, Victorine fingered, through her dress, a slight swelling just above her right knee. It was caused by fifty-four pounds fastened in the top of her stocking. She had little feeling, now, against balloons. They afforded temporary nourishment, till she had the few more pounds needful for their passage-money. Tony still believed he was going to screw salvation out of his blessed balloons: he was 'that hopeful – Tony', though their heads were only just above water on his takings. And she smiled. With her secret she could afford to be indifferent now to the stigma of gutter hawking. She had her story pat. From the evening paper, and from communion on buses with those interested in the national pastime, she had acquired the necessary information about racing. She even talked of it with Tony, who had street-corner knowledge. Already she had prepared chapter and verse of two imaginary coups; a sovereign made out of stitching imaginary blouses, invested on the winner of the Two Thousand Guineas, and the result on the dead-heater for the Jubilee at nice odds; this with a third winner, still to be selected, would bring her imaginary winnings up to the needed sixty pounds odd she would so soon have saved now out of 'the altogether'. This tale she would pitch to Tony in a week or two, reeling off by heart the wonderful luck she had kept from him until she had the whole of the money. She would slip her forehead against his eyes if he looked at her too hard, and kiss his lips till his head was no longer clear. And in the morning they would wake up and take their passages. Such was the plan of Victorine, with five ten-pound and four one-pound notes in her stocking, attached to the pink silk stays.

Afternoon of a Dryad had long been finished, and was on exhibition at the Dumetrius Gallery, with other works of Aubrey Greene. Victorine had paid a shilling to see it; had stood some furtive minutes gazing at that white body glimmering from among grass and spikey flowers, at the face, turned as if saying: 'I know a secret!'

'Bit of a genius, Aubrey Greene – that face is jolly good!' Scared, and hiding the face, Victorine had slipped away.

From the very day when she had stood shivering outside the studio of Aubrey Greene she had been in full work. He had painted her three times – always nice, always polite, quite the gentleman! And he had given her introductions. Some had painted her in clothes, some half-draped, some in that 'altogether', which no longer troubled her, with the money swelling her stocking and Tony without suspicion. Not everyone had been 'nice'; advances had been made to her, but she had nipped them in the bud. It would have meant the money quicker, but – Tony! In a fortnight now she could snap her fingers at it all. And often on the way home she stood by that plate-glass window, before the fruits, and the corn, and the blue butterflies. . . .

In the packed railway carriage they sat side by side, Bicket with tray on knee, debating where he had best stand.

'I favour the mokes,' he said at last, 'up by the pond. People'll have more money than when they get down among the swings and coconuts; and you can go and sit in a chair by the pond, like the seaside – I don't want you with me not till I've sold out.'

Victorine pressed his arm.

Along the top and over on to the heath to north and south

the holiday swarms surged, in perfect humour, carrying paper bags. Round the pond, children with thin, grey-white, spindly legs, were paddling and shrilly chattering, too content to smile. Elderly couples crawled slowly by, with jutting stomachs, and faces discoloured by the unaccustomed climb. Girls and young men were few, for they were dispersed already on the heath, in search of a madder merriment. On benches, in chairs of green canvas or painted wood, hundreds were sitting, contemplating their feet, as if imagining the waves of the sea. Now and again three donkeys would start, urged from behind, and slowly tittup their burdens along the pond's margin. Hawkers cried goods. Fat dark women told fortunes. Policemen stood cynically near them. A man talked and talked and took his hat round.

Tony Bicket unslung his tray. His cockney voice, wheedling and a little husky, offered his coloured airs without intermission. This was something like! It was brisk! And now and again he gazed through the throng away across the pond, to where Victorine would be seated in a canvas chair, looking different from everyone – he knew.

'Fine balloons – fine balloons! Six for a bob! Big one, Madam? Only sixpence. See the size! Buy, buy! Tyke one for the little boy!'

No 'aldermen' up here, but plenty in the mood to spend their money on a bit of brightness!

At five minutes before noon he snapped his tray to – not a bally balloon left! With six Bank Holidays a week he would make his fortune! Tray under arm, he began to tour the pond. The kiddies were all right, but – good Lord – how thin and pale! If he and Vic had a kid – but not they – not till they got out there! A fat brown kid, chysin' blue butterflies, and the sun oozin' out of him! Rounding the end of the pond, he walked slowly along the chairs. Lying back, elegant, with legs crossed, in brown stockings showing to the knees, and neat brown shoes with the flaps over – My! she looked a treat – in a world of her own, like that! Something caught Bicket by the throat. Gosh! He wanted things for her!

'Well, Vic! Penny!'

'I was thinkin' of Australia.'

'Ah! It's a gaudy long wait. Never mind – I've sold the bally lot. Which shall we do, go down among the trees, or get to the swings, at once?'

'The swings,' said Victorine.

The Vale of Health was in rhapsodic mood. The crowd flowed here in a slow, speechless stream, to the cries of the booth-keepers, and the owners of swings and coconuts. 'Roll – bowl – or pitch! Now for the milky ones! Penny a shy! ... Who's for the swings? ... Ices ... Ices ... Fine bananas!'

On the giant merry-go-round under its vast umbrella the thirty chain-hung seats were filled with girls and men. Round to the music – slowly – faster – whirling out to the full extent of the chain, bodies bent back, legs stuck forward, laughter and speech dying, faces solemn, a little lost, hands gripping the chains hard. Faster, faster; slowing, slowing to a standstill, and the music silent.

'My word!' murmured Victorine. 'Come on, Tony!'

They entered the enclosure and took their seats. Victorine, on the outside, locked her feet, instinctively, one over the other, and tightening her clasp on the chains, curved her body to the motion. Her lips parted:

'Lor, Tony!'

Faster, faster – every nerve and sense given to that motion! O-o-h! It *was* a feeling – flying round like that above the world! Faster – faster! Slower – slow, and the descent to earth.

'Tony, it's 'eaven!'

'Queer feelin' in yer inside, when you're swung right out!'

'I'd like it level with the top. Let's go once more!'

'Right-o!'

Twice more they went – half his profit on balloons! But who cared? He liked to see her face. After that, six shies at the milky ones without a hit, an ice apiece: then arm-in-arm to find a place to eat their lunch. That was the time Bicket enjoyed most, after the ginger-beer and sandwiches; smoking his fag, with his head on her lap, and the sky blue. A long time like that; till at last she stirred.

'Let's go and see the dancin' !'

In the grass enclosure ringed by the running path, some two dozen couples were jigging to a band.

Victorine pulled at his arm. 'I *would* love a turn !'

'Well, let's 'ave a go,' said Bicket. 'This one-legged bloke'll 'old my tray.'

They entered the ring.

'Hold me tighter, Tony !'

Bicket obeyed. Nothing he liked better; and slowly their feet moved – to this side and that. They made little way, revolving, keeping time, oblivious of appearances.

'You dance all right, Tony.'

'*You* dance a treat !' gasped Bicket.

In the intervals, panting, they watched ever the one-legged man; then to it again, till the band ceased for good.

'My word !' said Victorine. 'They dance on board ship, Tony !'

Bicket squeezed her waist.

'I'll do the trick yet, if I 'ave to rob the Bank. There's nothin' I wouldn't do for you, Vic.'

But Victorine smiled. She had done the trick already.

The crowd with parti-coloured faces, tired, good-humoured, frowsily scented, strolled over a battlefield thick-strewn with paper bags, banana peel, and newspapers.

'Let's 'ave tea, and one more swing,' said Bicket; 'then we'll get over on the other side among the trees.'

Away over on the far side were many couples. The sun went very slowly down. Those two sat under a bush and watched it go. A faint breeze swung and rustled the birch leaves. There was little human sound out here. All seemed to have come for silence, to be waiting for darkness in the hush. Now and then some stealthy spy would pass and scrutinize.

'Foxes !' said Bicket. 'Gawd ! I'd like to rub their noses in it !'

Victorine sighed, pressing closer to him.

Someone was playing on a banjo now; a voice singing. It grew dusk, but a moon was somewhere rising, for little shadows stole out along the ground.

They spoke in whispers. It seemed wrong to raise the voice, as though the grove were under a spell. Even their whisperings were scarce. Dew fell, but they paid no heed to it. With hands locked, and cheeks together, they sat very still. Bicket had a thought. This was poetry – this was! Darkness now, with a sort of faint and silvery glow, a sound of drunken singing on the Spaniard's Road, the whirr of belated cars returning from the north – and suddenly an owl hooted.

'My!' murmured Victorine, shivering. 'An owl! Fancy! I used to hear one at Norbiton. I 'ope it's not bad luck!'

Bicket rose and stretched himself.

'Come on!' he said: 'we've 'ad a dy. Don't you go catchin' cold!'

Arm-in-arm, slowly, through the darkness of the birch-grove, they made their way upwards – glad of the lamps, and the street, and the crowded station, as though they had taken an overdose of solitude.

Huddled in their carriage on the Tube, Bicket idly turned the pages of a derelict paper. But Victorine sat thinking of so much, that it was as if she thought of nothing. The swings and the grove in the darkness, and the money in her stocking. She wondered Tony hadn't noticed when it crackled – there wasn't a safe place to keep it in! What was he looking at, with his eyes so fixed? She peered, and read: '*Afternoon of a Dryad.* The striking picture by Aubrey Greene, on exhibition at the Dumetrius Gallery.'

Her heart stopped beating.

'Cripes!' said Bicket. 'Ain't that like you?'

'Like me? No!'

Bicket held the paper closer. 'It *is*. It's like you all over. I'll cut that out. I'd like to see that picture.'

The colour came up in her cheeks, released from a heart beating too fast now.

' 'Tisn't decent,' she said.

'Dunno about that; but it's awful like you. It's even got your smile.'

Folding the paper, he began to tear the sheet. Victorine's little finger pressed the notes beneath her stocking.

'Funny,' she said slowly, 'to think there's people in the world so like each other.'

'I never thought there could be one like you. Charin' Cross; we gotta change.'

Hurrying along the rat-runs of the Tube, she slipped her hand into his pocket, and soon some scraps of torn paper fluttered down behind her following him in the crush. If only he didn't remember where the picture was!

Awake in the night, she thought:

'I don't care; I'm going to get the rest of the money – that's all about it.'

But her heart moved queerly within her, like that of one whose feet have trodden suddenly the quaking edge of a bog.

Chapter Two

OFFICE WORK

◄◄·►►

Michael sat correcting the proofs of *Counterfeits* – the book left by Wilfrid behind him.

'Can you see Butterfield, sir?'

'I can.'

In Michael the word Butterfield excited an uneasy pride. The young man fulfilled with increasing success the function for which he had been engaged, on trial, four months ago. The head traveller had even called him 'a find'. Next to *Copper Coin* he was the finest feather in Michael's cap. The Trade were not buying, yet Butterfield was selling books, or so it was reported; he appeared to have a natural gift of inspiring confidence where it was not justified. Danby and Winter had even entrusted to him the private marketing of the vellum-bound 'Limited' of *A Duet*, by which they were hoping to recoup their losses on the ordinary edition. He was now engaged in working through a list of names considered likely to patronize the little masterpiece. This method of private approach had been suggested by himself.

'You see, sir,' he had said to Michael: 'I know a bit about Coué. Well, you can't work that on the Trade — they've got no capacity for faith. What can you expect? Every day they buy all sorts of stuff, always basing themselves on past sales. You can't find one in twenty that'll back the future. But with private gentlemen, and especially private ladies, you can leave a thought with them like Coué does — put it into them again and again that day by day in every way the author's gettin' better and better; and ten to one when you go round next, it's got into their subconscious, especially if you take 'em just after lunch or dinner, when they're a bit drowsy. Let me take my own time, sir, and I'll put that edition over for you.'

'Well,' Michael had answered, 'if you can inspire confidence in the future of my governor, Butterfield, you'll deserve more than your ten per cent.'

'I can do it, sir; it's just a question of faith.'

'But you haven't any, have you?'

'Well, not, so to speak, in the author — but I've got faith that I can give *them* faith in him; that's the real point.'

'I see — the three-card stunt; inspire the faith you haven't got, that the card is there, and they'll take it. Well, the disillusion is not immediate — you'll probably always get out of the room in time. Go ahead, then!'

The young man Butterfield had smiled. . . .

The uneasy part of the pride inspired in Michael now by the name was due to old Forsyte's continually saying to him that he didn't know — he couldn't tell — there was that young man and his story about Elderson, and they got no further. . . .

'Good morning, sir. Can you spare me five minutes?'

'Come in, Butterfield. Bunkered with *Duet*?'

'No, sir. I've placed forty already. It's another matter.' Glancing at the shut door, the young man came closer.

'I'm working my list alphabetically. Yesterday I was in the E's.' His voice dropped. 'Mr Elderson.'

'Phew !' said Michael. 'You can give *him* the go-by.'

'As a fact, sir, I haven't.'

'What ! Been over the top?'

'Yes, sir. Last night.'

'Good for you, Butterfield ! What happened?'

'I didn't send my name in, sir – just the firm's card.'

Michael was conscious of a very human malice in the young man's voice and face.

'Well?'

'Mr Elderson, sir, was at his wine. I'd thought it out, and I began as if I'd never seen him before. What struck me was – he took my cue !'

'Didn't kick you out?'

'Far from it, sir. He said at once: "Put my name down for two copies." '

Michael grinned. 'You both had a nerve.'

'No, sir; that's just it. Mr Elderson got it between wind and water. He didn't like it a little bit.'

'I don't twig,' said Michael.

'My being in this firm's employ, sir. He knows you're a partner here, and Mr Forsyte's son-in-law, doesn't he?'

'He does.'

'Well, sir, you see the connexion – two directors believing me – not *him*. That's why I didn't miss him out. I fancied it'd shake him up. I happened to see his face in the sideboard glass as I went out. *He's* got the wind up all right.'

Michael bit his forefinger, conscious of a twinge of sympathy with Elderson, as for a fly with the first strand of cobweb round his hind leg.

'Thank you, Butterfield,' he said.

When the young man was gone, he sat stabbing his blotting-paper with a paper-knife. What curious 'class' sensation was this? Or was it merely fellow-feeling with the hunted, a tremor

at the way things found one out? For, surely, this was real
evidence, and he would have to pass it on to his father, and
'Old Forsyte'. Elderson's nerve must have gone phut, or he'd
have said: 'You impudent young scoundrel – get out of here!'
That, clearly, was the only right greeting from an innocent,
and the only advisable greeting from a guilty man. Well! Nerve
did fail sometimes – even the best. Witness the very proof-sheet
he had just corrected:

THE COURT MARTIAL

'See 'ere! I'm myde o' nerves and blood
    The syme as you, not meant to be
Froze stiff up to me ribs in mud.
    You try it, like I 'ave, an' see!

'Aye, you snug beauty brass hat, when
    You stick what I stuck out that d'y,
An' keep yer ruddy 'earts up – then
    You'll learn, maybe, the right to s'y:

'Take aht an' shoot 'im in the snow,
    Shoot 'im for cowardice! 'E who serves
His King and Country's got to know
    There's no such bloody thing as nerves.'

Good old Wilfrid!

'Yes, Miss Perren?'

'The letter to Sir James Foggart, Mr Mont; you told me to
remind you. And will you see Miss Manuelli?'

'Miss Manu– Oh! Ah! Yes.'

Bicket's girl wife, whose face they had used on Storbert's
novel, the model for Aubrey Greene's – Michael rose, for the
girl was in the room already.

'I remember that dress!' he thought: 'Fleur never liked it.'

'What can I do for you, Mrs Bicket? How's Bicket, by the
way?'

'Fairly, sir, thank you.'

'Still in balloons?'

'Yes.'

'Well, we all are, Mrs Bicket.'

'Beg pardon?'

'In the air – don't you think? But you didn't come to tell me that?'

'No, sir.'

A slight flush in those sallow cheeks, fingers concerned with the tips of the worn gloves, lips uncertain; but the eyes steady – really an uncommon girl!

'You remember givin' me a note to Mr Greene, sir?'

'I do; and I've seen the result; it's topping, Mrs Bicket.'

'Yes. But it's got into the papers – my husband saw it there last night; and of course, he doesn't know about me.'

Phew! For what had he let this girl in?

'I've made a lot of money at it, sir – almost enough for our passage to Australia; but now I'm frightened. "Isn't it like you?" he said to me. I tore the paper up, but suppose he remembers the name of the Gallery and goes to see the picture! That's even much more like me! He might go on to Mr Greene. So would you mind, sir, speaking to Mr Greene, and beggin' him to say it was someone else, in case Tony did go?'

'Not a bit,' said Michael. 'But do you think Bicket would mind so very much, considering what it's done for you? It can be quite a respectable profession.'

Victorine's hands moved up to her breast.

'Yes,' she said, simply. 'I have been quite respectable. And I only did it because we do so want to get away, and I couldn't bear seein' him standin' in the gutter there sellin' those balloons in the fogs. But I'm ever so scared, sir, now.'

Michael stared.

'My God!' he said; 'money's an evil thing!'

Victorine smiled faintly. 'The want of it is, I know.'

'How much more do you need, Mrs Bicket?'

'Only another ten pound, about, sir.'

'I can let you have that.'

'Oh! thank you; but it's not that – I can easy earn it – I've got used to it; a few more days don't matter.'

'But how are you going to account for having the money?'

'Say I won it bettin'.'

'*Thin!*' said Michael. 'Look here! Say you came to me and I advanced it. If Bicket repays it from Australia, I can always put it to your credit again at a bank out there. I've got you into a hole, in a way, and I'd like to get you out of it.'

'Oh! no, sir; you did me a service. I don't want to put you about, telling falsehoods for me.'

'It won't worry me a bit, Mrs Bicket. I can lie to the umteenth when there's no harm in it. The great thing for you is to get away sharp. Are there many other pictures of you?'

'Oh! yes, a lot – not that you'd recognize them, I think, they're so square and funny.'

'Ah! well – Aubrey Greene has got you to the life!'

'Yes; it's like me all over, Tony says.'

'Quite. Well, I'll speak to Aubrey, I shall be seeing him at lunch. Here's the ten pounds! That's agreed then? You came to me today – see? Say you had a brain-wave. I quite understand the whole thing. You'd do a lot for him; and he'd do a lot for you. It's all right – don't cry!'

Victorine swallowed violently. Her hand in the worn glove returned his squeeze.

'I'd tell him tonight, if I were you,' said Michael, 'and I'll get ready.'

When she had gone he thought: 'Hope Bicket won't think I received value for that sixty pounds!' And, pressing his bell, he resumed the stabbing of his blotting-paper.

'Yes, Mr Mont?'

'Now let's get on with it, Miss Perren.'

'DEAR SIR JAMES FOGGART, – We have given the utmost consideration to your very interesting – er – production. While we are of opinion that the views so well expressed on the present condition of Britain in relation to the rest of the world are of great value to all – er – thinking persons, we do not feel that there are enough – er – thinking persons to make it possible to publish the book, except at a loss. The – er – thesis that Britain should now look for salvation through adjustment of markets, population, supply and demand, within the Empire, put with such exceedingly plain speech, will, we are afraid, get the goat of all the political parties; nor do we feel that your plan of emigrating boys and girls in large quantities before they are spoiled by British town life, can do otherwise than irritate a working-class which knows nothing of conditions outside its own country, and is notably averse to giving its children a chance in any other.'

'Am I to put that, Mr Mont?'

'Yes; but tone it in a bit. Er –

'Finally, your view that the land should be used to grow food is so very unusual in these days, that we feel your book would have a hostile Press except from the Old Guard and the Die-hard, and a few folk with vision.'

'Yes, Mr Mont?'

' "In a period of veering – er – transitions" – keep that, Miss Perren – "and the airy unreality of hopes that have gone up the spout" – almost keep that – "any scheme that looks forward and defers harvest for twenty years, must be extraordinarily un-popular. For all these reasons you will see how necessary it is for you to – er – seek another publisher. In short, we are not taking any.

' "With – er –" what you like – "dear Sir James Foggart,

' "We are your obedient servants,

DANBY AND WINTER." '

'When you've translated that, Miss Perren, bring it in, and I'll sign it.'

'Yes. Only, Mr Mont – I thought you were a Socialist. This almost seems – forgive my asking?'

'Miss Perren, it's struck me lately that labels are "off". How can a man be anything at a time when everything's in the air? Look at the Liberals. They can't see the situation whole because of Free Trade; nor can the Labour Party because of their Capital levy; nor can the Tories because of Protection; they're all hag-ridden by catch-words! Old Sir James Foggart's jolly well right, but nobody's going to listen to him. His book will be waste paper if anybody ever publishes it. The world's unreal just now, Miss Perren; and of all countries we're the most un-real.'

'Why, Mr Mont?'

'Why? Because with the most stickfast of all the national temperaments, we're holding on to what's gone more bust for us than for any other country. Anyway, Mr Danby shouldn't have left the letter to me, if he didn't mean me to enjoy myself. Oh! and while we're about it – I've got to refuse Harold Master's new book. It's a mistake, but they won't have it.'

'Why not, Mr Mont? *The Sobbing Turtle* was such a success!'

'Well, in this new thing Master's got hold of an idea which absolutely forces him to say something. Winter says those who hailed *The Sobbing Turtle* as such a work of art, are certain to be down on this for that; and Mr Danby calls the book an outrage on human nature. So there's nothing for it. Let's have a shot:

'MY DEAR MASTER, – In the exhilaration of your subject it has obviously not occurred to you that you've bust up the show. In *The Sobbing Turtle* you were absolutely in tune with half the orchestra, and that – er – the noisiest half. You were charmingly archaic, and securely cold-blooded. But now, what have you gone and done? Taken the last Marquesan islander for your hero and put him down in London town! This thing's a searching satire, a real criticism of life. I'm sure you didn't mean to be contemporary, or want to burrow into reality; but your subject has run off with you. Cold acid and cold blood are very different things, you know, to say nothing of your having had to drop the archaic. Personally, of course, I think this new thing miles better than *The Sobbing Turtle*, which was a nice little affair, but nothing to make a song about. But I'm not the public, and I'm not the critics. The young and thin will be aggrieved by your lack of modernity, they'll say you're moralizing; the old and fat will call you bitter and destructive; and the ordinary public will take your Marquesan seriously, and resent your making him superior to themselves. The prospects, you see, are not gaudy. How d'you think we're going to "get away" with such a book? Well, we're not! Such is the fiat of the firm. I don't agree with it. I'd publish it tomorrow; but needs must when Danby and Winter drive. So, with every personal regret, I return what is really a masterpiece.

Always yours,
MICHAEL MONT.'

'D'you know, Miss Perren, I don't think you need translate that?'

'I'm afraid it would be difficult.'

'Right-o, then; but do the other, please. I'm going to take my wife out to see a picture; back by four. Oh! and if a little chap called Bicket, that we used to have here, calls any time and asks to see me, he's to come up; but I want warning first. Will you let them know downstairs?'

'Yes, Mr Mont. Oh! didn't – wasn't that Miss Manuelli the model for the wrapper on Mr Storbert's novel?'

'She was, Miss Perren; alone I found her.'

'She's very interesting-looking, isn't she?'

'She's unique, I'm afraid.'

'She needn't mind that, I should think.'

'That depends,' said Michael; and stabbed his blotting-paper.

Chapter Three

'AFTERNOON OF A DRYAD'

◄◄─►►

FLEUR was still gracefully concealing most of what Michael called 'the eleventh baronet', now due in about two months' time. She seemed to be adapting herself, in mind and body, to the quiet and persistent collection of the heir. Michael knew that, from the first, following the instructions of her mother, she had been influencing his sex, repeating to herself, every evening before falling asleep, and every morning on waking the words: 'Day by day, in every way, he is getting more and more male,' to infect the subconscious which, everybody now said, controlled the course of events; and that she was abstaining from the words; 'I *will* have a boy,' for this, setting up a reaction, everybody said, was liable to produce a girl. Michael noted that she turned more and more to her mother, as if the French, or more naturalistic, side of her, had taken charge of a process which had to do with the body. She was frequently at Mapledurham, going down in Soames's car, and her mother was frequently in South Square. Annette's handsome presence, with its tendency to black lace was always pleasing to Michael, who had never forgotten her espousal of his suit in days when it was a forlorn hope. Though he still felt only on the threshold of Fleur's heart, and was preparing to play second fiddle to 'the eleventh baronet', he was infinitely easier in mind since Wilfrid had been gone. And he watched, with a sort of amused adoration, the way in which she focused her collecting powers on an object that had no epoch, a process that did not date.

Personally conducted by Aubrey Greene, the expedition to view his show at the Dumetrius Gallery left South Square after an early lunch.

'Your Dryad came to me this morning, Aubrey,' said Michael in the cab. 'She wanted me to ask you to put up a barrage if by any chance her husband blows round to accuse you of painting his wife. It seems he's seen a reproduction of the picture.'

'Umm!' murmured the painter: 'Shall I, Fleur?'

'Of course you must, Aubrey!'

Aubrey Greene's smile slid from her to Michael.

'Well, what's his name?'

'Bicket.'

Aubrey Greene fixed his eyes on space, and murmured slowly:

> 'An angry young husband called Bicket
> Said: "Turn yourself round and I'll kick it;
> You have painted my wife
> In the nude to the life.
> Do you think, Mr Greene, it was cricket?'

'Oh! Aubrey!'

'Chuck it!' said Michael, 'I'm serious. She's a most plucky little creature. She's made the money they wanted, and remained respectable.'

'So far as I'm concerned, certainly.'

'Well, I should think so.'

'Why, Fleur?'

'You're not a vamp, Aubrey!'

'As a matter of fact, she excited my aesthetic sense.'

'Much that'd save her from some aesthetes!' muttered Michael.

'Also, she comes from Putney.'

'There you have a real reason. Then, you *will* put up a barrage if Bicket blows in?'

Aubrey Greene laid his hand on his heart. 'And there we are!'

For the convenience of the eleventh baronet Michael had chosen the hour when the proper patrons of Aubrey Greene would still be lunching. A shock-headed young man and three pale-green girls alone wandered among the pictures. The painter led the way at once to his masterpiece; and for some minutes they stood before it in a suitable paralysis. To speak too soon in praise would never do; to speak too late would be equally tactless; to speak too fulsomely would jar; to mutter coldly: 'Very nice – very nice indeed!' would blight. To say bluntly: 'Well, old man, to tell you the truth, I don't like it a little bit!' would get his goat.

At last Michael pinched Fleur gently, and she said:

'It really is charming, Aubrey; and awfully like – at least –'

'So far as one can tell. But really, old man, you've done it in once. I'm afraid Bicket will think so, anyway.'

'Dash that!' muttered the painter. 'How do you find the colour values?'

'Jolly fine; especially the flesh; don't you think so, Fleur?'

'Yes; only I should have liked that shadow down the side a little deeper.'

'Yes?' murmured the painter: 'Perhaps!'

'You've caught the spirit,' said Michael. 'But I tell you what, old man, you're for it – the thing's got meaning. I don't know what the critics will do to you.'

Aubrey Greene smiled. 'That was the worst of her. She led me on. To get an idea's fatal.'

'Personally, I don't agree to that; do you, Fleur?'

'Of course not; only one doesn't say so.'

'Time we did, instead of kow-towing to the Café C'rillon. I say, the hair's all right, and so are the toes — they curl as you look at 'em.'

'And it *is* a relief not to get legs painted in streaky cubes. The asphodels rather remind one of the flowers in Leonardo's *Virgin of the Rocks*, Aubrey.'

'The whole thing's just a bit Leonardoish, old man. You'll have to live that down.'

'Oh! Aubrey, my father's seen it. I believe he's biting. Something you said impressed him — about our white monkey, d'you remember?'

Aubrey Greene threw up his hands. 'Ah! That white monkey — to have painted that! Eat the fruit and chuck the rinds around, and ask with your eyes what it's all about.'

'A moral!' said Michael: 'Take care, old man! Well! Our taxi's running up. Come along, Fleur; we'll leave Aubrey to his conscience.'

Once more in the cab, he took her arm.

'That poor little snipe, Bicket! Suppose I'd come on *you* as he'll come on his wife!'

'I shouldn't have looked so nice.'

'Oh! yes; much nicer; though she looks nice enough, I must say.'

'Then why should Bicket mind, in these days of emancipation?'

'Why? Good Lord, ducky! you don't suppose Bicket —! I mean, we emancipated people have got into the habit of thinking we're the world — well! we aren't; we're an excrescence, small, and noisy. We talk as if all the old values and prejudices had gone; but they've no more gone, really, you know, than the rows of villas and little grey houses.'

'Why this outburst, Michael?'

'Well, darling, I'm a bit fed-up with the attitude of our crowd. If emancipation were true, one could stick it; but it's not. There isn't ten per cent difference between now and thirty years ago.'

'How do you know? You weren't alive.'

'No; but I read the papers, and talk to the man in the street, and look at people's faces. Our lot think they're the tablecloth, but they're only the fringe. D'you know, only one hundred and fifty thousand people in this country have ever heard a Beethoven Symphony? How many, do you suppose, think old B. a back number? Five thousand, perhaps, out of forty-two millions. How's that for emancipation?'

He stopped, observing that her eyelids had drooped.

'I was thinking, Michael, that I should like to change my bedroom curtains to blue. I saw the exact colour yesterday at Harton's. They say blue has an effect on the mind – the present curtains really are too jazzy.'

The eleventh baronet!

'Anything you like, darling. Have a blue ceiling if it helps.'

'Oh, no! But I think I'll change the carpet, too; there's a lovely powder blue at Harton's.'

'Then get it. Would you like to go there now? I can take the Tube back to the office.'

'Yes, I think I'd better. I might miss it.'

Michael put his head out of the window. 'Harton's, please!' And, replacing his hat, he looked at her. Emancipated! Phew!

Chapter Four

AFTERNOON OF A BICKET

◄◄-►►

J U S T about that moment Bicket re-entered his sitting-room and deposited his tray. All the morning under the shadow of St Paul's he had re-lived Bank Holiday. Exceptionally tired in feet and legs, he was also itching mentally. He had promised himself a refreshing look from time to time at what was almost like a photo of Vic herself. And he had lost the picture! Yet he had taken nothing out of his pockets – just hung his coat up. Had it

jogged out in the crush at the station, or had he missed his
pocket opening and dropped it in the carriage? And he had
wanted to see the original, too. He remembered that the Gallery
began with a 'D', and at lunch-time squandered a penny-half-
penny to look up the names. Foreign, he was sure – the picture
being naked. 'Dumetrius?' Ah!

Back at his post, he had a bit of luck. 'That alderman',
whom he had not seen for months, came by. Intuition made him
say at once: 'Hope I see you well sir. Never forgotten your
kindness.'

The 'alderman', who had been staring up as if he saw a
magpie on the dome of St Paul's, stopped as though attacked
by cramp.

'Kindness?' he said; 'what kindness? Oh! Balloons! They
were no good to me!'

'No, sir, I'm sure,' said Bicket humbly.

'Well, here you are!' muttered the 'alderman'; 'don't expect
it again.'

Half a crown! A whole half-crown! Bicket's eyes pursued
the hastening form. 'Good luck!' he said softly to himself, and
began putting up his tray. 'I'll go home and rest my feet, and
tyke Vic to see that picture. It'll be funny lookin' at it together.'

But she was not in. He sat down and smoked a fag. He felt
aggrieved that she was out, this the first afternoon he had taken
off. Of course she couldn't stay in all day! Still –! He waited
twenty minutes, then put on Michael's suit and shoes.

'I'll go and see it alone,' he thought. 'It'll cost half as much.
They charge you sixpence, I expect.'

They charged him a shilling – a shilling! One fourth of his
day's earnings, to see a picture! He entered bashfully. There
were ladies who smelled of scent and had drawling voices but
not a patch on Vic for looks. One of them, behind him, said:

'See! There's Aubrey Greene himself! And that's the picture
they're talking of – *Afternoon of a Dryad*.'

They passed him and moved on. Bicket followed. At the end
of the room, between their draperies and catalogues, he glimpsed
the picture. A slight sweat broke out on his forehead. Almost

life-size, among the flowers and spiky grasses, the face smiled round at him – very image of Vic! Could someone in the world be as like her as all that? The thought offended him, as a collector is offended finding the duplicate of a unique possession.

'It's a wonderful picture, Mr Greene. What a type!'

A young man without hat, and fair hair sliding back, answered:

'A find, wasn't she?'

'Oh! perfect! the very spirit of a wood-nymph; so mysterious!'

The word that belonged to Vic! It was unholy. There she lay for all to look at, just because some beastly woman was made like her! A kind of rage invaded Bicket's throat, caused his cheeks to burn; and with it came a queer physical jealousy. That painter! What business had he to paint a woman so like Vic as that – a woman that didn't mind lyin' like that! They and their talk about cahryscuro and paganism, and a bloke called Leneardo! Blast their drawling and their tricks! He tried to move away, and could not, fascinated by that effigy, so uncannily resembling what he had thought belonged to himself alone. Silly to feel so bad over a 'coincidence', but he felt like smashing the glass and cutting the body up into little bits. The ladies and the painter passed on, leaving him alone before the picture. Alone, he did not mind so much. The face was mournful-like, and lonely, and – and teasing, with its smile. It sort of haunted you – it did! 'Well!' thought Bicket, 'I'll get home to Vic. Glad I didn't bring her, after all, to see herself-like. If I was an alderman, I'd buy the blinkin' thing, and burn it!'

And there, in the entrance-lobby, talking to a 'dago', stood – his very own 'alderman'! Bicket paused in sheer amazement.

'It's a rithing name, Mr Forthyte,' he heard the Dago say: 'hith prithes are going up.'

'That's all very well, Dumetrius, but it's not everybody's money in these days – too highly-finished, altogether!'

'Well, Mr Forthyte, to *you* I take off ten per thent.'

'Take off twenty and I'll buy it.'

That Dago's shoulders mounted above his hairy ears – they did; and what a smile!

'Mithter Forthyte! Fifteen, thir!'

'Well, you're doing me; but send it round to my daughter's in South Square – you know the number. When do you close?'

'Day after tomorrow, thir.'

So! The counterfeit of Vic had gone to that 'alderman', had it? Bicket uttered a savage little sound, and slunk out.

He walked with a queer feeling. Had he got unnecessary wind up? After all, it wasn't her. But to know that another woman could smile that way, have frizzy-ended short black hair, and be all curved the same! And at every woman's passing face he looked – so different, so utterly unlike Vic's!

When he reached home she was standing in the middle of the room, with her lips to a balloon. All around her, on the floor, chairs, table, mantelpiece, were the blown-out shapes of his stock; one by one they had floated from her lips and selected their own resting-places: puce, green, orange, purple, blue, enlivening with their colour the dingy little space. All his balloons blown up! And there, in her best clothes, she stood, smiling, queer, excited.

'What in thunder!' said Bicket.

Raising her dress, she took some crackling notes from the top of her stocking, and held them out to him.

'See! Sixty-four pounds, Tony! I've got it all. We can go.'

'*What!*'

'I had a brain-wave – went to that Mr Mont who gave us the clothes, and he's advanced it. We can pay it back, some day. Isn't it a marvel?'

Bicket's eyes, startled like a rabbit's, took in her smile, her excited flush, and a strange feeling shot through all his body, as if *they* were taking *him* in! She wasn't like Vic! No! Suddenly he felt her arms round him, felt her moist lips on his. She clung so tight, he could not move. His head went round.

'At last! At last! Isn't it fine? Kiss me, Tony!'

Bicket kissed; his vertigo was real, but behind it, for the moment stifled, what sense of unreality! ...

Was it before night, or in the night, that the doubt first came – ghostly, tapping, fluttering, haunting – then, in the dawn, jabbing through his soul, turning him rigid. The money – the picture – the lost paper – that sense of unreality! This story she had told him! Were such things possible? Why should Mr Mont advance that money? She had seen him – that was certain; the room, the secretary – you couldn't mistake her description of that Miss Perren. Why, then, feel this jabbing doubt? The money – such a lot of money! Not with Mr Mont – never – he was a gent! Oh! Swine that he was, to have a thought like that – of Vic! He turned his back to her and tried to sleep. But once you got a thought like that – sleep? No! Her face among the balloons, the way she had smothered his eyes and turned his head – so that he couldn't think, couldn't go into it and ask her questions! A prey to dim doubts, achings, uncertainty, thrills of hope, and visions of 'Austrylia', Bicket arose haggard.

'Well,' he said, over their cocoa and margarined bread: 'I must see Mr Mont, that's certain.' And suddenly he added: 'Vic?' looking straight into her face.

She answered his look – straight, yes, straight. Oh! he was a proper swine! ...

When he had left the house Victorine stood quite still, with hands pressed against her chest. She had slept less than he. Still as a mouse, she had turned and turned the thought: 'Did I take him in? Did I?' And if not – what? She took out the notes which had bought – or sold? – their happiness, and counted them once more. And the sense of injustice burned within her. Had she wanted to stand like that before men? Hadn't she been properly through it about that? Why, she could have had the sixty pounds three months ago from that sculptor, who was wild about her; or – so he said! But she had stuck it; yes, she had. Tony had nothing against her really – even if he knew it all. She had done it for him – Well! mostly – for him selling those balloons day after day in all weathers! But for her, they would still be stuck, and another winter coming, and unemployment – so they said in the paper – to be worse and worse! Stuck in the fogs and the cold, again! Ugh! Her chest was still funny sometimes; and he always hoarse. And this poky little room, and the bed so small that she couldn't stir without waking him. Why should Tony doubt her? For he did – she had felt it, heard it in his 'Vic?' Would Mr Mont convince him? Tony was sharp! Her head drooped. The unfairness of it all! Some had everything to their hand, like that pretty wife of Mr Mont's! And if one tried to find a way and get out to a new chance – then – then – this! She flung her hair back. Tony *must* believe – he should! If he wouldn't, let him look out. She had done nothing to be ashamed of! No, indeed! And with the longing to go in front and lead her happiness along, she got out her old tin trunk, and began with careful method to put things into it.

Chapter Five

MICHAEL GIVES ADVICE

◄◄►►

MICHAEL still sat, correcting the proofs of *Counterfeits*. Save 'Jericho', there had been no address to send them to. The East was wide, and Wilfrid had made no sign. Did Fleur ever think of Wilfrid – well, probably he was forgetting her already. Even passion required a little sustenance.

'A Mr Forsyte to see you, sir.'

Apparition in bookland!

'Ah! Show him in.'

Soames entered with an air of suspicion.

'This your place?' he said. 'I've looked in to tell you that I've bought that picture of young Greene's. Have you anywhere to hang it?'

'I should think we had,' said Michael. 'Jolly good, sir, isn't it?'

'Well,' muttered Soames, 'for these days, yes. He'll make a name.'

'He's an intense admirer of that White Monkey you gave us.'

'Ah! I've been looking into the Chinese. If I go on buying –'
Soames paused.

'They *are* a bit of an antidote, aren't they, sir?' That "Earthly
Paradise"! And those geese – they don't seem to mind your
counting their feathers, do they?'

Soames made no reply; he was evidently thinking: 'How on
earth I missed those things when they first came on the market!'
Then, raising his umbrella, and pointing it as if at the book
trade, he asked:

'Young Butterfield – how's he doing?'

'Ah! I was going to let you know, sir. He came in yesterday
and told me that he saw Elderson two days ago. He went to sell
him a copy of my father's "Limited"; Elderson said nothing and
bought two.'

'The deuce he did!'

'Butterfield got the impression that his visit put the wind up
him. Elderson knows, of course, that I'm in this firm, and your
son-in-law.'

Soames frowned. 'I'm not sure,' he said, 'that sleeping
dogs –! Well, I'm on my way there now.'

'Mention the book, sir, and see how Elderson takes it. Would
you like one yourself? You're on the list. E, F – Butterfield
should be reaching you today. It'll save you a refusal. Here it is
– nice get-up. One guinea.'

'*A Duet*,' read Soames. 'What's it about? Musical?'

'Not precisely. A sort of cat-calling between the ghosts of the
G.O.M. and Dizzy!'

'I'm not a reader,' said Soames. He pulled out a note. 'Why
didn't you make it a pound? Here's the shilling.'

'Thanks awfully, sir; I'm sure my father'll be frightfully
bucked to think you've got one.'

'Will he?' said Soames, with a faint smile. 'D'you ever do any
work here?'

'Well, we try to turn a doubtful penny.'

'What d'you make at it?'

'Personally, about five hundred a year.'

'That all?'

'Yes, but I doubt if I'm worth more than three.'

'H'm! I thought you'd got over your Socialism.'

'I fancy I have, sir. It didn't seem to go with my position.'

'No,' said Soames. 'Fleur seems well.'

'Yes, she's splendid. She does the Coué stunt, you know.'

Soames stared. 'That's her mother,' he said; 'I can't tell. Good-bye! Oh! I want to know; what's the meaning of that expression "got his goat"?'

' "Got his goat"? Oh, raised his dander, if you know what that means, it was before my time.'

'I see,' said Soames; 'I had it right, then. Well!' He turned. His back was very neat and real. It vanished through the doorway, and with it seemed to go the sense of definition.

Michael took up the proofs, and read two poems. Bitter as quinine! The unrest in them – the yearning behind the words! Nothing Chinese there! After all, the ancients – like Old Forsyte, and his father in a very different way – had an anchor down. 'What is it?' thought Michael. 'What's wrong with us? We're quick, and clever, cocksure, and dissatisfied. If only something would enthuse us, or get *our* goats! We've chucked religion, tradition, property, pity; and in their place we put – what? Beauty? Gosh! See Walter Nazing, and the Café C'rillon! and yet – we must be after something! Better world? Doesn't look like it. Future life? Suppose I ought to "look into" spiritualism, as Old Forsyte would say. But – half in this world, half in that – deuced odd if spirits are less restive than we are!'

To what – to what, then, was it all moving?

'Dash it!' thought Michael, getting up, 'I'll try dictating an advertisement!'

'Will you come in, please, Miss Perren? For the new Desert volume – Trade Journals: "Danby and Winter will shortly issue *Counterfeits*, by the author of *Copper Coin*, the outstanding success of the last publishing season." I wonder how many publishers have claimed that, Miss Perren, for how many books this year? "These poems show all the brilliancy of mood, and more than the technical accomplishment of the young author's first volume." How's that?'

'Brilliancy of mood, Mr Mont? Do you think?'

'No. But what am I to say? "All the pangs and pessimism"?'

'Oh, no! But possibly: "All the brilliancy of diction. The strangeness and variety of mood."'

'Good. But it'll cost more. Say: "All the brilliant strangeness"; that'll ring their bells in once. We're nuts on "the strange", but we're not getting it – the *outré*, yes, but not the strange.'

'Surely Mr Desert gets –'

'Yes, sometimes; but hardly anyone else. To be strange, you've got to have guts, if you'll excuse the phrase, Miss Perren.'

'Certainly, Mr Mont. That young man Bicket is waiting to see you.'

'He is, is he?' said Michael, taking out a cigarette. 'Give me time to tighten my belt, Miss Perren, and ask him up.'

'The lie benevolent,' he thought; 'now for it!'

The entrance of Bicket into a room where his last appearance had been so painful, was accomplished with a certain stolidity. Michael stood, back to the hearth, smoking; Bicket, back to a pile of modern novels, with the words 'This great new novel' on it. Michael nodded.

'Hallo, Bicket!'

Bicket nodded.

'Hope you're keeping well, sir?'

'Frightfully well, thank you.' And there was silence.

'Well,' said Michael at last, 'I suppose you've come about that little advance to your wife. It's quite all right; no hurry whatever.'

While saying this he had become conscious that the 'little snipe' was dreadfully disturbed. His eyes had a most peculiar look, those large, shrimp-like eyes which seemed, as it were, in advance of the rest of him. He hastened on:

'I believe in Australia myself. I think you're perfectly right, Bicket, and the sooner you go, the better. She doesn't look too strong.'

Bicket swallowed.

'Sir,' he said, 'you've been a gent to me, and it's hard to say things.'

'Then don't.'

Bicket's cheeks became suffused with blood: queer effect in that pale, haggard face.

'It isn't what you think,' he said: 'I've come to ask you to tell me the truth.' Suddenly he whipped from his pocket what Michael perceived to be a crumpled novel-wrapper.

'I took this from a book on the counter as I came by, downstairs. There! Is that my wife?' He stretched it out.

Michael beheld with consternation the wrapper of Storbert's novel. One thing to tell the lie benevolent already determined on – quite another to deny this!

Bicket gave him little time.

'I see it is, from your fyce,' he said. 'What's it all mean? I want the truth – I must 'ave it! I'm gettin' wild over all this. If that's 'er fyce there, then that's 'er body in the Gallery – Aubrey Greene; it's the syme nyme. What's it all mean?' His face had become almost formidable; his cockney accent very broad. 'What gyme 'as she been plyin'? You gotta tell me before I go aht of 'ere.'

Michael's heels came together. He said quietly:

'Steady, Bicket.'

'Steady! You'd be steady if *your* wife – ! All that money! *You* never advanced it – you never give it 'er – never! Don't tell me you did!'

Michael had taken his line. No lies!

'I lent her ten pounds to make a round sum of it – that's all; the rest she earned – honourably; and you ought to be proud of her.'

Bicket's mouth fell open.

'Proud? And how's she earned it? Proud! My Gawd!'

Michael said coldly:

'As a model. I myself gave her the introduction to my friend, Mr Greene, the day you had lunch with me. You've heard of models, I suppose?'

Bicket's hands tore the wrapper, and the pieces fell to the floor. 'Models!' he said: 'Pynters – yes, I've 'eard of 'em – Swines!'

'No more swine than you are, Bicket. Be kind enough not to insult my friend. Pull yourself together, man, and take a cigarette.'

Bicket dashed the proffered case aside.

'I – I – was stuck on her,' he said passionately, 'and she's put this up on me!' A sort of sob came out of his lungs.

'You were stuck on her,' said Michael; his voice had sting in it. 'And when she does her best for you, you turn her down – is that it? Do you suppose she liked it?'

Bicket covered his face suddenly.

'What should I know?' he muttered from behind his hands.

A wave of pity flooded up in Michael. Pity! Blurb!

He said dryly: 'When you've quite done, Bicket. D'you happen to remember what *you* did for *her*?'

Bicket uncovered his face and stared wildly. 'You've never told her that?'

'No; but I jolly well will if you don't pull yourself together.'

'What do I care if you do, now – lyin' like that, for all the men in the world! Sixty pounds! Honourably! D'you think I believe that?' His voice had desolation in it.

'Ah!' said Michael. 'You don't believe simply because you're ignorant, as ignorant as the swine you talk of. A girl can do what she did and be perfectly honest, as I haven't the faintest doubt she is. You've only to look at her, and hear the way she speaks of it. She did it because she couldn't bear to see you selling those balloons. She did it to get you out of the gutter, and give you both a chance. And now you've got the chance, you kick up like this. Dash it all, Bicket, be a sport! Suppose I tell her what you did for her – d'you think she's going to squirm and squeal? Not she! It was damned human of you, and it was damned human of her; and don't you forget it!'

Bicket swallowed violently again.

225

'It's all very well,' he said sullenly; 'it 'asn't 'appened to you.'

Michael was afflicted at once. No! It hadn't happened to him! And all his doubts of Fleur in the days of Wilfrid came hitting him.

'Look here, Bicket,' he said, 'do you doubt your wife's affection? The whole thing is there. I've only seen her twice, but I don't see how you can. If she weren't fond of you, why should she want to go to Australia, when she knows she can make good money here, and enjoy herself if she wants? I can vouch for my friend Greene. He's dashed decent, and I *know* he's played cricket.'

But, searching Bicket's face, he wondered: Were all the others she had sat to as dashed decent?

'Look here, Bicket! We all get up against it sometimes; and that's the test of us. You've just *got* to believe in her; there's nothing else to it.'

'To myke a show of herself for all the world to see!' The words seemed to struggle from the skinny throat. 'I saw that picture bought yesterday by a ruddy alderman.'

Michael could not conceal a grin at this description of 'Old Forsyte'.

'As a matter of fact,' he said, 'it was bought by my own father-in-law as a present to us, to hang in our house. And, mind you, Bicket, it's a fine thing.'

'Ah!' cried Bicket, 'it *is* a fine thing! Money! It's money bought her. Money'll buy anything. It'll buy the 'eart out of your chest.'

And Michael thought: 'I can't get away with it a bit! What price emancipation? He's never heard of the Greeks! And if he had, they'd seem to him a lot of loose-living foreigners. I must quit.' And, suddenly, he saw tears come out of those shrimp's eyes, and trickle down the hollowed cheeks.

Very disturbed, he said hastily:

'When you get out there, you'll never think of it again. Hang it all, Bicket, be a man! She did it for the best. If I were you, I'd never let on to her that I knew. That's what she'd do if I told her how you snooped those *Copper Coins*.'

Bicket clenched his fists – the action went curiously with the tears; then, without a word, he turned and shuffled out.

'Well,' thought Michael, 'giving advice is clearly not my stunt! Poor little snipe!'

Chapter Six

QUITTANCE

◄–►

BICKET stumbled, half-blind, along the Strand. Naturally good-tempered, such a nerve-storm made him feel ill, and bruised in the brain. Sunlight and motion slowly restored some power of thought. He had got the truth. But was it the whole and nothing but the truth? Could she have made all that money without –? If he could believe that, then, perhaps – out of this country where people could see her naked for a shilling – he might forget. But – all that money! And even if all earned 'honourable', as Mr Mont had put it, in how many days, exposed to the eyes of how many men? He groaned aloud in the street. The thought of going home to her – of a scene, of what he might learn if there *were* a scene, was just about unbearable. And yet – must do it, he supposed. He could have borne it better under St Paul's, standing in the gutter, offering his balloons. A man of leisure for the first time in his life, a blooming 'alderman' with nothing to do but step in and take a ticket to the ruddy butterflies! And he owed that leisure to what a man with nothing to take his thoughts off simply could not bear! He would rather have snaffled the money out of a shop till. Better that on his soul, than the jab of this dark fiendish sexual jealousy. 'Be a man!' Easy said! 'Pull yourself together! She did it for you!' He would a hundred times rather she had not. Blackfriars Bridge! A dive, and an end in the mud down there? But you had to rise three times; they would fish you out alive, and run you in for it – and nothing gained – not even the pleasure of thinking that Vic would see what she had done, when she came to identify the body. Dead was dead, anyway, and he would never know what she felt post-mortem! He trudged across the bridge, keeping his eyes before him. Little Ditch Street — how he used to scuttle down it, back to her, when she had pneumonia! Would he never feel like that again? He strode past the window, and went in.

Victorine was still bending over the brown tin trunk. She straightened herself, and on her face came a cold, tired look.

'Well,' she said, 'I see you know.'

Bicket had but two steps to take in that small room. He took them, and put his hands on her shoulders. His face was close, his eyes, so large and strained, searched hers.

'I know you've myde a show of yourself for all London to see; what I want to know is — the rest!'

Victorine stared back at him.

'The rest!' she said — it was not a question, just a repetition, in a voice that seemed to mean nothing.

'Ah!' said Bicket hoarsely; 'the rest — Well?'

'If you think there's a "rest", that's enough.'

Bicket jerked his hands away.

'Aoh! for the land's sake, daon't be mysterious. I'm 'alf orf me nut!'

'I see that,' said Victorine; 'and I see this: You aren't what I thought you. D'you think I liked doing it?' She raised her dress and took out the notes. 'There you are! You can go to Australia without me.'

Bicket cried hoarsely: 'And leave you to the blasted pynters?'

'And leave me to meself. Take them!'

But Bicket recoiled against the door, staring at the notes with horror. 'Not me!'

'Well, *I* can't keep 'em. I earned them to get you out of this.'

There was a long silence, while the notes lay between them on the table, still crisp if a little greasy — the long-desired, the dreamed-of means of release, of happiness together in the sunshine. There they lay; neither would take them! What then?

'Vic,' said Bicket at last, in a hoarse whisper, 'swear you never let 'em touch you!'

'Yes, I can swear that.'

And she could smile, too, saying it – that smile of hers! How believe her – living all these months, keeping it from him, telling him a lie about it in the end! He sank into a chair by the table and laid his head on his arms.

Victorine turned and began pulling an old cord round the trunk. He raised his head at the tiny sound. Then she really meant to go away! He saw his life devastated, empty as a coconut on Hampstead Heath; and all defence ran melted out of his cockney spirit. Tears rolled from his eyes.

'When you were ill,' he said, 'I stole for you. I got the sack for it.'

She spun round. 'Tony – you never told me! What did you steal?'

'Books. All your extra feedin' was books.'

For a long minute she stood looking at him, then stretched out her hands without a word. Bicket seized them.

'I don't care about anything,' he gasped, 'so 'elp me, so long as you're fond of me, Vic!'

'And I don't neither. Oh! let's get out of this, Tony! this awful little room, this awful country. Let's get out of it all!'

'Yes,' said Bicket; and put her hands to his eyes.

Chapter Seven

LOOKING INTO ELDERSON

★←→★

SOAMES had left Danby and Winter divided in thought between Elderson and the White Monkey. As Fleur surmised, he had never forgotten Aubrey Greene's words concerning that bit of salvage from the wreck of George Forsyte. 'Eat the fruits of life, scatter the rinds, and get copped doing it.' His application of them tended towards the field of business.

The country was still living on its capital. With the collapse

of the carrying trade and European markets, they were import-
ing food they couldn't afford to pay for. In his opinion they
would get copped doing it, and that before long. British credit
was all very well, the wonder of the world and that, but you
couldn't live indefinitely on wonder. With shipping idle, concerns making a loss all over the place, and the unemployed in
swarms, it was a pretty pair of shoes! Even insurance must
suffer before long. Perhaps that chap Elderson had foreseen
this already, and was simply feathering his nest in time. If one
was to be copped in any case, why bother to be honest? This was
cynicism so patent, that all the Forsyte in Soames rejected it;
and yet it would keep coming back. In a general bankruptcy,
why trouble with thrift, far-sightedness, integrity? Even the
Conservatives were refusing to call themselves Conservatives
again, as if there were something ridiculous about the word, and
they knew there was really nothing left to conserve. 'Eat the
fruit, scatter the rinds and get copped doing it.' That young
painter had said a clever thing – yes, and his picture was clever,
though Dumetrius had done one over the price – as usual!
Where would Fleur hang it? In the hall, he shouldn't be surprised – good light there; and the sort of people they knew
wouldn't jib at the nude. Curious – where all the nudes went to!
You never saw a nude – no more than you saw the proverbial
dead donkey! Soames had a momentary vision of dying donkeys
laden with pictures of the nude, stepping off the edge of the
world. Refusing its extravagance, he raised his eyes, just in time
to see St Paul's, as large as life. That little beggar with his balloons wasn't there today! Well – he'd nothing for him! At a
tangent his thoughts turned towards the object of his pilgrimage
– the P.P.R.S. and its half-year's accounts. At his suggestion,
they were writing off that German business wholesale – a dead
loss of two hundred and thirty thousand pounds. There would
be no interim dividend, and even then they would be carrying
forward a debit towards the next half-year. Well! better have a
rotten tooth out at once and done with; the shareholders would
have six months to get used to the gap before the general meeting. He himself had got used to it already, and so would they in

time. Shareholders were seldom nasty unless startled – a long-suffering lot!

In the board-room the old clerk was still filling his ink-pots from the magnum.

'Manager in?'

'Yes, sir.'

'Say I'm here, will you?'

The old clerk withdrew. Soames looked at the clock. Twelve! A little shaft of sunlight slanted down the wainscotting and floor. There was nothing else alive in the room save a bluebottle and the tick of the clock; not even a daily paper. Soames watched the bluebottle. He remembered how, as a boy, he had preferred bluebottles and greenbottles to the ordinary fly, because of their bright colour. It was a lesson. The showy things, the brilliant people, were the dangerous. Witness the Kaiser, and that precious Italian poet – what was his name! And this Jack-o'-lantern of their own! He shouldn't be surprised if Elderson were brilliant in private life. Why didn't the chap come? Was that encounter with young Butterfield giving him pause? The bluebottle crawled up the pane, buzzed down, crawled up again; the sunlight stole inward along the floor. All was vacuous in the board-room, as though embodying the principle of insurance: 'Keep things as they are.'

'Can't kick my heels here for ever,' thought Soames, and moved to the window. In that wide street leading to the river, sunshine illumined a few pedestrians and a brewer's dray, but along the main artery at the end the traffic streamed and rattled. London! A monstrous place! And all insured! 'What'll it be like thirty years hence?' he thought. To think that there would be London, without himself to see it! He felt sorry for the place, sorry for himself. Even old Gradman would be gone. He supposed the insurance societies would look after it, but he didn't know. And suddenly he became aware of Elderson. The fellow looked quite jaunty, in a suit of dittoes and a carnation.

'Contemplating the future, Mr Forsyte?'

'No,' said Soames. How had the fellow guessed his thoughts? 'I'm glad you've come in. It gives me a chance to say how grateful I am for the interest you take in the concern. It's rare. A manager has a lonely job.'

Was he mocking? He seemed altogether very spry and uppish. Light-heartedness always made Soames suspicious – there was generally some reason for it.

'If every director were as conscientious as you, one would sleep in one's bed. I don't mind telling you that the amount of help I got from the Board before you came on it was – well – negligible.'

Flattery! The fellow must be leading up to something!

Elderson went on:

'I can say to you what I couldn't say to any of the others: I'm not at all happy about business, Mr Forsyte. England is just about to discover the state she's really in.'

Faced with this startling confirmation of his own thoughts, Soames reacted.

'No good crying out before we're hurt,' he said; 'the pound's still high. We're good stayers.'

'In the soup, I'm afraid. If something drastic isn't done – we *shall* stay there. And anything drastic, as you know, means disorganization and lean years before you reap reward.'

How could the fellow talk like this, and look as bright and pink as a new penny? It confirmed the theory that he didn't care what happened. And, suddenly, Soames resolved to try a shot.

'Talking of lean years – I came in to say that I think we must call a meeting of the shareholders over this dead loss of the German business.' He said it to the floor, and looked quickly up. The result was disappointing. The manager's light-grey eyes met his without a blink.

'I've been expecting that from you,' he said.

'The deuce you have!' thought Soames, for it had but that moment come into his mind.

'By all means call one,' went on the manager; 'but I'm afraid the Board won't like it.'

Soames refrained from saying: 'Nor do I.'

'Nor the shareholders, Mr Forsyte. In a long experience I've found that the less you rub their noses in anything unpleasant, the better for everyone.'

'That may be,' said Soames, stiffening in contrariety; 'but it's all a part of the vice of not facing things.'

'I don't think, Mr Forsyte, that you will accuse *me* of not facing things, in the time to come.'

Time to come! Now, what on earth did the fellow mean by that?

'Well, I shall moot it at the next Board,' he said.

'Quite!' said the manager. 'Nothing like bringing things to a head, is there?'

Again that indefinable mockery, as if he had something up his sleeve. Soames looked mechanically at the fellow's cuffs – beautifully laundered, with a blue stripe; at his holland waistcoat, and his bird's-eye tie – a regular dandy. He would give him a second barrel!

'By the way,' he said, 'Mont's written a book. I've taken a copy.'

Not a blink! A little more show of teeth, perhaps – false, no doubt!

'I've taken two – poor, dear Mont!'

Soames had a sense of defeat. This chap was armoured like a crab, varnished like a Spanish table.

'Well,' he said, 'I must go.'

The manager held out his hand.

'Good-bye, Mr Forsyte. I'm so grateful to you.'

The fellow was actually squeezing his hand. Soames went out confused. To have his hand squeezed was so rare! It undermined him. And yet, it might be the crown of a consummate bit of acting. He couldn't tell. He had, however, less intention even than before of moving for a meeting of the shareholders. No, no! That had just been a shot to get a rise; and it had failed. But the Butterfield shot had gone home, surely! If innocent, Elderson must certainly have alluded to the impudence of the young man's call. And yet such a cool card was capable of failing to rise, just to tease you! No! nothing doing – as they said nowadays. He was as far as ever from a proof of guilt; and to speak

truth, glad of it. Such a scandal could serve no purpose save
that of blackening the whole concern, directors and all. People
were so careless, they never stopped to think, or apportion blame
where it was due. Keep a sharp eye open, and go on as they
were! No good stirring hornets' nests! He had got so far in
thought and progress, when a voice said:

'Well met, Forsyte! Are you going my way?'

'Old Mont', coming down the steps of 'Snooks'!

'I don't know,' said Soames.

'I'm off to the Aeroplane for lunch.'

'That new-fangled place?'

'Rising, you know, Forsyte – rising.'

'I've just been seeing Elderson. He's bought two copies of
your book.'

'Dear me! Poor fellow!'

Soames smiled faintly. 'That's what he said of you! And who
d'you think sold them to him? Young Butterfield.'

'Is he still alive?'

'He was this morning.'

Sir Lawrence's face took on a twist:

'I've been thinking, Forsyte. They tell me Elderson keeps two
women.'

Soames stared. The idea was attractive; would account for
everything.

'My wife says it's one too many, Forsyte. What do you say?'

'I?' said Soames. 'I only know the chap's as cool as a cucum-
ber. I'm going in here. Good-bye!'

One could get no help from that baronet fellow; he couldn't
take anything seriously. Two women! At Elderson's age! What
a life! There were always men like that, not content with one
thing at a time – living dangerously. It was mysterious to him.
You might look and look into chaps like that, and see nothing.
And yet, there they were! He crossed the hall, and went into the
room where connoisseurs were lunching. Taking down the
menu at the service table, he ordered himself a dozen oysters;
but, suddenly remembering that the month contained no 'r',
changed them to a fried sole.

Chapter Eight

LEVANTED

◄◄─►►

'No, dear heart, Nature's "off"!'

'How d'you mean, Michael?'

'Well, look at the Nature novels we get. Sedulous stuff pitched on Cornish cliffs or Yorkshire moors — ever been on a Yorkshire moor? — it comes off on you; and the Dartmoor brand. Gosh! Dartmoor, where the passions come from — ever been on Dartmoor? Well, they don't, you know. And the South Sea bunch! Oh, la la! And the poets, the splash-and-splutter school don't get within miles of Nature. The village idiot school is a bit better, certainly. After all, old Wordsworth made Nature, and she's a bromide. Of course, there's raw nature with the small "n"; but if you come up against that, it takes you all your time to keep alive — the Nature we gas about is licensed, nicely blended and bottled. She's not modern enough for contemporary style.'

'Oh! well, let's go on the river, anyway, Michael. We can have tea at "The Shelter".'

They were just reaching what Michael always called 'this desirable residence', when Fleur leaned forward, and, touching his knee, said:

'I'm not half as nice to you as you deserve, Michael.'

'Good Lord, darling! I thought you were.'

'I know I'm selfish; especially just now.'

'It's only the eleventh baronet.'

'Yes; it's a great responsibility. I only hope he'll be like you.'

Michael slid in to the landing-stage, shipped his sculls, and sat down beside her.

'If he's like me, I shall disown him. But sons take after their mothers.'

235

'I meant in character. I want him frightfully to be cheerful and not restless, and have the feeling that life's worth while.'

Michael stared at her lips – they were quivering; at her cheek, slightly browned by the afternoon's sunning; and, bending sideways, he put his own against it.

'He'll be a sunny little cuss, I'm certain.'

Fleur shook her head.

'I don't want him greedy and self-centred; it's in my blood, you know. I can see it's ugly, but I can't help it. How do you manage not to be?'

Michael ruffled his hair with his free hand.

'The sun isn't too hot for you, is it, ducky?'

'No. Seriously, Michael – how?'

'But I *am*. Look at the way I want you. Nothing will cure me of that.'

A slight pressure of her cheek on his own was heartening, and he said:

'Do you remember coming down the garden one night, and finding me in a boat just here? When you'd gone, I stood on my head, to cool it. I was on my uppers; I didn't think I'd got an earthly –' He stopped. No! He would not remind her, but that was the night when she said: 'Come again when I know I can't get my wish!' The unknown cousin!

Fleur said quietly:

'I was a pig to you, Michael, but I was awfully unhappy. That's gone. It's gone at last; there's nothing wrong now, except my own nature.'

Conscious that his feelings betrayed the period, Michael said: 'Oh! if that's all! What price tea?'

They went up the lawn arm-in-arm. Nobody was at home – Soames in London, Annette at a garden party.

'We'll have tea on the verandah, please,' said Fleur.

Sitting there, happier than he ever remembered being, Michael conceded a certain value to Nature, to the sunshine stealing down, the scent of pinks and roses, the sighing in the aspens. Annette's pet doves were cooing; and, beyond the quietly-flowing river, the spires of poplar trees rose along the further bank. But, after all, he was only enjoying them because of the girl beside him, whom he loved to touch and look at, and because, for the first time, he felt as if she did not want to get up and flutter off to someone or something else. Curious that there could be, outside oneself, a being who completely robbed the world of its importance, 'snooped', as it were, the whole 'bag of tricks' – and she one's own wife! Very curious, considering what one was! He heard her say:

'Of course, mother's a Catholic; only, living with father down here, she left off practising. She didn't even bother me much. I've been thinking, Michael – what shall we do about *him*?'

'Let him rip.'

'I don't know. He must be taught something, because of going to school. The Catholics, you know, really do get things out of their religion.'

'Yes; they go it blind; it's the only logical way now.'

'I think having no religion makes one feel that nothing matters.'

Michael suppressed the words: 'We could bring him up as a sun-worshipper,' and said, instead:

'It seems to me that whatever he's taught will only last till he can think for himself; then he'll settle down to what suits him.'

'But what do *you* think about things, Michael? You're as good as anyone I know.'

'Gosh!' murmured Michael, strangely flattered: 'Is that so?'

'What *do* you think? Be serious!'

'Well, darling, doctrinally nothing – which means, of course, that I haven't got religion. I believe one has to play the game – but that's ethics.'

'But surely it's a handicap not to be able to rely on anything but oneself? If there's something to be had out of any form of belief, one might as well have it.'

Michael smiled, but not on the surface.

'You're going to do just as you like about the eleventh baronet, and I'm going to abet you. But considering his breeding – I fancy he'll be a bit of a sceptic.'

'But I don't *want* him to be. I'd rather he were snug, and convinced and all that. Scepticism only makes one restless.'

'No white monkey in him? Ah! I wonder! It's in the air, I guess. The only thing will be to teach him a sense of other people, as young as possible, with a slipper, if necessary.'

Fleur gave him a clear look, and laughed.

'Yes,' she said: 'Mother used to try, but Father wouldn't let her.'

They did not reach home till past eight o'clock.

'Either your father's here, or mine,' said Michael, in the hall; 'there's a prehistoric hat.'

'It's Dad's. His is grey inside. Bart's is buff.'

In the Chinese room Soames indeed was discovered, with an opened letter, and Ting-a-ling at his feet. He held the letter out to Michael, without a word.

There was no date, and no address; Michael read:

DEAR MR FORSYTE. — Perhaps you will be good enough to tell the Board at the meeting on Tuesday that I am on my way to immunity from the consequences of any peccadillo I may have been guilty of. By the time you receive this, I shall be there. I have always held that the secret of life, no less than that of business, is to know when not to stop. It will be no use to proceed against me, for my person will not be attachable, as I believe you call it in the law, and I have left no property behind. If your object was to corner me, I cannot congratulate you on your tactics. If, on the other hand, you inspired that young man's visit as a warning that you were still pursuing the matter, I should like to add new thanks to those which I expressed when I saw you a few days ago.

Believe me, dear Mr Forsyte,

Faithfully yours,

ROBERT ELDERSON.

Michael said cheerfully:

'Happy release! Now you'll feel safer, sir.'

Soames passed his hand over his face, evidently wiping off its expression. 'We'll discuss it later,' he said. 'This dog's been keeping me company.'

Michael admired him at that moment. He was obviously swallowing his 'grief', to save Fleur.

'Fleur's a bit tired,' he said. 'We've been on the river, and had tea at "The Shelter"; Madame wasn't in. Let's have dinner at once, Fleur.'

Fleur had picked up Ting-a-ling, and was holding her face out of reach of his avid tongue.

'Sorry you've had to wait, Dad,' she murmured, behind the yellow fur; 'I'm just going to wash; shan't change.'

When she had gone, Soames reached for the letter.

'A pretty kettle of fish!' he muttered. 'Where it'll end, I can't tell!'

'But isn't this the end, sir?'

Soames stared. These young people! Here he was, faced with a public scandal, which might lead to he didn't know what – the loss of his name in the city, the loss of his fortune, perhaps; and they took it as if – ! They had no sense of responsibility – none! All his father's power of seeing the worst, all James' nervous pessimism, had come to the fore in him during the hour since, at the Connoisseur's Club, he had been handed that letter. Only the extra 'form' of the generation that succeeded James saved him, now that Fleur was out of the room, from making an exhibition of his fears.

'Your father in town?'

'I believe so, sir.'

'Good!' Not that he felt relief. That baronet chap was just as irresponsible – getting him to go on that Board! It all came of mixing with people brought up in a sort of incurable levity, with no real feeling for money.

'Now that Elderson's levanted,' he said, 'the whole thing must come out. Here's his confession in my hand –'

'Why not tear it up, sir, and say Elderson has developed consumption?'

The impossibility of getting anything serious from this young man afflicted Soames like the eating of heavy pudding.

'You think that would be honourable?' he said grimly.

'Sorry, sir!' said Michael, sobered. 'Can I help at all?'

'Yes; by dropping your levity, and taking care to keep wind of this matter away from Fleur.'

'I will,' said Michael earnestly: 'I promise you. I'll Dutch-oyster the whole thing. What's your line going to be?'

'We shall have to call the shareholders together and explain this dicky-dealing. They'll very likely take it in bad part.'

'I can't see why they should. How could you have helped it?'

Soames sniffed.

'There's no connexion in life between reward and your deserts. If the war hasn't taught you that, nothing will.'

'Well,' said Michael, 'Fleur will be down directly. If you'll excuse me a minute; we'll continue it in our next.'

Their next did not occur till Fleur had gone to bed.

'Now, sir,' said Michael, 'I expect my governor's at the Aeroplane. He goes there and meditates on the end of the world. Would you like me to ring him up, if your Board meeting's to-morrow?'

Soames nodded. He himself would not sleep a wink – why should 'Old Mont'?

Michael went to the Chinese tea-chest.

'Bart? This is Michael. Old For– my father-in-law is here; he's had a pill. ... No; Elderson. Could you blow in by any chance and hear? ... He's coming, sir. Shall we stay down, or go up to my study?'

'Down,' muttered Soames, whose eyes were fixed on the white monkey. 'I don't know what we're all coming to,' he added, suddenly.

'If we did, sir, we should die of boredom.'

'Speak for yourself. All this unreliability! I can't tell where it's leading.'

'Perhaps there's somewhere, sir, that's neither heaven nor hell.'

'A man of *his* age!'

'Same age as my dad; it was a bad vintage, I expect. If you'd been in the war, sir, it would have cheered you up no end.'

'Indeed!' said Soames.

'It took the linch-pins out of the cart – admitted; but, my

Lord! it did give you an idea of the grit there is about, when it comes to being up against it.'

Soames stared. Was this young fellow reading him a lesson against pessimism?

'Look at young Butterfield, the other day,' Michael went on, 'going over the top, to Elderson! Look at the girl who sat for "the altogether" in that picture you bought us! She's the wife of a packer we had, who got hoofed for snooping books. She made quite a lot of money by standing for the nude, and never lost her wicket. They're going to Australia on it. Yes, and look at that little snooper himself; he snooped to keep her alive after pneumonia, and came down to selling balloons.'

'I don't know what you're talking about,' said Soames.

'Only grit, sir. You said you didn't know what we were coming to. Well, look at the unemployed! Is there a country in the world where they stick it as they do here? I get awfully bucked at being English every now and then. Don't you?'

The words stirred something deep in Soames; but far from giving it away, he continued to gaze at the white monkey. The restless, inhuman, and yet so human, angry sadness of the creature's eyes! 'No whites to them!' thought Soames: 'that's what does it, I expect!' And George had liked that picture to hang opposite his bed! Well, George had grit – joked with his last breath: very English, George! Very English, all the Forsytes! Old Uncle Jolyon, and his way with shareholders; Swithin, upright, puffy, huge in a too little armchair at Timothy's: 'All these small fry!' he seemed to hear the words again; and Uncle Nicholas, whom that chap Elderson reproduced as it were unworthily, spry and all-there, and pretty sensual, but quite above suspicion of dishonesty. And old Roger, with his crankiness, and German mutton! And his own father, James – how he had hung on, long and frail as a reed, hung on and on! And Timothy, preserved in Consols, dying at a hundred! Grit and body in those old English boys, in spite of their funny ways. And there stirred in Soames a sort of atavistic will-power. He would see, and they would see – and that was all about it!

The grinding of a taxi's wheels brought him back from

reverie. Here came 'Old Mont', tittuppy, and light in the head as ever, no doubt. And, instead of his hand, Soames held out Elderson's letter.

'Your precious schoolfellow's levanted,' he said.

Sir Lawrence read it through, and whistled.

'What do you think, Forsyte – Constantinople?'

'More likely Monte Carlo,' said Soames gloomily. 'Secret commission – it's not an extraditable offence.'

The odd contortions of that baronet's face were giving him some pleasure – the fellow seemed to be feeling it, after all.

'I should think he's really gone to escape his women, Forsyte.'

The chap was incorrigible! Soames shrugged his shoulders almost violently.

'You'd better realize,' he said, 'that the fat is in the fire.'

'But surely, my dear Forsyte, it's been there ever since the French occupied the Ruhr. Elderson has cut his lucky; we appoint someone else. What more is there to it?'

Soames had the peculiar feeling of having overdone his own honesty. If an honourable man, a ninth baronet, couldn't see the implications of Elderson's confession, were they really there? Was any fuss and scandal necessary? Goodness knew, *he* didn't want it! He said heavily:

'We now have conclusive evidence of a fraud; we *know* Elderson was illegally paid for putting through business by which the shareholders have suffered a dead loss. How can we keep this knowledge from them?'

'But the mischief's done, Forsyte. How will the knowledge help them?'

Soames frowned.

'We're in a fiduciary position. I'm not prepared to run the risks of concealment. If we conceal, we're accessory after the fact. The thing might come out at any time.' If that was caution, not honesty, he couldn't help it.

'I should be glad to spare Elderson's name. We were at –'

'I'm aware of that,' said Soames, drily.

'But what risk is there of its coming out, Forsyte? Elderson won't mention it; nor young Butterfield, if you tell him not to.

Those who paid the commission certainly won't. And beyond us three here, no one else knows. It's not as if we profited in any way.'

Soames was silent. The argument was specious. Entirely unjust, of course, that he should be penalized for what Elderson had done!

'No,' he said, suddenly, 'it won't do. Depart from the law, and you can't tell where it'll end. The shareholders have suffered this loss and they have the right to all the facts within the directors' knowledge. There might be some means of restitution they could avail themselves of. We can't judge. It may be they've a remedy against ourselves.'

'If that's so, Forsyte, I'm with you.'

Soames felt disgust. Mont had no business to put it with a sort of gallantry that didn't count the cost; when the cost, if cost there were, would fall, not on Mont, whose land was heavily mortgaged, but on himself, whose property was singularly realizable.

'Well,' he said, coldly, 'remember that tomorrow. I'm going to bed.'

At his open window upstairs he felt no sense of virtue, but he enjoyed a sort of peace. He had taken his line, and there it was!

Chapter Nine

SOAMES DOESN'T GIVE A DAMN

-◄-►-

DURING the month following the receipt of Elderson's letter, Soames aged more than thirty days. He had forced his policy of disclosure on a doubting Board, the special meeting had been called, and, just as, twenty-three years ago, pursuing divorce from Irene, he had to face the public eye, so now he suffered day and night in dread of that undiscriminating optic. The French had a proverb: *'Les absents ont toujours tort!'* but

Soames had grave doubts about it. Elderson would be absent from that meeting of the shareholders, but – unless he was much mistaken – he himself, who would be present, would come in for the blame. The French were not to be relied on. What with his anxiety about Fleur, and his misgiving about the public eye, he was sleeping badly, eating little, and feeling below par. Annette had recommended him to see a doctor. That was probably why he did not. Soames had faith in doctors for other people; but they had never – he would say – done anything for *him*, possibly because, so far, there had not been anything to do.

Failing in her suggestion, and finding him every day less sociable, Annette had given him a book on Coué. After running it through, he had meant to leave it in the train, but the theory, however extravagant, had somehow clung to him. After all, Fleur was doing it; and the thing cost you nothing: there might be something in it! There was. After telling himself that night twenty-five times that he was getting better and better, he slept so soundly that Annette, in the next room, hardly slept at all.

'Do you know, my friend,' she said at breakfast, 'you were snoring last night so that I could not hear the cock crow.'

'Why should you want to?' said Soames.

'Well, never mind – if you had a good night. Was it my little Coué who gave you that nice dream?'

Partly from fear of encouraging Coué, and partly from fear of encouraging her, Soames avoided a reply; but he had a curious sense of power, as if he did not care what people said of him.

'I'll do it again tonight,' he thought.

'You know,' Annette went on, 'you are just the temperament for Coué, Soames. When you cure yourself of worrying, you will get quite fat.'

'Fat!' said Soames, looking at her curves. 'I'd as soon grow a beard.'

Fatness and beards were associated with the French. He would have to keep an eye on himself if he went on with this – er – what was one to call it? Tomfoolery was hardly the word to conciliate the process, even if it did require you to tie twenty-five knots in a bit of string: very French, that, like telling your beads! He himself had merely counted on his fingers. The sense of power lasted all the way up to London; he had the conviction that he could sit in a draught if he wanted to, that Fleur would have her boy all right; and as to the P.P.R.S. – ten to one he wouldn't be mentioned by name in any report of the proceedings.

After an early lunch and twenty-five more assurances over his coffee, he set out for the city.

This Board, held just a week before the special meeting of the shareholders, was in the nature of a dress rehearsal. The details of confrontation had to be arranged, and Soames was chiefly concerned with seeing that a certain impersonality should be preserved. He was entirely against disclosure of the fact that young Butterfield's story and Elderson's letter had been confided to himself. The phrase to be used should be a 'member of the Board'. He saw no need for anything further. As for explanations, they would fall, of course, to the chairman and the senior director, Lord Fontenoy. He found, however, that the Board thought he himself was the right person to bring the matter forward. No one else – they said – could supply the personal touch, the necessary conviction; the chairman should introduce the matter briefly, then call on Soames to give the evidence within his knowledge. Lord Fontenoy was emphatic.

'It's up to you, Mr Forsyte. If it hadn't been for you, Elderson would be sitting there today. From beginning to end you put the wind up him; and I wish the deuce you hadn't. The whole thing's a confounded nuisance. He was a very clever fellow, and we shall miss him. Our new man isn't a patch on him. If he did take a few thou. under the rose, he took 'em off the Huns.'

Old guinea-pig! Soames replied, acidly:

'And the quarter of a million he's lost the shareholders, for the sake of those few thou.? Bagatelle, I suppose?'

'Well, it might have turned out a winner; for the first year it did. We all back losers sometimes.'

Soames looked from face to face. They did not support this blatant attitude, but in them all, except perhaps 'Old Mont's', he felt a grudge against himself. Their expressions seemed to say:

'Nothing of this sort ever happened till you came on the Board.'
He had disturbed their comfort, and they disliked him for it.
They were an unjust lot! He said doggedly:

'You leave it to me, do you? Very well!'

What he meant to convey — or whether he meant to convey
anything, he did not know; but even that 'old guinea-pig' was
more civil afterwards. He came away from the Board, however,
without any sense of power at all. There he would be on Tuesday next, bang in the public eye.

After calling to inquire after Fleur, who was lying down
rather poorly, he returned home with a feeling of having been
betrayed. It seemed that he could not rely, after all, on this fellow with his twenty-five knots. However much better he might
become, his daughter, his reputation, and possibly his fortune,
were not apparently at the disposition of his subconscious self.
He was silent at dinner, and went up afterwards to his picture
gallery, to think things over. For half an hour he stood at the
open window, alone with the summer evening; and the longer
he stood there, the more clearly he perceived that the three were
really one. Except for his daughter's sake, what did he care for
his reputation or his fortune? His reputation! Lot of fools — if
they couldn't see that he was careful and honest so far as had
lain within his reach — so much the worse for them! His fortune
— well, he had better make another settlement on Fleur and her
child at once, in case of accidents; another fifty thousand. Ah!
if she were only through her trouble! It was time Annette
went up to her for good; and there was a thing they called twilight sleep. To have her suffering was not to be thought of!

The evening lingered out; the sun went down behind familiar
trees; Soames's hands, grasping the window-ledge, felt damp
with dew; sweetness of grass and river stole up into his nostrils.
The sky had paled, and now began to darken; a scatter of stars
came out. He had lived here a long time, through all Fleur's
childhood — best years of his life; still, it wouldn't break his
heart to sell. His heart was up in London. Sell? That was to run
before the hounds with a vengeance. No — no! — it wouldn't
come to *that*! He left the window and, turning up the lights,

began the thousand and first tour of his pictures. He had made some good purchases since Fleur's marriage, and without wasting his money on fashionable favourites. He had made some good sales, too. The pictures in this gallery, if he didn't mistake, were worth from seventy to a hundred thousand pounds; and, with the profits on his sales from time to time, they stood him in at no more than five-and-twenty thousand – not a bad result from a life's hobby, to say nothing of the pleasure! Of course, he might have taken up something – butterflies, photography, archaeology, or first editions; some other sport in which you backed your judgement against the field, and collected the results; but he had never regretted choosing pictures. Not he! More to show for your money, more kudos, more profit, and more risk! The thought startled him a little; had he really taken to pictures because of the risk? A risk had never appealed to him; at least, he hadn't realized it, so far. Had his 'subconscious' some part in the matter? He suddenly sat down and closed his eyes. Try the thing once more; very pleasant feeling, that morning, of not 'giving a damn'; he never remembered having it before! He had always felt it necessary to worry – kind of insurance against the worst; but worry was wearing, no doubt about it, wearing. Turn out the light! They said in that book, you had to relax. In the now dim and shadowy room, with the starlight, through many windows, dusted over its reality, Soames, in his easy chair, sat very still. A faint drone rose on the words: 'fatter and fatter' through his moving lips. 'No, no,' he thought: 'that's wrong!' And he began the drone again. The tips of his fingers ticked it off; on and on – he would give it a good chance. If only one needn't worry! On and on – 'better and better!' If only –! His lips stopped moving; his grey head fell forward into the subconscious. And the stealing starlight dusted over him, too, a little unreality.

Chapter Ten

BUT TAKES NO CHANCES

◀◆▶

MICHAEL knew nothing of the City; and, in the spirit of the old cartographers: 'Where you know nothing, place terrors', made his way through the purlieus of the Poultry, towards that holy of holies, the offices of Cuthcott, Kingson and Forsyte. His mood was attuned to meditation, for he had been lunching with Sibley Swan at the Café C'rillon. He had known all the guests – seven chaps even more modern than old Sib – save only a Russian so modern that he knew no French and nobody could talk to him. Michael had watched them demolish everything, and the Russian closing his eyes, like a sick baby, at mention of any living name. ... 'Carry on!' he thought, several of his favourites having gone down in the *mêlée*. 'Stab and bludge! Importance awaits you at the end of the alley.' But he had restrained his irreverence till the moment of departure.

'Sib,' he said, rising, 'all these chaps here are dead – ought they to be about in this hot weather?'

'What's that?' ejaculated Sibley Swan, amidst the almost painful silence of the chaps.

'I mean – they're alive – so they *must* be damned!' And avoiding a thrown chocolate which hit the Russian, he sought the door.

Outside, he mused: 'Good chaps, really! Not half so darned superior as they think they are. Quite a human touch – getting that Russian on the boko. Phew! It's hot!'

On that first day of the Eton and Harrow match all the forfeited heat of a chilly summer had gathered and shimmered over Michael, on the top of his Bank bus; shimmered over straw hats, and pale, perspiring faces, over endless other buses, business-men, policemen, shopmen at their doors, sellers of newspapers, laces, jumping toys, endless carts and cabs, letterings and wires, all the confusion of the greatest conglomeration in the world – adjusted almost to a hair's-breadth, by an unseen instinct. Michael stared and doubted. Was it possible that, with everyone pursuing his own business, absorbed in his own job, the thing could work out? An ant-heap was not busier, or more seemingly confused. Live wires crossed and crossed and crossed – inextricable entanglement, you'd say; and yet, life, the order needful to life, somehow surviving! 'No slouch of a miracle!' he thought, 'modern town life!' And suddenly it seemed to cease, as if demolished by the ruthless dispensation of some super Sibley Swan; for he was staring down a *cul-de-sac*. On both sides, flat houses, recently re-buffed, extraordinarily alike; at the end, a flat buff house, even more alike, and down to it, grey virgin pavement, unstained by horses or petrol; no cars, cats, carts, policemen, hawkers, flies, or bees. No sign of human life, except the names of legal firms to right and left of each open doorway.

' "Cuthcott, Kingson and Forsyte, Commissioners for Oaths: First Floor." '

'Rule Britannia!' thought Michael, ascending wide stone steps.

Entering the room to which he had been ushered, he saw an old and pug-faced fellow with a round grizzled beard, a black alpaca coat, and a roomy holland waistcoat round his roomy middle, who rose from a swivel chair.

'Aoh!' he said, 'Mr Michael Mont, I think. I've been expecting you. We shan't be long about it, after Mr Forsyte comes. He's just stepped round the corner. Mrs Michael well, I hope?'

'Thanks; as well as –'

'Ye-es; it makes you anxious. Take a seat. Perhaps you'd like to read the draft?'

Thus prescribed for, Michael took some foolscap from a pudgy hand, and sat down opposite. With one eye on the old fellow, and the other on the foolscap, he read steadily.

'It seems to mean something,' he said at last.

He saw a gape, as a frog at a fly, settle in the beard; and hastened to repair his error.

'Calculating what's going to happen if something else doesn't, must be rather like being a bookmaker.'

He felt at once that he had not succeeded. There was a grumpy mutter:

'We don't waste our time 'ere. Excuse me, I'm busy.'

Michael sat, compunctious, watching him tick down a long page of entries. He was like one of those old dogs which lie outside front doors, keeping people off the premises, and notifying their fleas. After less than five minutes of that perfect silence Soames came in.

'You're here, then?' he said.

'Yes, sir; I thought it best to come at the time you mentioned. What a nice cool room!'

'Have you read this?' asked Soames, pointing to the draft.

Michael nodded.

'Did you understand it?'

'Up to a point, I think.'

'The interest on *this* fifty thousand,' said Soames, 'is Fleur's until her eldest child, if it's a boy, attains the age of twenty-one, when the capital becomes his absolutely. If it's a girl, Fleur retains half the income for life, the rest of the income becomes payable to the girl when she attains the age of twenty-one or marries, and the capital of that half goes to her child or children lawfully begotten, at majority or marriage, in equal shares. The other half of the capital falls into Fleur's estate, and is disposable by her will, or follows the laws of intestacy.'

'You make it wonderfully clear,' said Michael.

'Wait!' said Soames. 'If Fleur has no children —'

Michael started.

'Anything is possible,' said Soames gravely, 'and my experience is that the contingencies not provided for are those which happen. In such a case the income of the whole is hers for life, and the capital hers at death to do as she likes with. Failing that, it goes to the next of kin. There are provisions against anticipation and so forth.'

'Ought she to make a fresh will?' asked Michael, conscious of sweat on his forehead.

'Not unless she likes. Her present will covers it.'

'Have I to do anything?'

'No. I wanted you to understand the purport before I sign; that's all. Give me the deed, Gradman, and get Wickson in, will you?'

Michael saw the old chap produce from a drawer a fine piece of parchment covered with copperplate writing and seals, look at it lovingly, and place it before Soames. When he had left the room, Soames said in a low voice:

'This meeting on Tuesday – I can't tell! But, whatever happens, so far as I can see, this ought to stand.'

'It's awfully good of you, sir.'

Soames nodded, testing a pen.

'I'm afraid I've got wrong with your old clerk,' said Michael; 'I like the look of him frightfully, but I accidentally compared him to a bookmaker.'

Soames smiled. 'Gradman,' he said, 'is a "character". There aren't many, nowadays.'

Michael was wondering: Could one be a 'character' under the age of sixty? – when the 'character' returned, with a pale man in dark clothes.

Lifting his nose sideways, Soames said at once:

'This is a post-nuptial settlement on my daughter. I deliver this as my act and deed.'

He wrote his name, and got up.

The pale person and Gradman wrote theirs, and the former left the room. There was a silence as of repletion.

'Do you want me any more?' asked Michael.

'Yes. I want you to see me deposit it at the bank with the marriage settlement. Shan't come back, Gradman!'

'Good-bye, Mr Gradman.'

Michael heard the old fellow mutter through his beard half buried in a drawer to which he was returning the draft, and followed Soames out.

'Here's where I used to be,' said Soames as they went along the Poultry; 'and my father before me.'

'More genial, perhaps,' said Michael.

'The trustees are meeting us at the bank; you remember them?'

'Cousins of Fleur's, weren't they, sir?'

'Second cousins; young Roger's eldest, and young Nicholas'. I chose them youngish. Very young Roger was wounded in the war – he does nothing. Very young Nicholas is at the Bar.'

Michael's ears stood up. 'What about the next lot, sir? Very, very young Roger would be almost insulting, wouldn't it?'

'There won't be one,' said Soames, 'with taxation where it is. He can't afford it; he's a steady chap. What are you going to call your boy, if it *is* one?'

'We think Christopher, because of St Paul's and Columbus. Fleur wants him solid, and I want him inquiring.'

'H'm. And if it's a girl?'

'Oh! – if it's a girl – Anne.'

'Yes,' said Soames: 'very neat. Here they are!'

They had reached the bank, and in the entrance Michael saw two Forsytes between thirty and forty, whose chinny faces he dimly remembered. Escorted by a man with bright buttons down his front, they all went to a room, where a man without buttons produced a japanned box. One of the Forsytes opened it with a key; Soames muttered an incantation, and deposited the deed. When he and the chinnier Forsyte had exchanged a few remarks with the manager on the question of the bank rate, they all went back to the lobby and parted with the words: 'Well, good-bye.'

'Now,' said Soames, in the din and hustle of the street, 'he's provided for, so far as I can see. When exactly do you expect it?'

'It should be just a fortnight.'

'Do you believe in this – this twilight sleep?'

'I should like to,' said Michael, conscious again of sweat on his forehead. 'Fleur's wonderfully calm; she does Coué night and morning.'

'That!' said Soames. He did not mention that he himself was doing it, thus giving away the state of his nerves. 'If you're going home, I'll come, too.'

'Good!'

He found Fleur lying down with Ting-a-ling on the foot of the sofa.

'Your father's here, darling. He's been anointing the future with another fifty thou. I expect he'd like to tell you all about it.'

Fleur moved restlessly.

'Presently. If it's going on as hot as this, it'll be rather a bore, Michael.'

'Oh! but it won't, ducky. Three days and a thunder-storm.'

Taking Ting-a-ling by the chin, he turned his face up.

'And how on earth is your nose going to be put out of joint, old man? There's no joint to put.'

'He knows there's something up.'

'He's a wise little brute, aren't you, old son?'

Ting-a-ling sniffed.

'Michael!'

'Yes, darling?'

'I don't seem to care about anything now – it's a funny feeling.'

'That's the heat.'

'No. I think it's because the whole business is too long. Everything's ready, and now it all seems rather stupid. One more person in the world or one more out of it – what does it matter?'

'Don't! It matters frightfully!'

'One more gnat to dance, one more ant to run about!'

Anguished, Michael said again:

'Don't, Fleur! That's just a mood.'

'Is Wilfrid's book out?'

'It comes out tomorrow.'

'I'm sorry I gave you such a bad time, there. I only didn't want to lose him.'

Michael took her hand.

'Nor did I – goodness knows!' he said.

'He's never written, I suppose?'

'No.'

'Well, I expect he's all right by now. Nothing lasts.'

Michael put her hand to his cheek.

'*I* do, I'm afraid,' he said.

The hand slipped round over his lips.

'Give Dad my love, and tell him I'll be down to tea. Oh! I'm so hot!'

Michael hovered a moment, and went out. Damn the heat, upsetting her like this!

He found Soames standing in front of the white monkey.

'I should take this down, if I were you,' he muttered, 'until it's over.'

'Why, sir?' asked Michael, in surprise.

Soames frowned.

'Those eyes!'

Michael went up to the picture. Yes! He was a haunting kind of brute!

'But it's such top-hole work, sir.'

Soames nodded.

'Artistically, yes. But at such times you can't be too careful what she sees.'

'I believe you're right. Let's have him down.'

'I'll hold him,' said Soames, taking hold of the bottom of the picture.

'Got him tight? Right-o. Now!'

'You can say I wanted an opinion on his period,' said Soames, when the picture had been lowered to the floor.

'There can hardly be a doubt of that, sir – the present!'

Soames stared. 'What? Oh! You mean –? Ah! H'm! Don't let her know he's in the house.'

'No. I'll lock him up.' Michael lifted the picture. 'D'you mind opening the door, sir?'

'I'll come back at tea-time,' said Soames. 'That'll look as if I'd taken him off. You can hang him again, later.'

'Yes. Poor brute!' said Michael, bearing the monkey off to limbo.

Chapter Eleven

WITH A SMALL 'n'

⤛⤜

On the night of the Monday following, after Fleur had gone to bed, Michael and Soames sat listening to the mutter of London coming through the windows of the Chinese room opened to the brooding heat.

'They say the war killed sentiment,' said Soames suddenly: 'Is that true?'

'In a way, yes, sir. We had so much reality that we don't want any more.'

'I don't follow you.'

'I meant that only reality really makes you feel. So if you pretend there *is* no reality, you don't have to feel. It answers awfully well, up to a point.'

'Ah!' said Soames. 'Her mother comes up tomorrow morning, to stay. This P.P.R.S. meeting of mine is at half-past two. Good night!'

Michael, at the window, watched the heat gathered black over the Square. A few tepid drops fell on his outstretched hand. A cat stole by under a lamp-post, and vanished into a shadow so thick that it seemed uncivilized.

Queer question of 'Old Forsyte's' about sentiment; odd that he should ask it! 'Up to a point! But don't we all get past that point?' he thought. Look at Wilfrid, and himself – after the war they had deemed it blasphemous to admit that anything mattered except eating and drinking, for tomorrow they died; even fellows like Nazing, and Master, who were never in the war, had felt like that ever since. Well, Wilfrid had got it in the neck; and he himself had got it in the wind; and he would bet that – barring one here and there whose blood was made of ink – they would all get it in the neck or wind soon or late. Why, he would cheerfully bear Fleur's pain and risk, instead of her! But if nothing mattered, why should he feel like that?

Turning from the window, he leaned against the lacquered back of the jade-green settee, and stared at the wall space between the Chinese tea-chests. Jolly thoughtful of the 'old man' to have that white monkey down! The brute was potent – symbolic of the world's mood: beliefs cancelled, faiths withdrawn! And, dash it! not only the young – but the old – were in that temper! 'Old Forsyte', or he would never have been scared by that monkey's eyes; yes, and his own governor, and Elderson, and all the rest. Young and old – no real belief in anything! And yet – revolt sprang up in Michael, with a whirr, like a covey of partridges. It *did* matter that some person or some principle outside oneself should be more precious than oneself – it dashed well did! Sentiment, then, wasn't dead – nor faith, nor belief, which were the same things. They were only shedding shells, working through chrysalis, into – butterflies, perhaps. Faith, sentiment, belief, had gone underground, possibly, but they were there, even in 'Old Forsyte' and himself. He had a good mind to put the monkey up again. No use exaggerating his importance! ... By George! Some flare! A jagged streak of vivid light had stripped darkness off the night. Michael crossed, to close the windows. A shattering peal of thunder blundered overhead; and down came the rain, slashing and sluicing. He saw a man running, black, like a shadow across a dark-blue screen; saw him by the light of another flash, suddenly made lurid and full of small meaning, with face of cheerful anxiety, as if he were saying: 'Hang it, I'm getting wet!' Another frantic crash!

'Fleur!' thought Michael; and clanging the last window down, he ran upstairs.

She was sitting up in bed, with a face all round, and young, and startled.

'Brutes!' he thought – guns and the heavens confounded in his mind: 'They've waked her up!'

'It's all right, darling! Just another little summer kick-up! Were you asleep?'

'I was dreaming!' He felt her hand clutching within his own, saw a sudden pinched look on her face, with a sort of rage. What infernal luck!

'Where's Ting?'

No dog was in the corner.

'Under the bed – you bet! Would you like him up?'

'No. Let him stay; he hates it.'

She put her head against his arm, and Michael curled his hand round her other ear.

'I never liked thunder much!' said Fleur, 'and now it – it hurts!'

High above her hair Michael's face underwent the contortions of an overwhelming tenderness. One of those crashes which seem just overhead sent her face burrowing against his chest, and, sitting on the bed, he gathered her in, close.

'I wish it were over,' came, smothered, from her lips.

'It will be directly, darling; it came on so suddenly!' But he knew she didn't mean the storm.

'If I come through, I'm going to be quite different to you, Michael.'

Anxiety was the natural accompaniment of such events, but the words: 'If I come through' turned Michael's heart right over. Incredible that one so young and pretty should be in even the remotest danger of extinction; incredibly painful that she should be in fear of it! He hadn't realized. She had been so calm, so matter-of-fact about it all.

'Don't!' he mumbled; 'of course you'll come through.'

'I'm afraid.'

The sound was small and smothered, but the words hurt horribly. Nature, with the small 'n', forcing fear into this girl he loved so awfully! Nature kicking up this godless din above her poor little head!

'Ducky, you'll have twilight sleep and know nothing about it; and be as right as rain in no time.'

Fleur freed her hand.

'Not if it's not good for him. Is it?'

'I expect so, sweetheart; I'll find out. What makes you think – ?'

'Only that it's not natural. I want to do it properly. Hold my hand hard, Michael. I – I'm not going to be a fool. Oh! Someone's knocking – go and see.'

Michael opened the door a crack. Soames was there – unnatural – in a blue dressing-gown and scarlet slippers!

'Is she all right?' he whispered.

'Yes, yes.'

'In this bobbery she oughtn't to be left.'

'No, sir, of course not. I shall sleep on the sofa.'

'Call me, if anything's wanted.'

'I will.'

Soames's eyes slid past, peering into the room. A string worked in his throat, as if he had things to say which did not emerge. He shook his head, and turned. His slim figure, longer than usual, in its gown, receded down the corridor, past the Japanese prints which he had given them. Closing the door again, Michael stood looking at the bed. Fleur had settled down; her eyes were closed, her lips moving. He stole back on tiptoe. The thunder, travelling away south, blundered and growled as if regretfully. Michael saw her eyelids quiver, her lips stop, then move again. 'Coué!' he thought.

He lay down on the sofa at the foot of the bed, whence, without sound, he could raise himself and see her. Many times he raised himself. She had dropped off, was breathing quietly. The thunder was faint now, the flashes imperceptible. Michael closed his eyes.

A faint last mutter roused him to look at her once more, high on her pillows by the carefully shaded light. Young – young! Colourless, like a flower in wax! No scheme in her brain, no dread – peaceful! If only she could stay like that and wake up with it all over! He looked away. And there she was at the far end, dim, reflected in a glass; and there to the right, again. She lay, as it were, all round him in the pretty room, the inhabiting spirit – of his heart.

It was quite still now. Through a chink in those powder-blue curtains he could see some stars. Big Ben chimed one.

He had slept, perhaps, dozed at least, dreamed a little. A

small sound woke him. A very little dog, tail down, yellow, low and unimportant, was passing down the room, trailing across it to the far corner. 'Ah!' thought Michael, closing his eyes again: 'You!'

Chapter Twelve

ORDEAL BY SHAREHOLDER

◄-◄-►-►

REPAIRING, next day, to the Aeroplane Club, where, notably spruce, Sir Lawrence was waiting in the lounge, Michael thought: 'Good old Bart! he's got himself up for the guillotine all right!'

'That white piping will show the blood!' he said. 'Old Forsyte's neat this morning, but not so gaudy.'

'Ah! How is "Old Forsyte"? In good heart?'

'One doesn't ask him, sir. How do you feel yourself?'

'Exactly as I used to before the Eton and Winchester match. I think I shall have shandy-gaff at lunch.'

When they had taken their seats, Sir Lawrence went on:

'I remember seeing a man tried for murder in Colombo; the poor fellow was positively blue. I think my favourite moment in the past, Michael, is Walter Raleigh asking for a second shirt. By the way, it's never been properly settled yet whether the courtiers of that day were lousy. What are you going to have, my dear fellow?'

'Cold beef, pickled walnuts, and gooseberry-tart.'

'Excellent for the character. I shall have curry; they give you a very good Bombay duck here. I rather fancy we shall be fired, Michael. "*Nous sommes trahis!*" used to be the prerogative of the French, but I'm afraid we're getting the attitude, too. The Yellow Press has made a difference.'

Michael shook his head.

'We say it, but we don't act on it; the climate's too uncertain.'

'That sounds deep. This looks very good curry – will you change your mind? Old Fontenoy sometimes comes in here; he has no inside. It'll be serious for him if we're shown the door.'

'Deuced rum,' said Michael suddenly, 'how titles still go down. There can't be any belief in their business capacity.'

'Character, my dear fellow – the good old English gentleman. After all, there's something in it.'

'I fancy, sir, it's more a case of complex in the shareholders. Their parents show them a lord when they're young.'

'Shareholders,' said Sir Lawrence; 'the word is comprehensive. Who are they, what are they, when are they?'

'This afternoon,' said Michael, 'and I shall have a good look at them.'

'They won't let you in, my dear.'

'No?'

'Certainly not.'

Michael frowned.

'What paper,' he said, 'is sure not to be represented?'

Sir Lawrence gave his whinnying laugh.

'The Field,' he said; *'The Horse and Hound; The Gardener's Weekly.'*

'I'll slide in on them.'

'You'll see us die game, I hope,' said Sir Lawrence, with sudden gravity.

They took a cab together to the meeting, but separated before reaching the door of the hotel.

Michael had thought better of the Press, and took up a position in the passage, whence he could watch for a chance. Stout men, in dark suits, with a palpable look of having lunched off turbot, joints, and cheese, kept passing him. He noticed that each handed the janitor a paper. 'I'll hand him a paper, too,' he thought, 'and scoot in.' Watching for some even stouter men, he took cover between two of them, and approached the door, with an announcement of *Counterfeits* in his left hand. Handing it across a neighbouring importance, he was quickly into a seat. He saw the janitor's face poked round the door. 'No,

my friend,' thought Michael, 'if you could tell duds from shareholders, you wouldn't be in that job!'

He found a report before him, and holding it up, looked at
other things. The room seemed to him to have been got by a
concert-hall out of a station waiting-room. It had a platform with
a long table, behind which were seven empty chairs, and seven
inkpots, with seven quill pens upright in them. 'Quills!'
thought Michael; 'symbolic, I suppose – they'll all use fountain-
pens!'

Back-centre of the platform was a door, and in front, below
it, a table, where four men were sitting, fiddling with notebooks. 'Orchestra,' thought Michael. He turned his attention to
the eight or ten rows of shareholders. They looked what they
were, but he could not tell why. Their faces were cast in an
infinity of moulds, but all had the air of waiting for something
they knew they would not get. What sort of lives did they lead,
or did their lives lead them? Nearly all wore moustaches. His
neighbours to right and left were the same stout shareholders
between whom he had slipped in; they both had thick lobes to
their ears, and necks even broader than the straight broad backs
of their heads. He was a good deal impressed. Dotted here and
there he noticed a woman, or a parson. There was practically
no conversation, from which he surmised that no one knew
his neighbour. He had a feeling that a dog somewhere would
have humanized the occasion. He was musing on the colour
scheme of green picked out with chocolate and chased with
gold, when the door behind the platform was thrown open,
and seven men in black coats filed in, and with little bows took
their seats behind the quills. They reminded him of people
getting up on horses, or about to play the piano – full of small
adjustments. That – on the chairman's right – would be old
Fontenoy, with a face entirely composed of features. Michael
had an odd conceit: a little thing in a white top-hat sat inside
the brain, driving the features eight-in-hand. Then came a face
straight from a picture of Her Majesty's Government in 1850,
round and pink, with a high nose, a small mouth, and little
white whiskers; while at the end on the right was a countenance

whose jaw and eyes seemed boring into a conundrum beyond the
wall at Michael's back. 'Legal!' he thought. His scrutiny passed
back to the chairman. Chosen? Was he – or was he not? A
bearded man, a little behind on the chairman's left, was already
reading from a book, in a rapid monotonous voice. That must
be the secretary letting off his minute guns. And in front of him
was clearly the new manager, on whose left Michael observed
his own father. The dark pothooks over Sir Lawrence's right
eye were slightly raised, and his mouth was puckered under the
cut line of his small moustache. He looked almost Oriental,
quick but still. His left hand held his tortoise-shell-rimmed
monocle between thumb and finger. 'Not quite in the scene!'
thought Michael; 'poor old Bart!' He had come now to the last
of the row. 'Old Forsyte' was sitting precisely as if alone in the
world; with one corner of his mouth just drawn down, and one
nostril just drawn up, he seemed to Michael quite fascinatingly
detached; and yet not out of the picture. Within that still neat
figure, whereof only one patent-leather boot seemed with a slight
movement to be living, was intense concentration, entire respect for the proceedings, and yet, a queer contempt for them;
he was like a statue of reality, by one who had seen that there
was precious little reality in it. 'He chills my soup,' thought
Michael, 'but – dash it! – I can't help half admiring him!'

The chairman had now risen. 'He *is*' – thought Michael;
'no, he isn't – yes – no – I can't tell!' He could hardly attend
to what the chairman said, for wondering whether he was
chosen or not, though well aware that it did not matter at all.
The chairman kept steadily on. Distracted, Michael caught
words and words: 'European situation – misguided policy –
French – totally unexpected – position disclosed – manager – unfortunate circumstances shortly to be explained to you – future
of this great concern – no reason to doubt –'

'Oil,' thought Michael, 'he is – and yet –!'

'I will now ask one of your directors, Mr Forsyte, to give you
at first hand an account of this painful matter.'

Michael saw Soames, pale and deliberate, take a piece of
paper from his breast-pocket, and rise. Was it to the occasion?

'I will give you the facts shortly,' he said in a voice which reminded Michael of a dry, made-up wine. 'On the eleventh of January last I was visited by a clerk in the employ of the Society —'

Familiar with these details, Michael paid them little attention, watching the shareholders for signs of reaction. He saw none, and it was suddenly borne in on him why they wore moustaches: They could not trust their mouths! Character was in the mouth. Moustaches had come in when people no longer went about, like the old Duke, saying: 'Think what you damned well like of my character!' Mouths had tried to come in again, of course, before the war; but what with majors, shareholders, and the working classes, they now had little or no chance! He heard Soames say: 'In these circumstances we came to the conclusion that there was nothing for it but to wait and see.' Michael saw a sudden quiver pass over the moustaches, as might wind over grass.

'Wrong phrase,' he thought; 'we all do it, but we can't bear being reminded of it.'

'Six weeks ago, however,' he heard Soames intone, 'an accidental incident seems to have warned your late manager that Sir Lawrence and I still entertained suspicions, for I received a letter from him practically admitting that he had taken this secret commission on the German business, and asking me to inform the Board that he had gone abroad and left no property behind him. This statement we have been at pains to verify. In these circumstances we had no alternative but to call you together, and lay the facts before you.'

The voice, which had not varied an iota, ceased its recital; and Michael saw his father-in-law return to his detachment — stork on one leg, about to apply beak to parasite, could have inspired no greater sense of loneliness. 'Too like the first account of the battle of Jutland!' he thought: 'He mentioned all the losses, and never once struck the human note.'

A pause ensued, such as occurs before an awkward fence, till somebody has found a gate. Michael rapidly reviewed the faces of the Board. Only one showed any animation. It was concealed in a handkerchief. The sound of the blown nose broke the spell. Two shareholders rose to their feet at once — one of them Michael's neighbour on the right.

'Mr Sawdry,' said the chairman, and the other shareholder sat down.

With a sonorous clearing of the throat, Michael's neighbour turned his blunt red face towards Soames.

'I wish to ask you, sir, why you didn't inform the Board when you first 'eard of this?'

Soames rose slightly.

'You are aware, I presume, that such an accusation, unless it can be fully substantiated, is a matter for criminal proceedings?'

'No; it would ha' been privileged.'

'As between members of the Board, perhaps; but any leakage would have rendered us liable. It was a mere case of word against word.'

'Perhaps Sir Lawrence Mont will give us 'is view of that?'

Michael's heart began to beat. There was an air of sprightliness about his father's standing figure.

'You must remember, sir,' he said, 'that Mr Elderson had enjoyed our complete confidence for many years; he was a gentleman, and, speaking for myself, an old school-fellow of his, I preferred, in common loyalty, to give his word preference, while — er — keeping the matter in mind.'

'Oh!' said Michael's neighbour: 'What's the chairman got to say about bein' kept in the dark?'

'We are all perfectly satisfied, sir, with the attitude of our co-directors, in a very delicate situation. You will kindly note that the mischief was already done over this unfortunate assurance, so that there was no need for undue haste.'

Michael saw his neighbour's neck grow redder.

'I don't agree,' he said. ' "Wait and see" — We might have 'ad that commission out of him, if he'd been tackled promptly.' And he sat down.

He had not reached mahogany before the thwarted shareholder had started up.

'Mr Botterill,' said the chairman.

Michael saw a lean and narrow head, with two hollows in a hairy neck, above a back slightly bent forward, as of a doctor listening to a chest.

'I take it from you, then, sir,' he said, 'that these two directors represent the general attitude of the Board, and that the Board were content to allow a suspected person to remain manager. The gentleman on your extreme left – Mr Forsyte, I think – spoke of an accidental incident. But for that, apparently, we should still be in the hands of an unscrupulous individual. The symptoms in this case are very disquieting. There appears to have been gross over-confidence; a recent instance of the sort must be in all our minds. The policy of assuring foreign business was evidently initiated by the manager for his own ends. We have made a severe loss by it. And the question for us shareholders would seem to be whether a Board who placed confidence in such a person, and continued it after their suspicions were aroused, are the right people to direct this important concern.'

Throughout this speech Michael had grown very hot. ' "Old Forsyte" was right,' he thought; 'they're on their uppers, after all.'

There was a sudden creak from his neighbour on the left.

'Mr Tolby,' said the chairman.

'It's a serious matter, this, gentlemen. I propose that the Board withdraw, an' leave us to discuss it.'

'I second that,' said Michael's neighbour on the right.

Searching the vista of the Board, Michael saw recognition gleam for a second in the lonely face at the end, and grinned a greeting.

The chairman was speaking.

'If that is your wish, gentlemen, we shall be happy to comply with it. Will those who favour the motion hold up their hands?'

All hands were held up, with the exception of Michael's, of two women whose eager colloquy had not permitted them to hear the request, and of one shareholder, just in front of Michael, so motionless that he seemed to be dead.

'Carried,' said the chairman, and rose from his seat.

Michael saw his father smiling, and speaking to 'Old Forsyte' as they both stood up. They all filed out, and the door was
closed.

'Whatever happens,' Michael thought, 'I've got to keep my
head shut, or I shall be dropping a brick.'

'Perhaps the Press will kindly withdraw, too,' he heard someone say.

With a general chinny movement, as if inquiring their rights
of no one in particular, the four Pressmen could be seen to clasp
their notebooks. When their pale reluctance had vanished,
there was a stir among the shareholders, like that of ducks when
a dog comes up behind. Michael saw why at once. They had
their backs to each other. A shareholder said:

'Perhaps Mr Tolby, who proposed the withdrawal, will act as
chairman.'

Michael's left-hand neighbour began breathing heavily.

'Right-o l' he said. 'Anyone who wants to speak, kindly ketch
my eye.'

Everyone now began talking to his neighbour, as though to
get at once a quiet sense of proportion, before speaking. Mr
Tolby was breathing so heavily that Michael felt a positive
draught.

''Ere, gentlemen,' he said suddenly, 'this won't do l We don't
want to be too formal, but we must preserve some order. I'll
open the discussion myself. Now, I didn't want to 'urt the
feelin's of the Board by plain speakin' in their presence. But, as
Mr What's-'is-name there, said: The public 'as got to protect
itself against sharpers, and against slackness. We all know what
'appened the other day, and what'll 'appen again in other concerns, unless we shareholders look after ourselves. In the first
place, then, what I say is: They ought never to 'ave touched
anything to do with the 'Uns. In the second place, I saw they
showed bad judgement. And in the third place I saw they were
too thick together. In my opinion, we should propose a vote of
no confidence.'

Cries of: 'Hear, hear l' mixed with indeterminate sounds,
were broken sharply by a loud: 'No l' from the shareholder who

had seemed dead. Michael's heart went out to him, the more so as he still seemed dead. The negative was followed by the rising of a thin, polished-looking shareholder, with a small grey moustache.

'If you'll forgive my saying so, sir,' he began, 'your proposal seems to me very rough-and-ready justice. I should be interested to know how you would have handled such a situation if you had been on the Board. It is extremely easy to condemn other people!'

'Hear, hear!' said Michael, astonished at his own voice.

'It is all very well,' the polished shareholder went on, 'when anything of this sort happens, to blame a directorate, but, speaking as a director myself, I should be glad to know whom one is to trust, if not one's manager. As to the policy of foreign insurance, it has been before us at two general meetings; and we have pocketed the profit from it for nearly two years. Have we raised a voice against it?'

The dead shareholder uttered a 'No!' so loud that Michael almost patted his head.

The shareholder, whose neck and back were like a doctor's, rose to answer.

'I differ from the last speaker in his diagnosis of the case. Let us admit all he says, and look at the thing more widely. The proof of pudding is in the eating. When a Government makes a bad mistake of judgement, the electorate turns against it as soon as it feels the effects. This is a very sound check on administration; it may be rough and ready, but it is the less of two evils. A Board backs its judgement; when it loses, it should pay. I think, perhaps, Mr Tolby, being our informal chairman, was out of order in proposing a vote of no confidence; if that be so, I should be happy to do so, myself.'

The dead shareholder's 'No!' was so resounding this time that there was a pause for him to speak; he remained, however, without motion. Both of Michael's neighbours were on their feet. They bobbed at each other over Michael's head, and Mr Tolby sat down.

'Mr Sawdry,' he said.

'Look 'ere gentlemen,' said Mr Sawdry, 'and ladies, this

267

seems to me a case for compromise. The directors that knew about the manager ought to go; but we might stop at that. The gentleman in front of me keeps on saying "No." Let 'im give us 'is views.'

'No,' said the dead shareholder, but less loudly.

'If a man can't give 'is views,' went on Mr Sawdry, nearly sitting down on Michael, ''e shouldn't interrupt, in my opinion.'

A shareholder in the front row now turned completely round so that he faced the meeting.

'I think,' he said, 'that to prolong this discussion is to waste time; we are evidently in two, if not three, minds. The whole of the business of this country is now conducted on a system of delegated trust; it may be good, it may be bad – but there it is. You've got to trust somebody. Now, as to this particular case, we've had no reason to distrust the Board, so far; and, as I take it, the Board had no previous reason to distrust the late manager. I think it's going too far, at present, to propose anything definite like a vote of no confidence; it seems to me that we should call the Board in and hear what assurances they have to give us against a repetition of anything of the sort in the future.'

The sounds which greeted this moderate speech were so inextricable that Michael could not get the sense of them. Not so with the speech which followed. It came from a shareholder on the right, with reddish hair, light eyelashes, a clipped moustache, and a scraped colour.

'I have no objection whatever to having the Board in,' he said in a rather jeering voice, 'and passing a vote of no confidence in their presence. There is a question, which no one has touched on, of how far, if we turn them out, we could make them liable for this loss. The matter is not clear, but there is a good sporting chance, if we like to take it. Whereas, if we don't turn them out, it's obvious we can't take it, even if we wish.'

The impression made by this speech was of quite a different order from any of the others. It was followed by a hush, as though something important had been said at last. Michael stared at Mr Tolby. The stout man's round, light, rather prominent eyes were extraordinarily reflective. 'Trout must look like that,' thought Michael, 'when they see a mayfly.' Mr Tolby suddenly stood up.

'All right,' he said, ''ave 'em in!'

'Yes,' said the dead shareholder. There was no dissent. Michael saw someone rise and ascend the platform.

'Let the Press know!' said Mr Tolby.

Chapter Thirteen

SOAMES AT BAY

◄◄·►►

WHEN the door had closed behind the departing directors, Soames sought a window as far as possible from the lunch eaten before the meeting.

'Funeral baked meats, eh, Forsyte?' said a voice in his ear. 'Our number's up, I think. Poor old Mothergill's looking very blue. I think he ought to ask for a second shirt!'

Soames's tenacity began wriggling within him.

'The thing wants tackling,' he grumbled; 'the chairman's not the man for the job!' Shades of old Uncle Jolyon! He would have made short work of this! It wanted a masterful hand.

'Warning to us all, Forsyte, against loyalty! It's not in the period. Ah! Fontenoy!'

Soames became conscious of features rather above the level of his own.

'Well, Mr Forsyte, hope you're satisfied? A pretty damned mess! If I'd been the chairman, I'd never have withdrawn. Always keep hounds under your eye, Mont. Take it off, and they'll go for you! Wish I could get among 'em with a whip; I'd give it those two heavy pug-faced chaps — they mean business! Unless you've got something up your sleeve, Mr Forsyte, we're dished.'

'What should I have up my sleeve?' said Soames coldly.

'Damn it, sir, you put the chestnuts in the fire, it's up to you to pull 'em out. I can't afford to lose these fees!'

Soames heard Sir Lawrence murmur: 'Crude, my dear Fontenoy!' and said with malice:

'You may lose more than your fees!'

'Can't! They may have Eaglescourt tomorrow, and take a loss off my hands.' A gleam of feeling burned up suddenly in the old eyes: 'The country drives you to the wall, skins you to the bone, and expects you to give 'em public service gratis. Can't be done, Mont – can't be done!'

Soames turned away; he had an utter disinclination for talk, like one standing before an open grave, watching a coffin slowly lowered. Here was his infallibility going – going! He had no illusions. It would all be in the papers, and his reputation for sound judgement gone for ever! Bitter! No more would the Forsytes say: 'Soames says –' No more would old Gradman follow him with eyes like an old dog's, grudging sometimes, but ever submitting to infallibility. It would be a nasty jar for the old fellow. His business acquaintances – after all, they were not many, now! – would no longer stare with envious respect. He wondered if the reverberations would reach Dumetrius, and the picture market! The sole comfort was: Fleur needn't know. Fleur! Ah! If only her business were safely over! For a moment his mind became empty of all else. Then with a rush the present filled it up again. Why were they all talking as if there were a corpse in the room? Well! There was – the corpse of his infallibility! As for monetary loss – that seemed secondary, remote, incre'ible – like a future life. Mont had said something about loyalty. He didn't know what loyalty had to do with it! But if they thought he was going to show any white feather, they were extremely mistaken. Acid courage welled up into his brain. Shareholders, directors – they might howl and shake their fists; he was not going to be dictated to. He heard a voice say:

'Will you come in, please, gentlemen?'

Taking his seat again before his unused quill, he noticed the silence – shareholders waiting for directors, directors for shareholders. 'Wish I could get among 'em with a whip!' Extravagant words of that 'old guinea-pig', but expressive, somehow!

At last the chairman, whose voice always reminded Soames of a raw salad with oil poured over it, said ironically:

'Well, gentlemen, we await your pleasure.'

That stout, red-faced fellow, next to Michael, stood up, opening his pug's mouth.

'To put it shortly, Mr Chairman, we're not at all satisfied; but before we take any resolution, we want to 'ear what you've got to say.'

Just below Soames, someone jumped up and added:

'We'd like to know, sir, what assurances you can offer us against anything of this sort in the future.'

Soames saw the chairman smile – no real backbone in that fellow!

'In the nature of things, sir,' he said, 'none whatever! You can hardly suppose that if we had known our manager was not worthy of our confidence, we should have continued him in the post for a moment!'

Soames thought: 'That won't do – he's gone back on himself!' Yes, and that other pug-faced chap had seen it!

'That's just the point, sir,' he was saying: 'Two of you *did* know, and yet, there the fellow was for months afterwards, playin' 'is own 'and, cheatin' the Society for all he was worth, I shouldn't wonder.'

One after another, they were yelping now:

'What about your own words?'

'You admitted collective responsibility.'

'You said you were perfectly satisfied with the attitude of your co-directors in the matter.' Regular pack!

Soames saw the chairman incline his head as if he wanted to shake it; old Fontenoy muttering, old Mothergill blowing his nose, Meyricke shrugged his sharp shoulders. Suddenly he was cut off from view of them – Sir Lawrence was standing up between.

'Allow me a word! Speaking for myself, I find it impossible to accept the generous attempt of the chairman to shoulder a responsibility which clearly rests on me. If I made a mistake of judgement in not disclosing our suspicions, I must pay the penalty; and I think it will clear the – er – situation if I tender my resignation to the meeting.'

Soames saw him give a little bow, place his monocle in his eye, and sit down.

A murmur greeted the words – approval, surprise, depre-cation, admiration? It had been gallantly done. Soames dis-trusted gallantry – there was always a dash of the peacock about it. He felt curiously savage.

'I, apparently,' he said, rising, 'am the other incriminated director. Very good! I am not conscious of having done any-thing but my duty from beginning to end of this affair. I am confident that I made no mistake of judgement. And I consider it entirely unjust that I should be penalized. I have had worry and anxiety enough, without being made a scapegoat by share-holders who accepted this policy without a murmur, before ever I came on the Board, and are now angry because they have lost by it. You owe it to me that the policy has been dropped: you owe it to me that you have no longer a fraudulent person for a manager. And you owe it to me that you were called together today to pass judgement on the matter. I have no intention what-ever of singing small. But there is another aspect to this affair. I am not prepared to go on giving my services to people who don't value them. I have no patience with the attitude displayed this afternoon. If anyone here thinks he has a grievance against me, let him bring an action. I shall be happy to carry it to the House of Lords, if necessary. I have been familiar with the City all my life, and I have not been in the habit of meeting with suspicions and ingratitude. If this is an instance of present manners, I have been familiar with the City long enough. I do not tender my resignation to the meeting; I resign.'

Bowing to the chairman, and pushing back his chair, he walked doggedly to the door, opened it and passed through.

He sought his hat. He had not the slightest doubt but that he had astonished their weak nerves! Those pug-faced fellows had their mouths open! He would have liked to see what he had left behind, but it was hardly consistent with dignity to open the door again. He took a sandwich instead, and began to eat it with his back to the door and his hat on. He felt better than he had for months. A voice said:

'"And the subsequent proceedings interested him no more!" I'd no idea, Forsyte, you were such an orator! You gave it 'em between the eyes! Never saw a meeting so knocked out! Well, you've saved the Board by focusing their resentment entirely on yourself. It was very gallant, Forsyte!'

Soames growled through his sandwich:

'Nothing of the sort! Are you out, too?'

'Yes. I pressed my resignation. That red-faced fellow was proposing a vote of confidence in the Board when I left – and they'll pass it, Forsyte – they'll pass it! Something was said about financial liability, by the way!'

'Was there?' said Soames, with a grim smile: 'That cock won't fight. Their only chance was to claim against the Board for initiating foreign assurance *ultra vires*; if they're re-affirming the Board, after the question's been raised in open meeting, they're dished. Nothing'll lie against you and me, for not disclosing our suspicions – that's certain.'

'A relief, I confess,' said Sir Lawrence, with a sigh. 'It was the speech of your life, Forsyte!'

Perfectly well aware of that, Soames shook his head. Apart from the horror of seeing himself in print, he was beginning to feel that he had been extravagant. It was always a mistake to lose your temper! A bitter little smile came on his lips. Nobody, not even Mont, would see how unjustly he had been treated.

'Well,' he said, 'I shall go.'

'I think I shall wait, Forsyte, and hear the upshot.'

'Upshot? They'll appoint two other fools, and slaver over each other. Shareholders! Good-bye!' He moved to the door.

Passing the Bank of England, he had a feeling of walking away from his own life. His acumen, his judgement, his manner of dealing with affairs – aspersed! They didn't like it; well – he would leave it! Catch him meddling, in future! It was all of a piece with the modern state of things. Hand to mouth, and the

273

steady men pushed to the wall! The men to whom a pound was a pound, and not a mess of chance and paper. The men who knew that the good of the country was the strict, straight conduct of their own affairs. They were not wanted. One by one, they would get the go-by – as he had got it – in favour of Jack-o'-lanterns, revolutionaries, restless chaps, or clever, unscrupulous fellows, like Elderson. It was in the air. No amount of eating your cake and wanting to have it could take the place of common honesty.

He turned into the Poultry before he knew why he had come there. Well, he might as well tell Gradman at once that he must exercise his own judgement in the future. At the mouth of the backwater he paused for a second, as if to print its buffness on his brain. He would resign his trusts, private and all! He had no notion of being sneered at in the family. But a sudden wave of remembrance almost washed his heart into his boots. What a tale of trust deeds executed, leases renewed, houses sold, investments decided on – in that back room up there; what a mint of quiet satisfaction in estates well managed! Ah! well! He would continue to manage his own. As for the others, they must look out for themselves, now. And a precious time they'd have of it, in face of the spirit there was about!

He mounted the stone steps slowly.

In the repository of Forsyte affairs, he was faced by the unusual – not Gradman, but, on the large ripe table, a large ripe melon alongside a straw bag. Soames sniffed. The thing smelled delicious. He held it to the light. Its greeny yellow tinge, its network of threads – quite Chinese! Was old Gradman going to throw its rind about, like that white monkey?

He was still holding it when a voice said:

'Aoh! I wasn't expecting you today, Mr Soames. I was going early; my wife's got a little party.'

'So I see!' said Soames, restoring the melon to the table. 'There's nothing for you to do at the moment, but I came in to tell you to draw my resignation from the Forsyte trusts.'

The old chap's face was such a study that he could not help a smile.

'You can keep me in Timothy's; but the rest must go. Young Roger can attend to them. He's got nothing to do.'

A gruff and deprecating: 'Dear me! They won't like it!' irritated Soames.

'Then they must lump it! I want a rest.'

He did not mean to enter into the reason – Gradman could read it for himself in the *Financial News*, or whatever he took in.

'Then I shan't be seeing you so often, Mr Soames; there's never anything in Mr Timothy's. Dear me! I'm quite upset. Won't you keep your sister's?'

Soames looked at the old fellow, and compunction stirred within him – as ever, at any sign that he was appreciated.

'Well,' he said, 'keep me in hers; I shall be in about my own affairs, of course. Good afternoon, Gradman. That's a fine melon.'

He waited for no more words. The old chap! *He* couldn't last much longer, anyway, sturdy as he looked! Well, they would find it hard to match him!

On reaching the Poultry, he decided to go to Green Street and see Winifred – queerly and suddenly home-sick for the proximity of Park Lane, for the old secure days, the efflorescent privacy of his youth under the wings of James and Emily. Winifred alone represented for him now, the past; her solid nature never varied, however much she kept up with the fashions.

He found her, a little youthful in costume, drinking China tea, which she did not like – but what could one do, other teas were 'common'! She had taken to a parrot. Parrots were coming in again. The bird made a dreadful noise. Whether under its influence or that of the China tea – which, made in the English way, of a brand the Chinese grew for foreign stomachs, always upset him – he was soon telling her the whole story.

When he had finished, Winifred said comfortably:

'Well, Soames, I think you did splendidly; it serves them right!'

275

Conscious that his narrative must have presented the truth as it would not appear to the public, Soames muttered:

'That's all very well; you'll find a very different version in the financial papers.'

'Oh! but nobody reads them. I shouldn't worry. Do you do Coué? Such a comfortable little man, Soames; I went to hear him. It's rather a bore sometimes, but it's quite the latest thing.'

Soames became inaudible – he never confessed a weakness.

'And how,' asked Winifred, 'is Fleur's little affair?'

' "Little affair!" ' echoed a voice above his head. That bird! It was clinging to the brocade curtains, moving its neck up and down.

'Polly!' said Winifred: 'don't be naughty!'

'Soames!' said the bird.

'I've taught him that. Isn't he rather sweet?'

'No,' said Soames. 'I should shut him up; he'll spoil your curtains.'

The vexation of the afternoon had revived within him suddenly. What was life, but parrotry? What did people see of the real truth? They just repeated each other, like a lot of shareholders, or got their precious sentiments out of *The Daily Liar*. For one person who took a line, a hundred followed on, like sheep!

'You'll stay and dine, dear boy!' said Winifred.

Yes! he would dine. Had she a melon, by any chance? He'd no inclination to go and sit opposite his wife at South Square. Ten to one Fleur would not be down. And as to young Michael – the fellow had been there that afternoon and witnessed the whole thing; he'd no wish to go over it again.

He was washing his hands for dinner, when a maid, outside, said:

'You're wanted on the phone, sir.'

Michael's voice came over the wire, strained and husky:

'That you, sir?'

'Yes. What is it?'

'Fleur. It began this afternoon at three. I've been trying to reach you.'

'What?' cried Soames. 'How? Quick!'

'They say it's all normal. But it's so awful. They say quite soon, now.' The voice broke off.

'My God!' said Soames. 'My hat!'

By the front door the maid was asking: 'Shall you be back to dinner, sir?'

'Dinner!' muttered Soames, and was gone.

He hurried along, almost running, his eyes searching for a cab. None to be had, of course! None to be had! Opposite the 'Iseeum' Club he got one, open in the fine weather after last night's storm. That storm! He might have known. Ten days before her time. Why on earth hadn't he gone straight back, or at least telephoned where he would be? All that he had been through that afternoon was gone like smoke. Poor child! Poor little thing! And what about twilight sleep? Why hadn't he been there? He might have – nature! Damn it! Nature – as if it couldn't leave even her alone!

'Get on!' he said, leaning out: 'Double fare!'

Past the Connoisseurs, and the Palace, and Whitehall; past all preserves whence nature was excluded, deep in the waters of primitive emotion Soames sat, grey, breathless. Past Big Ben – eight o'clock! Five hours! Five hours of it!

'Let it be over!' he muttered aloud: 'Let it be over, God!'

Chapter Fourteen

ON THE RACK

◄◄·►►

W H E N his father-in-law bowed to the chairman and withdrew, Michael had restrained a strong desire to shout: 'Bravo!' Who'd have thought the 'old man' could let fly like that? He had 'got their goats' with a vengeance. Quite an interval of fine mixed vociferation followed, before his neighbour, Mr Sawdry, made himself heard at last.

'Now that the director implicated has resigned, I shall 'ave pleasure in proposing a vote of confidence in the rest of the Board.'

Michael saw his father rise, a little finicky and smiling, and bow to the chairman. 'I take my resignation as accepted also; if you permit me, I will join Mr Forsyte in retirement.'

Someone was saying:

'I shall be glad to second that vote of confidence.'

And brushing past the knees of Mr Sawdry, Michael sought the door. From there he could see that nearly every hand was raised in favour of the vote of confidence; and with the thought: 'Thrown to the shareholders!' he made his way out of the hotel. Delicacy prevented him from seeking out those two. They had saved their dignity; but the dogs had had the rest.

Hurrying west, he reflected on the rough ways of justice. The shareholders had a grievance, of course; and someone had to get it in the neck to satisfy their sense of equity. They had pitched on Old Forsyte, who, of all, was least to blame; for if Bart had only held his tongue, they would certainly have lumped him into the vote of confidence. All very natural and illogical; and four o'clock already!

Counterfeits! The old feeling for Wilfrid was strong in him this day of publication. One must do everything one could for his book – poor old son! There simply must not be a frost.

After calling in at two big booksellers, he made for his club, and closeted himself in the telephone booth. In old days they 'took cabs and went about'. Ringing-up was quicker – was it? With endless vexations, he tracked down Sibley, Nazing, Upshire, Master, and half a dozen others of the elect. He struck a considered note likely to move them, the book – he said – was bound to 'get the goat of the old guard and the duds generally'; it would want a bit of drum-beating from the cognoscenti. To each of them he appealed as the only one whose praise really mattered. 'If you haven't reviewed the book, old chap, will you? It's you who count, of course.' And to each he added: 'I don't care two straws whether it sells, but I do want old Wilfrid to get his due.' And he meant it. The publisher in Michael was dead during that hour in the telephone booth, the friend alive and kicking hard. He came out with sweat running down his forehead, quite exhausted; and it was half-past five.

'Cup of tea – and home!' he thought. He reached his door at six. Ting-a-ling, absolutely unimportant, was cowering in the far corner of the hall.

'What's the matter, old man?'

A sound from above, which made his blood run cold, answered – a long, low moaning.

'Oh, God!' he rasped, and ran upstairs.

Annette met him at the door. He was conscious of her speaking in French, of being called '*mon cher*', of the words '*vers trois heures*. . . . The doctor says one must not worry – all goes for the best.' Again that moan, and the door shut in his face; she was gone. Michael remained standing on the rug with perfectly cold sweat oozing from him, and his nails dug deep into his palms.

'This is how one becomes a father!' he thought: 'This is how I became a son!' That moaning! He could not bear to stay there, and he could not bear to go away. It might be hours, yet! He kept repeating to himself: 'One must not worry – must not worry!' How easily said! How meaningless! His brain, his heart, ranging for relief, lighted on the strangest relief which could possibly have come to him. Suppose this child being born, had not been his – had been – been Wilfrid's; how would he have been feeling, here, outside this door? It might – it might so easily have been – since nothing was sacred, now! Nothing except – yes, just that which was dearer than oneself – just that which was in there, moaning. He could not bear it on the rug, and went downstairs. Across and across the copper floor, a cigar in his mouth, he strode in vague, rebellious agony. Why should birth be like this? And the answer was: It isn't – not in China! To have the creed that nothing mattered – and then run into it like this! Something born at such a cost, must matter, should matter. One must see to that! Speculation ceased in Michael's brain; he stood, listening terribly. Nothing! He could not bear it down there, and went up again. No sound at first, and then another moan! This time he fled into his study, and ranged round the room, looking at the cartoons of Aubrey Greene. He did not see a single one, and suddenly bethought him of 'Old Forsyte'. He ought to be told! He rang up the 'Connoisseurs', the 'Remove', and his own father's clubs, in case they might have gone there together after the meeting. He drew blank everywhere. It was half-past seven. How much longer was this going on? He went back to the bedroom door; could hear nothing. Then down again to the hall. Ting-a-ling was lying by the front door, now. 'Fed-up!' thought Michael, stroking his back, and mechanically clearing the letter-box. Just one letter – Wilfrid's writing! He took it to the foot of the stairs and read it with half his brain, the other half wondering – wandering up there.

DEAR MONT, – I start tomorrow to try and cross Arabia. I thought you might like a line in case Arabia crosses me. I have recovered my senses. The air here is too clear for sentiment of any kind; and passion in exile soon becomes sickly. I am sorry I made you so much disturbance. It was a mistake for me to go back to England after the war, and hang about writing drivel for smart young women and inky folk to read. Poor old England – she's in for a bad time. Give her my love; the same to yourselves.

> Yours ever,
> WILFRID DESERT

P.S. – If you've published the things I left behind, send any royalties to me care of my governor. – W.D.

Half Michael's brain thought: 'Well, that's that! And the book coming out today!' Queer! Was Wilfrid right – was it all a blooming gaff – the inky stream? Was one just helping on England's sickness? Ought they all to get on camels and ride the sun down? And yet, in books were comfort and diversion; and they were wanted! England had to go on – go on! 'No retreat, no retreat, they must conquer or die who have no retreat! ...' God! There it was again! Back he flew upstairs, with his ears covered and his eyes wild. The sounds ceased; Annette came out to him.

'Her father, *mon cher*; try to find her father!'

'I have – I can't,' gasped Michael.

'Try Green Street – Mrs Dartie. *Courage!* All is normal – it will be quite soon, now.'

When he had rung up Green Street and been answered at last, he sat with the door of his study open, waiting for 'Old Forsyte' to come. Half his sight remarked a round hole burnt in his trouser leg – he hadn't even noticed the smell; hadn't even realized that he had been smoking. He must pull himself together for the 'old man'. He heard the bell ring, and ran down to open.

'Well?' said Soames.

'Not yet, sir. Come up to my study. It's nearer.'

They went up side by side. That trim grey head, with the deep furrow between the eyes, and those eyes staring as if at pain behind them, steadied Michael. Poor old chap! He was 'for it', too! They were both on 'their uppers'!

'Have a peg, sir? I've got brandy here.'

'Yes,' said Soames. 'Anything.'

With the brandies in their hands, half-raised, they listened – jerked their hands up, drank. They were automatic, like two doll figures worked by the same string.

'Cigarette, sir?' said Michael.

Soames nodded.

With the lighted cigarettes just not in their mouths, they listened, put them in, took them out, puffed smoke. Michael had his right arm across his chest. Soames his left. They formed a pattern, thus, side by side.

'Bad to stick, sir. Sorry!'

Soames nodded. His teeth were clenched. Suddenly his hand relaxed.

'Listen!' he said. Sounds – different – confused!

Michael's hand seized something, gripped it hard; it was cold, thin – the hand of Soames. They sat thus, hand in hand, staring at the doorway, for how long neither knew.

Suddenly that doorway darkened; a figure in grey stood there – Annette!

'It is all r-right! A son!'

Chapter Fifteen

CALM

‹‹·›·›

On waking from deep sleep next morning, Michael's first thought was: 'Fleur is back!' He then remembered.

To his: 'O.K.?' whispered at her door, he received an emphatic nod from the nurse.

In the midst of excited expectation he retained enough modernity to think: 'No more blurb! Go and eat your breakfast quietly!'

In the dining-room Soames was despising the broken egg before him. He looked up as Michael entered, and buried his face in his cup. Michael understood perfectly; they had sat hand in hand! He saw, too, that the journal opened by his plate was of a financial nature.

'Anything about the meeting, sir? Your speech must read like one o'clock!'

With a queer little sound Soames held out the paper. The headlines ran: 'Stormy meeting – resignation of two directors – a vote of confidence.' Michael skimmed down till he came to:

'Mr Forsyte, the director involved, in a speech of some length, said he had no intention of singing small. He deprecated the behaviour of the shareholders; he had not been accustomed to meet with suspicions. He tendered his resignation.'

Michael dropped the sheet.

'By Jove!' he said – ' "Involved – suspicions". They've given it a turn, as though – !'

'The papers!' said Soames, and resumed his egg.

Michael sat down, and stripped the skin off a banana. ' "Nothing became him like his death",' he thought: 'Poor old boy!'

'Well, sir,' he said, 'I was there, and all I can say is: You and my father were the only two people who excited my respect.'

'That!' said Soames, putting down his spoon.

Michael perceived that he wished to be alone, and swallowing the banana, went to his study. Waiting for his summons, he rang up his father.

'None the worse for yesterday, sir?'

Sir Lawrence's voice came clear and thin, rather high.

'Poorer and wiser. What's the bulletin?'

'Top-hole.'

'Our love to both. Your mother wants to know if he has any hair?'

'Haven't seen him yet. I'm just going.'

Annette, indeed, was beckoning from the doorway.

'She wants you to bring the little dog, *mon cher.*'

With Ting-a-ling under his arm, and treading on tiptoe, Michael entered. The eleventh baronet! He did not seem to amount to much, beneath her head bent over him. And surely her hair was darker! He walked up to the bed, and touched it reverently.

Fleur raised her head, and revealed the baby sucking vigorously at her little finger. 'Isn't he a monkey?' said her faint voice.

Michael nodded. A monkey clearly – but whether white – that was the question!

'And you, sweetheart?'

'All right now, but it was –' She drew her breath in, and her eyes darkened: 'Ting, look!'

The Chinese dog, with nostrils delicately moving, drew backward under Michael's arm. His whole demeanour displayed a knowing criticism. 'Puppies,' he seemed to say, 'we do it in China. Judgement reserved!'

'What eyes!' said Michael: 'We needn't tell *him* that this was brought from Chelsea by the doctor.'

Fleur gave the tiniest laugh.

'Put him down, Michael.'

Michael put him down, and he went to his corner.

'I mustn't talk,' said Fleur, 'but I want to, frightfully; as if I'd been dumb for months.'

'Just as I felt,' thought Michael, 'she's been away, away somewhere, utterly away.'

'It was like being held down, Michael. Months of not being yourself.'

Michael said softly: 'Yes! the process *is* behind the times! Has he got any hair? My mother wants to know.'

Fleur revealed the head of the eleventh baronet, covered with dark down.

'Like my grandmother's; but it'll get lighter. His eyes are going to be grey. Oh! and, Michael, about godparents? Alison, of course – but men?'

Michael dwelled a little before answering:

'I had a letter from Wilfrid yesterday. Would you like him? He's still out there, but I could hold the sponge for him in church.'

'Is he all right again?'

'He says so.'

He could not read the expression of her eyes, but her lips were pouted slightly.

'Yes,' she said: 'and I think one's enough, don't you? Mine never gave me anything.'

'One of mine gave me a Bible, and the other gave me a wigging. Wilfrid, then.' And he bent over her.

Her eyes seemed to make him a little ironic apology. He kissed her hair, and moved hurriedly away.

By the door Soames was standing, awaiting his turn.

'Just a minute only, sir,' the nurse was saying.

Soames walked up to the bedside, and stood looking at his daughter.

'Dad, dear!' Michael heard her say.

Soames just touched her hand, nodded, as if implying approval of the baby, and came walking back, but, in a mirror, Michael saw his lips quivering.

On the ground floor once more, he had the most intense desire to sing. It would not do; and, entering the Chinese room, he stood staring out into the sunlit square. Gosh ! It was good to be alive ! Say what you liked, you couldn't beat it ! They might turn their noses up at life, and look down them at it; they might bolster up the future and the past, but – give him the present !

'I'll have that white monkey up again !' he thought. 'I'll see the brute further before he shall depress me !'

He went out to a closet under the stairs, and, from beneath four pairs of curtains done up in moth-preserver and brown paper, took out the picture. He held it away from him in the dim light. The creature's eyes ! It was all in those eyes !

'Never mind, old son !' he said : 'Up you go !' And he carried it into the Chinese room.

Soames was there.

'I'm going to put him up again, sir.'

Soames nodded.

'Would you hold him, while I hook the wire?'

Soames held the picture.

Returning to the copper floor, Michael said :

'All right, sir !' and stood back.

Soames joined him. Side by side they contemplated the white monkey.

'He won't be happy till he gets it,' said Michael at last : 'The only thing is, you see, he doesn't know what *it* is.'

THE SILVER SPOON

Contents

TO
John Fortescue

'But O, the thorns we stand upon!'
                        The Winter's Tale.

PART ONE

Chapter One

A STRANGER

→←→→

THE young man who, at the end of September, 1924, dismounted from a taxicab in South Square, Westminster, was so unobtrusively American that his driver had some hesitation in asking for double his fare. The young man had no hesitation in refusing it.

'Are you unable to read?' he said softly. 'Here's four shillings.'

With that he turned his back and looked at the house before which he had descended. This, the first private English house he had ever proposed to enter inspired him with a certain uneasiness, as of a man who expects to part with a family ghost. Comparing a letter with the number chased in pale brass on the door, he murmured: 'It surely is,' and rang the bell.

While waiting for the door to be opened, he was conscious of extreme quietude, broken by a clock chiming four as if with the voice of Time itself. When the last boom died, the door yawned inwards, and a man, almost hairless, said:

'Yes, sir?'

The young man removed a soft hat from a dark head.

'This is Mrs Michael Mont's house?'

'Correct, sir.'

'Will you give her my card, and this letter?'

' "Mr Francis Wilmot, Naseby, S.C." Will you wait in here, sir?'

Ushered through the doorway of a room on the right, Francis Wilmot was conscious of a commotion close to the ground, and some teeth grazing the calf of his leg.

'Dandie!' said the voice of the hairless man, 'you little devil!

293

That dog is a proper little brute with strangers, sir. Stand still!
I've known him bite clean through a lady's stockings.'

Francis Wilmot saw with interest a silver-grey dog nine
inches high and nearly as broad, looking up at him with lustrous eyes above teeth of extreme beauty.

'It's the baby, sir,' said the hairless man, pointing to a sort of
nest on the floor before the fireless hearth; 'he *will* go for people
when he's with the baby. But once he gets to smelling your
trousers, he's all right. Better not touch the baby, though. Mrs
Mont was here a minute ago; I'll take your card up to her.'

Francis Wilmot sat down on a settee in the middle of the
room; and the dog lay between him and the baby.

And while the young man sat he gazed around him. The
room was painted in panels of a sub-golden hue, with a silver-
coloured ceiling. A clavichord, little golden ghost of a piano,
stood at one end. Glass lustres, pictures of flowers and of a
silvery-necked lady swinging a skirt and her golden slippers,
adorned the walls. The curtains were of gold and silver. The
silver-coloured carpet felt wonderfully soft beneath his feet, the
furniture was of a golden wood.

The young man felt suddenly quite home-sick. He was back
in the living-room of an old 'Colonial house' in the bend of a
lonely South Carolina river, reddish in hue. He was staring at
the effigy of his high-collared, red-coated great-grandfather,
Francis Wilmot, Royalist major in the War of Independence.
They always said it was like the effigy he saw when shaving
every morning; the smooth dark hair drooping across his right
temple, the narrow nose and lips, the narrow dark hand on the
sword-hilt or the razor, the slits of dark eyes gazing steadily out.
Young Francis was seeing the darkies working in the cotton-
fields under a sun that he did not seem to have seen since he
came over here; he was walking with his setter along the swamp
edge, where Florida moss festooned the tall dolorous trees; he
was thinking of the Wilmot inheritance, ruined in the Civil
War, still decayed yet precious, and whether to struggle on with
it, or to sell it to the Yank who wanted a week-end run-to from
his Charleston dock job, and would improve it out of recogni-

tion. It would be lonely there, now that Anne had married that young Britisher, Jon Forsyte, and gone away north, to Southern Pines. And he thought of his sister, thus lost to him, dark, pale, vivid, 'full of sand'. Yes! this room made him home-sick, with its perfection, such as he had never beheld, where the only object out of keeping was that dog, lying on its side now, and so thick through that all its little legs were in the air. Softly he said:

'It's the prettiest room I ever was in.'

'What a perfectly charming thing to overhear!'

A young woman, with crinkly chestnut hair above a creamy face, with smiling lips, a short straight nose, and very white dark-lashed eyelids active over dark hazel eyes, stood near the door. She came towards him, and held out her hand.

Francis Wilmot bowed over it, and said gravely:

'Mrs Michael Mont?'

'So Jon's married your sister. Is she pretty?'

'She is.'

'Very?'

'Yes, indeed.'

'I hope baby has been entertaining you.'

'He's just great.'

'He is, rather. I hear Dandie bit you?'

'I reckon he didn't break the cuticle.'

'Haven't you looked? But he's quite healthy. Sit down, and tell me all about your sister and Jon. Is it a marriage of true minds?'

Francis Wilmot sat down.

'It certainly is. Young Jon is a pretty white man, and Anne –'

He heard a sigh.

'I'm very glad. He says in his letter that he's awfully happy. You must come and stay here. You can be as free as you like. Look on us as an hotel.'

The young man's dark eyes smiled.

'That's too good of you! I've never been on this side before. They got through the war too soon.'

Fleur took the baby out of its nest.

'This creature doesn't bite. Look – two teeth, but they don't antagonize – isn't that how you put it?'

'What is its name?'

'Kit – for Christopher. We agreed about his name luckily. Michael – my husband – will be in directly. He's in Parliament, you know. They're not sitting till Monday – Ireland, of course. We only came back for it from Italy yesterday. Italy's so wonderful – you must see it.'

'Pardon me, but is that the Parliament clock that chimes so loud?'

'Big Ben – yes. He marks time for them. Michael says Parliament is the best drag on Progress ever invented. With our first Labour Government, it's been specially interesting this year. Don't you think it's rather touching the way this dog watches my baby? He's got the most terrific jaw!'

'What kind of dog is he?'

'A Dandie Dinmont. We did have a Peke. It was a terrible tragedy. He *would* go after cats; and one day he struck a fighting Tom, and got clawed over both eyes – quite blinded – and so –'

The young man saw her eyes suddenly too bright. He made a soft noise, and said gently: 'That was too bad.'

'I had to change this room completely. It used to be Chinese. It reminded me too much.'

'This little fellow would chaw any cat.'

'Luckily he was brought up with kittens. We got him for his legs – they're so bowed in front that he can hardly run, so he just suits the pram. Dan, show your legs!'

The Dandie looked up with a negative sound.

'He's a terrible little "character". Do tell me, what's Jon like now? Is he still English?'

The young man was conscious that she had uttered at last something really in her mind.

'He is; but he's a dandy fellow.'

'And his mother? She used to be beautiful.'

'And is to this day.'

'She would be. Grey, I suppose, by now?'

'Yes. You don't like her?'

'Well, I hope she won't be jealous of your sister!'

'I think, perhaps, you're unjust.'

'I think, perhaps, I am.'

She sat very still, her face hard above the baby's. And the young man, aware of thoughts beyond his reach, got up.

'When you write to Jon,' she said suddenly, 'tell him that I'm awfully glad, and that I wish him luck. I shan't write to him myself. May I call you Francis?'

Francis Wilmot bowed. 'I shall be proud, ma'am.'

'Yes; but you must call me Fleur. We're sort of related, you know.'

The young man smiled, and touched the name with his lips.

'Fleur! It's a beautiful name!'

'Your room will be ready when you come back. You'll have a bathroom to yourself, of course.'

He put his lips to the hand held out.

'It's wonderful,' he said. 'I was feeling kind of homesick; I miss the sun over here.'

In going out, he looked back. Fleur had put her baby back in its nest, and was staring straight before her.

Chapter Two

CHANGE

<-<->->

BUT more than the death of a dog had caused the regarnishing of Fleur's Chinese room. On the evening of her twenty-second birthday Michael had come home saying:

'Well, my child, I've chucked publishing. With old Danby always in the right – it isn't a career.'

'Oh! Michael, you'll be bored to death.'

'I'll go into Parliament. It's quite usual, and about the same screw.'

He had spoken in jest. Six days later it became apparent that she had listened in earnest.

'You were absolutely right, Michael. It's the very thing for you. You've got ideas.'

'Other people's.'

'And the gift of the gab. We're frightfully handy for the House, here.'

'It costs money, Fleur.'

'Yes, I've spoken to Father. It was rather funny — there's never been a Forsyte, you know, anywhere near Parliament. But he thinks it'll be good for me; and that it's all baronets are fit for.'

'One has to have a Seat, unfortunately.'

'Well, I've sounded your father, too. He'll speak to people. They want young men.'

'Ah! And what are my politics?'

'My dear boy, you must know — at thirty.'

'I'm not a Liberal. But am I Labour or Tory?'

'You can think it out before the next election!'

Next day, while he was shaving, and she was in her bath, he cut himself slightly and said:

'The land and this unemployment is what I really care about. I'm a Foggartist.'

'What?'

'Old Sir James Foggart's book. You read it.'

'No.'

'Well, you said so.'

'So did others.'

'Never mind — his eyes are fixed on 1944, and his policy's according. Safety in the Air, the Land, and Child Emigration; adjustment of Supply and Demand within the Empire; cut our losses in Europe; and endure a worse Present for the sake of a better Future. Everything, in fact, that's unpopular, and said to be impossible.'

'Well, you could keep all that to yourself till you get in. You'll have to stand as a Tory.'

'How lovely you look!'

'If you get in, you can disagree with everybody. That'll give you a position from the start.'

'Some scheme!' murmured Michael.

'You can initiate this – this Foggartism. He isn't mad, is he?'

'No, only too sane, which is much the same thing, of course. You see we've got a higher wage-scale than any other country except America and the Dominions; and it isn't coming down again; we really group in with the new countries. He's for growing as much of our food as we can, and pumping British town children, before they're spoiled, into the Colonies, till Colonial demand for goods equals our supply. It's no earthly, of course, without wholehearted co-operation between the Governments within the Empire.'

'It sounds very sensible.'

'We published him, you know, but at his own expense. It's a "faith and the mountain" stunt. He's got the faith all right, but the mountain shows no signs of moving.'

Fleur stood up. 'Well,' she said, 'that's settled. Your father says he can get you a nomination as a Tory, and you can keep your own views to yourself. You'll get in on the human touch, Michael.'

'Thank you, ducky. Can I help dry you?' . . .

Before redecorating her Chinese room, however, Fleur had waited till after Michael was comfortably seated for a division which professed to be interested in agriculture. She chose a blend between Adam and Louis Quinze. Michael called it the 'bimetallic parlour'; and carried off 'The White Monkey' to his study. The creature's pessimism was not, he felt, suited to political life.

Fleur had initiated her 'salon' with a gathering in February. The soul of society had passed away since the Liberal *débâcle* and Lady Alison's politico-legal coterie no longer counted. Plainer people were in the ascendant. Her Wednesday evenings were youthful, with age represented by her father-in-law, two minor ambassadors, and Pevensey Blythe, editor of *The Outpost*. So unlike his literary style that he was usually mistaken for a Colonial Prime Minister, Blythe was a tall man with a beard, and grey bloodshot eyes, who expressed knowledge in paragraphs that few could really understand. 'What Blythe thinks today, the Conservative Party will not think tomorrow,' was said of him. He spoke in a small voice, and constantly used the impersonal pronoun.

'One is walking in one's sleep,' he would say of the political situation, 'and will wake up without any clothes on.'

A warm supporter of Sir James Foggart's book, characterizing it as 'the masterpiece of a blind archangel', he had a passion for listening to the clavichord, and was invaluable in Fleur's 'salon'.

Freed from poetry and modern music, from Sibley Swan, Walter Nazing and Hugo Solstis, Fleur was finding time for her son – the eleventh baronet. He represented for her the reality of things. Michael might have posthumous theories, and Labour predatory hopes, but for her the year 1944 would see the eleventh baronet come of age. That Kit should inherit an England worth living in was of more intrinsic importance than anything they proposed in the Commons and were unable to perform. All those houses they were going to build, for instance – very proper, but a little unnecessary if Kit still had Lippinghall Manor and South Square, Westminster, to dwell in. Not that Fleur voiced such cynical convictions, or admitted them even to herself. She did orthodox lip-service to the great god Progress.

The Peace of the World, Hygiene, Trade, and the End of Unemployment, preoccupied all, irrespective of Party, and Fleur was in the fashion; but instinct, rather than Michael and Sir James Foggart, told her that the time-honoured motto: 'Eat your cake and have it', which underlay the platforms of all Parties, was not 'too frightfully' sound. So long as Kit had cake, it was no good bothering too deeply about the rest; though, of course, one must seem to. Fluttering about her 'salon' – this to that person, and that to the other, and to all so pretty, she charmed by her grace, her common sense, her pliancy. Not infrequently she attended at the House, and sat, not listening too much to the speeches, yet picking up, as it were, by a sort of seventh sense (if women in Society all had six, surely Fleur had seven) what was necessary to the conduct of that 'salon' – the rise and fall of the Governmental barometer, the catchwords and clichés of policy; and, more valuable, impressions of personality, of the residuary man within the Member. She watched Michael's career, with the fostering eye of a godmother who has given her godchild a blue morocco prayer-book, in the hope that some day he may remember its existence. Although a sedulous attendant at the House all through the spring and summer, Michael had not yet opened his mouth, and so far she had approved of his silence, while nurturing his desire to know his own mind by listening to his wanderings in Foggartism. If it were indeed the only permanent cure for Unemployment, as he said, she too was a Foggartist; common sense assuring her that the only real danger to Kit's future lay in that national malady. Eliminate Unemployment, and nobody would have time to make a fuss. But her criticisms were often pertinent:

'My dear boy, does a country ever sacrifice the present for the sake of the future?' or: 'Do you really think country life is better than town life?' or: 'Can you imagine sending Kit out of England at fourteen to some God-forsaken end of the world?' or: 'Do you suppose the towns will have it?' And they roused Michael to such persistence and fluency that she felt he would really catch on in time – like old Sir Giles Snoreham, whom they would soon be making a peer, because he had always worn low-crowned hats and advocated a return to hansom cabs. Hats, buttonholes, an eye-glass – she turned over in her mind all such little realities as help a political career.

'Plain glass doesn't harm the sight; and it really has a focusing value, Michael.'

'My child, it's never done my Dad a bit of good; I doubt if it's sold three copies of any of his books. No! If I get on, it'll be by talking.'

But still she encouraged him to keep his mouth shut.

'It's no good starting wrong, Michael. These Labour people aren't going to last out the year.'

'Why not?'

'Their heads are swelling, and their tempers going. They're only on sufferance; people on sufferance have got to be pleasant or they won't be suffered. When they go out, the Tories will get in again and probably last. You'll have several years to be eccentric in, and by the time they're out again, you'll have your licence. Just go on working the human touch in your constituency; I'm sure it's a mistake to forget you've got constituents.'

Michael spent most week-ends that summer working the human touch in mid-Bucks; and Fleur spent most week-ends with the eleventh baronet at her father's house near Mapledurham.

Since wiping the dust of the city off his feet, after that affair of Elderson and the P.P.R.S., Soames had become almost too countrified for a Forsyte. He had bought the meadows on the far side of the river and several Jersey cows. Not that he was going in for farming or nonsense of that sort, but it gave him an interest to punt himself over and see them milked. He had put up a good deal of glass, too, and was laying down melons. The English melon was superior to any other, and every year's connexion with a French wife made him more and more inclined to eat what he grew himself. After Michael was returned for Parliament, Fleur had sent him Sir James Foggart's book, 'The Parlous State of England'. When it came, he said to Annette:

'I don't know what she thinks I want with this great thing!'

'To read it, Soames, I suppose.'

Soames sniffed, turning the pages.

'I can't tell what it's all about.'

'I will sell it at my bazaar, Soames. It will do for some good man who can read English.'

From that moment Soames began almost unconsciously to read the book. He found it a peculiar affair, which gave most people some good hard knocks. He began to enjoy them, especially the chapter deprecating the workman's dislike of parting with his children at a reasonable age. Having never been outside Europe, he had a somewhat sketchy idea of places like South Africa, Australia, Canada, and New Zealand; but this old fellow

Foggart, it appeared, had been there, and knew what he was talking about. What he said about their development seemed quite sensible. Children who went out there put on weight at once, and became owners of property at an age when in England they were still delivering parcels, popping in and out of jobs, hanging about street corners, and qualifying for unemployment and Communism. Get them out of England! There was a startling attraction in the idea for one who was English to a degree. He was in favour, too, of what was said about growing food and making England safe in the air. And then, slowly, he turned against it. The fellow was too much of a Jeremiah altogether. He complained to Fleur that the book dealt with nothing but birds in the bush; it was unpractical. What did 'Old Mont' say?

'He won't read it; he says he knows Old Foggart.'

'H'm!' said Soames, 'I shouldn't be surprised if there were something in it, then.' That little-headed baronet was old-fashioned! 'Anyway, it shows that Michael's given up those Labour fellows.'

'Michael says Foggartism will be Labour's policy when they understand all it means.'

'How's that?'

'He thinks it's going to do them much more good than anybody else. He says one or two of their leaders are beginning to smell it out, and that the rest of the leaders are bound to follow in time.'

'In that case,' said Soames, 'it'll never go down with their rank and file.' And for two minutes he sat in a sort of trance. Had he said something profound, or had he not?

Fleur's presence at week-ends with the eleventh baronet was extremely agreeable to him. Though at first he had felt a sort of disappointment that his grandchild was not a girl – an eleventh baronet belonged too definitely to the Monts – he began, as the months wore on, to find him 'an engaging little chap', and, in any case, to have him down at Mapledurham kept him away from Lippinghall. It tried him at times, of course, to see how the women hung about the baby – there was something very excessive about motherhood. He had noticed it with Annette; he noticed it now with Fleur. French – perhaps! He had not remembered his own mother making such a fuss; indeed, he could not remember anything that happened when he was one. A week-end, when Madame Lamotte, Annette and Fleur were all hanging over his grandson, three generations of maternity concentrated on that pudgy morsel, reduced him to a punt, fishing for what he felt sure nobody would eat.

By the time he had finished Sir James Foggart's book, the disagreeable summer of 1924 was over, and a more disagreeable September had set in. The mellow golden days that glow up out of a haze which stars with dewdrops every cobweb on a gate, simply did not come. It rained, and the river was so unnaturally full, that the newspapers were at first unnaturally empty – there was literally no news of drought; they filled up again slowly with reports of the wettest summer 'for thirty years'. Calm, greenish with weed and tree shadow, the river flowed unendingly between Soames's damp lawn and his damp meadows. There were no mushrooms. Blackberries tasted of rain. Soames made a point of eating one every year, and, by the flavour, could tell what sort of year it had been. There was a good deal of 'old-man's-beard'. In spite of all this, however, he was more cheerful than he had been for ages. Labour had been 'in', if not in real power, for months, and the heavens had only lowered. Forced by Labour-in-office to take some notice of politics, he would utter prophecies at the breakfast-table. They varied somewhat, according to the news; and, since he always forgot those which did not come true, he was constantly able to tell Annette that he had told her so. She took no interest, however, occupied, 'like a woman, with her bazaars and jam-making, running about in the car, shopping in London, attending garden-parties'; and, in spite of her tendency to put on flesh, still remarkably handsome. Jack Cardigan, his niece Imogen's husband, had made him a sixty-ninth-birthday present of a set of golf-clubs. This was more puzzling to Soames than anything that had ever happened to him. What on earth was he to do with them? Annette, with that French quickness which often annoyed him, suggested that he should use them. She was uncomfortable! At his age —! And then, one week-end in May the fellow himself had come down with Imogen and, teeing a ball up on half a molehill, had driven it across the river.

'I'll bet you a box of cigars, Uncle Soames, that you don't do that before we leave on Monday.'

'I never bet,' said Soames, 'and I don't smoke.'

'Time you began both. Look here, we'll spend tomorrow learning to knock the ball!'

'Absurd!' said Soames.

But in his room that night he had stood in his pyjamas swinging his arms in imitation of Jack Cardigan. The next day he sent the women out in the car with their lunch; he was not going to have them grinning at him. He had seldom spent more annoying hours than those which followed. They culminated in a moment when at last he hit the ball, and it fell into the river three yards from the near bank. He was so stiff next morning in arms and ribs, that Annette had to rub him till he said:

'Look out! you're taking the skin off!'

He had, however, become infected. After destroying some further portions of his lawn, he joined the nearest golf club, and began to go round by himself during the luncheon-hour, accompanied by a little boy. He kept at it with characteristic tenacity, till by July he had attained a certain proficiency; and he began to say to Annette that it would do her all the good in the world to take it up, and keep her weight down.

'*Merci*, Soames,' she would reply; 'I have no wish to be the figure of your English Misses, flat as a board before and behind.' She was reactionary, 'like her nation'; and Soames, who at heart had a certain sympathy with curves, did not seriously press the point. He found that the exercise jogged both his liver and his temper. He began to have colour in his cheeks. The day after his first nine-hole round with Jack Cardigan, who had given him three strokes a hole and beaten him by nine holes, he received a package which, to his dismay, contained a box of cigars. What the fellow was about, he could not imagine! He only discovered when, one evening a few days later, sitting at the window of his picture gallery, he found that he had one in his mouth. Curiously enough, it did not make him sick. It produced rather something of the feeling he used to enjoy after 'doing Coué' – now comparatively out of fashion, since an American, so his sister Winifred said, had found a shorter cut. A suspicion, however, that the family had set Jack Cardigan on, prevented him from indulging his new sensation anywhere but in his private gallery; so that cigars gathered the halo of a secret vice. He renewed his store stealthily. Only when he found that Annette, Fleur, and others had known for weeks, did he relax his rule, and say openly that the vice of the present day was cigarettes.

'My dear boy,' said Winifred, when she next saw him, 'everybody's saying you're a different man!'

Soames raised his eyebrows. He was not conscious of any change.

'That chap Cardigan,' he said, 'is a funny fellow! ... I'm going to dine and sleep at Fleur's; they're just back from Italy. The House sits on Monday.'

'Yes,' said Winifred; 'very fussy of them – sitting in the Long Vacation.'

'Ireland!' said Soames deeply. 'A pretty pair of shoes again!' Always had been; always would be!

Chapter Three

MICHAEL TAKES 'A LUNAR'

◄◄·◊·►►

MICHAEL had returned from Italy with the longing to 'get on with it', which results from Southern holidays. Countryman by up-bringing, still deeply absorbed by the unemployment problem and committed to Foggartism, as its remedy, he had taken up no other hobby in the House, and was eating the country's bread, if somewhat unbuttered, and doing nothing for it. He desired, therefore, to know where he stood, and how long he was going to stand there.

Bent on 'taking this lunar' — as 'Old Forsyte' would call it — at his own position, he walked away from the House that same day, after dealing with an accumulated correspondence. He walked towards Pevensey Blythe, in the office of that self-sufficing weekly: *The Outpost.* Sunburnt from his Italian holiday and thinned by Italian cookery, he moved briskly, and thought of many things. Passing down on to the Embankment, where a number of unemployed birds on a number of trees were also wondering, it seemed, where they stood and how long they were going to stand there, he took a letter from his pocket to read a second time.

> 12 Sapper's Row,
> Camden Town.

HONOURABLE SIR,

Being young in 'Who's Who', you will not be hard, I think, to those in suffering. I am an Austrian woman who married a German eleven years ago. He was an actor on the English stage, for his father and mother, who are no more living, brought him to England quite young. Interned he was, and his health broken up. He has the neurasthenie very bad so he cannot be trusted for any work. Before the war he was always in a part, and we had some good money; but this went partly when I was left with my child alone, and the rest was taken by the P.T., and we got very little back, neither of us being English. What we did get has all been to the doctor, and for our debts, and for burying our little child, which died happily, for though I loved it much this life which we have is not fit for a child to live. We live on my needle, and that is not earning much, a pound a week and sometimes nothing. The managers will not look at my husband all these years, because he shakes suddenly, so they think he drinks, but, Sir, he has not the money to buy it. We do not know where to turn, or what to do. So I thought, dear Sir, whether you could do anything for us with the P.T.; they have been quite sympatical; but they say they administrate an order and cannot do more. Or if you could get my husband some work where he will be in open air — the doctor say that is what he want. We have nowhere to go in Germany or in Austria, our well-beloved families being no more alive. I think we are like many, but I cannot help asking you, Sir, because we want to keep living if we can, and now we are hardly having any food. Please to forgive me my writing, and to believe your very anxious and humble

ANNA BERGFELD.

'God help them!' thought Michael, under a plane tree close to Cleopatra's Needle, but without conviction. For in his view God was not so much interested in the fate of individual aliens as the Governor of the Bank of England in the fate of a pound of sugar bought with the fraction of a Bradbury; He would not arbitrarily interfere with a ripple of the tides set loose by His arrangement of the Spheres. God, to Michael, was a monarch strictly limited by His own Constitution. He restored the letter to his pocket. Poor creatures! But really, with 1,200,000 and more English unemployed, mostly due to that confounded Kaiser and his Navy stunt —! If that fellow and his gang had not started their naval rivalry in 1899, England would have been out of the whole mess, or, perhaps, there never would have been a mess!

He turned up from the Temple station towards the offices of *The Outpost*. He had 'taken' that weekly for some years now. It knew everything, and managed to convey a slight impression that nobody else knew anything; so that it seemed more weighty than any other weekly. Having no particular Party to patronize, it could patronize the lot. Without Imperial bias, it professed a special knowledge of the Empire. Not literary, it made a point of reducing the heads of literary men – Michael, in his publishing days, had enjoyed every opportunity of noticing that. Professing respect for Church and the Law, it was an adept at giving them 'what-for'. It fancied itself on Drama, striking a somewhat Irish attitude towards it. But, perhaps above all, it excelled in neat detraction from political reputations, keeping them in their place, and that place a little lower than *The Outpost*'s. Moreover, from its editorials emanated that 'holy ghost' of inspired knowledge in periods just a little beyond average comprehension, without which no such periodical had real importance.

Michael went up the stairs two at a time, and entered a large square room, where Mr Blythe, back to the door, was pointing with a ruler to a circle drawn on a map.

'This is a bee map,' said Mr Blythe to himself. 'Quite the bee-est map I ever saw.'

Michael could not contain a gurgle, and the eyes of Mr Blythe came round, prominent, epileptic, richly encircled by pouches.

'Hallo!' he said defiantly. 'You? The Colonial Office prepared this map specially to show the best spots for Settlement schemes. And they've left out Baggersfontein – the very hub.'

Michael seated himself on the table.

'I've come in to ask what you think of the situation? My wife says Labour will be out in no time.'

'Our charming little lady!' said Mr Blythe; 'Labour will survive Ireland; they will survive Russia; they will linger on in their precarious way. One hesitates to predict their decease. Fear of their Budget may bring them down in February. After the smell of Russian fat has died away – say in November, Mont – one may make a start.'

'This first speech,' said Michael, 'is a nightmare to me. How, exactly, am I to start Foggartism?'

'One will have achieved the impression of a body of opinion before then.'

'But will there be one?'

'No,' said Mr Blythe.

'Oh!' said Michael. 'And, by the way, what about Free Trade?'

'One will profess Free Trade, and put on duties.'

'God and Mammon.'

'Necessary in England, before any new departure, Mont. Witness Liberal-Unionism, Tory-Socialism, and –'

'Other ramps,' said Michael gently.

'One will glide, deprecate Protection till there is more Protection than Free Trade, then deprecate Free Trade. Foggartism is an end, not a means; Free Trade and Protection are means, not the ends politicians have made them.'

Roused by the word 'politician', Michael got off the table; he was coming to have a certain sympathy with those poor devils. They were supposed to have no feeling for the country, and to be wise only after the event. But, really, who could tell what was good for the country, among the mists of talk? Not even old Foggart, Michael sometimes thought.

'You know, Blythe,' he said, 'that we politicians don't think ahead, simply because we know it's no earthly. Every elector thinks his own immediate good is the good of the country. Only their own shoes pinching will change elector's views. If Foggartism means adding to the price of living now, and taking wage-earning children away from workmen's families for the sake of benefit – ten or twenty years hence – who's going to stand for it?'

'My dear young man,' said Mr Blythe, 'conversion is our job. At present our trade-unionists despise the outside world. They've never seen it. Their philosophy is bounded by their smoky little streets. But five million pounds spent on the organized travel of a hundred thousand working men would do the trick in five years. It would infect the working class with a feverish desire for a place in the sun. The world is their children's for the taking. But who can blame them, when they know nothing of it?'

'Some thought!' said Michael. 'Only – what Government will think it? Can I take those maps? ... By the way,' he said at the door, 'there are Societies, you know, for sending out children.'

Mr Blythe grunted. 'Yes. Excellent little affairs! A few hundred children doing well – concrete example of what might be. Multiply it a hundredfold, and you've got a beginning. You can't fill pails with a teaspoon. Good-bye!'

Out on the Embankment Michael wondered if one could love one's country with a passion for getting people to leave it. But this over-bloated town condition, with its blight and smoky ugliness; the children without a chance from birth; these swarms of poor devils without work, who dragged about and hadn't an earthly, and never would, on present lines; this unbalanced, hand-to-mouth, dependent state of things – surely that wasn't to be for ever the state of the country one loved! He stared at the towers of Westminster, with the setting sun behind them. And there started up before him the thousand familiars of his past – trees, fields and streams, towers, churches, bridges; the English breeds of beasts, the singing birds, the owls, the jays and rooks at Lippinghall, the little differences from foreign sorts in shrub, flower, lichen, and winged life; the English scents, the English haze, the English grass; the eggs and bacon; the slow good humour, the moderation and the pluck; the smell of rain; the apple-blossom, the heather, and the sea. His country, and his breed – unspoilable at heart! He passed the Clock Tower. The House looked lacey and imposing, more beautiful than fashion granted. Did they spin the web of England's future in that House? Or were they painting camouflage – a screen over old England?

A familiar voice said: 'This is a monstrous great thing!'

And Michael saw his father-in-law staring up at the Lincoln statue. 'What did they want to put it here for?' said Soames. 'It's not English.' He walked along at Michael's side. 'Fleur well?'

'Splendid. Italy suited her like everything.'

Soames sniffed. 'They're a theatrical lot,' he said. 'Did you see Milan Cathedral?'

'Yes, sir. It's about the only thing we didn't take to.'

'H'm! Their cooking gave me the collywobbles in '82. I dare say it's better now. How's the boy?'

'A1, sir.'

Soames made a sound of gratification, and they turned the corner into South Square.

'What's this?' said Soames.

Outside the front door were two battered-looking trunks, a young man, grasping a bag, and ringing the bell, and a taxi-cab turning away.

'I can't tell you, sir,' murmured Michael. 'Unless it's the angel Gabriel.'

'He's got the wrong house,' said Soames, moving forward.

But just then the young man disappeared within.

Soames walked up to the trunks. 'Francis Wilmot,' he read out. ' "S.S. Amphibian." There's some mistake l'

Chapter Four

MERE CONVERSATION

◄◄►►

WHEN they came in, Fleur was returning downstairs from showing the young man to his room. Already fully dressed for the evening, she had but little on, and her hair was shingled. . . .

'My dear girl,' Michael had said, when shingling came in, 'to please me, don't l Your *nuque* will be too bristly for kisses.'

'My dear boy,' she had answered, 'as if one could help it l You're always the same with any new fashion l'

She had been one of the first twelve to shingle, and was just feeling that without care she would miss being one of the first twelve to grow some hair again. Marjorie Ferrar, 'the Pet of the Panjoys', as Michael called her, already had more than an inch. Somehow, one hated being distanced by Marjorie Ferrar. . . .

Advancing to her father, she said:

'I've asked a young American to stay, Dad; Jon Forsyte has married his sister, out there. You're quite brown, darling. How's mother?'

Soames only gazed at her.

And Fleur passed through one of those shamed moments, when the dumb quality of his love for her seemed accusing the glib quality of her love for him. It was not fair – she felt – that he should look at her like that; as if she had not suffered in that old business with Jon more than he; if she could take it lightly now, surely he could l As for Michael – not a word l – not even a joke l She bit her lips, shook her shingled head, and passed into the 'bimetallic parlour'.

Dinner began with soup and Soames deprecating his own

cows for not being Herefords. He supposed that in America they had plenty of Herefords?

Francis Wilmot believed that they were going in for Holsteins now.

'Holsteins!' repeated Soames. 'They're new since my young days. What's their colour?'

'Parti-coloured,' said Francis Wilmot. 'The English grass is just wonderful.'

'Too damp, with us,' said Soames. 'We're on the river.'

'The river Thames? What size will that be, where it hasn't a tide?'

'Just there – not more than a hundred yards.'

'Will it have fish?'

'Plenty.'

'And it'll run clear – not red; our Southern rivers have a red colour. And your trees will be willows, and poplars, and elms.'

Soames was a good deal puzzled. He had never been in America. The inhabitants were human, of course, but peculiar and all alike, with more face than feature, heads fastened upright on their backs, and shoulders too square to be real. Their voices clanged in their mouths; they pronounced the words 'very' and 'America' in a way that he tried to imitate without success; their dollar was too high, and they all had motor-cars; they despised Europe, came over in great quantities, and took back all they could; they talked all the time, and were not allowed to drink. This young man cut across all these preconceptions. He drank sherry and only spoke when he was spoken to. His shoulders looked natural; he had more feature than face; and his voice was soft. Perhaps, at least, he despised Europe.

'I suppose,' he said, 'you find England very small.'

'No, sir. I find London very large; and you certainly have the loveliest kind of a countryside.'

Soames looked down one side of his nose. 'Pretty enough!' he said.

Then came turbot and a silence, broken, low down, behind his chair.

'That dog!' said Soames, impaling a morsel of fish he had set aside as uneatable.

'No, no, Dad! He just wants to know you've seen him!'

Soames stretched down a finger, and the Dandie fell on his side.

'He never eats,' said Fleur; 'but he has to be noticed.'

A small covey of partridges came in, cooked.

'Is there any particular thing you want to see over here, Mr Wilmot?' said Michael. 'There's nothing very un-American left. You're just too late for Regent Street.'

'I want to see the Beefeaters; and Cruft's Dog Show; and your blood horses; and the Derby.'

'Darby!' Soames corrected. 'You can't stay for that – it's not till next June.'

'My cousin Val will show you race-horses,' said Fleur. 'He married Jon's sister, you know.'

A 'bombe' appeared. 'You have more of this in America, I believe,' said Soames.

'We don't have much ice-cream in the South, sir, but we have special cooking – very tasty.'

'I've heard of terrapin.'

'Well, *I* don't get frills like that. I live away back, and have to work pretty hard. My place is kind of homey; but I've got some mighty nice darkies that can cook fine – old folk that knew my grannies. The old-time darky is getting scarce, but he's the real thing.'

A Southerner!

Soames had been told that the Southerner was a gentleman. He remembered the 'Alabama', too; and his father, James, saying: 'I told you so' when the Government ate humble pie over that business.

In the savoury silence that accompanied soft roes on toast, the patter of the Dandie's feet on the parquet floor could be plainly heard.

'This is the only thing he likes,' said Fleur. 'Dan! go to your master. Give him a little bit, Michael.' And she stole a look at Michael, but he did not answer it.

On their Italian holiday, with Fleur in the throes of novelty, sun and wine warmed, disposed to junketing, amenable to his caresses, he had been having his real honeymoon, enjoying, for the first time since his marriage, a sense of being the chosen companion of his adored. And now had come this stranger, bringing reminder that one played but second fiddle to that young second cousin and first lover; and he couldn't help feeling the cup withdrawn again from his lips. She had invited this young man because he came from that past of hers whose tune one could not play. And, without looking up, he fed the Dandie with tid-bits of his favourite edible.

Soames broke the silence.

'Take some nutmeg, Mr Wilmot. Melon without nutmeg –'

When Fleur rose, Soames followed her to the drawing-room; while Michael led the young American to his study.

'You knew Jon?' said Francis Wilmot.

'No; I never met him.'

'He's a great little fellow; and some poet. He's growing dandy peaches.'

'Is he going on with that, now he's married?'

'Surely.'

'Not coming to England?'

'Not this year. They have a nice home – horses and dogs. They have some hunting there, too. Perhaps he'll bring my sister over for a trip, next fall.'

'Oh!' said Michael. 'And are you staying long, yourself?'

'Why! I'll go back for Christmas. I'd like to see Rome and Seville; and I want to visit the old home of my people, down in Worcestershire.'

'When did they go over?'

'William and Mary. Catholics – they were. Is it a nice part, Worcestershire?'

'Very; especially in the spring. It grows a lot of fruit.'

'Oh! You still grow things in this country?'

'Not many.'

'I thought that was so, coming on the cars, from Liverpool. I saw a lot of grass and one or two sheep, but I didn't see anybody working. The people all live in the towns, then?'

'Except a few unconsidered trifles. You must come down to my father's; they still grow a turnip or two thereabouts.'

'It's sad,' said Francis Wilmot.

'It is. We began to grow wheat again in the war; but they've let it all slip back – and worse.'

'Why was that?'

Michael shrugged his shoulders: 'No accounting for statesmanship. It lets the Land go to blazes when in office; and beats the drum of it when in opposition. At the end of the war we had the best air force in the world, and agriculture was well on its way to recovery. And what did they do? Dropped them both like hot potatoes. It was tragic. What do you grow in Carolina?'

'Just cotton, on my place. But it's mighty hard to make cotton pay nowadays. Labour's high.'

'High with you, too?'

'Yes, sir. Do they let strangers into your Parliament?'

'Rather. Would you like to hear the Irish debate? I can get you a seat in the Distinguished Strangers' gallery.'

'I thought the English were stiff; but it's wonderful the way you make me feel at home. Is that your father-in-law – the old gentleman?'

'Yes.'

'He seems kind of rarefied. Is he a banker?'

'No. But now you mention it – he ought to be.'

Francis Wilmot's eye roved round the room and came to rest on 'The White Monkey'.

'Well, now,' he said, softly, 'that, surely, is a wonderful picture. Could I get a picture painted by that man, for Jon and my sister?'

'I'm afraid not,' said Michael. 'You see, he was a Chink – not quite of the best period; but he must have gone West five hundred years ago at least.'

'Ah! Well, he had a great sense of animals.'

'We think he had a great sense of human beings.'

Francis Wilmot stared.

There was something, Michael decided, in this young man unresponsive to satire.

'So you want to see Cruft's Dog Show?' he said. 'You're keen on dogs, then?'

'I'll be taking a bloodhound back for John, and two for myself. I want to raise bloodhounds.'

Michael leaned back, and blew out smoke. To Francis Wilmot, he felt, the world was young, and life running on good tyres to some desirable destination. In England — l

'What is it you Americans want out of life?' he said abruptly.

'Well, I suppose you might say we want success — in the North at all events.'

'*We* wanted that in 1824,' said Michael.

'Oh! And nowadays?'

'We've had success, and now we're wondering whether it hasn't cooked our goose.'

'Well,' said Francis Wilmot, 'we're sort of thinly populated, compared with you.'

'That's it,' said Michael. 'Every seat here is booked in advance; and a good many sit on their own knees. Will you have another cigar, or shall we join the lady?'

Chapter Five

SIDE-SLIPS

⋘⋯⋙

IF Providence was completely satisfied with Sapper's Row, Camden Town, Michael was not. What could justify those twin dismal rows of three-storeyed houses, so begrimed that they might have been collars washed in Italy? What possible attention to business could make these little ground-floor shops do anything but lose money? From the thronged and tram-lined thoroughfare so pregnantly scented with fried fish, petrol, and old clothes, who would turn into this small backwater for sweetness or for profit? Even the children, made with heroic constancy on its second and third floors, sought the sweets of life outside its precincts; for in Sapper's Row they could neither be run over nor stare at the outside of cinemas. Hand-carts, bicycles, light vans which had lost their nerve and taxicabs which had lost their way, provided all the traffic; potted geraniums and spotted cats supplied all the beauty. Sapper's Row drooped and dithered.

Michael entered from its west end, and against his principles. Here was overcrowded England at its most dismal, and here was he, who advocated a reduction of its population, about to visit some broken-down aliens with the view of keeping them alive. He looked into three of the little shops. Not a soul! Which was worst! Such little shops frequented, or – deserted? He came to No. 12, and looking up, saw a face looking down. It was wax white, movingly listless, above a pair of hands sewing at a garment. 'That,' he thought, 'is my "obedient humble" and her needle.' He entered the shop below, a hairdresser's, containing a dirty basin below a dusty mirror, suspicious towels, bottles, and two dingy chairs. In his shirt-sleeves, astride one of them, reading *The Daily Mail*, sat a shadowy fellow with pale hollow cheeks, twisted moustache, lank hair, and the eyes, at once knowing and tragic, of a philosopher.

'Hair-cut, sir?'

Michael shook his head.

'Do Mr and Mrs Bergfeld live here?'

'Upstairs, top floor.'

'How do I get up?'

'Through there.'

Passing through a curtained aperture, Michael found a stairway, and at its top, stood, hesitating. His conscience was echoing Fleur's comment on Anna Bergfeld's letter: 'Yes, I dare say; but what's the good?' when the door was opened, and it seemed to him almost as if a corpse were standing there, with a face as though someone had come knocking on its grave, so eager and so white.

'Mrs Bergfeld? My name's Mont. You wrote to me.'

The woman trembled so, that Michael thought she was going to faint.

'Will you excuse me, sir, that I sit down?' And she dropped on to the end of the bed. The room was spotless, but besides the bed, held only a small deal washstand, a pot of geranium, a tin trunk with a pair of trousers folded on it, a woman's hat on a peg, and a chair in the window covered with her sewing.

The woman stood up again. She seemed not more than thirty, thin but prettily formed; and her oval face, without colour except in her dark eyes, suggested Rafael rather than Sapper's Row.

'It is like seeing an angel,' she said. 'Excuse me, sir.'

'Queer angel, Mrs Bergfeld. Your husband not in?'

'No, sir. Fritz has gone to walk.'

'Tell me, Mrs Bergfeld. If I pay your passages to Germany, will you go?'

'We cannot get a passport now; Fritz has been here twenty years, and never back; he has lost his German nationality, sir; they do not want people like us, you know.'

Michael stivered up his hair.

'Where are you from yourself?'

'From Salzburg.'

'What about going back there?'

'I would like to, but what would we do? In Austria everyone is poor now, and I have no relative left. Here at least we have my sewing.'

'How much is that a week?'

'Sometimes a pound; sometimes fifteen shillings. It is bread and the rent.'

'Don't you get the dole?'

'No, sir. We are not registered.'

Michael took out a five-pound note and laid it with his card on the washstand. 'I've got to think this over, Mrs Bergfeld. Perhaps your husband will come and see me.' He went out quickly, for the ghostly woman had flushed pink.

Repassing through the curtained aperture, he caught the hairdresser wiping out the basin.

'Find 'em, sir?'

'The lady.'

'Ah! Seen better days, I should say. The 'usband's a queer customer; 'alf off his nut. Wanted to come in here with me, but I've got to give this job up.'

'Oh! How's that?'

'I've got to have fresh air — only got one lung, and that's not very gaudy. I'll have to find something else.'

'That's bad, in these days.'

The hairdresser shrugged his bony shoulders. 'Ah!' he said. 'I've been a hairdresser from a boy, except for the war. Funny place this, to fetch up in after where I've been. The war knocked me out.' He twisted his little thin moustache.

'No pension?' said Michael.

'Not a bob. What I want to keep me alive is something in the open.'

Michael took him in from head to foot. Shadowy, narrow-headed, with one lung.

'But do you know anything about country life?'

'Not a blessed thing. Still, I've got to find something, or peg out.'

His tragic and knowing eyes searched Michael's face.

'I'm awfully sorry,' said Michael. 'Good-bye!'

The hairdresser made a queer jerky little movement.

Emerging from Sapper's Row into the crowded, roaring thoroughfare, Michael thought of a speech in a play he had seen a year or two before. 'The condition of the people leaves much to be desired. I shall make a point of taking up the cudgels in the House. I shall move –!' The condition of the people! What a remote thing! The sportive nightmare of a few dreaming nights, the skeleton in a well-locked cupboard, the discomforting rare howl of a hungry dog! And probably no folk in England less disturbed by it than the gallant six hundred odd who sat with him in 'that House'. For to improve the condition of the people was their job, and that relieved them of a sense of nightmare. Since Oliver Cromwell some sixteen thousand, perhaps, had sat there before them, to the same end. And was the trick done – not precisely! Still they were really working for it, and other people were only looking on and telling them how to do it!

Thus was he thinking when a voice said:

'Not got a job about you, sir?'

Michael quickened his steps, then stood still. He saw that the man who had spoken, having cast his eyes down again, had missed this sign of weakness; and he went back to him. They were black eyes in a face round and pasty like a mince-pie. Decent and shabby, quiet and forlorn, he wore an ex-Service-man's badge.

'You spoke to me?' said Michael.

'I'm sure I don't know why, sir; it just hopped out of me.'

'No work?'

'No; and pretty low.'

'Married?'

'Widower, sir; two children.'

'Dole?'

'Yes; and fair sick of it.'

'In the war, I see?'

'Yes, Mespot.'

'What sort of a job do you want?'

'Any mortal thing.'

'Give me your name and address.'

'Henry Boddick, 4 Waltham Buildings, Gunnersbury.'

Michael took it down.

'Can't promise anything,' he said.

'No, sir.'

'Good luck, anyway. Have a cigar?'

'Thank you, and good luck to *you*, sir.'

Michael saluted, and resumed his progress; once out of sight of Henry Boddick, he took a taxi. A little more of this, and he would lose the sweet reasonableness without which one could not sit in 'that House'!

'For Sale or to Let' recorded recurrently in Portland Place, somewhat restored his sense of balance.

That same afternoon he took Francis Wilmot with him to

the House, and leaving him at the foot of the Distinguished Strangers' stairway, made his way on to the floor.

He had never been in Ireland, so that the debate had for him little relation to reality. It seemed to illustrate, however, the obstacles in the way of agreement on any mortal subject. Almost every speech emphasized the paramount need for a settlement, but declared the impossibility of 'going back' on this, that, or the other factor which precluded such settlement. Still, for a debate on Ireland it seemed good-tempered; and presently they would all go out and record the votes they had determined on before it all began. He remembered the thrill with which he had listened to the first debates after his election; the impression each speech had given him that somebody must certainly be converted to something and the reluctance with which he had discovered that nobody ever was. Some force was at work far stronger than any eloquence, however striking or sincere. The clothes were washed elsewhere; in here they were but aired before being put on. Still, until people put thoughts into words, they didn't know what they thought, and sometimes they didn't know afterwards. And for the hundredth time Michael was seized by a weak feeling in his legs. In a few weeks he himself must rise on them. Would the House accord him its 'customary indulgence'! or would it say: 'Young fellow – teaching your grandmother to suck eggs – shut up!'

He looked around him.

His fellow members were sitting in all shapes. Chosen of the people, they confirmed the doctrine that human nature did not change, or so slowly that one could not see the process – he had seen their prototypes in Roman statues, in medieval pictures.... 'Plain but pleasant,' he thought, unconsciously reproducing George Forsyte's description of himself in his palmy days. But did they take themselves seriously, as under Burke, as under Gladstone even?

The words 'customary indulgence' roused him from reverie; for they meant a maiden speech. Ha! yes! the member for Cornmarket. He composed himself to listen. Delivering himself with restraint and clarity, the speaker seemed suggesting that the doctrine 'Do unto others as you would they should do unto you' need not be entirely neglected, even in Ireland; but it was long – too long – Michael watched the House grow restive. 'Alas! poor brother!' he thought, as the speaker somewhat hastily sat down. A very handsome man rose in his place. He congratulated his honourable friend on his able and well-delivered effort, he only regretted that it had nothing to do with the business in hand. Exactly! Michael slipped out. Recovering his 'distinguished stranger', he walked away with him to South Square.

Francis Wilmot was in a state of some enthusiasm.

'That was fine,' he said. 'Who was the gentleman under the curtains?'

'The Speaker?'

'No; I mean the one who didn't speak.'

'Exactly; he's the dignity of the House.'

'They ought to feed him oxygen; it must be sleepy under there. I liked the delegate who spoke last. He would "go" in America; he had big ideas.'

'The idealism which keeps you out of the League of Nations, eh?' said Michael with a grin.

Francis Wilmot turned his head rather sharply.

'Well,' he said, 'we're like any other people when it comes to bed-rock.'

'Quite so,' said Michael, 'idealism is just a by-product of geography – it's the haze that lies in the middle distance. The farther you are from bed-rock, the less quick you need to be to see it. We're twenty sea-miles more idealistic about the European situation than the French are. And you're three thousand sea-miles more idealistic than we are. But when it's a matter of niggers, we're three thousand sea-miles more idealistic than you; isn't that so?'

Francis Wilmot narrowed his dark eyes.

'It is,' he said. 'The farther North we go in the States, the more idealistic we get about the negro. Anne and I've lived all our life with darkies, and never had trouble; we love them, and they love us; but I wouldn't trust myself not to join in lynching

one that laid his hands on her. I've talked that over many times
with Jon. He doesn't see it that way; he says a darky should be
tried like a white man; but he doesn't know the real South. His
mind is still three thousand sea-miles away.'

Michael was silent. Something within him always closed up
at mention of a name which he still spelt mentally with an 'h'.

Francis Wilmot added ruminatively: 'There are a few saints
in every country proof against your theory; but the rest of us, I
reckon, aren't above human nature.'

'Talking of human nature,' said Michael, 'here's my father-
in-law!'

Chapter Six

SOAMES KEEPS HIS EYES OPEN

◄◄·►►

SOAMES, having prolonged his week-end visit, had been
spending the afternoon at the Zoological Gardens, removing his
great-nephews, the little Cardigans, from the too close proximity
of monkeys and cats. After standing them once more in Imogen's hall, he had roosted at his Club till, idly turning his evening paper, he had come on this paragraph, in the 'Chiff-chaff'
column:

'A surprise for the Coming Session is being confectioned at
the Wednesday gatherings of a young hostess not a hundred
miles from Westminster. Her husband, a prospective baronet
lately connected with literature, is to be entrusted with the
launching in Parliament of a policy which enjoys the peculiar
label of Foggartism, derived from Sir James Foggart's book
called *The Parlous State of England*. This amusing alarum is
attributed to the somewhat fantastic brain which guides a well-
known weekly. We shall see what comes of it. In the meantime
the enterprising little lady in question is losing no chance of
building up her 'salon' on the curiosity which ever surrounds
any buccaneering in politics.'

Soames rubbed his eyes; then read it again with rising anger. 'Enterprising little lady is losing no chance of building up her "salon".' Who had written that? He put the paper in his pocket – almost the first theft he had ever committed – and all the way across St James's Park in the gathering twilight he brooded on that anonymous paragraph. The allusion seemed to him unmistakable, and malicious into the bargain. 'Lion-hunter' would not have been plainer. Unfortunately, in a primary sense 'lion-hunter' was a compliment, and Soames doubted whether its secondary sense had ever been 'laid down' as libellous. He was still brooding deeply, when the young men ranged alongside.

'Well, sir?'

'Ah!' said Soames. 'I want to speak to you. You've got a traitor in the camp.' And without meaning to at all, he looked angrily at Francis Wilmot.

'Now, sir?' said Michael, when they were in the study.

Soames held out the folded paper.

Michael read the paragraph and made a face.

'Whoever wrote that comes to your evenings,' said Soames; 'that's clear. Who is he?'

'Very likely a she.'

'D'you mean to say they print such things by women?'

Michael did not answer. Old Forsyte was behind the times.

'Will they tell me who it is, if I go down to them?' asked Soames.

'No, fortunately.'

'How d'you mean "fortunately"?'

'Well, sir, the Press is a sensitive plant. I'm afraid you might make it curl up. Besides, it's always saying nice things that aren't deserved.'

'But this –' began Soames; he stopped in time, and substituted: 'Do you mean that we've got to sit down under it?'

'To lie down, I'm afraid.'

'Fleur has an evening tomorrow.'

'Yes.'

'I shall stay up for it, and keep my eyes open.'

Michael had a vision of his father-in-law, like a plain-clothes man in the neighbourhood of wedding-presents.

But in spite of assumed levity, Michael had been hit. The knowledge that his adored one had the collector's habit, and flitted, alluring, among the profitable, had, so far, caused him only indulgent wonder. But now it seemed more than an amusing foible. The swiftness with which she turned her smile off and on as though controlled by a switch under her shingled hair; the quick turns of her neck, so charming and exposed; the clever roving, disguised so well but not quite well enough, of the pretty eyes; the droop and flutter of their white lids; the expressive hands grasping, if one could so call such slim and dainty apprehensions, her career — all this suddenly caused Michael pain. Still she was doing it for him and Kit! French women, they said, co-operated with their husbands in the family career. It was the French blood in her. Or perhaps just idealism, the desire to have and be the best of whatever bunch there was about! Thus Michael, loyally. But his uneasy eyes roved from face to face of the Wednesday gathering, trying to detect signs of quizzicality.

Soames followed another method. His mind, indeed, was uncomplicated by the currents awash in that of one who goes to bed with the object of his criticism. For him there was no reason why Fleur should not know as many aristocrats, Labour members, painters, ambassadors, young fools, even writing fellows, as might flutter her fancy. The higher up they were, the less likely, he thought with a certain naïveté, they would be to borrow money or get her into a mess. His daughter was as good or better than any of them, and his deep pride was stung to the quick by the notion that people should think she had to claw and scrape to get them round her. It was not she who was after them, but they who were after her! Standing under the Fragonard which he had given her, grizzled, neatly moustached, close-faced, chinny, with a gaze concentrated on nothing in particular, as of one who has looked over much and found little in it, he might have been one of her ambassadors.

A young woman, with red-gold hair, about an inch long on her de-shingled neck, came and stood with her back to him, beside a soft man, who kept washing his hands. Soames could hear every word of their talk.

'Isn't the little Mont amusing? Look at her now, with "Don Fernando" – you'd think he was her only joy. Ah! There's young Bashly! Off she goes. She's a born little snob. But that doesn't make this a "salon", as she thinks. To found a "salon" you want personality, and wit, and the "don't care a damn" spirit. She hasn't got a scrap. Besides, who is she?'

'Money?' said the soft man.

'Not so very much. Michael's such dead nuts on her that he's getting dull; though it's partly Parliament, of course. Have you heard them talk this Foggartism? All food, children, and the future – the very dregs of dullness.'

'Novelty,' purred the soft man, 'is the vice of our age.'

'One resents a nobody like her climbing in on piffle like this Foggartism. Did you read the book?'

'Hardly. Did you?'

'No jolly fear! I'm sorry for Michael. He's being exploited by that little snob.'

Penned without an outlet, Soames had begun breathing hard. Feeling a draught, perhaps, the young woman turned to encounter a pair of eyes so grey, so cold, in a face so concentrated, that she moved away. 'Who was that old buffer?' she asked of the soft man; 'he gave me "the jim-jams." '

The soft man thought it might be a poor relation – he didn't seem to know anybody.

But Soames had already gone across to Michael.

'Who's the young woman with the red hair?'

'Marjorie Ferrar.'

'She's the traitress – turn her out!'

Michael stared.

'But we know her quite well – she's a daughter of Lord Charles Ferrar, and –'

'Turn her out!' said Soames again.

'How do you know that she's the traitress, sir?'

'I've just heard her use the very words of that paragraph, and worse.'

'But she's our guest.'

'Pretty guest!' growled Soames through his teeth.

'One can't turn a guest out. Besides, she is the granddaughter of a marquess and the pet of the Panjoys — it would make the deuce of a scandal.'

'Make it, then!'

'We won't ask her again; but really, that's all one can do.'

'Is it?' said Soames; and walking past his son-in-law, he went towards the object of his denunciation. Michael followed, much perturbed. He had never yet seen his father-in-law with his teeth bared. He arrived in time to hear him say in a low but quite audible voice:

'You were good enough, madam, to call my daughter a snob in her own house.'

Michael saw the de-shingled neck turn and rear, the hard blue eyes stare with a sort of outraged impudence; he heard her laugh, then Soames saying:

'You are a traitress; be so kind as to withdraw.'

Of the half-dozen people round, not a soul was missing it! Oh, hell! And he the master of the house! Stepping forward, he put his arm through that of Soames:

'That'll do, sir,' he said, quietly; 'this is not a Peace Conference.'

There was a horrid hush; and in all the group only the soft man's white hands, washing each other, moved.

Marjorie Ferrar took a step towards the door.

'I don't know who this person is,' she said; 'but he's a liar.'

'I reckon not.'

At the edge of the little group was a dark young man. His eyes were fixed on Marjorie Ferrar's, whose eyes in turn were fixed on his.

And suddenly, Michael saw Fleur, very pale, standing just behind him. She must have heard it all! She smiled, waved her hand, and said:

'Madame Carelli's going to play.'

Marjorie Ferrar walked on towards the door, and the soft man followed her, still washing those hands, as if trying to rid them of the incident. Soames, like a slow dog making sure, walked after them; Michael walked after him. The words 'How amusing!' floated back, and a soft echoing snigger. Slam! Both outer door and incident were closed.

Michael wiped his forehead. One half of the brain behind admired his father-in-law; the other thought: 'Well, the old man *has* gone and done it!' He went back into the drawing-room. Fleur was standing near the clavichord, as if nothing had happened. But Michael could see her fingers crisping at her dress; and his heart felt sore. He waited, quivering, for the last chord.

Soames had gone upstairs. Before 'The White Monkey' in Michael's study, he reviewed his own conduct. He regretted nothing. Red-headed cat! 'Born snob!' 'Money? Not very much.' Ha! 'A nobody like her!' Granddaughter of a marquess, was she? Well, he had shown the insolent baggage the door. All that was sturdy in his fibre, all that was acrid in his blood, all that resented patronage and privilege, the inherited spirit of his forefathers, moved within him. Who were the aristocracy, to give themselves airs? Jackanapes! Half of 'em descendants of those who had got what they had by robbery or jobbery! That one should call his daughter, *his* daughter, a snob! He wouldn't lift a finger, wouldn't cross a road, to meet the Duke of Seven Dials himself! If Fleur liked to amuse herself by having people round her, why shouldn't she? His blood ran suddenly a little cold. Would she say that he had spoiled her 'salon'? Well! He couldn't help it if she did; better to have had the thing out, and got rid of that cat, and know where they all were. 'I shan't wait up for her,' he thought. 'Storm in a tea-cup!'

The thin strumming of the clavichord came up to him out on the landing, waiting to climb to his room. He wondered if these evenings woke the baby. A gruff sound at his feet made him jump. That dog lying outside the baby's door! He wished the little beggar had been downstairs just now – he would have known how to put his teeth through that red-haired cat's nude stockings. He passed on up, looking at Francis Wilmot's door, which was opposite his own.

That young American chap must have overheard something too; but he shouldn't allude to the matter with him; not dignified. And, shutting his door on the strumming of the clavichord, Soames closed his eyes again as best he could.

Chapter Seven

SOUNDS IN THE NIGHT

◄◄·►►

MICHAEL had never heard Fleur cry, and to see her, flung down across the bed, smothering her sobs in the quilt, gave him a feeling akin to panic. She stopped at his touch on her hair, and lay still.

'Buck up, darling!' he said gently. 'If you aren't one, what does it matter?'

She struggled up, and sat cross-legged, her flushed face smudged with tears, her hair disordered.

'Who cares what one is? It's what one's labelled.'

'Well, we've labelled her "Traitress".'

'As if that made it better! We all talk behind people's backs. Who minds that? But how can I go on when everybody is sniggering and thinking me a lion-hunting snob? She'll cry it all over London in revenge. How can I have any more evenings?'

Was it for her career, or his, that she was sorrowing? Michael went round to the other side of the bed and put his arms about her from behind.

'Never mind what people think, my child. Sooner or later one's got to face that, anyway.'

'It's you who aren't facing it. If I'm not thought nice, I can't *be* nice.'

'Only the people who really know one matter.'

'Nobody knows one,' said Fleur sullenly. 'The fonder they are, the less they know, and the less it matters what they think.'

Michael withdrew his arms.

She sat silent for so long that he went back to the other side of the bed to see if he could tell anything from her face resting moodily on her hands. The grace of her body thus cramped was such that his senses ached. And since caresses would only worry her, he ached the more.

'I hate her,' she said at last; 'and if I can hurt her, I will.'

He would have liked to hurt the 'pet of the Panjoys' himself, but it did not console him to hear Fleur utter that sentiment; it meant more from her than from himself, who, when it came to the point, was a poor hand at hurting people.

'Well, darling,' he said, 'shall we sleep on it?'

'I said I wouldn't have any more evenings; but I shall.'

'Good!' said Michael; 'that's the spirit.'

She laughed. It was a funny hard little sound in the night. And with it Michael had to remain discontented.

All through the house it was a wakeful night. Soames had the three o'clock tremors, which cigars and the fresh air wherein he was obliged to play his golf had subdued for some time past. He was disturbed, too, by that confounded great clock from hour to hour, and by a stealthy noise between three and four, as of someone at large in the house.

This was, in fact, Francis Wilmot. Ever since his impulsive denial that Soames was a liar, the young man had been in a peculiar state of mind. As Soames surmised, he too had overheard Marjorie Ferrar slandering her hostess; but in the very moment of his refutation, like Saul setting forth to attack the Christians, he had been smitten by blindness. Those blue eyes, pouring into his the light of defiance, had finished with a gleam which seemed to say: 'Young man, you please me!' And it haunted him. That lissome nymph – with her white skin and red-gold hair, her blue eyes full of insolence, her red lips full of joy, her white neck fragrant as a pinewood in sunshine – the vision was abiding. He had been watching her all through the evening; but it was uncanny the way she had left her image on his senses in that one long moment, so that now he got no sleep. Though he had not been introduced, he knew her name to be

331

Marjorie Ferrar, and he thought it 'fine'. Countryman that he was and with little knowledge of women – she was unlike any woman he had known. And he had given her the lie direct! This made him so restless that he drank the contents of his water-bottle, put on his clothes, and stole downstairs. Passing the Dandie, who stirred as though muttering: 'Unusual! But I know those legs!' he reached the hall, where a milky glimmer came in through the fanlight. Lighting a cigarette, he sat down on the marble coat-sarcophagus. It cooled his anatomy, so that he got off it, turned up the light, saw a telephone directory resting beside him, and mechanically sought the letter 'F'. There she was! 'Ferrar, Marjorie, 3, River Studios, Wren Street.' Switching off the light, he slipped back the door-chain and stole out. He knew his way to the river, and went towards it.

It was the hour when sound, exhausted, has laid its head on the pillow, and one can hear a moth pass. London, in clear air, with no smoke going up, slept beneath the moon. Bridges, towers, water, all silvered, had a look as if withdrawn from man. Even the houses and the trees enjoyed their moony hour apart, and seemed to breathe out with Francis Wilmot a stanza from 'The Ancient Mariner':

> 'O Sleep, it is a gentle thing,
> Beloved from pole to pole!
> To Mary Queen the praise be given,
> She sent the gentle sleep from heaven
> That slid into my soul!'

He turned at random to the right along the river. Never in his life had he walked through a great city at the dead hour. Not a passion alive, nor a thought of gain; haste asleep, and terrors dreaming; here and there, no doubt, one turning on his bed; perhaps a soul passing. Down on the water lighters and barges lay shadowy and abandoned, with red lights burning; the lamps along the Embankment shone without purpose, as if they had been freed. Man was away. In the whole town only himself up and doing – what? Natively shrewd and resourceful in all active situations, the young Southerner had little power of diagnosis, and certainly did not consider himself ridiculous wandering about like this at night, not even when he suddenly felt that if he could 'locate' her windows, he could go home and sleep. He passed the Tate Gallery and saw a human being with moonlit buttons.

'Pardon me, officer,' he said, 'but where is Wren Street?'

'Straight on and fifth to the right.'

Francis Wilmot resumed his march. The 'moving' moon was heeling down, the stars were gaining light, the trees had begun to shiver. He found the fifth turning, walked down 'the block', and was no wiser; it was too dark to read names or numbers. He passed another buttoned human effigy and said:

'Pardon me, officer, but where are River Studios?'

'Comin' away from them; last house on the right.'

Francis Wilmot retraced his steps. There it was, then – by itself, back from the street. He stood before it and gazed at dark windows. She might be behind any one of them! Well! He had 'located' her, and, in the rising wind, he turned and walked home. He went upstairs stealthily as he had come down, past the Dandie, who again raised his head, muttered: 'Still more unusual, but the same legs!' entered his room, lay down, and fell asleep like a baby.

Chapter Eight

ROUND AND ABOUT

◄-►►

GENERAL reticence at breakfast concerning the incident of the night before, made little impression on Soames, because the young American was present, before whom, naturally, one would not discuss it; but he noted that Fleur was pale. In his early-morning vigil legal misgivings had assailed him. Could one call even a red-haired baggage 'traitress' in the hearing of some half-dozen persons with impunity? He went off to his

...

The Silver Spoon

sister Winifred's after breakfast, and told her the whole story.

'Quite right, my dear boy,' was her comment. 'They tell me that young woman is as fast as they're made. Her father, you know, owned the horse that didn't beat the French horse – I never can remember its name – in that race, the Something Stakes, at – dear me! what was the meeting?'

'I know nothing about racing,' said Soames.

But that afternoon at 'The Connoisseurs' Club' a card was brought to him:

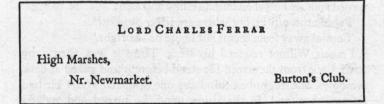

LORD CHARLES FERRAR

High Marshes,
    Nr. Newmarket.   Burton's Club.

For a moment his knees felt a little weak; but the word 'snob' coming to his assistance, he said drily: 'Show him into the strangers' room.' He was not going to hurry himself for this fellow, and finished his tea before repairing to that forlorn corner.

A tallish man was standing in the middle of the little room, thin and upright, with a moustache brushed arrogantly off his lips, and a single eye-glass which seemed to have grown over the right eye, so unaided was it. There were corrugations in his thin weathered cheeks, and in his thick hair flecked at the sides with grey. Soames had no difficulty in disliking him at sight.

'Mr Forsyte, I believe?'

Soames inclined his head.

'You made use of an insulting word to my daughter last night in the presence of several people.'

'Yes; it was richly deserved.'

'You were not drunk, then?'

'Not at all,' said Soames.

334

His dry precision seemed to disconcert the visitor, who twisted his moustache, frowned his eye-glass closer to his eye, and said:

'I have the names of those who overheard it. You will be good enough to write to each of them separately, withdrawing your expression unreservedly.'

'I shall do nothing of the kind.'

A moment's silence ensued.

'You are an attorney, I believe?'

'A solicitor.'

'Then you know the consequences of refusal.'

'If your daughter likes to go into Court, I shall be happy to meet her there.'

'You refuse to withdraw?'

'Absolutely.'

'Good-evening, then!'

'Good-evening!'

For two pins he would have walked round the fellow, the bristles rising on his back, but, instead, he stood a little to one side to let him out. Insolent brute! He could so easily hear again the voice of old Uncle Jolyon, characterizing some person of the eighties as 'a pettifogging little attorney'. And he felt that, some-how or other, he must relieve his mind. 'Old Mont' would know about this fellow – he would go across and ask him.

At 'The Aeroplane' he found not only Sir Lawrence Mont, looking almost grave, but Michael, who had evidently been detailing to his father last evening's incident. This was a relief to Soames, who felt the insults to his daughter too bitterly to talk of them. Describing the visit he had just received, he ended with the words:

'This fellow – Ferrar – what's his standing?'

'Charlie Ferrar? He owes money everywhere, has some useful horses, and is a very good shot.'

'He didn't strike me as a gentleman,' said Soames.

Sir Lawrence cocked his eyebrow, as if debating whether he ought to answer this remark about one who had ancestors, from one who had none.

'And his daughter,' said Soames, 'isn't a lady.'

Sir Lawrence wagged his head.

'Single-minded, Forsyte, single-minded; but you're right; there's a queer streak in that blood. Old Shropshire's a dear old man; it skipped his generation, but it's there. — it's there. His aunt —'

'He called me an attorney,' said Soames with a grim smile, 'and she called me a liar. I don't know which is worse.'

Sir Lawrence got up and looked into St James's Street. Soames had the feeling that the narrow head perched up on that straight thin back counted for more than his own, in this affair. One was dealing here with people who said and did what they liked and damned the consequences; this baronet chap had been brought up in that way himself, no doubt, he ought to know how their minds worked.

Sir Lawrence turned.

'She may bring an action, Forsyte; it was very public. What evidence have you?'

'My own ears.'

Sir Lawrence looked at the ears, as if to gauge their length.

'M'm! Anything else?'

'That paragraph.'

'She'll get at the paper. Yes?'

'The man she was talking to.'

Michael ejaculated: 'Philip Quinsey — put not your trust in Gath!'

'What more?'

'Well,' said Soames, 'there's what that young American overheard, whatever it was.'

'Ah!' said Sir Lawrence: 'Take care she doesn't get at *him*. Is that all?'

Soames nodded. It didn't seem much, now he came to think of it!

'You say she called you a liar. How would it be to take the offensive?'

There was a silence; then Soames said: 'Women? No!'

'Quite right, Forsyte! They have their privileges still. There's

nothing for it but to wait and see how the cat jumps. Traitress!
I suppose you know how much the word costs?'

'The cost,' said Soames, 'is nothing; it's the publicity!'

His imagination was playing streets ahead of him. He saw
himself already in 'the box', retailing the spiteful purring of that
cat, casting forth to the public and the papers the word 'snob', of
his own daughter; for if he didn't, he would have no defence.
Too painful!

'What does Fleur say?' he asked, suddenly, of Michael.

'War to the knife.'

Soames jumped in his chair.

'Ah!' he said: 'That's a woman all over – no imagination!'

'That's what I thought at first, sir, but I'm not so sure. She
says if Marjorie Ferrar is not taken by the short hairs, she'll put
it across everybody – and that the more public the thing is, the
less harm she can do.'

'I think,' said Sir Lawrence, coming back to his chair, 'I'll go
and see old Shropshire. My father and his shot woodcock together in Albania in 'fifty-four.'

Soames could not see the connexion, but did not snub the
proposal. A marquess was a sort of gone-off duke; even in
this democratic age, he would have some influence, one
supposed.

'He's eighty,' went on Sir Lawrence, 'and gets gout in the
stomach, but he's as brisk as a bee.'

Soames could not be sure whether it was a comfort.

'The grass shall not grow, Forsyte. I'll go there now.'

They parted in the street, Sir Lawrence moving north – towards Mayfair.

The Marquess of Shropshire was dictating to his secretary a
letter to his County Council, urging on them an item of his lifelong programme for the electrification of everything. One of the
very first to take up electricity, he had remained faithful to it all
his brisk and optimistic days. A short, bird-like old man, in
shaggy Lovat tweeds, with a blue tie of knitted silk passed
through a ring, bright cheeks and well-trimmed white beard
and moustache, he was standing in his favourite attitude, with

one foot on a chair, his elbow on his knee, and his chin on his hand.

'Ah! young Mont!' he said: 'Sit down.'

Sir Lawrence took a chair, crossed his knees, and threaded his finger-tips. He found it pleasing to be called 'young Mont', at sixty-six or so.

'Have you brought me another of your excellent books?'

'No, Marquess; I've come for your advice.'

'Ah! Go on, Mr Mersey: "In this way, gentlemen, you will save at least three thousand a year to your ratepayers; confer a blessing on the countryside by abolishing the smoke of four filthy chimneys; and make me your obliged servant,

"SHROPSHIRE."

Thank you, Mr Mersey. Now, my dear young Mont?'

Having watched the back of the secretary till it vanished, and noted the old peer pivoting his bright eyes, with their expression of one who means to see more every day, on his visitor, Sir Lawrence took his eyeglass between thumb and finger, and said:

'Your granddaughter, sir, and my daughter-in-law want to fight like billy-o.'

'Marjorie?' said the old man, and his head fell to one side like a bird's. 'I draw the line – a charming young woman to look at, but I draw the line. What has she done now?'

'Called my daughter-in-law a snob and a lion-hunter; and my daughter-in-law's father has called your granddaughter a traitress to her face.'

'Bold man,' said the marquess; 'bold man! Who is he?'

'His name is Forsyte.'

'Forsyte?' repeated the old peer; 'Forsyte? The name's familiar – now where would that be? Ah! Forsyte and Treffry – the big tea men. My father had his tea from them direct – real caravan; no such tea now. Is that the – ?'

'Some relation, perhaps. This man is a solicitor – retired; chiefly renowned from his pictures. A man of some substance, and probity.'

'Indeed! And is his daughter a – a lion-hunter?'

Sir Lawrence smiled.

'She's a charmer. Likes to have people about her. Very pretty. Excellent little mother; some French blood.'

'Ah!' said the marquess: 'the French! Better built round the middle than our people. What do you want me to do?'

'Speak to your son Charles.'

The old man took his foot off the chair, and stood nearly upright. His head moved sideways with a slight continuous motion.

'I never speak to Charlie,' he said gravely. 'We haven't spoken for six years.'

'I beg your pardon, sir. Didn't know. Sorry to have bothered you.'

'No, no; pleasure to see you. If I run across Marjorie, I'll see – I'll see. But, my dear Mont, what shall we do with these young women – no sense of service; no continuity; no hair; no figures? By the way, do you know this Power Scheme on the Severn?' He held up a pamphlet: 'I've been at them to do it for years. My colliery among others could be made to pay with electricity; but they won't move. We want some Americans over here.'

Sir Lawrence had risen; the old man's sense of service had so clearly taken the bit between its teeth again. He held out his hand.

'Good-bye, Marquess; delighted to see you looking so well.'

'Good-bye, my dear young Mont; command me at any time, and let me have another of your nice books.'

They shook hands; and from the Lovat clothes was disengaged a strong whiff of peat. Sir Lawrence, looking back, saw the old man back in his favourite attitude, foot on chair and chin on hand, already reading the pamphlet. 'Some boy!' he thought; 'as Michael would say. But what has Charlie Ferrar done not to be spoken to for six years? Old Forsyte ought to know . . . .'

In the meantime 'Old Forsyte' and Michael were walking homewards across St James's Park.

'That young American,' said Soames; 'What do you suppose made him put his oar in?'

'I don't know, sir; and I don't like to ask.'

'Exactly,' said Soames, glumly. There was, indeed something repulsive to him in treating with an American over a matter of personal dignity.

'Do they use the word "snob" over there?'

'I'm not sure; but, in the States to hunt lions is a form of idealism. They want to associate with what they think better than themselves. It's rather fine.'

Soames did not agree; but found difficulty in explaining why. Not to recognize anyone as better than himself or his daughter had been a sort of guiding principle, and guiding principles were not talked about. In fact, it was so deep in him that he hadn't known of it.

'I shan't mention it,' he said, 'unless he does. What more can this young woman do? She's in a set, I suppose?'

'The Panjoys –'

'Panjoys!'

'Yes, sir; out for a good time at any cost – they don't really count, of course. But Marjorie Ferrar is frightfully in the lime-light. She paints a bit; she's got some standing with the Press; she dances; she hunts; she's something of an actress; she goes everywhere week-ending. It's the week-ends that matter, where people have nothing to do but talk. Were you ever at a week-end party, sir?'

'I?' said Soames: 'Good Lord – no!'

Michael smiled – incongruity, indeed, could go no farther. 'We must get one up for you at Lippinghall.'

'No, thank you.'

'You're right, sir; nothing more boring. But they're the *coulisses* of politics. Fleur thinks they're good for me. And Marjorie Ferrar knows all the people we know, and lots more. It *is* awkward.'

'I should go on as if nothing had happened,' said Soames: 'But about that paper? They ought to be warned that this woman is venomous.'

Michael regarded his father-in-law quizzically.

On entering, they found the manservant in the hall.

'There's a man to see you, sir, by the name of Bugfill.'

'Oh | Ah | Where have you put him, Coaker?'

'Well, I didn't know what to make of him, sir, he shakes all over. I've stood him in the dining-room.'

'Excuse me, sir,' said Michael.

Soames passed into the 'parlour', where he found his daughter and Francis Wilmot.

'Mr Wilmot is leaving us, Father. You're just in time to say good-bye.'

If there were moments when Soames felt cordial, they were such as these. He had nothing against the young man; indeed, he rather liked the look of him; but to see the last of almost anybody was in a sense a relief; besides, there was this question of what he had overheard, and to have him about the place without knowing would be a continual temptation to compromise with one's dignity and ask him what it was.

'Good-bye, Mr Wilmot,' he said; 'if you're interested in pictures –' he paused, and holding out his hand, added, 'you should look in at the British Museum.'

Francis Wilmot shook the hand deferentially.

'I will. It's been a privilege to know you, sir.'

Soames was wondering why, when the young man turned to Fleur.

'I'll be writing to Jon from Paris, and I'll surely send your love. You've been perfectly wonderful to me. I'll be glad to have you and Michael visit me at any time you come across to the States; and if you bring the little dog, why – I'll just be honoured to let him bite me again.'

He bowed over Fleur's hand, and was gone, leaving Soames staring at the back of his daughter's neck.

'That's rather sudden,' he said, when the door was closed; 'anything upset him?'

She turned on him, and said coldly:

'Why did you make that fuss last night, Father?'

The injustice of her attack was so palpable, that Soames bit his moustache in silence. As if he could help himself, when she was insulted in his hearing!

'What good do you think you've done?'

Soames, who had no notion, made no attempt to enlighten her. He only felt sore inside.

'You've made me feel as if I couldn't look anybody in the face. But I'm going to, all the same. If I'm a lion-hunter and a snob, I'll do it thoroughly. Only I do wish you wouldn't go on thinking I'm a child and can't defend myself.'

And still Soames was silent, sore to the soles of his boots.

Fleur flashed a look at him, and said:

'I'm sorry, but I can't help it; everything's queered;' and she went out of the room.

Soames moved blindly to the window and stood looking out. He saw a cab with luggage drive away; saw some pigeons alight, peck at the pavement, and fly off again; he saw a man kissing a woman in the dusk; a policeman light his pipe and go off duty. He saw many human and interesting things; he heard Big Ben chime. Nothing in it all! He was staring at a silver spoon. He himself had put it in her mouth at birth.

Chapter Nine

POULTRY AND CATS

◄◄─►►

HE who had been stood in the dining-room, under the name of Bugfill, was still upright. Rather older than Michael, with an inclination to side-whisker, darkish hair, and a pale face stamped with that look of schooled quickness common to so many actors but unfamiliar to Michael, he was grasping the edge of the dining-table with one hand, and a wide-brimmed black hat with the other. The expression of his large, dark-circled eyes was such that Michael smiled and said:

'It's all right, Mr Bergfeld, I'm not a manager. Do sit down, and smoke.'

The visitor silently took the proffered chair and cigarette with an attempt at a fixed smile. Michael sat on the table.

'I gather from Mrs Bergfeld that you're on the rocks.'

'Fast,' said the shaking lips.

'Your health, and your name, I suppose?'

'Yes.'

'You want an open-air job, I believe? I haven't been able to think of anything very gaudy, but an idea did strike me last night in the stilly watches. How about raising poultry – everybody's doing it.'

'If I had my savings.'

'Yes, Mrs Bergfeld told me about them. I can inquire but I'm afraid –'

'It's robbery.' The chattered sound let Michael at once into the confidence of the many managers who had refused to employ him who uttered it.

'I know,' he said, soothingly, 'robbing Peter to pay Paul. That clause in the Treaty was a bit of rank barbarism, of course, camouflage it as they like. Still, it's no good to let it prey on your mind, is it?'

But his visitor had risen. 'To take from civilian to pay civilian! Then why not take civilian life for civilian life? What is the difference? And England does it – the leading nation to respect the individual. It is abominable.'

Michael began to feel that he was overdoing it.

'You forget,' he said, 'that the war made us all into barbarians, for the time being; we haven't quite got over it yet. And *your* country dropped the spark into the powder magazine, you know. But what about this poultry stunt?'

Bergfeld seemed to make a violent effort to control himself.

'For my wife's sake,' he said, 'I will do anything; but unless I get my savings back, how can I start?'

'I can't promise; but perhaps I could start you. That hairdresser below you wants an open-air job, too. What's his name, by the way?'

343

'Swain.'

'How do you get on with him?'

'He is an opinionated man, but we are good friends enough.'

Michael got off the table. 'Well, leave it to me to think it out. We shall be able to do something, I hope;' and he held out his hand.

Bergfeld took it silently, and his eyes resumed the expression with which they had first looked at Michael.

'That man,' thought Michael, 'will be committing suicide some day, if he doesn't look out.' And he showed him to the door. He stood there some minutes gazing after the German actor's vanishing form with a feeling as if the dusk were formed out of the dark stories of such as he and the hairdresser and the man who had whispered to him to stand and deliver a job. Well, Bart must lend him that bit of land beyond the coppice at Lippinghall. He would buy a war hut if there were any left and some poultry stock, and start a colony – the Bergfelds, the hairdresser, and Henry Boddick. They could cut the timber in the coppice, and put up the fowl-houses for themselves. It would be growing food – a practical experiment in Foggartism! Fleur would laugh at him. But was there anything one could do nowadays that somebody couldn't laugh at? He turned back into the house. Fleur was in the hall.

'Francis Wilmot has gone,' she said.

'Why?'

'He's off to Paris.'

'What was it he overheard last night?'

'Do you suppose I asked?'

'Well no,' said Michael, humbly. 'Let's go up and look at Kit, it's about his bath time.'

The eleventh baronet, indeed, was already in his bath.

'All right, nurse,' said Fleur, 'I'll finish him.'

'He's been in three minutes, ma'am.'

'Lightly boiled,' said Michael.

For one aged only fourteen months this naked infant had incredible vigour – from lips to feet he was all sound and motion. He seemed to lend a meaning to life. His vitality was absolute, not relative. His kicks and crows and splashings had the joy of a gnat's dance, or a jackdaw's gambols in the air. He gave thanks not for what he was about to receive, but for what he was receiving. White as a turtle-dove, with pink toes, darker in eyes and hair than he would be presently, he grabbed at the soap, at his mother, at the bath-towelling – he seemed only to need a tail. Michael watched him, musing. This manikin, born with all that he could possibly wish for within his reach – how were they to bring him up? Were they fit to bring him up, they who had been born – like all their generation in the richer classes – emancipated, to parents properly broken-in to worship the fetish – Liberty? Born to everything they wanted, so that they were at wits' end to invent something they could not get; driven to restive searching by having their own way? The war had deprived one of one's own way, but the war had over-done it, and left one grasping at licence. And for those, like Fleur, born a little late for the war, the tale of it had only low-ered what respect they could have for anything. With veneration killed, and self-denial 'off', with atavism buried, sentiment de-rided, and the future in the air, hardly a wonder that modernity should be a dance of gnats, taking itself damned seriously! Such were the reflections of Michael, sitting there above the steam, and frowning at his progeny. Without faith was one fit to be a parent? Well, people were looking for faith again. Only they were bound to hatch the egg of it so hard that it would be addled long before it was a chicken. 'Too self-conscious!' he thought. 'That's our trouble!'

Fleur had finished drying the eleventh baronet, and was dab-bing powder over him; her eyes seemed penetrating his skin, as if to gauge the state of health behind it. He watched her take the feet and hands one by one and examine each nail, lost in her scrutiny, unselfconscious in her momentary devotion! And oppressed by the difficulty, as a Member of Parliament, of being devoted, Michael snapped his fingers at the baby and left the nursery. He went to his study and took down a volume of the Encyclopaedia Britannica containing the word Poultry. He read about Leghorns, Orpingtons. White Sussex, Bramaputras, and was little the wiser. He remembered that if you drew a chalk-line to the beak of a hen, the hen thought it was tied up. He wished somebody would draw a chalk-line to his beak. Was Foggartism a chalk-line? A voice said:

'Tell Fleur I'm going to her aunt's.'

'Leaving us, sir?'

'Yes, I'm not wanted.'

What had happened?

'You'll see her before you go, sir?'

'No,' said Soames.

Had somebody rubbed out the chalk-line to Old Forsyte's nose?

'Is there any money in poultry-farming, sir?'

'There's no money in anything nowadays.'

'And yet the Income Tax returns continue to rise.'

'Yes,' said Soames; 'there's something wrong there.'

'You don't think people make their incomes out more than they are?'

Soames blinked. Pessimistic though he felt at the moment, he could not take quite that low view of human nature.

'You'd better see that Fleur doesn't go about abusing that red-haired baggage,' he said. 'She was born with a silver spoon in her mouth; she thinks she can do what she likes.' And he shut Michael in again.

Silver spoon in her mouth. How *à propos!* ...

After putting her baby into its cot Fleur had gone to the marqueterie bureau in the little sanctuary that would have been called a boudoir in old days. She sat there brooding. How could her father have made it all glaringly public! Couldn't he have seen that it was nothing so long as it was not public, but everything the moment it was? She longed to pour out her heart, and tell people her opinion of Marjorie Ferrar.

She wrote three letters — one to Lady Alison, and two to women in the group who had overheard it all last night. She concluded her third letter with the words: 'A woman like that, who pretends to be a friend and sneaks into one's house to sting one behind one's back is a snake of the first water. How Society can stick her, I can't think; she hasn't a moral about her nor a decent impulse. As for her charm — Good Lord!' Yes! And there was Francis Wilmot! She had not said all she wanted to say to him.

MY DEAR FRANCIS, she wrote:

I am so sorry you have to run away like this. I wanted to thank you for standing up for me last night. Marjorie Ferrar is just about the limit. But in London society one doesn't pay attention to back-biting. It has been so jolly to know you. Don't forget us; and do come and see me again when you come back from Paris.

Your very good friend,
FLEUR MONT.

In future she would have nothing but men at her evenings! But would they come if there were no women? And men like Philip Quinsey were just as snake-like. Besides, it would look as if she were really hurt. No! She would have to go on as before, just dropping people who were 'catty'. But who wasn't? Except Alison, and heavyweights like Mr Blythe, the minor Ambassadors, and three or four earnest politicians, she couldn't be sure about any of them. It was the thing to be 'catty'. They all scratched other people's backs, and their faces too when they weren't looking. Who in Society was exempt from scratches and who didn't scratch? Not to scratch a little was so dreadfully dull. She could not imagine a scratchless life except perhaps in Italy. Those Fra Angelico frescoes in the San Marco monastery! There was a man who did not scratch. St Francis talking to his birds, among his little flowers, with the sun and the moon and the stars for near relations. St Claire! St Fleur — little sister of St Francis! To be unworldly and quite good! To be one who lived to make other people happy! How new! How exciting, even — for about a week; and how dull afterwards! She drew aside the curtains and looked out into the Square. Two cats were standing in the light of a lamp — narrow, marvellously graceful, with their heads turned towards each other. Suddenly they began uttering horrible noises, and became all claws. Fleur dropped the curtain.

347

Chapter Ten

FRANCIS WILMOT REVERSES

─◄─►─

ABOUT that moment Francis Wilmot sat down in the lounge of the Cosmopolis Hotel, and as suddenly sat up. In the middle of the parquet floor, sliding and lunging, backing and filling, twisting and turning in the arms of a man with a face like a mask, was she, to avoid whom, out of loyalty to Fleur and Michael, he had decided to go to Paris. Fate! For he could hardly know that she came there most afternoons during the dancing hours. She and her partner were easily the show couple; and, fond of dancing, Francis Wilmot knew he was looking at something special. When they stopped, quite close to him, he said in his soft drawl:

'That was beautiful.'

'How do you do, Mr Wilmot?'

Why! She knew his name! This was the moment to exhibit loyalty! But she had sunk into a chair next his.

'And so you thought me a traitress last night?'

'I did.'

'Why?'

'Because I heard you call your hostess a snob.'

Marjorie Ferrar uttered an amused sound.

'My dear young man, if one never called one's friends anything worse than that — ! I didn't mean you to hear, or that poptious old person in the chin!'

'He was her father,' said Francis Wilmot, gravely. 'It hurt him.'

'Well! I'm sorry!'

A hand without a glove, warm but dry, was put into his. When it was withdrawn the whole of his hand and arm were tingling.

'Do you dance?'

348

'Yes, indeed, but I wouldn't presume to dance with you.'

'Oh! but you must.'

Francis Wilmot's head went round, and his body began going round too.

'You dance better than an Englishman, unless he's professional,' said her lips six inches from his own.

'I'm proud to hear you say so, ma'am.'

'Don't you know my name? or do you always call women ma'am? It's ever so pretty.'

'Certainly I know your name and where you live. I wasn't six yards from you this morning at four o'clock.'

'What were you doing there?'

'I just thought I'd like to be near you.'

Marjorie Ferrar said, as if to herself:

'The prettiest speech I ever heard. Come and have tea with me there to-morrow.'

Reversing, side-stepping, doing all he knew, Francis Wilmot said, slowly:

'I have to be in Paris.'

'Don't be afraid, I won't hurt you.'

'I'm not afraid, but —'

'Well, I shall expect you.' And transferring herself again to her mask-faced partner, she looked back at him over her shoulder.

Francis Wilmot wiped his brow. An astonishing experience, another blow to his preconception of a stiff and formal race! If he had not known she was the daughter of a lord, he would have thought her an American. Would she ask him to dance with her again? But she left the lounge without another glance.

An up-to-date young man, a typical young man, would have felt the more jaunty. But he was neither. Six months' training for the Air Service in 1918, one visit to New York and a few trips to Charleston and Savannah, had left him still a countryman, with a tradition of good manners, work, and simple living. Women, of whom he had known few, were to him worthy of considerable respect. He judged them by his sister, or by the friends of his dead mother, in Savannah, who were all of a

349

certain age. A Northern lady on the boat had told him that Southern girls measured life by the number of men they could attract; she had given him an amusing take-off of a Southern girl. It had been a surprise to this young Southerner. Anne was not like that; she had never had the chance to be, anyway, having married at nineteen the first young man who had asked her!

By the morning's post he received Fleur's little letter. 'Limit!' Limit of what? He felt indignant. He did not go to Paris, and at four o'clock he was at Wren Street.

In her studio Marjorie Ferrar, clad in a flax-blue overall, was scraping at a picture with a little knife. An hour later he was her slave. Cruft's Dog Show, the Beefeaters, the Derby — he could not even remember his desire to see them; he only desired to see one English thing — Marjorie Ferrar. He hardly remembered which way the river flowed, and by mere accident walked East instead of West. Her hair, her eyes, her voice — he 'had fallen for her!' He knew himself for a fool, and did not mind; farther man cannot go. She passed him in a little open car, driving it herself, on her way to a rehearsal. She waved her hand. Blood rushed to his heart and rushed away; he trembled and went pale. And, as the car vanished, he felt lost, as if in a world of shadow, grey and dreary! Ah! There was Parliament! And, near-by, the one spot in London where he could go and talk of Marjorie Ferrar, and that was where she had misbehaved herself! He itched to defend her from the charge of being 'the limit'. He could perceive the inappropriateness of going back there to talk to Fleur of her enemy, but anything was better than not talking of her. So, turning into South Square, he rang the bell.

Fleur was in her 'parlour', if not precisely eating bread and honey, at least having tea.

'Not in Paris? How nice! Tea?'

'I've had it,' said Francis Wilmot, colouring. 'I had it with *her.*'

Fleur stared.

'Oh!' she said, with a laugh. 'How interesting! Where did she pick you up?'

Without taking in the implication of the words, Francis Wilmot was conscious of something deadly in them.

'She was at the *thé dansant* at my hotel yesterday. She's a wonderful dancer. I think she's a wonderful person altogether; I'd like to have you tell me what you mean by calling her "the limit"?'

'I'd like to have you tell me why this *volte face* since Wednesday night?'

Francis Wilmot smiled: 'You people have been ever so kind to me, and I want you to be friends with her again. I'm sure she didn't mean what she said that night.'

'Indeed! Did she tell you that?'

'Why – not exactly! She said she didn't mean us to hear them.'

'No?'

He looked at her smiling face, conscious perhaps of deep waters, but youthfully, Americanly, unconscious of serious obstacle to his desire to smooth things out.

'I just hate to think you two are out after each other. Won't you come and meet her at my hotel, and shake hands?'

Fleur's eyes moved slowly over him from head to toe.

'You look as if you might have some French blood in you. Have you?'

'Yes. My grandmother was of French stock.'

'Well, I have more. The French, you know, don't forgive easily. And they don't persuade themselves into believing what they want to.'

Francis Wilmot rose, and spoke with a kind of masterfulness.

'You're going to tell me what you meant in your letter.'

'Am I? My dear young man, the limit of perfection, of course. Aren't you a living proof?'

Aware that he was being mocked, and mixed in his feelings, Francis Wilmot made for the door.

'Good-bye!' he said. 'I suppose you'll have no use for me in future.'

'Good-bye!' said Fleur.

He went out rueful, puzzled, lonelier even than when he

went in. He was guideless, with no one to 'put him wise' ! No directness and simplicity in this town. People did not say what they meant; and his goddess – as enigmatic and twisting as the rest ! More so – more so – for what did the rest matter?

Chapter Eleven

SOAMES VISITS THE PRESS

◄◄·►►

SOAMES had gone off to his sister's in Green Street thoroughly upset. That Fleur should have a declared enemy, powerful in Society, filled him with uneasiness; that she should hold him accountable for it, seemed the more unjust, because, in fact, he was.

An evening spent under the calming influence of Winifred Dartie's common sense, and Turkish coffee, which, though 'liverish stuff', he always drank with relish, restored in him something of the feeling that it was a storm in a tea-cup.

'But that paper paragraph,' he said, 'sticks in my gizzard.'

'Very tiresome, Soames, the whole thing; but I shouldn't bother. People skim those 'chiff-chaff' little notes and forget them the next moment. They're just put in for fun.'

'Pretty sort of fun ! That paper says it has a million readers.'

'There's no name mentioned.'

'These political people and whipper-snappers in Society all know each other,' said Soames.

'Yes, my dear boy,' said Winifred in her comfortable voice, so cosy, and above disturbance, 'but nobody takes anything seriously nowadays.'

She was sensible. He went up to bed in more cheerful mood.

But retirement from affairs had effected in Soames a deeper change than he was at all aware of. Lacking professional issues to anchor the faculty for worrying he had inherited from James Forsyte, he was inclined to pet any trouble that came along. The more he thought of that paragraph, the more he felt inclined for a friendly talk with the editor. If he could go to Fleur and say: 'I've made it all right with those fellows, anyway. There'll be no more of that sort of thing', he would wipe out her vexation. If you couldn't make people in private think well of your daughter, you could surely check public expression of the opposite opinion.

Except that he did not like to get into them, Soames took on the whole a favourable view of 'the papers'. He read *The Times;* his father had read it before him, and he had been brought up on its crackle. It had news – more news for his money than he could get through. He respected its leading articles; and if its great supplements had at times appeared to him too much of a good thing, still it was a gentleman's paper. Annette and Winifred took the *Morning Post*. That also was a gentleman's paper, but it had bees in its bonnet. Bees in bonnets were respectable things, but personally Soames did not care for them. He knew little of the other papers except that those he saw about had bigger headlines and seemed cut into little bits. Of the Press as a whole he took the English view: It was an institution. It had its virtues and its vices – anyway, you had to put up with it.

About eleven o'clock he was walking towards Fleet Street.

At the office of the *Evening Sun* he handed in his card and asked to see the editor. After a moment's inspection of his top-hat, he was taken down a corridor and deposited in a small room. It seemed a 'wandering great place'. Someone would see him, they said.

'Someone?'said Soames. 'I want the editor.'

The editor was very busy; could he come again when the rush was over?'

'No,' said Soames.

Would he state his business? Soames wouldn't.

The attendant again looked at his top-hat and went away.

Soames waited a quarter of an hour, and was then taken to an even smaller room, where a cheery-looking man in eye-glasses was turning over a book of filed cuttings. He glanced up as Soames entered, took his card from the table, and read from it:

'Mr Soames Forsyte? Yes?'

'Are you the editor?' asked Soames.

'One of them. Take a seat. What can I do for you?'

Impressed by a certain speed in the air, and desirous of making a good impression, Soames did not sit down, but took from his pocket-book the paragraph.

'I've come about this in your issue of last Thursday.'

The cheery man put it up to his eyes, seemed to chew the sense of it a little with his mouth, and said: 'Yes?'

'Would you kindly tell me who wrote it?'

'We never disclose the names of correspondents, sir.'

'Well, as a matter of fact, I know.'

The cheery man's mouth opened, as if to emit the words: 'Then why did you ask?' but closed in a smile instead.

'You'll forgive me,' said Soames; 'it quite clearly refers to my daughter, Mrs Michael Mont, and her husband.'

'Indeed! You have the advantage of me; but what's the matter with it? Seems rather a harmless piece of gossip.'

Soames looked at him. He was too cheery!

'You think so?' he said dryly. 'May I ask if you would like to have your daughter alluded to as an enterprising little lady?'

'Why not? It's quite a pleasant word. Besides, there's no name mentioned.'

'Do you put things in,' asked Soames shrewdly, 'in order that they may be Greek to all your readers?'

The cheery man laughed: 'Well,' he said, 'hardly. But really, sir, aren't you rather thin-skinned?'

This was an aspect of the affair that Soames had not foreseen. Before he could ask this editor chap not to repeat his offence, he had apparently to convince him that it *was* an offence; but to do that he must expose the real meaning of the paragraph.

'Well,' he said, 'if you can't see that the tone of the thing's unpleasant, I can't make you. But I beg you won't let any more such paragraphs appear. I happen to know that your correspondent is actuated by malevolence.'

The cheery man again ran his eye over the cutting.

'I shouldn't have judged that. People in politics are taking and giving knocks all the time – they're not mealy-mouthed. This seems perfectly innocuous as gossip goes.'

Thus back-handed by the words 'thin-skinned' and 'mealy-mouthed', Soames said testily:

'The whole thing's extremely petty.'

'Well, sir, you know, I rather agree. Good-morning!' and the cheery man blandly returned to his file.

The fellow was like an india-rubber ball! Soames clenched his top-hat. Now or never he must make him bound.

'If your correspondent thinks she can vent her spleen in print with impunity, she will find herself very much mistaken.' He waited for the effect. There was absolutely none. 'Good-morning!'' he said, and turned on his heel.

Somehow it had not been so friendly as he had expected. Michael's words 'The Press is a sensitive plant' came into his mind. He shouldn't mention his visit.

Two days later, picking up the *Evening Sun* at The Connoisseurs, he saw the word 'Foggartism'. H'm! A leader!

'Of the panaceas rife among the young hopefuls in politics, perhaps the most absurd is one which goes by the name of Foggartism. We are in a position to explain the nature of this patent remedy for what is supposed to be the national ill-health before it has been put on the market. Based on Sir James Foggart's book, *The Parlous State of England,* the main article of faith in this crazy creed would appear to be the depletion of British man-power. According to its prophets, we are to dispatch to the ends of the Empire hundreds of thousands of our boys and girls as soon as they leave school. Quite apart from the rank impossibility of absorbing them into the life of the slowly developing Dominions, we are to lose this vital stream of labour and defensive material, in order that twenty years hence the demand from our Dominions may equal the supplying power of Great Britain. A crazier proposition was never conceived in woolly brains. Well does the word Foggartism characterize such a proposition. Alongside this emigration 'stunt' – for there is no other term which suits its sensational character – rises a feeble back-to-the-land propaganda. The keystone of the whole professes to be the doctrine that the standard of British wages and living now preclude us from any attempt to rival German production, or to recover our trade with Europe. Such a turning of the tail on our industrial supremacy has probably never before been mooted in this country. The sooner these cheap-jack gerrymanders of British policy realize that the British voter will have nothing to do with so crack-brained a scheme, the sooner it will come to the still birth which is its inevitable fate.'

Whatever attention Soames had given to *The Parlous State of England*, he could not be accused of anything so rash as a faith in Foggartism. If Foggartism were killed to-morrow, he, with his inherent distrust of theories and ideas, his truly English pragmatism, could not help feeling that Michael would be well rid of a white elephant. What disquieted him, however, was the suspicion that he himself had inspired this article. Was this that too-cheery fellow's retort?

Decidedly, he should not mention his visit when he dined in South Square that evening.

The presence of a strange hat on the sarcophagus warned him of a fourth party. Mr Blythe, in fact, with a cocktail in his hand and an olive in his mouth, was talking to Fleur, who was curled up on a cushion by the fire.

'You know Mr Blythe, Dad?'

Another editor! Soames extended his hand with caution.

Mr Blythe swallowed the olive. 'It's of no importance;' he said.

'Well,' said Fleur, 'I think you ought to put it all off, and let them feel they've made fools of themselves.'

'Does Michael think that, Mrs Mont?'

'No; Michael's got his shirt out!' And they all looked round at Michael, who was coming in.

He certainly had a somewhat headstrong air.

According to Michael, they must take it by the short hairs and give as good as they got, or they might as well put up the shutters. They were sent to Parliament to hold their own opinions, not those stuck into them by Fleet Street. If they genuinely believed the Foggart policy to be the only way to cure unemployment, and stem the steady drain into the towns, they must say so, and not be stampeded by every little newspaper attack that came along. Common sense was on their side, and common sense, if you aired it enough, won through in the end. The opposition to Foggartism was really based on an intention to force lower wages and longer hours on Labour, only they daren't say so in so many words. Let the papers jump through their hoops as much as they liked. He would bet that when Foggartism had been six months before the public, they would be eating half their words with an air of eating someone else's! And suddenly he turned to Soames:

'I suppose, sir, you didn't go down about that paragraph?'

Soames, privately, and as a business man, had always so conducted himself that, if cornered, he need never tell a direct untruth. Lies were not English, not even good form. Looking down his nose, he said slowly:

'Well, I let them know that I knew that woman's name.'

Fleur frowned; Mr Blythe reached out and took some salted almonds.

'What did I tell you, sir?' said Michael. 'They always get back on you. The Press has a tremendous sense of dignity; and corns on both feet; eh, Mr Blythe?'

Mr Blythe said weightily: 'It's a very human institution, young man. It prefers to criticize rather than to be criticized.'

'I thought,' said Fleur icily, 'that I was to be left to my own cudgels.'

The discussion broke back to Foggartism, but Soames sat brooding. He would never again interfere in what didn't concern himself. Then, like all who love, he perceived the bitterness of his fate. He had only meddled with what *did* concern himself – her name, her happiness; and she resented it. Basket in which were all his eggs, to the end of his days he must go on walking gingerly, balancing her so that she was not upset, spilling his only treasure.

She left them over the wine that only Mr Blythe was drinking. Soames heard an odd word now and then, gathered that this great frog-chap was going to burst next week in *The Out-post*, gathered that Michael was to get on to his hind legs in the House at the first opportunity. It was all a muzz of words to him. When they rose, he said to Michael:

'I'll take myself off.'

'We're going down to the House, sir: won't you stay with Fleur?'

'No,' said Soames; 'I must be getting back.'

Michael looked at him closely.

'I'll just tell her you're going.'

Soames had wrapped himself into his coat, and was opening the door when he smelled violet soap. A bare arm had come round his neck. He felt soft pressure against his back. 'Sorry, Dad, for being such a pig.'

Soames shook his head.

'No,' said her voice; 'you're not going like that.'

She slipped between him and the door. Her clear eye looked into his; her teeth gleamed, very white. 'Say you forgive me!'

'There's no end to it,' said Soames.

She thrust her lips against his nose. 'There! Good-night, ducky! I know I'm spoiled!'

Soames gave her body a convulsive little squeeze, opened the door and went out without a word.

Under Big Ben boys were calling – political news, he sup-posed. Those Labour chaps were going to fall – some editor had got them into trouble. He would! Well – one down, t'other come on! It was all remote to him. She alone – she alone mat-tered.

Chapter Twelve

MICHAEL MUSES

➤➤➤

MICHAEL and Mr Blythe sought the Mother of Parliaments and found her in commotion. Liberalism had refused, and' Labour was falling from its back. A considerable number of people were in Parliament Square contemplating Big Ben and hoping for sensation.

'I'm not going in,' said Michael. 'There won't be a division tonight. General Election's a foregone conclusion, now. I want to think.'

'One will go up for a bit,' said·Mr Blythe; and they parted, Michael returning to the streets. The night was clear, and he had a longing to hear the voice of his country. But – where? For his countrymen would be discussing this pro and that con, would be mentioning each his personal 'grief' – here the Income Tax, there the dole, the names of leaders, the word Communism. Nowhere would he catch the echo of the uneasiness in the hearts of all. The Tories – as Fleur had predicted – would come in now. The country would catch at the anodyne of 'strong stable government'. But could strong stable government remove the inherent canker, the lack of balance in the top-heavy realm? Could it still the gnawing ache which everybody felt, and nobody would express?

'Spoiled,' thought Michael, 'by our past prosperity. We shall never admit it,' he thought, 'never I And yet in our bones we feel it I'

England with the silver spoon in her mouth and no longer the teeth to hold it there, or the will to part with it I And her very qualities – the latent 'grit', the power to take things smiling, the lack of nerves and imagination I Almost vices, now, perpetuating the rash belief that England could still 'muddle through' without special effort, although with every year there was less chance of recovering from shock, less time in which to exercise the British 'virtues'. 'Slow in the uptak',' thought Michael, 'it's a ghastly fault in 1924.'

Thus musing, he turned East. Mid-theatre-hour, and the 'Great Parasite' – as Sir James Foggart called it – was lying inert and bright. He walked the length of wakeful Fleet Street into the City so delirious by day, so dead by night. Here England's wealth was snoozing off the day's debauch. Here were all the frame and filaments of English credit. And based on – what? On food and raw material from which England, undefended in the air, might be cut off by a fresh war; on Labour, too big for European boots. And yet that credit stood high still, soothing all with its 'panache' – save, perhaps, receivers of the dole. With her promise to pay, England could still purchase anything, except a quiet heart.

And Michael walked on – through Whitechapel, busy still and coloured – into Mile End. The houses had become low, as if to give the dwellers a better view of stars they couldn't reach. He had crossed a frontier. Here was a different race almost; another England, but as happy-go-lucky and as hand-to-mouth as the England of Fleet Street and the City. Aye, and more! For the England in Mile End knew that whatever she felt could have no effect on policy. Mile on mile, without an end, the low grey streets stretched towards the ultimate deserted grass. Michael did not follow them, but coming to a cinema, turned in.

The show was far advanced. Bound and seated in front of the bad cowboy on a bronco, the heroine was crossing what Michael shrewdly suspected to be the film company's pet paddock. Every ten seconds she gave way to John T. Bronson, manager of the Tucsonville Copper Mine, devouring the road in his 60-h.p. Packard, to cut her off before she reached the Pima river. Michael contemplated his fellow gazers. Lapping it up! Strong stable government – not much! This was their anodyne and they could not have enough of it. He saw the bronco fall, dropped by a shot from John T. Bronson, and the screen disclose the words: 'Hairy Pete grows desperate. ...' 'You shall not have her, Bronson.' Quite! He was throwing her into the river

instead, to the words: 'John T. Bronson dives.' There he goes!
He has her by her flowing hair! But Hairy Pete is kneeling on
the bank. The bullets chip the water. Through the heroine's fair
perforated shoulder the landscape is almost visible. What is that
sound? Yes! John T. Bronson is setting his teeth! He lands,
he drags her out. From his cap he takes his automatic. Still dry
– thank God!

'Look to yourself, Hairy Pete!' A puff of smoke. Pete squirms
and bites the sand – he seems almost to absorb the desert. 'Hairy
Pete gets it for keeps!' Slow music, slower! John T. Bronson
raises the reviving form. Upon the bank of the Pima river they
stand embraced, and the sun sets. 'At last, my dinky love!'

'Pom, pom! that's the stuff!' thought Michael, returning to
the light of night: 'Back to the Land! "Plough the fields and
scatter" – when they can get this? Not much!' And he turned
West again, taking a seat on the top of a bus beside a man with
grease-stains on his clothes. They travelled in silence till Michael
said:

'What do you make of the political situation, sir?'

The possible plumber replied, without turning his head:

'I should say they've over-reached theirselves.'

'Ought to have fought on Russia – oughtn't they?'

'Russia – that cock won't fight either. No – ought to 'ave 'eld
on to the Spring, an' fought on a good stiff Budget.'

'Real class issue?'

'Yus!'

'But do you think class politics can wipe out unemployment?'

The man's mouth moved under his moustache as if mumbl-
ing a new idea.

'Ah! I'm fed up with politics; in work to-day and out tomorrow – what's the good of politics that can't give you a permanent job?'

'That's it.'

'Reparations,' said his neighbour; *'we're* not goin' to benefit
by reparations. The workin' classes ought to stand together in
every country.' And he looked at Michael to see how he liked
that.

'A good many people thought so before the war; and see what happened.'

'Ah!' said the man, 'and what good's it done us?'

'Have you thought of emigrating to the Dominions?'

The man shook his head.

'Don't like what I see of the Austrylians and Canydians.'

'Confirmed Englishman – like myself.'

'That's right,' said the man. 'So long, Mister,' and he got off.

Michael travelled till the bus put him down under Big Ben, and it was nearly twelve. Another election! Could he stand a second time without showing his true colours? Not the faintest hope of making Foggartism clear to a rural constituency in three weeks! If he spoke from now till the day of the election, they would merely think he held rather extreme views on Imperial Preference, which, by the way, he did. He could never tell the electorate that he thought England was on the wrong tack – one might just as well not stand. He could never buttonhole the ordinary voter, and say to him: 'Look here, you know, there's no earthly hope of any real improvement for another ten years; in the meantime we must face the music, and pay more for everything, so that twenty years hence we may be safe from possible starvation, and self-supporting within the Empire.' It wasn't done. Nor could he say to his Committee: 'My friends, I represent a policy that no one else does, so far.'

No! If he meant to stand again, he must just get the old wheezes off his chest. But did he mean to stand again? Few people had less conceit than Michael – he knew himself for a lightweight. But he had got this bee into his bonnet; the longer he lived the more it buzzed, the more its buzz seemed the voice of one crying in the wilderness, and that wilderness his country. To stop up that buzzing in his ears; to turn his back on old Blythe; to stifle his convictions, and yet remain in Parliament – he could not! It was like the war over again. Once in, you couldn't get out. And he was 'in' – committed to something deeper far than the top dressings of Party politics. Foggartism had a definite solution of England's troubles to work towards – an independent, balanced Empire; an England safe in the air, and free from unemployment – with Town and Country once more in some sort of due proportion! Was it such a hopeless dream? Apparently!

'Well,' thought Michael, putting his latch-key in his door, 'they may call me what kind of a bee fool they like – I shan't budge.' He went up to his dressing-room and, opening the window, leaned out.

The rumourous town still hummed; the sky was faintly coloured by reflection from its million lights. A spire was visible, some stars; the tree foliage in the Square hung flat, unstirred by wind. Peaceful and almost warm – the night. Michael remembered a certain evening – the last London air-raid of the war. From his convalescent hospital he had watched it for three hours.

'What fools we all are not to drop fighting in the air,' he thought. 'Well, if we don't, I shall go all out for a great air force – all hangs, for us, on safety from air attack. Even the wise can understand that.'

Two men had stopped beneath his window, talking. One was his next-door neighbour.

'Mark my words,' said his neighbour, 'the election'll see a big turnover.'

'Yes; and what are you going to do with it?' said the other.

'Let things alone; they'll right themselves. I'm sick of all this depressing twaddle. A shilling off the Income Tax, and you'll see.'

'How are you going to deal with the Land?'

'Oh! damn the Land! Leave it to itself, that's all the farmers really want. The more you touch it, the worse it gets.'

'Let the grass grow under your feet?'

The neighbour laughed. 'That's about it. Well, what else *can* you do – the Country won't have it. Good night!'

Sounds of a door, of footsteps. A car drove by; a moth flew in Michael's face. 'The Country won't have it!' Policies! What but mental yawns, long shrugs of the shoulders, trusting to Luck! What else could they be? *The Country wouldn't have it!* And Big Ben struck twelve.

Chapter Thirteen

INCEPTION OF THE CASE

◄-◄-►►

THERE are people in every human hive born to focus talk; perhaps their magnetism draws the human tongue, or their lives are lived at an acute angle. Of such was Marjorie Ferrar – one of the most talked-of young women in London. Whatever happened to her was rumoured at once in that collection of the busy and the idle called Society. That she had been ejected from a drawing-room was swiftly known. Fleur's letters about her became current gossip. The reasons for ejectment varied from truth to a legend that she had lifted Michael from the arms of his wife.

The origins of lawsuits are seldom simple. And when Soames called it all 'a storm in a tea-cup', he might have been right if Lord Charles Ferrar had not been so heavily in debt that he had withdrawn his daughter's allowance; if, too, a Member for a Scottish borough, Sir Alexander MacGown, had not for some time past been pursuing her with the idea of marriage. Wealth made out of jute, a rising Parliamentary repute, powerful phys-ique, and a determined character, had not advanced Sir Alex-ander's claims in twelve months so much as the withdrawal of her allowance advanced them in a single night. Marjorie Ferrar was, indeed, of those who can always get money at a pinch, but even to such come moments when they have seriously to con-sider what kind of pinch. In proportion to her age and sex, she was 'dipped' as badly as her father, and the withdrawal of her allowance was in the nature of a last straw. In a moment of dis-couragement she consented to an engagement, not yet to be made public. When the incident at Fleur's came to Sir Alexan-der's ears, he went to his betrothed flaming. What could he do?

'Nothing, of course; don't be silly, Alec! Who cares?'

'The thing's monstrous. Let me go and exact an apology from this old blackguard.'

364

'Father's been, and he wouldn't give it. He's got a chin you could hang a kettle on.'

'Now, look here, Marjorie, you've got to make our engagement public, and let me get to work on him. I won't have this story going about.'

Marjorie Ferrar shook her head.

'Oh! no, my dear. You're still on probation. I don't care a tuppeny ice about the story.'

'Well, I do, and I'm going to that fellow to-morrow.'

Marjorie Ferrar studied his face – its brown, burning eyes, its black, stiff hair, its jaw – shivered slightly, and had a brain-wave.

'You will do nothing of the kind, Alec, or you'll spill your ink. My father wants me to bring an action. He says I shall get swinging damages.'

The Scotsman in MacGown applauded, the lover quailed.

'That may be very unpleasant for you,' he muttered, 'unless the brute settles out of Court.'

'Of course he'll settle. I've got all his evidence in my vanity-bag.'

MacGown gripped her by the shoulders and gave her a fierce kiss.

'If he doesn't, I'll break every bone in his body.'

'My dear! He's nearly seventy, I should think.'

'H'm! Isn't there a young man in the same boat with him?'

'Michael? Oh! Michael's a dear. I couldn't have his bones broken.'

'Indeed!' said MacGown. 'Wait till he launches this precious Foggartism they talk of – dreary rot! I'll eat him!'

'Poor little Michael!'

'I heard something about an American boy, too.'

'Oh!' said Marjorie Ferrar, releasing herself from his grip. 'A bird of passage – don't bother about him.'

'Have you got a lawyer?'

'Not yet.'

'I'll send you mine. He'll make them sit up!'

She remained pensive after he had left her, distrusting her

own brain-wave. If only she weren't so hard up! She had learned during this month of secret engagement that 'Nothing for nothing and only fair value for sixpence' ruled North of the Tweed as well as South. He had taken a good many kisses and given her one trinket which she dared not take to 'her Uncle's'. It began to look as if she would have to marry him. The prospect was in some ways not repulsive – he was emphatically a man; her father would take care that she only married him on terms as liberal as his politics; and perhaps her motto 'Live dangerously' could be even better carried out with him than without. Resting inert in a long chair, she thought of Francis Wilmot. Hopeless as husband, he might be charming as lover, naïve, fresh, unknown in London, absurdly devoted, oddly attractive, with his lithe form, dark eyes, engaging smile. Too old-fashioned for words, he had made it clear already that he wanted to marry her. He was a baby. But until she was beyond his reach, she had begun to feel that he was beyond hers. After? Well, who knew? She lived in advance, dangerously, with Francis Wilmot. In the meantime this action for slander was a bore! and shaking the idea out of her head, she ordered her horse, changed her clothes, and repaired to the Row. After that she again changed her clothes, went to the Cosmopolis Hotel, and danced with her mask-faced partner and Francis Wilmot. After that she changed her clothes once more, went to a first night, partook of supper afterwards with the principal actor and his party, and was in bed by two o'clock.

Like most reputations, that of Marjorie Ferrar received more than its deserts. If you avow a creed of indulgence, you will be indulged by the credulous. In truth she had only had two love-affairs passing the limits of decorum; had smoked opium once, and been sick over it; and had sniffed cocaine just to see what it was like. She gambled only with discretion, and chiefly on race-horses; drank with strict moderation and a good head; smoked of course, but the purest cigarettes she could get, and through a holder. If she had learned suggestive forms of dancing, she danced them but once in a blue moon. She rarely rode at a five-bar gate, and that only on horses whose powers she knew.

To be in the know she read, of course, anything 'extreme', but would not go out of her way to do so. She had flown, but just to Paris. She drove a car well, and of course fast, but never to the danger of herself, and seldom to the real danger of the public. She had splendid health, and took care of it in private. She could always sleep at ten minutes' notice, and when she sat up half the night, slept half the day. She was 'in' with the advanced theatre, but took it as it came. Her book of poems, which had received praise because they emanated from one of a class supposed to be unpoetic, was remarkable not so much for irregularity of thought as for irregularity of metre. She was, in sum, credited with a too strict observance of her expressed creed: 'Take life in both hands, and eat it.'

This was why Sir Alexander MacGown's lawyer sat on the edge of his chair in her studio the following morning, and gazed at her intently. He knew her renown better than Sir Alexander. Messrs Settlewhite and Stark liked to be on the right side of a matter before they took it up. How far would this young lady, with her very attractive appearance and her fast reputation, stand fire? For costs – they had Sir Alexander's guarantee and the word 'traitress' was a good enough beginning; but in cases of word against word, it was ill predicting.

Her physiognomy impressed Mr Settlewhite favourably. She would not 'get rattled' in Court, if he was any judge; nor had she the Aubrey Beardsley cast of feature he had been afraid of, that might alienate a jury. No! an upstanding young woman with a good blue eye and popular hair. She would do, if her story were all right.

Marjorie Ferrar, in turn, scrutinized one who looked as if he might take things out of her hands. Long-faced, with grey deep eyes under long dark lashes, all his hair, and good clothes, he was as well preserved a man of sixty as she had ever seen.

'What do you want me to tell you, Mr Settlewhite?'

'The truth.'

'Oh! but naturally. Well, I was just saying to Mr Quinsey that Mrs Mont was very eager to form a "salon", and had none of the right qualities, and the old person who overheard me thought I was insulting her –'

'That all?'

'Well, I may have said she was fond of lions; and so she is.'

'Yes; but why did he call you a traitress?'

'Because she was his daughter and my hostess, I suppose.'

'Will this Mr Quinsey confirm you?'

'Philip Quinsey? – oh! rather! He's in my pocket.'

'Did anybody else overhear you running her down?'

She hesitated a second. 'No.'

'First lie!' thought Mr Settlewhite, with his peculiar sweet-sarcastic smile. 'What about an American?'

Marjorie Ferrar laughed. 'He won't say so, anyway.'

'An admirer?'

'No. He's going back to America.'

'Second lie!' thought Mr Settlewhite. 'But she tells them well.'

'You want an apology you can show to those who overheard the insult; and what we can get, I suppose?'

'Yes. The more the better.'

'Speaking the truth there,' thought Mr Settlewhite. 'Are you hard up?'

'Couldn't well be harder.'

Mr Settlewhite put one hand on each knee, and reared his slim body.

'You don't want it to come into Court?'

'No; though I suppose it might be rather fun.'

Mr Settlewhite smiled again.

'That entirely depends on how many skeletons you have in your cupboard.'

Marjorie Ferrar also smiled.

'I shall put everything in your hands,' she said.

'Not the skeletons, my dear young lady. Well, we'll serve him and see how the cat jumps; but he's a man of means and a lawyer.'

'I think he'll hate having anything about his daughter brought out in Court.'

'Yes,' said Mr Settlewhite, drily. 'So should I.'

'And she *is* a little snob, you know.'

'Ah! Did you happen to use that word?'

'N-no; I'm pretty sure I didn't.'

'Third lie!' thought Mr Settlewhite: 'not so well told.'

'It makes a difference. Quite sure?'

'Not quite.'

'He says you did?'

'Well, I told him he was a liar.'

'Oh! did you? And they heard you?'

'Rather!'

'That may be important.'

'I don't believe he'll say I called her a snob, in Court, anyway.'

'That's very shrewd, Miss Ferrar,' said Mr Settlewhite. 'I think we shall do.'

And with a final look at her from under his long lashes, he stalked, thin and contained, to the door.

Three days later Soames received a legal letter. It demanded a formal apology, and concluded with the words 'failing it, action will be taken'. Twice in his life he had brought actions himself; once for breach of contract, once for divorce; and now to be sued for slander! In every case he had been the injured party, in his own opinion. He was certainly not going to apologize. Under the direct threat he felt much calmer. He had nothing to be ashamed of. He would call that 'baggage' a traitress to her face again to-morrow, and pay for the luxury, if need be. His mind roved back to when, in the early 'eighties, as a very young lawyer, he had handled his Uncle Swithin's defence against a fellow member of the Walpole Club. Swithin had called him in public 'a little touting whipper-snapper of a parson'. He remembered how he had whittled the charge down to the word 'whipper-snapper', by proving the plaintiff's height to be five feet four, his profession the church, his habit the collection of money for the purpose of small-clothing the Fiji islanders. The jury had assessed 'whipper-snapper' at ten pounds — Soames always believed the small clothes had done it. His Counsel had made great game of them — Bobstay, Q.C. There *were* Counsel in those days; the Q.C.'s had been better than the K.C.'s were. Bobstay would have gone clean through this 'baggage' and come out on the other side. Uncle Swithin had asked him to dinner afterwards and given him York ham with Madeira sauce, and his special Heidsieck. He had never given anybody anything else. Well! There must still be cross-examiners who could tear a reputation to tatters, especially if there wasn't one to tear. And one could always settle at the last moment if one wished. There was no possibility anyway of Fleur being dragged in as witness or anything of that sort.

He was thunder-struck, a week later, when Michael rang him up at Mapledurham to say that Fleur had been served with a writ for libel in letters containing among others the expression 'a snake of the first water' and 'she hasn't a moral about her.'

Soames went cold all over. 'I told you not to let her go about abusing that woman.'

'I know; but she doesn't consult me every time she writes a letter to a friend.'

'Pretty friend!' said Soames into the mouthpiece. 'This is a nice pair of shoes!'

'Yes, sir; I'm very worried. She's absolutely spoiling for a fight — won't hear of an apology.'

Soames grunted so deeply that Michael's ear tingled forty miles away.

'In the meantime, what shall we do?'

'Leave it to me,' said Soames. 'I'll come up tonight. Has she any evidence to support those words?'

'Well, she says —'

'No,' said Soames, abruptly, 'don't tell me over the phone.' And he rang off. He went out on to the lawn. Women! Petted and spoiled — thought they could say what they liked! And so they could till they came up against another woman. He stopped by the boat-house and gazed at the river. The water was nice and clean, and there it was — flowing down to London to get all dirty! That feverish, quarrelsome business up there! Now he would have to set to and rake up all he could against this Ferrar woman, and frighten her off. It was distasteful. But nothing else for it, if Fleur was to be kept out of Court! Terribly petty. Society lawsuits — who ever got anything out of them, save heart-burning and degradation? Like the war, you might win and regret it ever afterwards, or lose and regret it more. All temper! Jealousy and temper!

In the quiet autumn light, with the savour of smoke in his nostrils from his gardener's first leaf bonfire, Soames felt moral. Here was his son-in-law, wanting to do some useful work in Parliament, and make a name for the baby, and Fleur beginning to settle down and take a position; and now this had come along, and all the chatterers and busy mockers in Society would be gnashing on them with their teeth — if they had any! He looked at his shadow on the bank, grotesquely slanting towards the water as if wanting to drink. Everything was grotesque, if it came to that! In Society, England, Europe — shadows scrimmaging and sprawling, scuffling and posturing; the world just marking time before another Flood! H'm! He moved towards the river. There went his shadow, plunging in before him! They would all plunge into that mess of cold water if they didn't stop their squabblings. And, turning abruptly, he entered his kitchen-garden. Nothing unreal there, and most things running to seed — stalks, and so on! How to set about raking up the past of this young woman? Where was it? These young sparks and fly-by-nights! They all had pasts, no doubt; but the definite, the concrete bit of immorality alone was of use, and when it came to the point, was unobtainable, he shouldn't wonder. People didn't like giving chapter and verse! It was risky, and not the thing! Tales out of school!

And, among his artichokes, approving of those who did not tell tales, disapproving of anyone who wanted them told, Soames resolved grimly that told they must be. The leaf-fire smouldered, and the artichokes smelled rank, the sun went down behind the high brick wall mellowed by fifty years of weather; all was peaceful and chilly, except in his heart. Often now, morning or evening, he would walk among his vegetables — they were real and restful, and you could eat them. They had better flavour than the greengrocer's and saved his bill —

middle-men's profiteering and all that. Perhaps they represented atavistic instincts in this great grandson of 'Superior Dosset's' father, last of a long line of Forsyte 'agriculturists'. He set more and more store by vegetables the older he grew. When Fleur was a little bit of a thing, he would find her when he came back from the City, seated among the sunflowers or blackcurrants, nursing her doll. He had once taken a bee out of her hair, and the little brute had stung him. Best years he ever had, before she grew up and took to this gadabout Society business, associating with women who went behind her back. Apology! So she wouldn't hear of one? She was in the right. But to be in the right and have to go into Court because of it, was one of the most painful experiences that could be undergone. The Courts existed to penalize people who were in the right – in divorce, breach of promise, libel and the rest of it. Those who were in the wrong went to the South of France, or if they did appear, defaulted afterwards and left you to pay your costs. Had he not himself had to pay them in his action against Bosinney? And in his divorce suit had not young Jolyon and Irene been in Italy when he brought it? And yet, he couldn't bear to think of Fleur eating humble-pie to that red-haired cat. Among the gathering shadows, his resolve hardened. Secure evidence that would frighten the baggage into dropping the whole thing like a hot potato – it was the only way!

Chapter Fourteen

FURTHER CONSIDERATION

⧏⧏⧐⧐

THE Government had 'taken their toss' over the Editor – no one could say precisely why – and Michael sat down to compose his address. How say enough without saying anything? And having impetuously written: 'Electors of mid-Bucks', he remained for many moments still as a man who has had too good a dinner. 'If' he traced words slowly – 'if you again return me as your representative, I shall do my best for the country according to my lights. I consider the limitations of armaments, and, failing that, the security of Britain through the enlargement of our air defences; the development of home agriculture; the elimination of unemployment through increased emigration to the Dominions; and the improvement of the national health particularly through the abatement of slums and smoke, to be the most pressing and immediate concerns of British policy. If I am returned, I shall endeavour to foster these ends with determination and coherence; and try not to abuse those whose opinions differ from my own. At my meetings I shall seek to give you some concrete idea of what is in my mind, and submit myself to your questioning.'

Dare he leave it at that? Could one issue an address containing no disparagement of the other side, no panegyric of his own? Would his Committee allow it? Would the electors swallow it? Well, if his Committee didn't like it – they could turn it down, and himself with it; only – they wouldn't have time to get another candidate!

The Committee, indeed, did not like it, but they lumped it; and the address went out with an effigy on it of Michael, looking, as he said, like a hairdresser. Thereon he plunged into a fray, which like every other, began in the general and ended in the particular.

During the first Sunday lull at Lippinghall, he developed his poultry scheme – by marking out sites, and deciding how water could be laid on. The bailiff was sulky. In his view it was throwing away money. 'Fellers like that!' Who was going to teach them the job? He had not time, himself. It would run into hundreds, and might just as well be poured down the gutter. 'The townsman's no mortal use on the land, Master Michael.'

'So everybody says. But, look here, Tutfield, here are three "down and outs", two of them ex-Service, and you've got to help me put this through. You say yourself this land's all right for poultry – well, it's doing no good now. Bowman knows every last thing about chickens, set him on to it until these chaps get the hang. Be a good fellow and put your heart into it; you wouldn't like being "down and out" yourself.'

The bailiff had a weakness for Michael, whom he had known from his bottle up. He knew the result, but if Master Michael liked to throw his father's money away, it was no business of his. He even went so far as to mention that he knew 'a feller' who had a hut for sale not ten miles away; and that there was 'plenty of wood in the copse for the cuttin'.'

On the Tuesday after the Government had fallen Michael went up to town and summoned a meeting of his 'down and outs'. They came at three the following day, and he placed them in chairs round the dining-table. Standing under the Goya, like a general about to detail a plan of attack which others would have to execute, he developed his proposal. The three faces expressed little, and that without conviction. Only Bergfeld had known anything of it, before, and his face was the most doubting.

'I don't know in the least,' went on Michael, 'what you think of it; but you all want jobs – two of you out of doors, and you, Boddick, don't mind what it is, I think.'

'That's right, sir,' said Boddick, 'I'm on.'

Michael instantly put him down as the best man of the three.

The other two were silent till Bergfeld said:

'If I had my savings –'

Michael interrupted quickly:

'I'm putting in the capital; you three put in the brains and labour. It's probably not more than a bare living, but I hope it'll be a healthy one. What do *you* say, Mr Swain?'

The hairdresser, more shadow-stricken than ever, in the glow of Fleur's Spanish room, smiled.

'I'm sure it's very kind of you. I don't mind havin' a try – only, who's goin' to boss the show?'

'Co-operation, Mr Swain.'

'Ah!' said the hairdresser; 'thought so. But I've seen a lot of tries at that, and it always ends in one bloke swallerin' the rest.'

'Very well,' said Michael, suddenly, 'I'll boss it. But if any of you crane at the job, say so at once, and have done with it. Otherwise I'll get that hut delivered and set up, and we'll start this day month.'

Boddick got up, and said: 'Right, sir. What about my children?'

'How old, Boddick?'

'Two little girls, four and five.'

'Oh! yes!' Michael had forgotten this item. 'We must see about that.'

Boddick touched his forelock, shook Michael's hand, went out. The other two remained standing.

'Good-bye, Mr Bergfeld; good-bye, Mr Swain!'

'If I might –'

'Could I speak to you for a minute?'

'Anything you have to say,' said Michael, astutely, 'had better be said in each other's presence.'

'I've always been used to hair.'

'Pity,' though Michael, 'that Life didn't drop that "h" for him – poor beggar!' 'Well, we'll get you a breed of birds that can be shingled,' he said. The hairdresser smiled down one side of his face. 'Beggars can't be choosers,' he remarked.

'*I* wished to ask you,' said Bergfeld, 'what system we shall adopt?'

'That's got to be worked out. Here are two books on poultry-keeping; you'd better read one each, and swop.'

He noted that Bergfeld took both without remonstrance on the part of Swain.

Seeing them out into the Square, he thought: 'Rum team! It won't work, but they've got their chance.'

A young man who had been standing on the pavement came forward.

'Mr Michael Mont, M.P.?'

'Yes.'

'Mrs Michael Mont at home?'

'I think so. What do you want?'

'I must see her personally, please.'

'Who are you from?'

'Messrs Settlewhite and Stark – a suit.'

375

'Dressmakers?'

The young man smiled.

'Come in,' said Michael. 'I'll see if she's at home.'

Fleur was in the 'parlour'.

'A young man from some dressmaker's for you, dear.'

'Mrs Michael Mont? In the suit of Ferrar against Mont – libel. Good-day, madam.'

Between those hours of four and eight, when Soames arrived from Mapledurham, Michael suffered more than Fleur. To sit and see a legal operation performed on her with all the scientific skill of the British Bar, it was an appalling prospect; and there would be no satisfaction in Marjorie Ferrar's also being on the table, with her inside exposed to the gaze of all! He was only disconcerted, therefore, when Fleur said:

'All right; if she wants to be opened up, she shall be. I know she flew to Paris with Walter Nazing last November; and I've always been told she was Bertie Curfew's mistress for a year.'

A Society case – cream for all the cats in Society, muck for all the blowflies in the streets – and Fleur the hub of it! He waited for Soames with impatience. Though 'Old Forsyte's' indignation had started this, Michael turned to him now, as to an anchor let go off a lee shore. The 'old man' had experience, judgement and a chin; he would know what, except bearing it with a grin, could be done. Gazing at a square foot of study wall which had escaped a framed caricature, he reflected on the underlying savagery of life. He would be eating a lobster tonight that had been slowly boiled alive! This study had been cleaned out by a charwoman whose mother was dying of cancer, whose son had lost a leg in the war, and who looked so jolly tired that he felt quite bad whenever he thought of her. The Bergfelds, Swains and Boddicks of the world – the Camden Towns, and Mile Ends – the devastated regions of France, the rock villages of Italy! Over it all what a thin crust of gentility! Members of Parliament and ladies of fashion, like himself and Fleur, simpering and sucking silver spoons, and now and then dropping spoons and simper, and going for each other like Kilkenny cats!

'What evidence has she got to support those words?' Michael

racked his memory. This was going to be a game of bluff. That Walter Nazing and Marjorie Ferrar had flown to Paris together appeared to him of next to no importance. People could still fly in couples with impunity; and as to what had happened afterwards in the great rabbit-warren Outre Manche – Pff! The Bertie Curfew affair was different. Smoke of a year's duration probably had fire behind it. He knew Bertie Curfew, the enterprising director of the 'Ne Plus Ultra Play Society', whose device was a stork swallowing a frog – a long young man, with long young hair that shone and was brushed back, and a long young record; a strange mixture of enthusiasm and contempt, from one to the other of which he passed with extreme suddenness. His sister, of whom he always spoke as 'Poor Norah', in Michael's opinion was worth ten of him. She ran a Children's House in Bethnal Green, and had eyes from which meanness and evil shrank away.

Big Ben thumped out eight strokes; the Dandie barked, and Michael knew that Soames had come.

Very silent during dinner, Soames opened the discussion over a bottle of Lippinghall Madeira by asking to see the writ.

When Fleur had brought it, he seemed to go into a trance.

'The old boy,' thought Michael, 'is thinking of his past. Wish he'd come to!'

'Well, Father?' said Fleur at last.

As if from long scrutiny of a ghostly Court of Justice, Soames turned his eyes on his daughter's face.

'You won't eat your words, I suppose?'

Fleur tossed her now de-shingled head. 'Do you want me to?'

'Can you substantiate them? You mustn't rely on what was told you – that isn't evidence.'

'I know that Amabel Nazing came here and said that she didn't mind Walter flying to Paris with Marjorie Ferrar, but that she did object to not having been told beforehand, so that she herself could have flown to Paris with somebody else.'

'We could subpoena that young woman,' said Soames.

Fleur shook her head. 'She'd never give Walter away in Court.'

'H'm! What else about this Miss Ferrar?'

'Everybody knows of her relationship with Bertie Curfew.'

'Yes,' Michael put in, 'and between "everybody knows" and "somebody tells" is a great gap fixed.'

Soames nodded.

'She just wants money out of us,' cried Fleur; 'she's always hard up. As if she cared whether people thought her moral or not! She despises morality – all her set do.'

'Ah! Her view of morality!' said Soames, deeply; he was suddenly seeing a British jury confronted by a barrister describing the modern view of morals: 'No need, perhaps, to go into personal details.'

Michael started up.

'By Jove, sir, you've hit it! If you can get her to admit that she's read certain books, seen or acted in certain plays, danced certain dances, worn certain clothes –' He fell back again into his chair; what if the other side started asking Fleur the same questions? Was it not the fashion to keep abreast of certain things, however moral one might really be? Who could stand up and profess to be shocked, today?'

'Well?' said Soames.

'Only that one's own point of view isn't quite a British jury's, sir. Even yours and ours, I expect, don't precisely tally.'

Soames looked at his daughter. He understood. Loose talk – afraid of being out of the fashion – evil communication corrupting all profession of good manners! Still, no jury could look at her face without – who could resist the sudden raising of those white lids? Besides, she was a mother, and the older woman wasn't; or if she was – she shouldn't be! No, he held to his idea. A clever fellow at the Bar could turn the whole thing into an indictment of the fast set and modern morality, and save all the invidiousness of exposing a woman's private life.

'You give me the names of her set and those books and plays and dancing clubs and things,' he said. 'I'll have the best man at the Bar.'

Michael rose from the little conference somewhat eased in mind. If the matter could be shifted from the particular to the general; if, instead of attacking Marjorie Ferrar's practice, the defence could attack her theory, it would not be so dreadful. Soames took him apart in the hall.

'I shall want all the information I can get about that young man and her.'

Michael's face fell.

'You can't get it from me, sir, I haven't got it.'

'She must be frightened,' said Soames. 'If I can frighten her, I can probably settle it out of Court without an apology.'

'I see; use the information out of Court, but not in.'

Soames nodded. 'I shall tell them that we shall justify. Give me the young man's address.'

'Macbeth Chambers, Bloomsbury. It's close to the British Museum. But do remember, sir, that to air Miss Ferrar's linen in Court will be as bad for us as for her.'

Again Soames nodded.

When Fleur and her father had gone up, Michael lit a cigarette, and passed back into the 'parlour'. He sat down at the clavichord. The instrument made very little noise – so he could strum on it without fear of waking the eleventh baronet. From a Spanish tune picked up three years ago on his honeymoon, whose savagery always soothed him, his fingers wandered on: 'I got a crown, you got a crown – all God's childern got a crown! Eb'ryone dat talk 'bout 'Eaben ain't goin' dere. All God's childern got a crown.'

Glass lustres on the wall gleamed out at him. As a child he had loved the colours of his aunt Pamela's glass chandeliers in the panelled rooms at Brook Street; but when he knew what was what, he and everyone had laughed at them. And now lustres had come in again; and Aunt Pamela had gone out! 'She had a crown – he had a crown –' Confound that tune! *'Auprès de ma blonde – il fait bon – fait bon – fait bon; Auprès de ma blonde, il fait bon dormir.'*

His 'blonde' – not so very blonde, either – would be in bed by now. Time to go up! But still he strummed on, and his mind wandered in and out – of poultry and politics, Old Forsyte, Fleur, Foggartism, and the Ferrar girl – like a man in a maelstrom whirling round with his head just above water. Who was it said the landing-place for modernity was a change of heart; the rebirth of a belief that life was worth while, and better life attainable? 'Better life?' Prerogative of priests? Not now. Humanity had got to save itself! To save itself — what was that, after all, but expression of 'the will to live'? But did humanity will to live as much as it used? That was the point. Michael stopped strumming and listened to the silence. Not even a clock ticking — time was inhospitable in 'parlours'; and England asleep outside. Was the English 'will to live' as strong as ever; or had they all become so spoiled, so sensitive to life, that they had weakened on it? Had they sucked their silver spoon so long that, threatened with a spoon of bone, they preferred to get down from table? 'I don't believe it,' thought Michael, 'I won't believe it. Only where are we going? Where am I going? Where are all God's children going? To bed, it seemed!

And Big Ben struck: One.

PART TWO

Chapter One

MICHAEL MAKES HIS SPEECH

◄─◄─►─►

WHEN in the new Parliament Michael rose to deliver his
maiden effort towards the close of the debate on the King's
Speech, he had some notes in his hand and not an idea in his
head. His heart was beating and his knees felt weak. The policy
he was charged to express, if not precisely new in concept, was
in reach and method so much beyond current opinion that he
awaited nothing but laughter. His would be a stray wind carrying the seed of a new herb into a garden, so serried and so full
that no corner would welcome its growth. There was a plant
called Chinese weed which having got hold never let go, and
spread till it covered everything. Michael desired for Foggartism the career of Chinese weed; but all he expected was the like
of what he had seen at Monterey on his tour round the world
after the war. Chance had once brought to that Californian
shore the seeds of the Japanese yew. In thick formation the little
dark trees had fought their way inland to a distance of some
miles. That battalion would never get farther now that native
vegetation had been consciously roused against it; but its thicket
stood – a curious and strong invader.

His first period had been so rehearsed that neither vacant
mind nor dry mouth could quite prevent delivery. Straightening
his waistcoat and jerking his head back, he regretted that the
speech from the throne foreshadowed no coherent and substantial policy such as might hope to free the country from its
present plague of under-employment and over-population. Econ-
omically speaking, any foreseeing interpretation of the course of
affairs must now place Britain definitely in the orbit of the overseas world.... ('Oh! oh!') Ironical laughter so soon and sudden

cleared Michael's mind and relaxed his lips; and, with the grin that gave his face a certain charm, he resumed:

Speakers on all sides of the House, dwelling on the grave nature of the Unemployment problem, had pinned their faith to the full recapture of European trade, some in one way, some in another. August as they were, he wished very humbly to remark that they could not eat cake and have it. (*Laughter.*) Did they contend that wages in Britain must come down and working hours be lengthened; or did they assert that European wages must go up, and European working hours be shortened? No, they had not had the temerity. Britain, which was to rid itself of unemployment in the ways suggested, was the only important country in the world which had to buy about seven-tenths of its food, and of whose population well-nigh six-sevenths lived in towns. It employed those six-sevenths in producing articles in some cases too dearly for European countries to buy, and yet it had to sell a sufficient surplus above the normal exchanges of trade to pay for seven-tenths of the wherewithal to keep its producers alive. (*A laugh.*) If this was a joke, it was a grim one. (*A voice: 'You have forgotten the carrying trade.'*) He accepted the honourable Member's correction, and hoped that he felt happy about the future of that trade. It was, he feared, a somewhat shrinking asset.

At this moment in his speech Michael himself became a somewhat shrinking asset, overwhelmed by a sudden desire to drop Foggartism and sit down. The cool attention, the faint smiles, the expression on the face of a past Prime Minister, seemed conspiring towards his subsidence. 'How young – oh! how young you are!' they seemed to say. 'We sat here before you were breeched.' And he agreed with them completely. Still there was nothing for it but to go on – with Fleur in the Ladies' Gallery, old Blythe in the Distinguished Strangers'; yes, and something stubborn in his heart! Clenching the notes in his hand, therefore, he proceeded:

In spite of the war, and because of the war, the population of their island had increased by 2,000,000. Emigration had fallen from over 200,000 to 100,000. And this state of things was to be remedied by the mere process of recapturing to the full European trade which, quite obviously, had no intention of being so recaptured. What alternative, then, was there? Some honourable Members, he was afraid not many, would be familiar with the treatise of Sir James Foggart, entitled *The Parlous State of England*. ('*Hear, hear!*' *from a back Labour bench*). He remembered to have read in a certain organ, or perhaps he should say harmonium, of the Press, for it was not a very deep-voiced instrument – (*laughter*) – that no such crack-brained policy had ever been devised for British consumption. ('*Hear, hear!*') Certainly Foggartism was mad enough to look ahead, to be fundamental, and to ask the country to face its own position and the music into the bargain. ...

About to go over 'the top' – with public confession of his faith trembling behind his lips – Michael was choked by the sudden thought: 'Is it all right – is it what I think, or am I an ignorant fool?' He swallowed vigorously, and staring straight before him, went on:

'Foggartism deprecates surface measures for a people in our position; it asks the country to fix its mind on a date – say twenty years hence – a minute in a nation's life – and to work steadily and coherently up to that date. It demands recognition of the need to make the British Empire, with its immense resources mostly latent, a self-sufficing unit. Imperialists will ask: What is there new in that? The novelty lies in degree and in method. Foggartism urges that the British people should be familiarized with the Empire by organized tours and propaganda on a great scale. It urges a vast increase – based on this familiarization – of controlled and equipped emigration from these shores. But it has been found impossible, as honourable members well know, to send out suitable grown folk in any adequate quantity, because confirmed town-dwellers with their town tastes and habits, and their physique already impaired by town life, are of little use in the Dominions, while the few still on the English land cannot be spared. Foggartism, therefore, would send out boys and girls, between the ages of fifteen, or perhaps sixteen, and eighteen, in great numbers. The House is aware that experiments in this direction have already been made, with conspicuous success, but such experiments are but a drop in the bucket. This is a matter which can only be tackled in the way that things were tackled during the war. Development of child emigration is wanted, in fact, on the same scale and with the same energy as was manifested in Munitions after a certain most honourable Member had put his shoulder to that wheel – multiplication a hundredfold. Although the idea must naturally prove abortive without the utmost good-will and co-operating energy on the part of the Dominions, I submit that this co-operation is not beyond the bounds of hope. The present hostility of people in the Dominions towards British immigrants is due to their very reasonable distrust of the usefulness of adult immigrants from this country. Once they have malleable youth to deal with, that drawback vanishes. In fact, the opening up of these vast new countries is like the progress of a rolling snow-ball, each little bit of "all right" – I beg the House's pardon – picks up another little bit; and there is no limit to the cumulative possibilities if a start is made at the right end and the scheme pushed and controlled by the right people.' Someone behind him said: 'Talking through his hat.' Michael paused, disconcerted; then, snatching at his bit, went on: 'A job of this sort half done is better left alone, but in the war, when something was found necessary, it *was* done, and men were always available for the doing of it. I put it to the House that the condition of our country now demands efforts almost as great as then.'

He could see that some members were actually listening to him with attention, and, taking a deep breath, he went on:

'Leaving out Ireland –' (*A voice: 'Why?'*) 'I prefer not to touch on anything that does not like to be touched –' (*laughter*) 'the present ratio of white population between Britain and the rest of the Empire is roughly in the nature of five to two. Child Emigration on a great scale will go far to equalize this ratio within twenty years; the British character of the British Empire will be established for ever, and supply and demand between the Mother Country and the Dominions will be levelled up.' (*A voice*

'*The Dominions will then supply themselves.*') 'The honourable
Member will forgive me if I doubt that, for some time to come.
We have the start in the machinery of manufacture. It may, of
course, be five, seven, ten years before unemployment here
comes down even to the pre-war rate, but can you point to any
other plan which will really decrease it? I am all for good wages
and moderate working hours. I believe the standard in Britain
and the new countries, though so much higher than the European, is only a decent minimum, and in some cases does not
reach it; I want better wages, even more moderate working
hours; and the want is common among working men wherever
the British flag flies.' ('*Hear, hear!*') 'They are not going back
on that want; and it is no good supposing that they are!' ('*Hear,
hear!*' '*Oh! oh!*') 'The equalization of demand and supply *within the Empire* is the only way of preserving and improving the
standards of life, which are now recognized as necessary on
British soil. The world has so changed that the old maxim "buy
in the cheapest, sell in the dearest market" is standing on its
head so far as England is concerned. Free trade was never a
principle –' ('*Oh! oh!*' '*Hear, hear!*' *and laughter.*) 'Oh! well, it
was born twins with expediency, and the twins have got mixed,
and are both looking uncommonly peeky.' (*Laughter.*) 'But I
won't go into that. ...' (*A voice: 'Better not!'*) Michael could
see the mouth it came from below a clipped moustache in a red
black-haired face turned round at him from a Liberal bench. He
could not put a name to it, but he did not like the unpolitical
expression it wore. Where was he? Oh! yes. ... 'There is another
point in the Foggart programme: England as she now is, in-
sufficiently protected in the air, and lamentably devoid of food-
producing power, is an abiding temptation to the aggressive feeling of other nations. And here I must beg the House's pardon
for a brief reference to Cinderella – in other words, the Land.
The speech from the throne gave no lead in reference to that
vexed question, beyond implying that a conference of all interested will be called. Well, without a definite intention in the
minds of all the political Parties to join in some fixed and long-
lasting policy for rehabilitation, such a conference is bound to

fail. Here again Foggartism –' ('*Ho! ho!*') 'Here again Foggartism steps in. Foggartism says: Lay down your Land policy *and don't change it.* Let it be as sacred as the Prohibition Law in America.' (*A voice: 'And as damned!' Laughter.*) 'The sacred and damned – it sounds like a novel by Dostoievski.' (*Laughter.*) 'Well, we shall get nowhere without this damned sanctity. On our Land policy depends, not only the prosperity of farmers, landlords, and labourers, desirable and important though that is, but the very existence of England, if unhappily there should come another war under the new conditions. Yes, and in a fixed land policy lies the only hope of preventing the permanent deterioration of the British type. Foggartism requires that we lay down our land policy, so that within ten years we may be growing up to seventy per cent of our food. Estimates made during the war showed that as much as eighty-two per cent could be grown at a pinch; and the measures then adopted went a long way to prove that this estimate was no more than truth. Why were those measures allowed to drop? Why was all that great improvement allowed to run to seed and grass? What is wanted is complete confidence in every branch of home agriculture; and nothing but a policy guaranteed over a long period can ever produce that confidence.' Michael paused. Close by, a member yawned; he heard a shuffle of feet; another old Prime Minister came in; several members were going out. There was nothing new about 'the Land'. Dared he tackle the air – that third plank in the Foggart programme? There was nothing new about the air either! Besides, he would have to preface it by a plea for the abolition of air fighting, or at least for the reduction of armaments. It would take too long! Better leave well alone! He hurried on:

'Emigration! The Land! Foggartism demands for both the same sweeping attention as was given to vital measures during the war. I feel honoured in having been permitted to draw the attention of all Parties to this – I will brave an honourable Member's disposition to say "Ho, ho!" – great treatise of Sir James Foggart. And I beg the House's pardon for having been so long in fulfilling my task.'

He sat down, after speaking for thirteen minutes. Off his chest! An honourable Member rose.

'I must congratulate the Member for mid-Bucks on what, despite its acquaintanceship with the clouds, and its Lewis Carrolian appeal for less bread, more taxes, we must all admit to be a lively and well-delivered first effort. The Member for Tyne and Tees, earlier in the Debate, made an allusion to the Party to which I have the honour to belong, which – er –'

'Exactly!' thought Michael, and after waiting for the next speech, which contained no allusion whatever to his own, he left the House.

Chapter Two

RESULTS

━◄─◄─►─►━

HE walked home, lighter in head and heart. That was the trouble – a light weight! No serious attention would be paid to him. He recollected the maiden speech of the Member of Cornmarket. At least he had stopped, today, as soon as the House began to fidget. He felt hot, and hungry. Opera-singers grew fat through their voices, Members of Parliament thin. He would have a bath.

He was half clothed again when Fleur came in.

'You did splendidly, Michael. That beast!'

'Which?'

'His name's MacGown.'

'Sir Alexander MacGown? What about him?'

'You'll see tomorrow. He insinuated that you were interested in the sale of the Foggart book, as one of its publishers.'

'That's rather the limit.'

'And all the rest of his speech was a cut-up; horrid tone about the whole thing. Do you know him?'

'MacGown? No. He's Member for some Scottish borough.'

'Well, he's an enemy. Blythe is awfully pleased with you, and wild about MacGown; and so is Bart. I've never seen him so angry. You'll have to write to *The Times* and explain that you've had no interest in Danby & Winter's since before you were elected. Bart and your mother are coming to dinner. Did you know she was with me?'

'Mother? She abhors politics.'

'All she said was: "I wish dear Michael would brush his hair back before speaking. I like to see his forehead." And when MacGown sat down, she said: "My dear, the back of that man's head is perfectly straight. D'you think he's a Prussian? And he's got thick lobes to his ears. I shouldn't like to be married to him!" She had her opera-glasses.'

Sir Lawrence and Lady Mont were already in the 'parlour' when they went down, standing opposite each other like two storks, if not precisely on one leg, still very distinguished. Pushing Michael's hair up, Lady Mont pecked his forehead, and her dove-like eyes gazed at the top of his head from under their arched brows. She was altogether a little Norman in her curves; she even arched her words. She was considered 'a dear; but not too frightfully all there'.

'How did you manage to stick it, Mother?'

'My dear boy, I was thrilled; except for that person in jute. I thought the shape of his head insufferable. Where did you get all that knowledge? It was so sensible.'

Michael grinned. 'How did it strike you, sir?'

Sir Lawrence grimaced.

'You played the *enfant terrible*, my dear. Half the party won't like it because they've never thought of it; and the other half won't like it because they *have*.'

'What! Foggartists at heart?'

'Of course; but in Office. You mustn't support your real convictions in Office – it's not done.'

'This nice room,' murmured Lady Mont. 'When I was last here it was Chinese. And where's the monkey?'

'In Michael's study, Mother. We got tired of him. Would you like to see Kit before dinner?'

Left alone, Michael and his father stared at the same object, a Louis Quinze snuff-box picked up by Soames.

'Would you take any notice of MacGown's insinuation, Dad?'

'Is that his name – the hairy haberdasher I I should.'

'How?'

'Give him the lie.'

'In private, in the Press, or in the House?'

'All three. In private I should merely call him a liar. In the Press you should use the words: "Reckless disregard for truth." And in Parliament – that you regret he "should have been so misinformed." To complete the crescendo you might add that men's noses have been pulled for less.'

'But you don't suppose,' said Michael, 'that people would believe a thing like that?'

'They will believe anything, my dear, that suggests corruption in public life. It's one of the strongest traits in human nature. Anxiety about the integrity of public men would be admirable, if it wasn't so usually felt by those who have so little integrity themselves that they can't give others credit for it.' Sir Lawrence grimaced, thinking of the P.P.R.S. 'And talking of that – why wasn't Old Forsyte in the House today?'

'I offered him a seat, but he said he hadn't been in the House since Gladstone moved the Home Rule Bill, and then only because he was afraid his father would have a fit.'

Sir Lawrence screwed his eye-glass in.

'That's not clear to me,' he said.

'His father had a pass, and didn't like to waste it.'

'I see. That was noble of Old Forsyte.'

'He said that Gladstone had been very windy.'

'Ah I They were even longer in those days. You covered your ground very quickly, Michael. I should say with practice you would do. I've a bit of news for Old Forsyte. Shropshire doesn't speak to Charlie Ferrar because the third time the old man paid his debts to prevent his being posted, he made that a condition, for fear of being asked again. It's not so lurid as I'd hoped. How's the action?'

'The last I heard was something about administering what they call interrogatories.'

'Ah! I know. They answer you in a way nobody can make head or tail of, and that without prejudice. Then they administer them to you, and you answer in the same way; it all helps the lawyers. What is there for dinner?'

'Fleur said we'd kill the fatted calf when I'd got my speech off.'

Sir Lawrence sighed.

'I'm glad. Your mother has Vitamins again rather badly; we eat little but carrots, generally raw. French blood in a family is an excellent thing – prevents faddiness about food. Ah! here they come! ...'

It has often been remarked that the breakfast-tables of people who avow themselves indifferent to what the Press may say of them are garnished by all the newspapers on the morning when there is anything to say. In Michael's case this was a waste of almost a shilling. The only allusions to his speech were contained in four out of the thirteen dailies. *The Times* reported it (including the laughter) with condensed and considered accuracy. The *Morning Post* picked out three imperial bits, prefaced by the words: 'In a promising speech.' The *Daily Telegraph* remarked: 'Among the other speakers was Mr Michael Mont.' And the *Manchester Guardian* observed: 'The Member for Mid-Bucks in a maiden speech advocated the introduction of children into the Dominions.'

Sir Alexander MacGown's speech received the added attention demanded by his extra years of Parliamentary service, but there was no allusion to the insinuation. Michael turned to Hansard. His own speech seemed more coherent than he had hoped. When Fleur came down he was still reading MacGown's.

'Give me some coffee, old thing.'

Fleur gave him the coffee and leaned over his shoulder.

'This MacGown is after Marjorie Ferrar,' she said; 'I remember now.'

Michael stirred his cup. 'Dash it all! The House is free from that sort of pettiness.'

'No. I remember Alison telling me – I didn't connect him up yesterday. Isn't it a disgusting speech?'

'Might be worse,' said Michael, with a grin.

'"As a member of the firm who published this singular production, he is doubtless interested in pressing it on the public, so that we may safely discount the enthusiasm displayed." Doesn't that make your blood boil?'

Michael shrugged his shoulders.

'Don't you ever feel angry, Michael?'

'My dear, I was through the war. Now for *The Times*. What shall I say?

'SIR,

'May I trespass upon your valuable space (that's quite safe), in the interests of public life – (that keeps it impersonal) – to – er – Well?'

'To say that Sir Alexander MacGowan in his speech yesterday told a lie when he suggested that I was interested in the sale of Sir James Foggart's book.'

'Straight,' said Michael, 'but they wouldn't put it in. How's this?

'To draw attention to a misstatement in Sir Alexander MacGown's speech of yesterday afternoon. As a matter of fact (always useful) I ceased to have any interest whatever in the firm which published Sir James Foggart's book, *The Parlous State of England*, even before I became a member of the late Parliament; and am therefore in no way interested, as Sir Alexander MacGown suggested, in pressing it upon the public. I hesitate to assume that he meant to impugn my honour (must get in 'honour') but his words might bear that construction. My interest in the book is simply my interest in what is truly the "parlous state of England".

Faithfully, etc.

That do?'

'Much too mild. Besides, I shouldn't say that you really believe the state of England is parlous. It's all nonsense, you know. I mean it's exaggerated.'

'Very well,' said Michael, 'I'll put the state of the country instead. In the House I suppose I rise to a point of order. And in the Lobby to a point of disorder, probably. I wonder what the *Evening Sun* will say?'

The *Evening Sun*, which Michael bought on his way to the House, gave him a leader, headed: 'Foggartism again,' beginning as follows: 'Young Hopeful, in the person of the Member for Mid-Bucks, roused the laughter of the House yesterday by his championship of the insane policy called Foggartism, to which we have already alluded in these columns'; and so on for twenty lines of vivid disparagement. Michael gave it to the doorkeeper.

In the House, after noting that MacGown was present, he rose at the first possible moment.

'Mr Speaker, I rise to correct a statement in yesterday's debate reflecting on my personal honour. The honourable member for Greengow, in his speech said –' He then read the paragraph from Hansard. 'It is true that I was a member of the firm which published Sir James Foggart's book in August, 1923, but I retired from all connexion with that firm in October, 1923, before ever I entered this House. I have therefore no pecuniary or other interest whatever in pressing the claims of the book, beyond my great desire to see its principles adopted.'

He sat down to some applause; and Sir Alexander MacGown rose. Michael recognized the face with the unpolitical expression he had noticed during his speech.

'I believe,' he said, 'that the honourable Member for Mid-Bucks was not sufficiently interested in his own speech to be present when I made my reply to it yesterday. I cannot admit that my words bear the construction which he has put on them. I said, and I still say, that one of the publishers of a book must necessarily be interested in having the judgement which induced him to publish it vindicated by the public. The Honourable Member has placed on his head a cap which I did not intend for it.' His face came round toward Michael, grim, red, provocative.

Michael rose again.

'I am glad the honourable Member has removed a construction which others besides myself had put on his words.'

A few minutes later, with a certain unanimity, both left the House.

The papers not infrequently contain accounts of how Mr
Swash, the honourable Member for Topcliffe, called Mr Buckler,
the honourable Member for Tooting, something unparliamen-
tary. (*'Order!'*) And of how Mr Buckler retorted that Mr Swash
was something worse. (*'Hear, hear!' and 'Order!'*) And of how
Mr Swash waved his fists (*uproar*), and Mr Buckler threw himself upon the Chair, or threw some papers (*'Order! order!
order!'*) And of how there was great confusion, and Mr Swash,
or Mr Buckler, was suspended, and led vociferous out of the
Mother of Parliaments by the Serjeant-at-Arms, with other edifying details. The little affair between Michael and Sir Alexander
went off in other wise. With an instinct of common decency,
they both made for the lavatory; nor till they reached those
marble halls did either take the slightest notice of the other. In
front of a roller towel Michael said:

'Now, sir, perhaps you'll tell me why you behaved like a dirty
dog. You knew perfectly well the construction that would be
placed on your words.'

Sir Alexander turned from a hair-brush.

'Take that!' he said, and gave Michael a swinging box on the
ear. Staggering, Michael came up wildly with his right, and
caught Sir Alexander on the nose. Their movements then became intensive. Michael was limber, Sir Alexander stocky;
neither was over proficient with his fists. The affair was cut short
by the honourable Member for Wasbaston, who had been in retirement. Coming hastily out of a door, he received simultaneously a black eye, and a blow on the diaphragm, which
caused him to collapse. The speaker, now, was the Member for
Wasbaston, in language stronger than those who knew the honourable gentleman would have supposed possible.

'I'm frightfully sorry, sir,' said Michael. 'It's always the
innocent party who comes off worst.'

'I'll dam' well have you both suspended,' gasped the Member
for Wasbaston.

Michael grinned, and Sir Alexander said: 'To hell!'

'You're a couple of brawling cads!' said the Member for Wasbaston. 'How the devil am I to speak this afternoon?'

'If you went in bandaged', said Michael, dabbing the damaged eye with cold water, 'and apologized for a motor accident, you would get a special hearing, and a good Press. Shall I take the silver lining out of my tie for a bandage?'

'Leave my eye alone,' bellowed the Member for Wasbaston, 'and get out, before I lose my temper!'

Michael buttoned the top of his waistcoat loosened by Sir Alexander's grip, observed in the glass that his ear was very red, his cuff bloodstained, and his opponent still bleeding from the nose, and went out.

'Some scrap!' he thought, entering the fresher air of Westminster. 'Jolly lucky we were tucked away in there! I don't think I'll mention it!' His ear was singing and he felt rather sick, physically and mentally. The salvational splendour of Foggartism already reduced to a brawl in a lavatory! It made one doubt one's vocation. Not even the Member for Wasbaston, however, had come off with dignity, so that the affair was not likely to get into the papers.

Crossing the road towards home, he sighted Francis Wilmot walking west.

'Hallo!'

Francis Wilmot looked up, and seemed to hesitate. His face was thinner, his eyes deeper set; he had lost his smile.

'How is Mrs Mont?'

'Very well, thanks. And you?'

'Fine,' said Francis Wilmot. 'Will you tell her I've had a letter from her cousin Jon. They're in great shape. He was mighty glad to hear I'd seen her, and sent his love.'

'Thanks,' said Michael, drily. 'Come and have tea with us.'

The young man shook his head.

'Have you cut your hand?'

Michael laughed. 'No, somebody's nose.'

Francis Wilmot smiled wanly. 'I'm wanting to do that all the time. Whose was it?'

'A man called MacGown's.'

Francis Wilmot seized Michael's hand. 'It's the very nose!' Then, apparently disconcerted by his frankness, he turned on his

394

heel and made off, leaving Michael putting one and one together.

Next morning's papers contained no allusion to the bloodletting of the day before, except a paragraph to the effect that the Member for Wasbaston was confined to his house by a bad cold. The Tory journals preserved a discreet silence about Foggartism; but in two organs – one Liberal and one Labour – were little leaders, which Michael read with some attention.

The Liberal screed ran thus: 'The debate on the King's speech produced one effort which at least merits passing notice. The policy alluded to by the Member for mid-Bucks under the label of Foggartism, because it emanates from that veteran Sir James Foggart, has a certain speciousness in these unsettled times, when everyone is looking for quack specifics. Nothing which departs so fundamentally from all that Liberalism stands for will command for a moment the support of any truly Liberal vote. The risk lies in its appeal to backwoodism in the Tory ranks. Loose thought and talk of a pessimistic nature always attracts a certain type of mind. The state of England is not really parlous. It in no way justifies any unsound or hysterical departure from our traditional policy. But there is no disguising the fact that certain so-called thinkers have been playing for some time past with the idea of reviving a 'splendid isolation', based (whether they admit it or not) on the destruction of Free Trade. The young Member for mid-Bucks in his speech handled for a moment that corner-stone of Liberalism, and then let it drop; perhaps he thought it too weighty for him. But reduced to its elements, Foggartism is a plea for the abandonment of Free Trade, and a blow in the face of the League of Nations.'

Michael sighed and turned to the Labour article, which was signed, and struck a more human note:

'And so we are to have our children carted off to the Antipodes as soon as they can read and write, in order that the capitalist class may be relieved of the menace lurking in Unemployment. I know nothing of Sir James Foggart, but if he was correctly quoted in Parliament yesterday by a member for an agricultural constituency, I smelled Prussianism about that old gentleman. I wonder what the working man is saying over his breakfast-table? I fear the words: "To Hell!" are not altogether absent from his discourse. No, Sir James Foggart, English Labour intends to call its own hand; and with all the old country's drawbacks, still prefers it for itself and its children. We are not taking any, Sir James Foggart.'

'There it is naked,' thought Michael. 'The policy ought never to have been entrusted to me. Blythe ought to have found a Labour townsman.'

Foggartism, whittled to a ghost by jealousy and class-hatred, by shibboleth, section and Party – he had a vision of it slinking through the purlieus of the House and the corridors of the Press, never admitted to the Presence, nor accepted as flesh and blood!

'Never mind,' he muttered; 'I'll stick it. If one's a fool, one may as well be a blazing fool. Eh, Dan?'

The Dandie, raising his head from his paws, gave him a lustrous glance.

Chapter Three

MARJORIE FERRAR AT HOME

◄◄–►►

FRANCIS WILMOT went on his way to Chelsea. He had a rendezvous with Life. Over head and ears in love, and old-fashioned to the point of marriage, he spent his days at the tail of a petticoat as often absent as not. His simple fervour had wrung from Marjorie Ferrar confession of her engagement. She had put it bluntly: she was in debt, she wanted shekels and she could not live in the backwoods.

He had promptly offered her all his shekels. She had refused them with the words:

'My poor dear, I'm not so far gone as that.'

Often on the point of saying 'Wait until I'm married', the look on his face had always deterred her. He was primitive; would never understand her ideal: Perfection, as wife, mistress, and mother, all at once. She kept him only by dangling the hope that she would throw MacGown over; taking care to have him present when MacGown was absent, and absent when MacGown was present. She had failed to keep them apart on two occasions, painful and productive of more lying than she was at all accustomed to. For she was really taken with this young man; he was a new flavour. She 'loved' his dark 'slinky' eyes, his grace, the way his 'back-chat' grew, dark and fine, on his slim comely neck. She 'loved' his voice and his old-fashioned way of talking. And, rather oddly, she 'loved' his loyalty. Twice she had urged him to find out whether Fleur wasn't going to 'climb down' and 'pay up'. Twice he had refused, saying: 'They were mighty nice to me; and I'd never tell you what they said, even if I did go and find out.'

She was painting his portrait, so that a prepared canvas with a little paint on it chaperoned their almost daily interviews, which took place between three and four when the light had already failed. It was an hour devoted by MacGown to duty in the House. A low and open collar suited Francis Wilmot's looks. She liked him to sit lissom on a divan with his eyes following her; she liked to come close to him, and see the tremor of his fingers touching her skirt or sleeve, the glow in his eyes, the change in his face when she moved away. His faith in her was inconvenient. P's and Q's were letters she despised. And yet, to have to mind them before him gave her a sort of pleasure, made her feel good. One did not shock children!

That day, since she expected MacGown at five, she had become uneasy, before the young man came in saying:

'I met Michael Mont; his cuff was bloody. Guess whose blood!'

'Not Alec's?'

Francis Wilmot dropped her hands.

'Don't call that man "Alec" to me.'

397

'My dear child, you're too sensitive. I thought they'd have a row – I read their speeches. Hadn't Michael a black eye? No? Tt – tt! Al – er – "that man" will be awfully upset. Was the blood fresh?'

'Yes,' said Francis Wilmot, grimly.

'Then he won't come. Sit down, and let's do some serious work for once.'

But throwing himself on his knees, he clasped his hands behind her waist.

'Marjorie, Marjorie!'

Disciple of Joy, in the forefront of modern mockery, she was yet conscious of pity, for him and for herself. It was hard not to be able to tell him to run out, get licence and ring, or whatever he set store by, and have done with it! Not even that she was ready to have done with it without ring or licence! For one must keep one's head. She had watched one lover growing tired, kept her head, and dismissed him before he knew it; grown tired of another, kept her head, and gone on till he was tired too. She had watched favourites she had backed go down, kept her head and backed one that didn't; had seen cards turn against her, and left off playing before her pile was gone. Time and again she had earned the good mark of Modernity.

So she kissed the top of his head, unclasped his hands, and told him to be good; and, in murmuring it, felt that she had passed her prime.

'Amuse me while I paint,' she said. 'I feel rotten.'

And Francis Wilmot, like a dark ghost, amused her.

Some believe that a nose from which blood has been drawn by a blow swells less in the first hour than it does later. This was why Sir Alexander MacGown arrived at half-past four to say that he could not come at five. He had driven straight from the House with a little bag of ice held to it. Having been led to understand that the young American was 'now in Paris', he stood stock still, staring at one whose tie was off and whose collar was unbuttoned. Francis Wilmot rose from the divan, no less silent. Marjorie Ferrar put a touch on the canvas.

'Come and look, Alec; it's only just begun.'

'No, thanks,' said MacGown.

Crumpling his tie into his pocket, Francis Wilmot bowed and moved towards the door.

'Won't you stay for tea, Mr Wilmot?'

'I believe not, thank you.'

When he was gone Marjorie Ferrar fixed her eyes on the nose of her betrothed. Strong and hard, it was, as yet, little differentiated from the normal.

'Now,' said MacGown, 'why did you lie about that young blighter? You said he was in Paris. Are you playing fast and loose with me, Marjorie?'

'Of course! Why not?'

MacGown advanced to within reach of her.

'Put down that brush.'

Marjorie Ferrar raised it; and suddenly it hit the wall opposite.

'You'll stop that picture, and you'll not see that fellow again; he's in love with you.'

He had taken her wrists.

Her face, quite as angry as his own, was reined back.

'Let go! I don't know if you call yourself a gentleman?'

'No, a plain man.'

'Strong and silent – out of a dull novel. Sit down, and don't be unpleasant.'

The duel of their eyes, brown and burning, blue and icy, endured for quite a minute. Then he did let go.

'Pick up that brush and give it to me.'

'I'm damned if I will!'

'Then our engagement is off. If you're old-fashioned, I'm not. You want a young woman who'll give you a whip for a wedding present.'

MacGown put his hands up to his head.

'I want you too badly to be sane.'

'Then pick up the brush.'

MacGown picked it up.

'What have you done to your nose?'

MacGown put his hand to it.

'Ran it against a door.'

Marjorie Ferrar laughed. 'Poor door!'

MacGown gazed at her in genuine astonishment.

'You're the hardest woman I ever came across; and why I love you, I don't know.'

'It hasn't improved your looks or your temper, my dear. You were rash to come here today.'

MacGown uttered a sort of groan. 'I can't keep away, and you know it.'

Marjorie Ferrar turned the canvas face to the wall, and leaned there beside it.

'I don't know what you think of the prospects of our happiness, Alec; but I think they're pretty poor. Will you have a whisky and soda? It's in that cupboard. Tea, then? Nothing? We'd better understand each other. If I marry you, which is very doubtful, I'm not going into purdah, I shall have what friends I choose. And until I marry you, I shall even see them. If you don't like it, you can leave it.'

She watched his clenched hands, and her wrists tingled. To be perfect wife to him would 'take a bit of doing!' If only she knew of a real 'good thing' instead, and had a 'shirt to put on it!' If only Francis Wilmot had money and did not live where the cotton came from and darkies crooned in the fields; where rivers ran red, Florida moss festooned the swamps and the sun shone; where grapefruit grew — or didn't? — and mocking-birds sang sweeter than the nightingale. South Carolina, described to her with such enthusiasm by Francis Wilmot! A world that was not her world stared straight into the eyes of Marjorie Ferrar. South Carolina! Impossible! It was like being asked to be ancient!

MacGown came up to her. 'I'm sorry,' he said. 'Forgive me, Marjorie.'

On her shrugging shoulders he put his hands, kissed her lips, and went away.

And she sat down in her favourite chair, listless, swinging her foot. The sand had run out of her dolly — life was a bore! It was like driving tandem, when the leader would keep turning round, or the croquet party in *Alice in Wonderland*, read in the buttercup-fields at High Marshes not twenty years ago that felt like twenty centuries!

What did she want? Just a rest from men and bills? Or that fluffy something called 'real love'? Whatever it was, she hadn't got it! And so! Dress, and go out, and dance; and later dress again, and go out and dine; and the dresses not paid for!

Well, nothing like an egg-nog for 'the hump'!

Ringing for the ingredients, she made one with plenty of brandy, capped it with nutmeg, and drank it down.

Chapter Four

'FONS ET ORIGO'

◄◄─►►

T w o mornings later Michael received two letters. The first, which bore an Australian post-mark, ran thus:

D e a r S i r ,

I hope you are well and the lady. I thought perhaps you'd like to know how we are. Well, Sir, we're not much to speak of out here after a year and a half. I consider there's too much gilt on the ginger-bread as regards Australia. The climate's all right when it isn't too dry or too wet – it suits my wife fine, but Sir when they talk about making your fortune all I can say is tell it to the marines. The people here are a funny lot they don't seem to have any use for us and I don't seem to have any use for them. They call us Pommies and treat us as if we'd took a liberty in coming to their blooming country. You'd say they wanted a few more out here, but they don't seem to think so. I often wish I was back in the old Country. My wife says we're better off here, but I don't know. Anyway they tell a lot of lies as regards emigration.

Well, Sir, I've not forgotten your kindness. My wife says please to remember her to you and the lady.

Yours faithfully,
A n t h o n y B i c k e t .

With that letter in his hand, Michael, like some psycho-metric medium, could see again the writer, his thin face, prominent eyes, large ears, a shadowy figure of the London streets behind his coloured balloons. Poor little snipe – square peg in round hole wherever he might be; and all those other pegs – thousands upon thousands, that would never fit in. Pommies! Well! He wasn't recommending emigration for them; he was recommending it for those who could be shaped before their wood had set. Surely they wouldn't put that stigma on to children! He opened the other letter.

Roll Manor,
Nr. Huntingdon.

My Dear Sir,

The disappointment I have felt since the appearance of my book was somewhat mitigated by your kind allusions to it in Parliament, and your championship of its thesis. I am an old man, and do not come to London now, but it would give me pleasure to meet you. If you are ever in this neighbourhood, I should be happy if you would lunch with me, or stay the night, as suits you best.

With kind regards.

Faithfully yours,
Jas: Foggart.

He showed it to Fleur.

'If you go, my dear, you'll be bored to tears.'

'I must go,' said Michael; '*Fons et Origo!*'

He wrote that he would come to lunch the following day.

He was met at the station by a horse drawing a vehicle of a shape he had never before beheld. The green-liveried man to whose side he climbed introduced it with the words: 'Sir James thought, sir, you'd like to see about you; so 'e sent the T cart.'

It was one of those grey late autumn days, very still, when the few leaves that are left hang listless, waiting to be wind-swept. The puddled road smelled of rain, rooks rose from the stubbles as if in surprise at the sound of horses' hoofs; and the turned earth of ploughed fields had the sheen that betokened clay. To the flat landscape poplars gave a certain spirituality; and the russet-tiled farmhouse roofs a certain homeliness.

'That's the manor, sir,' said the driver, pointing with his whip. Between an orchard and a group of elms, where was obviously a rookery, Michael saw a long low house of deeply weathered brick covered by Virginia creeper whose leaves had fallen. At a little distance were barns, out-houses, and the wall of a kitchen-garden. The T cart turned into an avenue of limes and came suddenly on the house unprotected by a gate. Michael pulled an old iron bell. Its lingering clang produced a lingering man, who, puckering his face, said: 'Mr Mont? Sir James is expecting you. This way, sir.'

Through an old low hall smelling pleasantly of wood-smoke, Michael reached a door which the puckered man closed in his face.

Sir James Foggart! Some gaitered old countryman with little grey whiskers, neat, weathered and firm-featured; or one of those short-necked John Bulls, still extant, square and weighty, with a flat top to his head, and a flat white topper on it?

The puckered man reopened the door, and said:

'Sir James will see you, sir.'

Before the fire in a large room with a large hearth and many books was a huge old man, grey-bearded and grey-locked, like a superannuated British lion, in an old velvet coat with whitened seams.

He appeared to be trying to rise.

'Please don't, sir,' said Michael.

'If you'll excuse me, I won't. Pleasant journey?'

'Very.'

'Sit down. Much touched by your speech. First speech, I think?'

Michael bowed.

'Not the last, I hope.'

The voice was deep and booming; the eyes looked up keenly, as if out of thickets, so bushy were the eyebrows, and the beard grew so high on the cheeks. The thick grey hair waved across the forehead and fell on to the coat collar. A primeval old man in a high state of cultivation. Michael was deeply impressed.

'I've looked forward to this honour, sir,' he said, 'ever since we published your book.'

'I'm a recluse – never get out now. Tell you the truth, don't want to – see too many things I dislike. I write, and smoke my pipe. Ring the bell, and we'll have lunch. Who's this Sir Alexander MacGown? His head wants punching!'

'No longer, sir,' said Michael.

Sir James Foggart leaned back and laughed. His laugh was long, deep, slightly hollow, like a laugh in a trombone.

'Capital! And how did those fellows take your speech? Used to know a lot of 'em at one time – fathers of these fellows, grandfathers, perhaps.'

'How do you know so well what England wants, sir,' said Michael, suavely, 'now that you never leave home?'

Sir James Foggart pointed with a large thin hand covered with hair to a table piled with books and magazines.

'Read,' he said; 'read everything – eyes as good as ever – seen a good deal in my day.' And he was silent, as if seeing it again.

'Are you following your book up?'

'M'm. Something for 'em to read when I'm gone. Eighty-four, you know.'

'I wonder,' said Michael, 'that you haven't had the Press down.'

'Have – had 'em yesterday; three by different trains; very polite young men; but I could see they couldn't make head or tail of the old creature – too far gone, eh?'

At this moment the door was opened, and the puckered man came in, followed by a maid and three cats. They put a tray on Sir James's knees and another on a small table before Michael. On each tray was a partridge with chipped potatoes, spinach and bread sauce. The puckered man filled Sir James's glass with barley-water, Michael's with claret, and retired. The three cats, all tortoise-shells, began rubbing themselves against Sir James's trousers, purring loudly.

'Don't mind cats, I hope? No fish today, pussies!'

Michael was hungry and finished his bird. Sir James gave most of his to the cats. They were then served with fruit salad, cheese, coffee and cigars, and everything removed except the cats, who lay replete before the fire curled up in a triangle.

Michael gazed through the smoke of two cigars at the fount and origin, eager, but in doubt whether it would stand pumping – it seemed so very old.¹ Well¹ anyway, he must have a shot¹

'You know Blythe, sir, of *The Outpost*? He's your great supporter; I'm only a mouthpiece.'

'Know his paper – best of the weeklies; but too clever by half.'

'Now that I've got the chance,' said Michael, 'would you mind if I asked you one or two questions?'

Sir James Foggart looked at the lighted end of his cigar. 'Fire ahead.'

'Well, sir, can England really stand apart from Europe?'

'Can she stand *with* Europe? Alliances based on promise of assistance that won't be forthcoming – worse than useless.'

'But suppose Belgium were invaded again, or Holland?'

'The one case, perhaps. Let that be understood. Knowledge in Europe, young man, of what England will or will not do in given cases is most important. And they've never had it. *Perfide Albion!* Heh¹ We always wait till the last moment to declare our policy. Great mistake. Gives the impression that we serve Time – which, with our democratic system, by the way, we generally do.'

'I like that, sir,' said Michael, who did not. 'About wheat? How would you stabilize the price so as to encourage our growth of it?'

'Ha¹ My pet lamb. We want a wheat loan, Mr Mont, and Government control. Every year the Government should buy in advance all the surplus we need and store it; then fix a price for the home farmers that gives them a good profit; and sell to the public at the average between the two prices. You'd soon see plenty of wheat grown here, and a general revival of agriculture.'

'But wouldn't it raise the price of bread, sir?'

'Not it.'

'And need an army of officials?'

405

'No. Use the present machinery properly organized.'

'State trading, sir?' said Michael, with diffidence.

Sir James Foggart's voice boomed out. 'Exceptional case – basic case – why not?'

'I quite agree,' said Michael, hastily. 'I never thought of it, but why not? ... Now as to the opposition to child emigration in this country. Do you think it comes from the affection of parents for their children?'

'More from dislike of losing the children's wages.'

'Still, you know,' murmured Michael, 'one might well kick against losing one's children for good at fifteen!'

'One might; human nature's selfish, young man. Hang on to 'em and see 'em rot before one's eyes, or grow up to worse chances than one's own – as you say, that's human nature.'

Michael who had not said it, felt somewhat stunned.

'The child emigration scheme will want an awful lot of money, and organization.'

Sir James stirred the cats with his slippered foot.

'Money! There's still a mint of money – misapplied. Another hundred million loan – four and a half millions a year in the Budget; and a hundred thousand children at least sent out every year. In five years we should save the lot in unemployment dole.' He waved his cigar, and its ash spattered on his velvet coat.

'Thought it would,' said Michael to himself, knocking his own off into a coffee-cup. 'But can children sent out wholesale like that be properly looked after, and given a real chance, sir?'

'Start gradually; where there's a will there's a way.'

'And won't they just swell the big towns out there?'

'Teach 'em to want land, and give it 'em.'

'I don't know if it's enough,' said Michael, boldly; 'the lure of the towns is terrific.'

Sir James nodded. 'A town's no bad thing till it's overdone, as they are here. Those that go to the towns will increase the demand for our supplies.'

'Well,' thought Michael, 'I'm getting on. What shall I ask him next?' And he contemplated the cats, who were stirring uneasily. A peculiar rumbling noise had taken possession of the silence. Michael looked up. Sir James Foggart was asleep! In repose he was more tremendous than ever – perhaps rather too tremendous; for his snoring seemed to shake the room. The cats tucked their heads farther in. There was a slight smell of burning. Michael picked a fallen cigar from the carpet. What should he do now? Wait for a revival, or clear out? Poor old boy! Foggartism had never seemed to Michael a more forlorn hope than in this sanctum of its fount and origin. Covering his ears, he sat quite still. One by one the cats got up. Michael looked at his watch. 'I shall lose my train,' he thought, and tiptoed to the door, behind a procession of deserting cats. It was as though Foggartism was snoring the little of its life away! 'Good-bye, sir!' he said softly, and went out. He walked to the station very thoughtful. Foggartism! That vast if simple programme seemed based on the supposition that human beings could see two inches before their noses. But was that supposition justified; if so would England be so town-ridden and over-populated? For one man capable of taking a far and comprehensive view and going to sleep on it, there were nine – if not nine-and-ninety – who could take near and partial views and remain wide awake. Practical politics! The answer to all wisdom however you might boom it out. 'Oh! Ah! Young Mont – not a practical politician!' It was public death to be so labelled. And Michael, in his railway carriage, with his eyes on the English grass, felt like a man on whom everyone was heaping earth. Had pelicans crying in the wilderness a sense of humour? If not, their time was poor. Grass, grass, grass! Grass and the towns! And, nestling his chin into his heavy coat, he was soon faster asleep than Sir James Foggart.

Chapter Five

PROGRESS OF THE CASE

◄─‹─›─►

WHEN Soames said 'Leave it to me,' he meant it, of course; but it was really very trying that whenever anything went wrong, he, and not somebody else, had to set it right!

To look more closely into the matter he was staying with his sister Winifred Dartie in Green Street. Finding his nephew Val at dinner there the first night, he took the opportunity of asking him whether he knew anything of Lord Charles Ferrar.

'What do you want to know, Uncle Soames?'

'Anything unsatisfactory. I'm told his father doesn't speak to him.'

'Well,' said Val, 'it's generally thought he'll win the Lincolnshire with a horse that didn't win the Cambridgeshire.'

'I don't see the connexion.'

Val Dartie looked at him through his lashes. He was not going to enter for the slander stakes. 'Well, he's got to bring off a *coup* soon, or go under.'

'Is that all?'

'Except that he's one of those chaps who are pleasant to you when you can be of use, and unpleasant when you can't.'

'So I gathered from his looks,' said Soames. 'Have you had any business dealings with him?'

'Yes; I sold him a yearling by Torpedo out of Banshee.'

'Did he pay you?'

'Yes,' said Val, with a grin; 'and she turned out no good.'

'H'm! I suppose he was unpleasant afterwards? That all you know?'

Val nodded. He knew more, if gossip can be called 'more'; but what was puffed so freely with the smoke of racing-men's cigars was hardly suited to the ears of lawyers.

For so old a man of the world Soames was singularly unaware how in that desirable sphere, called Society, everyone is slandered daily, and no bones broken; slanderers and slandered dining and playing cards together with the utmost good feeling and the intentions of re-slandering each other the moment they are round the corner. Such genial and hair-raising reports reach no outside ears, and Soames really did not know where to begin investigation.

'Can you ask this Mr Curfew to tea?' he said to Fleur.

'What for, Father?'

'So that I can pump him.'

'I thought there were detectives for all that sort of thing.'

Soames went a special colour. Since his employment of Mr Polteed, who had caught him visiting his own wife's bedroom in Paris, at the beginning of the century, the word detective produced a pain in his diaphragm. He dropped the subject. And yet, without detectives, what was he to do?

One night, Winifred having gone to the theatre, he sat down with a cigar, to think. He had been provided by Michael with a list of 'advanced' books and plays which 'modern' people were reading, attending and discussing. He had even been supplied with one of the books: *Canthar*, by Perceval Calvin. He fetched it from his bedroom, and, turning up a lamp, opened the volume. After reading the first few pages, in which he could see nothing, he turned to the end and read backwards. In this way he could skip better, and each erotic passage, to which he very soon came, led him insensibly on to the one before it. He had reached the middle of the novel, before he had resort in wonder to the title-pages. How was it that the publisher and author were at large? Ah! The imprint was of a foreign nature. Soames breathed more freely. Though sixty-nine, and neither judge, juryman nor otherwise professionally compelled to be shocked, he was shaken. If women were reading this sort of thing, then there really was no distinction between men and women nowadays. He took up the book again, and read steadily on to the beginning. The erotic passages alone interested him. The rest seemed rambling, disconnected stuff. He rested again. What was this novel written for? To make money, of course. But was there another purpose? Was the author one of these 'artist' fellows who thought that to give you 'life' — wasn't that the phrase? they must put down every visit to a bedroom, and some besides? 'Art for Art's sake', 'realism' — what did they call it? In Soames's comparatively bleak experience 'life' did not consist wholly of visiting bedrooms, so that he was unable to admit that this book was life, the whole of life, and nothing but life. 'Calvin's a crank, sir,' Michael had said, when he handed him the novel. 'He thinks people can't become continent except through being excessively incontinent; so he shows his hero and heroine arriving gradually at continence.' 'At Bedlam,' thought Soames. They would see what a British jury had to say to that, anyway. But how elicit a confession that this woman and her set had read it with gusto? And then an idea occurred to him, so brilliant that he had to ponder deeply before he could feel any confidence in it. These 'advanced' young people had any amount of conceit; everyone who didn't share their views was a 'dud', or a 'grundy'. Suppose the book were attacked in the Press, wouldn't it draw their fire? And if their fire could be drawn in print, could it not be used afterwards as evidence of their views on morality? H'm! This would want very nice handling. And first of all, how was he to prove that Marjorie Ferrar had read this book? Thus casting about him, Soames was rewarded by another brilliant thought: Young Butterfield — who had helped him to prove the guilt of Elderson in that matter of the P.P.R.S. and owed his place at Danby & Winter's, the publishers, to Soames's recommendation! Why not make use of him? Michael always said the young man was grateful. And obscuring the title of the book against his flank, in case he should meet a servant, Soames sought his own bedroom.

His last thought that night was almost diagnostic.

'In my young days we read that sort of book if we could get hold of it, and didn't say so; now, it seems, they make a splash of reading it, and pretend it does them good!'

Next morning from 'the Connoisseurs' he telephoned to Danby & Winter's, and asked to speak to Mr Butterfield.

'Yes?'

'Mr Forsyte speaking. Do you remember me?'

'Yes, indeed, sir.'

'Can you step round to the Connoisseurs' Club this morning some time?'

'Certainly, sir. Will twelve-thirty suit you?'

Secretive and fastidious in matters connected with sex, Soames very much disliked having to speak to a young man about an 'immoral' book. He saw no other way of it, however, and, on his visitor's arrival, shook hands and began at once.

'This is confidential, Mr Butterfield.'

Butterfield, whose dog-like eyes had glowed over the handshake, answered:

'Yes, sir. I've not forgotten what you did for me, sir.'

Soames held out the book.

'Do you know that novel?'

Butterfield smiled slightly.

'Yes, sir. It's printed in Brussels. They're paying five pounds a copy for it.'

'Have you read it?'

The young man shook his head. 'It's not come my way, sir.'

Soames was relieved. 'Well, don't! But just attend a moment. Can you buy ten copies of it, at my expense, and post them to ten people whose names I'll give you? They're all more or less connected with literature. You can put in slips to say the copies are complimentary, or whatever you call it. But mention no names.'

The young man Butterfield said deprecatingly:

'The price is rising all the time, sir. It'll cost you well on sixty pounds.'

'Never mind that.'

'You wish the book boomed, sir?'

'Good Gad – no! I have my reasons, but we needn't go into them.'

'I see, sir. And you want the copies to come – as if – as if from heaven?'

'That's it,' said Soames. 'I take it that publishers often send

411

doubtful books to people they think will support them. There's just one other thing. Can you call a week later on one of the people to whom you've sent the books, and offer to sell another copy as if you were an agent for it? I want to make quite sure it's already reached that person, and been read. You won't give your name, of course. Will you do this for me?'

The eyes of the young man Butterfield again glowed.

'Yes, sir. I owe you a great deal, sir.'

Soames averted his eyes; he disliked all expression of gratitude.

'Here's the list of names, then, with their addresses. I've underlined the one you call on. I'll write you a cheque to go on with; and you can let me know later if there's anything more to pay.'

He sat down, while the young man Butterfield scrutinized the list.

'I see it's a lady, sir, that I'm to call on.'

'Yes; does that make any difference to you?'

'Not at all, sir. Advanced literature is written for ladies nowadays.'

'H'm!' said Soames. 'I hope you're doing well?'

'Splendidly, sir. I was very sorry that Mr Mont left us; we've been doing better ever since.'

Soames lifted an eyebrow. The statement confirmed many an old suspicion. When the young man had gone, he took *Canthar*. Was he capable of writing an attack on it in the Press, over the signature 'Paterfamilias'? He was not. The job required someone used to that sort of thing. Besides, a real signature would be needed to draw fire. It would not do to ask Michael to suggest one; but Old Mont might know some fogey at the 'Parthenæum,' who carried metal. Sending for a bit of brown paper, he disguised the cover with it, put the volume in his overcoat pocket, and set out for 'Snooks'.

He found Sir Lawrence about to lunch, and they sat down together. Making sure that the waiter was not looking over his shoulder, Soames, who had brought the book in with him, pushed it over, and said:

'Have you read that?'

Sir Lawrence whinnied.

'My dear Forsyte, why this morbid curiosity? Everybody's reading it. They say the thing's unspeakable.'

'Then you haven't?' said Soames, keeping him to the point.

'Not yet, but if you'll lend it me, I will. I'm tired of people who've enjoyed it asking me if I've read "that most disgusting book". It's not fair, Forsyte. Did *you* enjoy it?'

'I skimmed it,' said Soames, looking round his nose. 'I had a reason. When you've read it, I'll tell you.'

Sir Lawrence brought it back to him at 'the Connoisseurs' two days later.

'Here you are, my dear Forsyte,' he said. 'I never was more glad to get rid of a book! I've been in a continual stew for fear of being overseen with it! Perceval Calvin – *quel sale Monsieur!*'

'Exactly!' said Soames. 'Now, I want to get that book attacked.'

'You! Is Saul also among the prophets? Why this sudden zest?'

'It's rather roundabout,' said Soames, sitting on the book. He detailed the reason, and ended with:

'Don't say anything to Michael, or Fleur.'

Sir Lawrence listened with his twisting smile.

'I see,' he said, 'I see. Very cunning, Forsyte. You want me to get someone whose name will act like a red rag. It mustn't be a novelist, or they'll say he's jealous – which he probably is: the book's selling like hot cakes – I believe that's the expression. Ah! I think – I rather think Forsyte, that I have the woman.'

'Woman!' said Soames. 'They won't pay any attention to that.'

Sir Lawrence cocked his loose eyebrow. 'I believe you're right – the only women they pay attention to nowadays are those who go one better than themselves. Shall I do it myself, and sign "Outraged Parent"?'

'I believe it wants a real name.'

'Again right, Forsyte; it does. I'll drop into the "Parthenæum", and see if anyone's alive.'

Two days later Soames received a note.

The Parthenæum,
Friday.

MY DEAR FORSYTE,

I've got the man – the editor of the *Protagonist*; and he'll do it under his own name. What's more, I've put him on to the right line. We had a spirited argument. He wanted to treat it *de haut en bas* as the work of a dirty child. I said: 'No. This thing is symptomatic. Treat it seriously; show that it represents a school of thought, a deliberate literary attitude; and make it a plea for censorship.' Without the word censorship, Forsyte, they will never rise. So he's leaving his wife and taking it into the country for the week-end. I admire your conduct of the defence, my dear Forsyte; it's very subtle. But if you'll forgive me for saying so, it's more important to prevent the case coming into Court than to get a verdict if it does.

Sincerely yours,
LAWRENCE MONT.

With which sentiment Soames so entirely agreed, that he went down to Mapledurham, and spent the next two afternoons going round and round with a man he didn't like, hitting a ball, to quiet his mind.

Chapter Six

MICHAEL VISITS BETHNAL GREEN

THE feeling of depression with which Michael had come back from the fount and origin was somewhat mitigated by letters he was receiving from people of varying classes, nearly all young. They were so nice and earnest. They made him wonder whether after all practical politicians were not too light-hearted, like the managers of music-halls who protected the public carefully from

414

their more tasteful selves. They made him feel that there might be a spirit in the country that was not really represented in the House, or even in the Press. Among these letters was one which ran:

Sunshine House,
Bethnal Green.

DEAR MR MONT,

I was so awfully glad to read your speech in *The Times*. I instantly got Sir James Foggart's book. I think the whole policy is simply splendid. You've no idea how heart-breaking it is for us who try to do things for children, to know that whatever we do is bound to be snowed under by the life they go to when school age ends. We have a good opportunity here of seeing the realities of child life in London. It's wonderful to see the fondness of the mothers for the little ones, in spite of their own hard lives – though not all, of course, by any means; but we often notice, and I think it's common experience, that when the children get beyond ten or twelve, the fondness for them begins to assume another form. I suppose it's really the commercial possibilities of the child making themselves felt. When money comes in at the door, disinterested love seems to move towards the window. I suppose it's natural, but it's awfully sad, because the commercial possibilities are generally so miserable; and the children's after-life is often half ruined for the sake of the few shillings they earn. I do fervently hope something will come of your appeal; only – things move so slowly, don't they? I wish you would come down and see our House here. The children are adorable, and we try to give them sunshine.

Sincerely yours,
NORAH CURFEW

Bertie Curfew's sister! But surely that case would not really come to anything! Grateful for encouragement, and seeking light on Foggartism, he decided to go. Perhaps Norah Curfew would take the little Boddicks! He suggested to Fleur that she should accompany him, but she was afraid of picking up something unsuitable to the eleventh baronet, so he went alone.

The house, facing the wintry space called Bethnal Green, consisted of three small houses converted into one, with their

three small back yards, trellised round and gravelled, for a play-
ground. Over the door were the words: SUNSHINE HOUSE
in gold capitals. The walls were cream-coloured, the woodwork
dark, and the curtains of gay chintz. Michael was received in
the entrance-lobby by Norah Curfew herself. Tall, slim and
straight, with dark hair brushed back from a pale face, she had
brown eyes, clear, straight and glowing.

'Gosh!' thought Michael, as she wrung his hand. 'She *is*
swept and garnished. No basement in her soul!'

'It *was* good of you to come, Mr Mont. Let me take you over
the house. This is the play-room.'

Michael entered a room of spotless character, which had evidently been formed from several knocked into one. Six small
children dressed in blue linen were seated on the floor, playing
games. They embraced the knees of Norah Curfew when she
came within reach. With the exception of one little girl Michael
thought them rather ugly.

'These are our residents. The others only come out of
school hours. We have to limit them to fifty, and that's a
pretty good squeeze. We want funds to take the next two
houses.'

'How many of you are working here?'

'Six. Two of us do the cooking; one the accounts; and the
rest washing, mending, games, singing, dancing and general
chores. Two of us live in.'

'I don't see your harps and crowns.'

Norah Curfew smiled.

'Pawned,' she said.

'What do you do about religion?' asked Michael, thinking of
the eleventh baronet's future.

'Well, on the whole we don't. You see, they're none of them
more than twelve; and the religious age, when it begins at all,
begins with sex about fourteen. We just try to teach kindness
and cheerfulness. I had my brother down the other day. He's
always laughed at me; but he's going to do a matinée for us,
and give us the proceeds.'

'What play?'

'I think it's called "The Plain Dealer". He says he's always wanted to do it for a good object.'

Michael stared. 'Do you know "The Plain Dealer"?'

'No; it's by one of the Restoration people, isn't it?'

'Wycherley.'

'Oh! yes!' Her eyes remaining clearer than the dawn, Michael thought: 'Poor dear! It's not my business to queer the pitch of her money-getting; but Master Bertie likes his little joke!'

'I must bring my wife down here,' he said; 'she'd love your walls and curtains. And I wanted to ask you. You haven't room, have you, for two more little girls, if we pay for them? Their father's down and out, and I'm starting him in the country – no mother.'

Norah Curfew wrinkled her straight brows, and on her face came the look Michael always connected with haloes, an anxious longing to stretch good-will beyond power and pocket.

'Oh; we must!' she said. 'I'll manage somehow. What are their names?'

'Boddick – Christian, I don't know. I call them by their ages – Four and Five.'

'Give me the address. I'll go and see them myself; if they haven't got anything catching, they shall come.'

'You really are an angel,' said Michael simply.

Norah Curfew coloured, and opened a door. 'That's silly,' she said, still more simply. 'This is our mess-room.'

It was not large, and contained a girl working a typewriter, who stopped with her hands on the keys and looked round; another girl beating up eggs in a bowl, who stopped reading a book of poetry; and a third, who seemed practising a physical exercise, and stopped with her arms extended.

'This is Mr Mont,' said Norah Curfew, 'who made that splendid speech in the House. Miss Betts, Miss La Fontaine, Miss Beeston.'

The girls bowed, and the one who continued to beat the eggs, said: 'It was bully.'

Michael also bowed. 'Beating the air, I'm afraid.'

'Oh! but, Mr Mont, it must have an effect. It said what so many people are really thinking.'

'Ah!' said Michael, 'but their thoughts are so deep, you know.'

'Do sit down.'

Michael sat on the end of a peacock-blue divan.

'I was born in South Africa,' said the egg-beater, 'and I know what's waiting.'

'My father was in the House,' said the girl, whose arms had come down to her splendid sides. 'He was very much struck. Anyway, we're jolly grateful.'

Michael looked from one to the other.

'I suppose if you didn't all believe in things, you wouldn't be doing this? *You* don't think the shutters are up in England, anyway?'

'Good Lord, no!' said the girl at the typewriter; 'you've only to live among the poor to know that.'

'The poor haven't got every virtue, and the rich haven't got every vice – that's nonsense!' broke in the physical exerciser.

Michael murmured soothingly.

'I wasn't thinking of that. I was wondering whether something doesn't hang over our heads too much?'

'D'you mean poison-gas?'

'Partly; and town blight, and a feeling that Progress had been found out.'

'Well, I don't know,' replied the egg-beater, who was dark and pretty. 'I used to think so in the war. But Europe isn't the world. Europe isn't even very important, really. The sun hardly shines there, anyway.'

Michael nodded. 'After all, if the Millennium comes and we do blot each other out in Europe, it'll only mean another desert about the size of the Sahara, and the loss of a lot of people obviously too ill-conditioned to be fit to live. It'd be a jolly good lesson to the rest of the world, wouldn't it? Luckily the other continents are far off each other.'

'Cheerful!' exclaimed Norah Curfew.

Michael grinned.

'Well, one can't help catching the atmosphere of this place. I admire you all frightfully, you know, giving up everything, to come and do this.'

'That's tosh,' said the girl at the typewriter. 'What is there to give up – bunny-hugging? One got used to doing things in the war.'

'If it comes to that,' said the egg-beater, 'we admire you much more for not giving up Parliament.'

Again Michael grinned.

'Miss La Fontaine – wanted in the kitchen !'

The egg-beater went towards the door.

'Can you beat eggs? D'you mind – shan't be a minute.' Handing Michael the bowl and fork, she vanished.

'What a shame !' said Norah Curfew. 'Let me !'

'No,' said Michael; 'I can beat eggs with anybody. What do you all feel about cutting children adrift at fifteen?'

'Well, of course, it'll be bitterly opposed,' said the girl at the typewriter. 'They'll call it inhuman, and all that. It's much more inhuman really to keep them here.'

'The real trouble,' said Norah Curfew, 'apart from the shillings earned, is the class-interference idea. Besides, Imperialism isn't popular.'

'I should jolly well think it isn't,' muttered the physical exerciser.

'Ah !' said the typist, 'but this isn't Imperialism, is it, Mr Mont? It's all on the lines of making the Dominions the equal of the Mother Country.'

Michael nodded. 'Commonwealth.'

'That won't prevent their camouflaging their objection to losing the children's wages,' said the physical exerciser.

A close discussion ensued between the three young women as to the exact effect of children's wages on the working-class budget. Michael beat his eggs and listened. It was, he knew, a point of the utmost importance. The general conclusion seemed to be that children earned on the whole rather more than their keep, but that it was 'very shortsighted in the long run', because it fostered surplus population and unemployment, and a 'great

419

shame' to spoil the children's chances for the sake of the parents.

The re-entrance of the egg-beater put a stop to it.

'They're beginning to come in, Norah.'

The physical exerciser slipped out, and Norah Curfew said:

'Now, Mr Mont, would you like to see them?'

Michael followed her. He was thinking: 'I wish Fleur had come!' These girls seemed really to believe in things.

Downstairs the children were trickling in from school. He stood and watched them. They seemed a queer blend of anaemia and vitality, of effervescence and obedience. Unselfconscious as puppies, but old beyond their years; and yet, looking as if they never thought ahead. Each movement, each action was as if it were their last. They were very quick. Most of them carried something to eat in a paper bag or a bit of grease-paper. They chattered, and didn't laugh. Their accent struck Michael as deplorable. Six or seven at most were nice to look at; but nearly all looked good-tempered, and none seemed to be selfish. Their movements were jerky. They mobbed Norah Curfew and the physical exerciser; obeyed without question, ate without appetite, and grabbed at the house cat. Michael was fascinated.

With them came four or five mothers, who had questions to ask, or bottles to fill. They too were on perfect terms with the young women. Class did not exist in this house; only personality was present. He noticed that the children responded to his grin, that the women didn't, though they smiled at Norah Curfew and the physical exerciser; he wondered if they would give him a bit of their minds if they knew of his speech.

Norah Curfew accompanied him to the door.

'Aren't they ducks?'

'I'm afraid if I saw much of them, I should give up Foggartism.'

'Oh! but why?'

'Well, you see, it designs to make them men and women of property.'

'You mean that would spoil them?'

Michael grinned. 'There's something dangerous about silver

spoons. Here's my initiation fee.' He handed her all his money.

'Oh! Mr Mont, we didn't – !'

'Well, give me back sixpence, otherwise I shall have to walk home.'

'It's frightfully kind of you. Do come again; and please don't give up Foggartism.'

He walked to the train thinking of her eyes; and, on reaching home, said to Fleur:

'You absolutely must come and see that place. It's quite clean, and the spirit's topping. It's bucked me up like anything. Norah Curfew's perfectly splendid.'

Fleur looked at him between her lashes.

'Oh!' she said. 'I will.'

Chapter Seven

CONTRASTS

◄─◆─►

THE land beyond the coppice at Lippinghall was a ten-acre bit of poor grass, chalk and gravel, fenced round, to show that it was property. Except for one experiment with goats, abandoned because nobody would drink their milk in a country that did not demean itself by growing food, nothing had been done with it. By December this poor relation of Sir Lawrence Mont's estate was being actively exploited. Close to the coppice the hut had been erected, and at least an acre converted into a sea of mud. The coppice itself presented an incised and draggled appearance, owing to the ravages of Henry Boddick and another man, who had cut and stacked a quantity of timber, which a contractor was gradually rejecting for the fowl-house and granary. The incubator-house was at present in the nature of a prophecy. Progress, in fact, was somewhat slow, but it was hoped that fowls might be asked to begin their operations soon after the New Year. In the meantime Michael had decided that the colony had better get the worst over and go into residence. Scraping the Manor House for furniture, and sending in a store of groceries, oil-lamps, and soap, he installed Boddick on the left, earmarked the centre for the Bergfelds, and the right hand for Swain. He was present when the Manor car brought them from the station. The murky day was turning cold, the trees dripped, the car-wheels splashed up the surface water. From the doorway of the hut Michael watched them get out, and thought he had never seen three more untimely creatures. Bergfeld came first; having only one suit, he had put it on, and looked what he was – an actor out of a job. Mrs Bergfeld came second, and having no outdoor coat, looked what she was – nearly frozen. Swain came last. On his shadowy face was nothing quite so spirited as a sneer; but he gazed about him, and seemed to say: 'My hat!'

Boddick, with a sort of prescience, was absent in the coppice. 'He,' thought Michael, 'is my only joy!'

Taking them into the kitchen mess-room of the hut, he deployed a thermos of hot coffee, a cake, and a bottle of rum.

'Awfully sorry things look so dishevelled; but I think the hut's dry, and there are plenty of blankets. These oil-lamps smell rather. You were in the war, Mr Swain; you'll feel at home in no time. Mrs Bergfeld, you look so cold, do put some rum into your coffee; we always do when we go over the top.'

They all put rum into their coffee, which had a marked effect. Mrs Bergfeld's cheeks grew pink, and her eyes darkened. Swain remarked that the hut was a 'bit of all right'; Bergfeld began making a speech. Michael checked him. 'Boddick knows all the ropes. I'm afraid I've got to catch a train; I've only just time to show you round.'

While whirling back to town afterwards he felt that he had, indeed, abandoned his platoon just as it was going over the top. That night he would be dining in Society; there would be light and warmth, jewels and pictures, wine and talk; the dinner would cost the board of his 'down and outs' for a quarter at least; and nobody would give them and their like a thought. If he ventured to draw Fleur's attention to the contrast, she would say:

'My dear boy, that's like a book by Gurdon Minho; you're getting sentimental.' And he would feel a fool. Or would he? Would he not, perhaps, look at her small distinguished head and think: 'Too easy a way out, my dear; those who take it have little heads!' And, then, his eyes, straying farther down to that white throat and all the dainty loveliness below, would convey a warmth to his blood and a warning to his brain not to give way to blasphemy, lest it end by disturbing bliss. For what with Foggartism, poultry, and the rest of it, Michael had serious thoughts sometimes that Fleur had none; and with wisdom born of love, he knew that if she hadn't, she never would have, and he must get used to it. She was what she was, and could be converted only in popular fiction. Excellent business for the self-centred heroine to turn from interest in her own belongings to interest in people who had no belongings; but in life it wasn't done. Fleur at least camouflaged her self-concentration gracefully; and with Kit – ! Ah ! but Kit was herself !

So he did not mention his 'down and outs' on their way to dinner in Eaton Square. He took instead a lesson in the royal Personage named on their invitation card, and marvelled at Fleur's knowledge. 'She's interested in social matters. And do remember, Michael, not to sit down till she asks you to, and not to go away before her, and to say "ma'am".'

Michael grinned. 'I suppose they'll all be nobs, or sn – er – why the deuce did they ask us?'

But Fleur was silent, thinking of her curtsey.

Royalty was affable, the dinner short but superb, served and eaten off gold plate, at a rate which suited the impression that there really wasn't a moment to spare. Fleur took a mental note of this new necessity. She knew personally five of the twenty-four diners, and the rest as in an illustrated paper, darkly. She had seen them all there at one time or another, stepping hideously in paddocks, photographed with their offspring or their dogs, about to reply for the Colonies, or 'taking a lunar' at a flying grouse. Her quick instinct apprehended almost at once the reason why she and Michael had been invited. His speech ! Like some new specimen at the Zoo, he was an object of curiosity, a stunt. She saw people nodding in the direction of him, seated opposite her between two ladies covered with flesh and pearls. Excited and very pretty, she flirted with the Admiral on her right, and defended Michael with spirit from the Under-Secretary on her left. The Admiral grew warm, the Under-Secretary, too young for emotion, cold.

'A little knowledge, Mrs Mont,' he said at the end of his short second innings, 'is a dangerous thing.'

'Now where have I heard that?' said Fleur. 'Is it in the Bible?'

The Under-Secretary tilted his chin.

'We who have to work departments know too much, perhaps; but your husband certainly doesn't know enough. Foggartism is an amusing idea, but there it stops.'

'We shall see!' said Fleur. 'What do you say, Admiral?'

'Foggartism! What's that — new kind of death ray? I saw a fellow yesterday, Mrs Mont — give you my word! — who's got a ray that goes through three bullocks, a nine-inch brick wall, and gives a shock to a donkey on the other side; and only at quarter strength.'

Fleur flashed a look round towards the Under-Secretary, who had turned his shoulder, and, leaning towards the Admiral, murmured:

'I wish you'd give a shock to the donkey on *my* other side; he wants it, and I'm not nine inches thick.'

But before the Admiral could shoot his death ray, Royalty had risen.

In the apartment to which Fleur was withdrawn, she had been saying little for some minutes, and noticing much, when her hostess came up and said:

'My dear, Her Royal Highness —'

Fleur followed, retaining every wit.

A frank and simple hand patted the sofa beside her. Fleur sat down. A frank and simple voice said:

'What an interesting speech your husband made! It was so refreshing, I thought.'

'Yes, ma'am,' said Fleur; 'but there it will stop, I am told.'

A faint smile curled lips guiltless of colouring matter.

'Well, perhaps. Has he been long in Parliament?'

'Only a year.'

'Ah! I liked his taking up the cudgels for the children.'

'Some people think he's proposing a new kind of child slavery.'

'Oh! really! Have you any children?'

'One,' said Fleur, and added honestly: 'And I must say I wouldn't part with him at fourteen.'

'Ah! And have you been long married?'

'Four years.'

At this moment the royal lady saw someone else she wished to speak to, and was compelled to break off the conversation, which she did very graciously, leaving Fleur with the feeling that she had been disappointed with the rate of production.

In the cab trailing its way home through the foggy night, she felt warm and excited, and as if Michael wasn't.

'What's the matter, Michael?'

His hand came down on her knee at once.

'Sorry, old thing! Only, really – when you think of it – eh?'

'Of what? You were quite a li – object of interest.'

'The whole thing's a game. Anything for novelty!'

'The Princess was very nice about you.'

'Ah! Poor thing! But I suppose you get used to anything!'

Fleur laughed. Michael went on:

'Any new idea gets seized and talked out of existence. It never gets farther than the brain, and the brain gets bored; and there it is, already a back number!'

'That can't be true, Michael. What about Free Trade, or Woman Suffrage?'

Michael squeezed her knee. 'All the women say to me: "But how interesting, Mr Mont; I think it's most thrilling!" And the men say: "Good stunt, Mont! But not practical politics, of course." And I've only one answer: "Things as big got done in the war." By George, it's foggy!'

They were going, indeed, at a snail's pace, and through the

windows could see nothing but the faint glow of the street lamps emerging slowly, high up, one by one. Michael let down a window and leaned out.

'Where are we?'

'Gawd knows, sir.'

Michael coughed, put up the window again, and resumed his clutch of Fleur.

'By the way, Wastwater asked me if I'd read *Canthar*. He says there's a snorting cut-up of it in *The Protagonist*. It'll have the usual effect – sends sales up.'

'They say it's very clever.'

'Horribly out of drawing – not fit for children, and tells adults nothing they don't know. I don't see how it can be justified.'

'Genius, my dear. If it's attacked, it'll be defended.'

'Sib Swan won't have it – he says it's muck.'

'Oh! yes; but Sib's getting a back number.'

'That's very true,' said Michael, thoughtfully. 'By Jove! how fast things move, except in politics, and fog.'

Their cab had come to a standstill. Michael let down the window again.

'I'm fair lost, sir,' said the driver's hoarse voice. 'Ought to be near the Embankment, but for the life of me I can't find the turning.' Michael buttoned his coat, put up the window again, and got out on the near side.

The night was smothered, alive only with the continual hootings of creeping cars. The black vapour, acrid and cold, surged into Michael's lungs.

'I'll walk beside you; we're against the kerb; creep on till we strike the river, or a bobby.'

The cab crept on, and Michael walked beside it, feeling with his foot for the kerb.

The refined voice of an invisible man said: 'This is sanguinary!'

'It is,' said Michael. 'Where are we?'

'In the twentieth century, and the heart of civilization.'

Michael laughed, and regretted it; the fog tasted of filth.

'Think of the police!' said the voice, 'having to be out in this all night!'

'Splendid force, the police!' replied Michael. 'Where are you, sir?'

'Here, sir. Where are you?'

It was the exact position. The blurred moon of a lamp glowed suddenly above Michael's head. The cab ceased to move.

'If I could only smell the 'Ouses of Parliament,' said the cabman. 'They'll be 'avin' supper there be now.'

'Listen!' said Michael – Big Ben was striking. 'That was to our left.'

'At our back,' said the cabman.

'Can't be, or we should be in the river; unless you've turned right round!'

'Gawd knows where I've turned,' said the cabman, sneezing. 'Never saw such a night!'

'There's only one thing for it – drive on until we hit something. Gently does it.'

The cabman started the cab, and Michael, with his hand on it, continued to feel for the kerb with his foot.

'Steady!' he said, suddenly. 'Car in front.' There was a slight bump.

'Nah then!' said a voice. 'Where yer comin'? Cawn't yer see?'

Michael moved up alongside of what seemed to be another taxi.

'Comin' along at that pice!' said its driver; 'and fool moon, too!'

'Awfully sorry,' said Michael. 'No harm done. You got any sense of direction left?'

'The pubs are all closed – worse luck! There's a bloomin' car in front o' me that I've hit three times. Can't make any impression on it. The driver's dead, I think. Would yer go and look, Guv'nor?'

Michael moved towards the loom in front. But at that moment it gave way to the more universal blackness. He ran four steps to hail the driver, stumbled off the kerb, fell, picked himself up and spun round. He moved along the kerb to his right, felt he was going wrong, stopped and called: 'Hallo!' A faint 'Hallo!' replied from – where? He moved what he thought was back, and called again. No answer! Fleur would be frightened. He shouted. Half a dozen faint hallos replied to him; and someone at his elbow said: 'Don't cher know where y'are?'

'No; do you?'

'What do you think? Lost anything?'

'Yes; my cab.'

'Left anything in it?'

'My wife.'

'Lawd! You won't get 'er back tonight.' A hoarse laugh, ghostly and obscene, floated by. A bit of darkness loomed for a moment, and faded out. Michael stood still. 'Keep your head!' he thought. 'Here's the kerb – either they're in front, or they're behind; or else I've turned a corner.' He stepped forward along the kerb. Nothing! He stepped back. Nothing! 'What the blazes have I done?' he muttered: 'or have they moved on!' Sweat poured down him in spite of the cold. Fleur would be really scared! And the words of his election address sprang from his lips: 'Chiefly by the elimination of smoke!'

'Ah!' said a voice, 'got a cigarette, Guv'nor?'

'I'll give you all I've got and half a crown, if you'll find a cab close by with a lady in it. What street's this?'

'Don't arst me! The streets 'ave gone mad, I think.'

'Listen!' said Michael sharply.

'That's right, "Someone callin' so sweet." '

'Hallo!' cried Michael. 'Fleur!'

'Here! Here!'

It sounded to his right, to his left, behind him, in front. Then came the steady blowing of a cab's horn.

'Now we've got 'em,' said the bit of darkness. 'This way, Guv'nor, step slow, and mind my corns!'

Michael yielded to a tugging at his coat.

'It's like no-man's-land in a smoke barrage!' said his guide.

'You're right. Hallo! Coming!'

The horn sounded a yard off. A voice said: 'Oh! Michael!'

His face touched Fleur's in the window of the cab.

'Just a second, darling. There you are, my friend, and thanks
awfully! Hope you'll get home!'

'I've 'ad worse nights out than this. Thank you, Captain!
Wish you and the lady luck.' There was a sound of shuffling on,
and the fog sighed out: 'So long!'

'All right, sir,' said the hoarse voice of Michael's cabman. 'I
know where I am now. First on the left, second on the right.
I'll bump the kerb till I get there. Thought you was swallered
up, sir!'

Michael got into the cab, and clasped Fleur close. She uttered
a long sigh, and sat quite still.

'Nothing more scaring than a fog!' he said.

'I thought you'd been run over!'

Michael was profoundly touched.

'Awfully sorry, darling. And you've got all that beastly fog
down your throat. We'll drown it out when we get in. That
poor chap was an ex-service man. Wonderful the way the English keep their humour and don't lose their heads.'

'I lost mine!'

'Well, you've got it back,' said Michael, pressing it against his
own to hide the emotion he was feeling. 'Fog's our sheet-anchor,
after all. So long as we have fog, England will survive.' He felt
Fleur's lips against his.

He belonged to her, and she couldn't afford to have him
straying about in fogs or Foggartism! Was that the — ? And
then, he yielded to the thrill.

The cabman was standing by the opened door. 'Now, sir, I'm
in your Square. P'r'aps you know your own 'ouse.'

Wrenched from the kiss, Michael stammered: 'Righto!' The
fog was thinner here; he could consult the shape of trees. 'On and
to your right, third house.'

There it was — desirable — with its bay trees in its tubs and its
fanlight shining. He put his latch-key in the door.

'A drink?' he said.

The cabman coughed: 'I won't say no, sir.'

Michael brought the drink.

'Far to go?'

'Near Putney Bridge. Your 'ealth, sir!'

Michael watched his pinched face drinking.

'Sorry you've got to plough into that again!'

The cabman handed back the glass.

'Thank'ee, sir; I shall be all right now; keep along the river, and down the Fulham Road. Thought they couldn't lose me in London. Where I went wrong was trying for a short cut instead of takin' the straight road round. 'Ope the young lady's none the worse, sir. She was properly scared while you was out there in the dark. These fogs ain't fit for 'uman bein's. They ought to do somethin' about 'em in Parliament.'

'They ought!' said Michael, handing him a pound note. 'Good-night, and good luck!'

'It's an ill wind!' said the cabman, starting his cab. 'Good-night, sir, and thank you kindly.'

'Thank *you*!' said Michael.

The cab ground slowly away, and was lost to sight.

Michael went into the Spanish room. Fleur, beneath the Goya, was boiling a silver kettle, and burning pastilles. What a contrast to the world outside – its black malodorous cold reek, its risk and fear! In this pretty glowing room, with this pretty glowing woman, why think of its tangle, lost shapes, and straying cries?

Lighting his cigarette, he took his drink from her by its silver handle, and put it to his lips.

'I really think we ought to have a car, Michael!'

Chapter Eight

COLLECTING EVIDENCE

❖

THE editor of *The Protagonist* had so evidently enjoyed himself that he caused a number of other people to do the same.

'There's no more popular sight in the East, Forsyte,' said Sir

Lawrence, 'than a boy being spanked; and the only difference
between East and West is that in the East the boy at once offers
himself again at so much a spank. I don't see Mr Perceval
Calvin doing that.'

'If he defends himself,' said Soames, gloomily, 'other people
won't.'

They waited, reading daily denunciations signed: 'A mother
of Three'; 'Roger: Northampton'; 'Victorian'; 'Alys St Maurice'; 'Plus Fours'; 'Arthur Whiffkin'; 'Sportsman if not Gentleman'; and 'Pro Patria'; which practically all contained the
words: 'I cannot say that I have read the book through, but I
have read enough to –'

It was five days before the defence fired a shot. But first came
a letter above the signature: 'Swishing Block', which, after
commenting on the fact that a whole school of so-called literature had been indicted by the editor of *The Protagonist* in his
able letter of the 14th inst, noted with satisfaction that the said
school had grace enough to take its swishing without a murmur.
Not even an anonymous squeak had been heard from the whole
apostolic body.

'Forsyte,' said Sir Lawrence, handing it to Soames, 'That's
my very own mite, and if it doesn't draw them – nothing will!'

But it did. The next issue of the interested journal in which
the correspondence was appearing contained a letter from the
greater novelist L.S.D. which restored everyone to his place.
This book might or might not be Art, he hadn't read it; but
the editor of *The Protagonist* wrote like a pedagogue, and there
was an end of him. As to the claim that literature must always
wear a flannel petticoat, it was 'piffle', and that was that. From
under the skirts of this letter the defence, to what of exultation
Soames ever permitted himself, moved out in force. Among the
defenders were as many as four of the selected ten associates to
whom young Butterfield had purveyed copies. They wrote over
their own names that *Canthar* was distinctly LITERATURE;
they were sorry for people who thought in these days that
LITERATURE had any business with morals. The work must
be approached aesthetically or not at all. ART was ART, and

431

morality was morality, and never the twain could, would, or should meet. It was monstrous that a work of this sort should have to appear with a foreign imprint. When would England recognize genius when she saw it?

Soames cut the letters out one after the other, and pasted them in a book. He had got what he wanted, and the rest of the discussion interested him no more. He had received, too, a communication from young Butterfield.

SIR,

I called on the lady last Monday, and was fortunately able to see her in person. She seemed rather annoyed when I offered her the book. 'That book,' she said: 'I read it weeks ago.' 'It's exciting a great deal of interest, Madam,' I said. 'I know,' she said. 'Then you won't take a copy; the price is rising steadily, it'll be very valuable in time?' 'I've got one,' she said. That's what you told me to find out, sir; so I didn't pursue the matter. I hope I have done what you wanted. But if there is anything more, I shall be most happy. I consider that I owe my present position entirely to you.

Soames didn't know about that, but as to his future position – he might have to put the young man into the box. The question of a play remained. He consulted Michael.

'Does that young woman still act in the advanced theatre place you gave me the name of?'

Michael winced. 'I don't know, sir; but I could find out.'

Inquiry revealed that she was cast for the part of Olivia in Bertie Curfew's matinée of 'The Plain Dealer'.

' "The Plain Dealer"?' said Soames. 'Is that an advanced play?'

'Yes, sir, two hundred and fifty years old.'

'Ah!' said Soames; 'they were a coarse lot in those days. How is it she goes on there if she and the young man have split?'

'Oh! well, they're very cool hands. I do hope you're going to keep things out of Court, sir?'

'I can't tell. When's this performance?'

'January the seventh.'

Soames went to his club library and took down 'Wycherley'. He was disappointed with the early portions of 'The Plain

432

Dealer', but it improved as it went on, and he spent some time making a list of what George Forsyte would have called the 'nubbly bits'. He understood that at that theatre they did not bowdlerize. Excellent! There were passages that would raise hair on any British jury. Between *Canthar* and this play, he felt as if he had a complete answer to any claim by the young woman and her set to having 'morals about them'. Old professional instincts were rising within him. He had retained Sir James Foskisson, K.C., not because he admired him personally, but because if he didn't, the other side might. As junior he was employing very young Nicholas Forsyte; he had no great opinion of him, but it was as well to keep the matter in the family, especially if it wasn't to come into Court.

A conversation with Fleur that evening contributed to his intention that it should not.

'What's happened to that young American?' he said.

Fleur smiled acidly. 'Francis Wilmot? Oh! he's "fallen for" Marjorie Ferrar.'

' "Fallen for her"?' said Soames. 'What an expression!'

'Yes, dear; it's American.'

' "For" her? It means nothing, so far as I can see.'

'Let's hope not, for his sake! She's going to marry Sir Alexander MacGown, I'm told.'

'Oh!'

'Did Michael tell you that he hit him on the nose?'

'Which – who?' said Soames testily. 'Whose nose?'

'MacGown's, dear; and it bled like anything.'

'Why on earth did he do that?'

'Didn't you read his speech about Michael?'

'Oh!' said Soames. 'Parliamentary fuss – that's nothing. They're always behaving like schoolboys, there. And so she's going to marry him. Has he been putting her up to all this?'

'No; *she's* been putting him.'

Soames discounted the information with a sniff; he scented the hostility of woman for woman. Still, chicken and egg – political feeling and social feeling, who could say which first promoted which? In any case, this made a difference. Going to be married – was she? He debated the matter for some time, and then decided that he would go and see Settlewhite and Stark. If they had been a firm of poor repute or the kind always employed in '*causes célèbres*', he wouldn't have dreamed of it; but, as a fact, they stood high, were solid family people, with an aristocratic connexion and all that.

He did not write, but took his hat and went over from 'The Connoisseurs' to their offices in King Street, St James's. The journey recalled old days – to how many such negotiatory meetings had he not gone or caused his adversaries to come! He had never cared to take things into Court if they could be settled out of it. And always he had approached negotiation with the impersonality of one passionless about to meet another of the same kidney – two calculating machines, making their livings out of human nature. He did not feel like that today; and, aware of this handicap, stopped to stare into the print and picture shop next door. Ah! There were those first proofs of the Roussel engravings of the Prince Consort Exhibition of '51, that Old Mont had spoken of – he had an eye for an engraving, Old Mont. Ah! and there was a Fred Walker, quite a good one! Mason, and Walker – they weren't done for yet by any means. And the sensation that a man feels hearing a blackbird sing on a tree just coming into blossom, stirred beneath Soames's ribs. Long – long since he had bought a picture! Let him but get this confounded case out of the way, and he could enjoy himself again. Riving his glance from the window, he took a long breath, and walked into Settlewhite and Stark's.

The chief partner's room was on the first floor, and the chief partner standing where chief partners stand.

'How do you do, Mr Forsyte? I've not met you since "Bobbin against the L. & S.W." That must have been 1900!'

'1899,' said Soames. 'You were for the Company.'

Mr Settlewhite pointed to a chair.

Soames sat down and glanced up at the figure before the fire. H'm! a long-lipped, long-eyelashed, long-chinned face; a man of his own calibre, education, and probity! He need not beat about the bush.

'This action,' he said, 'is a very petty business. What can we do about it?'

Mr Settlewhite frowned.

'That depends, Mr Forsyte, on what you have to propose? My client has been very grossly libelled.'

Soames smiled sourly.

'She began it. And what is she relying on – private letters to personal friends of my daughter's, written in very natural anger! I'm surprised that a firm of your standing –'

Mr Settlewhite smiled.

'Don't trouble to compliment my firm! I'm surprised myself that you are acting for your daughter. You can hardly see all round the matter. Have you come to offer an apology?'

'That!' said Soames. 'I should have thought it was for your client to apologize.'

'If such is your view, I'm afraid it's no use continuing this discussion.'

Soames regarded him fixedly.

'How do you think you're going to prove damage? She belongs to the fast set.'

Mr Settlewhite continued to smile.

'I understand she's going to marry Sir Alexander MacGown,' said Soames.

Mr Settlewhite's lips tightened.

'Really, Mr Forsyte, if you have come to offer an apology and a substantial sum in settlement, we can talk. Otherwise –'

'As a sensible man,' said Soames, 'you know that these Society scandals are always dead sea fruit – nothing but costs and vexations, and a feast for all the gossips about town. I'm prepared to offer you a thousand pounds to settle the whole thing, but an apology I can't look at. A mutual expression of regret – perhaps; but an apology's out of the question.'

'Fifteen hundred I might accept – the insults have had wide currency. But an apology is essential.'

Soames sat silent, chewing the injustice of it all. Fifteen hundred! Monstrous! Still he would pay even that to keep Fleur out of Court. But humble-pie! She wouldn't eat it, and he couldn't make her, and he didn't know that he wanted to. He got up.

'Look here, Mr Settlewhite, if you take this into Court, you will find yourself up against more than you think. But the whole thing is so offensive to me, that I'm prepared to meet you over the money, though I tell you frankly I don't believe a jury would award a penny piece. As to an apology, a "formula" could be found perhaps' – why the deuce was the fellow smiling? – 'Something like this: "We regret that we have said hasty things about each other", to be signed by both parties.'

Mr Settlewhite caressed his chin.

'Well, I'll put your proposition before my client. I join with you in wishing to see the matter settled, not because I'm afraid of the result' – 'Oh, no!' thought Soames – 'but because these cases, as you say, are not edifying.' He held out his hand.

Soames gave it a cold touch.

'You understand that this is entirely "without prejudice",' he said, and went out. 'She'll take it!' he thought. Fifteen hundred pounds of his money thrown away on that baggage, just because for once she had been labelled what she was; and all his trouble to get evidence wasted! For a moment he resented his devotion to Fleur. Really it was fatuous to be so fond as that! Then his heart rebounded. Thank God! He had settled it.

Christmas was at hand. It did not alarm him, therefore, that he received no answering communication. Fleur and Michael were at Lippinghall with the ninth and eleventh baronets. He and Annette had Winifred and the Cardigans down at 'The Shelter'. Not till the 6th of January did he receive a letter from Messrs Settlewhite and Stark.

DEAR SIR,
In reference to your call of the 17th ultimo, your proposition was duly placed before our client, and we are instructed to say that she will accept the sum of £1,500 – fifteen hundred pounds – and an apology, duly signed by your client, copy of which we enclose.
We are, dear Sir,
Faithfully yours,
SETTLEWHITE AND STARK

Soames turned to the enclosure. It ran thus:

I, Mrs Michael Mont, withdraw the words concerning Miss Marjorie Ferrar contained in my letters to Mrs Ralph Ppynrryn and Mrs Edward Maltese of October 4th last, and hereby tender a full and free apology for having written them.

(SIGNED)

Pushing back the breakfast-table, so violently that it groaned, Soames got up.

'What is it, Soames?' said Annette. 'Have you broken your plate again? You should not bite so hard.'

'Read that!'

Annette read.

'You would give that woman fifteen hundred pounds? I think you are mad, Soames. I would not give her fifteen hundred pence! Pay this woman, and she tells her friends. That is fifteen hundred apologies in all their minds. Really, Soames – I am surprised. A man of business, a clever man! Do you not know the world better than that? With every pound you pay, Fleur eats her words!'

Soames flushed. It was so French, and yet somehow it was so true. He walked to the window. The French – they had no sense of compromise, and every sense of money!

'Well,' he said, 'that ends it anyway. She won't sign. And I shall withdraw my offer.'

'I should hope so. Fleur has a good head. She will look very pretty in Court. I think that woman will be sorry she ever lived! Why don't you have her what you call shadowed? It is no good to be delicate with women like that.'

In a weak moment he had told Annette about the book and the play; for, unable to speak of them to Fleur and Michael, he had really had to tell someone; indeed, he had shown her *Canthar*, with the words: 'I don't advise you to read it, it's very French.'

Annette had returned it to him two days later, saying: 'It is not French at all; it is disgusting. You English are so coarse. It has no wit. It is only nasty. A serious nasty book – that is the

437

limit. You are so old-fashioned, Soames. Why do you say this book is French?'

Soames, who really didn't know why, had muttered:

'Well, they can't get it printed in England.' And with the words: 'Bruxelles, Bruxelles, you call Bruxelles —' buzzing about his ears, had left the room. He had never known any people so touchy as the French!

Her remark about 'shadowing', however, was not easily forgotten. Why be squeamish, when all depended on frightening this woman? And on arriving in London he visited an office that was not Mr Polteed's, and gave instructions for the shadowing of Marjorie Ferrar's past, present, and future.

His answer to Settlewhite and Stark, too, was brief, determined, and written on the paper of his own firm.

Jan. 6th, 1925

DEAR SIRS,

I have your letter of yesterday's date, and note that your client has rejected my proposition, which, as you know, was made entirely without prejudice, and is now withdrawn *in toto*.

Yours faithfully,

SOAMES FORSYTE

If he did not mistake, they would be sorry. And he gazed at the words '*in toto*'; somehow they looked funny. *In toto!* And now for 'The Plain Dealer'!

The theatre of the 'Ne Plus Ultra' Play-Producing Society had a dingy exterior, a death-mask of Congreve in the hall, a peculiar smell, and an apron stage. There was no music. They hit something three times before the curtain went up. There were no footlights. The scenery was peculiar — Soames could not take his eyes off it till, in the first Entr'acte, its principle was revealed to him by the conversation of two people sitting just behind.

'The point of the scenery here is that no one need look at it, you see. They go farther than anything yet done.'

'They've gone farther in Moscow.'

'I believe not. Curfew went over there. He came back raving about the way they speak their lines.'

'Does he know Russian?'

'No. You don't need to. It's the timbre. I think he's doing pretty well here with that. You couldn't give a play like this if you took the words in.'

Soames, who had been trying to take the words in – it was, indeed, what he had come for – squinted round at the speakers. They were pale and young and went on with a strange unconcern.

'Curfew's doing great work. He's shaking them up.'

'I see they've got Marjorie Ferrar as Olivia.'

'Don't know why he keeps on an amateur like that.'

'Box office, dear boy; she brings the smart people. She's painful, I think.'

'She did one good thing – the dumb girl in that Russian play. But she can't speak for nuts; you're following the sense of her words all the time. She doesn't rhythmatize you a little bit.'

'She's got looks.'

'M'yes.'

At this moment the curtain went up again. Since Marjorie Ferrar had not yet appeared, Soames was obliged to keep awake; indeed, whether because she couldn't 'speak for nuts', or merely from duty, he was always awake while she was on the stage, and whenever she had anything outrageous to say he noted it carefully; otherwise he passed an excellent afternoon, and went away much rested. In his cab he mentally rehearsed Sir James Foskisson in the part of cross-examiner:

'I think, madam, you played Olivia in a production of 'The Plain Dealer' by the 'Ne Plus Ultra' Play-Producing Society? ... Would it be correct to say that the part was that of a modest woman? ... Precisely. And did it contain the following lines (Quotation of nubbly bits.) ... Did that convey anything to your mind, madam? ... I suppose that you would not say it was an immoral passage? ... No? Nor calculated to offend the ears and debase the morals of a decent-minded audience? ... No. In fact, you don't take the same view of morality that I, or, I venture to think, the jury do? ... No. The dark scene – you did not remonstrate with the producer for not omitting that scene? ... Quite. Mr Curfew, I think was the producer? Yes. Are you on such terms with that gentleman as would have made a remonstrance easy? ... Ah! Now, madam, I put it to you that throughout 1923 you were seeing this gentleman nearly every day. ... Well, say three or four times a week. And yet you say that you were not on such terms as would have made it possible for you to represent to him that no modest young woman should be asked to play a scene like that. ... Indeed! The jury will form their own opinion of your answer. You are not a professional actress, dependent for your living on doing what you are told to do? ... No. And yet you have the face to come here and ask for substantial damages because of the allegation in a private letter that you haven't a moral about you? ... Have you? ...' And so on, and so on. Oh! no. Damages! She wouldn't get a farthing.

Chapter Nine

'VOLTE FACE'

◄─◆─►

KEEPING Sir Alexander MacGown and Francis Wilmot in the air, fulfilling her week-end and other engagements, playing much bridge in the hope of making her daily expenses, getting a day's hunting when she could, and rehearsing the part of Olivia, Marjorie Ferrar had almost forgotten the action, when the offer of fifteen hundred pounds and the formula were put before her by Messrs Settlewhite and Stark. She almost jumped at it. The money would wipe out her more pressing debts; she would be able to breathe, and reconsider her future.

She received their letter on the Friday before Christmas, just as she was about to go down to her father's, near Newmarket, and wrote hastily to say she would call at their office on her way home on Monday. The following evening she consulted her father. Lord Charles was of opinion that if this attorney fellow would go as far as fifteen hundred, he must be dead keen on settling, and she had only to press for the apology to get it. Anyway, she should let them stew in their juice for a bit. On Monday he wanted to show her his yearlings. She did not, therefore, return to Town till the 23rd, and found the office closed for Christmas. It had never occurred to her that solicitors had holidays. On Christmas Eve she herself went away for ten days; so that it was January the 4th before she was again able to call. Mr Settlewhite was still in the South of France, but Mr Stark would see her. Mr Stark knew little about the matter, but thought Lord Charles's advice probably sound; he proposed to write accepting the fifteen hundred pounds if a formal apology were tendered; they could fall back on the formula if necessary, but it was always wise to get as much as you could. With some misgiving Marjorie Ferrar agreed.

Returning from the matinée on January 7th, tired and elated by applause, by Bertie Curfew's words: 'You did quite well, darling,' and almost the old look on his face, she got into a hot bath, and was just out when her maid announced Mr Wilmot.

'Keep him, Fanny; say I'll be with him in twenty minutes.'

Feverish and soft, as if approaching a crisis, she dressed hastily, put essence of orange-blossom on her neck and hands, and went to the studio. She entered without noise. The young man, back to the door, in the centre of the room, evidently did not hear her. Approaching within a few feet, she waited for the effect on him of orange-blossom. He was standing like some Eastern donkey, that with drooped ears patiently awaits the fresh burdening of a sore back. And suddenly he spoke: 'I'm all in.'

'Francis!'

The young man turned.

'Oh! Marjorie!' he said, 'I never heard.' And taking her hands, he buried his face in them.

She was hampered at that moment. To convert his mouth from despairing kissing of her hands to triumphal flame upon her lips would have been so easy if he had been modern, if his old-fashioned love had not complimented her so subtly; if, too, she were not feeling for him something more – or was it less? –

than passion. Was she to know at last the sensations of the simple – a young girl's idyll – something she had missed? She led him to the divan, sat down by his side, and looked into his eyes. Fabled sweetness, as of a spring morning – Francis and she, children in the wood, with the world well lost! She surrendered to the innocence of it; deliberately grasped something delicious, new. Poor boy! How delightful to feel him happy at last – to promise marriage and mean to perform it! When? Oh! when he liked – Soon, quite soon; the sooner the better! Almost unconscious that she was 'playing' a young girl, she was carried away by his amazement and his joy. He was on fire, on air; yet he remained delicate – he was wonderful! For an hour they sat – a fragrant hour for memory to sniff – before she remembered that she was dining out at half-past eight. She put her lips to his, and closed her eyes. And thought ran riot. Should she spoil it, and make sure of him in modern fashion? What was his image of her but a phlizz, but a fraud? She saw his eyes grow troubled, felt his hands grow fevered. Something seemed drowning before her eyes. She stood up.

'Now, my darling, you must fly!'

When he had flown, she threw off her dress and brushed out her hair that in the mirror seemed to have more gold than red. ... Some letters on her dressing-table caught her eye. The first was a bill, the second a bill; the third ran thus:

DEAR MADAM,

We regret to say that Cuthcott Kingson & Forsyte have refused to give the apology we asked for, and withdrawn their verbal offer *in toto*. We presume, therefore, that the action must go forward. We have every hope, however, that they may reconsider the matter before it comes into Court.

Your obedient servants,

SETTLEWHITE & STARK.

She dropped it and sat very still, staring at a little hard line on the right side of her mouth and a little hard line on the left. ...

Francis Wilmot, flying, thought of steamship lines and staterooms, of registrars and rings. An hour ago he had despaired; now it seemed he had always known she was 'too fine not to

442

give up this fellow whom she didn't love'. He would make her the queen of South Carolina – he surely would! But if she didn't like it out there, he would sell the 'old home', and they would go and live where she wished – in Venice; he had heard her say Venice was wonderful; or New York, or Sicily; with her he wouldn't care! And London in the cold dry wind seemed beautiful, no longer a grey maze of unreality and shadows, but a city where you could buy rings and steamship passages. The wind cut him like a knife and he did not feel it. That poor devil Mac-Gown! He hated the sight, the thought of him, and yet felt sorry, thinking of him with the cup dashed from his lips. And all the days, weeks, months himself had spent circling round the flame, his wings scorched and drooping, seemed now but the natural progress of the soul towards Paradise. Twenty-four – his age and hers; an eternity of bliss before them! He pictured her on the porch at home. Horses! A better car than the old Ford! The darkies would adore her – kind of grand, and so white! To walk with her among the azaleas in the spring, that he could smell already; no – it was his hands where he had touched her! He shivered, and resumed his flight under the bare trees, well-nigh alone in the east wind; the stars of a bitter night shining.

A card was handed to him as he entered his hotel.

'Mr Wilmot, a gentleman to see you.'

Sir Alexander was seated in a corner of the lounge, with a crush hat in his hand. He rose and came towards Francis Wilmot, grim and square.

'I've been meaning to call on you for some time, Mr Wilmot.'

'Yes sir. May I offer you a cocktail, or a glass of sherry?'

'No, thank you. You are aware of my engagement to Miss Ferrar?'

'I was, sir.'

This red aggressive face, with its stiff moustache and burning eyes, revived his hatred; so that he no longer felt sorry.

'You know that I very much object to your constant visits to that young lady. In this country it is not the part of a gentleman to pursue an engaged young woman.'

'That,' said Francis Wilmot coolly, 'is for Miss Ferrar herself to say.'

MacGown's face grew even redder.

'If you hadn't been an American, I should have warned you to keep clear a long time ago.'

Francis Wilmot bowed.

'Well! Are you going to?'

'Permit me to decline an answer.'

MacGown thrust forward his face.

'I've told you,' he said. 'If you trespass any more, look out for yourself.'

'Thank you; I will,' said Francis Wilmot softly.

MacGown stood for a moment swaying slightly. Was he going to hit out? Francis Wilmot put his hands into his trouser pockets.

'You've had your warning,' said MacGown, and turned on his heel.

'Good-night!' said Francis Wilmot to that square receding back. He had been gentle, he had been polite, but he hated the fellow, yes, indeed! Save for the triumphal glow within him, there might have been a fuss!

Chapter Ten

PHOTOGRAPHY

SUMMONED to the annual Christmas covert-shooting at Lippinghall, Michael found there two practical politicians and one member of the Government.

In the mullion-windowed smoking-room, where men retired, and women too sometimes, into chairs old, soft, leathery, the ball of talk was lightly tossed, and naught so devastating as Foggartism mentioned. But in odd minutes and half-hours Michael gained insight into political realities, and respect for practical politicians. Even on this holiday they sat up late, got up early, wrote letters, examined petitions, dipped into Blue Books. They were robust, ate heartily, took their liquor like men, never seemed fatigued. They shaved clean, looked healthy, and shot badly with enjoyment. The member of the Government played golf instead, and Fleur went round with him. Michael learned the lesson : have so much on your mind that you have practically nothing in it; no time to pet your schemes, fancies, feelings. Carry on, and be careful that you don't know to what end.

As for Foggartism, they didn't – *à la Evening Sun* – poohpooh it; they merely asked, as Michael had often asked himself: 'Yes, but how are you going to work it? Your scheme might be very good, if it didn't hit people's pockets. Any addition to the price of living is out of the question – the country's taxed up to the hilt. Your Foggartism's going to need money in every direction. You may swear till you're blue in the face that ten or twenty years hence it'll bring fivefold return; nobody will listen. You may say: "Without it we're all going to the devil"; but we're accustomed to that – some people think we're there already, and they resent its being said. Others, especially manufacturers, believe what they want to. They can't bear anyone who cries "stinking fish", whatever his object. Talk about reviving trade, and less taxation, or offer more wages and talk of a capital levy, and, according to Party, we shall believe you've done the trick – until we find you haven't. But you're talking of less trade and more taxation in the present with a view to a better future. Great Scott! In politics you can shuffle the cards, but you mustn't add or substract. People only react to immediate benefit, or, as in the war, to imminent danger. You must cut out sensationalism.'

In short, they were intelligent, and completely fatalistic.

After these quiet talks, Michael understood, much better than before, the profession of politics. He was greatly attracted by the member of the Government; his personality was modest, his manner pleasant, he had Departmental ideas, and was doing his best with his own job according to those ideas; if he had others he kept them to himself. He seemed to admire Fleur, and he listened better than the other two. He said, too, some things they hadn't. 'Of course, what we're able to do may be found so inadequate that there'll be a great journalistic outcry, and under cover of it we may bring in some sweeping measures that people will swallow before they know what they're in for.'

'The Press,' said Michael; 'I don't see them helping.'

'Well! It's the only voice there is. If you could get fast hold of the vociferous papers, you might even put Foggartism over. What you're really up against is the slow town growth of the last hundred and fifty years, an ingrained state of mind which can only see England in terms of industrialism and the carrying trade. And in the town-mind, of course, hope springs eternal. They don't like calamity talk. Some genuinely think we can go on indefinitely on the old lines, and get more and more prosperous into the bargain. Personally, I don't. It's possible that much of what old Foggart advocates may be adopted bit by bit, even child emigration, from sheer practical necessity; but it won't be called Foggartism. Inventor's luck! *He'll* get no credit for being the first to see it. And,' added the Minister gloomily, 'by the time it's adopted, it'll probably be too late.'

Receiving the same day a request for an interview from a Press syndicate whose representative would come down to suit his convenience, Michael made the appointment, and prepared an elaborate exposition of his faith. The representative, however, turned out to be a camera, and a photograph entitled: 'The Member for mid-Bucks expounding Foggartism to our Representative,' became the only record of it. The camera was active. It took a family group in front of the porch: 'Right to left, Mr Michael Mont, M.P., Lady Mont, Mrs Michael Mont, Sir Lawrence Mont, Bt.' It took Fleur: 'Mrs Michael Mont, with Kit and Dandie.' It took the Jacobean wing. It took the Minister, with his pipe, 'enjoying a Christmas rest'. It took a corner of the walled garden: 'In the grounds'. It then had lunch. After lunch it took the whole house-party: 'At Sir Lawrence Mont's, Lippinghall Manor, Bucks'; with the Minister on Lady Mont's right and the Minister's wife on Sir Lawrence's left. This photograph would have turned out better if the Dandie, inadvertently left out, had not made a sudden onslaught on the camera legs. It took a photograph of Fleur alone: 'Mrs Michael Mont – a charming young Society hostess.' It understood that Michael was making an interesting practical experiment – could it take Foggartism in action? Michael grinned and said: 'Yes, if it would take a walk, too.'

They departed for the coppice. The colony was in its normal state – Boddick, with two of the contractor's men cheering him on, was working at the construction of the incubator-house; Swain, smoking a cigarette, was reading the *Daily Mail*; Bergfeld was sitting with his head in his hands, and Mrs Bergfeld was washing up.

The camera took three photographs. Michael, who had noted that Bergfeld had begun shaking, suggested to the camera that it would miss its train. It at once took a final photograph of Michael in front of the hut, two cups of tea at the Manor, and its departure.

As Michael was going upstairs that night, the butler came to him.

'The man Boddick's in the pantry, Mr Michael; I'm afraid something's happened, sir.'

'Oh!' said Michael blankly.

Where Michael had spent many happy hours, when he was young, was Boddick, his pale face running with sweat, and his dark eyes very alive.

'The German's gone, sir.'

'Gone?'

'Hanged hisself. The woman's in an awful state. I cut him down and sent Swain to the village.'

'Good God! Hanged! But why?'

'He's been very funny these last three days; and that camera upset him properly. Will you come, sir?'

They set out with a lantern, Boddick telling his tale.

'As soon as ever you was gone this afternoon he started to shake and carry on about having been made game of. I told 'im not to be a fool, and went out to get on with it. But when I

447

came in to tea, he was still shakin', and talkin' about his honour and his savin's; Swain had got fed up and was jeerin' at him, and Mrs Bergfeld was as white as a ghost in the corner. I told Swain to shut his head; and Fritz simmered down after a bit, and sat humped up as he does for hours together. Mrs Bergfeld got our tea. I had some chores to finish, so I went out after. When I come in at seven, they was at it again hammer and tongs, and Mrs Bergfeld cryin' fit to bust her heart. "Can't you see," I said, "how you're upsettin' your wife?" "Henry Boddick," he said, "I've nothing against *you*, you've always been decent to me. But this Swain," he said, "'is name is Swine!" and he took up the bread-knife. I got it away from him, and spoke him calm. "Ah!" he said, "but *you've* no pride." Swain was lookin' at him with that sort o' droop in his mouth he's got. "Pride," he says, "you silly blighter, what call 'ave *you* to 'ave any pride?" Well, I see that while we was there he wasn't goin' to get any better, so I took Swain off for a glass at the pub. When we came back at ten o'clock, Swain went straight to bed, and I went into the mess-room, where I found his wife alone. "Has he gone to bed?" I said. "No," she said, "he's gone out to cool his head. Oh! Henry Boddick," she said, "I don't know what to do with him!" We sat there a bit, she tellin' me about 'im brooding, and all that – nice woman she is, too; till suddenly she said: "Henry Boddick," she said, "I'm frightened. Why don't he come?" We went out to look for him, and where d'you think he was, sir? You know that big tree we're just goin' to have down? There's a ladder against it, and the guidin' rope all fixed. He'd climbed up that ladder in the moonlight, put the rope round his neck, and jumped off; and there he was, six feet from the ground, dead as a duck. I roused up Swain, and we got him in, and – Well, we 'ad a proper time! Poor woman, I'm sorry for her, sir – though really I think it's just as well he's gone – he couldn't get upsides with it, anyhow. That camera chap would have given something for a shot at what we saw there in the moonlight.'

'Foggartism in action!' thought Michael bitterly. 'So endeth the First Lesson!'

The hut looked lonely in the threading moonlight and the bitter wind. Inside, Mrs Bergfeld was kneeling beside the body placed on the deal table, with a handkerchief over its face. Michael put a hand on her shoulder. She gave him a wild look, bowed her head again, and her lips began moving. 'Prayer!' thought Michael. 'Catholic – of course!' He took Boddick aside. 'Don't let her see Swain. I'll talk to him.'

When the police and the doctor came in, he button-holed the hairdresser, whose shadowy face looked ghastly in the moonlight. He seemed much upset.

'You'd better come down to the house for the night, Swain.'

'All right, sir. I never meant to hurt the poor beggar. But he did carry on so, and I've got my own trouble. I couldn't stand 'im monopolisin' misfortune the way he does. When the inquest's over, I'm off. If I can't get some sun soon, I'll be as dead as 'im.'

Michael was relieved. Boddick would be left alone.

When at last he got back to the house with Swain, Fleur was asleep. He did not wake her to tell her the news, but lay a long time trying to get warm, and thinking of that great obstacle to all salvation – the human element. And, mingled with his visions of the woman beside that still, cold body were longings for the warmth of the young body close to him.

The photographs were providential. For three days no paper could be taken up which did not contain some allusion, illustrated, to 'The Tragedy on a Buckinghamshire estate' 'German actor hangs himself'; 'The drama at Lippinghall'; 'Tragic end of an experiment'; 'Right to Left: Mr Michael Mont, Member for mid-Bucks; Bergfeld, the German actor who hanged himself; Mrs Bergfeld.'

The *Evening Sun* wrote more in sorrow than in anger:

'The suicide of a German actor on Sir Lawrence Mont's estate at Lippinghall has in it a touch of the grotesquely moral. The unfortunate man seems to have been one of three "out-of-works" selected by the young Member for mid-Bucks, recently conspicuous for his speech on "Foggartism", for a practical experiment in that peculiar movement. Why he should have chosen a German to assist the English people to return to the Land is not perhaps very clear; but, largely speaking, the incident illustrates the utter unsuitability of all amateur attempts to solve this problem, and the futility of pretending to deal with the unemployment crisis while we still tolerate among us numbers of aliens who take the bread out of the mouths of our own people.' The same issue contained a short leader entitled: 'The Alien in Our Midst.' The inquest was well attended. It was common knowledge that three men and one woman lived in the hut, and sensational developments were expected. A good deal of disappointment was felt that the evidence disclosed nothing at all of a sexual character.

Fleur, with the eleventh baronet, returned to town after it was over. Michael remained for the funeral – in a Catholic cemetery some miles away. He walked with Henry Boddick behind Mrs Bergfeld. A little sleet was drifting out of a sky the colour of the gravestones, and against that whitish sky the yew trees looked very stark. He had ordered a big wreath laid on the grave, and when he saw it thus offered up, he thought: 'First human beings, then rams, now flowers! Progress? I wonder!'

Having arranged that Norah Curfew should take Mrs Bergfeld as cook in Bethnal Green, he drove her up to London in the Manor car. During that long drive he experienced again feelings that he had not had since the war. Human hearts, dressed-up to the nines in circumstances, interests, manners, accents, race, and class, when stripped by grief, by love, by hate, by laughter were one and the same heart. But how seldom were they stripped! Life was a clothed affair! A good thing too, perhaps – the strain of nakedness was too considerable! He was, in fact, infinitely relieved to see the face of Norah Curfew, and hear her cheerful words to Mrs Bergfeld:

'Come in, my dear, and have some tea!' She was the sort who stripped to the heart without strain or shame.

Fleur was in the drawing-room when he got home, furred up to her cheeks, which were bright as if she had just come in from the cold.

'Been out, my child?'

'Yes. I –' She stopped, looked at him rather queerly, and said: 'Well, have you finished with that business?'

'Yes; thank God. I've dropped the poor creature on Norah Curfew.'

Fleur smiled. 'Ah! Yes, Norah Curfew! *She* lives for everybody but herself, doesn't she?'

'She does,' said Michael, rather sharply.

'The new woman. One's getting clean out of fashion.'

Michael took her cheeks between his hands.

'What's the matter, Fleur?'

'Nothing.'

'There is.'

'Well, one gets a bit fed up with being left out, as if one were fit for nothing but Kit, and looking appetizing.'

Michael dropped his hands, hurt and puzzled. Certainly he had not consulted her about his 'down and outs'; had felt sure it would only bore or make her laugh – No future in it! And had there been?

'Any time you like to go shares in any mortal thing, Fleur, you've only to say so.'

'Oh! I don't want to poke into your affairs. I've got my own. Have you had tea?'

'Do tell me what's the matter?'

'My dear boy, you've already asked me that, and I've already told you – nothing.'

'Won't you kiss me?'

'Of course. And there's Kit's bath – would you like to go up?'

Each short jab went in a little farther. This was a spiritual crisis, and he did not know in the least how to handle it. Didn't she want him to admire her, to desire her? What did she want? Recognition that she was as interested as he in – in the state of the country? Of course! Only – was she?

'Well,' she said, '*I* want tea, anyway. Is the new woman dramatic?'

Jealousy? The notion was absurd. He said quietly:

'I don't quite follow you.'

Fleur looked up at him with very clear eyes.

'Good God!' said Michael, and left the room.

He went upstairs and sat down before 'The White Monkey'. In that strategic position he better perceived the core of his domestic moment. Fleur had to be first – had to take precedence. No object in her collection must live a life of its own! He was appalled by the bitterness of that thought. No, no! It was only that she had a complex – a silver spoon, and it had become natural in her mouth. She resented his having interests in which she was not first; or rather, perhaps, resented the fact that they were not her interests too. And that was to her credit, when you came to think of it. She was vexed with herself for being egocentric. Poor Child! 'I've got to mind my eye,' thought Michael, 'or I shall make some modern-novel mess of this in three parts.' And his mind strayed naturally to the science of dishing up symptoms as if they were roots – Ha! He remembered his nursery governess locking him in; he had dreaded being penned up ever since. The psycho-analysts would say that was due to the action of his governess. It wasn't – many small boys wouldn't have cared a hang; it was due to a nature that existed before that action. He took up the photograph of Fleur that stood on his desk. He loved the face, he would always love it. If she had limitations – well! So had he – lots! This was comedy, one mustn't make it into tragedy! Surely she had a sense of humour, too! Had she? Had she not? And Michael searched the face he held in his hands. ...

But, as usual with husbands, he had diagnosed without knowledge of all the facts.

Fleur had been bored at Lippinghall, even collection of the Minister had tried her. She had concealed her boredom from Michael. But self-sacrifice takes its revenge. She reached home in a mood of definite antagonism to public affairs. Hoping to feel better if she bought a hat or two, she set out for Bond Street. At the corner of Burlington Street, a young man bared his head.

'Fleur!'

Wilfrid Desert! Very lean and very brown!

'You!'

'Yes. I'm just back. How's Michael?'

'Very well. Only he's in Parliament.'

'Great Scott! And how are you?'

'As you see. Did you have a good time?'

'Yes. I'm only perching. The East has got me!'

'Are you coming to see us?'

'I think not. The burnt child, you know.'

'Yes; you *are* brown!'

'Well, good-bye, Fleur! You look just the same, only more so. I'll see Michael somewhere.'

'Good-bye!' She walked on without looking back, and then regretted not having found out whether Wilfrid had done the same.

She had given Wilfrid up for – well, for Michael, who – who had forgotten it! Really she was too self-sacrificing!

And then at three o'clock a note was brought her:

'By hand, ma'am; answer waiting.'

She opened an envelope, stamped 'Cosmopolis Hotel.'

MADAM,

We apologize for troubling you, but are in some perplexity. Mr Francis Wilmot, a young American gentleman, who has been staying in this hotel since early October, has, we are sorry to say, contracted pneumonia. The doctor reports unfavourably on his condition. In these circumstances we thought it right to examine his effects, in order that we might communicate with his friends; but the only indication we can find is a card of yours. I venture to ask you if you can help us in the matter.

Believe me to be, Madam,
Your faithful servant,
(for the Management)

Fleur stared at an illegible signature, and her thoughts were bitter. Jon had dumped Francis on her as a herald of his happiness; her enemy had lifted him! Well, then, why didn't that Cat look after him herself? Oh! well, poor boy! Ill in a great hotel – without a soul!

'Call me a taxi, Coaker.'

On her way to the hotel she felt slight excitement of the 'ministering angel' order.

Giving her name at the bureau, she was taken up to Room 209. A chambermaid was there. The doctor, she said, had ordered a nurse, who had not yet come.

Francis Wilmot, very flushed, was lying back, propped up; his eyes were closed.

'How long has he been ill like this?'

'I've noticed him looking queer, ma'am; but we didn't know how bad he was until today. I think he's just neglected it. The doctor says he's got to be packed. Poor gentleman, it's very sad. You see, he's hardly there!'

Francis Wilmot's lips were moving; he was evidently on the verge of delirium.

'Go and make some lemon tea in a jug as weak and hot as you can; quick!'

When the maid had gone, she went up and put her cool hand to his forehead.

'It's all right, Francis. Much pain?'

Francis Wilmot's lips ceased to move; he looked up at her and his eyes seemed to burn.

'If you cure me,' he said, 'I'll hate you. I just want to get out, quick!'

She changed her hand on his forehead, whose heat seemed to scorch the skin of her palm. His lips resumed their almost soundless movement. The meaningless, meaningful whispering frightened her, but she stood her ground, constantly changing her hand, till the maid came back with the tea.

'The nurse has come, miss; she'll be up in a minute.'

'Pour out the tea. Now, Francis, drink!'

His lips sucked, chattered, sucked. Fleur handed back the cup, and stood away. His eyes had closed again.

'Oh! ma'am,' whispered the maid, 'he *is* bad! Such a nice young gentleman, too.'

'What was his temperature; do you know?'

'I did hear the doctor say nearly 105. Here is the nurse, ma'am.'

Fleur went to her in the doorway.

'It's not just ordinary, nurse – he *wants* to go. I think a love-affair's gone wrong. Shall I stop and help you pack him?'

When the pneumonia jacket had been put on, she lingered, looking down at him. His eyelashes lay close and dark against his cheeks, long and innocent, like a little boy's.

Outside the door, the maid touched her arm.

'I found this letter, ma'am; ought I to show it to the doctor?'

Fleur read:

MY POOR DEAR BOY,
We were crazy yesterday. It isn't any good, you know. Well, I haven't got a breakable heart; nor have you really, though you may think so when you get this. Just go back to your sunshine and your darkies, and put me out of your thoughts. I couldn't stay the course. I couldn't possibly stand being poor. I must just go through it with my Scotsman and travel the appointed road. What is the good of thinking we can play at children in the wood, when one of them is

Your miserable (at the moment)
MARJORIE

I mean this – I mean it. Don't come and see me any more, and make it worse for yourself. M.

'Exactly!' said Fleur. 'I've told the nurse. Keep it and give it him back if he gets well. If he doesn't, burn it. I shall come to-morrow.' And, looking at the maid with a faint smile, she added: '*I* am not that lady!'

'Oh! no, ma'am – miss – no, I'm sure! Poor young gentleman! Isn't there nothing to be done?'

'I don't know. I should think not....'

She had kept all these facts from Michael with a sudden retaliatory feeling. He couldn't have private – or was it public – life all to himself!

After he had gone out with his 'Good God!' she went to the window. Queer to have seen Wilfrid again! Her heart had not fluttered, but it tantalized her not to know whether she could

455

attract him back. Out in the Square it was as dark as when last she had seen him before he fled to the East – a face pressed to this window that she was touching with her fingers. 'The burnt child!' No! She did not want to reduce him to that state again; to copy Marjorie Ferrar, who had copied her. If, instead of going East, Wilfrid had chosen to have pneumonia like poor Francis! What would she have done? Let him die for want of her? And what ought she to do about Francis, having seen that letter? Tell Michael? No, he thought her frivolous and irresponsible. Well! She would show him! And that sister – who had married Jon? Ought she to be cabled to? But this would have a rapid crisis, the nurse had said, and to get over from America in time would be impossible! Fleur went back to the fire. What kind of girl was this wife of Jon's? Another in the new fashion – like Norah Curfew; or just one of those Americans out for her own way and the best of everything? But they would have the new fashion in America, too – even though it didn't come from Paris. Anne Forsyte! – Fleur gave a little shiver in front of the hot fire.

She went upstairs, took off her hat, and scrutinized her image. Her face was coloured and rounded, her eyes were clear, her brow unlined, her hair rather flattened. She fluffed it out, and went across into the nursery.

The eleventh baronet, asleep, was living his private life with a very determined expression on his face; at the foot of his cot lay the Dandie, with his chin pressed to the floor, and at the table the nurse was sewing. In front of her lay an illustrated paper with the photograph inscribed: 'Mrs Michael Mont, with Kit and Dandie.'

.'What do you think of it, nurse?'

'I think it's horrible, ma'am; it makes Kit look as if he hadn't any sense – giving him a stare like that!'

Fleur took up the paper; her quick eyes had seen that it concealed another. There on the table was a second effigy of herself: 'Mrs Michael Mont, the pretty young London hostess, who, rumour says, will shortly be defendant in a Society lawsuit.' And, above, yet another effigy, inscibed: 'Miss Marjorie Ferrar, the brilliant granddaughter of the Marquis of Shropshire, whose engagement to Sir Alexander MacGown, M.P., is announced.'

Fleur dropped paper back on paper.

Chapter Eleven

SHADOWS

THE dinner, which Marjorie Ferrar had so suddenly recollected, was MacGown's, and when she reached the appointed restaurant, he was waiting in the hall.

'Where are the others, Alec?'

'There are no others,' said MacGown.

Marjorie Ferrar reined back. 'I can't dine with you alone in a place like this!'

'I had the Ppynrryns, but they fell through.'

'Then I shall go to my club.'

'For God's sake, no, Marjorie. We'll have a private room. Go and wait in there, while I arrange it.'

With a shrug she passed into a little 'lounge'. A young woman whose face seemed familiar idled in, looked at her, and idled out again, the ormolu clock ticked, the walls of striped pale grey stared blankly in the brilliant light, and Marjorie Ferrar stared blankly back – she was still seeing Francis Wilmot's ecstatic face.

'Now!' said MacGown. 'Up those stairs, and third on the right. I'll follow in a minute.'

She had acted in a play, she had passed an emotional hour, and she was hungry. At least she could dine before making the necessary scene. And while she drank the best champagne MacGown could buy, she talked and watched the burning eyes of her adorer. That red-brown visage, square, stiff-haired head, and powerful frame – what a contrast to the pale, slim face and form of Francis! This was a man, and when he liked, agreeable. With him she would have everything she wanted except – what Francis could give her. And it was one or the other – not both, as she had thought it might be. She had once crossed the 'striding edge' on Helvellyn, with a precipice on one side and a precipice on the other, and herself, doubting down which to fall, in the middle. She hadn't fallen, and – she supposed – she wouldn't now! One didn't, if one kept one's head!

Coffee was brought; and she sat, smoking, on the sofa. Her knowledge of private rooms taught her that she was now as alone with her betrothed as money could make them. How would he behave?

He threw his cigar away, and sat down by her side. This was the moment to rise and tell him that he was no longer her betrothed. His arm went round her, his lips sought her face. 'Mind my dress; it's the only decent one I've got.'

And, suddenly, not because she heard a noise, but because her senses were not absorbed like his, she perceived a figure in the open doorway. A woman's voice said: 'Oh! I beg your pardon; I thought –' Gone!

Marjorie Ferrar started up.

'Did you see that young woman?'

'Yes. Damn her!'

'She's shadowing me.'

'What?'

'I don't know her, and yet I know her perfectly. She had a good look at me downstairs, when I was waiting.'

MacGown dashed to the door and flung it open. Nobody was there! He shut it, and came back.

'By heaven! Those people, I'll —' Well, that ends it! Marjorie, I shall send our engagement to the papers tomorrow.'

Marjorie Ferrar, leaning her elbows on the mantelpiece, stared at her own face in the glass above it. 'Not a moral about her!' What did it matter? If only she could decide to marry Francis out of hand, slide away from them all – debts, lawyers, Alec! And then the 'You be damned' spirit in her blood revolted. The impudence of it! Shadowing her! No! She was not going to leave Miss Fleur triumphant – the little snob; and that old party with the chin !

MacGown raised her hand to his lips; and somehow the caress touched her.

'Oh ! well,' she said, 'I suppose you'd better.'

'Thank God !'

'Do you really think that to get me is a cause for gratitude?'

'I would go through Hell to get you.'

'And after? Well, as we're public property, let's go down and dance.'

For an hour she danced. She would not let him take her home, and in her cab she cried. She wrote to Francis when she got in. She went out again to post it. The bitter stars, the bitter wind, the bitter night ! At the little slurred thump of her letter dropping, she laughed. To have played at children ! It was too funny ! So that was done with ! 'On with the dance !'

Extraordinary, the effect of a little paragraph in the papers ! Credit, like new-struck oil, spurted sky-high. Her post contained, not bills for dresses, but solicitations to feed, frizz, fur, flower, feather, furbelow, and photograph her. London offered itself. To escape that cynical avalanche she borrowed a hundred pounds and flew to Paris. There, every night, she went to the theatre. She had her hair done in a new style, she ordered dresses, ate at places known to the few – living it up to Michael's nickname for her; and her heart was heavy.

She returned after a week, and burned the avalanche – fortunately all letters of congratulation contained the phrase 'of course you won't think of answering this.' She didn't. The weather was mild; she rode in the Row; she prepared to hunt. On the eve of departure, she received an anonymous communication.

'Francis Wilmot is very ill with pneumonia at the Cosmopolis Hotel. He is not expected to live.'

Her heart flurried round within her breast and flumped; her knees felt weak; her hand holding the note shook; only her head stayed steady. The handwriting was 'that little snob's'. Had Francis caused this message to be sent? Was it his appeal? Poor boy! And must she go and see him if he were going to die? She so hated death. Did this mean that it was up to her to save him? What did it mean? But indecision was not her strong point. In ten minutes she was in a cab, in twenty at the hotel. Handing her card, she said:

'You have a Mr Wilmot here — a relative of mine. I've just heard of his serious illness. Can I go up and see the nurse?'

The management looked at the card, inquisitively at her face, touched a bell, and said:

'Certainly, madam. ... Here, you — take this lady up to room — er — 209.'

Led by what poor Francis called a 'bell-boy' into the lift, she walked behind his buttons along a pale-grey river of corridor carpet, between pale-grey walls, past cream-coloured after cream-coloured door in the bright electric light, with her head a little down.

The 'bell-boy' knocked ruthlessly on a door.

It was opened and in the lobby of the suite stood Fleur. . . .

Chapter Twelve

DEEPENING

-<-·->-

HOWEVER untypically American according to Soames, Francis Wilmot seemed to have the national passion for short cuts.

In two days from Fleur's first visit he had reached the crisis, hurrying towards it like a man to his bride. Yet, compared with the instinct to live, the human will is limited, so that he failed to die. Fleur, summoned by telephone, went home cheered by the doctor's words: 'He'll do now, if we can coax a little strength into him.' That, however, was the trouble. For three afternoons she watched his exhausted indifference seeming to increase. And she was haunted by cruel anxiety. On the fourth day she had been sitting for more than an hour when his eyes opened.

'Yes, Francis?'

'I'm going to quit all right, after all.'

'Don't talk like that – it's not American. Of course you're not going to quit.'

He smiled, and shut his eyes. She made up her mind then.

Next day he was about the same, more dead than alive. But her mind was at rest; her messenger had brought back word that Miss Ferrar would be in at four o'clock. She would have had the note by now; but would she come? How little one knew of other people, even when they were enemies!

He was drowsing, white and strengthless, when she heard the 'bell-boy's' knock. Passing into the lobby, she closed the door softly behind her, and opened the outer door. So she *had* come!

If this meeting of two declared enemies had in it something dramatic, neither perceived it at the moment. It was just intensely unpleasant to them both. They stood for a moment looking at each other's chins. Then Fleur said:

'He's extremely weak. Will you sit down while I tell him you're here?'

Having seen her settled where Francis Wilmot put his clothes out to be valeted in days when he had worn them, Fleur passed back into the bedroom, and again closed the door.

'Francis,' she said, 'someone is waiting to see you.'

Francis Wilmot did not stir, but his eyes opened and cleared strangely. To Fleur they seemed suddenly the eyes she had known; as if all these days they had been 'out', and someone had again put a match to them.

'You understand what I mean?'

The words came clear and feeble: 'Yes; but if I wasn't good enough for her before, I surely am not now. Tell her I'm through with that fool business.'

A lump rose in Fleur's throat.

'Thank her for coming!' said Francis Wilmot, and closed his eyes again.

Fleur went back into the lobby. Marjorie Ferrar was standing against the wall with an unlighted cigarette between her lips.

'He thanks you for coming; but he doesn't want to see you. I'm sorry I brought you down.'

Marjorie Ferrar took out the cigarette. Fleur could see her lips quivering. 'Will he get well?'

'I don't know. I think so – now. He says he's "Through with that fool business."'

Marjorie Ferrar's lips tightened. She opened the outer door, turned suddenly, and said:

'Will you make it up?'

'No,' said Fleur.

There was a moment of complete stillness: then Marjorie Ferrar gave a little laugh, and slipped out.

Fleur went back. He was asleep. Next day he was stronger. Three days later Fleur ceased her visits; he was on the road to recovery. She had become conscious moreover, that she had a little lamb which, wherever Mary went, was sure to go. She was being shadowed! How amusing! And what a bore that she couldn't tell Michael; because she had not yet begun again to tell him anything.

On the day that she ceased her visits he came in while she was dressing for dinner, with a 'weekly' in his hand.

'Listen to this,' he said:

FONDOUK

' "When to God's fondouk the donkeys are taken –
  Donkeys of Africa, Sicily, Spain –
If peradventure the Deity waken,
  He shall not easily slumber again.

Where in the sweet of God's straw they have laid them
  Broken and dead of their burdens and sores,
He, for a change, shall remember He made them –
  One of the best of His numerous chores –

Order from someone a sigh of repentance –
  Donkeys of Araby, Syria, Greece –
Over the fondouk distemper the sentence:
  God's own forsaken – the stable of peace." '

'Who's that by? It sounds like Wilfrid.'

'It is by Wilfrid,' said Michael, and did not look at her. 'I met him at the Hotch-Potch.'

'And how is he?'

'Very fit.'

'Have you asked him here?'

'No. He's going East again soon.'

Was he fishing? Did he know that she had seen him? And she said:

'I'm going down to father's, Michael. He's written twice.'

Michael put her hand to his lips.

'All right, darling.'

Fleur reddened; her strangled confidence seemed knotted in her throat. She went next day with Kit and Dandie. The 'little lamb' would hardly follow to 'The Shelter'.

Annette had gone with her mother to Cannes for a month; and Soames was alone with the English winter. He was paying little attention to it, for the 'case' was in the list, and might be reached in a few weeks' time. Deprived of French influence, he was again wavering towards compromise. The announcement of Marjorie Ferrar's engagement to MacGown had materially changed the complexion of affairs. In the eyes of a British jury, the character of a fast young lady, and the character of the same young lady publicly engaged to a Member of Parliament, with wealth and a handle to his name, would not be at all the same thing. They were now virtually dealing with Lady MacGown, and nothing, Soames knew, was so fierce as a man about to be married. To libel his betrothed was like approaching a mad dog.

He looked very grave when Fleur told him of her 'little lamb'. It was precisely the retaliation he had feared; nor could he tell her that he had 'told her so', because he hadn't. He had certainly urged her to come down to him, but delicacy had forbidden him to give her the reason. So far as he could tell through catechism, there had been nothing 'suspect' in her movements since Lippinghall, except those visits to the Cosmopolis Hotel. But they were bad enough. Who was going to believe that she went to this sick young man out of pure kindness? Such a motive was not current in a Court of Law. He was staggered when she told him that Michael didn't know of them. Why not?

'I didn't feel like telling him.'

'Feel? Don't you see what a position you've put yourself in? Here you are, running to a young man's bedside, without your husband's knowledge.'

'Yes, darling; but he was terribly ill.'

'I dare say,' said Soames; 'so are lots of people.'

'Besides, he was head over heels in love with *her*.'

'D'you think he's going to admit that, even if we could call him?'

Fleur was silent, thinking of Francis Wilmot's face.

'Oh! I don't know,' she said at last. 'How horrid it all is!'

'Of course it's horrid,' said Soames. 'Have you had a quarrel with Michael?'

'No; not a quarrel. Only he doesn't tell *me* things.'

'What things?'

'How should I know, dear?'

Soames grunted. 'Would he have minded your going?'

'Of course not. He'd have minded if I hadn't. He likes that boy.'

'Well, then,' said Soames, 'either you or he, or both, will have to tell a lie, and say that he did know. I shall go up and talk to him. Thank goodness we can prove the illness. If I catch anybody coming down here after you – !'

He went up the following afternoon. Parliament being in recess, he sought the Hotch-Potch Club. He did not like a place always connected in his mind with his dead cousin, that fellow young Jolyon, and said to Michael at once: 'Can we go somewhere else?'

'Yes, sir; where would you like?'

'To your place, if you can put me up for the night. I want to have a talk with you.'

Michael looked at him askance.

'Now,' said Soames, after dinner, 'what's this about Fleur – she says you don't tell her things?'

Michael gazed into his glass of port.

'Well, sir,' he said slowly, 'I'd be only too glad to, of course, but I don't think they really interest her. She doesn't feel that public things matter.'

'Public! I meant private.'

'There aren't any private things. D'you mean that she thinks there are?'

Soames dropped his scrutiny.

'I don't know – she said "things".'

'Well, you can put that out of your head, and hers.'

'H'm! Anyway, the result's been that she's been visiting that young American with pneumonia at the Cosmopolis Hotel, without letting you know. It's a mercy she hasn't picked it up.'

'Francis Wilmot?'

'Yes. He's out of the wood, now. That's not the point. She's been shadowed.'

'Good God!' said Michael.

'Exactly! This is what comes of not talking to your wife. Wives are funny – they don't like it.'

Michael grinned.

'Put yourself in my place, sir. It's my profession, now, to fuss about the state of the country, and all that; and you know how it is – one gets keen. But to Fleur, it's all a stunt. I quite understand that; but, you see, the keener I get, the more I'm afraid of boring her, and the less I feel I can talk to her about it. In a sort of way she's jealous.'

Soames rubbed his chin. The state of the country was a curious sort of co-respondent. He himself was often worried by the state of the country, but as a source of division between husband and wife it seemed to him cold-blooded; he had known other sources in his time!

'Well, you mustn't let it go on,' he said. 'It's trivial.'

Michael got up.

'Trivial! Well, sir, I don't know, but it seems to me very much the sort of thing that happened when the war came. Men had to leave their wives then.'

'Wives put up with that,' said Soames, 'the country was in danger.'

'Isn't it in danger now?'

With his inveterate distrust of words, it seemed to Soames almost indecent for a young man to talk like that. Michael was a politician, of course; but politicians were there to keep the country quiet, not to go raising scares and talking through their hats.

'When you've lived a little longer,' he said, 'you'll know that there's always something to fuss about if you like to fuss. There's nothing in it really; the pound's going up. Besides, it doesn't matter what you tell Fleur, so long as you tell her something.'

'She's intelligent, sir,' said Michael.

Soames was taken aback. He could not deny the fact, and answered:

'Well, national affairs are too remote; you can't expect a woman to be interested in them.'

'Quite a lot of women are.'

'Blue-stockings.'

'No, sir; they nearly all wear "nude".'

'H'm! Those! As to interest in national affairs – put a tax on stockings, and see what happens!'

Michael grinned.

'I'll suggest it, sir.'

'If you expect,' said Soames, 'that people – women or not – are going to put themselves out of the way for any scheme like this – this Foggartism of yours, you'll be very much disappointed.'

'So everybody tells me. It's just because I don't like cold water at home as well as abroad, that I've given up worrying Fleur.'

'Well, if you take my advice, you'll take up something practical – the state of the traffic, or penny postage. Drop pessimism; people who talk at large like that, never get trusted in this country. In any case you'll have to say you knew about her visits to that young man.'

466

'Certainly, sir, wife and husband are one. But you don't really mean to let them make a circus of it in Court?'

Soames was silent. He did not *mean* them to; but what if they did?

'I can't tell,' he said, at last. 'The fellow's a Scotchman. What did you go hitting him on the nose for?'

'He gave me a thick ear first. I know it was an excellent opportunity for turning the other cheek, but I didn't think of it in time.'

'You must have called him something.'

'Only a dirty dog. As you know, he suggested a low motive for my speech.'

Soames stared. In his opinion this young man was taking himself much too seriously.

'Your speech! You've got to get it out of your mind,' he said, 'that anything you can say or do will make any difference.'

'Then what's the good of my being in Parliament?'

'Well, you're in the same boat with everybody else. The country's like a tree; you can keep it in order, but you can't go taking it up by the roots to look at them.'

Michael looked at him, impressed.

'In public matters,' said Soames, 'the thing is to keep a level head, and do no more than you're obliged.'

'And what's to govern one's view of necessity?'

'Common sense. One can't have everything.'

And rising, he began scrutinizing the Goya.

'Are you going to buy another Goya, sir?'

'No; if I buy any more pictures, I shall go back to the English School.'

'Patriotism?'

Soames gave him a sharp look.

'There's no patriotism,' he said, 'in fussing. And another thing you've got to remember is that foreigners like to hear that we've got troubles. It doesn't do to discuss our affairs out loud.'

Michael took these sayings to bed with him. He remembered, when he came out of the war, thinking: 'If there's another war, nothing will induce me to go.' But now, if one were to come, he knew he *would* be going again. So Old Forsyte thought he was just 'fussing'! Was he? Was Foggartism a phlizz? Ought he to come to heel, and take up the state of the traffic? Was everything unreal? Surely not his love for Fleur? Anyway he felt hungry for her lying there. And Wilfrid back, too! To risk his happiness with her for the sake of — what? *Punch* had taken a snap at him this week, grinning and groping at a surrounding fog. Old England, like Old Forsyte, had no use for theories. Self-conscious national efforts were just pomposity. Pompous! He? The thought was terribly disturbing. He got out of bed and went to the window. Foggy! In fog all were shadows; and he the merest shadow of them all, an unpractical politician, taking things to heart! One! Two! Big Ben! How many hearts had he turned to water! How many dreams spoiled, with his measured resonance! Line up with the top-dressers, and leave the country to suck its silver spoon!

PART THREE

Chapter One

'CIRCUSES'

<del>+←→+</del>

IN his early boyhood Soames had been given to the circus. He had outgrown it; 'Circuses' were now to him little short of an abomination. Jubilees and Pageants, that recurrent decimal, the Lord Mayor's Show, Earl's Court, Olympia, Wembley – all he disliked. He could not stand a lot of people with their mouths open. Dressing up was to him a symptom of weak-mindedness, and the collective excitement of a crowd an extravagance that offended his reticent individualism. Though not deeply versed in history, he had an idea, too, that nations who went in for 'circuses' were decadent. Queen Victoria's funeral, indeed, had impressed him – there had been a feeling in the air that day; but, ever since, things had gone from bad to worse. They made everything into a 'circus' now! A man couldn't commit a murder without the whole paper-reading population – himself included – looking over each other's shoulders; and as to these football-matches, and rodeos – they interfered with the traffic and the normal course of conversation; people were so crazy about them!

Of course, 'circuses' had their use. They kept the people quiet. Violence by proxy, for instance, was obviously a political principle of some value. It was difficult to gape at the shedding of blood and shed it at the same time; the more people stood in rows to see others being hurt, the less trouble would they take to hurt others, and the sounder Soames could sleep by night. Still sensation-hunting had become a disease, in his opinion, and no one was being inoculated for it, so far as he could see!

As the weeks went on and the cases before it in the List went off, the 'circus' they were proposing to make of his daughter

appeared to him more and more monstrous. He had an instinctive distrust of Scotchmen – they called themselves Scotsmen
nowadays, as if it helped their character! – they never let go,
and he could not approve in other people a quality native to
himself. Besides, 'Scotchmen' were so – so exuberant – always
either dour or else hearty – extravagant chaps! Towards the
middle of March, with the case in the List for the following week,
he took an extreme step and entered the Lobby of the House of
Commons. He had spoken to no one of his determination to
make this last effort, for it seemed to him that all – Annette,
Michael, Fleur herself – had done their best to spoil the chance of
settlement.

Having sent in his card, he waited a long while in that lofty
purlieu. 'Lobbying', he knew the phrase, but had never realized
the waste of time involved in it. The statues consoled him somewhat. Sir Stafford Northcote – a steady chap; at old Forsyte
dinner-parties in the 'eighties his character had been as much a
standby as the saddle of mutton. He found even 'that fellow
Gladstone' bearable in stucco, or whatever it was up there. You
might dislike, but you couldn't sneeze at him, as at some of
these modern chaps. He was sunk in coma before Lord Granville
when at last he heard the words:

'Sir Alexander MacGown,' and saw a square man with a
ruddy face, stiff black hair, and clipped moustache, coming between the railings, with a card in his hand.

'Mr Forsyte?'

'Yes. Can we go anywhere that's not quite so public?'

The 'Scotchman' nodded, and led him down a corridor to a
small room.

'Well?'

Soames smoothed his hat. 'This affair,' he said, 'can't be any
more agreeable to you than it is to me.'

'Are you the individual who was good enough to apply the
word "traitress" to the lady I'm engaged to?'

'That is so.'

'Then I don't see how you have the impudence to come and
speak to me.'

Soames bit his lips.

'I spoke under the provocation of hearing your fiancée call my daughter a snob, in her own house. Do you want this petty affair made public?'

'If you think that you and your daughter can get away with calling the lady I'm going to marry "a snake", "a traitress", "an immoral person", you're more mistaken than you ever were in your life. An unqualified apology that her Counsel can announce in Court is your only way out.'

'That you won't get; mutual regret is another thing. As to the question of damages –'

'Damn the damages!' said MacGown violently. And there was that in Soames which applauded.

'Well,' he said, 'I'm sorry for you and her.'

'What the devil do you mean, sir?'

'You will know by the end of next week, unless you revise your views in between. If it comes into Court, we shall justify.'

The 'Scotchman' went so red that for a moment Soames was really afraid he would have an apoplectic fit.

'You'd better look out what you say in Court.'

'We pay no attention to bullies in Court.'

MacGown clenched his fists.

'Yes,' said Soames, 'it's a pity I'm not your age. Good evening!'

He passed the fellow and went out. He had noted his way in this 'rabbit warren', and was soon back among the passionless statues. Well! He had turned the last stone and could do no more, except make that overbearing fellow and his young woman sorry they'd ever been born. He came out into the chilly mist of Westminster. Pride and temper! Sooner than admit themselves in the wrong, people would turn themselves into an expensive 'circus' for the gaping and the sneers, the japing and the jeers of half the town! To vindicate her 'honour', that 'Scotchman' would have his young woman's past dragged out! And fairly faced by the question whether to drag it out or not, Soames stood still. If he didn't, she might get a verdict; if he did, and didn't convince the jury, the damages would be shockingly increased. They might run into thousands. He felt the need of definite decision. One had been drifting in the belief that the thing wouldn't come into Court! Four o'clock! Not too late, perhaps, to see Sir James Foskisson. He would telephone to very young Nicholas to arrange a conference at once, and if Michael was at South Square, he would take him down to it. . . .

In his study, Michael had been staring with lugubrious relish at Aubrey Greene's cartoon of himself in a Society paper. On one leg, like Guy – or was it Slingsby? – in the Edward Lear 'Nonsense' book, he was depicted crying in a wilderness where a sardonic smile was rising on the horizon. Out of his mouth the word 'Foggartism' wreathed like the smoke of a cigar. Above a hole in the middle distance, a meercat's body supported the up-turned face and applauding forepaws of Mr Blythe. The thing was devastating in treatment and design – not unkind, merely killing. Michael's face had been endowed with a sort of after-dinner rapture, as if he were enjoying the sound of his own voice. Ridicule! Not even a personal friend, an artist, could see that the wilderness was at least as deserving of ridicule as the pelican! The cartoon seemed to write the word 'futility' large across his page. It recalled to him Fleur's words at the outset: 'And by the time the Tories go out you'll have your licence.' She was a born realist! From the first she had foreseen for him the position of an eccentric, picturesquely beating a little private drum! A dashed good cartoon! And no one could appreciate it so deeply as its victim. But why did everyone smile at Foggart-ism? Why? Because among a people who naturally walked, it leaped like a grasshopper; to a nation that felt its way in fog, it seemed a will-o'-the-wisp. Yes, he was a fool for his pains! And – just then, Soames arrived.

'I've been to see that Scotchman,' he said. 'He means to take it into Court.'

'Oh! Not really, sir! I always thought you'd keep it out.'

'Only an unqualified apology will do that. Fleur can't give it; she's in the right. Can you come down with me now and see Sir James Foskisson?'

They set out in a taxi for the Temple.

The chambers of a very young Nicholas Forsyte were in Paper Buildings. Chinny, mild and nearly forty, he succeeded within ten minutes in presenting to them every possible doubt.

'He seems to enjoy the prospect of getting tonked,' murmured Michael while they were going over to Sir James.

'A poor thing,' Soames responded; 'but careful. Foskisson must attend to the case himself.'

After those necessary minutes during which the celebrated K.C. was regathering from very young Nicholas what it was all about, they were ushered into the presence of one with a large head garnished by small grey whiskers, and really obvious brains. Since selecting him, Soames had been keeping an eye on the great advocate; had watched him veiling his appeals to a jury with an air of scrupulous equity; very few – he was convinced – and those not on juries, could see Sir James Foskisson coming round a corner. Soames had specially remarked his success in cases concerned with morals or nationality – no one so apt at getting a co-respondent, a German, a Russian, or anybody at all bad, non-suited! At close quarters his whiskers seemed to give him an intensive respectability – difficult to imagine him dancing, dicing, or in bed. In spite of his practice, too, he enjoyed the reputation of being thorough; he might be relied on to know more than half the facts of any case by the time he went into Court, and to pick up the rest as he went along – or at least not to show that he hadn't. Very young Nicholas, knowing all the facts, had seemed quite unable to see what line could possibly be taken. Sir James, on the other hand, appeared to know only just enough. Sliding his light eyes from Soames to Michael, he retailed them, and said: 'Eminently a case for an amicable settlement.'

'Indeed!' said Soames.

Something in his voice seemed to bring Sir James to attention.

'Have you attempted that?'

'I have gone to the limit.'

'Excuse me, Mr Forsyte, but what do you regard as the limit?'

'Fifteen hundred pounds, and a mutual expression of regret. They'd accept the money, but they ask for an unqualified apology.'

The great lawyer rested his chin. 'Have you tried the unqualified apology without the money?'

'No.'

'I would almost be inclined. MacGown is a very rich man. The shadow and the substance, eh? The expressions in the letters are strong. What do you say, Mr Mont?'

'Not so strong as those she used of my wife.'

Sir James Foskisson looked at the very young Nicholas.

'Let me see,' he said, 'those were – ?'

'Lion-huntress and snob,' said Michael curtly.

Sir James wagged his head precisely as if it were a pair of scales.

'Immoral, snake, traitress, without charm – you think those weaker?'

'They don't make you snigger, sir, the others do. In Society it's the snigger that counts.'

Sir James smiled.

'The jury won't be in Society, Mr Mont.'

'My wife doesn't feel like making an apology, anyway, unless there's an expression of regret on the other side; and I don't see why she should.'

Sir James Foskisson seemed to breathe more freely.

'In that case,' he said, 'we have to consider whether to use the detective's evidence or not. If we do, we shall need to subpoena the hall porter and the servants at Mr – er – Curfew's flat.'

'Exactly,' said Soames; 'that's what we're here to decide.' It was as if he had said: 'The conference is now opened.'

Sir James perused the detective's evidence for five silent minutes.

'If this is confirmed, even partially,' he said at last, 'we win.'

Michael had gone to the window. The trees in the garden had tiny buds; some pigeons were strutting on the grass below. He heard Soames say:

'I ought to tell you that they've been shadowing my daughter.

There's nothing, of course, except some visits to a young American dangerously ill of pneumonia at his hotel.'

'Of which I knew and approved,' said Michael, without turning round.

'Could we call him?'

'I believe he's still at Bournemouth. But he was in love with Miss Ferrar.'

Sir James turned to Soames.

'If there's no question of a settlement, we'd better go for the gloves. Merely to cross-examine as to books and play and clubs is very inconclusive.'

'Have you read the dark scene in "The Plain Dealer"?' asked Soames; 'and that novel, *Canthar*?'

'All very well, Mr Forsyte, but impossible to say what a jury would make of impersonal evidence like that.'

Michael had come back to his seat.

'I've a horror,' he said, 'of dragging in Miss Ferrar's private life.'

'No doubt. But do you want me to win the case?'

'Not that way. Can't we go into Court, say nothing, and pay up?'

Sir James Foskisson smiled and looked at Soames. 'Really,' he seemed to say, 'why did you bring me this young man?'

Soames, however, had been pursuing his own thoughts.

'There's too much risk about that flat; if we failed there, it might be a matter of twenty thousand pounds. Besides, they would certainly call my daughter. I want to prevent that at all costs. I thought you could turn the whole thing into an indictment of modern morality.'

Sir James Foskisson moved in his chair, and the pupils of his light-blue eyes became as pin-points. He nodded almost imperceptibly three times, precisely as if he had seen the Holy Ghost.

'When shall we be reached?' he said to very young Nicholas.

'Probably next Thursday – Mr Justice Brane.'

'Very well. I'll see you again on Monday. Good evening.' And he sank back into an immobility, which neither Soames nor Michael felt equal to disturbing.

They went away silent – very young Nicholas tarrying in conversation with Sir James's devil.

Turning at the Temple station, Michael murmured:

'It was just as if he'd said: "Some stunt!" wasn't it? I'm looking in at *The Outpost*, sir. If you're going back to Fleur, will you tell her?'

Soames nodded. There it was! He had to do everything that was painful.

Chapter Two

'NOT GOING TO HAVE IT'

◄◄‹·›►►

I N the office of *The Outpost* Mr Blythe had just been in conversation with one of those great business men who make such deep impression on all to whom they voice their views in strict confidence. If Sir Thomas Lockit did not precisely monopolize the control of manufacture in Great Britain, he, like others, caused almost anyone to think so – his knowledge was so positive and his emphasis so cold. In his view the country must resume the position held before the Great War. It all hinged on coal – a question of this seven hours a day; and they were 'not going to have it'. A shilling, perhaps two shillings, off the cost of coal. They were 'not going to have' Europe doing without British produce. Very few people knew Sir Thomas Lockit's mind; but nearly all who did were extraordinarily gratified.

Mr Blythe, however, was biting his finger, and spitting out the result.

'Who was that fellow with the grey moustache?' asked Michael.

"Lockit. He's "not going to have it".'

'Oh!' said Michael, in some surprise.

'One sees more and more, Mont, that the really dangerous people are not the politicians, who want things with public passion – that is, mildly, slowly; but the big business men, who want things with private passion, strenuously, quickly. They know their own minds; and if we don't look out they'll wreck the country.'

'What are they up to now?' said Michael.

'Nothing for the moment; but it's brewing. One sees in Lockit the futility of will-power. He's not going to have what it's entirely out of his power to prevent. He'd like to break Labour and make it work like a nigger from sheer necessity. Before that we shall be having civil war. Some of the Labour people, of course, are just as bad – they want to break everybody. It's a bee nuisance. If we're all to be plunged into industrial struggles again, how are we to get on with Foggartism?'

'I've been thinking about the country,' said Michael. 'Aren't we beating the air, Blythe? Is it any good telling a man who's lost a lung that what he wants is a new one?'

Mr Blythe puffed out one cheek.

'Yes,' he said, 'the country had a hundred very settled years – Waterloo to the War – to get into its present state; it's got its line of life so fixed and its habits so settled that nobody – neither editors, politicians nor business men – can think except in terms of its bloated town industrialism. The country's got beyond the point of balance in that hundred settled years, and it'll want fifty settled years to get back to that point again. The real trouble is that we're not going to get fifty settled years. Some bee thing or other – war with Turkey or Russia, trouble in India, civil ructions, to say nothing of another general flare-up – may knock the bottom out of any settled plans at any time. We've struck a disturbed patch of history, and we know it in our bones, and live from hand to mouth, according.'

'Well, then!' said Michael glumly, thinking of what the Minister had said to him at Lippinghall.

Mr Blythe puffed out the other cheek.

'No backsliding, young man! In Foggartism we have the best goods we can see before us, and we must bee well deliver them, as best we can. We've outgrown all the old hats.'

'Have you seen Aubrey Greene's cartoon?'

'I have.'

'Good — isn't it? But what I really came in to tell you is that this beastly libel case of ours will be on next week.'

Mr Blythe's ears moved.

'I'm sorry for that. Win or lose — nothing's worse for public life than private ructions. You're not going to have it, are you?'

'We can't help it. But our defence is to be confined to an attack on the new morality.'

'One can't attack what isn't,' said Mr Blythe.

'D'you mean to say,' said Michael, grinning, 'that you haven't noticed the new morality?'

'Certainly not. Formulate it if you can.'

' "Don't be stupid, don't be dull." '

Mr Blythe grunted. 'The old morality used to be: "Behave like a gentleman." '

'Yes! But in modern thought there ain't no sich an animal.'

'There are fragments lying about; they reconstructed Neanderthal man from half a skull.'

'A word that's laughed at can't be used, Blythe.'

'Ah!' said Mr Blythe. 'The chief failings of your generation, young Mont, are sensitiveness to ridicule and terror of being behind the times. It's bee weak-minded.'

Michael grinned.

'I know it. Come down to the House. Parsham's Electrification Bill is due. We may get some lights on Unemployment.'

Having parted from Mr Blythe in the Lobby, Michael came on his father walking down a corridor with a short bright old man in a trim grey beard.

'Ah! Michael, we've been seeking you. Marquess, my hopeful son! The marquess wants to interest you in electricity.'

Michael removed his hat.

'Will you come to the reading-room, my lord?'

This, as he knew, was Marjorie Ferrar's grandfather, and might be useful. In a remote corner of a room lighted so that nobody could see anyone else reading, they sat down in triangular formation.

'You know about electricity, Mr Mont?' said the marquess.

'No, sir, except that more of it would be desirable in this room.'

'Everywhere, Mr Mont. I've read about your Foggartism; if you'll allow me to say so, it's quite possibly the policy of the future; but nothing will be done with it till you've electrified the country. I should like you to start by supporting this Bill of Parsham's.'

And, with an engaging distinction of syllable, the old peer proceeded to darken Michael's mind.

'I see, sir,' said Michael at last. 'This Bill ought to add considerably to Unemployment.'

'Temporarily.'

'I wonder if I ought to take on any more temporary trouble. I'm finding it difficult enough to interest people in the future as it is – they seem to think the present so important.'

Sir Lawrence whinnied.

'You must give him time and pamphlets, Marquess. But, my dear fellow, while your Foggartism is confined to the stable, you'll want a second horse.'

'I've been advised already to take up the state of the traffic or penny postage. And, by the way, sir, that case of ours *is* coming into Court next week.'

Sir Lawrence's loose eyebrow shot up:

'Oh!' he said. 'Do you remember, Marquess – your granddaughter and my daughter-in-law? I came to you about it.'

'Something to do with lions? A libel, was it?' said the old peer. 'My aunt –'

While Michael was trying to decide whether this was an ejaculation or the beginning of a reminiscence, his father broke in:

'Ah! yes, an interesting case that, Marquess – it's all in Betty Montecourt's Memoirs.'

'Libels,' resumed the marquess, 'had flavour in those days. The words complained of were: "Her crinoline covers her considerable obliquity."'

'If anything's to be done to save scandal,' muttered Michael, 'it must be done now. We're at a deadlock.'

'Could *you* put in a word, sir?' said Sir Lawrence.

The marquess's beard quivered.

'I see from the papers that my granddaughter is marrying a man called MacGown, a Member of this House. Is he about?'

'Probably,' said Michael. 'But I had a row with him. I think, sir, there would be more chance with her.'

The marquess rose. 'I'll ask her to breakfast. I dislike publicity. Well, I hope you'll vote for this Bill, Mr Mont, and think over the question of electrifying the country. We want young men interested. I'm going to the Peers' Gallery now. Good-bye!'

When briskly he had gone, Michael said to his father: 'If he's not going to have it, I wish he'd ask Fleur to breakfast, too. There are two parties to this quarrel.'

Chapter Three

SOAMES DRIVES HOME

→-≺≺

Soames in the meantime was seated with one of those parties in her 'parlour'. She had listened in silence, but with a stubborn and resentful face. What did he know of the loneliness and frustration she had been feeling? Could he tell that the thrown stone had started her mirrored image of herself; that the words 'snob' and 'lion-huntress' had entered her very soul? He could not understand the spiritual injury she had received, the sudden deprivation of that self-importance, and hope of rising, necessary to all. Concerned by the expression on her face, preoccupied with the practical aspects of the 'circus' before them, and desperately involved in thoughts of how to keep her out of it as much as possible, Soames was reduced to the closeness of a fish.

'You'll be sitting in front, next to me,' he said. 'I shouldn't wear anything too bright. Would you like your mother there, too?'

Fleur shrugged her shoulders.

'Just so,' said Soames. 'But if she wants to come, she'd better, perhaps. Brane is not a joking judge, thank goodness. Have you ever been in a Court?'

'No.'

'The great thing is to keep still and pay no attention to anything. They'll all be behind you, except the jury – and there's nothing in them, really. If you look at them, don't smile!'

'Why? Aren't they safe, Dad?'

Soames put the levity aside.

'I should wear a small hat. Michael must sit on your left. Have you got over that – er – not telling each other things?'

'Yes.'

'I shouldn't begin it again. He's very fond of you.'

Fleur nodded.

'Is there anything you want to tell *me*? You know I – I worry about you.'

Fleur got up and sat on the arm of his chair; he had at once a feeling of assuagement.

'I really don't care now. The harm's done. I only hope *she'll* have a bad time.'

Soames, who had the same hope, was somewhat shocked by its expression.

He took leave of her soon after and got into his car for the dark drive back to Mapledurham. The spring evening was cold and he had the window up. At first he thought of very little; and then of still less. He had passed a tiring afternoon, and was glad of the slight smell of stephanotis provided by Annette. The road was too familiar to rouse his thoughts, beyond wonder at the lot of people there always seemed to be in the world between six and seven. He dozed his way into the new cut, woke, and dozed again. What was this – Slough? Before going to Marlborough he had been at school there with young Nicholas and St John Heyman, and after his time, some other young Forsytes. Nearly sixty years ago! He remembered his first day – a brand-new little boy in a brand-new little top-hat, with a play-box stored by his mother with things to eat, and blessed with the words: 'There, Summy dear, that'll make you popular.' He had reckoned on having command of that corruption for some weeks; but no sooner had he produced a bit of it than they had taken the box, and suggested to him that it would be a good thing to eat the lot. In twenty-two minutes twenty-two boys had materially increased their weight, and he himself, in handing out the contents, had been obliged to eat less than a twenty-third. They had left him one packet of biscuits, and those had caraway seeds, for which he had constitutionally no passion whatever. Afterwards, three other new boys had complained that he was a fool for having it all eaten up like that, instead of saving it for them, and he had been obliged to sit on their heads one by one. His popularity had lasted twenty-two minutes, and, so far as he knew, had never come back. He had been against Communism ever since.

Bounding a little on the cushioned seat, he remembered poignantly his own cousin St John Heyman pushing him into a gorse-bush and holding him there for an appreciable minute. Horrid little brutes, boys! For a moment he felt quite grateful to Michael for trying to get them out of England. And yet –! He had some pleasant memories even of boys. There was his collection of butterflies – he had sold two Red Admirals in poor condition to a boy for one-and-threepence. To be a boy again – h'm – and shoot peas at passengers in a train that couldn't stop, and drink cherry brandy going home, and win a prize by reciting two hundred lines of 'The Lady of the Lake' better than 'Cherry-Tart' Burroughes – Um? What had become of 'Cherry-Tart' Burroughes, who had so much money at school that his father went bankrupt! 'Cherry-Tart' Burroughes!

The loom of Slough faded. One was in rank country now, and he ground the handle of the window to get a little fresh air. A smell of trees and grass came in. Get boys out of England! They had funny accents in those great places overseas. Well, they had funny accents here, too. The accent had been all right at Slough – for if it wasn't a boy got lammed. He remembered the first time his father and mother – James and Emily – came down; very genteel (before the word was fly-blown), all whiskers and crinoline; the beastly boys had made personal remarks

which had hurt him! Get 'em out of England! But in those
days there had been nowhere for boys to go. He took a long
breath of the wayside air. They said England was changed,
spoiled, some even said 'done for'. Bosh! It still smelt the same!
His great-uncle, one of 'Superior Dosset's' brothers, had gone as
a boy to Bermuda at the beginning of the last century, and had
he been heard of since? Not he. Young Jon Forsyte and his
mother — his own first, unfaithful, still not quite forgotten wife
— had gone to the States — would they be heard of again? He
hoped not. England! Some day, when he had time and the car
was free, he would go and poke round on the border of Dorset
and Devon where the Forsytes came from. There was nothing
there — he understood, and he wouldn't care to let anybody
know of his going; but the earth must be some sort of colour,
and there would be a graveyard, and — ha! Maidenhead! These
sprawling villas and hotels and gramophones spoiled the river.
Funny that Fleur had never been very fond of the river; too slow
and wet, perhaps — everything was quick and dry now, like
America. But had they such a river as the Thames anywhere out
of England? Not they! Nothing that ran green and clear and
weedy, where you could sit in a punt and watch the cows, and
those big elms, and the poplars. Nothing that was safe and
quiet, where you called your soul your own and thought of
Constable and Mason and Walker.

His car bumped something slightly, and came to a stand.
That fellow Riggs was always bumping something! He looked
out. The chauffeur had got down and was examining his mudguard.

'What was that?' said Soames.

'I think it was a pig, sir.'

'Where?'

'Shall I drive on, or see?'

Soames looked round. There seemed no inhabitants in sight.

'Better see.'

The chauffeur disappeared behind the car. Soames remained
seated. He had never had any pigs. They said the pig was a
clean animal. People didn't treat pigs properly. It was very

quiet! No cars on the road; in the silence the wind was talking a little in the hedgerow. He noticed some stars.

'It *is* a pig, sir; he's breathing.'

'Oh!' said Soames. If a cat had nine, how many lives had a pig? He remembered his father James's only riddle: 'If a herring and a half cost three-ha'pence, what's the price of a grid-iron?' When still very small, he had perceived that it was unanswerable.

'Where is he?' he said.

'In the ditch, sir.'

A pig was property, but if in the ditch, nobody would notice it till after he was home. 'Drive on,' he said. 'No! Wait!' And, opening the near door, he got out. After all, the pig was in distress. 'Show me,' he said, and moved in the tail-light of his car to where the chauffeur stood pointing. There, in the shallow ditch, was a dark object emitting cavernous low sounds, as of a man asleep in a club chair.

'It must belong to one of them cottages we passed a bit back,' said the chauffeur.

Soames looked at the pig.

'Anything broken?'

'No sir; the mudguard's all right. I fancy it copped him pretty fair.'

'In the pig, I meant.'

The chauffeur touched the pig with his boot. It squealed, and Soames quivered. Someone would hear! Just like that fellow, drawing attention to it – no gumption whatever! But how, without touching, did you find out whether anything was broken in a pig? He moved a step and saw the pig's eyes; and a sort of fellow-feeling stirred in him. What if it had a broken leg! Again the chauffeur touched it with his foot. The pig uttered a lamentable noise, and, upheaving its bulk, squealing and grunting, trotted off. Soames hastily resumed his seat. 'Drive on!' he said. Pigs! They never thought of anything but themselves; and cottagers were just as bad – very unpleasant about cars. And he wasn't sure they weren't right – tearing great things! The pig's eye seemed looking at him again from where his feet were resting. Should he keep some, now that he had those meadows on the other side of the river? Eat one's own bacon, cure one's own hams! After all, there was something in it – clean pigs, properly fed! That book of old Foggart said one must grow more food in England, and be independent if there were another war. He sniffed. Smell of baking – Reading town already! They still grew biscuits in England! Foreign countries growing his food – something unpleasant about living on sufferance like that! After all, English meat and English wheat – as for a potato, you couldn't get one fit to eat in Italy, or France. And now they wanted to trade with Russia again! Those Bolshevists hated England. Eat their wheat and eggs, use their tallow and skins? *Infra dig,* he called it! the car swerved and he was jerked against the side cushions. The village church! – that fellow Riggs was always shying at something. Pretty little old affair, too, with its squat spire and its lichen – couldn't see that out of England – graves, old names, yew trees. And that reminded him: One would have to be buried, some day. Here, perhaps. Nothing flowery! Just his name, 'Soames Forsyte', standing out on rough stone, like that grave he had sat on at Highgate; no need to put 'Here lies' – of course he'd lie! As to a cross, he didn't know. Probably they'd put one, whatever he wished. He'd like to be in a corner, though, away from people – with an apple tree or something, over him. The less they remembered him, the better. Except Fleur – and she would have other things to think of!

The car turned down the last low hill to the level of the river. He caught a glimpse of it flowing dark between the poplars, like the soul of England, running hidden. The car rolled into the drive, and stopped before the door. He shouldn't tell Annette yet about this case coming into Court – she wouldn't feel as he did – she had no nerves!

Chapter Four

CATECHISM

◄─►

MARJORIE FERRAR's marriage was fixed for the day of the Easter Recess; her honeymoon to Lugano; her trousseau with Clothilde; her residence in Eaton Square; her pin-money at two thousand a year; and her affections on nobody. When she received a telephone message: Would she come to breakfast at Shropshire House? she was surprised. What could be the matter with the old boy?

At five minutes past nine, however, on the following day she entered the ancestral precincts, having left almost all powder and pigment on her dressing-table. Was he going to disapprove of her marriage? Or to give her some of her grandmother's lace, which was only fit to be in a museum?

The marquess was reading the paper in front of an electric fire. He bent on her his bright, shrewd glance.

'Well, Marjorie? Shall we sit down, or do you like to breakfast standing? There's porridge, scrambled eggs, fish – ah! and grapefruit – very considerate of them! Pour out the coffee, will you?'

'What'll *you* have, Grandfather?'

'Thank you, I'll roam about and peck a bit. So you're going to be married. Is that fortunate?'

'People say so.'

'He's in Parliament, I see. Do you think you could interest him in this Electricity Bill of Parsham's?'

'Oh! yes. He's dead keen on electricity.'

'Sensible man. He's got Works, I suppose. Are they electrified?'

'I expect so.'

The marquess gave her another glance.

'You know nothing about it,' he said. 'But you're looking very charming. What's this I hear of a libel?'

She might have known! Grandfather was too frightfully spry! He missed nothing!

'It wouldn't interest you, dear.'

'I disagree. My father and *old* Sir Lawrence Mont were great friends. Why do you want to wash linen in Court?'

'I don't.'

'Are you the plaintiff?'

'Yes.'

'What do you complain of?'

'They've said things about me.'

'Who?'

'Fleur Mont and her father.'

'Ah! the relation of the tea-man. What have they said?'

'That I haven't a moral about me.'

'Well, have you?'

'As much as most people.'

'Anything else?'

'That I'm a snake of the first water.'

'I don't like that. What made them say so?'

'Only that I was heard calling her a snob; and so she is.'

The marquess, who had resigned a finished grapefruit, placed his foot on a chair, his elbow on his knee, his chin on his hand, and said:

'No divinity hedges our Order in these days, Marjorie; but we still stand for something. It's a mistake to forget that.'

She sat very still. Everybody respected grandfather; even her father, to whom he did not speak. But to be told that she stood for something was really too dull for anything! All very well for grandfather at his age, and with his lack of temptations! Besides, *she* had no handle to her name, owing to the vaunted nature of British institutions. Even if she felt that – by Lord Charles out of Lady Ursula – she ought not to be dictated to, she had never put on frills – had always liked to be thought a mere Bohemian. And, after all, she did stand – for not being stuffy, and not being dull.

'Well, Grandfather, I tried to make it up, but she wouldn't. Coffee?'

'Yes, coffee. But tell me, are you happy about yourself?'

Marjorie Ferrar handed him the cup.

'No. Who is?'

'A hit,' said the marquess. 'You're going to be very well off, I hear. That means power. It's worth using well, Marjorie. He's a Scotsman, isn't he? Do you like him?' Again the shrewd bright glance.

'At times.'

'I see. With your hair, you must be careful. Red hair is extraordinarily valuable on occasion. In the Eton and Harrow Match, or for speaking after dinner; but don't let it run away with you after you're married. Where are you going to live?'

'In Eaton Square. There's a Scotch place, too.'

'Have your kitchens electrified. I've had it done here. It saves the cook's temper. I get very equable food. But about this libel. Can't you all say you're sorry – why put money into the lawyers' pockets?'

'She won't, unless I do, and I won't, unless she does.'

The marquess drank off his coffee.

'Then what is there in the way? I dislike publicity, Marjorie. Look at that suit the other day. Anything of this nature in Society, nowadays, is a nail in our coffins.'

'I'll speak to Alec, if you like.'

'Do! Has he red hair?'

'No; black.'

'Ah! What would you like for a wedding-present – lace?'

'Oh! no, please, dear. Nobody's wearing lace.'

With his head on one side, the marquess looked at her. 'I can't get that lace off,' he seemed to say.

'Perhaps you'd like a colliery. Electrified, it would pay in no time.'

Marjorie Ferrar laughed. 'I know you're hard up, Grandfather; but I'd rather not have a colliery, thanks. They're so expensive. Just give me your blessing.'

'I wonder,' said the marquess, 'if I could sell blessings? Your uncle Dangerfield has gone in for farming; he's ruining me. If only he'd grow wheat by electricity; it's the only way to make it pay at the present price. Well, if you've finished breakfast, good-bye. I must go to work.'

Marjorie Ferrar, who had indeed begun breakfast, stood up and pressed his hand. He was a dear old boy, if somewhat rapid! ...

That same evening, in a box at the St Anthony, she had her opportunity, when MacGown was telling her about Soames's visit.

'Oh, dear! Why on earth didn't you settle it, Alec? The whole thing's a bore. I've had my grandfather at me about it.'

'If they'll apologize,' said MacGown, 'I'll settle it tomorrow. But an apology they must make.'

'And what about me? I don't want to stand up to be shot at.'

'There are some things one can't sit down under, Marjorie. Their whole conduct has been infamous.'

Visited by a reckless impulse, she said:

'What d'you suppose I'm really like, Alec?'

MacGown put his hand on her bare arm.

'I don't suppose I know.'

'Well?'

'Defiant.'

Curious summary! Strangely good in a way – only – !

'You mean that I like to irritate people till they think I'm – what I'm not. But suppose' – her eyes confronted his – 'I really am.'

MacGown's grasp tightened.

'You're not; and I won't have it said.'

'You think this case will whitewash my – defiance?'

'I know what gossip is; and I know it buzzes about you. People who say things are going to be taught, once for all, that they can't.'

Marjorie Ferrar turned her gaze towards the still life on the dropped curtain, laughed and said:

'My dear man, you're dangerously provincial.'

'I know a straight line when I see one.'

'Yes; but there aren't any in London. You'd better hedge, Alec, or you'll be taking a toss over me.'

MacGown said, simply: 'I believe in you more than you believe in yourself.'

She was glad that the curtain rose just then, for she felt confused and rather touched.

Instead of confirming her desire to drop the case, that little talk gave her a feeling that by the case her marriage stood or fell. Alec would know where he was when it was over, and so would she! There would be precious little secret about her and she would either not be married to him, or at least not married under false pretences. Let it rip! It was, however, a terrible bore; especially the preparatory legal catechism she had now to undergo. What effect, for instance, had been produced among her friends and acquaintances by those letters? From the point of view of winning, the point was obviously not without importance. But how was she to tell? Two hostesses had cancelled week-end invitations: a rather prim countess, and a Canadian millionairess married to a decaying baronet. It had not occurred to her before that this was the reason, but it might have been. Apart from them she would have to say she didn't know, people didn't tell you to your face what they heard or thought of you. They were going to try and make her out a piece of injured innocence! Good Lord! What if she declared her real faith in Court, and left them all in the soup! Her real faith – what was it? Not to let a friend down; not to give a man away; not to funk; to do things differently from other people; to be always on the go; not to be 'stuffy'; not to be dull! The whole thing was topsy-turvy! Well, she must keep her head!

Chapter Five

THE DAY

◄-◄-►-►

ON the day of the case Soames rose, in Green Street, with a sort of sick impatience. Why wasn't it the day after?

Renewed interviews with very young Nicholas and Sir James Foskisson had confirmed the idea of defence by attack on modern morality. Foskisson was evidently going to put his heart into attacking that from which he had perhaps suffered; and if he were at all like old Bobstay, who, aged eighty-two, had just published his reminiscences, that cat would lose her hair and give herself away. Yesterday afternoon Soames had taken an hour's look at Mr Justice Brane, and been very favourably impressed; the learned judge, though younger than himself – he had often briefed him in other times – looked old-fashioned enough now for anything.

Having cleaned his teeth, put in his plate, and brushed his hair, Soames went into the adjoining room and told Annette she would be late. She always looked terribly young and well in bed, and this, though a satisfaction to him, he could never quite forgive. When he was gone, fifteen years hence, perhaps, she would still be under sixty, and might live another twenty years.

Having roused her sufficiently to say: 'You will have plenty of time to be fussy in that Court, Soames,' he went back and looked out of his window. The air smelled of spring – aggravating! He bathed and shaved with care – didn't want to go into the Box with a cut on his chin! – then went back to see that Annette was not putting on anything bright. He found her in pink underclothes.

'I should wear black,' he said.

Annette regarded him above her hand-mirror.

'Whom do you want me to fascinate, Soames?'

'These people will bring their friends, I shouldn't wonder; anything conspicuous –'

'Don't be afraid; I shall not try to be younger than my daughter.'

Soames went out again. The French! Well, she had good taste in dress.

After breakfast he went off to Fleur's. Winifred and Imogen would look after Annette – they too were going to the Court, as if there were anything to enjoy about this business!

Spruce in his silk hat, he walked across the Green Park, conning over his evidence. No buds on the trees – a late year; and the Royal Family out of town! Passing the Palace, he thought: 'They're very popular!' He supposed they liked this great Empire group in front of them, all muscle and flesh and large animals! The Albert Memorial, and this – everybody ran them down; but, after all, peace and plenty – nothing modern about them! Emerging into Westminster, he cut his way through a smell of fried fish into the Parliamentary backwater of North Street, and, between its pleasant little houses, gazed steadily at the Wren Church. Never going inside any church except St. Paul's, he derived a sort of strength from their outsides – churches were solid and stood back, and didn't seem to care what people thought of them! He felt a little better, rounding into South Square. The Dandie met him in the hall. Though he was not over-fond of dogs, the breadth and solidity of this one always affected Soames pleasurably – better than that little Chinese abortion they used to have! This dog was a character – masterful and tenacious – you would get very little out of *him* in a witness-box! Looking up from the dog, he saw Michael and Fleur coming down the stairs. After hurriedly inspecting Michael's brown suit and speckled tie, his eyes came to anchor on his daughter's face. Pale but creamy, nothing modern – thank goodness! no rouge, salve, powder, or eye-blacking; perfectly made-up for her part! In a blue dress, too, very good taste, which must have taken some finding! The desire that she should not feel nervous stilled Soames's private qualms.

'Quite a smell of spring!' he said: 'Shall we start?'

While a cab was being summoned, he tried to put her at ease.

'I had a look at Brane yesterday; he's changed a good deal from when I used to know him. I was one of the first to give him briefs.'

'That's bad, isn't it, sir?' said Michael.

'How?'

'He'll be afraid of being thought grateful.'

Flippant, as usual!

'Our judges,' he said, 'are a good lot, take them all round.'

'I'm sure they are. Do you know if he ever reads, sir?'

'How d'you mean – reads?'

'Fiction. We don't, in Parliament.'

'Nobody reads novels, except women,' said Soames. And he felt Fleur's dress. 'You'll want a fur; that's flimsy.'

While she was getting the fur, he said to Michael: 'How did she sleep?'

'Better than I did, sir.'

'That's a comfort, anyway. Here's the cab. Keep away from that Scotchman.'

'I see him every day in the House, you know.'

'Ah!' said Soames; 'I forgot. You make nothing of that sort of thing there, I believe.' And taking his daughter's arm, he led her forth.

'I wonder if old Blythe will turn up,' he heard Michael say, when they passed the office of *The Outpost*. It was the first remark made in the cab, and, calling for no response, it was the last.

The Law Courts had their customary air, and people, in black and blue, were hurrying into them. 'Beetle-trap!' muttered Michael. Soames rejected the simile with his elbow – for him they were just familiar echoing space, concealed staircases, stuffy corridors, and the square enclosures of one voice at a time.

Too early, they went slowly up the stairs. Really, it was weak-minded! Here they had come – they and the other side – to get – what? He was amazed at himself for not having insisted on Fleur's apologizing. Time and again in the case of others, all this had appeared quite natural – in the case of his own daughter, it now seemed almost incredibly idiotic. He hurried her on, however, past lingering lawyers' clerks, witnesses, what not. A few low words to an usher, and they were inside, and sitting down. Very young Nicholas was already in his place, and Soames so adjusted himself that there would be a thickness of Sir James, when he materialized, between them. Turning to confer, he lived for a cosy moment in the past again, as might some retired old cricketer taking block once more. Beyond young Nicholas he quartered the assemblage with his glance. Yes, people had got wind of it! He knew they would – with that cat always in the public eye – quite a lot of furbelows up there at the back, and more coming. He reversed himself abruptly; the jury were filing in – special, but a common-looking lot! Why were juries always common-looking? He had never been on one himself. He glanced at Fleur. There she sat, and what she was feeling he couldn't tell. As for young Michael, his ears looked very pointed. And just then he caught sight of Annette. She'd better not come and sit down here, after all – the more there were of them in front, the more conspicuous it would be! So he shook his head at her, and waved towards the back. Ah! She was going! She and Winifred and Imogen would take up room – all rather broad in the beam; but there were still gaps up there. And suddenly he saw the plaintiff and her lawyer and Mac-Gown; very spry they looked, and that insolent cat was smiling! Careful not to glance in their direction, Soames saw them sit down, some six feet off. Ah! and here came Counsel – Foskisson and Bullfry together, thick as thieves. They'd soon be calling each other 'my friend' now, and cutting each other's throats! He wondered if he wouldn't have done better after all to let the other side have Foskisson, and briefed Bullfry – an ugly-looking customer, broad, competent and leathery. He and Michael with Fleur between them, and behind – Foskisson and his junior; Settlewhite and the Scotchman with 'that cat' between them, and behind – Bullfry and his junior! Only the Judge wanted now to complete the pattern! And here he came! Soames gripped Fleur's arm and raised her with himself. Bob! Down again! One side of Brane's face seemed a little fuller than the other; Soames wondered if he had toothache, and how it would affect the proceedings.

And now came the usual 'shivaree' about such and such a case, and what would be taken next week, and so on. Well! that was over, and the Judge was turning his head this way and that, as if to see where the field was placed. Now Bullfry was up:

'If it please Your Lordship –'

He was making the usual opening, with the usual flowery description of the plaintiff – granddaughter of a marquess, engaged to a future Prime Minister ... or so you'd think! ... prominent in the most brilliant circles, high-spirited, perhaps a thought too high-spirited.... Baggage! ... the usual smooth and subacid description of the defendant! ... Rich and ambitious young married lady.... Impudent beggar! ... Jury would bear in mind that they were dealing in both cases with members of advanced Society, but they would bear in mind, too, that primary words had primary meanings and consequences, whatever the Society in which they were uttered. H'm! Very sketchy reference to the incident in Fleur's drawing-room – minimized, of course – ha! an allusion to himself – man of property and standing – thank you for nothing! Reading the libellous letter now! Effect of them ... very made-up, all that! ... Plaintiff obliged to take action.... Bunkum! 'I shall now call Mrs Ralph Ppynrryn.'

'How do you spell that name, Mr Bullfry?'

'With two p's two y's, two n's and two r's, my lord.'

'I see.'

Soames looked at the owner of the name. Good-looking woman of the flibberty-gibbet type! He listened to her evidence with close attention. Her account of the incident in Fleur's drawing-room seemed substantially correct. She had received the libellous letter two days later; had thought it her duty, as a friend, to inform Miss Ferrar. Should say, as a woman in Society, that this incident and these letters had done Miss Ferrar harm. Had talked it over with a good many people. A public incident. Much feeling excited. Had shown her letter to Mrs

Maltese, and been shown one that she had received. Whole matter had become current gossip. H'm!

Bullfry down, and Foskisson up!

Soames adjusted himself. Now to see how the fellow shaped – the manner of a cross-examiner was so important! Well, he had seen worse – the eye, like frozen light, fixed on unoccupied space while the question was being asked, and coming round on to the witness for the answer; the mouth a little open, as if to swallow it; the tongue visible at times on the lower lip, the unoccupied hand clasping something under the gown behind.

'Now, Mrs – er – Ppynrryn. This incident, as my friend has called it, happened at the house of Mrs Mont, did it not? And how did you come there? As a friend. Quite so! And you have nothing against Mrs Mont? No. And you thought it advisable and kind, madam, to show this letter to the plaintiff and to other people – in fact, to foment this little incident to the best of your ability?' Eyes round!

'If a friend of mine received such a letter about me, I should expect her to tell me that the writer was going about abusing me.'

'Even if your friend knew of the provocation and was also a friend of the letter-writer?'

'Yes.'

'Now, madam, wasn't it simply that the sensation of this little quarrel was too precious to be burked? It would have been so easy, wouldn't it, to have torn the letter up and said nothing about it? You don't mean to suggest that it made *you* think any the worse of Miss Ferrar – you knew her too well, didn't you?'

'Ye-es.'

'Exactly. As a friend of both parties you knew that the expressions were just spleen and not to be taken seriously?'

'I can't say that.'

'Oh! You regard them as serious? Am I to take it that you thought they touched the hambone? In other words, that they were true?'

'Certainly not.'

'Could they do Miss Ferrar any harm if they were palpably untrue?'

'I think they could.'

'Not with you – you were a friend?'

'Not with me.'

'But with other people, who would never have heard of them but for you. In fact, madam, you enjoyed the whole thing. Did you?'

'Enjoyed? No.'

'You regarded it as your duty to spread this letter? Don't you enjoy doing your duty?'

The dry cackle within Soames stopped at his lips.

Foskisson down, and Bullfry up!

'It is, in fact, your experience, Mrs Ppynrryn, as well as that of most of us not so well constituted, perhaps, as my learned friend, that duty is sometimes painful.'

'Yes.'

'Thank you. Mrs Edward Maltese.'

During the examination of this other young woman, who seemed to be dark and solid, Soames tried to estimate the comparative effect produced by Fleur and 'that cat' on the four jurymen whose eyes seemed to stray towards beauty. He had come to no definite conclusion, when Sir James Foskisson rose to cross-examine.

'Tell me, Mrs Maltese, which do you consider the most serious allegation among those complained of?'

'The word "treacherous" in my letter, and the expression "a snake of the first water" in the letter to Mrs Ppynrryn.'

'More serious than the others?'

'Yes.'

'That is where you can help me madam. The circle you move in is not exactly the plaintiff's, perhaps?'

'Not exactly.'

'Intersecting, um?'

'Yes.'

'Now, in which section, yours or the plaintiff's, would you

say the expression "she hasn't a moral about her" would be the more, or shall we say the less, damning?'

'I can't say.'

'I only want your opinion. Do you think your section of Society as advanced as Miss Ferrar's?'

'Perhaps not.'

'It's well known, isn't it, that her circle is very free and easy?'

'I suppose so.'

'Still, *your* section is pretty advanced – I mean, you're not "stuffy"?'

'Not what, Sir James?'

'Stuffy, my lord; it's an expression a good deal used in modern Society.'

'What does it mean?'

'Strait-laced, my lord.'

'I see. Well, he's asking you if you're stuffy?'

'No, my lord. I hope not.'

'You hope not. Go on, Sir James.'

'Not being stuffy, you wouldn't be exactly worried if somebody said to you : "My dear, you haven't a moral about you"?'

'Not if it was said as charmingly as that.'

'Now come, Mrs Maltese, does such an expression, said charmingly or the reverse, convey any blame to you or to your friends?'

'If the reverse, yes.'

'Am I to take it that the conception of morality in your circle is the same as in – my lord's?'

'How is the witness to answer that, Sir James?'

'Well, in your circle are you shocked when your friends are divorced, or when they go off together for a week in Paris, say, or wherever they find convenient?'

'Shocked? Well, I suppose one needn't be shocked by what one wouldn't do oneself.'

'In fact, you're not shocked?'

'I don't know that I'm shocked by anything.'

'That would be being stuffy, wouldn't it?'

'Perhaps.'

'Well, will you tell me then – if that's the state of mind in your circle; and you said, you know, that your circle is less free and easy than the plaintiff's – how it is possible that such words as "she hasn't a moral about her" can have done the plaintiff any harm?'

'The whole world isn't in our circles.'

'No. I suggest that only a very small portion of the world is in your circles. But do you tell me that you or the plaintiff pay any –?'

'How can she tell, Sir James, what the plaintiff pays?'

'That *you*, then, pay attention to what people outside your circle think?'

Soames moved his head twice. The fellow was doing it well. And his eye caught Fleur's face turned towards the witness; a little smile was curling her lip.

'I don't personally pay much attention even to what anybody *in* my circle thinks.'

'Have you more independence of character than the plaintiff, should you say?'

'I dare say I've got as much.'

'Is she notoriously independent?'

'Yes.'

'Thank you, Mrs Maltese.'

Foskisson down, Bullfry up!

'I call the plaintiff, my lord.'

Soames uncrossed his legs.

Chapter Six

IN THE BOX

<<->>

MARJORIE FERRAR stepped into the Box, not exactly nervous, and only just 'made-up'. The papers would record a black costume with chinchilla fur and a black hat. She kissed the air in front of the book, took a deep breath, and turned to Mr Bullfry.

For the last five days she had resented more and more the way this case had taken charge of her. She had initiated it, and it had completely deprived her of initiative. She had, in fact, made the old discovery, that when the machinery of quarrel is once put in motion, much more than pressure of the starting button is required to stop its revolutions. She was feeling that it would serve Alec and the lawyers right if all went wrong.

The voice of Mr Bullfry, carefully adjusted, soothed her. His questions were familiar, and with each answer her confidence increased, her voice sounded clear and pleasant in her ears. And she stood at ease, making her figure as boyish as she could. Her performance, she felt, was interesting to the Judge, the jury, and all those people up there, whom she could dimly see. If only 'that little snob' had not been seated, expressionless, between her and her Counsel! When at length Mr Bullfry sat down and Sir James Foskisson got up, she almost succumbed to the longing to powder her nose. Clasping the Box, she resisted it, and while he turned his papers, and hitched his gown, the first tremor of the morning passed down her spine. At least he might look at her when he spoke!

'Have you ever been a party to an action before, Miss Ferrar?'
'No.'

'You quite understand, don't you, that you are on your oath?'
'Quite.'

'You have told my friend that you had no animus against Mrs Mont. Look at this marked paragraph in *The Evening Sun* of October 3rd. Did you write that?'

Marjorie Ferrar felt exactly as if she had stepped out of a conservatory into an east wind. Did they know everything, then?

'Yes; I wrote it.'

'It ends thus: "The enterprising little lady is losing no chance of building up her 'salon' on the curiosity which ever surrounds any buccaneering in politics." Is the reference to Mrs Mont?'

'Yes.'

'Not very nice, is it – of a friend?'

'I don't see any harm in it.'

'The sort of thing, in fact, you'd like written about yourself?'

'The sort of thing I should expect if I were doing the same thing.'

'That's not quite an answer, but let me put it like this: The sort of thing your father would like to read about. you, is it?'

'My father would never read that column.'

'Then it surprises you to hear that Mrs Mont's father did? Do you write many of these cheery little paragraphs about your friends?'

'Not many.'

'Every now and then, eh? And do they remain your friends?'

'It's not easy in Society to tell who's a friend and who isn't.'

'I quite agree, Miss Ferrar. You have admitted making one or two critical – that was your word, I think – remarks concerning Mrs Mont, in her own house. Do you go to many houses and talk disparagingly of your hostess?'

'No; and in any case I don't expect to be eavesdropped.'

'I see; so long as you're not found out, it's all right, eh? Now, on this first Wednesday in October last, at Mrs Mont's, in speaking to this gentleman, Mr Philip – er – Quinsey, did you use the word "snob" of your hostess?'

'I don't think so.'

'Be careful. You heard the evidence of Mrs Ppynrryn and Mrs Maltese. Mrs Maltese said, you remember, that Mr Forsyte – that is Mrs Mont's father – said to you on that occasion: "You called my daughter a snob in her own house, madam – be so kind as to withdraw; you are a traitress." Is that a correct version?'

'Probably.'

'Do you suggest that he invented the word "snob"?'

'I suggest he was mistaken.'

'Not a nice word, is it – "snob"? Was there any other reason why he should call you a traitress?'

'My remarks weren't meant for his ears. I don't remember exactly what I said.'

'Well, we shall have Mr Forsyte in the Box to refresh your memory as to exactly what you said. But I put it to you that you called her a snob, not once but twice, during that little conversation?'

'I've told you I don't remember; he shouldn't have listened.'

'Very well! So you feel quite happy about having written that paragraph and said nasty things of Mrs Mont behind her back in her own drawing-room?'

Marjorie Ferrar grasped the Box till the blood tingled in her palms. His voice was maddening.

'Yet it seems, Miss Ferrar, that you object to others saying nasty things about you in return. Who advised you to bring this action?'

'My father first; and then my fiancé.'

'Sir Alex MacGown. Does he move in the same circles as you?'

'No; he moves in Parliamentary circles.'

'Exactly; and he wouldn't know, would he, the canons of conduct that rule in your circle?'

'There are no circles so definite as that.'

'Always willing to learn, Miss Ferrar. But tell me, do you know what Sir Alexander's Parliamentary friends think about conduct and morality?'

'I can guess. I don't suppose there's much difference.'

'Are you suggesting, Miss Ferrar, that responsible public men take the same light-hearted view of conduct and morals as you?'

'Aren't you rather assuming, Sir James, that her view *is* light-hearted?'

'As to conduct, my lord, I submit that her answers have shown the very light-hearted view she takes of the obligations incurred by the acceptance of hospitality, for instance. I'm coming to morals now.'

'I think you'd better, before drawing your conclusions. What have public men to do with it?'

'I'm suggesting, my lord, that this lady is making a great to-do about words which a public man, or any ordinary citizen, would have a perfect right to resent, but which she, with her views, has no right whatsoever to resent.'

'You must prove her views then. Go on!'

Marjorie Ferrar, relaxed for a moment, gathered herself again. Her views!

'Tell me, Miss Ferrar — we all know now the meaning of the word "stuffy" — are public men "stuffier" than you?'

'They may say they are.'

'You think them hypocrites?'

'I don't think anything at all about them.'

'Though you're going to marry one? You are complaining of the words: "She hasn't a moral about her." Have you read this novel *Canthar?*' He was holding up a book.

'I think so.'

'Don't you know?'

'I've skimmed it.'

'Taken off the cream, eh? Read it sufficiently to form an opinion?'

'Yes.'

'Would you agree with the view of it expressed in this letter to a journal? "The book breaks through the British 'stuffiness', which condemns any frank work of art — and a good thing, too!" Is it a good thing?'

'Yes. I hate Grundyism.'

'"It is undoubtedly Literature." The word is written with a large L. Should you say it was?'

'Literature – yes. Not great literature, perhaps.'

'But it ought to be published?'

'I don't see why not.'

'You know that it is not published in England?'

'Yes.'

'But it ought to be?'

'It isn't everybody's sort of book, of course.'

'Don't evade the question, please. In your opinion ought this novel *Canthar* to be published in England? ... Take your time, Miss Ferrar.'

The brute lost nothing! Just because she had hesitated a moment trying to see where he was leading her.

'Yes. I think literature should be free.'

'You wouldn't sympathize with its suppression if it were published?'

'No.'

'You wouldn't approve of the suppression of any book on the ground of mere morals?'

'I can't tell you unless I see the book. People aren't bound to read books, you know.'

'And you think your opinion generally on this subject is that of public men and ordinary citizens?'

'No; I suppose it isn't.'

'But your view would be shared by most of your own associates?'

'I should hope so.'

'A contrary opinion would be "stuffy", wouldn't it?'

'If you like to call it so. It's not my word.'

'What is your word, Miss Ferrar?'

'I think I generally say "ga-ga".'

'Do you know, I'm afraid the Court will require a little elaboration of that.'

'Not for me, Sir James; I'm perfectly familiar with the word; it means "in your dotage".'

'The Bench is omniscient, my lord. Then anyone, Miss Ferrar, who didn't share the opinion of yourself and your associates in the matter of this book would be "ga-ga", that is to say, in his or her dotage?'

'Æsthetically.'

'Ah! I thought we should arrive at that word. You, I suppose, don't connect art with life?'

'No.'

'Don't think it has any effect on life?'

'It oughtn't to.'

'When a man's theme in a book is extreme incontinence, depicted with all due emphasis, that wouldn't have any practical effect on his readers, however young?'

'I can't say about other people, it wouldn't have any effect on me.'

'You are emancipated, in fact.'

'I don't know what you mean by that.'

'Isn't what you are saying about the divorce of art from life the merest clap-trap; and don't you know it.'

'I certainly don't.'

'Let me put it another way: Is it possible for those who believe in current morality to hold your view that art has no effect on life?'

'Quite possible; if they are cultured.'

'Cultured! Do you believe in current morality yourself?'

'I don't know what you call current morality.'

'I will tell you, Miss Ferrar. I should say, for instance, it was current morality that women should not have *liaisons* before they're married, and should not have them after.'

'What about men?'

'Thank you; I was coming to men. And that men should at least not have them after.'

'I shouldn't say that was *current* morality at all.'

In yielding to that satiric impulse she knew at once she had made a mistake – the judge had turned his face towards her. He was speaking.

'Do I understand you imply that in your view it is moral for women to have *liaisons* before marriage, and for men and women to have them after?'

'I think it's current morality, my lord.'

'I'm not asking you about current morality; I'm asking whether in *your* view it is moral?'

'I think many people think it's all right who don't say it, yet.'

She was conscious of movement throughout the jury; and of a little flump in the well of the Court. Sir Alexander had dropped his hat. The sound of a nose being loudly blown broke the stillness, the face of Bullfry, K.C., was lost to her view. She felt the blood mounting in her cheeks.

'Answer my question, please. Do *you* say it's all right?'

'I – I think it depends.'

'On what?'

'On – on circumstances, environment, temperament; all sorts of things.'

'Would it be all right for *you*?'

Marjorie Ferrar became very still. 'I can't answer that question, my lord.'

'You mean – you don't want to!'

'I mean I don't know.'

And, with a feeling as if she had withdrawn her foot from a bit of breaking ice, she saw Bullfry's face re-emerge from his handkerchief.

'Very well. Go on, Sir James!'

'Anyway, we may take it, Miss Ferrar, that those of us who say we don't believe in these irregularities are hypocrites in your view?'

'Why can't you be fair?'

He was looking at her now; and she didn't like him any the better for it.

'I shall prove myself fair before I've done, Miss Ferrar.'

'You've got your work cut out, haven't you?'

'Believe me, madam, it will be better for you not to indulge in witticism. According to you, there is no harm in a book like *Canthar*?'

'There ought to be none.'

'You mean if we were all as aesthetically cultured – as you.' – Sneering beast! – 'But are we?'

'No.'

'Then there is harm. But you wouldn't mind that harm being done. I don't propose, my lord, to read from this very unpleasant novel. Owing apparently to its unsavoury reputation, a copy of it now costs nearly seven pounds. And I venture to think that is in itself an answer to the plaintiff's contention that "art" so called has no effect on life. We have gone to the considerable expense of buying copies, and I shall ask that during the luncheon interval the jury may read some dozen marked passages.'

'Have you a copy for me, Sir James?'

'Yes, my lord.'

'And one for Mr Bullfry? ... If there is any laughter, I shall have the Court cleared. Go on.'

'You know the "Ne Plus Ultra" Play-Producing Society, Miss Ferrar? It exists to produced advanced plays, I believe.'

'Plays – I don't know about "advanced".'

'Russian plays, and the Restoration dramatists?'

'Yes.'

'And you have played in them?'

'Sometimes.'

'Do you remember a play called "The Plain Dealer", by Wycherly, given at a matinée on January 7th last – did you play in that the part of Olivia?'

'Yes.'

'A nice part?'

'A very good part.'

'I said "nice".'

'I don't like the word.'

'Too suggestive of "prunes and prisms", Miss Ferrar? Is it the part of a modest woman?'

'No.'

'Is it, towards the end, extremely immodest? I allude to the dark scene.'

'I don't know about extremely.'

'Anyway, you felt no hesitation about undertaking and playing the part – a little thing like that doesn't worry you?'

'I don't know why it should. If it did, I shouldn't act.'

'You don't act for money?'

'No; for pleasure.'

'Then, of course, you can refuse any part you like?'

'If I did, I shouldn't have any offered me.'

'Don't quibble, please. You took the part of Olivia not for money but for pleasure. You enjoyed playing it?'

'Pretty well.'

'I'm afraid I shall have to ask the jury, my lord, to run their eyes over the dark scene in "The Plain Dealer".'

'Are you saying, Sir James, that a woman who plays an immoral part is not moral – that would asperse a great many excellent reputations.'

'No, my lord; I'm saying that here is a young lady so jealous of her good name in the eyes of the world, that she brings a libel action because someone has said in a private letter that she 'hasn't a moral about her'. And at the same time she is reading and approving books like this *Canthar*, playing parts like that of Olivia in "The Plain Dealer", and, as I submit, living in a section of Society that really doesn't know the meaning of the word morals, that looks upon morals, in fact, rather as we look upon measles. It's my contention, my lord, that the saying in my client's letter: "She hasn't a moral about her", is rather a compliment to the plaintiff than otherwise.'

'Do you mean that it was intended as a compliment?'

'No, no, my lord.'

'Well, you want the jury to read that scene. You will have a busy luncheon interval, gentlemen. Go on, Sir James.'

'Now, Miss Ferrar – my friend made a point of the fact that you are engaged to a wealthy and highly respected Member of Parliament. How long have you been engaged to him?'

'Six months.'

'You have no secrets from him, I suppose?'

'Why should I answer that?'

'Why should she, Sir James?'

'I am quite content to leave it to her reluctance, my lord.'

Sneering brute! As if everybody hadn't secrets from everybody!

'Your engagement was not made public till January, was it?'

'No.'

'May I take it that you were not sure of your own mind till then?'

'If you like.'

'Now, Miss Ferrar, did you bring this action because of your good name? Wasn't it because you were hard up?'

She was conscious again of blood in her cheeks.

'No.'

'*Were* you hard up when you brought it?'

'Yes.'

'Very?'

'Not worse than I have been before.'

'I put it to you that you owed a great deal of money, and were hard pressed.'

'If you like.'

'I'm glad you've admitted that, Miss Ferrar; otherwise I should have had to prove it. And you didn't bring this action with a view to paying some of your debts?'

'No.'

'Did you in early January become aware that you were not likely to get any sum in settlement of this suit?'

'I believe I was told that an offer was withdrawn.'

'And do you know why?'

'Yes, because Mrs Mont wouldn't give the apology I asked for.'

'Exactly! And was it a coincidence that you thereupon made up your mind to marry Sir Alexander MacGown?'

'A coincidence?'

'I mean the announcement of your engagement, you know?'

Brute!

'It had nothing to do with this case.'

'Indeed! Now when you brought this action, did you really care one straw whether people thought you moral or not?'

'I brought it chiefly because I was called "a snake".'

'Please answer my question.'

'It isn't so much what *I* cared, as what my friends cared.'

'But their view of morality is much what yours is — thoroughly accommodating?'

'Not my *fiancé's*.'

'Ah! no. He doesn't move in your circle, you said. But the rest of your friends. You're not ashamed of your own accommodating philosophy, are you?'

'No.'

'Then why be ashamed of it for them?'

'How can I tell what *their* philosophy is?'

'How can she, Sir James?'

'As your lordship pleases. Now, Miss Ferrar! You like to stand up for your views, I hope. Let me put your philosophy to you in a nutshell: You believe, don't you, in the full expression of your personality; it would be your duty, wouldn't it, to break through any convention — I don't say law — but any so-called moral convention that cramped you?'

'I never said I had a philosophy.'

'Don't run away from it, please.'

'I'm not in the habit of running away.'

'I'm so glad of that. You believe in being the sole judge of your own conduct?'

'Yes.'

'You're not alone in that view, are you?'

'I shouldn't think so.'

'It's the view, in fact, of what may be called the forward wing of modern Society, isn't it — the wing you belong to, and are proud of belonging to? And in that section of Society — so long as you don't break the actual law — you think and do as you like, eh?'

'One doesn't always act up to one's principles.'

'Quite so. But among your associates, even if you and they don't always act up to it, it *is* a principle, isn't it, to judge for yourselves and go your own ways without regard to convention?'

'More or less.'

'And, living in that circle, with that belief, you have the effrontery to think the words: "She hasn't a moral about her", entitle you to damages?'

Her voice rang out angrily: 'I have morals. They may not be yours, but they may be just as good, perhaps better. I'm not a hypocrite, anyway.'

Again she saw him look at her, there was a gleam in his eyes; and she knew she had made another mistake.

'We'll leave my morals out of the question, Miss Ferrar. But we'll go a little farther into what you say are yours. In your own words, it should depend on temperament, circumstances, environment, whether you conform to morality or not?'

She stood silent, biting her lip.

'Answer, please.'

She inclined her head. 'Yes.'

'Very good!' He had paused, turning over his papers, and she drew back in the box. She had lost her temper – had made him lose his; at all costs she must keep her head now! In this moment of search for her head she took in everything – expressions, gestures, even the atmosphere – the curious dramatic emanation from a hundred and more still faces; she noted the one lady juryman, the judge breaking the nib of a quill, with his eyes turned away from it as if looking at something that had run across the well of the Court. Yes, and down there, the lengthening lip of Mr Settlewhite, Michael's face turned up at her with a rueful frown, Fleur Mont's mask with red spots in the cheeks, Alec's clenched hands, and his eyes fixed on her. A sort of comic intensity about it all! If only she were the size of Alice in 'Wonderland', and could take them all in her hands and shake them like a pack of cards – so motionless, there, at her expense! That sarcastic brute had finished fiddling with his papers, and she moved forward again to attention in the box.

'Now, Miss Ferrar, his lordship put a general question to you which you did not feel able to answer. I am going to put it in a way that will be easier for you. Whether or no it was right for you to have one' – she saw Michael's hand go up to his face –

'have you *in fact* had a – *liaison*?' And from some tone in his voice, from the look on his face, she could tell for certain that her persecutor knew she had.

With her back to the wall, she had not even a wall to her back. Ten, twenty, thirty seconds – judge, jury, that old fox with his hand under the tail of his gown, and his eyes averted! Why did she not spit out the indignant: No! which she had so often rehearsed? Suppose he proved it – as he had said he would prove her debts?

'Take your time, Miss Ferrar. You know what a *liaison* is, of course.'

Brute! On the verge of denial, she saw Michael lean across, and heard his whisper: 'Stop this!' And then 'that little snob' looked up at her – the scrutiny was knowing and contemptuous: 'Now hear her lie!' it seemed to say. And she answered quickly: 'I consider your question insulting.'

'Oh! come, Miss Ferrar, after your own words! After what –'

'Well! I shan't answer it.'

A rustle, a whispering in the Court.

'You won't answer it?'

'No.'

'Thank you, Miss Ferrar.' Could a voice be more sarcastic? The brute was sitting down.

Marjorie Ferrar stood defiant, with no ground under her feet. What next? Her counsel was beckoning. She descended from the box and, passing her adversaries, resumed her seat next her betrothed. How red and still he was! She heard the judge say:

'I shall break for lunch now, Mr Bullfry,' saw him rise and go out, and the jury getting up. The whispering and rustling in the Court swelled to a buzz. She stood up. Mr Settlewhite was speaking to her.

Chapter Seven

'FED UP'

<><>

GUIDED by him into a room designed to shelter witnesses, Marjorie Ferrar looked at her lawyer.

'Well?'

'An unfortunate refusal, Miss Ferrar – very. I'm afraid the effect on the jury may be fatal. If we can settle it now, I should certainly say we'd better.'

'It's all the same to me.'

'In that case you may take it I shall settle. I'll go and see Sir Alexander and Mr Bullfry at once.'

'How do I get out quietly?'

'Down those stairs. You'll find cabs in Lincoln's Inn Fields. Excuse me.' He made her a grave little bow and stalked away.

Marjorie Ferrar did not take a cab; she walked. If her last answer had been fatal, on the whole she was content. She had told no lies to speak of, had stood up to 'that sarcastic beast', and given him sometimes as good as she had got. Alec! Well, she couldn't help it! He had insisted on her going into Court; she hoped he liked it now she'd been! Buying a newspaper, she went into a restaurant and read a description of herself, accompanied by a photograph. She ate a good lunch, and then continued her walk along Piccadilly. Passing into the Park, she sat down under a tree coming into bud, and drew the smoke of a cigarette quietly into her lungs. The Row was almost deserted. A few persons of little or no consequence occupied a few chairs. A riding mistress was teaching a small boy to trot. Some sparrows and a pigeon alone seemed to take a distant interest in her. The air smelled of spring. She sat some time with the pleasant feeling that nobody in the world knew where she was. Odd, when you thought of it – millions of people every day, leaving their houses, offices, shops, on their way to the next place, were as lost to the world as stones in a pond! Would it be nice to disappear permanently, and taste life incognita? Bertie Curfew was going to Moscow again. Would he take her as secretary, and *bonne amie*? Bertie Curfew – she had only pretended to be tired of him! The thought brought her face to face with the future. Alec! Explanations! It was hardly the word! He had a list of her debts, and had said he would pay them as a wedding-present. But – if there wasn't to be a wedding? Thank God, she had some ready money. The carefully 'laid-up' four-year-old in her father's stable had won yesterday. She had dribbled 'a pony' on at a nice price. She rose and sauntered along, distending her bust – in defiance of the boy-like fashion, which, after all, was on the wane – to take in the full of a sweet wind.

Leaving the Park, she came to South Kensington station and bought another paper. It had a full account under the headlines: 'Modern Morality Attacked.' 'Miss Marjorie Ferrar in the Box.' It seemed funny to stand there reading those words among people who were reading the same without knowing her from Eve, except, perhaps, by her clothes. Continuing her progress towards Wren Street, she turned her latch-key in the door, and saw a hat. Waiting for her already! She took her time; and, pale from powder, as though she had gone through much, entered the studio.

MacGown was sitting with his head in his hands. She felt real pity for him – too strong, too square, too vital for that attitude! He raised his face.

'Well, Alec!'

'Tell me the truth, Marjorie. I'm in torment.'

She almost envied him the depth of his feeling, however unreasonable after her warnings. But she said ironically:

'Who was it knew me better than I knew myself?'

In the same dull voice he repeated:

'The truth, Marjorie, the truth!'

But why should she go into the confessional? Was he entitled to her past? His rights stopped at her future. It was the old business – men expecting more from women than they could give them. Inequality of the sexes. Something in that, perhaps, in the old days when women bore children, and men didn't; but now that women knew all about sex and only bore children when they wanted to, and not always even then, why should men be freer?

And she said slowly: 'In exchange for your adventures I'll tell you mine.'

'For God's sake don't mock me; I've had hell these last hours.'

His face showed it, and she said with feeling:

'I said you'd be taking a toss over me, Alec. Why on earth did you insist on my bringing this case? You've had your way, and now you don't like it.'

'It's true, then?'

'Yes. Why not?'

He uttered a groan, recoiling till his back was against the wall, as if afraid of being loose in the room.

'Who was he?'

'Oh! no! That I can't possibly tell you. And how many affairs have you had?'

He paid no attention. He wouldn't! He knew she didn't love him; and such things only mattered if you loved! Ah! well! His agony was a tribute to her, after all!

'You're well out of me,' she said sullenly; and, sitting down, she lighted a cigarette. A scene! How hateful! Why didn't he go? She'd rather he'd be violent than deaf and dumb and blind like this.

'Not that American fellow?'

She could not help a laugh.

'Oh! no, poor boy!'

'How long did it last?'

'Nearly a year.'

'My God!'

He had rushed to the door. If only he would open it and go! That he could feel so violently! That figure by the door was just not mad! His stuffy passions!

And then he did pull the door open and was gone.

She threw herself at full length on the divan; not from

lassitude, exactly, nor despair – from a feeling rather as if nothing mattered. How stupid and pre-war! Why couldn't he, like her, be free, be supple, take life as it came? Passions, prejudices, principles, pity – old-fashioned as the stuffy clothes worn when she was a tot. Well! Good riddance! Fancy living in the same house, sharing the same bed, with a man so full of the primitive that he could 'go off his chump' with jealousy about her! Fancy living with a man who took life so seriously, that he couldn't even see himself doing it! Life was a cigarette to be inhaled and thrown away, a dance to be danced out. On with that dance! ... Yes, but she couldn't let him pay her debts, now, even if he wanted to. Married, she would have repaid him with her body; as it was – no! Oh! why didn't someone die and leave her something? What a bore it all was! And she lay still, listening to the tea-time sounds of a quiet street – taxis rounding the corner from the river; the dog next door barking at the postman; that one-legged man – ex-Service – who came most afternoons and played on a poor fiddle. He expected her shilling – unhappy fellow! she'd have to get up and give it him. She went to the little side window that looked on to the street, and suddenly recoiled. Francis Wilmot in the doorway with his hand up to the bell! Another scene! No, really! This was too much! There went the bell! No time to say 'Not at home!' Well, let them all come – round her past, like bees round a honeypot!

'Mr Francis Wilmot.'

He stood there, large as the life he had nearly resigned – a little thinner, that was all.

'Well, Francis,' she said, 'I thought you were "through with that fool business"?'

Francis Wilmot came gravely up and took her hand. 'I sail to-morrow.'

Sail! Well, she could put up with that. He seemed to her just a thin, pale young man with dark hair and eyes and no juices in his system.

'I read the evening papers. I wondered if, perhaps, you'd wish to see me.'

Was he mocking her? But he wore no smile; there was

no bitterness in his voice; and, though he was looking at her intently, she could not tell from his face whether he still had any feeling. She said:

'You think I owe you something? I know I treated you very badly.'

He looked rather as if she'd hit him.

'For heaven's sake, Francis, don't say you've come out of chivalry. That'd be too funny.'

'I don't follow you; I just thought, perhaps, you didn't like to answer that question about a love affair – because of me.'

Marjorie Ferrar broke into hysterical laughter.

'Senor Don Punctilio! Because of you! No, no, my dear!'

Francis Wilmot drew back and made her a little bow.

'I shouldn't have come,' he said.

She had a sudden return of feeling for that slim unusual presence, with its grace and its dark eyes.

'I'm a free-lance again now, Francis, anyway.'

A long moment went by, and then he made her another little bow. It was a clear withdrawal.

'Then for God's sake,' she said, 'go away! I'm fed up!' And she turned her back on him.

When she looked round, he *had* gone, and that surprised her. He was a new variety, or a dead one, dug up! He didn't know the rudiments of life – old-fashioned, *à faire rire!* And, back at full length on the divan, she brooded. Well, her courage was 'not out'! To-morrow was Bella Magussie's 'At Home' to meet – some idiot. Everybody would be there, and so would she!

Chapter Eight

FANTOCHES

→←→→

WHEN Michael, screwed towards Sir James Foskisson's averted face, heard the words: 'Well, I shan't answer', he spun round. It was just as if she had said: 'Yes, I have.' The judge was looking at her, everyone looking at her. Wasn't Bullfry going to help her? No! He was beckoning her out of the box. Michael half rose, as she passed him. By George! He was sorry for Mac-Gown! There he sat, poor devil! with everyone getting up all round him, still, and red as a turkey-cock.

Fleur! Michael looked at her face, slightly flushed, her gloved hands clasped in her lap, her eyes fixed on the ground. Had his whisper: 'Stop this!' his little abortive bow, offended her? How could one have helped sympathizing with the 'Pet of the Panjoys' in so tight a place! Fleur must see that! The Court was emptying – fine birds, many – he could see her mother and her aunt and cousin, and Old Forsyte, talking with Foskisson. Ah! he had finished; was speaking: 'We can go now.'

They followed him along the corridor, down the stairs, into the air.

'We've time for a snack,' Soames was saying. 'Come in here!'

In one of several kennels without roofs in a celebrated room with a boarded floor, they sat down.

'Three chump chops, sharp,' said Soames, and staring at the cruet-stand, added: 'She's cooked her goose. They'll drop it like a hot potato. I've told Foskisson he can settle, with both sides paying their own costs. It's more than they deserve.'

'He ought never to have asked that question, sir.'

Fleur looked up sharply.

'Really, Michael!'

'Well, darling, we agreed he shouldn't. Why didn't Bullfry help her out, sir?'

'Only too glad to get her out of the box; the judge would have asked her himself in another minute. It's a complete fiasco, thank God!'

'Then we've won?' said Fleur.

'Unless I'm a Dutchman,' answered Soames.

'I'm not so sure,' muttered Michael.

'I tell you it's all over; Bullfry'll never go on with it.'

'I didn't mean that, sir.'

Fleur said acidly; 'Then what *do* you mean, Michael?'

'I don't think we shall be forgiven, that's all.'

'What for?'

'Well, I dare say I'm all wrong. Sauce, sir?'

'Worcester – yes. This is the only place in London where you can rely on a floury potato. Waiter – three glasses of port, quick!'

After fifteen minutes of concentrated mastication, they returned to the Court.

'Wait here,' said Soames, in the hall; 'I'll go and find out.'

In that echoing space, where a man's height was so inconsiderable, Fleur and Michael stood, not speaking, for some time.

'She couldn't know that Foskisson had been told not to follow it up, of course,' he said at last. 'Still, she must have expected the question. She should have told a good one and have done with it. I couldn't help feeling sorry for her.'

'You'd feel sorry for a flea that bit you, Michael. What do you mean by our not being forgiven?'

'Well! The drama was all on her side, and it's drama that counts. Besides, there's her engagement!'

'That'll be broken off.'

'Exactly! And if it is, she'll have sympathy; while if it isn't, he'll have it. Anyway, we shan't. Besides, you know, she stood up for what we all really believe nowadays.'

'Speak for yourself.'

'Well, don't we talk of everyone being free?'

'Yes, but is there any connexion betwen what we say and what we do?'

'No,' said Michael.

And just then Soames returned.

'Well, sir?'

'As I told you, Bullfry caught at it. They've settled. It's a moral victory.'

'Oh! not moral, I hope, sir.'

'It's cost a pretty penny, anyway,' said Soames, looking at Fleur. 'Your mother's quite annoyed – she's no sense of proportion. Very clever the way Foskisson made that woman lose her temper.'

'He lost his, at the end. That's his excuse, I suppose.'

'Well,' said Soames, 'it's all over! Your mother's got the car; we'll take a taxi.'

On the drive back to South Square, taking precisely the same route, there was precisely the same silence.

When a little later Michael went over to the House, he was edified by posters.

'Society Libel Action.'

'Marquess's Granddaughter and K.C.'

'Dramatic evidence.'

'Modern Morality!'

All over – was it? With publicity – in Michael's opinion – it had but just begun! Morality! What was it – who had it, and what did they do with it? How would he have answered those questions himself? Who could answer them, nowadays, by rote or rule? Not he, nor Fleur! They had been identified with the Inquisition, and what was their position now? False, if not odious! He passed into the House. But, try as he would, he could not fix his attention on the Purity of Food, and passed out again. With a curious longing for his father, he walked rapidly down Whitehall. Drawing blank at 'Snooks' and 'The Aeroplane', he tried the 'Parthenæum' as a last resort. Sir Lawrence was in a corner of a forbidden room, reading a life of Lord Palmerston. He looked up at his son.

'Ah! Michael! They don't do justice to old Pam. A man without frills, who worked like a nigger. But we mustn't talk here!' And he pointed to a member who seemed awake. 'Shall we take a turn before the old gentleman over there has a fit? The books here are camouflage; it's really a dormitory.'

He led the way, with Michael retailing the events of the morning.

'Foskisson?' said Sir Lawrence, entering the Green Park. 'He was a nice little chap when I left Winchester. To be professionally in the right is bad for a man's character – counsel, parsons, policemen, they all suffer from it. Judges, High Priests, Arch-Inspectors, aren't so bad – they've suffered from it so long that they've lost consciousness.'

'It was a full house,' said Michael glumly, 'and the papers have got hold of it.'

'They would.' And Sir Lawrence pointed to the ornamental water. 'These birds,' he said, 'remind me of China. By the way, I met your friend Desert yesterday at the 'Aeroplane' – he's more interesting now that he's dropped Poetry for the East. Everybody ought to drop something. I'm too old now, but if I'd dropped baronetcy in time, I could have made quite a good contortionist.'

'What would you recommend for Members of Parliament?' asked Michael, with a grin.

'Postmanship, my dear – carrying on, you know; a certain importance, large bags, dogs to bark at you, no initiative, and conversation on every door-step. By the way, do you see Desert?'

'I have seen him.'

Sir Lawrence screwed up his eyes.

'The providential,' he said, 'doesn't happen twice.'

Michael coloured; he had not suspected his father of such shrewd observation. Sir Lawrence swung his cane.

'Your man Boddick,' he said, 'has persuaded some of his hens to lay; he's giving us quite good eggs.'

Michael admired his reticence. But somehow that unexpected slanting allusion to a past domestic crisis roused the feeling that for so long now had been curled like a sleepy snake in his chest, that another crisis was brewing and must soon be faced.

'Coming along for tea, sir? Kit had tummy-ache this morning. How's your last book doing? Does old Danby advertise it properly?'

'No,' said Sir Lawrence, 'no; he's keeping his head wonderfully; the book is almost dead.'

'I'm glad I dropped *him*, anyway,' said Michael, with emphasis. 'I suppose, sir, you haven't got a tip to give us, now this case is over?'

Sir Lawrence gazed at a bird with a long red bill.

'When victorious,' he said at last, 'lie doggo. The triumphs of morality are apt to recoil on those who achieve them.'

'That's what I feel, sir. Heaven knows *I* didn't want to achieve one. My father-in-law says my hitting MacGown on the boko really brought it into Court.'

Sir Lawrence whinnied.

'The tax on luxuries. It gets you everywhere. I don't think I will come along, Michael — Old Forsyte's probably there. Your mother has an excellent recipe for child's tummy-ache; you almost lived on it at one time. I'll telephone it from Mount Street. Good-bye!'

Michael looked after that thin and sprightly figure moving North. Had he troubles of his own? If so, he disguised them wonderfully. Good old Bart! And he turned towards South Square.

Soames was just leaving.

'She's excited,' he said, on the door-step. 'It's the reaction. Give her a Seidlitz powder to-night. Be careful, too; I shouldn't talk about politics.'

Michael went in. Fleur was at the open window of the drawing-room.

'Oh! here you are!' she said. 'Kit's all right again. Take me to the Café Royal tonight, Michael, and if there's anything funny anywhere, for goodness' sake, let's see it. I'm sick of feeling solemn. Oh! And, by the way, Francis Wilmot's coming in to say good-bye. I've had a note. He says he's all right again.'

At the window by her side, Michael sniffed the unaccountable scent of grass. There was a south-west wind, and slanting from over the house-tops, sunlight was sprinkling the soil, the buds, the branches. A blackbird sang; a piano-organ round a corner was playing 'Rigoletto'. Against his own, her shoulder was soft, and to his lips her cheek was warm and creamy. . . .

When Francis Wilmot left them that evening after dinner at the Café Royal, Fleur said to Michael:

'Poor Francis! Did you ever see anyone so changed? He might be thirty. I'm glad he's going home to his river and his darkies. What are live oaks? Well! Are we going anywhere?'

Michael cloaked her shoulders.

' "Great Itch", I think; there's no other scream so certain.'

After their scream they came out into a mild night. High up in red and green the bright signs fled along the air: 'Tomber's Tires for Speed and Safety', 'Milkoh Makes Mothers Merry.' Through Trafalgar Square they went and down Whitehall, all moonlight and Portland stone.

'The night's unreal,' said Fleur. ' "*Fantoches*" !'

Michael caught her waist.

'Don't! Suppose some Member saw you!'

'He'd only sympathize. How nice and solid you feel!'

'No. *Fantoches* have no substance.'

'Then give me shadow.'

'The substance is in Bethnal Green.'

Michael dropped his arm.

'That's a strange thought.'

'I have intuitions, Michael.'

'Because I can admire a good woman, can I not love you?'

'*I* shall never be "good"; it isn't in me.'

'Whatever you are's enough for me.'

'Prettily said. The Square looks jolly to-night! Open the doll's house.'

The hall was dark, with just a glimmer coming through the fanlight. Michael took off her cloak and knelt down. He felt her fingers stir his hair; real fingers, and real all this within his arms; only the soul elusive. Soul?

'*Fantoches*!' came her voice, soft and mocking. 'And so to bed!'

Chapter Nine

ROUT AT MRS MAGUSSIE'S

◄──►►

THERE are routs social, political, propagandic; and routs like Mrs Magussie's. In one of Anglo-American birth, inexhaustible wealth, unimpeachable widowhood, and catholic taste, the word hostess had found its highest expression. People might die, marry, and be born with impunity so long as they met, preferably in her house, one of the largest in Mayfair. If she called in a doctor, it was to meet another doctor; if she went to church, it was to get Canon Forant to meet Dean Kimble at lunch afterwards. Her cards of invitation had the words: 'To meet' printed on them; and she never put 'me'. She was selfless. Once in a way she had a real rout, because once in a way a personality was available, whose name everybody, from poets to prelates, must know. In her intimate belief people loved to meet anybody sufficiently distinguished; and this was where she succeeded, because almost without exception they did. Her two husbands had 'passed on', having met in their time nearly everybody. They had both been distinguished, and had first met in her house; and she would never have a third for Society was losing its landmarks, and she was too occupied. People were inclined to smile at mention of Bella Magussie, and yet, how do without one who performed the function of cement? Without her, bishops could not place their cheeks by the jowls of ballet girls, or Home Secretaries be fertilized by disorderly dramatists. Except in her house, the diggers-up of old civilization in Beluchistan never encountered the levellers of modern civilization in London. Nor was there any chance for lights of the Palace to meet those lights of the Halls – Madame Nemesia and Top Nobby. Nowhere else could a Russian dancer go to supper with Sir Walter Peddel, M.D., F.R.S.T.R., P.M.V.S., 'R.I.P.' as Michael would add. Even a bowler with the finest collection of ducks' eggs in first-class cricket was not without a chance of wringing the hand of the great Indian economist Sir Banerjee Bath Babore. Mrs Magussie's, in fine, was a house of chief consequence; and her long face, as of the guardian of some first principle, moving about the waters of celebrity, was wrinkled in a great cause. To meet or not to meet? She had answered the question for good and all.

The 'met' or 'meetee' for her opening rout in 1925 was the great Italian violinist Luigi Sporza, who had just completed his remarkable tour of the world, having in half the time played more often than any two previous musicians. The prodigious feat had been noted in the Press of all countries with every circumstance – the five violins he had tired out, the invitation he had received to preside over a South American Republic, the special steamer he had chartered to keep an engagement in North America, and his fainting fit in Moscow after the Beethoven and Brahms concertos, the Bach chaconne, and seventeen encores. During the lingering year of his great effort, his fame had been established. As an artist he had been known to a few, as an athlete he was now known to all.

Michael and Fleur, passing up the centre stairway, saw a man 'not 'arf like a bull' – Michael muttered – whose hand people were seizing, one after the other, to move away afterwards with a look of pain.

'Only Italy can produce men like that,' said Michael in Fleur's ear. 'Give him the go-by. He'll hurt you.'

But Fleur moved forward.

'Made of sterner stuff,' murmured Michael. It was not the part of his beloved to miss the hand of celebrity, however horny! No portion of her charming face quivered as the great athlete's grip closed on hers, and his eyes, like those of a tired minotaur, traversed her supple body with a gleam of interest.

'Hulking brute!' thought Michael, disentangling his own grasp, and drifting with her over shining space. Since yesterday's ordeal and its subsequent spring-running, he had kept his unacceptable misgivings to himself; he did not even know whether, at this rout, she was deliberately putting their position to the test, or merely, without forethought, indulging her liking to be in the swim. And what a swim! In that great pillared 'salon', Members of Parliament, poets, musicians, very dry in the smile, as who should say: 'I could have done it better,' or 'Imagine doing that!' Peers, physicians, dancers, painters, Labour Leaders, cricketers, lawyers, critics, ladies of fashion, and ladies who 'couldn't bear it' – every mortal person that Michael knew or didn't know seemed present. He watched Fleur's eyes quartering them, busy as bees beneath the white lids he had kissed last night. He envied her that social curiosity; to live in London without it was like being at the sea without bathing. She was quietly – he could tell – making up her mind whom she wanted to speak to among those she knew, and whom, among those she didn't yet know, she wanted to speak to her. 'I hope to God she's not in for a snubbing,' he thought, and when she was engaged in talk, he slipped towards a pillar. A small voice behind him said: 'Well, young Mont!' Mr Blythe, looking like a Dover sole above Kew Bridge, was squeezed against the same pillar, his eyes goggling timorously above his beard.

'Stick to me!' he said. 'These bees are too bee busy.'

'Were you in Court yesterday?' asked Michael.

'No; one read about it. You did well.'

'She did better.'

'H'm!' said Mr Blythe. 'By the way, *The Evening Sun* was at us again this afternoon. They compared us to kittens playing with their tails. It's time for your second barrel, Mont.'

'I thought – on the agricultural estimates.'

'Good! Governmental purchase and control of wheat. Stress use of the present machinery. No more officials than are absolutely necessary.'

'Blythe,' said Michael suddenly, 'where were you born?'

'Lincolnshire.'

'You're English, then?'

'Pure,' said Mr Blythe.

'So am I; so's old Foggart – I looked him up in the studbook. It's lucky, because we shall certainly be assailed for lack of patriotism.'

'We *are*,' said Mr Blythe ' "People who can see no good in their own country. . . . Birds who foul their own nest. . . . Gentry never happy unless running England down in the eyes of the world. . . . Calamity-mongers. . . . Pessimists. . . ." You don't mind that sort of gup, I hope?'

'Unfortunately,' said Michael, 'I do; it hurts me inside. It's so damned unjust. I simply can't bear the idea of England being in a fix.'

Mr Blythe's eyes rolled.

'She's bee well not going to be, if we can help it.'

'If only I amounted to something,' murmured Michael; 'but I always feel as if I could creep into one of my back teeth.'

'Have it crowned. What you want is brass, Mont. And talking of brass: There's your late adversary! *She's* got it all right. Look at her!'

Michael saw Marjorie Ferrar moving away from the great Italian, in not too much of a sea-green gown, with her red-gold head held high. She came to a stand a small room's length from Fleur, and swept her eyes this way and that. Evidently she had taken up that position in deliberate challenge.

'I must go to Fleur.'

'So must I,' said Mr Blythe, and Michael gave him a grateful look.

And now it would have been so interesting to one less interested than Michael. The long, the tapering nose of Society could be seen to twitch, to move delicately upwards, and like the trunk of some wild elephant scenting man, writhe and snout this way and that, catching the whiff of sensation. Lips were smiling and moving closer to ears; eyes turning from that standing figure to the other; little reflective frowns appeared on foreheads, as if beneath cropped and scented scalps, brains were trying to make choice. And Marjorie Ferrar stood smiling and composed; and Fleur talked and twisted the flower in her hand; and both went on looking their best. So began a battle without sign of war declared, without even seeming recognition of each other's presence. Mr Blythe, indeed, stood pat between the two of them. Bulky and tall, he was an effective screen. But Michael on the other side of her, could see and grimly follow. The Nose was taking time to apprehend the full of the aroma; the Brain to make its choice. Tide seemed at balance, not moving in or out. And then, with the slow implacability of tides, the water moved away from Fleur and lapped round her rival. Michael chattered, Mr Blythe goggled, using the impersonal pronoun with a sort of passion; Fleur smiled, talked, twisted the flower. And, over there, Marjorie Ferrar seemed to hold a little court. Did people admire, commiserate, approve of, or sympathize with her? Or did they disapprove of himself and Fleur? Or was it just that the 'Pet of the Panjoys' was always the more sensational figure? Michael watched Fleur growing paler, her smile more nervous, the twitching of the flower spasmodic. And he dared not suggest going; for she would see in it an admission of defeat. But on the faces, turned their way, the expression became more and more informative. Sir James Foskisson had done his job too well; he had slavered his clients with his own self-righteousness. Better the confessed libertine than those who brought her to judgement! And Michael thought: 'Dashed natural, after all! Why didn't the fellow take my tip, and let us pay and look pleasant.'

And just then close to the great Italian he caught sight of a tall young man with his hair brushed back, who was looking at his fingers. By George! It was Bertie Curfew! And there behind him, waiting for his turn 'to meet', who but MacGown himself! The humour of the gods had run amok! Head in air, soothing his mangled fingers, Bertie Curfew passed them, and strayed into the group around his former flame. Her greeting of him was elaborately casual. But up went the tapering Nose, for here came MacGown! How the fellow had changed – grim, greyish, bitter! The great Italian had met his match for once. And he too, stepped into that throng.

A queer silence was followed by a burst of speech, and then by dissolution. In twos and threes they trickled off, and there were MacGown and his betrothed standing alone. Michael turned to Fleur.

'Let's go.'

Silence reigned in their homing cab. He had chattered himself out on the field of battle, and must wait for fresh supplies of camouflage. But he slipped his hand along till he found hers, which did not return his pressure. The card he used to play at times of stress – the eleventh baronet – had failed for the last three months; Fleur seemed of late to resent his introduction as a remedy. He followed her into the dining-room, sore at heart, bewildered in mind. He had never seen her look so pretty as in that oyster-coloured frock, very straight and simply made, with a swing out above the ankles. She sat down at the narrow dining-table, and he seated himself opposite, with the costive feeling of one who cannot find words that will ring true. For social discomfiture he himself didn't care a tinker's curse; but she – !

And suddenly, she said:

'And you don't mind?'

'For myself – not a bit.'

'Yes, you've still got your Foggartism and your Bethnal Green.'

'If *you* care, Fleur, I care a lot.'

'*If* I care !'

'How – exactly?'

'I'd rather not increase your feeling that I'm a snob.'

'I never had any such feeling.'

'Michael !'

'Hadn't you better say what you mean by the word?'

'You know perfectly well.'

'I know that you appreciate having people about you, and like them to think well of you. That isn't being a snob.'

'Yes; you're very kind, but you don't admire it.'

'I admire *you*.'

'You mean, desire me. You admire Norah Curfew.'

'Norah Curfew! For all I care, she might snuff out to-morrow.'

And from her face he had the feeling that she believed him.

'If it isn't her, it's what she stands for – all that I'm not.'

'I admire a lot in you,' said Michael, fervently; 'your intelligence, your flair; I admire you with Kit and your father; your pluck; and the way you put up with me.'

'No, I admire you much more than you admire me. Only, you see, I'm not capable of devotion.'

'What about Kit?'

'I'm devoted to myself – that's all.'

He reached across the table and touched her hand.

'Morbid, darling.'

'No. I see too clearly to be morbid.'

She was leaning back, and her throat, very white and round, gleamed in the alabaster-shaded light; little choky movements were occurring there.

'Michael, I want you to take me round the world.'

'And leave Kit?'

'He's too young to mind. Beside, my mother would look after him.'

If she had got as far as that, this was a deliberate desire!

'But your father –'

'He's not really old yet, and he'd have Kit.'

'When we rise in August, perhaps –'

'No, now.'

'It's only five months to wait. We'd have time in the vacation to do a lot of travelling.'

Fleur looked straight at him.

'I knew you cared more for Foggartism now than for me.'

'Be reasonable, Fleur.'

'For five months – with the feeling I've got here!' she put her hand to her breast. 'I've had six months of it already. You don't realize, I suppose, that I'm down and out?'

'But, Fleur, it's all so –'

'Yes, it's always petty to mind being a dead failure, isn't it?'

'But, my child –'

'Oh! If you can't feel it – !'

'I can – I felt wild this evening. But all you've got to do is to let them see that you don't care; and they'll come buzzing round again like flies. It would be running away, Fleur.'

'No,' said Fleur, coldly, 'it's not that – I don't try twice for the same prize. Very well, I'll stay and be laughed at.'

Michael got up.

'I know you don't think there's anything to my job. But there is, Fleur, and I've put my hand to it. Oh I don't look like that. Dash it I This is dreadful I'

'I suppose I could go by myself. That would be more thrilling.'

'Absurd I Of course you couldn't I You're seeing blue to-night, old thing. It'll all seem different to-morrow.'

'To-morrow and to-morrow I No, Michael, mortification has set in, my funeral can take place any day you like I'

Michael's hands went up. She meant what she was saying I To realize, he must remember how much store she had set on her powers as hostess; how she had worked for her collection and shone among it I Her house of cards all pulled about her ears I Cruel I But would going round the world help her? Yes I Her instinct was quite right. He had been round the world himself, nothing else would change her values in quite that way; nothing else would so guarantee oblivion in others and herself I Lippinghall, her father's, the sea for the five months till vacation came – they wouldn't meet her case I She needed what would give her back her importance. And yet, how could he go until vacation? Foggartism – that lean and lonely plant – unwatered and without its only gardener, would wither to its roots, if, indeed, it had any. There was some movement in it now, interest here and there – this Member and that were pecking at it. Private efforts in the same direction were gathering way. And time was going on – Big Ben had called no truce; unemployment swelling, trade dawdling, industrial trouble brewing – brewing, hope losing patience I And what would old Blythe say to his desertion now?

'Give me a week,' he muttered. 'It's not easy. I must think it over.'

Chapter Ten

THE NEW LEAF

→←→→

WHEN MacGown came up to her, Marjorie Ferrar thought:
'Does he know about Bertie?' Fresh from her triumph over 'that
little snob', fluttered by the sudden appearance of her past, and
confronted with her present, she was not in complete possession
of her head. When they had moved away into an empty side
room, she faced him.

'Well, Alec, nothing's changed. I still have a past as lurid as
yesterday. I'm extremely sorry I ever kept it from you. But I did
practically tell you, several times; only you wouldn't take it.'

'Because it was hell to me. Tell me everything, Marjorie!'

'You want to revel in it?'

'Tell me everything, and I'll marry you still.'

She shook her head. 'Marry! Oh! no! I don't go out of my
depth any more. It was absurd anyway. I never loved you, Alec.'

'Then you loved that — you still —'

'My dear Alec, enough!'

He put his hands to his head, and swayed. And she was
touched by genuine compassion.

'I'm awfully sorry, I really am. You've got to cut me out;
that's all.'

She had turned to leave him, but the misery in his face
stopped her. She had not quite realized. He was burnt up! He
was — ! And she said quickly:

'Marry you I won't; but I'd like to pay up, if I could —'
He looked at her.

Quivering all over from that look, she shrugged her shoulders, and walked away. Men of an old fashion! Her own fault
for stepping outside the charmed circle that took nothing too
seriously. She walked over the shining floor, conscious of many
eyes, slipped past her hostess, and soon was in a cab.

She lay awake, thinking. Even without announcement the return of presents would set London by the ears and bring on her again an avalanche of bills. Five thousand pounds! She got up and rummaged out the list, duplicate of that which Alec had. He might still want to pay them! After all, it was he who had spilled the ink by making her go into Court! But then his eyes came haunting her. Out of the question! And, shivering a little, she got back into bed. Perhaps she would have a brainwave in the morning. She had so many in the night, that she could not sleep. Moscow with Bertie Curfew? The stage? America and the 'movies'? All three? She slept at last, and woke languid and pale. With her letters was one from Shropshire House.

DEAR MARJORIE,

If you've nothing better to do, I should like to see you this morning.

Affectionately,

SHROPSHIRE

What now? She looked at herself in the glass, and decided that she *must* make-up a little. At eleven o'clock she was at Shropshire House. The marquess was in his work-room at the top, among a small forest of contraptions. With coat off, he was peering through a magnifying-glass at what looked like nothing.

'Sit down, Marjorie,' he said : 'I'll have done in a minute.'

Except the floor, there seemed nowhere to sit, so she remained standing.

'I thought so,' said the marquess; 'the Italians are wrong.'

He put the spy-glass down, ran his hand through his silvery hair, and drew his ruffled beard into a peak. Then, taking an eyebrow between finger and thumb, he gave it an upward twist, and scratched himself behind one ear.

'They're wrong; there's no reaction whatever.'

Turning towards his granddaughter, he screwed up his eyes till they were bright as pins. 'You've never been up here before. Sit in the window.'

She seated herself on a broad window-ledge covering some sort of battery, with her back to the light.

533

'So you brought that case, Marjorie?'

'I had to.'

'Now why?' He was standing with his head a little to one side, his cheeks very pink, and his eyes very shrewd. And she thought: 'After all, I'm his granddaughter. I'll plunge.'

'Common honesty, if you want to know.'

The marquess pouted, as if trying to understand the words.

'I read your evidence,' he said, 'if you mean that.'

'No. I meant that I wanted to find out where I stood.'

'And did you?'

'Very much so.'

'Are you still going to be married?'

Really, he was a spry old boy!

'No.'

'Whose doing? Yours or his?'

'He still says he'll marry me if I tell him everything. But I don't choose to.'

The marquess moved two steps, placed his foot on a box, and assumed his favourite attitude. He had a red silk tie this morning which floated loose; his tweed trousers were of a blue-green, his shirt of a green-blue. He looked wonderfully bright.

'Is there much to tell?'

'A good deal.'

'Well, Marjorie, you know what I said to you.'

'Yes, Grandfather, but I don't quite see it. *I* don't want to stand for anything.'

'Ah! you're an exception in our class – luckily! But it's the exceptions that do the harm.'

'If people took one as any better than themselves, perhaps. But they don't nowadays.'

'Not quite honest, that,' interrupted the marquess; 'what about the feeling in your bones?'

She smiled.

'It's good to mortify oneself, Grandfather.'

'By having a better time than you ought, um? So your marriage is off?'

'Very much so.'

534

'Are you in debt?'

'Yes.'

'How much do you owe?'

Marjorie Ferrar hesitated. Should she compromise, or blurt it out?

'No heel-taps, Marjorie.'

'Well, then, five thousand about.'

The old peer screwed up his lips, and a melancholy little whistle escaped.

'A good deal of it, of course, is due to my engagement.'

'Your father won a race the other day, I see.'

The old boy knew everything!

'Yes; but I believe it's all gone.'

'It would be,' said the marquess. 'What are you going to do now?'

She had a strong desire to answer: 'What are *you*?' but restrained it, and said:

'I thought of going on the stage.'

'Well, I suppose that might be suitable. Can you act?'

'I'm not a Duse.'

'Duse?' The marquess shook his head. 'One must go back to Ristori for really great acting. Duse! Very talented, of course, but always the same. So you don't choose to marry him now?' He looked at her intently. 'That, I think, is right. Have you a list of your debts?'

Marjorie Ferrar rummaged in her vanity bag. 'Here it is.'

She could see his nose wrinkling above it, but whether at its scent, or its contents, she could not tell.

'Your grandmother,' he said, 'spent about a fifth of what you seem to on about five times the acreage of clothes. You wear nothing nowadays, and yet it costs all this.'

'The less there is, Grandfather, the better it has to be cut, you know.'

'Have you sent your presents back?'

'I've had them packed.'

'They must all go,' said the marquess. 'Keep nothing he or anyone else gave you.'

'Of course not.'

'To frank you,' he said, suddenly, 'I should have to sell the Gainsborough.'

'Oh, no!'

Gainsborough's picture of his own grandmother as a little girl – that beautiful thing! She stretched out her hand for the list. Still holding it, he put his foot to the ground, and stood peering at her with his bright, intent old eyes.

'The question is, Marjorie, how far it's possible to strike a bargain with you. Have you a "word" to keep?'

She felt the blood mounting in her cheeks.

'I think so. It depends on what I've got to promise. But Grandfather, I don't *want* you to sell the Gainsborough.'

'Unfortunately,' said the marquess, 'without doing your uncle Dangerfield in the eye, I've nothing else. It's been my fault, I suppose, for having had expensive children. Other people don't seem to have had them to the same degree.'

She stifled a smile.

'Times are hard,' went on the marquess. 'Land costs money, collieries cost money, Shropshire House costs money; and where's the money? I've got an invention here that ought to make my fortune, but nobody will look at it.'

The poor old boy – at his age! She said with a sigh:

'I really didn't mean to bother you with this, Grandfather. I'll manage somehow.'

The old peer took several somewhat hampered steps, and she noticed that his red slippers were heel-less. He halted, a wonderfully bright spot among the contraptions.

'To come back to what we were saying, Marjorie. If your idea of life is simply to have a good time, how can you promise anything?'

'What did you want me to promise?'

He came and stood before her again, short and a little bent.

'You look as if you had stuff in you, too, with your hair. Do you really think you could earn your living?'

'I believe I can; I know a lot of people.'

'If I clear you, will you give me your word to pay ready money

in future? Now don't say "Yes", and go out and order yourself a
lot of fallals. I want the word of a lady, if you understand what
that implies.'

She stood up.

'I suppose you've every right to say that. But I don't want you
to clear me if you have to sell the Gainsborough.'

'You must leave that to me. I might manage, perhaps, to
scrape it up without. About that promise?'

'Yes; I promise that.'

'Meaning to keep it?'

'Meaning to keep it.'

'Well, that's something.'

'Anything else, Grandfather?'

'I should have liked to ask you not to cheapen our name any
more, but I suppose that would be putting the clock back. The
spirit of the age is against me.'

Turning from his face, she stood looking out of the window.
The spirit of the age! It was all very well, but he didn't understand what it was. Cheapen? Why! she had *raised* the price of
the family name; hoicked it out of a dusty cupboard, and made
of it a current coin. People sat up when they read of her. Did
they sit up when they read of grandfather? But he would never
see that! And she murmured:

'All right, dear, I'll be careful. I think I shall go to America.'

His eyes twinkled.

'And start a fashion of marrying American husbands? It's
not yet been done, I believe. Get one who's interested in electricity, and bring him over. There are great things for an
American to do here. Well, I'll keep this list and work it off
somehow. Just one thing, Marjorie: I'm eighty, and you're –
what are you – twenty-five? Don't get through life so fast –
you'll be dreadfully bored by the time you're fifty, and there's
no greater bore than a bored person. Good-bye!' He held out his
hand.

She took a long breath. Free!

And seizing his hand, she put it to her lips. Oh! He was gazing
at it – oh! Had her lips come off? And she hurried out. The old

boy! He was a darling to have kept that list! A new leaf! She
would go at once to Bertie Curfew and get him to turn it over
for her! The expression in his eye last night!

Chapter Eleven

OVER THE WINDMILL

◄◄·►►

DURING his period of indecision Michael struck no attitudes,
and used practically no words; the thing was too serious. Perhaps
Kit would change Fleur's mood, or she would see other dis-
advantages, such as her father. The complete cessation, however,
of any social behaviour on her part – no invitation issued, or
received, no function attended, or even discussed, during that
rather terrible week, proved that the iron had really seared her
spirit. She was not sulky, but she was mum and listless. And she
was always watching him, with a wistful expression on her face,
and now and then a resentful look, as if she had made up her
mind that he was going to refuse. He could consult no one, too,
for to any who had not lived through this long episode, Fleur's
attitude would seem incomprehensible, even ridiculous. He
could not give her away; could not even go to old Blythe, until
he had decided. Complicating his mental conflict was the habi-
tual doubt whether he was really essential to Foggartism. If
only his head would swell! He had not even the comfort of feeling that a sturdy negative would impress Fleur; she thought his
job a stunt, useful to make him conspicuous, but of no real importance to the country. She had the political cynicism of the
woman in the street; only that which threatened property or Kit
would really ruffle her. He knew that his dilemma was comic.
The future of England against the present of a young woman
socially snubbed! But, after all, only Sir James Foggart and old
Blythe so far seriously connected Foggartism with the future of

England; and if, now, he went off round the world, even they would lose their faith.

On the last morning of that week, Michael, still in doubt, crossed Westminster Bridge and sought the heart of the Surrey side. It was unfamiliar, and he walked with interest. Here, he remembered, the Bickets had lived; the Bickets who had failed, and apparently were failing in Australia, too. Street after mean street! Breeding-ground of Bickets! Catch them early, catch them often, catch them before they were Bickets, spoiled for the land; make them men and women of property, give them air and give them sun – the most decent folk in the world, give them a chance! Ugly houses, ugly shops, ugly pubs! No, that wouldn't do! Keep Beauty out of it; Beauty never went down in 'the House'! No sentiment went down! At least, only such as was understood – 'British stock', 'Patriotism', 'Empire', 'Moral Fibre'. Thews and productive power – stick to the clichés! He stood listening outside a school to the dull hum of education. The English breed with its pluck and its sense of humour and its patience, all mewed-up in mean streets!

He had a sudden longing for the country. His motor-cycle! Since taking his seat in Parliament he had not been on a machine so inclined to bump his dignity. But he would have it out now, and go for a run – it might shake him into a decision!

Fleur was not in, and no lunch ordered. So he ate some ham, and by two o'clock had started.

With spit and bluster he ran out along the road past Chiswick, Slough and Maidenhead; crossed the river and sputtered towards Reading. At Caversham he crossed again, and ran on to Pangbourne. By the towing path he tipped his machine into some bushes and sat down to smoke a pipe. Quite windless! The river between the bare poplars had a grey, untroubled look; the catkins were forming on the willows. He plucked a twig, and stirred it round the bowl of his pipe before pressing in tobacco. The shaking had done him good; his mind was working freely. The war! One had no hesitations then; but then – one had no Fleur. Besides, that was a clear, a simple issue. But now, beyond this 'to stay or not to stay', Michael seemed seeing the future of his married life. The decision that he made would affect what might last another fifty years. To put your hand to the plough, and at the first request to take it off again! You might be ploughing crooked, and by twilight; but better plough by dim light than no light; a crooked furrow than none at all! Foggartism was the best course he could see, and he must stick to it! The future of England! A blackbird, close by, chuckled. Quite so! But, as old Blythe said, one must stand up to laughter! Oh! Surely Fleur would see in the long run that he couldn't play fast and loose; see that if she wanted him to remain in Parliament — and she did — he must hang on to the line he had taken, however it amused the blackbirds. She wouldn't like him to sink to the nonentity of a turntail. For after all she was his wife, and with his self-respect her own was bound up.

He watched the smoke from his pipe, and the low grey clouds, the white-faced Herefords grazing beyond the river, and a man fishing with a worm. He took up the twig and twirled it, admiring the yellowish-grey velvet of its budding catkins. He felt quiet in the heart, at last, but very sorry. How to make up to Fleur? Beside this river not two miles away, he had wooed — queer word — if not won her! And now they had come to this snag. Well, it was up to her now, whether or no they should come to grief on it. And it seemed to him, suddenly, that he would like to tell Old Forsyte. ...

When he heard the splutter of Michael's motor-cycle, Soames was engaged in hanging the Fred Walker he had bought at the emporium next to Messrs Settlewhite and Stark, memorializing his freedom from the worry of that case, and soothing his itch for the British School. Fred Walker! The fellow was old-fashioned; he and Mason had been succeeded by a dozen movements. But — like old fiddles, with the same agreeable glow — there they were, very good curiosities such as would always command a price.

Having detached a Courbet, early and about ripe, he was standing in his shirt-sleeves, with a coil of wire in his hand, when Michael entered.

'Where have you sprung from?' he said, surprised.

'I happened to be passing, sir, on my old bike. I see you've kept your word about the English School.'

Soames attached the wire.

'I shan't be happy,' he said, 'till I've got an old Crome – best of the English landscapists.'

'Awfully rare, isn't he, old Crome?'

'Yes, that's why I want him.'

The smile on Michael's face, as if he were thinking: 'You mean that's why you consider him the best,' was lost on Soames giving the wire a final twist.

'I haven't seen your pictures for a long time, sir. Can I look round?'

Observing him sidelong, Soames remembered his appearance there one summer Sunday, after he had first seen Fleur in that Gallery off Cork Street. Only four years? It seemed an age! The young fellow had worn better than one had hoped; looked a good deal older, too, less flighty; an amiable chap, considering his upbringing, and that war! And suddenly he perceived that Michael was engaged in observing him. Wanted something, no doubt – wouldn't have come down for nothing! He tried to remember when anybody had come to see him without wanting something; but could not. It was natural!

'Are you looking for a picture to go with that Fragonard?' he said. 'There's a Chardin in the corner.'

'No, no, sir; you've been much too generous to us already.'

Generous! How could one be generous to one's only daughter?

'How is Fleur?'

'I wanted to tell you about her. She's feeling awfully restless.'

Soames looked out of the window. The spring was late!

'She oughtn't to be, with that case out of the way.'

'That's just it, sir.'

Soames gimleted the young man's face. 'I don't follow you.'

'We're being cold-shouldered.'

'How? You won.'

541

'Yes, but you see, people resent moral superiority.'

'What's that? Who —?' Moral superiority — he resented it himself!

'Foskisson, you know; we're being tarred with his brush. I told you I was afraid of it. It's the being laughed at Fleur feels so bitterly.'

'Laughed at? Who has the impudence —?'

'To attack modern morality was a good stunt, sir, with the judge and the jury, and anyone professionally pompous; but it makes one ridiculous nowadays in Society, you know, when everybody prides himself on lack of prejudice.'

'Society!'

'Yes, sir; but it's what we live in. *I* don't mind, got used to it over Foggartism; but Fleur's miserable. It's natural, if you think of it — Society's her game.'

'She ought to have more strength of mind,' said Soames. But he was gravely perturbed. First she'd been looked on as a snob, and now there was this!

'What with that German actor hanging himself at Lipping-hall,' Michael went on, 'and my Foggartism, and this Ferrar rumpus, our pitch is badly queered. We've had a wretched week of it since the case. Fleur feels so out of her plate, that she wants me to take her round the world.'

A bomb bursting on the dove-cote down there could not have been more startling. Round the world! He heard Michael murmuring on:

'She's quite right, too. It might be the very best thing for her; but I simply can't leave my job until the long vacation. I've taken up this thing, and I must stick to it while Parliament's sitting.'

Sitting! As if it were a hen, addling its precious eggs! Round the world!

But Michael ran on:

'It's only today I've quite decided. I should feel like a deserter, and that wouldn't be good for either of us in the long run. But she doesn't know yet.'

For Soames the dove-cote was solidifying again, now that he

knew Michael was not going to take her away for goodness knew how long!

'Round the world!' he said. 'Why not – er – Pontresina?'

'I think,' answered Michael slowly, like a doctor diagnosing, 'that she wants something dramatic. Round the world at twenty-three! She feels somehow that she's lost caste.'

'How can she think of leaving that little chap?'

'Yes, that show's it's pretty desperate with her. I wish to goodness I *could* go.'

Soames stared. The young fellow wasn't expecting him to do anything about it, was he? Round the world? A crazy notion!

'I must see her,' he said. 'Can you leave that thing of yours in the garage and come up with me in the car? I'll be ready in twenty minutes. You'll find tea going downstairs.'

Left alone with the Fred Walker still unhung, Soames gazed at his pictures. He saw them with an added clarity, a more penetrating glance, a sort of ache in his heart, as if – Well! A good lot they were, better than he had thought, of late! *She* had gone in for collecting people! And now she'd lost her collection! Poor little thing! All nonsense, of course – as if there were any satisfaction in people! Suppose he took her up that Chardin? It was a good Chardin. Dumetrius had done him over the price, but not too much. And, before Chardin was finished with, he would do Dumetrius. Still – if it would give her any pleasure! He unhooked the picture and, carrying it under his arm, went downstairs.

Beyond certain allusions to the characteristics of the eleventh baronet, and the regrettable tendencies of the police to compel slow travelling over the new cut constructed to speed up traffic, little was said in the car. They arrived in South Square about six o'clock to wait for her. The Dandie, having descended to look for strange legs, had almost immediately ascended again, and the house was very quiet. Michael was continually looking at his watch.

'Where do you think she's got to?' said Soames at last.

'Haven't an idea, sir; that's the worst of London, it swallows people up.'

He had begun to fidget; Soames, who also wanted to fidget, was thinking of saying 'Don't!' when from the window Michael cried:

'Here she is!' and went quickly to the door.

Soames sat on, with the Chardin resting against his chair.

They were a long time out there! Minute after minute passed, and still they did not come.

At last Michael reappeared. He looked exceedingly grave.

'She's in her little room upstairs, sir. I'm afraid it's upset her awfully. Perhaps you wouldn't mind going up.'

Soames grasped the Chardin.

'Let's see, that's the first door on the left, isn't it?' He mounted slowly, his mind blank, and without waiting for her to answer his mild knock, went in.

Fleur was sitting at the satinwood bureau, with her face buried on her arms. Her hair, again in its more natural 'bob', gleamed lustrously under the light. She seemed unconscious of his entry. This sight of private life affected Soames, unaccustomed to give or receive undefended glimpses of self, and he stood, uncertain. Had he the right to surprise her, with her ears muffled like that, and her feelings all upset? He would have gone out and come in again, but he was too concerned. And, moving to her side, he put his finger on her shoulder and said:

'Tired, my child?'

Her face came round — queer, creased, not like her face; and Soames spoke the phrase of her childhood:

'See what I've brought you!'

He raised the Chardin; she gave it just a glance and he felt hurt. After all, it was worth some hundreds of pounds! Very pale, she had crossed her arms on her chest as if shutting herself up. He recognized the symptom. A spiritual crisis! The sort of thing his whole life had been passed in regarding as extravagant; like a case of appendicitis that will not wait decently.

'Michael,' he said, 'tells me you want him to take you round the world.'

'Well, he can't; so that ends it.'

544

If she had said: 'Yes, and why can't he?' Soames would have joined the opposition automatically. But her words roused his natural perversity. Here she was, and here was her heart's desire – and she wasn't getting it! He put the Chardin down and took a walk over the soft carpet.

'Tell me,' he said, coming to a halt, 'where do you feel it exactly?'

Fleur laughed: 'In my head, and my eyes, and my ears, and my heart.'

'What business,' muttered Soames, 'have they to look down their confounded noses!' And he set off again across the room. All the modern jackanapes whom from time to time he had been unable to avoid in her house, seemed to have come sniggering round him with lifted eyebrows, like a set of ghosts. The longing to put them in their places – a shallow lot – possessed him at that moment to the exclusion of a greater sanity.

'I – I don't see how *I* can take you,' he said, and stopped short.

What was that he was saying? Who had asked him to take her? Her eyes, widely open, were fixed on him.

'But of course not, Dad!'

Of course not! He didn't know about that!

'I shall get used to being laughed at, in time.'

Soames growled.

'I don't see why you should,' he said. 'I suppose people do go round the world.'

Fleur's pallor had gone, now.

'But not you, dear; why, it would bore you stiff! It's very sweet of you, even to think of it; but of course I couldn't let you – at your age!'

'At my age?' said Soames. 'I'm not so very old.'

'No, no, Dad; I'll just dree my weird.'

Soames took another walk, without a sound. Dree her weird, indeed!

'I won't have it,' he ejaculated; 'if people can't behave to you, I – I'll show them!'

She had got up, and was breathing deeply, with her lips parted and her cheeks very flushed. So she had stood, before her first party, holding out her frock for him to see.

'We'll go,' he said gruffly. 'Don't make a fuss! That's settled.'

Her arms were round his neck; his nose felt wet. What nonsense! as if – ! ...

He stood unbuttoning his braces that night in the most peculiar state of mind. Going round the world – was he? Preposterous! It had knocked that young fellow over, anyway – he was to join them in August wherever they were by that time! Good Lord! It might be China! The thing was fantastic; and Fleur behaving like a kitten! The words of a comic ditty, sung by a clergyman, in his boyhood, kept up a tattoo within him:

> 'I see Jerusalem and Madagascar,
> And North and South Amerikee....'

Yes! Indeed! His affairs were in apple-pie order, luckily! There was nothing to do, in Timothy's or Winifred's Trusts – the only two he had on his hands now; but how things would get on without him, he couldn't tell. As to Annette! She wouldn't be sorry, he supposed. There was no one else to care, except Winifred, a little. It was, rather, the intangible presence of England that troubled him, about to forsake her for months on end! Still, the cliffs of Dover would be standing, he supposed, and the river still running past his lawn, when he came back, if he ever came back! You picked up all sorts of things out there – microbes, insects, snakes – never knew what you'd run into! Pretty business, steering Fleur clear of all that. And the sightseeing he would have to do! For *she* wouldn't miss anything! Trust her! Going round among a lot of people with their mouths open – he couldn't stand that; but he would have to! H'm! A relief when that young fellow could join them. And yet – to have her to himself; he hadn't, for a long time now. But she would pick up with everybody, of course. He would have to make himself agreeable to Tom, Dick, and Harry. A look at Egypt, then to India, and across to China and Japan, and back through that great sprawling America – God's own country, didn't they call it! She had it all mapped out. Thank goodness, no question of Russia! She hadn't even proposed that – it was all to pieces now, they said! Communism! Who knew what would happen at home before they got back? It seemed to Soames as if England, too, must all go to pieces, if he left it. Well, he'd said he would take her! And she had cried over it. Phew! He threw the window up, and in the Jaeger dressing-gown, kept there for stray occasions, leaned into the mild air. No Westminster Square did he seem to see out there, but his own river and its poplars, with the full moon behind them, a bright witness – the quiet beauty he had never put into words, the green tranquility he had felt for thirty years, and only permitted to seep into the back of his being. He would miss it – the scents, the sighs of the river under the wind, the chuckle down at the weir, the stars. They had stars out there, of course, but not English stars. And the grass – those great places had no grass, he believed! The blossom, too, was late this year – no blossom before they left! Well, the milk was spilled! And that reminded him: The dairyman would be certain to let the cows go out of milk – he was a 'natural', that chap! He would have to warn Annette. Women never seemed to understand that a cow didn't go on giving milk for ever, without being attended to. If he only had a man to rely on in the country, like old Gradman in Town! H'm! Old Gradman's eyes would drop out when he heard this news! Bit of old England there; and wouldn't be left long, now! It would be queer to come back and find old Gradman gone. One – Two – Three – Eleven! That clock! It had kept him awake before now; still – it was a fine old clock! That young fellow was to go on sitting under it. And was there anything in the notions that kept him sitting there, or were they just talk? Well, he was right to stick to his guns, anyway. But five months away from his young wife – great risk in that! 'Youth's a stuff' – Old Shakespeare knew the world. Well! Risk or no risk, there was! After all, Fleur had a good head; and young Michael had a good heart. Fleur had a good heart, too; he wouldn't have said that she hadn't! She would feel leaving the baby when it came to the point. She didn't realize, yet. And Soames felt within him the stir of a curious conflict, between hope that, after all, she

might give it up, and apprehension lest she should. Funny –
that! His habits, his comfort, his possessions . . . and here he was,
flinging them all over the windmill! Absurd! And yet –!

Chapter Twelve

ENVOI

◂◂·▸▸

A w a y from Fleur five months at least!

Soames's astounding conduct had indeed knocked Michael
over. And yet, after all, they had come to a crisis in their life together, the more serious because concerned with workaday feelings. Perhaps out there she would become afflicted, like himself,
with an enlarged prospect; lose her idea that the world consisted
of some five thousand people of advanced tastes, of whom she
knew at the outside five hundred. It was she who had pushed
him into Parliament, and until he was hoofed therefrom as a
failure, their path was surely conjoined along the crest of a large
view. In the fortnight before her departure he suffered and kept
smiling; wryly thankful that she was behaving 'like a kitten', as
her father called it. Her nerves had been on edge ever since the
autumn over that wretched case – what more natural than this
reaction? At least she felt for him sufficiently to be prodigal of
kisses – great consolation to Michael while it lasted. Once or twice
he caught her hanging with wet eyes over the eleventh baronet;
once found her with a wet face when he awoke in the morning.
These indications were a priceless assurance to him that she
meant to come back. For there were moments when possibilities
balled into a nightmare. Absurd! She was going with her father,
that embodiment of care and prudence! Who would have
thought old Forsyte could uproot himself like this? He, too,
was leaving a wife, though Michael saw no signs of it. One didn't
know much about old Forsyte's feelings, except that they
centred round his daughter, and that he was continually asking

questions about labels and insects. He had bought himself, too, a life-saving waistcoat and one for Fleur. Michael held with him only one important conversation.

'I want you,' Soames said, 'to keep an eye on my wife, and see she doesn't go getting into a mess with the cows. She'll have her mother with her, but women are so funny. You'll find her first-rate with the baby. How will you be off for money?'

'Perfectly all right, sir.'

'Well, if you want some for any good purpose, go to old Gradman in the City; you remember him, perhaps?'

'Yes, and I'm afraid he'll remember me.'

'Never mind; he's a faithful old fellow.' And Michael heard him sigh. 'I'd like you to look in at Green Street, too, now and then. Your aunt-in-law may feel my being away a little. I'll let you have news of Fleur from time to time – now they've got this wireless she'll want to know about the baby. I'm taking plenty of quinine. Fleur says she's a good sailor. There's nothing like champagne for that, I'm told. And, by the way, you know best, but I shouldn't press your notions too far in Parliament; they're easily bored there, I believe. We'll meet you at Vancouver, at the end of August. She'll be tired of travelling by then. She's looking forward to Egypt and Japan, but I don't know. Seems to me it'll be all travelling.'

'Have you plenty of ducks, sir? You'll want them at this time of year in the Red Sea; and I should take a helmet.'

'I've got one,' said Soames; 'they're heavy great things,' and, looking suddenly at Michael, he added:

'I shall look after her, and you'll look after yourself, I hope.'

Michael understood him.

'Yes, sir. And thank you very much. I think it's most frightfully sporting of you.'

'It's to be hoped it'll do her good; and that the little chap won't miss her.'

'Not if I can help it.'

Soames, who was seated in front of 'The White Monkey', seemed to go into a trance. At last he stirred in his chair and said:

'The war's left everything very unsettled. I suppose people believe in something nowadays, but *I* don't know what it is.'

Michael felt a fearful interest.

'Do you mind telling me sir, what you believe in yourself?'

'What was good enough for my father is good enough for me. They expect too much now; there's no interest taken in being alive.'

'Interest taken in being alive!' The words were singularly comprehensive. Were they the answer to all modern doubt?

The last night, the last kiss came; and the glum journey to the Docks in Soames's car. Michael alone went to see them off! The gloomy dockside, and the grey river; the bustle with baggage, and the crowded tender. An aching business! Even for her, he almost believed — an aching business. And the long desultory minutes, on the ship; the initiation of Soames into its cramped, shining, strangely odoured mysteries. The ghastly smile one had to keep on the lips, the inane jokes one had to make. And then that moment, apart, when she pressed her breast to his and gave him a clinging kiss.

'Good-bye, Michael; it's not for very long.'

'Good-bye, darling! Take care of yourself. You shall have all the news I can send you, and don't worry about Kit.'

His teeth were clenched, and her eyes — he saw — were wet! And, then, once more:

'Good-bye!'

'Good-bye!'

Back on the tender, with the strip of grey water opening, spreading between him and the ship's side, and that high line of faces above the bulwark — Fleur's face under the small fawn hat, her waving hand; and, away to the left, seen out of the tail of his eyes, old Forsyte's face alone — withdrawn so that they might have their parting to themselves — long, chinny, grey-moustached, very motionless; absorbed and lonely, as might be that of some long-distance bird arrived on an unknown shore, and looking back towards the land of its departure. Smaller and smaller they grew, merged in blur, vanished.

For the whole journey back to Westminster, Michael smoked cigarette on cigarette, and read the same sentence over and over in the same journal, and the sentence was:

'Robbery at Highgate, Cat Burglar gets clear away.'

He went straight into the House of Commons. And all the afternoon sat listening and taking in a few words now and then, of a debate on education. What chance – what earthly chance – had his skyscraping in this place, where they still talked with calm disagreement, as if England were the England of 1906, and the verdict on him was: 'Amiable but very foolish young man!' National unity – national movement! No jolly fear! The country wouldn't have it! One was battering at a door which everybody said must be opened, but through which nobody could pass. And a long strip of grey water kept spreading between him and the talkers; the face under the fawn hat confused itself with that of the Member for Wasbaston; the face of Old Forsyte above the bulwark rail appeared suddenly between two Labour Leaders; and the lines of faces faded to a blur on a grey river where gulls were flighting.

Going out, he passed a face that had more reality – Mac-Gown's! Grim! It wasn't the word. No one had got any change out of that affair. *Multum ex parvo! Parvum ex multo!* That was the modern comedy!

Going home to have a look at Kit and send Fleur a wireless, he passed four musicians playing four instruments with a sort of fury. They had able bodies in shabby clothes. 'By Jove!' thought Michael, 'I know that chap's face! – surely he was in my company in France!' He watched till the cheeks collapsed. Yes! A good man, too! But they had all been good men. By George, they had been wonders! And here they were! And he within an ace of abandoning them! Though everybody had his nostrum, and one perhaps was as good as another, still one could only follow what light one had! And if the Future was unreadable, and Fate grinned, well – let it grin!

How empty the house felt! Tomorrow Kit and the dog were to go down to 'The Shelter' in the car, and it would be still emptier. From room after room he tried to retrieve some sight or scent of Fleur. Too painful: His dressing-room, his study were the only places possible – in them he would abide.

He went to the nursery and opened the door softly. Whiteness and dimity; the dog on his fat silver side, the Magicoal fire burning; the prints on the white walls so carefully selected for the moment when the eleventh baronet should begin to take notice – prints slightly comic, to avoid a moral; the high and shining fender-guard that even Magicoal might not be taken too seriously; the light coming in between bright chintz. A charming room! The nurse, in blue, was standing with her back to the door, and did not see him. And, in his little high chair, the eleventh baronet was at table; on his face, beneath its dark chestnut curls, was a slight frown; and in his tiny hand he held a silver spoon, with which over the bowl before him he was making spasmodic passes.

Michael heard the nurse saying:

'Now that mother's gone, you must be a little man, Kit, and learn to use your spoon.'

Michael saw his offspring dip at the bowl and throw some of its contents into the air.

'That's not the way at all.'

The eleventh baronet repeated the performance, and looked for applause, with a determined smile.

'Naughty!'

'A – a!' said the eleventh baronet, plopping the spoon. The contents spurted wastefully.

'Oh! you spoiled boy!'

'"England, my England!"' thought Michael, 'as the poet said.'

SWAN SONG

Contents

TO
F. N. Doubleday

We are such stuff
As dreams are made on; and our little life
Is rounded with a sleep.

The Tempest.

PART ONE

Chapter One

INITIATION OF THE CANTEEN

⤆⟡⤇

In modern Society, one thing after another, this spice on that, ensures a kind of memoristic vacuum, and Fleur Mont's passage of arms with Marjorie Ferrar was, by the spring of 1926, well-nigh forgotten. Moreover, she gave Society's memory no encouragement, for after her tour round the world, she was interested in the Empire – a bent so out of fashion as to have all the flavour and excitement of novelty with a sort of impersonality guaranteed.

Colonials, Americans, and Indian students, people whom nobody could suspect of being lions, now encountered each other in the 'bimetallic parlour', and were found by Fleur 'very interesting', especially the Indian students, so supple and enigmatic, that she could never tell whether she were 'using' them or they were 'using' her.

Perceiving the extraordinary uphill nature of Foggartism, she had been looking for a second string to Michael's Parliamentary bow, and, with her knowledge of India, where she had spent six weeks of her tour, she believed that she had found it in the idea of free entrance for the Indians into Kenya. In her talks with these Indian students, she learned that it was impossible to walk in a direction unless you knew what it was. These young men might be complicated and unpractical, meditative and secret, but at least they appeared to be convinced that the molecules in an organism mattered less than the organism itself – that they, in fact, mattered less than India. Fleur, it seemed, had encountered faith – a new and 'intriguing' experience. She mentioned the fact to Michael.

'It's all very well,' he answered, 'but our Indian friends didn't live four years in the trenches, or the fear thereof, for the sake of their faith. If they had, they couldn't possibly have the feeling that it matters as much as they think it does. They might want to, but their feelers would be blunted. That's what the war really did to all of us in Europe who were in the war.'

'That doesn't make "faith" any less interesting,' said Fleur, dryly.

'Well, my dear, the prophets abuse us for being at loose ends, but can you have faith in a life force so darned extravagant that it makes mincemeat of you by the million? Take it from me, Victorian times fostered a lot of very cheap and easy faith, and our Indian friends are in the same case – their India has lain doggo since the Mutiny, and that was only a surface upheaval. So you needn't take 'em too seriously.'

'I don't; but I like the way they believe they're serving India.'

And at his smile she frowned, seeing that he thought she was only increasing her collection.

Her father-in-law, who had really made some study of Orientalism, lifted his eyebrow over these new acquaintances.

'My oldest friend,' he said, on the first of May, 'is a judge in India. He's been there forty years. When he'd been there two, he wrote to me that he was beginning to know something about the Indians. When he'd been there ten, he wrote that he knew all about them. I had a letter from him yesterday, and he says that after forty years he knows nothing about them. And they know as little about us. East and West – the circulation of the blood is different.'

'Hasn't forty years altered the circulation of your friend's blood?'

'Not a jot,' replied Sir Lawrence. 'It takes forty generations. Give me another cup of your nice Turkish coffee, my dear. What does Michael say about the general strike?'

'That the Government won't budge unless the T.U.C. withdraw the notice unreservedly.'

'Exactly! And but for the circulation of English blood there'd be "a pretty mess", as old Forsyte would say.'

'Michael's sympathies are with the miners.'

'So are mine, young lady. Excellent fellow, the miner – but

unfortunately cursed with leaders. The mine-owners are in the same case. Those precious leaders are going to grind the country's nose before they've done. Inconvenient product — coal; it's blackened our faces, and now it's going to black our eyes. Not a merry old soul ! Well, good-bye ! My love to Kit, and tell Michael to keep his head."

This was precisely what Michael was trying to do. When 'the Great War' broke out, though just old enough to fight, he had been too young to appreciate the fatalism which creeps over human nature with the approach of crisis. He was appreciating it now before 'the Great Strike', together with the peculiar value which the human being attaches to saving face. He noticed that both sides had expressed the intention of meeting the other side in every way, without, of course, making any concessions whatever; the slogans, 'Longer hours, less wages', 'Not a minute more, not a bob off', curtsied, and got more and more distant as they neared each other. And now, with the ill-disguised impatience of his somewhat mercurial nature, Michael was watching the sober and tentative approaches of the typical Britons in whose hands any chance of mediation lay. When, on that memorable Monday, not merely the faces of the gentlemen with slogans, but the very faces of the typical Britons were suddenly confronted with the need for being saved, he knew that all was up; and returning from the House of Commons at midnight, he looked at his sleeping wife. Should he wake Fleur and tell her that the country was 'for it', or should he not? Why spoil her beauty sleep? She would know soon enough. Besides, she wouldn't take it seriously. Passing into his dressing-room, he stood looking out of the window at the dark Square below. A general strike at a few hours' notice ! 'Some' test of the British character ! The British character? Suspicion had been dawning on Michael for years that its appearances were deceptive; that Members of Parliament, theatre-goers, trotty little ladies with dresses tight blown about trotty little figures, plethoric generals in armchairs, pettish and petted poets, parsons in pulpits, posters in the street — above all, the Press, were not representative of the national disposition. If the papers were not to come out, one would at least get a chance of feeling and seeing the British character; owing to the papers, one never had seen or felt it clearly during the war, at least not in England. In the trenches, of course, one had – there, sentiment and hate, advertisement and moonshine, had been 'taboo', and with a grim humour the Briton had just 'carried on', unornamental and sublime, in the mud and the blood, the stink and the racket, and the endless nightmare of being pitchforked into fire without rhyme or reason! The Briton's defiant humour that grew better as things grew worse, would – he felt – get its chance again now. And, turning from the window, he undressed and went back into the bedroom.

Fleur was awake.

'Well, Michael?'

'The strike's on.'

'What a bore!'

'Yes; we shall have to exert ourselves.'

'What did they appoint that Commission for, and pay all that subsidy, if not to avoid this?'

'My dear girl, that's mere common sense – no good at all.'

'Why can't they come to an agreement?'

'Because they've got to save face. Saving face is the strongest motive in the world.'

'How do you mean?'

'Well, it caused the war; it's causing the strike now; without "saving face" there'd probably be no life on the earth at all by this time.'

Michael kissed her.

'I suppose you'll have to do something,' she said, sleepily. 'There won't be much to talk about in the House while this is on.'

'No; we shall sit and glower at each other, and use the word "formula" at stated intervals.'

'I wish we had a Mussolini.'

'I don't. You pay for him in the long run. Look at Diaz and Mexico; or Lenin and Russia; or Napoleon and France; or Cromwell and England, for the matter of that.'

'Charles the Second,' murmured Fleur into her pillow 'was rather a dear.'

Michael stayed awake a little, disturbed by the kiss, slept a little, woke again. To save face! No one would make a move because of their faces. For nearly an hour he lay trying to think out a way of saving them all, then fell asleep. He woke at seven with the feeling that he had wasted his time. Under the appearance of concern for the country, and professions of anxiety to find a 'formula', too many personal feelings, motives, and prejudices were at work. As before the war, there was a profound longing for the humiliation and dejection of the adversary; each wished his face saved at the expense of the other fellow's!

He went out directly after breakfast.

People and cars were streaming over Westminster Bridge, no buses ran, no trams; but motor-lorries, full or empty, rumbled past. Some 'specials' were out already, and everybody had a look as if they were going to a tea party, cloaked in a kind of defiant jollity. Michael moved on towards Hyde Park. Over night had sprung up this amazing mish-mash of lorries and cans and tents! In the midst of all the mental and imaginative lethargy which had produced this national crisis – what a wonderful display of practical and departmental energy! 'They say we can't organize!' thought Michael; 'can't we just – *after the event*!'

He went on to a big railway station. It was picketed, but they were running trains already, with volunteer labour. Poking round, he talked here and there among the volunteers. 'By George!' he thought, 'these fellows'll want feeding! What about a canteen!' And he returned post haste to South Square.

Fleur was in.

'Will you help me run a railway canteen for volunteers?' He saw the expression: 'Is that a good stunt?' rise on her face, and hurried on:

'It'll mean frightfully hard work; and getting anybody we can to help. I daresay I could rope in Norah Curfew and her gang from Bethnal Green for a start. But it's your quick head that's wanted, and your way with men.'

563

Fleur smiled. 'All right,' she said.

They took the car – a present from Soames on their return from round the world – and went about, picking people up and dropping them again. They recruited Norah Curfew and 'her gang' in Bethnal Green; and during this first meeting of Fleur with one whom she had been inclined to suspect as something of a rival, Michael noted how, within five minutes, she had accepted Norah Curfew as too 'good' to be dangerous. He left them at South Square in conference over culinary details, and set forth to sap the natural oppositions of officialdom. It was like cutting barbed wide on a dark night before an 'operation'. He cut a good deal, and went down to the 'House'. Humming with unformulated 'formulas', it was, on the whole, the least cheerful place he had been in that day. Everyone was talking of the 'menace to the Constitution'. The Government's long face was longer than ever, and nothing – they said – could be done until it had been saved. The expressions 'Freedom of the Press' and 'At the pistol's mouth', were being used to the point of tautology! He ran across Mr Blythe brooding in the Lobby on the temporary decease of his beloved weekly, and took him over to South Square 'for a bite' at nine o'clock. Fleur had come in for the same purpose. According to Mr Blythe, the solution was to 'form a group' of right-thinking opinion.

'Exactly, Blythe! But what is right-thinking, at "the present time of speaking"?'

'It all comes back to Foggartism,' said Mr Blythe.

'Oh!' said Fleur, 'I do wish you'd both drop that. Nobody will have anything to say to it. You might as well ask the people of today to live like St Francis d'Assisi.'

'My dear young lady, suppose St Francis d'Assisi had said that, we shouldn't be hearing today of St Francis.'

'Well, what real effect has he had? He's just a curiosity. All those great spiritual figures are curiosities. Look at Tolstoi now, or Christ, for that matter!'

'Fleur's rather right, Blythe.'

'Blasphemy!' said Mr Blythe.

'I don't know, Blythe; I've been looking at the gutters lately, and I've come to the conclusion that they put a stopper on Foggartism. Watch the children there, and you'll see how attractive gutters are! So long as a child can have a gutter, he'll never leave it. And, mind you, gutters are a great civilizing influence. We have more gutters here than any other country and more children brought up in them; and we're the most civilized people in the world. This strike's going to prove that. There'll be less bloodshed and more good humour than there could be anywhere else; all due to the gutter.'

'Renegade!' said Mr Blythe.

'Well,' said Michael, 'Foggartism, like all religions, is the over-expression of a home truth. We've been too wholesale, Blythe. What converts have we made?'

'None,' said Mr Blythe. 'But if we can't take children from the gutter, Foggartism is no more.'

Michael wriggled; and Fleur said promptly: 'What never was can't be no more. Are you coming with me to see the kitchens, Michael – they've been left in a filthy state. How does one deal with black beetles on a large scale?'

'Get a beetle-man – sort of pied piper, who lures them to their fate.'

Arrived on the premises of the canteen-to-be, they were joined by Ruth La Fontaine, of Norah Curfew's 'gang', and descended to the dark and odorous kitchen. Michael struck a match, and found the switch. Gosh! In the light, surprised, a brown-black scuttling swarm covered the floor, the walls, the tables. Michael had just sufficient control of his nerves to take in the faces of those three – Fleur's shuddering frown, Mr Blythe's open mouth, the dark and pretty Ruth La Fontaine's nervous smile. He felt Fleur clutch his arm.

'How *disgusting*!'

The disturbed creatures were finding their holes or had ceased to scuttle; here and there, a large one, isolated, seemed to watch them.

'Imagine!' cried Fleur. 'And food's been cooked here all these years! Ugh!'

'After all,' said Ruth La Fontaine, with a shivery giggle, 'they're not so b-bad as b-bugs.'

Mr Blythe puffed hard at his cigar. Fleur muttered:

'What's to be done, Michael?'

Her face was pale; she was drawing little shuddering breaths; and Michael was thinking: 'It's too bad; I must get her out of this!' when suddenly she seized a broom and rushed at a large cockroach on the wall. In a minute they were all at it – swabbing and sweeping, and flinging open door and windows.

Chapter Two

ON THE 'PHONE

◄-→►

WINIFRED DARTIE had not received her *Morning Post*. Now in her sixty-eighth year, she had not followed too closely the progress of events which led up to the general strike – they were always saying things in the papers, and you never knew what was true; those Trades Union people, too, were so interfering, that really one had no patience. Besides, the Government always did something in the end. Acting, however, on the advice of her brother Soames, she had filled her cellars with coal and her cupboards with groceries, and by ten o'clock on the second morning of the strike, was seated comfortably at the telephone.

'Is that you, Imogen? Are you and Jack coming for me this evening?'

'No, Mother. Jack's sworn in, of course. He has to be on duty at five. Besides, they say the theatres will close. We'll go later. *Dat Lubly Lady's* sure to run.'

'Very well, dear. But what a fuss it all is! How are the boys?'

'Awfully fit. They're both going to be little "specials". I've made them tiny badges. D'you think the child's department at Harridge's would have toy truncheons?'

'Sure too, if it goes on. I shall be there today; I'll suggest it. They'd look too sweet, wouldn't they? Are you all right for coal?'

'Oh, yes. Jack says we mustn't hoard. He's fearfully patriotic.'

'Well, good-bye, dear! My love to the boys!'

She had just begun to consider whom she should call up next when the telephone bell rang.

'Yes?'

'Mr Val Dartie living there?'

'No. Who is speaking?'

'My name is Stainford. I'm an old college friend of his. Could you give me his address, please?'

Stainford? It conveyed nothing.

'I'm his mother. My son is not in town; but I daresay he will be before long. Can I give him any message?'

'Well, thanks! I want to see him. I'll ring up again; or take my chance later. Thanks!'

Winifred replaced the receiver.

Stainford! The voice was distinguished. She hoped it had nothing to do with money. Odd, how often distinction was connected with money! Or, rather, with the lack of it. In the old Park Lane days they had known so many fashionables who had ended in the bankruptcy or divorce courts. Emily – her mother – had never been able to resist distinction. That had been the beginning of Monty – he had worn such perfect waistcoats and gardenias, and had known so much about all that was fast – impossible not to be impressed by him. Ah, well! She did not regret him now. Without him she would never have had Val, or Imogen's two boys, or Benedict (almost a colonel), though she never saw him now, living as he did, in Guernsey, to grow cucumbers, away from the income tax. They might say what they liked about the age, but could it really be more up-to-date than it was in the 'nineties and the early years of the century, when income tax was at a shilling, and that considered high! People now just ran about and talked, to disguise the fact that they were not so 'chic' and up-to-date as they used to be.

Again the telephone bell rang. 'Will you take a trunk call from Wansdon?' ...

'Hallo! That you, Mother?'

'Oh, Val, how nice! Isn't this strike absurd?'

'Silly asses! I say: we're coming up.'

'Really, dear. But why? You'll be so much more comfortable in the country.'

'Holly says we've got to do things. Who d'you think turned up last night? – her brother – young Jon Forsyte. Left his wife and mother in Paris – said he'd missed the war and couldn't afford to miss this. Been travelling all the winter – Egypt, Italy, and that – chucked America, I gather. Says he wants to do something dirty – going to stoke an engine. We're driving up to the "Bristol" this afternoon.'

'Oh, but why not come to me, dear, I've got plenty of everything?'

'Well, there's young Jon – I don't think –'

'But he's a nice boy, isn't he?'

'Uncle Soames isn't with you, is he?'

'No, dear. He's at Mapledurham. Oh, and by the way, Val, someone has just rung up for you – a Mr Stainford.'

'Stainford? What! Aubrey Stainford – I haven't seen him since Oxford.'

'He said he would ring up again or take his chance of finding you here.'

'Oh, I'd love to see old Stainford again. Well, if you don't mind putting us up, Mother. Can't leave young Jon out, you know – he and Holly are very thick after six years; but I expect he'll be out all the time.'

'Oh, that'll be quite all right, dear; and how is Holly?'

'Topping.'

'And the horses?'

'All right. I've got a snorting two-year-old, rather backward. Shan't run him till Goodwood, but he ought to win then.'

'That'll be delightful. Well, dear boy, I'll expect you. But you won't be doing anything rash, with your leg?'

'No; just drive a bus, perhaps. Won't last, you know. The

Government's all ready. Pretty hot stuff. We've *got* 'em this time.'

'I'm so glad. It'll be such a good thing to have it over; it's dreadfully bad for the season. Your uncle will be very upset.'

An indistinguishable sound; then Val's voice again:

'I say, Holly says *she'll* want a job – you might ask young Mont. He's in with people. See you soon, then – good-bye!'

Replacing the receiver, Winifred had scarcely risen from the satinwood chair on which she had been seated, when the bell rang again.

'Mrs Dartie? ... That you, Winifred? Soames speaking. What did I tell you?'

'Yes; it's very annoying, dear. But Val says it'll soon be over.'

'What's he know about it?'

'He's very shrewd.'

'Shrewd? H'm! I'm coming up to Fleur's.'

'But why, Soames? I should have thought –'

'Must be on the spot, in case of – accidents. Besides, the car'll be eating its head off down here – may as well be useful. Do that fellow Riggs good to be sworn in. This thing may lead to something.'

'Oh! Do you think –'

'Think? It's no joke. Comes of playing about with subsidies.'

'But you told me last summer –'

'They don't look ahead. They've got no more *nous* than a tom-cat. Annette wants to go to her mother's in France. I shan't stop her. She can't gad about while this is on. I shall take her to Dover with the car today, and come up tomorrow.'

'Ought one to sell anything, Soames?'

'Certainly not.'

'People seem dreadfully busy about it all. Val's going to drive a bus. Oh! and, Soames – that young Jon Forsyte is back. He's left his wife and mother in Paris, and come over to be a stoker.'

A deep sound, and then:

'What's he want to do that for? Much better keep out of England.'

'Ye-es. I suppose Fleur —'

'Don't you go putting things into *her* head!'

'Of course not, Soames. So I shall see you? Good-bye.'

Dear Soames was always so fussy about Fleur! Young Jon
Forsyte and she — of course — but that was ages ago! Calf love!
And Winifred smiled, sitting very still. This strike was really
most 'intriguing'. So long as they didn't break any windows —
because, of course, the milk supply would be all right, the
Government always saw to that; and as to the newspapers —
well, after all, they were a luxury! It would be very nice to have
Val and Holly. The strike was really something to talk about;
there had been nothing so exciting since the war. And, obeying
an obscure instinct to do something about it, Winifred again
took up the receiver. 'Give me Westminster 0000 ... Is that Mrs
Michael Mont's? Fleur? Aunt Winifred speaking. How are you,
dear?'

The voice which answered had that quick little way of
shaping words that was so amusing to Winifred, who in her
youth had perfected a drawl, which effectually dominated both
speed and emotion. All the young women in Society nowadays
spoke like Fleur, as if they had found the old way of speaking
English slow and flat, and were gingering it with little pinches.

'Perfectly all right, thanks. Anything I can do for you,
Auntie?'

'Yes, my dear — your cousin Val and Holly are coming up to
me about this strike. And Holly — I think it's very unnecessary,
but she wants to *do* something. She thought perhaps Michael
would know —'

'Oh, well, of course there are lots of things. We've started a
canteen for railway workers; perhaps she'd like to help in that.'

'My dear, that would be awfully nice.'

'It won't, Aunt Winifred; it's pretty strenuous.'

'It can't last, dear, of course. Parliament are bound to do
something about it. It must be a greater comfort to you to have
all the news at first hand. Then, may I send Holly to you?'

'But of course. She'll be very useful. At her age she'd better do
supplies, I think, instead of standing about, serving. I get on

with her all right. The great thing is to have people that get on together, and don't fuss. Have you heard from Father?'

'Yes; he's coming up to you tomorrow.'

'Oh! But why?'

'He says he must be on the spot, in case of –'

'That's so silly. Never mind. It'll make two cars.'

'Holly will have hers, too. Val's going to drive a bus, he says – and – er – young – well, dear, that's all! My love to Kit. There are a tremendous lot of milk-cans in the Park already, Smither says. She went out this morning into Park Lane to have a look. It's all rather thrilling, don't you think?'

'At the House they say it'll mean another shilling on the income tax before it's over.'

'Oh dear!'

At this moment a voice said: 'Have they answered?' And, replacing the receiver, Winifred again sat, placid. Park Lane! From the old house there – house of her youth – one would have had a splendid view of everything – quite the headquarters! But how dreadfully the poor old Pater would have felt it! James! She seemed to see him again with his plaid over his shoulders, and his nose glued to a window-pane, trying to cure with the evidence of his old grey eyes the fatal habit they all had of not telling him anything. She still had some of his wine. And Warmson, their old butler, still kept 'The Pouter Pigeon', on the river at Moulsbridge. He always sent her a Stilton cheese at Christmas, with a memorandum of the exact amount of the old Park Lane port she was to pour into it. His last letter had ended thus: 'I often think of the master, and how fond he was of going down the cellar right up to the end. As regards wine, ma'am, I'm afraid the days are not what they were. My duty to Mr Soames and all. Dear me, it seems a long time since I first came to Park Lane.

'Your obedient servant,
'GEORGE WARMSON

'P.S. – I had a pound or two on that colt Mr Val bred, please to tell him – and came in useful.'

The old sort of servant! And now she had Smither, from Timothy's, Cook having died – so mysteriously, or, as Smither

put it: 'Of hornwee, ma'am, I verily believe, missing Mr
Timothy as we did' — Smither as a sort of supercargo — didn't
they call it, on ships? and really very capable, considering she
was sixty, if a day, and the way her corsets creaked. After all, to
be with the family again was a great comfort to the poor old
soul – eight years younger than Winifred, who, like a true Forsyte, looked down on the age of others from the platform of
perennial youth. And a comfort, too, to have about the house
one who remembered Monty in his prime – Montague Dartie,
so long dead now, that he had a halo as yellow as his gills had
so often been. Poor, dear Monty! Was it really forty-seven years
since she married him, and came to live in Green Street? How
well those satinwood chairs with the floral green design on their
top rails, had worn – furniture of times before this seven-hour
day and all the rest of it! People thought about their work then,
and not about the cinema! And Winifred, who had never had
any work to think about, sighed. It had all been great fun –
and, if they could only get this little fuss over, the coming season
would be most enjoyable. She had seats already for almost everything. Her hand slipped down to what she was sitting on. Yes,
she had only had those chairs re-covered twice in all her forty-
seven years in Green Street, and, really, they were quite respectable still. True! no one ever sat on them now, because they
were straight up without arms; and in these days, of course,
everybody sprawled, so restless, too, that no chair could stand it.
She rose to judge the degree of respectability beneath her, tilting
the satinwood chair forward. The year Monty died they had
been re-covered last – 1913, just before the war. Really that had
been a marvellous piece of grey-green silk!

Chapter Three

HOME-COMING

◄─┼─►

JON FORSYTE'S sensations on landing at Newhaven, by the
last possible boat, after five and a half years' absence, had been
most peculiar. All the way by car to Wansdon under the Sussex
Downs he was in a sort of excited dream. England! What wonderful chalk, what wonderful green! What an air of having
been there for ever! The sudden dips into villages, the old
bridges, the sheep, the beech clumps! And the cuckoo – not
heard for six years! A poet, somewhat dormant of late, stirred
within this young man. Delicious old country! Anne would be
crazy about this countryside – it was so beautifully finished.
When the general strike was over she could come along, and he
would show her everything. In the meantime she would be all
right with his mother in Paris, and he would be free for any
job he could get. He remembered this bit, and Chanctonbury
Ring up there, and his walk over from Worthing. He remembered very well. Fleur! His brother-in-law, Francis Wilmot,
had come back from England with much to say about Fleur; she
was very modern now, and attractive, and had a boy. How
deeply one could be in love; and how completely get over it!
Considering what his old feelings down here had been, it was
strange but pleasant to be just simply eager to see Holly and
'old Val'.

Beyond a telegram from Dieppe, he had made no announcement of his coming; but they would surely be here because of the
horses. He would like to have a look at Val's racing stable, and
get a ride, perhaps, on the Downs before taking on a strike job.
If only Anne were with him, and they could have that ride together! And Jon thought of his first ride with Anne in the
South Carolinian woods – that ride from which they had neither
of them recovered. There it was! The jolly old house! And here

573

at the door — Holly herself! And at sight of his half-sister, slim and dark-haired in a lilac dress, Jon was visited by a stabbing memory of their father as he had looked that dreadful afternoon, lying dead in the old arm-chair at Robin Hill. Dad — always lovable — and so good to him!

'Jon! How wonderful to see you!'

Her kiss, he remembered, had always lighted on his eyebrow — she hadn't changed a bit. A half-sister was nicer than a full-sister, after all. With full sisters you were almost bound to fight a little.

'What a pity you couldn't bring Anne and your mother! But perhaps it's just as well, till this is over. You look quite English still, Jon; and your mouth's as nice and wide as ever. Why do Americans and naval men have such small mouths?'

'Sense of duty, I think. How's Val?'

'Oh, Val's all right. You haven't lost your smile. D'you remember your old room?'

'Rather. And how are *you*, Holly?'

'So-so. I've become a writer, Jon.'

'Splendid!'

'Not at all. Hard labour and no reward.'

'Oh!'

'The first book was born too still for anything. A sort of "African Farm", without the spiritual frills — if you remember it.'

'Rather! But I always left the frills out.'

'Yes, we get our objection to frills from Dad, Jon. He said to me once: "It'll end in calling all matter spirit or all spirit matter — I don't know which."'

'It won't,' said Jon; 'people love to divide things up. I say, I remember every stick in this room. How are the horses? Can I have a look at them and a ride tomorrow?'

'We'll go forth early and see them at exercise. We've only got three two-year-olds, but one of them's most promising.'

'Fine! After that I must go up and get a good, dirty job. I should like to stoke an engine. I've always wanted to know how stokers feel.'

'We'll all go. We can stay with Val's mother. It *is* so lovely to see you, Jon. Dinner's in half an hour.'

Jon lingered five minutes at his window. That orchard in full bloom – not mathematically planted, like his just-sold North Carolinian peach trees – was as lovely as on that long-ago night when he chased Fleur therein. That was the beauty of England – nothing was planned! How home-sick he had been over there; yes, and his mother, too! He would never go back! How wonderful that sea of apple blossom! Cuckoo again! That alone was worth coming home for. He would find a place and grow fruit, down in the West, Worcestershire or Somerset, or near here – they grew a lot of figs and things at Worthing, he remembered. Turning out his suit-case, he began to dress. Just where he was sitting now, pulling on his American socks, had he sat when Fleur was showing him her Goya dress. Who would have believed then that, six years later, he would want Anne, not Fleur, beside him on this bed! The gong! Dabbing at his hair, bright and stivery, he straightened his tie and ran down.

Val's views on the strike, Val's views on everything, shrewd and narrow as his horseman's face! Those Labour johnnies were up against it this time with a vengeance; they'd have to heel up before it was over. How had Jon liked the Yanks? Had he seen 'Man of War'? No? Good Lord! The thing best worth seeing in America! Was the grass in Kentucky really blue? Only from the distance? Oh! What were they going to abolish over there next? Wasn't there a place down South where you were only allowed to cohabit under the eyes of the town watch? Parliament here were going to put a tax on betting; why not introduce the 'Tote' and have done with it? Personally he didn't care, he'd given up betting! And he glanced at Holly. Jon, too, glanced at her lifted brows and slightly parted lips – a charming face – ironical and tolerant! She drove Val with silken reins!

Val went on: Good job Jon had given up America; if he must farm out of England, why not South Africa, under the poor old British flag; though the Dutch weren't done with yet! A tough lot! They had gone out there, of course, so bright and early that they were real settlers – none of your adventurers, failures-at-home, remittance-men. He didn't like the beggars, but they were stout fellows, all the same. Going to stay in England? Good! What about coming in with them and breeding racing stock?

After an awkward little silence, Holly said slyly:

'Jon doesn't think that's quite a man's job, Val.'

'Why not?'

'Luxury trade.'

'Blood stock – where would horses be without it?'

'Very tempting,' said Jon. 'I'd like an interest in it. But I'd want to grow fruit and things for a main line.'

'All right, my son; you can grow apples they eat on Sundays.'

'You see, Jon,' said Holly, 'nobody believes in growing anything in England. We talk about it more and more, and do it less and less. Do you see any change in Jon, Val?'

The cousins exchanged a stare.

'A bit more solid; nothing American, anyway.'

Holly murmured thoughtfully: 'Why can one always tell an American?'

'Why can one always tell an Englishman?' said Jon.

'Something guarded, my dear. But a national looks the most difficult thing in the world to define. Still, you can't mistake the American expression.'

'I don't believe you'll take Anne for one.'

'Describe her, Jon.'

'No. Wait till you see her.'

When, after dinner, Val was going his last round of the stables, Jon said:

'Do you ever see Fleur, Holly?'

'I haven't for eighteen months, I should think. I like her husband; he's an awfully good sort. You were well out of that, Jon. She isn't your kind – not that she isn't charming; but she has to be plump centre of the stage. I suppose you knew that, really.'

Jon looked at her and did not answer.

'Of course,' murmured Holly, 'when one's in love, one doesn't know much.'

Up in his room again, the house began to be haunted. Into it seemed to troop all his memories, of Fleur, of Robin Hill – old trees of his boyhood, his father's cigars, his mother's flowers and music; the nursery of his games, Holly's nursery before his, with its window looking out over the clock tower above the stables, the room where latterly he had struggled with rhyme. In through his open bedroom window came the sweet-scented air – England's self – from the loom of the Downs in the moon-scattered dusk, this first night of home for more than two thousand nights. With Robin Hill sold, this was the nearest he had to home in England now. But they must make one of their own – he and Anne. Home! On the English liner he had wanted to embrace the stewards and stewardesses just because they spoke with an English accent. It was, still, as music to his ears. Anne would pick it up faster now – she was very receptive! He had liked the Americans, but he was glad Val had said there was nothing American about him. An owl hooted. What a shadow that barn cast – how soft and old its angle! He got into bed. Sleep – if he wanted to be up to see the horses exercised! Once before, here, he had got up early – for another purpose! And soon he slept; and a form – was it Anne's, was it Fleur's – wandered in the corridors of his dreams.

Chapter Four

SOAMES GOES UP TO TOWN

◄‹·›►

HAVING seen his wife off from Dover on the Wednesday, Soames Forsyte motored towards town. On the way he decided to make a considerable detour and enter London over Hammersmith, the farthest westerly bridge in reason. There was for him a fixed connexion between unpleasantness and the East End, in times of industrial disturbance. And feeling that, if he encountered a threatening proletariat, he would insist on going through with it, he acted in accordance with the other side of a Forsyte's temperament, and looked ahead. Thus it was that he found his car held up in Hammersmith Broadway by the only threatening conduct of the afternoon. A number of persons had collected to interfere with a traffic of which they did not seem to approve. After sitting forward, to say to his chauffeur, 'You'd better go round, Riggs,' Soames did nothing but sit back. The afternoon was fine, and the car – a landaulette – open, so that he had a good view of the total impossibility of 'going round'. Just like that fellow Riggs to have run bang into this! A terrific pack of cars crammed with people trying to run out of town; a few cars like his own, half empty, trying to creep past them into town; a motor-omnibus, not overturned precisely, but with every window broken, standing half across the road; and a number of blank-looking people eddying and shifting before a handful of constables! Such were the phenomena which Soames felt the authorities ought to be handling better.

The words, 'Look at that blighted plutocrat!' assailed his ears; and in attempting to see the plutocrat in question, he became aware that it was himself. The epithets were unjust! He was modestly attired in a brown overcoat and soft felt hat; that fellow Riggs was plain enough in all conscience, and the car was an ordinary blue. True, he was alone in it, and all the other cars seemed full of people; but he did not see how he was to get over that, short of carrying into London persons desirous of going in the opposite direction. To shut the car, at all events, would look too pointed – so there was nothing for it but to sit still and take no notice! For this occupation no one could have been better framed by Nature than Soames, with his air of slightly despising creation. He sat, taking in little but his own nose, with the sun shining on his neck behind, and the crowd eddying round the police. Such violence as had been necessary to break the windows of the bus had ceased, and the block was rather what might have been caused by the Prince of Wales. With every appearance of not encouraging it by seeming to take notice, Soames was observing the crowd. And a vacant-looking lot they were, in his opinion; neither their eyes nor their hands had any

of that close attention to business which alone made revolutionary conduct formidable. Youths, for the most part, with
cigarettes drooping from their lips – they might have been
looking at a fallen horse.

People were born gaping nowadays. And a good thing, too!
Cinemas, fags, and football matches – there would be no real
revolution while they were on hand; and as there seemed to be
more and more on hand every year, he was just feeling that the
prospect was not too bleak, when a young woman put her head
over the window of his car.

'Could you take me into town?'

Soames automatically consulted his watch. The hands pointing to seven o'clock gave him extraordinarily little help. Rather
a smartly-dressed young woman, with a slight cockney accent
and powder on her nose! That fellow Riggs would never have
done grinning. And yet he had read in the *British Gazette* that
everybody was doing it. Rather gruffly he said:

'I suppose so. Where do you want to go?'

'Oh, Leicester Square would do me all right.'

Great Scott!

The young woman seemed to sense his emotion. 'You see,'
she said, 'I got to get something to eat before my show.'

Moreover, she was getting in! Soames nearly got out. Re-
straining himself, he gave her a sidelong look; actress or something – young – round face, made up, naturally – nose a little
snub – eyes grey, rather goggly – mouth – h'm, pretty mouth,
slightly common! Shingled – of course.

'It's awf'ly kind of you!'

'Not at all!' said Soames; and the car moved.

'Think it's going to last, the strike?'

Soames leaned forward.

'Go on, Riggs,' he said; 'and put this young lady down in –
er – Coventry Street.'

'It's frightf'ly awk for us, all this,' said the young lady. 'I
should never've got there in time. You seen our show, *Dat
Lubly Lady*?'

'No.'

'It's rather good.'

'Oh!'

'We shall have to close, though, if this lasts.'

'Ah!'

The young lady was silent, seeming to recognize that she was not in the presence of a conversationalist.

Soames re-crossed his legs. It was so long since he had spoken to a strange young woman, that he had almost forgotten how it was done. He did not want to encourage her, and yet was conscious that it was his car.

'Comfortable?' he said suddenly.

The young lady smiled.

'What d'you think?' she said. 'It's a lovely car.'

'I don't like it,' said Soames.

The young lady's mouth opened.

'Why?'

Soames shrugged his shoulders; he had only been keeping the conversation alive.

'I think it's rather fun, don't you?' said the young lady. 'Carrying on – you know, like we're all doing.'

The car was now going at speed, and Soames began to calculate the minutes necessary to put an end to this juxtaposition.

The Albert Memorial, already; he felt almost an affection for it – so guiltless of the times!

'You *must* come and see our show,' said the young lady.

Soames made an effort and looked into her face.

'What do you do in it?' he asked.

'Sing and dance.'

'I see.'

'I've rather a good bit in the third act, where we're all in our nighties.'

Soames smiled faintly.

'You've got no one like Kate Vaughan now,' he said.

'Kate Vaughan? Who was she?'

'Who was Kate Vaughan?' repeated Soames; 'greatest dancer that was ever in burlesque. Dancing was graceful in those days; now it's all throwing your legs about. The faster you can move your legs, the more you think you're dancing.' And, disconcerted by an outburst that was bound to lead to something, he averted his eyes.

'You don't like jazz?' queried the young lady.

'I do not,' said Soames.

'Well, I don't either — not reelly; it's getting old-fashioned, too.'

Hyde Park Corner already! And the car going a good twenty!

'My word! Look at the lorries; it's marvellous, isn't it?'

Soames emitted a confirmatory grunt. The young lady was powdering her nose now, and touching up her lips, with an almost staggering frankness. 'Suppose anyone sees me?' thought Soames. And he would never know whether anyone had or not. Turning up the high collar of his overcoat, he said:

'Draughty things, these cars! Shall I put you down at Scott's?'

'Oh no. Lyons, please; I've only time f'r a snack; got to be on the stage at eight. It's been awf'ly kind of you. I only hope somebody'll take me home!' Her eyes rolled suddenly, and she added: 'If you know what I mean.'

'Quite!' said Soames, with a certain delicacy of perception. 'Here you are. Stop — Riggs!'

The car stopped, and the young lady extended her hand to Soames.

'Good-bye, and thank you!'

'Good-bye!' said Soames. Nodding and smiling, she got out.

'Go on, Riggs, sharp! South Square.'

The car moved on. Soames did not look back; in his mind the thought formed like a bubble on the surface of water: 'In the old days anyone who looked and talked like that would have left me her address.' And she hadn't! He could not decide whether or no this marked an advance.

At South Square, on discovering that Michael and Fleur were out, he did not dress for dinner, but went to the nursery. His grandson, now nearly three years old, was still awake, and said: 'Hallo!'

'Hallo!' Soames produced a toy watchman's rattle. There followed five minutes of silent and complete absorption, broken fitfully by guttural sounds from the rattle. Then his grandson lay back in his cot, fixed his blue eyes on Soames and said: 'Hallo!'

'Hallo!' replied Soames.

'Ta, ta!' said his grandson.

'Ta, ta!' said Soames, backing to the door and nearly falling over the silver dog. The interview then terminated, and Soames went downstairs. Fleur had telephoned to say he was not to wait dinner.

Opposite the Goya he sat down. No good saying he remembered the Chartist riots of '48, because he had been born in '55; but he knew his Uncle Swithin had been a 'special' at the time. This general strike was probably the most serious internal disturbance that had happened since; and, sitting over his soup, he bored further and further into its possibilities. Bolshevism round the corner – that was the trouble! That and the fixed nature of ideas in England. Because a thing like coal had once been profitable, they thought it must always be profitable. Political leaders, Trades Unionists, newspaper chaps – they never looked an inch before their noses! They'd had since last August to do something about it, and what had they done? Drawn up a report that nobody would look at!

'White wine, sir, or claret?'

'Anything that's open.' To have said that in the 'eighties, or even the 'nineties, would have given his father a fit! The idea of drinking claret already opened was then almost equivalent to atheism. Another sign of the slump in ideals.

'What do *you* think about this strike, Coaker?'

The almost hairless man lowered the Sauterne.

'Got no body in it, sir, if you ask me.'

'What makes you say that?'

'If it had any body in it, sir, they'd have had the railings of Hyde Park up by now.'

Soames poised a bit of his sole. 'Shouldn't be surprised if you were right,' he said, with a certain approval.

'They make a lot of fuss, but no – there's nothing to it. The dole – that was a clever dodge, sir. *Pannus et circesses,* as Mr Mont says, sir.'

'Ha! Have you seen this canteen they're running?'

'No, sir; I believe they've got the beetle man in this evening. I'm told there's a proper lot of beetles.'

'Ugh!'

'Yes, sir; it's a nahsty insect.'

Having finished dinner, Soames lighted the second of his two daily cigars and took up the ear-pieces of the wireless. He had resisted this invention as long as he could – but in times like these! 'London calling!' Yes, and the British Isles listening! Trouble in Glasgow? There would be – lot of Irish there. More 'specials' wanted? There'd soon be plenty of those. He must tell that fellow Riggs to enlist. This butler chap, too, could well be spared. Trains! They seemed to be running a lot of trains already. After listening with some attention to the Home Secretary, Soames put the ear-pieces down and took up the *British Gazette.* It was his first sustained look at this tenuous production, and he hoped it would be his last. The paper and printing were deplorable. Still, he supposed it was something to have got it out at all. Tampering with the freedom of the Press! Those fellows were not finding it so easy as they thought. They had tampered, and the result was a Press much more definitely against them than the Press they had suppressed. Burned their fingers there! And quite unnecessary – old-fashioned notion now – influence of the Press. The war had killed it. Without confidence in truth there was no influence. Politicians or the Press – if you couldn't believe them, they didn't count! Perhaps they would re-discover that some day. In the meantime the papers were like cocktails – titivators mostly of the appetite and the nerves. How sleepy he was! He hoped Fleur wouldn't be very late coming in. Mad thing, this strike, making everybody do things they weren't accustomed to, just as Industry, too, was beginning – or at least pretending – to recover. But that was it! With every year, in these times, it was more difficult to do what you said you would. Always something or other turning up!

The world seemed to live from hand to mouth, and at such a pace, too! Sitting back in the Spanish chair, Soames covered his eyes from the light, and the surge of sleep mounted to his brain; strike or no strike, the soft, inexorable tide washed over him.

A tickling, and over his hand, thin and rather brown, the fringe of a shawl came dangling. Why! With an effort he climbed out of an abyss of dreams. Fleur was standing beside him. Pretty, bright, her eyes shining, speaking quickly, excitedly, it seemed to him.

'Here you are, then, Dad!' Her lips felt hot and soft on his forehead, and her eyes – What was the matter with her? She looked so young – she looked so – how express it?

'So you're in!' he said. 'Kit's getting talkative. Had anything to eat?'

'Heaps!'

'This canteen –'

She flung off her shawl.

'I'm enjoying it frightfully.'

Soames noted with surprise the rise and fall of her breast, as if she had been running. Her cheeks, too, were very pink.

'You haven't caught anything, have you – in that place?'

Fleur laughed. A sound – delicious and unwarranted.

'How funny you are, Dad! I hope the strike lasts!'

'Don't be foolish!' said Soames. 'Where's Michael?'

'Gone up. He called for me, after the House. Nothing doing there, he says.'

'What's the time?'

'Past twelve, dear. You must have had a real good sleep.'

'Just nodding.'

'We saw a tank pass, on the Embankment – going east. It looked awfully queer. Didn't you hear it?'

'No,' said Soames.

'Well, don't be alarmed if you hear another. They're on their way to the docks, Michael says.'

'Glad to hear it – shows the Government means business. But you must go up. You're overtired.'

She gazed at him over the Spanish shawl on her arm – whistling some tune.

'Good night!' he said. 'I shall be coming up in a minute.'

She blew him a kiss, twirled round, and went.

'I don't like it,' murmured Soames to himself; 'I don't know why, but I don't like it.'

She had looked too young. Had the strike gone to her head? He rose to squirt some soda-water into a glass – that nap had left a taste in his mouth.

Um – dum – bom – um – dum – bom – um – dum – bom! A grunching noise! Another of those tanks? He would like to see one of those great things! For the idea that they were going down to the docks gave him a feeling almost of exhilaration. With them on the spot the country was safe enough. Putting on his motoring coat and hat, he went out, crossed the empty Square, and stood in the street, whence he could see the Embankment. There it came! Like a great primeval monster in the lamplit darkness, growling and gruntling along, a huge, fantastic tortoise – like an embodiment of inexorable power. 'That'll astonish their weak nerves!' thought Soames, as the tank crawled, grunching, out of sight. He could hear another coming; but with a sudden feeling that it would be too much of a good thing, he turned on his heel. A sort of extravagance about them, when he remembered the blank-looking crowd around his car that afternoon, not a weapon among the lot, nor even a revolutionary look in their eyes!

'No *body* in the strike!' These great crawling monsters! Were the Government trying to pretend that there was? Playing the strong man! Something in Soames revolted slightly. Hang it! This was England, not Russia, or Italy! They might be right, but he didn't like it! Too – too military! He put his latchkey into the keyhole. Um – dum – bom – um – dum – bom! Well, not many people would see or hear them – this time of night! He supposed they had got here from the country somewhere – he wouldn't care to meet them wandering about in the old lanes and places. Father and mother and baby tanks – like – like a family of mastodons, m – m? No sense of proportion in things like that! And no sense of humour! He stood on the stairs listening. It was to be hoped they wouldn't wake the baby!

Chapter Five

JEOPARDY

◄—►

When, looking down the row of faces at her canteen table, Fleur saw Jon Forsyte's, it was within her heart as if, in winter, she had met with honeysuckle. Recovering from that faint intoxication, she noted his appearance from farther off. He was sitting seemingly indifferent to food; and on his face, which was smudged with coal-dust and sweat, was such a smile as men wear after going up a mountain or at the end of a long run – tired, charming, and as if they had been through something worth while. His lashes – long and dark as in her memory – concealed his eyes, and quarrelled with his brighter hair, tousled to the limit of its shortness.

Continuing to issue instructions to Ruth La Fontaine, Fleur thought rapidly. Jon! Dropped from the skies into her canteen, stronger-looking, better knit, with more jaw, and deeper eyes, but frightfully like Jon! What was to be done about it? If only she could turn out the lights, steal up behind, lean over and kiss him on that smudge above his left eye! Yes! And then – what? Silly! And now, suppose he came out of his faraway smile and saw her! As likely as not he would never come into her canteen again. She remembered his conscience! And she took a swift decision. Not tonight! Holly would know where he was staying. At her chosen time, on her chosen ground, if – on second thoughts, she wanted to play with fire. And, giving a mandate to Ruth La Fontaine concerning buns, she looked back over her shoulder at Jon's absorbed and smiling face, and passed out into her little office.

And second thoughts began. Michael, Kit, her father; the solid security of virtue and possessions; the peace of mind into which she had passed of late! All jeopardized for the sake of a smile, and a scent of honeysuckle! No! The account was closed. To reopen it was to tempt Providence. And if to tempt Providence was the practice of Modernity, she wasn't sure whether she was modern. Besides, who knew whether she *could* reopen that account? And she was seized by a gust of curiosity to see that wife of his — that substitute for herself. Was she in England? Was she dark, like her brother Francis? Fleur took up her list of purchases for the morrow. With so much to do, it was idiotic even to think about such things! The telephone! All day its bell had been ringing; since nine o'clock that morning she had been dancing to its pipe.

'Yes...? Mrs Mont speaking. What? But I've ordered them. ... Oh! But really I *must* give them bacon and eggs in the morning. They can't start on cocoa only.... How? The Company can't afford? ... Well! Do you want an effective service or not? ... Come round to see you about it? I really haven't time.... Yes, yes ... now please do be nice to me and tell the manager that they simply must be properly fed. They look so tired. He'll understand ... Yes.... Thank you ever so!' She hung up the receiver. 'Damn!'

Someone laughed. 'Oh! it's you, Holly! Cheeseparing and red tape as usual! This is the fourth time today. Well, I don't care — I'm going ahead. Look! Here's Harridge's list for tomorrow. It's terrific, but it's got to be. Buy it all; I'll take the risk, if I have to go round and slobber on him.' And beyond the ironic sympathy on Holly's face she seemed to see Jon's smile. He should be properly fed — all of them should! And, without looking at her cousin, she said:

'I saw Jon in there. Where has he dropped from?'

'Paris. He's putting up with us in Green Street.'

Fleur stuck her chin forward, and gave a little laugh.

'Quaint to see him again, all smudgy like that! His wife with him?'

'Not yet,' said Holly; 'she's in Paris still, with his mother.'

'Oh! It'd be fun to see him some time!'

'He's stoking an engine on the local service – goes out at six, and doesn't get in till about midnight.'

'Of course; I meant after, if the strike ever ends.'

Holly nodded. 'His wife wants to come over and help; would you like her in the canteen?'

'If she's the right sort.'

'Jon says : Very much so.'

'I don't see why an American should worry herself. Are they going to live in England?'

'Yes.'

'Oh! Well, we're both over the measles.'

'If you get them again grown-up, Fleur, they're pretty bad.'

Fleur laughed. 'No fear!' And her eyes, hazel, clear, glancing, met her cousin's eyes, deep, steady, grey.

'Michael's waiting for you with the car,' said Holly.

'All right! Can you carry on till they've finished? Norah Curfew's on duty at five tomorrow morning. I shall be round at nine, before you start for Harridge's. If you think of anything else, stick it on the list – I'll make them stump up somehow. Good night, Holly.'

'Good night, my dear.'

Was there a gleam of pity in those grey eyes? Pity, indeed!

'Give Jon my love. I do wonder how he likes stoking! We must get some more wash-basins in.'

Sitting beside Michael, who was driving their car, she saw again, as it were, Jon's smile in the glass of the windscreen, and in the dark her lips pouted as if reaching for it. Measles – they spotted you, and raised your temperature! How empty the streets were, now that the taxis were on strike! Michael looked round at her.

'Well, how's it going?'

'The beetle-man was a caution, Michael. He had a face like a ravaged wedge, a wave of black hair, and the eyes of a lost soul; but he was frightfully efficient.'

'Look! There's a tank; I was told of them. They're going

down to the docks. Rather provocative! Just as well there are no papers for them to get into.'

Fleur laughed.

'Father'll be at home. He's come up to protect me. If there really was shooting, I wonder what he'd do – take his umbrella?'

'Instinct. How about you and Kit? It's the same thing.'

Fleur did not answer. And when, after seeing her father, she went upstairs, she stood at the nursery door. The tune that had excited Soames's surprise made a whiffling sound in the empty passage. *'L'amour est enfant de Bohême; il n'a jamais jamais connu de loi; si tu ne m'aimes pas, je t'aime, et si je t'aime, prends garde à toi!'* Spain, and the heartache of her honeymoon! 'Voice in the night crying!' Close the shutters, muffle the ears – keep it out! She entered her bedroom and turned up the light. It had never seemed to her so pretty, with its many mirrors, its lilac and green, its shining silver. She stood looking at her face, into which had come two patches of red, one in each cheek. Why wasn't she Norah Curfew – dutiful, uncomplicated, selfless, who would give Jon eggs and bacon at half-past five to-morrow morning – Jon with a clean face! Quickly she undressed. Was that wife of his her equal undressed? To which would he award the golden apple if she stood side by side with Anne? And the red spots deepened in her cheeks. Overtired – she knew that feeling! She would not sleep! But the sheets were cool. Yes, she preferred the old smooth Irish linen to that new rough French grass-bleached stuff. Ah! Here was Michael coming in, coming up to her! Well! No use to be unkind to him – poor old Michael! And in his arms, she saw – Jon's smile.

The first day spent stoking an engine had been enough to make anyone smile. An engine-driver almost as youthful, but in private life partner in his own engineering works, had put Jon 'wise' to the mystery of getting level combustion. 'A tricky job, and very tiring!' Their passengers had behaved well. One had even come up and thanked them. The engine-driver had winked at Jon. There had been some hectic moments. Supping pea soup, Jon thought of them with pleasure. It had been great sport, but his hands and arms felt wrenched. 'Oil them tonight,' the engine-driver had said.

A young woman was handing him 'jacket' potatoes. She had marvellously clear, brown eyes, something like Anne's — only Anne's were like a water nymph's. He took a potato, thanked her, and returned to a stoker's dreams. Extraordinary pleasure in being up against it — being in England again, doing something for England! One had to leave one's country to become conscious of it. Anne had telegraphed that she wanted to come over and join him. If he wired back 'no', she would come all the same. He knew that much after nearly two years of marriage. Well, she would see England at its best. Americans didn't really know what England was. Her brother had seen nothing but London; he had spoken bitterly — a girl, Jon supposed, though nothing had been said of her. In Francis Wilmot's history of England the gap accounted for the rest. But everybody ran down England, because she didn't slop over, or blow her own trumpet.

'Butter?'

'Thanks, awfully. These potatoes are frightfully good.'

'So glad.'

'Who runs this canteen?'

'Mr and Mrs Michael Mont mostly; he's a Member of Parliament.'

Jon dropped his potato.

'Mrs Mont? Gracious! She's a cousin of mine. Is she here?'

'Was. Just gone, I think.'

Jon's far-sighted eyes travelled round the large and dingy room. Fleur! How amazing!

'Treacle pudding?'

'No, thanks. Nothing more.'

'There'll be coffee, tea, or cocoa, and eggs and bacon, tomorrow at 5.45.'

'Splendid! I think it's wonderful.'

'It is, rather, in the time.'

'Thank you awfully. Good Night!'

Jon sought his coat. Outside were Val and Holly in their car.

'Hallo, young Jon ! You're a nice object.'

'What job have *you* caught, Val?'

'Motor-lorry – begin tomorrow.'

'Fine !'

'This'll knock out racing for a bit.'

'But not England.'

'England? Lord – no ! What did you think?'

'Abroad they were saying so.'

'Abroad !' growled Val. 'They would !'

And there was silence at thirty miles an hour.

From his bedroom door Jon said to his sister :

'They say Fleur runs that canteen. Is she really so old now?'

'Fleur has a very clear head, my dear. She saw you there. No second go of measles, Jon.'

Jon laughed.

'Aunt Winifred,' said Holly, 'will be delighted to have Anne here on Friday, she told me to tell you.'

'Splendid ! That's awfully good of her.'

'Well, good night; bless you. There's still hot water in the bathroom.'

In his bath Jon lay luxuriously still. Sixty hours away from his young wife, he was already looking forward with impatience to her appearance on Friday. And so Fleur ran that canteen ! A fashionable young woman with a clear and, no doubt, shingled head – he felt a great curiosity to see her again, but nothing more. Second go of measles ! Not much ! He had suffered too severely from the first. Besides, he was too glad to be back – result, half-acknowledged home-sickness. His mother had been homesick for Europe; but *he* had felt no assuagement in Italy and France. It was England he had wanted. Something in the way people walked and talked; in the smell and the look of everything; some good-humoured, slow, ironic essence in the air, after the tension of America, the shrillness of Italy, the clarity of Paris. For the first time in five years his nerves felt coated. Even those features of his native land which offended the æsthetic soul were comforting. The approaches to London, the countless awful little houses, of brick and slate which his own great-grandfather 'Superior Dosset' Forsyte, had helped, so his father had once told him, to build; the many little new houses, rather better but still bent on compromise; the total absence of symmetry or plan; the ugly railway stations; the cockney voices, the lack of colour, taste, or pride in people's dress – all seemed comfortable, a guarantee that England would always be England.

And so Fleur was running that canteen! He would be seeing her! He would like to see her! Oh, yes!

Chapter Six

SNUFF-BOX

-<->-

I N the next room Val was saying to Holly:

'Had a chap I knew at college to see me today. Wanted me to lend him money. I once did, when I was jolly hard up myself, and never got it back. He used to impress me frightfully – such an awfully good-looking, languid beggar. I thought him top notch as a "blood". You should see him now!'

'I did. I was coming in as he was going out; I wondered who he was. I never saw a more bitterly contemptuous expression on a face. Did you lend him money?'

'Only a fiver.'

'Well, don't lend him any more.'

'Hardly. D'you know what he's done? Gone off with that Louis Quinze snuff-box of mother's that's worth about two hundred. There's been nobody else in that room.'

'Good heavens!'

'Yes, it's pretty thick. He had the reputation of being the fastest man up at the 'Varsity in my time – in with the gambling set. Since I went out to the Boer war I've never heard of him.'

'Isn't your mother very annoyed, Val?'

'She wants to prosecute – it belonged to my granddad. But how can we – a college pal! Besides, we shouldn't get the box back.'

Holly ceased to brush her hair.

'It's rather a comfort to me – this,' she said.

'What is?'

'Why, everybody says the standard of honesty's gone down. It's nice to find someone belonging to our generation that had it even less.'

'Rum comfort!'

'Human nature doesn't alter, Val. I believe in the younger generation. We don't understand them – brought up in too settled times.'

'That may be. My own dad wasn't too particular. But what am I to do about this?'

'Do you know his address?'

'He said the Brummell Club would find him – pretty queer haunt, if I remember. To come to sneaking things like that! It's upset me frightfully.'

Holly looked at him lying on his back in bed. Catching her eyes on him, he said:

'But for you, old girl, I might have gone a holy mucker myself.'

'Oh, no, Val! You're too open-air. It's the indoor people who go really wrong.'

Val grinned.

'Something in that – the only exercise I ever saw that fellow take was in a punt. He used to bet like anything, but he didn't know a horse from a hedgehog. Well, Mother must put up with it, I can't do anything.'

Holly came up to his bed.

'Turn over, and I'll tuck you up.'

Getting into bed herself, she lay awake, thinking of the man who had gone a holy mucker, and the contempt on his face – lined, dark, well-featured, with prematurely greying hair, and prematurely faded rings round the irises of the eyes; of his clothes, too, so preternaturally preserved, and the worn, careful school tie. She felt she knew him. No moral sense, and ingrained contempt for those who had. Poor Val ! He hadn't so much moral sense that he need be despised for it ! And yet –! With a good many risky male instincts, Val had been a loyal comrade all these years. If in philosophic reach or æsthetic taste he was not advanced, if he knew more of the horses than of poetry, was he any the worse? She sometimes thought he was the better. The horse didn't change shape or colour every five years and start reviling its predecessor. The horse was a constant, kept you from going too fast, and had a nose to stroke – more than you could say of a poet. They had, indeed, only one thing in common – a liking for sugar. Since the publication of her novel Holly had become member of the 1930 Club. Fleur had put her up, and whenever she came to town, she studied modernity there. Modernity was nothing but speed ! People who blamed it might as well blame telephone, wireless, flying machine, and quick lunch counter. Beneath that top-dressing of speed, modernity was old. Women had worn fewer clothes when Jane Austen began to write. Drawers – the historians said – were only nineteenth-century productions. And take modern talk ! After South Africa the speed of it certainly took one's wind away; but the thoughts expressed were much her own thoughts as a girl, cut into breathless lengths, by car and telephone bell. The modern courtships ! They resulted in the same thing as under George the Second, but took longer to reach it, owing to the motor-cycle and the standing lunch. Take modern philosophy ! People had no less real philosophy than Martin Tupper or Izaak Walton; only, unlike those celebrated ancients, they had no time to formulate it. As to a future life – modernity lived in hope, and not too much of that, as everyone had done, from immemorial time. In fact, as a novelist naturally would, Holly jumped to conclusions. Scratch – she thought – the best of modern youth, and you would find Charles James Fox and Perdita in golf sweaters ! A steady sound retrieved her thoughts. Val was asleep. How long and dark his eyelashes still were, but his mouth was open !

'Val,' she said, very softly; 'Val ! Don't snore, dear !' ...

A snuff-box may be precious, not so much for its enamel, its period, and its little brilliants, as because it has belonged to one's father. Winifred, though her sense of property had been well proved by her retention of Montague Dartie 'for poorer', throughout so many years, did not possess her brother Soames's collecting instinct, nor, indeed, his taste in objects which George Forsyte had been the first to call of 'bigotry and virtue'. But the further Time removed her father James – a quarter of a century by now – the more she revered his memory. As some ancient general or philosopher, secured by age from competition, is acclaimed year by year a greater genius, so with James! His objection to change, his perfect domesticity, his power of saving money for his children, and his dread of not being told anything, were haloed for her more and more with every year that he spent underground. Her fashionable aspirations waning with the increase of adipose, the past waxed and became a very constellation of shining memories. The removal of this snuff-box – so tangible a reminder of James and Emily – tried her considerable equanimity more than anything that had happened to her for years. The thought that she had succumbed to the distinction of a voice on the telephone, caused her positive discomfort. With all her experience of distinction, she ought to have known better! She was, however, one of those women who, when a thing is done, admit the fact with a view to having it undone as soon as possible; and, having failed with Val, who merely said: 'Awfully sorry, Mother, but there it is – jolly bad luck!' she summoned her brother.

Soames was little less than appalled. He remembered seeing James buy the box at Jobson's for hardly more than one-tenth of what it would fetch now. Everything seemed futile if, in such a way, one could lose what had been nursed for forty years into so really magnificent a state of unearned increment. And the fellow who had taken it was of quite good family, or so his nephew said! Whether the honesty of the old Forsytes, in the atmosphere of which he had been brought up and turned out into the world, had been inherited or acquired – derived from their blood or their banks – he had never considered. It had been in their systems just as the proverb 'Honesty is the best policy' was in that of the private banking which then obtained. A slight reverie on banking was no uncommon affection of the mind in one who could recall the repercussion of 'Understart and Darnett's' failure, and the disappearance one by one of all the little, old banks with legendary names. These great modern affairs were good for credit and bad for novelists – run on a bank – there had been no better reading! Such monster concerns couldn't 'go broke', no matter what their clients did; but whether they made for honesty in the individual, Soames couldn't tell. The snuffbox was gone, however; and if Winifred didn't take care, she wouldn't get it back. How, precisely, she was to take care he could not at present see; but he should advise her to put it into the hands of somebody at once.

'But whose, Soames?'

'There's Scotland Yard,' answered Soames, gloomily. 'I believe they're very little good, except to make a fuss. There's that fellow I employed in the Ferrar case. He charges very high.'

'I shouldn't care so much,' said Winifred, 'if it hadn't belonged to the dear Dad.'

'Ruffians like that,' muttered Soames, 'oughtn't to be at large.'

'And to think,' said Winifred, 'that it was especially to see him that Val came to stay here.'

'Was it?' said Soames, gloomily. 'I suppose you're sure that fellow took it?'

'Quite. I'd had it out to polish only a quarter of an hour before. After he went, I came back into the room at once, to put it away, and it was gone. Val had been in the room the whole time.'

Soames dwelled for a moment, then rejected a doubt about his nephew, for, though connected by blood with that precious father of his, Montague Dartie, and a racing man to boot, he was half a Forsyte after all.

'Well,' he said, 'shall I send you this man – his name's Becroft – always looks as if he'd over-shaved himself, but he's got a certain amount of *nous*. I should suggest his geting in touch with that fellow's club.'

'Suppose he's already sold the box?' said Winifred.

'Yesterday afternoon? Should doubt that; but it wants immediate handling. I'll see Becroft as I go away. Fleur's overdoing it, with this canteen of hers.'

'They say she's running it very well. I do think all these young women are so smart.'

'Quick enough,' grumbled Soames, 'but steady does it in the long run.'

At that phrase – a maxim never far away from the lips of the old Forsytes in her youthful days – Winifred blinked her rather too light eyelashes.

'That was always rather a bore, you know, Soames. And in these days, if you're not quick, things move past you, so.'

Soames gathered his hat. 'That snuff-box will, if we don't look sharp.'

'Well, thank you, dear boy. I do hope we get it back. The dear Pater was so proud of it, and when he died it wasn't worth half what it is now.'

'Not a quarter,' said Soames, and the thought bored into him as he walked away. What was the use of having judgement, if anybody could come along and pocket the results! People sneered at property nowadays; but property was a proof of good judgement – it was one's *amour propre* half the time. And he thought of the *amour propre* Bosinney had stolen from him in those far-off days of trouble. Yes, even marriage – was an exercise of judgement – a pitting of yourself against other people. You 'spotted a winner', as they called it, or you didn't – Irene hadn't been 'a winner' – not exactly! Ah! And he had forgotten to ask Winifred about that young Jon Forsyte who had suddenly come back into the wind. But about this snuff-box! The Brummell Club was some sort of betting place, he had heard; full of gamblers, and people who did and sold things on commission, he shouldn't wonder. That was the vice of the day; that and the dole. Work? No! Sell things on commission – motor-cars, for choice. Brummell Club! Yes! This was the place! It had a window – he remembered. No harm, anyway, in asking if the fellow really belonged there! And entering, he enquired:

'Mr Stainford a member here?'

'Yes. Don't know if he's in. Mr Stainford been in, Bob?'

'Just come in.'

'Oh!' said Soames, rather taken aback.

'Gentleman to see him, Bob.'

A rather sinking sensation occurred within Soames.

'Come with me, sir.'

Soames took a deep breath, and his legs moved. In an alcove off the entrance – somewhat shabby and constricted – he could see a man lolling in an old armchair, smoking a cigarette through a holder. He had a little red book in one hand and a small pencil in the other, and held them as still as if he were about to jot down a conviction that he had not got. He wore a dark suit with little lines; his legs were crossed, and Soames noted that one foot in a worn brown shoe, treed and polished against age to the point of pathos, was slowly moving in a circle.

'Gemman to see you, sir.'

Soames now saw the face. Its eyebrows were lifted in a V reversed, its eyelids nearly covered its eyes. Together with the figure, it gave an impression of really remarkable languor. Thin to a degree, oval and pale, it seemed all shadow and slightly aquiline feature. The foot had become still, the whole affair still. Soames had the curious feeling of being in the presence of something arrogantly dead. Without time for thought, he began:

'Mr Stainford, I think? Don't disturb yourself. My name is Forsyte. You called at my sister's in Green Street yesterday afternoon.'

A slight contraction of the lines round that small mouth was followed by the words:

'Will you sit down?'

The eyes had opened now, and must once have been beautiful. They narrowed again, so that Soames could not help feeling that their owner had outlived everything except himself. He swallowed a qualm and resumed:

'I just wanted to ask you a question. During your call, did you by any chance happen to notice a Louis Quinze snuff-box on the table? It's – er – disappeared, and we want to fix the time of its loss.'

As a ghost might have smiled, so did the man in the chair; his eyes disappeared still further.

'Afraid not.'

With the thought: 'He's got it!' Soames went on:

'I'm sorry – the thing had virtue as an heirloom. It has obviously been stolen. I wanted to narrow down the issue. If you'd noticed it, we could have fixed the exact hour – on the little table just where you were sitting – blue enamel.'

The thin shoulders wriggled slightly, as though resenting this attempt to place responsibility on them.

'Sorry I can't help you; I noticed nothing but some rather good marqueterie.'

'Coolest card I ever saw,' thought Soames. 'Wonder if it's in his pocket.'

'The thing's unique,' he said slowly. 'The police won't have much difficulty. Well, thanks very much. I apologize for troubling you. You knew my nephew at college, I believe. Good-morning.'

'Good-morning.'

From the door Soames took a stealthy glance. The figure was perfectly motionless, the legs still crossed, and above the litle red book the pale forehead was poised under the smooth grizzling hair. Nothing to be made of that! But the fellow had it, he was sure.

He went out and down to the Green Park with a most peculiar feeling. Sneak thief! A gentleman to come to that! The Elderson affair had been bad, but somehow not pitiful like this. The whitened seams of the excellent suit, the traversing creases in the once admirable shoes, the faded tie exactly tied, were evidence of form preserved, day by day, from hand to mouth. They afflicted Soames. That languid figure! What *did* a chap do when he had no money and couldn't exert himself to save his life? Incapable of shame – that was clear! He must talk to

Winifred again. And, turning on his heel, Soames walked back towards Green Street. Debouching from the Park, he saw on the opposite side of Piccadilly the languid figure. It, too, was moving in the direction of Green Street. Phew! He crossed over and followed. The chap had an air. He was walking like someone who had come into the world from another age – an age which set all its store on 'form'. He felt that 'this chap' would sooner part with life itself than exhibit interest in anything. Form! Could you carry contempt for emotion to such a pitch that you could no longer feel emotion? Could the lifted eyebrow become more important to you than all the movements of the heart and brain? Threadbare peacock's feathers walking, with no peacock inside! To show feeling was perhaps the only thing of which that chap would be ashamed. And, a little astonished at his own powers of diagnosis, Soames followed round corner after corner, till he was actually in Green Street. By George! The chap *was* going to Winifred's 'I'll astonish his weak nerves!' thought Soames. And, suddenly hastening, he said, rather breathlessly, on his sister's very doorstep:

'Ah! Mr Stainford! Come to return the snuff-box?'

With a sigh, and a slight stiffening of his cane on the pavement, the figure turned. Soames felt a sudden compunction – as of one who has jumped out at a child in the dark. The face, unmoved, with eyebrows still raised and lids still lowered, was greenishly pale, like that of a man whose heart is affected; a faint smile struggled on his lips. There was fully half a minute's silence, then the pale lips spoke.

'Depends. How much?'

What little breath was in Soames' body left him. The impudence! And again the lips moved.

'You can have it for ten pounds.'

'I can have it for nothing,' said Soames, 'by asking a policeman to step here.'

The smile returned. 'You won't do that.'

'Why not?'

'Not done.'

'Not done!' repeated Soames. 'Why on earth not? Most barefaced thing I ever knew.'

'Ten pounds,' said the lips. 'I want them badly.'

Soames stood and stared. The thing was so sublime; the fellow as easy as if asking for a match; not a flicker on a face which looked as if it might pass into death at any moment. Great art! He perceived that it was not the slightest use to indulge in moral utterance. The choice was between giving him the ten pounds or calling a policeman. He looked up and down the street.

'No – there isn't one in sight. I have the box here – ten pounds.'

Soames began to stammer. The fellow was exercising on him a sort of fascination. And suddenly the whole thing tickled him. It was rich!

'Well!' he said, taking out two five-pound notes. 'For brass – !'

A thin hand removed a slight protuberance from a side pocket.

'Thanks very much. Here it is! Good-morning!'

The fellow was moving away. He moved with the same incomparable languor; he didn't look back. Soames stood with the snuff-box in his hand, staring after him.

'Well,' he said aloud, 'that's a specimen they can't produce now,' and he rang Winifred's bell.

Chapter Seven

MICHAEL HAS QUALMS

✦←→✦

DURING the eight days of the General Strike, Michael's somewhat hectic existence was relieved only by the hours spent in a House of Commons so occupied in meditating on what it could do, that it could do nothing. He had formed his own opinion of how to settle the matter, but as no one else had formed it, the result was inconspicuous. He watched, however, with a very deep satisfaction the stock of British character daily quoted higher at home and abroad; and with a certain uneasiness the stock of British intelligence becoming almost unsaleable. Mr Blythe's continual remark: 'What the bee aitch are they all about?' met with no small response in his soul. What *were* they about? He had one conversation with his father-in-law on the subject.

Over his egg Soames had said:

'Well, the Budget's dished.'

Over his marmalade Michael answered:

'Used you to have this sort of thing in your young days, sir?'

'No,' said Soames; 'no Trade Unionism then, to speak of.'

'People are saying this'll be the end of it. What's your opinion of the strike as a weapon, sir?'

'For the purposes of suicide, perfect. It's a wonder they haven't found that out long ago.'

'I rather agree, but what's the alternative?'

'Well,' said Soames, 'they've got the vote.'

'Yes, that's always said. But somehow Parliament seems to matter less and less; there's a directive sense in the country now, which really settles things before we get down to them in Parliament. Look at this strike, for instance; we can do nothing about it.'

'There must be government,' said Soames.

'Administration – of course. But all we seem able to do in Parliament is to discuss administration afterwards without much effect. The fact is, things swop around too quick for us nowadays.'

'Well,' said Soames, 'you know your own business best. Parliament always was a talking shop.' And with that unconscious quotation from Carlyle – an extravagant writer whom he curiously connected with revolution – he looked up at the Goya, and added: 'I shouldn't like to see Parliament done away with, though. Ever heard any more of that red-haired young woman?'

'Marjorie Ferrar? Oddly enough, I saw her yesterday in Whitehall. She told me she was driving for Downing Street.'

'She spoke to you?'

'Oh yes. No ill feeling.'

'H'm!' said Soames. 'I don't understand this generation. Is she married?'

'No.'

'That chap MacGown had a lucky escape – not that he deserved it. Fleur doesn't miss her evenings?'

Michael did not answer. He did not know. Fleur and he were on such perfect terms that they had no real knowledge of each other's thoughts. Then, feeling his father-in-law's grey eye gimletting into him, he said hastily:

'Fleur's all right, sir.'

Soames nodded. 'Don't let her overdo this canteen.'

'She's thoroughly enjoying it – gives her head a chance.'

'Yes,' said Soames, 'she's got a good little head, when she doesn't lose it.' He seemed again to consult the Goya, and added:

'By the way, that young Jon Forsyte is over here – they tell me – staying at Green Street, and stoking an engine or something. A boy-and-girl affair; but I thought you ought to know.'

'Oh!' said Michael, 'thanks. I hadn't heard.'

'I don't suppose she's heard, either,' said Soames guardedly; 'I told them not to tell her. D'you remember, in America, up at Mount Vernon, when I was taken ill?'

'Yes, sir; very well.'

'Well, I wasn't. Fact is, I saw that young man and his wife talking to you on the stairs. Thought it better that Fleur shouldn't run up against them. These things are very silly, but you never can tell.'

'No,' said Michael dryly; 'you never can tell. I remember liking the look of him a good deal.'

'Hm!' muttered Soames. 'He's the son of his father, I expect.'

And, from the expression on his face, Michael formed the notion that this was a doubtful advantage.

No more was said, because of Soames's lifelong conviction that one did not say any more than one need say; and of Michael's prejudice against discussing Fleur seriously, even with

her father. She had seemed to him quite happy lately. After five
and a half years of marriage, he was sure that mentally Fleur
liked him, that physically she had no objection to him, and that
a man was not sensible if he expected much more. She con-
sistently declined, of course, to duplicate Kit, but only because
she did not want to be put out of action again for months at a
time. The more active, the happier she was – over this canteen,
for instance she was in her glory. If, indeed, he had realized that
Jon Forsyte was being fed there, Michael would have been
troubled; as it was, the news of the young man's reappearance
in England made no great impression. The country held the
field of one's attention those strenuous days. The multiple evidence of patriotism exhilarated him – undergraduates at the
docks, young women driving cars, shopfolk walking cheerfully
to their work, the swarms of 'specials', the general 'carrying-
on'. Even the strikers were good-humoured. A secret conviction
of his own concerning England was being reinforced day by
day, in refutation of the pessimists. And there was no place so
un-English at the moment, he felt, as the House of Commons,
where people had nothing to do but pull long faces and talk over
'the situation'.

The news of the General Strike's collapse caught him as he
was going home after driving Fleur to the canteen. A fizz and
bustle in the streets, and the words: 'Strike Over' scrawled extem-
pore at street corners, preceded the 'End of the Strike – Official'
of the hurrying newsvendors. Michael stopped his car against the
kerb and bought a news-sheet. There it was! For a minute he
sat motionless with a choky feeling, such as he had felt when
the news of the Armistice came through. A sword lifted from
over the head of England! A source of pleasure to her enemies
dried up! People passed and passed him, each with a news-sheet,
or a look in the eye. They were taking it almost as soberly as
they had taken the strike itself. 'Good old England! We're a
great people when we're up against it!' he thought, driving his
car slowly on into Trafalgar Square. A group of men, who had
obviously been strikers, stood leaning against the parapet. He
tried to read their faces. Glad, sorry, ashamed, resentful, re-

lieved? For the life of him he could not tell. Some defensive joke seemed going the round of them.

'No wonder we're a puzzle to foreigners!' thought Michael. 'The least understood people in the world!'

He moved on slowly round the square, into Whitehall. Here were some slight evidences of feeling. The block was thick around the Cenotaph and the entrance to Downing Street; and little cheers kept breaking out. A 'special' was escorting a lame man across the street. As he came back, Michael saw his face. Why, it was Uncle Hilary! His mother's youngest brother, Hilary Charwell, Vicar of St Augustine's-in-the-Meads.

'Hallo, Michael!'

'You a "special", Uncle Hilary? Where's your cloth?'

'My dear! Are you one of those who think the Church debarred from mundane pleasure? You're not getting old-fashioned, Michael?'

Michael grinned. He had a real affection for Uncle Hilary, based on admiration for his thin, long face, so creased and humorous, on boyish recollection of a jolly uncle, on a suspicion that in Hilary Charwell had been lost a Polar explorer, or other sort of first-rate adventurer.

'That reminds me, Michael; when are you coming round to see us? I've got a topping scheme for airing "The Meads".'

'Ah!' said Michael; 'overcrowding's at the bottom of everything, even this strike.'

'Right you are, my son. Come along, then, as soon as you can. You fellows in Parliament ought always to see things at first hand. You suffer from auto-intoxication in that House. And now pass on, young man, you're impeding the traffic.'

Michael passed on, grinning. Good old Uncle Hilary! Humanizing religion, and living dangerously – had climbed all the worst peaks in Europe; no sense of his own importnace and a real sense of humour. Quite the best type of Englishman! They had tried to make him a dignitary, but he had jibbed at the gaiters and hat-ropes. He was what they called a 'live wire', and often committed the most dreadful indiscretions; but everybody liked him, even his own wife. Michael dwelt for a moment on his Aunt May. Forty – he supposed – with three children and fourteen hundred things to attend to every day; shingled, and cheerful as a sandboy. Nice-looking woman, Aunt May!

Having garaged his car, he remembered that he had not lunched. It was three o'clock. Munching a biscuit, he drank a glass of sherry, and walked over to the House of Commons. He found it humming in anticipation of a statement. Sitting back, with his legs stretched out, he had qualms. What things had been done in here! The abolitions of Slavery and of Child Labour, the Married Woman's Property Act, Repeal of the Corn Laws; but could they be done nowadays? And if not – was it a life? He had said to Fleur that you couldn't change your vocation twice and survive. But did he want to survive? Failing Foggartism – and Foggartism hadn't failed only because it hadn't started – what did he really care about?

Leaving the world better than he found it? Sitting there, he couldn't help perceiving a certain vagueness about such an aspiration, even when confined to England. It was the aspiration of the House of Commons; but in the ebb and flow of Party, it didn't seem to make much progress. Better to fix on some definite bit of administrative work, stick to it, and get something done. Fleur wanted him to concentrate on Kenya for the Indians. Again rather remote, and having little to do with England. What definite work was most needed in connexion with England? Education? Bunkered again! How tell what was the best direction into which to turn education? When they brought in State Education, for instance, they had thought the question settled. Now people were saying that State education had ruined the State. Emigration? Attractive, but negative. Revival of agriculture? Well, the two combined were Foggartism, and he knew by now that nothing but bitter hardship would teach those lessons; you might talk till you were blue in the face without convincing anyone but yourself.

What then?

'I've got a topping scheme for airing "The Meads".' 'The Meads' was one of the worst slum parishes in London. 'Clear the slums!' thought Michael; 'that's practical, anyway!' You could smell the slums, and feel them. They stank and bit and bred corruption. And yet the dwellers therein loved them; or at least preferred them to slums they knew not of! And slum-dwellers were such good sorts! Too bad to play at shuttlecock with them! He must have a talk with Uncle Hilary. Lots of vitality in England still – numbers of red-haired children! But the vitality got sooted as it grew up – like plants in a back garden. Slum clearance, smoke abolition, industrial peace, emigration, agriculture, and safety in the air! 'Them's my sentiments!' thought Michael. 'And if that isn't a large enough policy for any man, I'm – !'

He turned his face towards the statement, and thought of his uncle's words about this 'House'. Were they all really in a state of auto-intoxication here – continual slow poisoning of the tissues? All these chaps around him thought they were doing things. And he looked at the chaps. He knew most of them, and had great respect for many, but collectively he could not deny that they looked a bit dazed. His neighbour to the right was showing his front teeth in an asphyxiated smile. 'Really,' he thought; 'it's heroic how we all keep awake day after day!'

Chapter Eight

SECRET

> ⋘⋙

I⊤ would not have been natural that Fleur should rejoice in the collapse of the General Strike. A national outlook over such a matter was hardly in her character. Her canteen was completing the re-establishment in her of the social confidence which the Marjorie Ferrar affair had so severely shaken; and to be thoroughly busy with practical matters suited her. Recruited by Norah Curfew, by herself, Michael, and his Aunt Lady Alison Charwell, she had a first-rate crew of helpers of all ages, most of them in Society. They worked in the manner popularly attributed to Negroes; they craned at nothing – not even cockroaches. They got up at, or stayed up to, all hours. They were never cross and always cheery. In a word, they seemed inspired. The difference they had made in the appearance of the railway's culinary premises was startling to the Company. Fleur herself was 'on the bridge' all the time. On her devolved the greasing of the official wheels, the snipping off of red tape in numberless telephonic duels, and the bearding of the managerial face. She had even opened her father's pocket to supplement the shortcomings she encountered. The volunteers were fed to repletion, and – on Michael's inspiration – she had undermined the pickets with surreptitious coffee dashed with rum, at odd hours of their wearisome vigils. Her provisioning car, entrusted to Holly, ran the blockade, by leaving and arriving, as though Harridge's, whence she drew her supplies, were the last place in its thoughts.

'Let us give the strikers,' said Michael, 'every possible excuse to wink the other eye.'

The canteen, in fact, was an unqualified success. She had not seen Jon again, but she lived in that peculiar mixture of fear and hope which signifies a real interest in life. On the Friday Holly announced to her that Jon's wife had arrived – might she bring her down next morning?

'Oh! yes,' said Fleur. 'What is she like?'

'Attractive – with eyes like a water-nymph's, or so Jon thinks; but it's quite the best type of water-nymph.'

'M-m!' said Fleur.

She was checking a list on the telephone next day when Holly brought Anne. About Fleur's own height, straight and slim, darker in the hair, browner in complexion, browner in the eye (Fleur could see what Holly had meant by 'water-nymph'), her nose a little too sudden, her chin pointed and her teeth very white, her successor stood. Did she know that Jon and she – ?

And stretching out her free hand, Fleur said:

'I think it's awfully sporting of you as an American. How's your brother Francis?'

The hand she squeezed was brown, dry, warm; the voice she heard only faintly American, as if Jon had been at it.

'You were just too good to Francis. He always talks of you. If it hadn't been for you –'

'That's nothing. Excuse me. ... Ye-es? ... No! If the Princess comes, ask her to be good enough to come when they're feeding. Yes – yes – thank you! To-morrow? Certainly. ... Did you have a good crossing?'

'Frightful!' I was glad Jon wasn't with me. I do so hate being green, don't you?'

'I never am,' said Fleur.

That girl had Jon to bend above her when she was green! Pretty? Yes. The browned face was very alive – rather like Francis Wilmot's, but with those enticing eyes, much more eager. What was it about those eyes that made them so unusual and attractive? – surely the suspicion of a squint! She had a way of standing, too – a trick of the neck, the head was beautifully poised. Lovely clothes, of course! Fleur's glance swept swiftly down to calves and ankles. Not thick, not crooked! No luck!

'I think it's just wonderful of you to let me come and help.'

'Not a bit. Holly will put you wise.'

'That sounds nice and homey.'

'Oh! We all use your expressions now. Will you take her provisioning, Holly?'

When the girl had gone, under Holly's wing, Fleur bit her lip. By the uncomplicated glance of Jon's wife she guessed that Jon had not told her. How awfully young! Fleur felt suddenly as if she herself had never had a youth. Ah! If Jon had not been caught away from her! Her bitten lip quivered, and she buried it in the mouthpiece of the telephone.

Whenever again – three or four times – before the canteen was closed, she saw the girl, she forced herself to be cordial. Instinctively she felt that she must shut no doors on life just now. What Jon's reappearance meant to her she could not yet tell; but no one should put a finger this time in whatever pie she chose to make. She was mistress of her face and movements now, as she had never been when she and Jon were babes in the wood. With a warped pleasure she heard Holly's: 'Anne thinks you wonderful, Fleur!' No! Jon had not told his wife about her. It was like him, for the secret had not been his alone! But how long would that girl be left in ignorance? On the day the canteen closed she said to Holly:

'No one has told Jon's wife that he and I were once in love, I suppose?'

Holly shook her head.

'I'd rather they didn't, then.'

'Of course not, my dear. I'll see to it. The child's nice, I think.'

'Nice,' said Fleur, 'but not important.'

'You've got to allow for the utter strangeness of everything. Americans are generally important, sooner or later.'

'To themselves,' said Fleur, and saw Holly smile. Feeling that she had revealed a corner of her feelings, she smiled too.

'Well, so long as they get on. They do, I suppose?'

'My dear, I've hardly seen Jon, but I should say it's perfectly successful. Now the strike's over they're coming down to us at Wansdon.'

'Good! Well, this is the end of the old canteen. Let's powder our noses and get out; Father's waiting for me with the car. Can we drop you?'

'No, thanks; I'll walk.'

'What? The old *gêne*? Funny how hard things die!'

'Yes; when you're a Forsyte,' murmured Holly. 'You see, we don't show our feelings. It's airing them that kills feelings.'

'Ah!' said Fleur. 'Well, God bless you, as they say, and give Jon my love. I'd ask them to lunch, but you're off to Wansdon?'

'The day after to-morrow.'

In the little round mirror Fleur saw her face mask itself more thoroughly, and turned to the door.

'I *may* look in at Aunt Winifred's, if I've time. So long!'

Going down the stairs she thought: 'So it's air that kills feelings!'

Soames, in the car, was gazing at Riggs's back. The fellow was as lean as a rail.

'Finished with that?' he said to her.

'Yes, dear.'

'Good job, too. Wearing yourself to a shadow.'

'Why? Do I look thin, Dad?'

'No,' said Soames, 'no. That's your mother. But you can't keep on at that rate. Would you like some air? Into the Park, Riggs.'

Passing into that haven, he murmured:

'I remember when your grandmother drove here every day, regular as clockwork. People had habits then. Shall we stop and have a look at that Memorial affair they made such a fuss about?'

'I've seen it, Dad.'

'So have I,' said Soames. 'Stunt sculpture! Now, that St Gaudens statue at Washington *was* something.' And he looked at her sidelong. Thank goodness she didn't know of the way he had fended her off from young Jon Forsyte over there. She must have heard by now that the fellow was in London, and staying at her aunt's, too! And now the strike was off, and normal railway services beginning again, he would be at a loose end! But perhaps he would go back to Paris; his mother was there still, he understood. It was on the tip of his tongue to ask. Instinct, however, potent only in his dealings with Fleur, stopped him. If she had seen the young man, she wouldn't tell him of it. She was looking somehow secret – or was that just imagination?

No! He couldn't see her thoughts. Good thing, perhaps! Who could afford to have his thoughts seen? The recesses, ramifications, excesses of thought! Only when sieved and filtered was thought fit for exposure. And again Soames looked sidelong at his daughter.

She was thinking, indeed, to purposes that would have upset him. How was she going to see Jon alone before he left for Wansdon? She could call to-morrow, of course, openly at Green Street, and probably *not* see him. She could ask him to lunch in South Square, but hardly without his wife or her own husband. There was in fact, no way of seeing him alone except by accident. And she began trying to plan one. On the point of perceiving that the essence of an accident was that it could not be planned, she planned it. She would go to Green Street at nine in the morning to consult Holly on the canteen accounts. After such strenuous days Holly and Anne might surely be breakfasting in bed. Val had gone back to Wansdon, Aunt Winifred never got up! Jon *might* be alone! And she turned to Soames:

'Awfully sweet of you, Dad, to be airing me; I *am* enjoying it.'

'Like to get out and have a look at the ducks? The swans have got a brood at Mapledurham again this year.'

The swans! How well she remembered the six little grey destroyers following the old swans over the green-tinged water, that six-year-gone summer of her love! Crossing the grass down to the Serpentine, she felt a sort of creeping sweetness. But nobody – nobody should know of what went on inside her. Whatever happened – and, after all, most likely nothing would happen – she would save face this time – strongest motive in the world, as Michael said.

'Your grandfather used to bring me here when I was a shaver,' said her father's voice beside her. It did not add: 'And I used to bring that wife of mine when we were first married.' Irene! She had liked water and trees. She had liked all beauty, and she hadn't liked him!

'Eton jackets. Sixty years ago and more. Who'd have thought it then?'

'Who'd have thought what, Dad? That Eton jackets would still be in?'

'That chap – Tennyson, wasn't it? – "The old order changeth, giving place to new." I can't see *you* in high necks and skirts down to your feet, to say nothing of bustles. Women then were defended up to the nines, but you knew just as much about them as you do now – and that's precious little.'

'I wonder. Do you think people's passions are what they used to be, Dad?'

Soames brooded into his hand. Now, why had she said that? He had once told her that a grand passion was a thing of the past, and she had replied that she had one. And suddenly he was back in steamy heat, redolent of earth and potted pelargonium, kicking a hot water-pipe in a greenhouse at Maple-durham. Perhaps she'd been right; there was always a lot of human nature about.

'Passions!' he said. 'Well, you still read of people putting their heads under the gas. In old days they used to drown themselves. Let's go and have tea at that kiosk place.'

When they were seated, and the pigeons were enjoying his cake, he took a long look at her. She had her legs crossed – and very nice they were! – and just that difference in her body from the waist up, from so many young women he saw about. She didn't sit in a curve, but with a slight hollow in her back giving the impression of backbone and a poise to her head and neck. She was shingled again – the custom had unexpected life – but, after all, her neck was remarkably white and round. Her face – short, with its firm rounded chin, very little powder and no rouge, with its dark-lashed white lids, clear-glancing hazel eyes, short, straight nose and broad low brow, with the chestnut hair over its ears, and its sensibly kissable mouth – really it was a credit!

'I should think,' he said, 'you'd be glad to have more time for Kit again. He's a rascal. What d'you think he asked me for yesterday – a hammer!'

'Yes; he's always breaking things up. I smack him as little as possible, but it's unavoidable at times – nobody else is allowed to. Mother got him used to it while we were away, so he looks on it as all in the day's work.'

'Children,' said Soames, 'are funny things. We weren't made such a fuss of when I was young.'

'Forgive me, Dad, but I think *you* make more fuss of him than anybody.'

'What?' said Soames. 'I?'

'You do exactly as he tells you. Did you give him the hammer?'

'Hadn't one – what should I carry hammers about for?'

Fleur laughed. 'No; but you take him so seriously. Michael takes him ironically.'

'The little chap's got a twinkle,' said Soames.

'Mercifully. Didn't you spoil *me*, Dad?'

Soames gaped at a pigeon.

'Can't tell,' he said. 'Do you feel spoiled?'

'When I want things, I want things.'

He knew that; but so long as she wanted the right things!

'And when I don't get them, I'm not safe.'

'Who says that?'

'No one ever says it, but I know it.'

H'm! What was she wanting now? Should he ask? And, as if attending to the crumbs on his lapel, he took 'a lunar'. That face of hers, whose eyes for a moment were off guard, was dark with some deep — he couldn't tell! Secret! That's what it was!

Chapter Nine

RENCOUNTER

◄—►—►

WITH the canteen accounts in her hand, Fleur stepped out between her tubbed bay trees. A quarter to nine by Big Ben! Twenty odd minutes to walk across the Green Park! She had drunk her coffee in bed to elude questions — and there, of course, was Dad with his nose glued to the dining-room window. She waved the accounts and he withdrew his face as if they had flicked him. He was ever so good, but he shouldn't always be dusting her — she wasn't a piece of china!

She walked briskly. She had no honeysuckle sensations this morning, but felt hard and bright. If Jon had come back to England to stay, she must get him over. The sooner the better, without fuss! Passing the geraniums in front of Buckingham Palace, just out and highly scarlet, she felt her blood heating. Not walk so fast or she would arrive damp! The trees were far advanced; the Green Park under breeze and sun, smelled of grass and leaves. Spring had not smelled so good for years. A longing for the country seized on Fleur. Grass and trees and water – her hours with Jon had been passed among them – one hour in this very Park, before he took her down to Robin Hill! Robin Hill had been sold to some peer or other, and she wished him joy of it – she knew its history as of some unlucky ship! That house had 'done in' her father, and Jon's father, yes – and his grandfather, she believed, to say nothing of herself. One would not be 'done in' again so easily! And, passing into Piccadilly, Fleur smiled at her green youth. In the early windows of the club, nicknamed by George Forsyte the 'Iseeum', no one of his compeers sat as yet, above the moving humours of the street, sipping from glass or cup, and puffing his conclusions out in smoke. Fleur could just remember him, her old Cousin George Forsyte, who used to sit there, fleshy and sardonic behind the curving panes; Cousin George, who had owned the 'White Monkey' up in Michael's study. Uncle Montague Dartie, too, whom she remembered because the only time she had seen him he had pinched her in a curving place, saying: 'What are little girls made of?' so that she had clapped her hands when she heard that he had broken his neck, soon after; a horrid man, with fat cheeks and a dark moustache, smelling of scent and cigars. Rounding the last corner, she felt breathless. Geraniums were in her aunt's window-boxes – but not the fuchsias yet. Was *their* room the one she herself used to have? And, taking her hand from her heart, she rang the bell.

'Ah! Smither, anybody down?'

'Only Mr Jon's down yet, Miss Fleur.'

Why did hearts wobble? Sickening – when one was perfectly cool!

'He'll do for the moment, Smither. Where is he?'

'Having breakfast, Miss Fleur.'

'All right; show me in. I don't mind having another cup myself.'

Under her breath, she declined the creaking noun who was preceding her to the dining-room: 'Smither: O Smither: Of a Smither: To a Smither: A Smither.' Silly!

'Mrs Michael Mont, Mr Jon. Shall I get you some fresh coffee, Miss Fleur?'

'No, thank you, Smither.' Stays creaked, the door was shut. Jon was standing up.

'Fleur!'

'Well, Jon?'

She could hold his hand and keep her pallor, though the blood was in *his* cheeks, no longer smudged.

'Did I feed you nicely?'

'Splendidly. How are you, Fleur? Not tired after all that?'

'Not a bit. How did you like stoking?'

'Fine! My engine-driver was a real brick. Anne will be so disappointed; she's having a lie-off.'

'She was quite a help. Nearly six years, Jon; you haven't changed much.'

'Nor you.'

'Oh! *I* have. Out of knowledge.'

'Well, I don't see it. Have you had breakfast?'

'Yes. Sit down and go on with yours. I came round to see Holly about some accounts. Is she in bed, too?'

'I expect so.'

'Well, I'll go up directly. How does England feel, Jon?'

'Topping. Can't leave it again. Anne says she doesn't mind.'

'Where are you going to settle?'

'Somewhere near Val and Holly, if we can get a place to grow things.'

'Still keen on growing things?'

'More than ever.'

'How's the poetry?'

'Pretty dud.'

Fleur quoted:

' "Voice in the night crying, down in the old sleeping Spanish city darkened under her white stars." '

'Good Lord! Do you remember that?'

'Yes.'

His eyes were as straight, his lashes as dark as ever.

'Would you like to meet Michael, Jon, and see my infant?'

'Rather!'

'When do you go down to Wansdon?'

'To-morrow or the day after.'

'Then, won't you both come and lunch to-morrow?'

'We'd love to.'

'Half-past one. Holly and Aunt Winifred, too. Is your mother still in Paris?'

'Yes. She thinks of settling there.'

'Well, Jon – things fall on their feet, don't they?'

'They do.'

'Shall I give you some more coffee? Aunt Winifred prides herself on her coffee.'

'Fleur, you do look splendid.'

'Thank you! Have you been down to see Robin Hill?'

'Not yet. Some potentate's got it now.'

'Does your – does Anne find things amusing here?'

'She's terribly impressed – says we're a nation of gentlemen. Did you ever think that?'

'Positively – no; comparatively – perhaps.'

'It all smells so good here.'

'The poet's nose. D'you remember our walk at Wansdon?'

'I remember everything, Fleur.'

'That's honest. So do I. It took me some time to remember that I'd forgotten. How long did it take you?'

'Still longer, I expect.'

'Well, Michael's the best male I know.'

'Anne's the best female.'

'How fortunate – isn't it? How old is she?'

'Twenty-one.'

'Just right for you. Even if we hadn't been star-crossed, I was always too old for you. God! Weren't we young fools?'

'I don't see that. It was natural – it was beautiful.'

'Still got ideals? Marmalade? It's Oxford.'

'Yes. They can't make marmalade out of Oxford.'

'Jon, your hair grows exactly as it used to. Have you noticed mine?'

'I've been trying to.'

'Don't you like it?'

'Not so much, quite; and yet –'

'You mean I shouldn't look well out of the fashion. Very acute! You don't mind *her* being shingled, apparently.'

'It suits Anne.'

'Did her brother tell you much about me?'

'He said you had a lovely house; and nursed him like an angel.'

'Not like an angel; like a young woman of fashion. There's still a difference.'

'Anne was awfully grateful for that. She's told you?'

'Yes. But I'm afraid, between us, we sent Francis home rather cynical. Cynicism grows here; d'you notice it in me?'

'I think you put it on.'

'My dear! I take it off when I talk to you. You were always an innocent. Don't smile – you were! That's why you were well rid of me. Well, I never thought I should see you again.'

'Nor I. I'm sorry Anne's not down.'

'You've never told her about me.'

'How did you know that?'

'By the way she looks at me.'

'Why should I tell her?'

'No reason in the world. Let the dead past – It's fun to see you again, though. Shake hands. I'm going up to Holly now.'

Their hands joined over the marmalade on his plate.

'We're not children now, Jon. Till to-morrow, then! You'll like my house. *A rivederci*!'

Going up the stairs she thought with resolution about nothing.

'Can I come in, Holly?'

'Fleur! My dear!'

That thin, rather sallow face, so charmingly intelligent, was propped against a pillow. Fleur had the feeling that, of all people, it was most difficult to keep one's thoughts from Holly.

'These accounts,' she said. 'I'm to see that official ass at ten. Did you order all these sides of bacon?'

The thin sallow hand took the accounts, and between the large grey eyes came a furrow.

'Nine? No – yes; that's right. Have you seen Jon?'

'Yes; he's the only early bird. Will you all come to lunch with us to-morrow?'

'If you think it'll be wise, Fleur.'

'I think it'll be pleasant.'

She met the search of the grey eyes steadily, and with secret anger. No one should see into her – no one should interfere!

'All right then, we'll expect you all four at one-thirty. I must run now.'

She did run; but since she really had no appointment with any 'official ass', she went back into the Green Park and sat down.

So that was Jon – now! Terribly like Jon – then! His eyes deeper, his chin more obstinate – that perhaps was all the difference. He still had his sunny look; he still believed in things. He still – admired her. Ye-es! A little wind talked above her in a tree. The day was surprisingly fine – the first really fine day since Easter! What should she give them for lunch? How should she deal with Dad? He must not be there! To have perfect command of oneself was all very well; to have perfect command of one's father was not so easy. A pattern of leaves covered her short skirt, the sun warmed her knees; she crossed them and leaned back. Eve's first costume – a pattern of leaves. ... 'Wise?' Holly had said. Who knew? Shrimp cocktails? No! English food. Pancakes – certainly! ... To get rid of Dad, she must propose herself with Kit at Mapledurham for the day after; then he would go, to prepare for them. Her mother was still in France. The others would be gone to Wansdon. Nothing to wait for in town. A nice warm sun on her neck. A scent of grass – of honeysuckle! Oh! dear!

Chapter Ten

AFTER LUNCH

◄─►

THAT the most pregnant function of human life is the meal, will be admitted by all who take part in these recurrent crises. The impossibility of getting down from table renders it the most formidable of human activities among people civilized to the point of swallowing not only their food but their feelings.

Such a conclusion at least was present to Fleur during that lunch. That her room was Spanish, reminded her that it was not with Jon that she had spent her honeymoon in Spain. There had been a curious moment, too, before lunch; for, the first words Jon had spoken on seeing Michael had been :

'Hallo! This is queer! Was Fleur with you that day at Mount Vernon?'

What was this? Had she been kept in the dark?

Then Michael had said:

'You remember, Fleur? The young Englishman I met at Mount Vernon.'

'"Ships that pass in the night!"' said Fleur.

Mount Vernon! So *they* had met there! And she had not!

'Mount Vernon is lovely. But you ought to see Richmond, Anne. We could go after lunch. You haven't been to Richmond for ages, I expect, Aunt Winifred. We could take Robin Hill on the way home, Jon.'

'Your old home, Jon? Oh! Do let's!'

At that moment she hated the girl's eager face at which Jon was looking.

'There's the potentate,' he said.

'Oh!' said Fleur, quickly, 'he's at Monte Carlo. I read it yesterday. Could *you* come, Michael?'

'Afraid I've got a Committee. And the car can only manage five.'

'It would be just too lovely!'

Oh! that American enthusiasm! It was comforting to hear her aunt's flat voice opining that it would be a nice little run – the chestnuts would be out in the Park.

Had Michael really a Committee? She often knew what Michael really had, she generally knew more or less what he was thinking, but now she did not seem to know. In telling him last night of this invitation to lunch, she had carefully obliterated the impression by an embrace warmer than usual – he must not get any nonsense into his head about Jon! When, too, to her father she had said:

'Couldn't Kit and I come down to you the day after to-morrow: but you'll want a day there first, I'm afraid, if Mother's not there,' how carefully she had listened to the tone of his reply:

'H'm! Ye – es! I'll go down to-morrow morning.'

Had he scented anything: had Michael scented anything? She turned to Jon.

'Well, Jon, what d'you think of my house?'

'It's very like you.'

'Is that a compliment?'

'To the house? Of course.'

'Francis didn't exaggerate then?'

'Not a bit.'

'You haven't seen Kit yet. We'll have him down. Coaker, please ask Nurse to bring Kit down, unless he's asleep. ... He'll be three in July; quite a good walker already. It makes one frightfully old!'

The entrance of Kit and his silver dog caused a sort of cooing sound, speedily checked, for three of the women were of Forsyte stock, and the Forsytes did not coo. He stood there, blue and rather Dutch, with a slight frown and his hair bright, staring at the company.

'Come here, my son. This is Jon – your second cousin once removed.'

Kit advanced.

'S'all I bwing my 'orse in?'

'Horse, Kit. No; shake hands.'

The small hand went up; Jon's hand came down.

'You got dirty nails.'

She saw Jon flush, heard Anne's: 'Isn't he just too cunning?' and said:

'Kit, you're very rude. So would you have, if you'd been stoking an engine.'

'Yes, old man, I've been washing them ever since, but I can't get them clean.'

'Why?'

'It's got into the skin.'

'Le' me see.'

'Go and shake hands with your great-aunt, Kit.'

'No.'

'Dear little chap,' said Winifred. 'Such a bore, isn't it, Kit?'

'Very well, then, go out again, and get your manners, and bring them in.'

'All wight.'

His exit, closed in by the silver dog, was followed by a general laugh; Fleur said, softly:

'Little wretch – poor Jon!' And through her lashes she saw Jon give her a grateful look.

In this mid-May fine weather the view from Richmond Hill had all the width and leafy charm which had drawn so many Forsytes in phaeton's and barouches, in hansom cabs and motor-cars from immemorial time, or at least from the days of George the Fourth. The winding river shone discreetly, far down there, and the trees of the encompassing landscape, though the oaks were still goldened, had just began to have a brooding look; in July they would be heavy and blueish. Curiously, few houses showed among the trees and fields; very scanty evidence of man, within twelve miles of London! The spirit of an older England seemed to have fended jerry-builders from a prospect sacred to the ejaculations of four generations.

Of those five on the terrace Winifred best expressed that guarding spirit, with her:

'Really, it's a very pretty view!'

A view – a view! And yet a view was not what it had been when old Jolyon travelled the Alps with that knapsack of brown leather and square shape, still in his grandson Jon's possession; or Swithin above his greys, rolling his neck with consequence towards the lady by his side, had pointed with his whip down at the river and pouted: 'A pooty little view!' Or James, crouched over his long knees in some gondola, had examined the Grand Canal at Venice with doubting eyes, and muttered: 'They never told me the water was this colour!' Or Nicholas, taking his constitutional at Matlock, had opined that the gorge was the finest in England. No, a view was not what it had been! George Forsyte and Montague Dartie, with their backs to it, quizzically contemplating the Liberty ladies brought down to be fed, had started that rot; and now the young folk didn't use the expression, but just ejaculated: 'Christ!' or words to that effect.

But there was Anne, of course, like an American, with clasped hands, and:

'Isn't it too lovely, Jon? It's sort of romantic!'

And so to the Park, where Winifred chanted automatically at sight of the chestnuts, and every path and patch of fern and fallen tree drew from Holly or Jon some riding recollection.

'Look, Anne, that's where I threw myself off my pony as a kid when I lost my stirrup and got so bored with being bumped.'

Or: 'Look, Jon! Val and I had a race down that avenue. Oh! and there's the log we used to jump. Still there!'

And Anne was in ecstasies over the deer and the grass, so different from the American varieties.

To Fleur the Park meant nothing.

'Jon,' she said, suddenly, 'what are you going to do to get in at Robin Hill?'

'Tell the butler that I want to show my wife where I lived as a boy; and give him a couple of good reasons. I don't want to see the house, all new furniture and that.'

'Couldn't we go in at the bottom, through the coppice?' and her eyes added: 'As we did that day.'

'We might come on someone, and get turned back.'

The couple of good reasons secured their top entrance to the grounds; the 'family' was not 'in residence'.

Bosinney's masterpiece wore its mellowest aspect. The sunblinds were down, for the sun was streaming on its front, past the old oak tree, where was now no swing. In Irene's rosegarden which had replaced old Jolyon's fernery, buds were forming, but only one rose was out.

' "Rose, you Spaniard!" ' Something clutched Fleur's heart. What was Jon thinking – what remembering, with those words and that frown? Just here she had sat between his father and his mother, believing that she and Jon would live here some day; together watch the roses bloom, the old oak drop its leaves; together say to their guests: 'Look! There's the grandstand at Epsom – see? Just above those poplars!'

And now she could not even walk beside him, who was playing guide to that girl, his wife! Beside her aunt she walked instead. Winifred was extremely intrigued. She had never yet seen this house, which Soames had built with the brains of young Bosinney; which Irene, with 'that unfortunate little affair of hers' had wrecked; this house where Old Uncle Jolyon and Cousin Jolyon had died; and Irene, so ironically, had lived and had this boy Jon – a nice boy, too; this house of Forsyte song and story. It was very distinguished and belonged to a peer now, which, since it had gone out of the family, seemed suitable. In the walled fruit-garden, she said to Fleur:

'Your grandfather came down here once, to see how it was getting on. I remember his saying: "It'll cost a pretty penny to keep up." And I should think it does. But it was a pity to sell it. Irene's doing, of course! She never cared for the family. Now, if only –' But she stopped short of the words: 'you and Jon had made a match of it.'

'What on earth would Jon have done, Auntie, with a great place like this so near London? He's a poet.'

'Yes,' murmured Winifred – not very quick, because in her youth quickness had not been fashionable: 'There's too much glass, perhaps.' And they went down through the meadow.

The coppice! Still there at the bottom of the field! But Fleur lingered now, stood by the fallen log, waited till she could say:

'Listen! The cuckoo, Jon!'

The cuckoo's song, and the sight of bluebells under the larch trees! Beside her Jon stood still! Yes, and the spring stood still. There went the song – over and over!

'It was *here* we came on your mother, Jon, and our stars were crossed. Oh, Jon!'

Could so short a sound mean so much, say so much, be so startling? His face! She jumped on to the log at once.

'No ghosts, my dear!'

And, with a start, Jon looked up at her.

She put her hands on his shoulders and jumped down. And among the bluebells they went on. And the bird sang after them.

'That bird repeats himself,' said Fleur.

Chapter Eleven

PERAMBULATION

◄‹∙›►

THE instinct in regard to his daughter, which by now formed part of his protective covering against the machinations of Fate, had warned Soames, the day before, that Fleur was up to something when she went out while he was having breakfast. Seen through the window waving papers at him, she had an air of unreality, or at least an appearance of not telling him anything. As something not quite genuine in the voice warns a dog that he is about to be left, so was Soames warned by the ostentation of those papers. He finished his breakfast, therefore, too abruptly for one constitutionally given to marmalade, and set forth to Green Street. Since that young fellow Jon was staying there, this fashionable locality was the seat of any reasonable uneasiness. If, moreover, there was a place in the world where Soames could still unbutton his soul, it was his sister Winifred's drawing-room, on which in 1879 he himself had impressed so deeply the personality of Louis Quinze that, in spite of jazz and Winifred's desire to be in the heavier modern fashion, that monarch's incurable levity was still to be observed.

Taking a somewhat circuitous course and looking in at the Connoisseur's Club on the way, Soames did not arrive until after Fleur's departure. The first remark from Smither confirmed the uneasiness which had taken him forth.

'Mr Soames! Oh! What a pity – Miss Fleur's just gone! And nobody down yet but Mr Jon.'

'Oh!' said Soames. 'Did she see him?'

'Yes, sir. He's in the dining-room, if you'd like to go in.'

Soames shook his head.

'How long are they staying, Smither?'

'Well, I did hear Mrs Val say they were all going back to Wansdon the day after to-morrow. We shall be all alone again in case you were thinking of coming to us, Mr Soames.'

Again Soames shook his head. 'Too busy,' he said.

'What a beautiful young lady Miss Fleur 'as grown, to be sure; such a colour she 'ad this morning!'

Soames gave vent to an indeterminate sound. The news was not to his liking, but he could hardly say so in front of an institution. One could never tell how much Smither knew. She had creaked her way through pretty well every family secret in her time, from the days when his own matrimonial relations supplied Timothy's with more than all the gossip it required. Yes, and were not his own matrimonial relations, twice-laid, still supplying the raw material? Curiously sinister it seemed to him just then, that the son of his supplanter Jolyon should be here in this house, the nearest counterfeit of that old homing centre of the Forsytes, Timothy's in the Bayswater Road. What perversity there was in things! And, repeating the indeterminate sound, he said:

'By the way, I suppose that Mr Stainford never came here again?'

'Oh, yes, Mr Soames; he called yesterday to see Mr Val; but Mr Val was gone.'

'He did – did he?' said Soames, round-eyed. 'What did he take this time?'

'Oh! Of course I knew better than to let him in.'

'You didn't give him Mr Val's address in the country?'

'Oh, no, sir; he knew it.'

'Deuce he did!'

'Shall I tell the mistress you're here, Mr Soames? She must be nearly down by now.'

'No; don't disturb her.'

'I'm that sorry, sir; it's always such a pleasure to see you.'

Old Smither bridling! A good soul! No such domestics nowadays! And, putting on his hat, Soames touched its brim, murmuring:

'Well, good-bye, Smither. Give her my love!' and went out.

'So!' he thought, 'Fleur's seen that boy!' The whole thing would begin over again! He had known it! And, very slowly, with his hat rather over his eyes, he made for Hyde Park Corner. This was for him a moment in deep waters, when the heart must be hardened to this dangerous decision or to that. With the tendency for riding past the hounds inherited from his father James in all matters which threatened the main securities of life, Soames rushed on in thought to the ruin of his daughter's future, wherein so sacredly was embalmed his own.

'Such a colour she 'ad this morning!' When she waved those papers at him, she was pale enough – too pale! A confounded chance! Breakfast time, too – worst time in the day – most intimate! His naturally realistic nature apprehended all the suggestions that lay in breakfast. Those who breakfasted alone together slept together as often as not. Putting things into her head! Yes; and they were not boy and girl now! Well, it all depended on what their feelings were, if they still had any. And who was to know? Who, in heaven's name, was to know? Automatically he had begun to encompass the Artillery Memorial. A great white thing which he had never yet taken in properly, and didn't know that he wanted to. Yet somehow it was very real, and suited to his mood – faced things; nothing high-flown about that gun – short, barking brute of a thing; or those dark men – drawn and devoted under their steel hats ! Nothing pretty-pretty about that memorial – no angels' wings there ! No Georges and no dragons, nor horses on the prance; no panoply, and no *panache* ! There it 'sot' – as they used to say – squatted like a great white toad on the nation's life. Concreted thunder. Not an illusion about it ! Good thing to look at once a day, and see what you'd got to avoid. 'I'd like to rub the noses of those Crown Princes and military cocks-o'-the-walk on it,' thought Soames, 'with their – what was it? – "fresh and merry wars!" ' And, crossing the road in the sunshine, he passed into the Park, moving towards Knightsbridge.

But about Fleur? Was he going to take the bull by the horns, or to lie low? Must be one thing or the other. He walked rapidly now, concentrated in face and movement, stalking as it were his own thoughts with a view to finality. He passed at Knightsbridge, and after unseeing scrutiny of two or three small shops where in his time he had picked up many a bargain, for himself or shopman, he edged past Tattersall's. That hung on – they still sold horses there, he believed ! Horses had never been in his line, but he had not lived in Montpelier Square without knowing the *habitués* of Tattersall's by sight. Like everything else that was crusted, they'd be pulling it down before long, he shouldn't wonder, and putting up some motor place or cinema !

Suppose he talked to Michael? No ! Worse than useless. Besides he couldn't talk about Fleur and that boy to anyone – thereby hung too long a tale; and the tale was his own. Montpelier Square ! He had turned into the very place, whether by design he hardly knew. It hadn't changed – but was all slicked up since he was last there, soon after the war. Builders and decorators must have done well lately – about the only people who had. He walked along the right side of the narrow square, where he had known turbulence and tragedy. There the house was, looking much as it used to, not quite so neat, and a little more florid. Why had he ever married that woman? What had made him so set on it? Well ! She had done her best to deter him. But — God! — how he had wanted her! To this day he could recognize that. And at first — at first, he had thought, and perhaps she had thought — but who could tell? — *he* never could! And then slowly — or was it quickly? — the end; a ghastly business! He stood still by the square railings, and stared at the doorway that had been his own, as if from its green paint and its brass number he might receive inspiration how to choke love in his own daughter for the son of his own wife — yes, how to choke it before it spread and choked her!

And as, on those days and nights of his first married life, returning home, he had sought in vain for inspiration how to awaken love, so now no inspiration came to tell him how to strangle love. And, doggedly, he turned out of the little square.

In a way it was ridiculous to be fussing about the matter; for, after all, Michael was a good young fellow, and her marriage far from unhappy, so far as he could see. As for young Jon, presumably he had married for love; there hadn't been anything else to marry for, he believed — unless he had been misinformed, the girl and her brother had been museum pieces, two Americans without money to speak of. And yet — there was the moon, and he could not forget how Fleur had always wanted it. A desire to have what she hadn't yet got was her leading characteristic. Impossible, too, to blink his memory of her, six years ago — to forget her body crumpled and crushed into the sofa in the dark night when he came back from Robin Hill and broke the news to her. Perusing with his mind the record since, Soames had an acute and comfortless feeling that she had, as it were, been marking time, that all her fluttering activities, even the production of Kit, had been in the nature of a makeshift. Like the age to which she belonged, she had been lifting her feet up and down without getting anywhere, because she didn't know where she wanted to get. And yet, of late, since she had been round the world, he had seemed to notice something quieter and more solid in her conduct, as if settled purposes were pushing up, and she were coming to terms at last with her daily life. Look, for instance, at the way she had tackled this canteen! And, turning his face homeward, Soames had a vision of a common not far from Mapledurham, where some fool had started a fire which had burned the gorse, and of the grass pushing up almost impudently green and young, through the charred embers of that conflagration. Rather like things generally, when you thought of it! The war had burned them all out, but things, yes, and people, too – one noticed – were beginning to sprout a bit, as if they felt again it might be worth while. Why, even he himself had regained some of his old connoisseur's desire to have nice things! It all depended on what you saw ahead, on whether you could eat and drink because tomorrow you didn't die. With this Dawes Settlement and Locarno business and the General Strike broken, there might even be another long calm, like the Victorian, which would make things possible. He was seventy-one, but one could always dwell on Timothy, who had lived to be a hundred, fixed star in shifting skies. And Fleur – only twenty-four – might almost outlive the century if she, or, rather the century, took care and bottled up its unruly passions, its disordered longings, and all that silly rushing along to nowhere in particular. If they steadied down, the age might yet become a golden, or a platinum, age at any rate. Even he might live to see the income tax at half a crown. 'No,' he thought, confused between his daughter and the age; 'she mustn't go throwing her cap over the windmill. It's short-sighted!' And, his blood warmed by perambulation, he became convinced that he would not speak to her, but lie low, and trust to that common sense, of which she surely had her share – oh, yes! 'Just keep my eyes open, and speak to no one,' he thought; 'least said, soonest mended.'

He had come again to the Artillery Memorial; and for the second time he moved around it. No! A bit of a blot – it seemed to him, now – so literal and heavy! Would that great white thing help Consols to rise? Some thing with wings might, after all, have been preferable. Some encouragement to people to take shares or go into domestic service; help, in fact, to make life liveable, instead of reminding them all the time that they had already once been blown to perdition and might again be. Those Artillery fellows – he had read somewhere – loved their guns, and wanted to be reminded of them. But did anybody else love their guns, or want reminder? Not those Artillery fellows would look at this every day outside St George's Hospital, but Tom, Dick, Harry, Peter, Gladys, Joan and Marjorie. 'Mistake!' thought Soames; 'and a pretty heavy one. Something sedative, statue of Vulcan, or somebody on a horse; that's what's wanted!' And remembering George III on a horse, he smiled grimly. Anyway, there the thing was, and would have to stay! But it was high time artists went back to nymphs and dolphins, and other evidences of a settled life.

When at lunch Fleur suggested that he would want a day's law at Mapledurham before she and Kit came down, he again felt there was something behind; but, relieved enough at getting her, he let 'the sleeping dog' lie; nor did he mention his visit to Green Street.

'The weather looks settled,' he said. 'You want some sun after that canteen. They talk about these ultra-violet rays. Plain sunshine used to be good enough. The doctors'll be finding something extra-pink before long. If they'd only let things alone!'

'Darling, it amuses them.'

'Re-discovering what our grandmothers knew so well that we've forgotten 'em, and calling 'em by fresh names! A thing isn't any more wholesome to eat for instance, because they've invented the word "vitamin". Why, your grandfather ate an orange every day of his life, because his old doctor told him to, at the beginning of the last century. Vitamins! Don't you let Kit get faddy about his food. It's a long time before he'll go to school – that's one comfort. School feeding!'

'Did they feed you so badly, Dad?'

'Badly! How we grew up, I don't know. We ate our principal meal in twenty minutes, and were playing football ten minutes after. But nobody thought about digestion, then.'

'Isn't that an argument for thinking of it now?'

'A good digestion,' said Soames, 'is the whole secret of life.' And he looked at his daughter. Thank God! *She* wasn't peaky. So far as he knew, her digestion was excellent. She might fancy herself in love, or out of it; but so long as she was unconscious of her digestion, she would come through. 'The thing is to walk as much as you can, in these days of cars,' he added.

'Yes,' said Fleur, 'I had a nice walk this morning.'

Was she challenging him over her apple charlotte? If so, he wasn't going to rise.

'So did I,' he said. 'I went all about. We'll have some golf down there.'

She looked at him for a second, then said a surprising thing:

'Yes, I believe I'm getting middle-aged enough for golf.'

Now what did she mean by that?

Chapter Twelve

PRIVATE FEELINGS

◄◄─►►

On the day of the lunch party and the drive to Robin Hill, Michael really had a Committee, but he also had his private feelings and wanted to get on terms with them. There are natures in which discovery of what threatens happiness perverts to prejudice all judgement of the disturbing object. Michael's was not such. He had taken a fancy to the young Englishman met at the home of that old American George Washington, partly, indeed, because he *was* English; and, seeing him now seated next to Fleur, second cousin and first love – he was unable to revise the verdict. The boy had a nice face, and was better-looking than himself; he had attractive hair, a strong chin, straight eyes, and a modest bearing; there was no sense in blinking facts like those. The Free Trade in love, which obtained amongst pleasant people, forbade Michael to apply the cruder principles of Protection even in thoughts. Fortunately, the boy was married to this slim and attractive girl, who looked at one – as Mrs Val had put it to him – like a guaranteed-pure water-nymph! Michael's private feelings were therefore more concerned with Fleur than with the young man himself. But hers was a difficult face to read, a twisting brain to follow, a heart hard to get at; and – was Jon Forsyte the reason why? He remembered how in Cork Street this boy's elderly half-sister – that fly-away little lady, June Forsyte – had blurted out to him that Fleur ought to have married her young brother – first he had ever heard of it. How painfully it had affected him with its intimation that he played but second fiddle in the life of his beloved! He remembered, too, some cautious and cautionary allusions by 'old Forsyte'. Coming from that model of secrecy and suppressed feelings, they, too, had made on Michael a deep and lasting impression reinforced by his own failure to get at the bottom of Fleur's heart. He went to his Committee with but half his mind on public matters. What had nipped that early love affair in the bud and given him his chance? Not sudden dislike, lack of health, or lack of money – not relationship, for Mrs Val Dartie had married her second cousin apparently with everyone's consent. Michael, it will be seen, had remained quite ignorant of the skeleton in Soames's cupboard. Such Forsytes as he had met, reticent about family affairs, had never mentioned it; and Fleur had never spoken of her first love, much less of the reason why it had come to naught. Yet, there must have been some reason; and it was idle to try and understand her present feelings without knowing what it was!

His Committee was on birth control in connexion with the Ministry of Health; and, while listening to arguments why he should not support for other people what he practised himself, he was visited by an idea. Why not go and ask June Forsyte? He could find her in the telephone book – there could be but one with such a name.

'What do *you* say, Mont?'

'Well, sir, if we won't export children to the Colonies or speed up emigration somehow, there's nothing for it but birth control. In the upper and middle classes we're doing it all the time, and blinking the moral side, if there is one; and I really don't see how we can insist on a moral side for those who haven't a quarter of our excuse for having lots of children.'

'My dear Mont,' said the chairman, with a grin, 'aren't you cutting there at the basis of all privilege?'

'Very probably,' said Michael, with an answering grin. 'I think, of course, that child emigration is much better, but nobody else does, apparently.'

Everybody knew that 'young Mont' had a 'bee in his bonnet' about child emigration, and there was little disposition to encourage it to buzz. And, since no one was more aware than Michael of being that crank in politics, one who thought you could not eat your cake and have it, he said no more. Presently, feeling that they would go round and round the mulberry bush for some time yet, and sit on the fence after, he excused himself and went away.

He found the address he wanted: 'Miss June Forsyte, Poplar House, Chiswick', and mounted a Hammersmith bus.

How fast things seemed coming back to the normal! Extraordinarily difficult to upset anything so vast, intricate, and elastic as a nation's life. The bus swung along among countless vehicles and pedestrian myriads, and Michael realized how firm were those two elements of stability in the modern state, the common need for eating, drinking, and getting about; and the fact that so many people could drive cars. 'Revolution?' he thought. 'There never was a time when it had less chance. Machinery's dead agin it.' Machinery belonged to the settled state of things, and every day saw its reinforcement. The unskilled multitude and the Communistic visionaries, their leaders, only had a chance now where machinery and means of communication were still undeveloped, as in Russia. Brains, ability and technical skill, were by nature on the side of capital and individual enterprise, and were gaining even more power.

'Poplar House' took some finding, and, when found, was a little house supporting a large studio with a north light. It stood, behind two poplar trees, tall, thin, white, like a ghost. A foreign woman opened to him. Yes. Miss Forsyte was in the studio with Mr Blade! Michael sent up his card, and waited in a draught, extremely ill at ease; for now that he was here he could not imagine why he had come. How to get the information he wanted without seeming to have come for it, passed his comprehension; for it was the sort of knowledge that could only be arrived at by crude questioning.

Finding that he was to go up, he went, perfecting his first lie. On entering the studio, a large room with green canvassed walls, pictures hung or stacked, the usual daïs, a top light half curtained, and some cats, he was conscious of a fluttering movement. A little light lady in flowing green, with short silver hair, had risen from a footstool, and was coming towards him.

'How do you do? You know Harold Blade, of course?'

The young man, at whose feet she had been sitting, rose and stood before Michael, square, somewhat lowering with a dun-coloured complexion and heavily charged eyes.

'You must know his wonderful Rafaelite work.'

'Oh yes!' said Michael, whose conscience was saying: 'Oh no!'

The young man said grimly: 'He doesn't know me from Adam.'

'No, really,' muttered Michael. 'But do tell me, why Rafaelite? I've always wanted to know.'

'Why?' exclaimed June. 'Because he's the only man who's giving us the old values; he's rediscovered them.'

'Forgive me, I'm such a dud in art matters – I thought the academicians were still in perspective!'

They!' cried June, and Michael winced at the passion in the word. 'Oh, well – if you still believe in them –'

'But I don't,' said Michael.

'Harold is the only Rafaelite; people are grouping round him, of course, but he'll be the last, too. It's always like that. Great painters make a school, but the schools never amount to anything.'

Michael looked with added interest at the first and last Rafaelite. He did not like the face, but it had a certain epileptic quality.

'Might I look round? Does my father-in-law know your work, I wonder? He's a great collector, and always on the lookout.'

'Soames!' said June, and again Michael winced. 'He'll be collecting Harold when we're all dead. Look at that!'

Michael turned from the Rafaelite, who was shrugging his thick shoulders. He saw what was clearly a portrait of June. It was entirely recognizable, very smooth, all green and silver, with a suggestion of halo round the head.

'Pure primary line and colour – d'you think they'd hang *that* in the Academy?'

'Seems to me exactly what they would hang,' thought Michael, careful to keep the conclusion out of his face.

'I like the suggestion of a halo,' he murmured.

The Rafaelite uttered a short, sharp laugh.

'I'm going for a walk,' he said; 'I'll be in to supper. Goodbye!'

'Good-bye!' said Michael, with a certain relief.

'Of course,' said June when they were alone, 'he's the *only* person who could paint Fleur. He'd get her modern look so perfectly. Would she sit to him? With everybody against him, you know, he has *such* a struggle.'

'I'll ask her. But do tell me – why is everybody against him?'

'Because he's been through all these empty modern crazes, and come back to pure form and colour. They think he's a traitor, and call him academic. It's always the way when a man has the grit to fly against fashion and follow his own genius. I can see exactly what he'd do with Fleur. It would be a great chance for him, because he's very proud, and this would be a proper commission from Soames. Splendid for her, too, of course. She ought to jump at it – in ten years' time he'll be *the* man.'

Michael, who doubted if Fleur would 'jump at it', or Soames give the commission, replied cautiously: 'I'll sound her. ... By the way, your sister Holly and your young brother and his wife were lunching with us today.'

'Oh!' said June, 'I haven't seen Jon yet.' And looking at Michael with her straight blue eyes, she added:

'Why did you come to see me?'

Under that challenging stare Michael's diplomacy wilted.

636

'Well,' he said, 'frankly, I want you to tell me why Fleur and your young brother came to an end with each other.'

'Sit down,' said June, and resting her pointed chin on her hand, she looked at him with eyes moving a little from side to side, as might a cat's.

'I'm glad you asked me straight out; I hate people who beat about the bush. Don't you know about his mother? She was Soames's first wife, of course.'

'Oh!' said Michael.

'Irene,' and, as she spoke the name, Michael was aware of something deep and primitive stirring in that little figure. 'Very beautiful – they didn't get on; she left him – and years later she married my father, and Soames divorced her. I mean Soames divorced her and she married my father. They had Jon. And then, when Jon and Fleur fell in love, Irene and my father were terribly upset, and so was Soames – at least, he ought to have been.'

'And then?' asked Michael, for she was silent.

'The children were told; and my father died in the middle of it all; and Jon sacrificed himself and took his mother away, and Fleur married you.'

So that was it! In spite of the short, sharp method of the telling, he could feel tragic human feeling heavy in the tale. Poor little devils!

'I always thought it was too bad,' said June suddenly. 'Irene ought to have put up with it. Only – only –' and she stared at Michael, 'they wouldn't have been happy. Fleur's too selfish. I expect she saw that.'

Michael raised an indignant voice.

'Yes,' said June; 'you're a good sort, I know – too good for her.'

'I'm not,' said Michael sharply.

'Oh yes, you are. She isn't bad, but she's a selfish little creature.'

'I wish you'd remember –'

'Sit down! Don't mind what I say. I only speak the truth, you know. Of course, it was all horrible; Soames and my father were first cousins. And those children were awfully in love.'

Again Michael was conscious of the deep and private feeling within the little figure; conscious, too, of something deep and private stirring within himself.

'Painful!' he said.

'I don't know,' June went on abruptly, 'I don't know; perhaps it was all for the best. You're happy, aren't you?'

With that pistol to his head, he stood and delivered.

'I am. But is she?'

The little green-and-silver figure straightened up. She caught his hand and gave it a squeeze. There was something almost terribly warm-hearted about the action, and Michael was touched. He had only seen her twice before!

'After all, Jon's married. What's his wife like?'

'Looks charming – nice, I think.'

'An American!' said June deeply. 'Well, Fleur's half French. I'm glad you've got a boy.'

Never had Michael known anyone whose words conveyed so much unintended potency of discomfort! Why was she glad he had a boy? Because it was an insurance – against what?

'Well,' he mumbled, 'I'm very glad to know at last what it was all about.'

'You ought to have been told before; but you don't know still. Nobody can know what family feuds and feelings are like, who hasn't had them. Though I was angry about those children, I admit that. You see, I was the first to back Irene against Soames in the old days. I wanted her to leave him at the beginning of everything. She had a beastly time; he was such a – such a slug about his precious rights, and no proper pride either. Fancy forcing yourself on a woman who didn't want you!'

'Ah!' Michael muttered. 'Fancy!'

'People in the 'eighties and 'nineties didn't understand how disgusting it was. Thank goodness, they do now!'

'Do they?' murmured Michael. 'I wonder!'

'Of course they do.'

Michael sat corrected.

'Things are much better in that way than they were – not

nearly so stuffy and farmyardy. I wonder Fleur hasn't told you all about it.'

'She's never said a word.'

'Oh!'

That sound was as discomforting as any of her more elaborate remarks. Clearly she was thinking what he himself was thinking: that it had gone too deep with Fleur to be spoken of. He was not even sure that Fleur knew whether he had ever heard of her affair with Jon.

And, with a sudden shrinking from any more discomforting sounds, he rose.

'Thanks awfully for telling me. I must buzz off now, I'm afraid.'

'I shall come and see Fleur about sitting to Harold. It's too good a chance for him to miss. He simply must get commissions.'

'Of course!' said Michael; he could trust Fleur's powers of refusal better than his own.

'Good-bye, then!'

But when he got to the door and looked back at her standing alone in that large room, he felt a pang – she seemed so light, so small, so fly-away, with her silver hair and her little intent face – still young from misjudged enthusiasm. He had got something out of her, too, left nothing with her; and he had stirred up some private feeling of her past, some feeling as strong, perhaps stronger, than his own.

She looked dashed lonely! He waved his hand to her.

Fleur had returned when he got home, and Michael realized suddenly that in calling on June Forsyte he had done a thing inexplicable, save in relation to her and Jon!

'I must write and ask that little lady not to mention it,' he thought. To let Fleur know that he had been fussing about her past would never do.

'Had a good time?' he said.

'Very. Young Anne reminds me of Francis, except for her eyes.'

'Yes; I liked the looks of those two when I saw them at Mount Vernon. That was a queer meeting, wasn't it?'

'The day father was unwell?'

He felt that she knew the meeting had been kept from her. If only he could talk to her freely; if only she would blurt out everything!

But all she said was: 'I feel at a bad loose end, Michael, without the canteen.'

Chapter Thirteen

SOAMES IN WAITING

◄◄─►►

To say that Soames preferred his house by the river when his wife was not there, would be a crude way of expressing a far from simple equation. He was glad to be still married to a handsome woman and very good housekeeper, who really could not help being French and twenty-five years younger than himself. But the fact was, that when she was away from him, he could see her good points so much better than when she was not. Though fond of mocking him in her French way, she had, he knew, lived into a certain regard for his comfort, and her own position as his wife. Affection? No, he did not suppose she had affection for him, but she liked her home, her bridge, her importance in the neighbourhood, and doing things about the house and garden. She was like a cat. And with money she was admirable – making it go further and buy more than most people. She was getting older, too, all the time, so that he had lost serious fear that she would overdo some friendship or other, and let him know it. That Prosper Profond business of six years ago, which had been such a squeak, had taught her discretion.

It had been quite unnecessary really for him to go down a day before Fleur's arrival; his household ran on wheels too well geared and greased. On his fifteen acres, with the new dairy and cows across the river, he grew everything now except flour, fish and meat of which he was but a sparing eater. Fifteen acres, if hardly 'land', represented a deal of produce. The establishment was, in fact, typical of countless residences of the unlanded well-to-do.

Soames had taste, and Annette, if anything, had more, especially in food, so that a better fed household could scarcely have been found.

In this bright weather, the leaves just full, the mayflower in bloom, bulbs not yet quite over, and the river re-learning its summer smile, the beauty of the prospect was not to be sneezed at. Soames on his green lawn walked a little and thought of why gardeners seemed always on the move from one place to another. He couldn't seem to remember ever having seen an English gardener otherwise than about to work. That was, he supposed, why people so often had Scotch gardeners. Fleur's dog came out and joined him. The fellow was getting old, and did little but attack imaginary fleas. Soames was very particular about real fleas, and the animal was washed so often that his skin had become very thin – a golden brown retriever, so rare that he was always taken for a mongrel. The head gardener came by with a spud in his hand.

'Good afternoon, sir.'

'Good afternoon,' replied Soames. 'So the strike's over !'

'Yes, sir. If they'd attend to their business, it'd be better.'

'It would. How's your asparagus?'

'Well, I'm trying to make a third bed, but I can't get the extra labour.'

Soames gazed at his gardener, who had a narrow face, rather on one side, owing to the growth of flowers. 'What?' he said. 'When there are about a million and a half people out of employment?'

'And where they get to, I can't think,' said the gardener.

'Most of them,' said Soames, 'are playing instruments in the streets.'

'That's right, sir – my sister lives in London. I could get a boy, but I can't trust him.'

'Why don't you do it yourself?'

'Well, sir, I expect it'll come to that; but I don't want to let the garden down, you know.' And he moved the spud uneasily.

'What have you got that thing for? There isn't a weed about the place.'

The gardener smiled. 'It's something cruel,' he said, 'the way they spring up when you're not about.'

'Mrs Mont will be down tomorrow,' muttered Soames. 'I shall want some good flowers in the house.'

'Very little at this time of year, sir.'

'I never knew a time of year when there was much. You must stir your stumps and find something.'

'Very good, sir,' said the gardener, and walked away.

'Where's he going now?' thought Soames. 'I never knew such a chap. But they're all the same.' He supposed they did work some time or other; in the small hours, perhaps – precious small hours! Anyway, he had to pay 'em a pretty penny for it! And, noticing the dog's head on one side, he said:

'Want a walk?'

They went out of the gate together, away from the river. The birds were in varied song, and the cuckoos obstreperous.

They walked up to the bit of common land where there had been a conflagration in the exceptionally fine Easter weather. From there one could look down at the river winding among poplars and willows. The prospect was something like that in a long river landscape by Daubigny which he had seen in an American's private collection – a very fine landscape, he never remembered seeing a finer. He could mark the smoke from his own kitchen chimney, and was more pleased than he would have been marking the smoke from any other. He had missed it a lot last year – all those months, mostly hot – touring the world with Fleur from one unhomelike place to another. Young Michael's craze for emigration! Soames was Imperialist enough to see the point of it in theory; but in practice every place out of England seemed to him so raw, or so extravagant. An Englishman was entitled to the smoke of his own kitchen chimney. Look at the Ganges – monstrous great thing, compared with that winding silvery thread down there! The St

Lawrence, the Hudson, the Pótomac – as he still called it in thought – had all pleased him, but, comparatively, they were sprawling pieces of water. And the people out there were a sprawling lot. They had to be, in those big places. He moved down from the common through a narrow bit of wood where rooks were in a state of some excitement. He knew little about the habits of birds, not detached enough from self for the study of creatures quite unconnected with him; but he supposed they would be holding a palaver about food – worm-currency would be depressed, or there had been some inflation or other – fussy as the French over their wretched franc. Emerging, he came down opposite the lock-keeper's cottage. There, with the scent of the wood-smoke threading from its low and humble chimney, the weir murmuring, the blackbirds and the cuckoos calling, Soames experienced something like asphyxiation of the proprietary instincts. Opening the handle of his shooting-stick, he sat down on it, to contemplate the oozy green on the sides of the emptied lock and dabble one hand in the air. Ingenious things – locks! Why not locks in the insides of men and women, so that their passions could be dammed to the proper moment, then used, under control, for the main traffic of life, instead of pouring to waste over weirs and down rapids? The tongue of Fleur's dog licking his dabbled hand interrupted this somewhat philosophic reflection. Animals were too human nowadays, always wanting to have notice taken of them; only that afternoon he had seen Annette's black cat look up into the plaster face of his Naples Psyche, and mew faintly – wanting to be taken up into its lap, he supposed.

The lock-keeper's daughter came out to take some garments off a line. Women in the country seemed to do nothing but hang clothes on lines and take them off again! Soames watched her, neat-handed, neat-ankled, in neat light-blue print, with a face like a Botticelli – lots of faces like that in England! She would have a young man or perhaps two – and they would walk in that wood, and sit in damp places and all the rest of it, and imagine themselves happy, he shouldn't wonder; or she would get up behind him on one of those cycle things and go tearing about the country with her dress up to her knees. And her name would be Gladys or Doris, or what not! She saw him, and smiled. She had a full mouth that looked pretty when it smiled. Soames raised his hat slightly.

'Nice evening!' he said.

'Yes, sir.'

Very respectful.

'River's still high.'

'Yes, sir.'

Rather a pretty girl! Suppose he had been a lock-keeper, and Fleur had been a lock-keeper's daughter – hanging clothes on a line, and saying: 'Yes, sir!' Well, he would as soon be a lock-keeper as anything else in a humble walk of life – watching water go up and down, and living in that pretty cottage, with nothing to worry about, except – except his daughter! And he checked an impulse to say to the girl: 'Are you a good daughter?' Was there such a thing nowadays – a daughter that thought of you first, and herself after?

'These cuckoos!' he said, heavily.

'Yes, sir.'

She was taking a somewhat suggestive garment off the line now, and Soames lowered his eyes, he did not want to embarrass the girl – not that he saw any signs. Probably you couldn't embarrass a girl nowadays! And, rising, he closed the handle of his shooting-stick.

'Well, it'll keep fine, I shouldn't wonder.'

'Yes, sir.'

'Good evening.'

'Good evening, sir.'

Followed by the dog, he moved along towards home. Butter wouldn't melt in her mouth; but how would she talk to her young man? Humiliating to be old! On an evening like this, one should be young again, and walk in a wood with a girl like that; and all that had been faun-like in his nature pricked ears for a moment, licked lips, and with a shrug and a slight sense of shame, died down.

It had always been characteristic of Soames, who had his full share of the faun, to keep the fact carefully hidden. Like all his family, except, perhaps, his cousin George and his uncle Swithin, he was secretive in matters of sex; no Forsyte talked sex, or liked to hear others talk it; and when they felt its call, they gave no outward sign. Not the Puritan spirit, but a certain refinement in them forbade the subject, and where they got it from they did not know!

After his lonely dinner he lit his cigar and strolled out again. It was really warm for May, and still light enough for him to see his cows in the meadow beyond the river. They would soon be sheltering for the night, under that hawthorn hedge. And here came the swans, with their grey brood in tow; handsome birds, going to bed on the island!

The river was whitening; the dusk seemed held in the trees, waiting to spread and fly up into a sky just drained of sunset. Very peaceful, and a little eerie – the hour between! Those starlings made a racket – disagreeable beggars; there could be no real self-respect with such short tails! The swallows went by, taking 'night-caps' of gnats and early moths; and the poplars stood so still – just as if listening – that Soames put up his hand to feel for the breeze. Not a breath! And then, all at once – no swallows flying, no starlings; a chalky hue over river, over sky! The lights sprang up in the house. A night-flying beetle passed over him, booming. The dew was falling – he felt it; must go in. And, as he turned, quickly, dusk softened the trees, the sky, the river. And Soames thought: 'Hope to goodness there'll be no mysteries when she comes down tomorrow. I don't want to be worried!' Just she and the little chap; it might be so pleasant, if that old love trouble with its gnarled roots in the past and its bitter fruits in the future were not present, to cast a gloom....

He slept well, and next morning could settle to nothing but the arrangement of things already arranged. Several times he stopped dead in the middle of this task to listen for the car and remind himself that he must not fuss, or go asking things. No doubt she had seen young Jon again yesterday, but he must not ask.

He went up to his picture gallery and unhooked from the

wall a little Watteau, which he had once heard her admire. He took it downstairs and stood it on an easel in her bedroom – a young man in full plum-coloured skirts and lace ruffles, playing a tambourine to a young lady in blue, with a bare bosom, behind a pet lamb. Charming thing! She could take it away when she went, and hang it with the Fragonards and Chardin in her drawing-room. Standing by the double-poster, he bent down and sniffed at the bed-linen. Not quite as fragrant as it ought to be. That woman, Mrs Edger – his housekeeper – had forgotten the pot-pourri bags; he knew there would be something! And, going to a store closet, he took four little bags with tiny mauve ribbons from a shelf, and put them into the bed. He wandered thence into the bathroom. He didn't know whether she would like those salts – they were Annette's new speciality, and smelt too strong for *his* taste. Otherwise it seemed all right; the soap was 'Roger and Gallet', and the waste worked. All these new gadgets – half of them didn't; there was nothing like the old-fashioned thing that pulled up with a chain! Great change in washing during his lifetime. He couldn't quite remember pre-bathroom days; but he could well recall how his father used to say regularly: 'They never gave me a bath when I was a boy. First house of my own, I had one put in – people used to come and stare at it – in 1840. They tell me the doctors are against washing now; but I don't know.' James had been dead a quarter of a century, and the doctors had turned their coats several times since. Fact was, people enjoyed baths; so it didn't really matter what views the doctors took! Kit enjoyed them – some children didn't. And, leaving the bathroom, Soames stood in front of the flowers the gardener had brought in – among them, three special early roses. Roses were the fellow's forte, or rather his weak point – he cared for nothing else; that was the worst of people nowadays, they specialized so that there was no relativity between things, in spite of its being the fashionable philosophy, or so they told him. He took up a rose and sniffed at it deeply. So many different kinds now – he had lost track! In his young days one could tell them – La France, Maréchal Neil, and Gloire de Dijon – nothing else to speak of; you never heard of *them* now. And at this reminder of the mutability of flowers and the ingenuity of human beings, Soames felt slightly exhausted. There was no end to things!

She was late, too! That fellow Riggs – for he had left the car to bring her down, and had come by train himself – would have got punctured, of course; he was always getting punctured if there was any reason why he shouldn't. And for the next half-hour Soames fidgeted about so that he was deep in nothing in his picture gallery at the very top of the house and did not hear the car arrive. Fleur's voice roused him from thoughts of her.

'Hallo!' he said, peering down the stairs, 'where have *you* sprung from? I expected you an hour ago.'

'Yes, dear, we had to get some things on the way. How lovely it all looks! Kit's in the garden.'

'Ah!' said Soames, descending. 'Did you get a rest yester –' and he pulled up in front of her.

She bent her face forward for a kiss, and her eyes looked beyond him. Soames put his lips on the edge of her cheek-bone. She was away somewhere! And, as his lips mumbled her soft skin slightly, he thought: 'She's not thinking of me – why should she? She's young!'

PART TWO

Chapter One

SON OF SLEEPING DOVE

❦

WHETHER or not the character of Englishmen in general is based on chalk, it is undeniably present in the systems of our jockeys and trainers. Living for the most part on downs, drinking a good deal of water, and concerned with the joints of horses, they are almost professionally calcareous, and at times distinguished by bony noses and chins.

The chin of Greenwater, the retired jockey in charge of Val Dartie's stable, projected, as if in years of race-riding it had been bent on prolonging the efforts of his mounts and catching the judge's eye. His thin, commanding nose dominated a mask of brown skin and bone, his narrow brown eyes glowed slightly, his hair was smooth and brushed back; he was five feet seven inches in height, and long seasons, during which he had been afraid to eat, had laid a look of austerity over such natural liveliness, as may be observed in – say – a water-wagtail. A married man with two children, he was endeared to his family by the taciturnity of one who had been intimate with horses for thirty-five years. In his leisure hours he played the piccolo. No one in England was more reliable.

Val, who had picked him up on his retirement from the pigskin in 1921, thought him an even better judge of men than of horses, incapable of trusting them farther than he could see them, and that not very far. Just now it was particularly necessary to trust no one, for there was in the stable a two-year-old colt, Rondavel, by Kaffir out of Sleeping Dove, of whom so much was expected, that nothing whatever had been said about him. On the Monday of Ascot week Val was the more surprised, then, to hear his trainer remark:

'Mr Dartie, there was a son of a gun watching the gallop this morning.'

'The deuce there was!'

'Someone's been talking. When they come watching a little stable like this – something's up. If you take my advice, you'll send the colt to Ascot and let him run his chance on Thursday – won't do him any harm to smell a racecourse. We can ease him after, and bring him again for Goodwood.'

Aware of his trainer's conviction that the English race-horse, no less than the English man, liked a light preparation nowadays, Val answered:

'Afraid of overdoing him?'

'Well, he's fit now, and that's a fact. I had Sinnet shake him up this morning, and he just left 'em all standing. Fit to run for his life, he is; wish you'd been there.'

'Oho!' said Val, unlatching the door of the box. 'Well, my beauty?'

The Sleeping Dove colt turned his head, regarding his owner with a certain lustrous philosophy. A dark grey, with one white heel and a star, he stood glistening from his morning toilet. A good one! The straight hocks and ranginess of St Simon crosses in his background! Scope, and a rare shoulder for coming down a hill. Not exactly what you'd call a 'picture' – his lines didn't quite 'flow', but great character. Intelligent as a dog, and game as an otter! Val looked back at his trainer's intent face.

'All right, Greenwater. I'll tell the missus – we'll go in force. Who can you get to ride at such short notice?'

'Young Lamb.'

'Ah!' said Val, with a grin; 'you've got it all cut and dried, I see.'

Only on his way back to the house did he recollect a possible 'hole in the ballot' of secrecy. ... Three days after the General Strike collapsed, before Holly and young Jon and his wife had returned, he had been smoking a second pipe over his accounts, when the maid had announced:

'A gentleman to see you, sir.'

'What name?'

'Stainford, sir.'

Checking the impulse to say: 'And you left him in the hall!'
Val passed hurriedly into that part of the house.

His old college pal was contemplating a piece of plate over
the stone hearth.

'Hallo!' said Val.

His unemotional visitor turned round.

Less threadbare than in Green Street, as if something had restored his credit, his face had the same crow's-footed, contemptuous calm.

'Ah, Dartie!' he said. 'Joe Lightson, the bookie, told me you
had a stable down here. I thought I'd look you up on my way to
Brighton. How has your Sleeping Dove yearling turned out?'

'So-so,' said Val.

'When are you going to run him? I thought, perhaps you'd
like me to work your commission. I could do it much better than
the professionals.'

Really, the fellow's impudence was sublime!

'Thanks very much; but I hardly bet at all.'

'Is that possible? I say, Dartie, I didn't mean to bother you
again, but if you could let me have a "pony", it would be a great
boon.'

'Sorry, but I don't keep "ponies" about me down here.'

'A cheque —'

Cheque – not if he knew it!

'No,' said Val firmly. 'Have a drink?'

'Thanks very much!'

Pouring out the drink at the sideboard in the dining-room,
with one eye on the stilly figure of his guest, Val took a resolution.

'Look here, Stainford –' he began, then his heart failed him.
'How did you get here?'

'By car, from Horsham. And that reminds me. I haven't a
soū with me to pay for it.'

Val winced. There was something ineffably wretched about
the whole thing.

'Well,' he said, 'here's a fiver, if that's any use to you; but really I'm not game for any more.' And, with a sudden outburst, he added : 'I've never forgotten, you know, that I once lent you all I had at Oxford when I was deuced hard-pressed myself, and you never paid it back, though you came into shekels that very term.'

The well-shaped hand closed on the fiver; a bitter smile opened the thin lips.

'Oxford ! Another life ! Well, good-bye, Dartie – I'll get on; and thanks ! Hope you'll have a good season.'

He did not hold out his hand. Val watched his back, languid and slim, till it was out of sight. . . .

Yes ! That memory explained it ! Stainford must have picked up some gossip in the village – not likely that they would let a 'Sleeping Dove' lie ! It didn't much matter; since Holly would hardly let him bet at all. But Greenwater must look sharp after the colt. Plenty of straight men racing; but a lot of blackguards hanging about the sport. Queer how horses collected black-guards – most beautiful creatures God ever made ! But beauty was like that – look at the blackguards hanging round pretty women ! Well, he must let Holly know. They could stay, as usual, at old Warmson's Inn, on the river; from there it was only a fifteen-mile drive to the course. . . .

The 'Pouter Pigeon' stood back a little from the river Thames, on the Berkshire side, above an old-fashioned garden of roses, stocks, gillyflowers, poppies, phlox drummondi, sweet-williams. In the warm June weather the scents from that garden and from sweet-briar round the windows drifted into an old brick house painted cream-colour. Late Victorian service in Park Lane under James Forsyte, confirmed by a later marriage with Emily's maid Fifine, had induced in Warmson, indeed, such complete know-ledge of what was what, that no river inn had greater attrac-tions for those whose taste had survived modernity. Spotless linen, double beds warmed with copper pans, even in summer; cider, home-made from a large orchard, and matured in rum casks – the inn was a veritable feather-bed to all the senses. Prints of 'Mariage à la Mode', 'Rake's Progress', 'The Nightshirt Steeplechase', 'Run with the Quorn', and large functional groupings of Victorian celebrities with their names attached to blank faces on a key chart, decorated the walls. Its sanitation and its port were excellent. Pot-pourri lay in every bedroom, old pewter round the coffee-room, clean napkins at every meal. And a poor welcome was assured to earwigs, spiders, and the wrong sort of guest ... Warmson, one of those self-contained men who spread when they take inns, pervaded the house, with a red face set in small, grey whiskers, like a sun of just sufficient warmth.

To young Anne Forsyte all was 'just too lovely'. Never in her short life, confined to a large country, had she come across such defiant cosiness – the lush peace of the river, the songs of birds, the scents of flowers, the rustic arbour, the drifting lazy sky, now blue, now white, the friendly fat spaniel, and the feeling that tomorrow and tomorrow and tomorrow would for ever be the same as yesterday.

'It's a poem, Jon.'

'Slightly comic. When everything's slightly comic, you don't tire.'

'I'd certainly never tire of this.'

'We don't grow tragedy in England, Anne.'

'Why?'

'Well, tragedy's extreme; and we don't like extremes. Tragedy's dry and England's damp.'

She was leaning her elbows on the wall at the bottom of the garden, and, turning her chin a little in her hand, she looked round and up at him.

'Fleur Mont's father lives on the river, doesn't he? Is that far from here?'

'Mapledurham? I should think about ten miles.'

'I wonder if we shall see her at Ascot. I think she's lovely.'

'Yes,' said Jon.

'I wonder you didn't fall in love with her, Jon.'

'We were kids when I knew her.'

'I think she fell in love with you.'

'Why?'

'By the way she looks at you. ... She isn't in love with Mr Mont; she just likes him.'

'Oh!' said Jon.

Since in the coppice at Robin Hill Fleur had said 'Jon!' in so strange a voice, he had known queer moments. There was that in him which could have caught her, balanced there on the log with her hands on his shoulders, and gone straight back into the past with her. There was that in him which abhorred the notion. There was that in him which sat apart and made a song about them both, and that in him which said: 'Get to work and drop all these silly feelings!' He was, in fact, confused. The past, it seemed, did not die, as he had thought, but lived on beside the present, and sometimes, perhaps, became the future. Did one live for what one had not got? There was wrinkling in his soul, and feverish draughts crept about within him. The whole thing was on his conscience – for if Jon had anything, he had a conscience.

'When we get our place,' he said, 'we'll have all these old-fashioned flowers. They're much the sweetest!'

'Ah! Yes, do let's get a home, Jon. Only are you sure you want one? Wouldn't you like to travel and write poetry?'

'It's not a job. Besides, my verse isn't good enough. You want the mood of Hatteras J. Hopkins:

> Now, severed from my kind by my contempt,
> I live apart and beat my lonely drum.'

'I wish you weren't modest, Jon.'

'It's not modesty, Anne; it's a sense of the comic.'

'Couldn't we get a swim before dinner? It would be fine.'

'I don't know what the regulations are here.'

'Let's bathe first and find out afterwards.'

'All right. You go and change. I'll get this gate open.'

A fish splashed, a long white cloud brushed the poplar tops beyond the water. Just such an evening, six years ago, he had walked the towing-path with Fleur, had separated from her, waited to see her look back and wave her hand. He could see her still – that special grace, which gave her movements a lingering solidity within the memory. And now – it was Anne! And Anne in water was a dream! ...

Above the 'Pouter Pigeon' the sky was darkening; cars in their garages were still; no boats passed, only the water moved, and the river wind talked vaguely in the rushes and among the leaves. All within was cosy. On their backs lay Warmson and his Fifine, singing a little through their noses. By a bedside light Holly read *The Worst Journey in the World*, and beside her Val dreamed that he was trying to stroke a horse's nose, shortening under his hand to the size of a leopard's. And Anne slept with her eyes hidden against Jon's shoulder, and Jon lay staring at the crannies through which the moonlight eddied.

And in his stable at Ascot the son of Sleeping Dove, from home for the first time, pondered on the mutability of equine affairs, closing and opening his eyes and breathing without sound in the strawy dark above the black cat he had brought to bear him company.

Chapter Two

SOAMES GOES RACING

To Winifred Dartie the début of her son's Sleeping Dove colt on Ascot Cup Day seemed an occasion for the gathering of such members of her family as were permitted to go racing by the primary caution in their blood; but it was almost a shock to her when Fleur telephoned: 'Father's coming; he's never been to Ascot, and doesn't know that he wants to go.'

'Oh!' she said, 'it's too late to get any more Enclosure tickets. But Jack can see to him. What about Michael?'

'Michael can't come; he's deep in slums – got a new slogan: "Broader gutters!"'

'He's so good,' said Winifred. 'Let's go down early enough to lunch before racing, dear. I think we'd better drive.'

'Father's car is up – we'll call for you.'

'Delightful!' said Winifred. 'Has your father got a grey top hat? No? Oh! But he simply must wear one; they're all the go this year. Don't say anything, just get him one. He wears seven-and-a-quarter; and, dear, tell them to heat the hat and squash it in at the sides — otherwise they're always too round for him. And he needn't bring any money to speak of; Jack will do all our betting for us.'

Fleur thought that it was not likely father would have a bet; he had said he just wanted to see what the thing was like.

'He's so funny about betting,' said Winifred, 'like your grandfather.'

Not that it had been altogether funny in the case of James, who had been called on to pay the racing debts of Montague Dartie three times over.

With Soames and Winifred on the back seats, Fleur and Imogen on the front seats, and Jack Cardigan alongside Riggs, they took a circuitous road by way of Harrow to avoid the traffic, and emerged into it just at the point where for the first time it became thick. Soames, who had placed his grey top hat on his knee, put it on, and said:

'Just like Riggs!'

'Oh no, Uncle!' said Imogen. 'It's Jack's doing. When he's got to go through Eton, he always likes to go through Harrow first.'

'Oh! Ah!' said Soames. 'He was there. I should like Kit's name put down.'

'How nice!' said Imogen. 'Our boys will have left when he goes. You look so well in that hat, Uncle.'

Soames took it off again.

'White elephant,' he said. 'Can't think what made Fleur get me the thing!'

'My dear,' said Winifred, 'it'll last you for years. Jack's had his ever since the war. The great thing is to prevent the moth getting into it, between seasons. What a lot of cars! I do think it's wonderful that so many people should have the money in these days.'

The sight of so much money flowing down from town would have been more exhilarating to Soames if he had not been wondering where on earth they all got it. With the coal trade at a standstill and factories closing down all over the place, this display of wealth and fashion, however reassuring, seemed to him almost indecent.

Jack Cardigan, from his front seat, had been explaining a thing he called the 'tote'. It seemed to be a machine that did your betting for you. Jack Cardigan was a funny fellow; he made a life's business of sport; there wasn't another country that could have produced him! And, leaning forward, Soames said to Fleur:

'You're not got a draught there?'

She had been very silent all the way, and he knew why. Ten to one if young Jon Forsyte wouldn't be at Ascot! Twice over at Mapledurham he had noticed letters addressed by her to:

'Mrs Val Dartie,
Wansdon,
Sussex.'

She had seemed to him very fidgety or very listless all that fortnight. Once, when he had been talking to her about Kit's future, she had said: 'I don't think it matters, Dad, whatever one proposes – he'll dispose; parents don't count now: look at me!'

And he had looked at her, and left it at that.

He was still contemplating the back of her head when they drew into an enclosure and he was forced to expose his hat to the public gaze. What a crowd! Here, on the far side of the course, were rows of people all jammed together, who, so far as he could tell, would see nothing, and be damp one way or another throughout the afternoon. If that was pleasure! He followed the others across the course, in front of the grandstand. So those were 'the bookies'! Funny lot, with their names 'painted clearly on each', so that people could tell them apart, just as well, for they all seemed to him the same, with large necks and red faces, or scraggy necks and lean faces, one of each kind in every firm, like a couple of music-hall comedians. And, every now and then, in the pre-racing hush, one of them gave a sort of circular howl and looked hungrily at space. Funny fellows! They passed alongside the Royal Enclosure where bookmakers did not seem to be admitted. Numbers of grey top hats there! This was the place – he had heard – to see pretty women. He was looking for them when Winifred pressed his arm.

'Look, Soames – the Royal Procession!'

Thus required to gape at those horse-drawn carriages at which everybody else would be gaping, Soames averted his eyes, and became conscious that Winifred and he were alone!

'What's become of the others?' he said.

'Gone to the paddock, I expect.'

'What for?'

'To look at the horses, dear.'

Soames had forgotten the horses.

'Fancy driving up like that, at this time of day!' he muttered.

'I think it's so amusing!' said Winifred. 'Shall we go to the paddock, too?'

Soames, who had not intended to lose sight of his daughter, followed her towards whatever the paddock might be.

It was one of those days when nobody could tell whether it was going to rain, so that he was disappointed by the dresses and the women's looks. He saw nothing to equal his daughter and was about to make a disparaging remark when a voice behind him said:

'Look, Jon! There's Fleur Mont!'

Placing his foot on Winifred's, Soames stood still. There, and wearing a grey top hat, too, was that young chap between his wife and his sister. A memory of tea at Robin Hill with his cousin Jolyon, that boy's father, twenty-seven years ago, assailed Soames – and of how Holly and Val had come in and sat looking at him as if he were a new kind of bird. There they went, those three, into a ring of people who were staring at nothing so far as he could see. And there, close to them, were those other three, Jack Cardigan, Fleur and Imogen.

'My dear,' said Winifred, 'you *did* tread on my toe.'

'I didn't mean to,' muttered Soames. 'Come over to the other side – there's more room.'

It seemed horses were being led around; but it was at his

daughter that Soames wanted to gaze from behind Winifred's shoulder. She had not yet seen the young man, but was evidently looking for him – her eyes were hardly ever on the horses – no great wonder in that, perhaps, for they all seemed alike to Soames, shining and snakey, quiet as sheep, with boys holding on to their heads. Ah! A stab went through his chest, for Fleur had suddenly come to life; and, as suddenly, seemed to hide her resurrection even from herself! How still she stood – ever so still – gazing at that young fellow talking to his wife.

'That's the favourite, Soames. At least, Jack said he would be. What do you think of him?'

'Much like the others – got four legs.'

Winifred laughed. Soames was so amusing!

'Jack's moving; if we're going to have a bet, I think we'd better go back, dear. I know what I fancy.'

'I don't fancy anything,' said Soames. 'Weak-minded, I call it; as if they could tell one horse from another!'

'Oh! but you'd be surprised,' said Winifred; 'you must get Jack to –'

'No, thank you.'

He had seen Fleur move and join those three. But faithful to his resolve to show no sign, he walked glumly back into the grandstand. What a monstrous noise they were making now in the ring down there! And what a pack of people in this great stand! Up there, on the top of it, he could see what looked like half a dozen lunatics frantically gesticulating – some kind of signalling, he supposed. Suddenly, beyond the railings at the bottom of the lawn, a flash of colour passed. Horses – one, two, three; a dozen or more – all labelled wtih numbers, and with little bright men sitting on their necks like monkeys. Down they went – and soon they'd come back, he supposed; and a lot of money would change hands. And then they'd do it again, and the money would change back. And what satisfaction they all got out of it, he didn't know! There were men who went on like that all their lives, he believed – thousands of them: must be lots of time and money to waste in the country! What was it Timothy had said: 'Consols are going up!' They hadn't; on the contrary, they were down a point, at least, and would go lower before the Coal Strike was over. Jack Cardigan's voice said in his ear:

'What are you going to back, Uncle Soames?'

'How should I know?'

'You must back something, to give you an interest.'

'Put something on for Fleur, and leave me alone,' said Soames; 'I'm too old to begin.'

And, opening the handle of his racing-stick, he sat down on it. 'Going to rain,' he added gloomily. He sat there alone; Winifred and Imogen had joined Fleur down by the rails with Holly and her party – Fleur and that young man side by side. And he remembered how, when Bosinney had been hanging round Irene, he, as now, had made no sign, hoping against hope that by ignoring the depths beneath him he could walk upon the waters. Treacherously they had given way then and engulfed him; would they again – would they again? His lip twitched; and he put out his hand. A little drizzle fell on the back of it.

'They're off!'

Thank goodness – the racket had ceased! Funny change from din to hush. The whole thing funny – a lot of grown-up children! Somebody called out shrilly at the top of his voice – there was a laugh – then noise began swelling from the stand; heads were craning round him. 'The favourite wins!' 'Not he!' More noise; a thudding – a flashing past of colour! And Soames thought: 'Well, that's over!' Perhaps everything was like that really. A hush – a din – a flashing past – a hush! All life a race, a spectacle – only you couldn't see it! A venture and a paying-up! And beneath his new hat he passed his hand down over one flat cheek, and then the other. A paying-up! He didn't care who paid up, so long as it wasn't Fleur! But there it was – some debts could not be paid by proxy! What on earth was Nature about when she made the human heart!

The afternoon wore on, and he saw nothing of his daughter. It was as if she suspected his design of watching over her. There was the 'horse of the century' running in the Gold Cup, and he positively mustn't miss that — they said. So again Soames was led to the ring where the horses were moving round.

'That the animal?' he said, pointing to a tall mare, whom, by reason of two white ankles, he was able to distinguish from the others. Nobody answered him, and he perceived that he was separated from Winifred and the Cardigans by three persons, all looking at him with a certain curiosity.

'Here he comes!' said one of them. Soames turned his head. Oh! So *this* was the horse of the century, was it? — this bay fellow — same colour as the pair they used to drive in the Park Lane barouche. His father always had bays, because old Jolyon had browns, and Nicholas blacks, and Swithin greys, and Roger — he didn't remember what Roger used to have — something a bit eccentric — piebalds, he shouldn't wonder. Sometimes they would talk about horses, or, rather, about what they had given for them: Swithin had been a judge, or so he said — Soames had never believed it, he had never believed in Swithin at all. But he could perfectly well remember George being run away with by his pony in the Row, and pitched into a flower-bed — no one had ever been able to explain how; just like George, with his taste for the grotesque! He himself had never taken any interest in horses. Irene, of course, had loved riding — she would! She had never had any after she married him. ... A voice said:

'Well, what do you think of him, Uncle Soames?'

Val, with his confounded grin; Jack Cardigan, too, and a thin, brown-faced man with a nose and chin. Soames said guardedly:

'Nice enough nag.'

If they thought they were going to get a rise out of him!

'Think he'll stay, Val? It's the deuce of a journey.'

'He'll stay all right.'

'Got nothing to beat,' said the thin brown man.

'The Frenchman, Greenwater.'

'No class, Captain Cardigan. He's not all the horse they think him, but he can't lose today.'

'Well, I hope to God he beats the Frenchman; we want a cup or two left in the country.'

Something responded within Soames's breast. If it was against a Frenchman, he would do his best to help.

'Put me five pounds on him,' he said suddenly to Jack Cardigan.

'Good for you, Uncle Soames. He'll start about evens. See his head and his forehead and the way he's let down – lots of heart room. Not quite so good behind the saddle, but a great horse, I think.'

'Which is the Frenchman?' asked Soames. 'That! Oh! Ah! I don't like *him*. I want to see this race.'

Jack Cardigan gripped his arm – the fellow's fingers were like iron.

'You come along with me!' he said. Soames went, was put up higher than he had been yet, given Imogen's glasses – a present from himself – and left there. He was surprised to find how well and far he could see. What a lot of cars, and what a lot of people! 'The national pastime' – didn't they call it? Here came the horses walking past, each led by a man. Well! They were pretty creatures, no doubt! An English horse against a French horse – that gave the thing some meaning. He was glad Annette was still with her mother in France, otherwise she'd have been here with him. Now they were cantering past. Soames made a real effort to tell one from the other, but except for their numbers, they were so confoundedly alike. 'No,' he said to himself, 'I'll just watch those two, and that tall horse' – its name had appealed to him, Pons Asinorum. Rather painfully he got the colours of the three by heart and fixed his glasses on the wheeling group out there at the starting-point. As soon as they were off, however, all he could see was that one horse was in front of the others. Why had he gone to the trouble of learning the colours? On and on and on he watched them, worried because he could make nothing of it, and everybody else seemed making a good deal. Now they were round into the straight. 'The favourite's coming up!' 'Look at the Frenchman!' Soames could see the colours now. Those two! His hand shook a little and he dropped his glasses. Here they came – a regular ding-dong! Dash it – he wasn't – England wasn't! Yes, by George! No!

Yes! Entirely without approval his heart was beating painfully. 'Absurd!' he thought. 'The Frenchman!' 'No! the favourite wins! He wins!' Almost opposite the horse was shooting out. Good horse! Hooray! England for ever! Soames covered his mouth just in time to prevent the words escaping. Somebody said something to him. He paid no attention; and, carefully putting Imogen's glasses into their case, took off his grey hat and looked into it. There was nothing there except a faint discoloration of the buff leather where he had perspired.

Chapter Three

THE TWO-YEAR-OLDS

◄◄─►►

THE toilet of the two-year-olds was proceeding in the more unfrequented portions of the paddock.

'Come and see Rondavel saddled, Jon,' said Fleur.

And, when he looked back, she laughed.

'No, you've got Anne all day and all night. Come with me for a change.'

On the far side of the paddock the son of Sleeping Dove was holding high his intelligent head, and his bit was being gently jiggled, while Greenwater with his own hands adjusted the saddle.

'A race-horse has about the best time of anything on earth,' she heard Jon say. 'Look at his eye – wise, bright, not bored. Draft horses have a cynical, long-suffering look – race-horses never. He likes his job; that keeps him spirity.'

'Don't talk like a pamphlet, Jon. Did you expect to see me here?'

'Yes.'

'And it didn't keep you away? How brave!'

'Must you say that sort of thing?'

'What then? You notice, Jon, that a race-horse never stands

over at the knee; the reason is, of course, that he isn't old enough. By the way, there's one thing that spoils your raptures about them. They're not free agents.'

'Is anyone?'

How set and obstinate his face!

They joined Val, who said gloomily:

'D'you want to have anything on?'

'Do *you*, Jon?' said Fleur.

'Yes; a tenner.'

'So will I then. Twenty pounds between us, Val.'

Val sighed.

'Look at him! Ever see a two-year-old more self-contained? I tell you that youngster's going far. And I'm confined to a miserable "pony"! Damn!'

He left them and spoke to Greenwater.

'More self-contained,' said Fleur. 'Not a modern quality, is it, Jon?'

'Perhaps, underneath.'

'Oh! You've been in the backwoods too long. Francis, too, was wonderfully primitive; so, I suppose, is Anne. You should have tried New York, judging by their literature.'

'I don't judge by literature; I don't believe there's any relation between it and life.'

'Let's hope not, anyway. Where shall we see the race from?'

'The rails over there. It's the finish I care about. I don't see Anne.'

Fleur closed her lips suddenly on the words: 'Damn Anne.'

'We can't wait for them,' she said. 'The rails soon fill up.'

On the rails they were almost opposite the winning-post, and they stood there silent, in a queer sort of enmity – it seemed to Fleur.

'Here they come!'

Too quickly and too close to be properly taken in, the two-year-olds come cantering past.

'Rondavel goes well,' said Jon. 'And I like that brown.'

Fleur noted them languidly, too conscious of being alone with him – really alone, blocked off by strangers from any knowing eye. To savour that loneliness of so few minutes was tasking all her faculties. She slipped her hand through his arm, and forced her voice.

'I'm awfully worked up, Jon. He simply must win.'

Did he know that in focusing his glasses he left her hand uncaged?

'I can't make them out from here.' Then his arm recaged her hand against his side. Did he know? What did he know?

'They're off!'

Fleur pressed closer.

Silence – din – shouting of this name – that name! But pressure against him was all it meant to Fleur. Past they came, a flourishing flash of colour; but she saw nothing of it, for her eyes were closed.

'By Gosh!' she heard him say: 'He's won.'

'Oh, Jon!'

'I wonder what price we got?'

Fleur looked at him, a spot of red in each pale cheek, and her eyes very clear.

'Price? Did you really mean that, Jon?'

And, though he was behind her, following to the paddock she knew from the way his eyes were fixed on her, that he had not meant it.

They found their party reunited, all but Soames. Jack Cardigan was explaining that the price obtained was unaccountably short, since there was no stable money on to speak of; somebody must have known something; he seemed to think that this was extremely reprehensible.

'I suppose Uncle Soames hasn't been going for the gloves,' he said. 'Nobody's seen him since the Gold Cup. Wouldn't it be ripping if we found he'd kicked over and had a "monkey" on?'

Fleur said uneasily:

'I expect Father got tired and went to the car. We'd better go too, Auntie, and get away before the crowd.'

She turned to Anne. 'When shall we see you again?' She saw the girl look at Jon, and heard him say glumly:

'Oh! sometime.'

'Yes, we'll fix something up. Good-bye, my dear! Good-bye, Jon! Tell Val I'm very glad.' And, with a farewell nod, she led the way. Of a sort of rage in her heart she gave no sign, preparing normality for her father's eyes.

Soames, indeed, was in the car. Excitement over the Gold Cup – so contrary to his principles – had caused him to sit down in the stand. And there he had remained during the next two races, idly watching the throng below, and the horses going down fast and coming back faster. There, quietly, in the isolation suited to his spirit, he could, if not enjoy, at least browse on a scene strikingly unfamiliar to him. The national pastime – he knew that everybody had 'a bit on' something nowadays. For one person who ever went racing there were twenty –it seemed – who didn't, and yet knew at least enough to lose their money. You couldn't buy a paper, or have your hair cut, without being conscious of that. All over London, and the South, the Midlands and the North, in all classes, they were at it, supporting horses with their bobs and dollars and sovereigns. Most of them – he believed – had never seen a race-horse in their lives – hardly a horse of any sort; racing was a sort of religion, he supposed, and now that they were going to tax it, an orthodox religion. Some primeval nonconformity in the blood of Soames shuddered a little. He had no sympathy, of course, with those leather-lunged chaps down there under their queer hats, and their umbrellas, but the feeling that they were now made free of heaven – or at least of that synonym of heaven the modern state – ruffled him. It was almost as if England were facing realities at last – Very dangerous! They would be licensing prostitution next! To tax what were called vices was to admit that they were part of human nature. And though, like a Forsyte, he had long known them to be so, to admit it was, he felt, too French. To acknowledge the limitations of human nature was a sort of defeatism; when you once began that, you didn't know where you'd stop. Still, from all he could see, the tax would bring in a pretty penny – and pennies were badly needed; so, he didn't know, he wasn't sure. He wouldn't have done it himself, but he wasn't prepared to turn out the Government for having done it. They had recognized, too, no doubt, as he did, that gambling was the greatest make-weight there was against revolution; so long as a man could bet he had always a chance of getting something for nothing, and that desire was the real driving force behind any attempt to turn things upside down. Besides you had to move with the times uphill or downhill, and it was difficult to tell one from the other. The great thing was to avoid extremes.

From this measured reflection he was abruptly transferred to feelings unmeasured. Fleur and that young fellow were walking across there down to the rails! From under the brim of his grey hat he watched them painfully, reluctantly admitting that they made as pretty a couple as any there. They came to a stand on the rails – not talking; and to Soames, who, when moved, was exceptionally taciturn, this seemed a bad sign. Were things really going wrong, then – was passion forming within its still cocoon to fly on butterfly wings for its brief hour? What was going on within the silence of those two? The horses were passing now; and the grey, they said, was his own nephew's? Why did the fellow have horses? He had known how it would be when Fleur said he was going to Ascot. He regretted now having come. No, he didn't! Better to know what there was to be known. In the press of people to the rails he could no longer see more than the young man's grey hat, and the black-and-white covering of his daughter's head. For a minute the race diverted him: might as well see Val's horse well beaten. They said he thought a lot of it; and Soames thought the less of its chance for that. Here they came, all in a bunch – thundering great troop, and that grey – a handy colour, you couldn't miss it. Why, he was winning! Hang it – he had won!

'H'm!' he said aloud: 'that's my nephew's horse!'

Since nobody replied, he hoped they hadn't heard. And back went his eyes to those two on the rails. Yes, they were coming away silently – Fleur a little in front. Perhaps – perhaps, after all, they didn't get on, now! Must hope for the best. By George, but he felt tired! He would go to the car, and wait.

And there in the dusk of it he was sitting when they came, full of bubble and squeak – something very little-headed about

667

people when they'd won money. For they had all won money, it seemed!

'And you didn't back him, Uncle Soames?'

'I was thinking of other things,' said Soames, gazing at his daughter.

'We thought you were responsible for the shockin' bad price.'

'Why!' said Soames, gloomily. 'Did you expect me to bet against him?'

Jack Cardigan threw back his head and laughed.

'I don't see anything funny,' muttered Soames.

'Nor do I, Jack,' said Fleur. 'Why should Father know anything about racing?'

'I beg your pardon, sir, I'll tell you all about it.'

'God forbid!' said Soames.

'No, but it's rather queer. D'you remember that chap Stainford, who sneaked the Mater's snuff-box?'

'I do.'

'Well, it seems he paid Val a visit at Wansdon, and Val thinks he picked up the idea that Rondavel was a real good one. There was a chap watching the gallop last Monday. That's what decided them to run the colt today. They were going to wait for Goodwood. Too late, though; somebody's made a pot over him. We only got fours.'

It was all Greek to Soames, except that the languid ruffian Stainford had somehow been responsible a *second* time for bringing about a meeting between Fleur and Jon; for he knew from Winifred that Val and his *ménage* had gone to stay at Green Street during the strike on purpose to see Stainford. He wished to goodness he had called a policeman that day, and had the fellow shut up.

They were a long time getting out of the traffic – owing to the perversity of 'that chap Riggs', and did not reach South Square till seven o'clock. They were greeted by the news that Kit had a temperature. Mr Mont was with him. Fleur flew up. Having washed off his day, Soames settled himself in the 'parlour' to wait uneasily for their report. Fleur used to have temperatures, and not infrequently they led to something. If Kit's didn't lead to anything serious, it might be good for her – keeping her thoughts at home. He lay back in his chair opposite the Fragonard – a delicate thing, but with no soul in it, like all the works of that period – wondering why Fleur had changed the style of this room from Chinese to Louise Quinze. Just for the sake of change, he supposed. These young people had no continuity; some microbe in the blood – of the 'idle rich', and the 'idle poor', and everybody else, so far as he could see. Nobody could be got to stay anywhere – not even in their graves, judging by all those séances. If only people would attend quietly to their business, even to that of being dead! They had such an appetite for living, that they had no life. A beam of sunlight, smoky with dust-motes, came slanting in on to the wall before him – pretty thing, a beam of sunlight, but a terrible lot of dust, even in a room spick-and-spandy as this. And to think that a thing smaller than one of those dust-motes could give a child a temperature. He hoped to goodness Kit had nothing catching. And his mind went over the illnesses of childhood – mumps, measles, chicken-pox, whooping-cough. Fleur had caught them all, but never scarlet fever. And Soames began to fidget. Surely Kit was too young to have got scarlet fever. But nurses were so careless – you never knew! And suddenly he began to wish for Annette. What was she doing in France all this time? She was useful in illness; had some very good prescriptions. He *would* say that for the French – their doctors were clever when you could get them to take an interest. The stuff they had given him for his lumbago at Deauville had been first-rate. And after his visit the little doctor chap had said: 'I come for the money tomorrow!' or so it had sounded. It seemed he had meant: 'I come in the morning tomorrow.' They never could speak anything but their own confounded language, and looked aggrieved when you couldn't speak it yourself.

They had kept him a long time there without news before Michael came in.

'Well?'

'Well, sir, it looks uncommonly like measles.'

'H'm! Now, how on earth did he get that?'

'Nurse has no idea; but Kit's awfully sociable. If there's another in sight, he goes for him.'

'That's bad,' said Soames. 'You've got slums at the back here.'

'Ah!' said Michael: 'Slums to the right of us, slums to the left of us, slums to the front of us – how can you wonder?'

Soames stared. 'They're not notifiable,' he said, 'thank goodness!'

'Slums?'

'No. Measles.' If he had a dread, it was a notifiable disease, with the authorities poking their noses in, and having up the drains as likely as not. 'How's the little chap feeling?'

'Very sorry for himself.'

'In my opinion,' said Soames, 'there's a great deal more in fleas than they think. That dog of his may have picked up a measley flea. I wonder the doctors don't turn their attention to fleas.'

'I wonder they don't turn their attention to slums,' said Michael; 'that's where the fleas come from.'

Again Soames stared. Had his son-in-law got slums in his bonnet now? His manifestations of public spirit were very disturbing. Perhaps he'd been going round those places, and brought the flea in himself, or some infection or other.

'Have you sent for the doctor?'

'Yes; he'll be here any minute.'

'Is he any good, or just the ordinary cock-and-bull type?'

'The same man we had for Fleur.'

'Oh! Ah! I remember – too much manner, but shrewd. Doctors!'

There was silence in the polished room, while they waited for the bell to ring; and Soames brooded. Should he tell Michael about the afternoon? His mouth opened once, but nothing came out. Over and over again his son-in-law had surprised him by the view he took of things. And he only stared at Michael, who was gazing out of the window – queer face the young fellow had; plain, and yet attractive with those pointed ears and eyebrows running up on the outside – wasn't always thinking of himself like good-looking young men seemed to be. Good-

looking men were always selfish; got spoiled, he supposed. He
would give a penny for the young fellow's thoughts.

'Here he is!' said Michael, jumping up.

Soames was alone again. How long alone, he didn't know, for
he was tired, and, in spite of his concern, he dozed. The opening of the door roused him in time to assume anxiety before
Fleur spoke.

'It's almost certainly measles, Dad.'

'Oh!' said Soames, blankly. 'What about nursing?'

'Nurse and I, of course.'

'That'll mean you can't get about.'

'And aren't you glad?' her face seemed to say. How she read
his thoughts!

God knew he wasn't glad of anything that troubled her – and
yet –!

'Poor little chap!' he said, evasively: 'Your mother must
come back. I must try and find him something that'll take his
attention off.'

'Don't trouble, Dad; he's too feverish, poor darling. Dinner's
ready. I'm having mine upstairs.'

Soames rose and went up to her.

'Don't you be worrying,' he said. 'All children –'

Fleur put her arm out.

'Not too near, Dad. No, I won't worry.'

'Give him my love,' said Soames. 'He won't care for it.'

Fleur looked at him. Her lips smiled a very little. Her eyelids
winked twice. Then she turned and went out, and Soames
thought:

'She – poor little thing! I'm no use!' It was of her, not of his
grandson, that he thought.

Chapter Four

IN THE MEADS

⤛⬦⤜

THE Meads of St Augustine had, no doubt, once on a time been flowery, and burgesses had walked there of a Sunday, plucking nosegays. If there were a flower now, it would be found on the altar of the Reverend Hilary's church, or on Mrs Hilary's dining-table. The rest of a numerous population had heard of these unnatural products, and, indeed, seeing them occasionally in baskets, would utter the words: 'Aoh! Look at the luv-ly flahers!'

When Michael visited his uncle, according to promise, on Ascot Cup Day, he was ushered hurriedly into the presence of twenty little Augustinians on the point of being taken in a covered motor-van for a fortnight among flowers in a state of nature. His Aunt May was standing among them. She was a tall woman with bright brown shingled hair going grey, and the slightly rapt expression of one listening to music. Her smile was very sweet, and this, with the puzzled twitch of her delicate eyebrows, as who should say placidly: 'What next, I wonder?' endeared her to everyone. She had emerged from a rectory in Huntingdonshire, in the early years of the century, and had married Hilary at the age of twenty. He had kept her busy ever since. Her boys and girl were all at school now, so that in term time she had merely some hundreds of Augustinians for a family. Hilary was wont to say: 'May's a wonder. Now that she's had her hair off, she's got so much time on her hands that we're thinking of keeping guinea-pigs. If she'd only let me grow a beard, we could really get a move on.'

She greeted Michael with a nod and a twitch.

'Young London, my dear,' she said, privately, 'just off to Leatherhead. Rather sweet, aren't they?'

Michael, indeed, was surprised by the solidity and neatness of

672

the twenty young Augustinians. Judging by the streets from which they came and the mothers who were there to see them off, their families had evidently gone 'all out' to get them in condition for Leatherhead.

He stood grinning amiably, while they were ushered out on to the glowing pavement between the unrestrained appreciation of their mothers and sisters. Into the van, open only at the rear, they piled, with four young ladies to look after them.

'Four-and-twenty blackbirds baked in a pie,' murmured Michael.

His aunt laughed.

'Yes, poor little dears, won't they be hot! But aren't they good?' She lowered her voice. 'And d'you know what they'll say when they come back after their fortnight? "Oh! yes, we like it all very much, thank you, but it was rather slow. We like the streets better." Every year it's the same.'

'Then, what's the use of sending them, Aunt May?'

'It does them good physically; they look sturdy enough, but they aren't really strong. Besides, it seems so dreadful they should never see the country. Of course we country-bred folk, Michael, never can realize what London streets are to children — very nearly heaven, you know.'

The motor-van moved to an accompaniment of fluttered handkerchiefs and shrill cheering.

'The mothers love them to go,' said his aunt; 'it's kind of distinguished. Well, that's that! What would you like to see next? The street we've just bought, to gut and re-gut? Hilary'll be there with the architect.'

'Who owned the street?' asked Michael.

'He lived in Capri. I don't suppose he ever saw it. He died the other day, and we got it rather reasonably, considering how central we are, here. Sites are valuable.'

'Have you paid for it?'

'Oh! no.' Her eyebrows twitched. 'Post-dated a cheque on Providence.'

'Good Lord!'

'We had to have the street. It was such a chance. We've

paid the deposit, and we've got till September to get the rest.'

'How much?' said Michael.

'Thirty-two thousand.'

Michael gasped.

'Oh! We shall get it, dear, Hilary's wonderful in that way. Here's the street.'

It was a curving street of which, to Michael, slowly passing, each house seemed more dilapidated than the last. Grimy and defaced, with peeling plaster, broken rails and windows, and a look of having been abandoned to its fate – like some half-burnt-out ship – it hit the senses and the heart with its forlornness.

'What sort of people live here, Aunt May?'

'All sorts – three or four families to each house. Covent Garden workers, hawkers, girls in factories, out-of-works – every kind. The unmentionable insect abounds, Michael. The girls are wonderful – they keep their clothes in paper bags. Many of them turn out quite neat. If they didn't, of course, they'd get the sack, poor dears.'

'But is it possible,' said Michael, 'that people can *want* to go on living here?'

His aunt's brows became intricate.

'It isn't a question of want, my dear. It's a simple economic proposition. Where else *can* they live so cheaply? It's more than that, even; where else can they go at all, if they're turned out? The authorities demolished a street not long ago up there, and built that great block of workmen's flats; but the rents were prohibitive to the people who had been living in the street, and they simply melted away to other slums. Besides, you know, they don't like those barracky flats, and I don't wonder. They'd much rather have a little house, if they can; or the floor of a house if they can't. Or even a room. That's in the English nature, and it will be till they design workmen's dwellings better. The English like to live low down: I suppose because they always have. Oh! here's Hilary!'

Hilary Charwell, in a dark-grey Norfolk suit, a turn-down collar open at the neck, and no hat, was standing in the doorway of a house, talking to another spare man with a thin, and, to Michael, very pleasant face.

'Well, Michael, my boy, what think you of Slant Street? Each one of these houses is going to be gutted and made as bright as a new pin.'

'How long will they keep bright, Uncle Hilary?'

'Oh ! That's all right,' said Hilary, 'judging by our experiments so far. Give 'em a chance, and the people are only too glad to keep their houses clean. It's wonderful what they do, as it is. Come in and see, but don't touch the walls. May, you stay and talk to James. An Irish lady in here; we haven't many. Can I come in, Mrs Corrigan?'

'Sure an' ye can. Plased to see your rivirence, though ut's not tidy I am this mornin'.'

A broad woman, with grizzled black hair and brawny arms, had paused in whatever she was doing to a room inconceivably crowded and encrusted. Three people evidently slept in the big bed, and one in a cot; cooking seemed to go on at the ordinary small black hearth, over which, on a mantel-board, were the social trophies of a lifetime. Some clothes were hung on a line. The patched and greasy walls had no pictures.

'My nephew, Mr Michael Mont, Mrs Corrigan; he's a Member of Parliament.'

The lady put her arms akimbo.

'Indeed, an' is he, then?'

It was said with an infinite indulgence that went to Michael's heart. 'An is ut true your rivirence has bought the street? An' what would ye be doing with ut? Ye wont' be afther turning us out, I'm thinking.'

'Not for the world, Mrs Corrigan.'

'Well, an' I knew that. I said to them: "It's cleaning our in-sides he'll maybe doing, but he'll never be afther putting us out."'

'When the turn of this house comes, Mrs Corrigan — I hope before very long — we'll find you good lodgings till you can come back here to new walls and floors and ceilings, a good range, no more bugs, and proper washing arrangements.'

'Well, an' wouldn't that be the day I'd like to see!'

'You'll see it fast enough. Look, Michael, if I put my finger through there, the genuine article will stalk forth! It's you that can't knock holes in your walls, Mrs Corrigan.'

'An' that's the truth o' God,' replied Mrs Corrigan. 'The last time Corrigan knocked a peg in, 'twas terrible – the life there was in there!'

'Well, Mrs Corrigan, I'm delighted to see you looking so well. Good-morning, and tell Corrigan if his donkey wants a rest any time, there'll be room in our paddock. Will you be going hopping this year?'

'We will that,' replied Mrs Corrigan. 'Good-day to your rivirence; good-day, sorr!'

On the bare, decrepit landing Hilary Charwell said: 'Salt of the earth, Michael. But imagine living in that atmosphere! Luckily they're all "snoof".'

'What?' said Michael, taking deep breaths of the somewhat less complicated air.

'It's a portmanteau syllable for "Got no sense of smell to speak of". And wanted too. One says "deaf", "blind", "dumb" – why not "snoof"?'

'Excellent! How long do you reckon it'll take you to convert this street, Uncle Hilary?'

'About three years.'

'And how are you going to get the money?'

'Win, wangle, and scrounge it. In here there are three girls who serve in "Petter and Poplins". They're all out, of course. Neat, isn't it? See their paper bags?'

'I say, Uncle, would you blame a girl for doing anything to get out of a house like this?'

'No,' said the Reverend Hilary, 'I would not, and that's the truth o' God.'

'That's why I love you, Uncle Hilary. You restore my faith in the Church.'

'My dear boy,' said Hilary, 'the old Reformation was nothing to what's been going on in the Church lately. You wait and see! Though I confess a little wholesome Disestablishment would do us all no harm. Come and have lunch, and we'll talk about my slum conversion scheme. We'll bring James along.'

'You see,' he resumed, when they were seated in the Vicarage dining-room, 'there must be any amount of people who would be glad enough to lay out a small portion of their wealth at two-and-a-half per cent, with prospect of a rise to four as time went on, if they were certain that it meant the elimination of the slums. We've experimented and we find that we can put slum houses into proper living condition for their existing population at a mere fraction over the old rents, and pay two-and-a-half on our outlay. If we can do that here, it can be done in all slum centres, by private Slum Conversion Societies such as ours, working on the principle of not displacing the existing slum population. But what's wanted, of course, is money – a General Slum Conversion fund – Bonds at two per cent, with bonuses, repayable in twenty years, from which the Societies could draw funds as they need them for buying and converting slum property.'

'How will you repay the Bonds in twenty years?'

'Oh! Like the Government – by issuing more.'

'But,' said Michael, 'the local authorities have very wide powers, and much more chance of getting the money.'

Hilary shook his head.

'Wide powers, yes; but they're slow, Michael – the snail is a fast animal compared with them; besides, they only displace, because the rents they charge are too high. Also it's not in the English character, my dear. Somehow we don't like being "done for" by officials, or being answerable to them. There's lots of room, of course, for slum area treatment by Borough Councils, and they do lots of good work, but by themselves, they'll never scotch the evil. You want the human touch; you want a sense of humour, and faith; and that's a matter for private effort in every town where there are slums.'

'And who's going to start this general fund?' asked Michael, gazing at his aunt's eyebrows, which had begun to twitch.

'Well,' said Hilary, twinkling, 'I thought that might be where you came in. That's why I asked you down to-day, in fact.'

'The deuce!' said Michael almost leaping above the Irish stew on his plate.

'Exactly!' said his uncle; 'but couldn't you get together a committee of both Houses to issue an appeal? From the work we've done James can give you exact figures. They could see for themselves what's happened here. Surely, Michael, there must be ten just men who could be got to move in a matter like this —'

' "Ten Apostles," ' said Michael faintly.

'Well, but there's no real need to bring Christ in — nothing remote or sentimental; you could approach them from any angle. Old Sir Timothy Fanfield, for example, would love to have a "go" at slum landlordism. Then we've electrified all the kitchens so far, and mean to go on doing it — so you could get old Shropshire on that. Besides, there's no need to confine the committee to the two Houses — Sir Thomas Morsell, or, I should think, any of the big doctors, would come in; you could pinch a brace of bankers with Quaker blood in them; and there are always plenty of retired governor generals with their tongues out. Then if you could rope in a member of the Royal Family to head it — the trick would be done.'

'Poor Michael!' said his aunt's soft voice: 'Let him finish his stew, Hilary.'

But Michael had dropped his fork for good; he saw another kind of stew before him.

'The General Slum Conversion Fund,' went on Hilary, 'affiliating every Slum Conversion Society in being or to be, so long as it conforms to the principle of not displacing the present inhabitant. Don't you see what a pull that gives over the inhabitants? — we start them straight, and we jolly well see that they don't let their houses down again.'

'But can you?' said Michael.

'Ah! you've heard stories of baths being used for coal and vegetables, and all that. Take it from me, they're exaggerated, Michael. Anyway, that's where we private workers come in with a big advantage over municipal authorities. They have to drive, we try to lead.'

'Let me hot up your stew, dear?' said his aunt.

Michael refused. He perceived that it would need no hotting up! Another crusade! His Uncle Hilary had always fascinated him with his crusading blood – at the time of the Crusades the name had been Kéroual, and now spelt Charwell, was pronounced Cherwell, in accordance with the sound English custom of worrying foreigners.

'I'm not approaching you, Michael, with the inducement that you should make your name at this, because, after all, you're a gent!'

'Thank you!' murmured Michael; 'always glad of a kind word.'

'No. I'm suggesting that you ought to do something, considering your luck in life.'

'I quite agree,' said Michael humbly. 'The question seems to be: Is this the something?'

'It is, undoubtedly,' said his uncle, waving a salt-spoon on which was engraved the Charwell crest. 'What else can it be?'

'Did you ever hear of Foggartism, Uncle Hilary?'

'No; what's that?'

'My aunt!' said Michael.

'Some blanc-mange, dear?'

'Not you, Aunt May! But did you really never hear of it, Uncle Hilary?'

'Foggartism? Is it that fog-abating scheme one reads about?'

'It is not,' said Michael. 'Of course, you're sunk in misery and sin here. Still, it's almost too thick. You've heard of it, Aunt May?'

His aunt's eyebrows became intricate again.

'I think,' she said, 'I do remember hearing someone say it was balderdash!'

Michael groaned: 'And you, Mr James?'

'It's to do with the currency, isn't it?'

'And here,' said Michael, 'we have three intelligent, public-spirited persons, who've never heard of Foggartism – and I've heard of nothing else for over a year.'

'Well,' said Hilary, 'had you heard of my slum-conversion scheme?'

'Certainly not.'

'I think,' said his aunt, 'it would be an excellent thing if you'd smoke while I make the coffee. Now I do remember, Michael: your mother did say to me that she wished you would get over it. I'd forgotten the name. It had to do with taking town children away from their parents.'

'Partly,' said Michael, with gloom.

'You have to remember, dear, that the poorer people are, the more they cling to their children.'

'Vicarious joy in life,' put in Hilary.

'And the poorer children are, the more they cling to their gutters, as I was telling you.'

Michael buried his hands in his pockets.

'There is no good in me,' he said stonily. 'You've pitched on a stumer, Uncle Hilary.'

Both Hilary and his wife got up very quickly, and each put a hand on his shoulder.

'My dear boy!' said his aunt.

'God bless you!' said Hilary. 'Have a "gasper".'

'All right,' said Michael, grinning, 'it's wholesome.'

Whether or not it was the 'gasper' that was wholesome, he took and lighted it from his uncle's.

'What is the most pitiable sight in the world, Aunt May – I mean, next to seeing two people dance the Charleston?'

'The most pitiable sight?' said his aunt dreamily.

'Oh! I think – a rich man listening to a bad gramophone.'

'Wrong!' said Michael. 'The most pitiable sight in the world is a politician barking up the right tree. Behold him!'

'Look out, May! Your machine's boiling. She makes very good coffee, Michael – nothing like it for the grumps. Have some, and then James and I will show you the houses we've converted. James – come with me a moment.'

'Noted for his pertinacity,' muttered Michael, as they disappeared.

'Not only noted, Michael – dreaded.'

'Well, I would rather be Uncle Hilary than anybody I know.'

'He *is* rather a dear,' murmured his aunt. 'Coffee?'

'What does he really believe, Aunt May?'

'Well, he hardly has time for that.'

'Ah! that's the new hope of the Church. All the rest is just as much an attempt to improve on mathematics as Einstein's theory. Orthodox religion was devised for the cloister, Aunt May, and there aren't any cloisters left.'

'Religion,' said his aunt dreamily, 'used to burn a good many people, Michael, not in cloisters.'

'Quite so, when it emerged from cloisters, religion used to be red-hot politics, then it became caste feeling, and now it's a crossword puzzle – You don't solve *them* with your emotions.'

His aunt smiled.

'You have a dreadful way of putting things, my dear.'

'In our "suckles", Aunt May, we do nothing but put things – it destroys all motive power. But about this slum business: do you really advise me to have "a go"?'

'Not if you want a quiet life.'

'I don't know that I do. I did after the war; but not now. But, you see, I've tried Foggartism and everybody's too sane to look at it. I really can't afford to back another loser. Do you think there's a chance of getting a national move on?'

'Only a sporting chance, dear.'

'Would you take it up then, if you were me?'

'My dear, I'm prejudiced – Hilary's heart is so set on it; but it does seem to me that there's no other cause I'd so gladly fail in. Well, not exactly; but there really is nothing so important as giving our town dwellers decent living conditions.'

'It's rather like going over to the enemy,' muttered Michael. 'Our future oughtn't to be so bound up in the towns.'

'It *will* be, whatever's done. "A bird in the hand", and such a big bird, Michael. Ah! Here's Hilary!'

Hilary and his architect took Michael forth again into 'The Meads'. The afternoon had turned drizzly, and the dismal character of that flowerless quarter was more than ever apparent. Up street, down street, Hilary extolled the virtues of his parishioners. They drank, but not nearly so much as was natural in the circumstances; they were dirty, but he would be dirtier under their conditions. They didn't come to church – who on earth would expect them to? They assaulted their wives to an almost negligible extent; were extraordinarily good, and extremely unwise, to their children. They had the most marvellous faculty for living on what was not a living wage. They helped each other far better than those who could afford to; never saved a bean, having no beans to save, and took no thought for a morrow which might be worse than to-day. Institutions they abominated. They were no more moral than was natural in their overcrowded state. Of philosophy they had plenty, of religion none that he could speak of. Their amusements were cinemas, streets, gaspers, public houses, and Sunday papers. They liked a tune, and would dance if afforded a chance. They had their own brand of honesty which required special study. Unhappy? Not precisely, having given up a future state in this life or in that – realist to their encrusted finger-nails. English? Well, nearly all, and mostly London-born. A few country folk had come in young, and would never go out old.

'You'd like them, Michael; nobody who really knows them can help liking them. And now, my dear fellow, good-bye, and think it over. The hope of England lies in you young men. God bless you !'

And with these words in his ears, Michael went home, to find his little son sickening for measles.

Chapter Five

MEASLES

◄◄─►►

THE diagnosis of Kit's malady was soon verified, and Fleur went into purdah.

Soames's efforts to distract his grandson arrived almost every day. One had the ears of a rabbit, with the expression of a dog, another the tail of a mule detachable from the body of a lion, the third made a noise like many bees; the fourth, though designed for a waistcoat, could be pulled out tall. The procuring of these rarities, together with the choicest mandarine oranges, muscatel grapes, and honey that was not merely 'warranted' pure, occupied his mornings in town. He was staying at Green Street, whereto the news, judiciously wired, had brought Annette. Soames, who was not yet entirely resigned to a spiritual life, was genuinely glad to see her. But after one night, he felt he could spare her to Fleur. It would be a relief to feel that she had her mother with her. Perhaps by the end of her seclusion that young fellow would be out of her reach again. A domestic crisis like this might even put him out of her head. Soames was not philosopher enough to gauge in-round the significance of his daughter's yearnings. To one born in 1855 love was a purely individual passion, or if it wasn't it ought to be. It did not occur to him that Fleur's longing for Jon might also symbolize the craving in her blood for life, the whole of life, and nothing but life; that Jon had represented her first serious defeat in the struggle for the fullness of perfection; a defeat that might yet be wiped out. The modern soul, in the intricate turmoil of its sophistication, was to Soames a book which, if not sealed, had its pages still uncut. 'Crying for the moon' had become a principle when he was already much too old for principles. Recognition of the limits of human life and happiness was in his blood, and had certainly been fostered by his experience. Without, exactly, defining existence as 'making the best of a bad job', he would have contended that though, when you had almost everything, you had better ask for more, you must not fash yourself if you did not get it. The virus of a time-worn religion which had made the really irreligious old Forsytes say their prayers to the death, in a muddled belief that they would get something for them after death, still worked inhibitively in the blood of their prayerless offspring, Soames, so that, although fairly certain that he would get nothing after death, he still believed that he would not get everything before death. He lagged, in fact, behind the beliefs of a new century in whose 'make-up' resignation played no part — a century which either believed, with spiritualism, that there were plenty of chances to get things after death, or that, since one died for good and all, one must see to it that one had everything before death. Resignation! Soames would have denied, of course, that he believed in any such thing; and certainly he thought nothing too good for his daughter! And yet, somehow, he felt in his bones that there *was* a limit, and Fleur did not – this little distinction, established by the difference in their epochs, accounted for his inability to follow so much of her restive search.

Even in the nursery, grieved and discomforted by the feverish miseries of her little son, Fleur continued that search. Sitting beside his cot, while he tossed and murmured and said he was 'so 'ot', her spirit tossed and murmured and said so, too. Except that, by the doctor's orders, bathed and in changed garments, she went for an hour's walk each day, keeping to herself, she was entirely out of the world, so that the heart from which she suffered had no anodyne but that of watching and ministering to Kit. Michael was 'ever so sweet' to her; and the fact that she wanted another in his place could never have been guessed from her manner. Her resolution to give nothing away was as firm as ever, but it was a real relief not to encounter the gimletting affection of her father's eye. She wrote to no one; but she received from Jon a little letter of condolence.

> Wansdon.
> June 22

DEAR FLEUR,

We are so awfully sorry to hear of Kit's illness. It must be wretched for you. We do hope the poor little chap is over the painful part by now. I remember my measles as two beastly days, and then lots of th'ngs that felt nice and soothing all the way down. But I expect he's too young to be conscious of anything much except being thoroughly uncomfy.

Rondavel, they say, is all the better for his race. It was jolly seeing it together.

Good-bye, Fleur; with all sympathy,

> Your affectionate friend,
> JON

She kept it – as she had kept his old letters – but not like them, about her; there had come to be a dim, round mark on the 'affectionate friend' which looked as if it might have dropped from an eye; besides, Michael was liable to see her in any stage of costume. So she kept it in her jewel-box, whereof she alone had the key.

She read a good deal to Kit in those days, but still more to herself, conscious that of late she had fallen behind the forward march of literature, and seeking for distraction in an attempt to be up-to-date, rather than in the lives of characters too lively to be alive. They had so much soul, and that so contortionate that she could not even keep her attention on them long enough to discover why they were not alive. Michael brought her book after book, with the words: 'This is supposed to be clever,' or 'Here's the last Nazing,' or 'Our old friend Calvin again – not quite so near the ham-bone this time, but as near as makes no matter.' And she would sit with them on her lap and feel gradually that she knew enough to be able to say: 'Oh! yes, I've read *The Gorgons* – it's marvellously Proustian.' Or '*Love – the Chamelon?* – well, it's better than her *Green Cave*, but not up to *Souls in the Nude*.' Or, 'You *must* read *The Whirligig*, my dear – it gets quite marvellously nowhere.'

She held some converse with Annette, but of the guarded character, suitable between mothers and daughters after a certain age; directed, in fact, towards elucidating problems not unconnected with garb. The future – according to Annette – was dark. Were skirts to be longer or shorter by the autumn? If shorter, she herself would pay no attention; it might be all very well for Fleur, but she had reached the limit – at her age she would *not* go above the knee. As to the size of hats – again there was no definite indication. The most distinguished cocotte in Paris was said to be in favour of larger hats, but forces were working in the dark against her – motoring and Madame de Michel-Ange '*qui est toute pour la vieille cloche*'. Fleur wanted to know whether she had heard anything fresh about shingling. Annette, who was not yet shingled, but whose neck for a long time had trembled on the block, confessed herself '*désespérée*'. Everything now depended on the Basque cap. If woman took to them, shingling would stay; if not, hair might come in again.

In any case, the new tint would be pure gold; '*Et cela sera impossible. Ton père aurait une apoplexie.*' In any case, Annette feared that she was condemned to long hair till the day of judgement. Perhaps, the good God would give her a good mark for it.

'If you want to shingle, Mother, I should. It's just father's conservatism – he doesn't really know what he likes. It would be a new sensation for him.'

Annette grimaced. '*Ma chère; je n'en sais rien.* Your father is capable of anything.'

The man 'capable of anything' came every afternoon for half an hour, and would remain seated before the Fragonard, catechising Michael or Annette, and then say, rather suddenly:

'Well, give my love to Fleur; I'm glad the little chap's better!' Or: 'That pain he's got will be wind, I expect. But I should have what's-his-name see to it. Give my love to Fleur.' And in the hall he would stand a moment by the coat-sarcophagus, listening. Then, adjusting his hat, he would murmur what sounded like: 'Well, there it is!' or: 'She doesn't get enough air,' and go out.

And from the nursery window Fleur would see him, departing at his glum and measured gait, with a compunctious relief. Poor old Dad! Not his fault that he symbolized for her just now the glum and measured paces of domestic virtue. Soames's hope, indeed, that enforced domesticity might cure her, was not being borne out. After the first two or three anxious days, while Kit's temperature was still high, it worked to opposite ends. Her feeling for Jon, in which now was an element of sexual passion, lacking before her marriage, grew, as all such feelings grow, without air and exercise for the body and interest for the mind. It flourished like a plant transferred into a hot-house. The sense of having been defrauded fermented in her soul. Were they never to eat of the golden apple – she and Jon? Was it to hang there, always out of reach – amid dark, lustrous leaves, quite unlike an apple tree's? She took out her old water-colour box – long now since it had seen the light – and coloured a fantastic tree with large golden fruits.

Michael caught her at it.

'That's jolly good,' he said. 'You ought to keep up your water-colours, old thing.'

Rigid, as if listening for something behind the words, Fleur answered: 'Sheer idleness!'

'What's the fruit?'

Fleur laughed.

'Exactly! But this is the soul of a fruit-tree, Michael – not its body!'

'I might have known,' said Michael ruefully. 'Anyway, may I have it for my study when it's done? It's got real feeling.'

Fleur felt a queer gratitude. 'Shall I label it "The Uneatable Fruit"?'

'Certainly not – it looks highly luscious; you'd have to eat it over a basin, though, like a mango.'

Fleur laughed again.

'Steward!' she said. And, to Michael bending down to kiss her, she inclined her cheek. At least he should guess nothing of her feelings. And indeed, the French blood in her never ran cold at one of whom she was fond but did not love; the bitter spice which tinctured the blood of most of the Forsytes preserved the jest of her position. She was still the not unhappy wife of a good comrade and best of fellows, who, whatever she did herself, would never do anything ungenerous or mean. Fastidious recoilings from unloved husbands of which she read in old-fashioned novels, and of which she knew her father's first wife had been so guilty, seemed to her rather ludicrous. Promiscuity was in the air; a fidelity of the spirit so logical that it extended to the motions of the body, was paleolithic, or at least Victorian and 'middle class'. Fullness of life could never be reached on those lines. And yet the frank paganism, advocated by certain masters of French and English literature, was also debarred from Fleur, by its austerely logical habit of going the whole hog. There wasn't enough necessary virus in her blood, no sex mania about Fleur; indeed, hereunto, that obsession had hardly come her way at all. But now – new was the feeling, as well as old, that she had for Jon; and the days went by in scheming how, when she was free again, she could see him and hear his voice and touch him as she had touched him by the enclosure rails while the horses went flashing by.

Chapter Six

FORMING A COMMITTEE

◄◄·►►

IN the meantime Michael was not so unconscious as she thought, for when two people live together, and one of them is still in love, he senses change as a springbok will scent drought. Memories of that lunch, and of his visit to June, were still unpleasantly green. In his public life – that excellent anodyne for its private counterpart – he sought distraction, and made up his mind to go 'all out' for his Uncle Hilary's slum-conversion scheme. Having amassed the needed literature, he began considering to whom he should go first, well aware that public bodies are centrifugal. Round what fine figure of a public man should he form his committee? Sir Timothy Fanfield and the Marquess of Shropshire would come in usefully enough later, but, though well known for their hobbies, they 'cut no ice' with the general public. A certain magnetism was needed. There was none in any banker he could think of, less in any lawyer or cleric, and no reforming soldier could be otherwise than discredited, until he had carried his reforms, by which time he would be dead. He would have liked an admiral, but they were all out of reach. Retired Prime Ministers were in too lively request, besides being tarred with the brush of Party; and literary idols would be too old, too busy with themselves, too lazy, or too erratic. There remained doctors, business men, governor-generals, dukes, and newspaper proprietors. It was at this point that he consulted his father.

Sir Lawrence, who had also been coming to South Square almost daily during Kit's illness, focused the problem with his eye-glass, and said nothing for quite two minutes.

'What do you mean by magnetism, Michael? The rays of a setting or of a rising sun?'

'Both, if possible, Dad.'

'Difficult,' said his progenitor, 'difficult. One thing's certain – you can't afford cleverness.'

'How?'

'The public have suffered from it too much. Besides, we don't really like it in this country, Michael. Character, my dear, character!'

Michael groaned.

'Yes, I know,' said Sir Lawrence, 'awfully out of date with you young folk.' Then raising his loose eyebrow abruptly so that his eye-glass fell on to the problem, he added: 'Eureka! Wilfred Bentworth! The very man – last of the squires – re-forming the slums. It's what you'd call a stunt.'

'Old Bentworth?' repeated Michael dubiously.

'He's only my age – sixty-eight, and got nothing to do with politics.'

'But isn't he stupid?'

'There speaks your modern! Rather broad in the beam, and looking a little like a butler with a moustache, but – stupid? No. Refused a peerage three times. Think of the effect of that on the public!'

'Wilfred Bentworth? I should never have thought of him – always looked on him as the professional honest man,' murmured Michael.

'But he *is* honest!'

'Yes, but when he speaks, he always alludes to it.'

'That's true,' said Sir Lawrence, 'but one must have a defect. He's got twenty thousand acres, and knows all about fatting stock. He's on a railway board; he's the figurehead of his county's cricket, and chairman of a big hospital. Everybody knows him. He has Royalty to shoot; goes back to Saxon times; and is the nearest thing to John Bull left. In any other country he'd frighten the life out of any scheme, but in England – well, if you can get him, Michael, your job's half done.'

Michael looked quizzically at his parent. Did Bart quite

understand the England of to-day? His mind roved hurriedly over the fields of public life. By George! He did!

'How shall I approach him, Dad? Will you come on the committee yourself? You know him; and we could go together.'

'If you'd really like to have me,' said Sir Làwrence, almost wistfully, 'I will. It's time I did some work again.'

'Splendid! I think I see your point about Bentworth. Beyond suspicion – has too much already to have anything to gain, and isn't clever enough to take in anyone if he wanted to.'

Sir Lawrence nodded. 'Add his appearance; that counts tremendously in a people that have given up the land as a bad job. We still love to think of beef. It accounts for a good many of our modern leaderships. A people that's got away from its base, and is drifting after it knows not what, wants beam, beef, beer – or at least port – in its leaders. There's something pathetic about that, Michael. What's to-day – Thursday? This'll be Bentworth's board day. Shall we strike while the iron's hot? We'll very likely catch him at Burton's.'

'Good!' said Michael, and they set forth.

'This club,' murmured Sir Lawrence, as they were going up the steps of Burton's Club, 'is confined to travellers, and I don't suppose Bentworth's ever travelled a yard. That shows how respected he is. No, I'm wronging him. I remember he commanded his yeomanry in the Boer War. "The Squire" in the club, Smileman?'

'Yes, Sir Lawrence; just come in.'

The 'last of the squires' was, indeed, in front of the tape. His rosy face, with clipped white moustache, and hard, little, white whiskers, was held as if the news had come to him, not he to the news. Banks might inflate and Governments fall, wars break out and strikes collapse, but there would be no bending of that considerable waist, no flickering in the steady blue stare from under eyebrows a little raised at their outer ends. Rather bald, and clipped in what hair was left, never did man look more perfectly shaved; and the moustache ending exactly where the lips ended, gave an extreme firmness to the general good humour of an open-air face.

Looking from him to his own father – thin, quick, twisting, dark, as full of whims as a bog is of snipe – Michael was impressed. A whim, to Wilfred Bentworth, would be strange fowl indeed! 'How ever he's managed to keep out of politics,' thought Michael, 'I can't conceive.'

' "Squire" – my son – a sucking statesman. We've come to ask you to lead a forlorn hope. Don't smile! You're "for it", as they say in this Bonzoid age. We propose to shelter ourselves behind you in the breach.'

'Eh! What? Sit down! What's all this?'

'It's a matter of the slums, "if you know what I mean," as the lady said. But go ahead, Michael!'

Michael went ahead. Having developed his uncle's thesis and cited certain figures, he embroidered them with as much picturesque detail as he could remember, feeling rather like a fly attacking the flanks of an ox and watching his tail.

'When you drive a nail into the walls, sir,' he ended, 'things come out.'

'Good God!' said the squire suddenly. 'Good God!'

'One doubts the "good", there,' put in Sir Lawrence.

The squire stared.

'Irreverent beggar,' he said. 'I don't know Charwell, they say he's cracked.'

'Hardly that,' murmured Sir Lawrence; 'merely unusual, like most members of really old families.'

The early English specimen in the chair before him twinkled.

'The Charwells, you know,' went on Sir Lawrence, 'were hoary when that rascally lawyer, the first Mont, founded us under James the First.'

'Oh!' said the squire. 'Are you one of *his* precious creations? I didn't know.'

'You're not familiar with the slums, sir?' said Michael, feeling that they must not wander in the mazes of descent.

'What! No. Ought to be, I suppose. Poor devils!'

'It's not so much,' said Michael, cunningly, 'the humanitarian side, as the deterioration of stock, which is so serious.'

'M'm?' said the squire. 'Do you know anything about stock-breeding?'

Michael shook his head.

'Well, you can take it from me that it's nearly all heredity. You could fat a slum population, but you can't change their character!'

'I don't think there's anything very wrong with their character,' said Michael. 'The children are predominantly fair, which means, I suppose that they've still got the Anglo-Saxon qualities.'

He saw his father cock an eye. 'Quite the diplomat!' he seemed saying.

'Whom have you got in mind for this committee?' asked the squire, abruptly.

'My father,' said Michael; 'and we'd thought of the Marquess of Shropshire –'

'Very long in the tooth.'

'But very spry,' said Sir Lawrence. 'Still game to electrify the world.'

'Who else?'

'Sir Timothy Fanfield –'

'That fire-eating old buffer! Yes?'

'Sir Thomas Morsell –'

'M'm!'

Michael hurried on: 'Or any other medical man you thought better of, sir.'

'There are none. Are you sure about the bugs?'

'Absolutely!'

'Well, I should have to see Charwell. I'm told he can gammon the hind-leg off a donkey.'

'Hilary's a good fellow,' put in Sir Lawrence; 'a really good fellow, "squire".'

'Well, Mont, if I take to him, I'll come in. I don't like vermin.'

'A great national movement, sir,' began Michael, 'and nobody –'

The squire shook his head.

'Don't make any mistake,' he said. 'May get a few pounds,

perhaps – get rid of a few bugs; but national movements – no such things in this country.' . . .

'Stout fellow,' said Sir Lawrence when they were going down the steps again; 'never been enthusiastic in his life. He'll make a splendid chairman. I think we've got him, Michael. You played your bugs well. We'd better try the Marquess next. Even a duke will serve under Bentworth, they know he's of older family than themselves, and there's something about him.'

'Yes, what is it?'

'Well, he isn't thinking about himself; he never gets into the air; and he doesn't give a damn for anyone or anything.'

'There must be something more than that,' said Michael.

'Well, there is. The fact is, he thinks as England really thinks, and not as it thinks it thinks.'

'By Jove!' said Michael. '"Some" diagnosis! Shall we dine, sir?'

'Yes, let's go to the Parthenaeum! When they made me a member there, I used to think I should never go in, but d'you know, I use it quite a lot. It's more like the East than anything else in London. A Yogi could ask for nothing better. I go in and I sit in a trance until it's time for me to come out again. There's no vulgar material comfort. The prevailing colour is that of the Ganges. And there's more inaccessible wisdom in the place than you could find anywhere else in the West. We'll have the club dinner. It's calculated to moderate all transports. Lunch, of course, you can't get if you've a friend with you. One must draw the line somewhere at hospitality.'

'Now,' he resumed, when they had finished moderating their transports, 'let's go and see the Marquess! I haven't set eyes on the old boy since that Marjorie Ferrar affair. We'll hope he hasn't got gout . . .'

In Curzon Street, they found that the Marquess had finished dinner and gone back to his study.

'Don't wake him if he's asleep,' said Sir Lawrence.

'His lordship is never asleep, Sir Lawrence.'

He was writing when they were ushered in, and stopped to peer at them round the corner of his bureau.

'Ah, young Mont!' he said. 'How pleasant!' Then paused rather abruptly. 'Nothing to do with my granddaughter, I trust?'

'Far from it, Marquess. We just want your help in a public work on behalf of the humble. It's a slum proposition, as the Yanks say.'

The Marquess shook his head.

'I don't like interfering with the humble; the humbler people are, the more one ought to consider their feelings.'

'We're absolutely with you there, sir; but let my son explain.'

'Sit down, then.' And the Marquess rose, placed his foot on his chair, and, leaning his elbow on his knee, inclined his head to one side. For the second time that evening Michael plunged into explanation.

'Bentworth?' said the Marquess. 'His shorthorns are good; a solid fellow, but behind the times.'

'That's why we want you, Marquess.'

'My dear young Mont, I'm too old.'

'It's precisely because you're so young that we came to you.'

'Frankly, sir,' said Michael, 'we thought you'd like to be on the committee of appeal, because in my uncle's policy there's electrification of the kitchens; we must have someone who's an authority on that and keep it to the fore.'

'Ah!' said the Marquess. 'Hilary Charwell – I once heard him preach in St Paul's – most amusing! What do the slum-dwellers say to electrification?'

'Nothing till it's done, of course, but once it's done, it's everything to them.'

'H'm!' said the Marquess. 'H'm! It would appear that there are no flies on your uncle.'

'We hope' pursued Michael, 'that, with electrification, there will soon be no flies on anything else.'

The Marquess nodded. 'It's the right end of the stick. I'll think of it. My trouble is that I've no money; and I don't like appealing to others without putting down something substantial myself.'

The two Monts looked at each other; the excuse was patent, and they had not foreseen it.

'I suppose,' went on the Marquess, 'you don't know anyone who would buy some lace – *point de Venise*, the real stuff? Or,' he added, 'I've a Morland –'

'Have you?' cried Michael. 'My father-in-law was saying only the other day that he wanted a Morland.'

'Has he a good home for it?' said the Marquess, rather wistfully. 'It's a white pony.'

'Oh, yes, sir; he's a real collector.'

'Any chance of its going to the nation, in time?'

'Quite a good chance, I think.'

'Well, perhaps he'd come and look at it. It's never changed hands so far. If he would give me the market price, whatever that may be, it might solve the problem.'

'That's frightfully good of you.'

'Not at all,' said the Marquess. 'I believe in electricity, and I detest smoke; this seems a movement in the right direction. It's a Mr Forsyte, I think. There was a case – my granddaughter; but that's a past matter. I trust you're friends again?'

'Yes, sir; I saw her about a fortnight ago, and it was quite O.K.'

'Nothing lasts with you modern young people,' said the Marquess; 'the younger generation seems to have forgotten the war already. Is that good, I wonder? What do *you* say, Mont?'

' "*Tout casse, tout passe,*" Marquess.'

'Oh! I don't complain,' said the Marquess; 'rather the contrary. By the way – on this committee you'll want a new man with plenty of money.'

'Can you suggest one?'

'My next-door neighbour – a man called Montross – I think his real name is shorter – might possibly serve. He's made millions, I believe, out of the elastic band – has some patent for making them last only just long enough. I see him sometimes gazing longingly at me – I don't use them, you know. Perhaps if you mention my name. He has a wife, and no title at present. I should imagine he might be looking for a public work.'

'He sounds,' said Sir Lawrence, 'the very man. Do you think we might venture now?'

'Try!' said the Marquess, 'try. A domestic character, I'm told. It's no use doing things by halves; an immense amount of money will be wanted if we are to electrify any considerable number of kitchens. A man who would help substantially towards that would earn his knighthood much better than most people.'

'I agree,' said Sir Lawrence; 'a real public service. I suppose we mustn't dangle the knighthood?'

The Marquess shook the head that was resting on his hand.

'In these days – no,' he said. 'Just the names of his colleagues. We can hardly hope that he'll take an interest in the thing for itself.'

'Well, thank you ever so much. We'll let you know whether Wilfred Bentworth will take the chair, and how we progress generally.'

The Marquess took his foot down and inclined his head at Michael.

'I like to see young politicians interesting themselves in the future of England, because, in fact, no amount of politics will prevent her having one. By the way, have you had your own kitchen electrified?'

'My wife and I are thinking of it, sir.'

'Don't think! said the Marquess. 'Have it done!'

'We certainly shall, now.'

'We must strike while the strike is on,' said the Marquess. 'If there is anything shorter than the public's memory, I am not aware of it.'

'Phew!' said Sir Lawrence, on the next doorstep; 'the old boy's spryer than ever. I take it we may assume that the name here was originally Moss. If so, the question is: "Have we the wits for this job?"'

And, in some doubt, they scrutinized the mansion before them.

'We had better be perfectly straightforward,' said Michael. 'Dwell on the slums, mention the names we hope to get, and leave the rest to him.'

'I think,' said his father, 'we had better say "got", not "hope to get".'

'The moment we mention the names, Dad, he'll know we're after his dibs.'

'He'll know that in any case, my boy.'

'I suppose there's no doubt about the dibs?'

'"Montross, Ltd !" They're not confined to elastic bands.'

'I should like to make a perfectly plain appeal to his generosity, Dad. There's a lot of generosity in that blood, you know.'

'We can't stand just here, Michael, discussing the make-up of the chosen. Ring the bell !'

Michael rang.

'Mr Montross at home? Thank you. Will you give him these cards, and ask if we might see him for a moment?'

The room into which they were ushered was evidently accustomed to that sort of thing, for, while there was nothing that anyone could take away, there were chairs in which it was possible to be quite comfortable, and some valuable but large pictures and busts.

Sir Lawrence was examining a bust, and Michael a picture, when the door was opened, and a voice said : 'Yes, gentlemen?'

Mr Montross was of short stature, and somewhat like a thin walrus who had once been dark but had gone grey; his features were slightly aquiline, he had melancholy brown eyes, and big drooping grizzly moustaches and eyebrows.

'We were advised to come to you, sir,' began Michael at once, 'by your neighbour, the Marquess of Shropshire. We're trying to form a committee to issue an appeal for a national fund to convert the slums.' And for the third time he plunged into detail.

'And why do you come to *me*, gentlemen?' said Mr Montross, when he had finished.

Michael subdued a stammer.

'Because of your wealth, sir,' he said, simply.

'Good !' said Mr Montross. 'You see, I began in the slums, Mr Mont – is it? – yes, Mr Mont – I began there – I know a lot about those people, you know. I thought perhaps you came to me because of that.'

'Splendid, sir,' said Michael, 'but of course we hadn't an idea.'

697

'Well, those people are born without a future.'

'That's just what we're out to rectify, sir.'

'Take them away from their streets and put them in a new country, then – perhaps; but leave them in the streets –' Mr Montross shook his head. 'I know them, you see, Mr Mont; if these people thought about the future, they could not go on living. And if you do not think about the future, you cannot have one.'

'How about yourself?' said Sir Lawrence.

Mr Montross turned his gaze from Michael to the cards in his hand, then raised his melancholy eyes.

'Sir Lawrence Mont, isn't it? I am a Jew – that is different. A Jew will rise from any beginnings, if he is a real Jew. The reason the Polish and the Russian Jews do not rise so easily you can see from their faces – they have too much Slav or Mongol blood. The pure Jew like me rises.'

Sir Lawrence and Michael exchanged a glance. 'We like this fellow,' it seemed to say.

'I was a poor boy in a bad slum,' went on Mr Montross, intercepting the glance, 'and I am now – well, a millionaire; but I have not become that, you know, by throwing away my money. I like to help people that will help themselves.'

'Then,' said Michael, with a sigh, 'there's nothing in this scheme that appeals to you, sir?'

'I will ask my wife,' answered Mr Montross, also with a sigh. 'Good-night, gentlemen. Let me write to you.'

The two Monts moved slowly towards Mount Street in the last of the twilight.

'Well?' said Michael.

Sir Lawrence cocked his eyebrow.

'An honest man,' he said: 'it's fortunate for us he has a wife.'

'You mean – ?'

'The potential Lady Montross will bring him in. There was no other reason why he should ask her. That makes four, and Sir Timothy's a "sitter"; slum landlords are his *bêtes noires*. We only want three more. A bishop one can always get, but I've forgotten which it is for the moment; we *must* have a big doctor, and we ought to have a banker, but perhaps your uncle, Lionel Charwell, will do; he knows all about the shady side of finance in the courts, and we could make Alison work for us. And now, my dear, good-night! I don't know when I've felt more tired.'

They parted at the corner, and Michael walked towards Westminster. He passed under the spikes of Buckingham Palace Gardens, and along the stables leading to Victoria Street. All this part had some very nice slums, though of late he knew the authorities had been 'going for them'. He passed an area where they had 'gone' for them to the extent of pulling down a congery of old houses. Michael stared up at the remnants of walls mosaicked by the unstripped wallpapers. What had happened to the tribe out-driven from these ruins; whereto had they taken the tragic lives of which they made such cheerful comedy? He came to the broad river of Victoria Street and crossed it, and, taking a route that he knew was to be avoided, he was soon where women encrusted with age sat on doorsteps for a breath of air, and little alleys led off to unplumbed depths. Michael plumbed them in fancy, not in fact. He stood quite a while at the end of one, trying to imagine what it must be like to live there. Not succeeding, he walked briskly on, and turned into his own Square, and to his own habitat with its bay-treed tubs, its Danish roof, and almost hopeless cleanliness. And he suffered from the feeling which besets those who are sensitive about their luck.

'Fleur would say,' he thought, perching on the coat-sarcophagus, for he, too, was tired, 'that those people having no aesthetic sense and no tradition to wash up to, are at least as happy as we are. She'd say that they get as much pleasure out of living from hand to mouth (and not too much mouth), as we do from baths, jazz, poetry and cocktails; and she's generally right.' Only, what a confession of defeat! If that were really so, to what end were they all dancing? If life with bugs and flies were as good as life without bugs and flies, why Keating's powder and all the other aspirations of the poets? Blake's New Jerusalem was, surely, based on Keating, and Keating was based on a sensitive skin. To say, then, that civilization was skin-deep, wasn't cynical at all. People possibly had souls, but they certainly had skins, and progress was real only if thought of in terms of skin!

So ran the thoughts of Michael, perched on the coat-sarcopha-gus; and meditating on Fleur's skin, so clear and smooth, he went upstairs.

She had just had her final bath, and was standing at her bed-room window. Thinking of – what? The moon over the Square?

'Poor prisoner!' he said, and put his arm round her.

'What a queer sound the town makes at night, Michael. And, if you think, it's made up of the seven million separate sounds of people going their own ways.'

'And yet – the whole lot are going one way.'

'We're not going any way,' said Fleur, 'there's only pace.'

'There must be direction, my child, underneath.'

'Oh! of course, change.'

'For better or worse; but that's direction in itself.'

'Perhaps only to the edge, and over we go.'

'Gadarene swine!'

'Well, why not?'

'I admit,' said Michael unhappily, 'it's all hair-triggerish; but there's always common sense.'

'Common sense – in face of passions!'

Michael slackened his embrace. 'I thought you were always on the side of common sense. Passion? The passion to have? Or the passion to know?'

'Both,' said Fleur. 'That's the present age, and I'm a child of it. You're not, you know, Michael.'

'Query!' said Michael, letting go her waist. 'But if you want to have or know anything particular, Fleur, I'd like to be told.'

There was a moment of stillness, before he felt her arm slip-ping through his, and her lips against his ear.

'Only the moon, my dear. Let's go to bed.'

Chapter Seven

TWO VISITS

❖

O N the very day that Fleur was freed from her nursing she received a visit from the last person in her thoughts. If she had not altogether forgotten the existence of one indelibly associated with her wedding day, she had never expected to see her again. To hear the words: 'Miss June Forsyte, ma'am,' and find her in front of the Fragonard, was like experiencing a very slight earthquake.

The silvery little figure had turned at her entrance, extending a hand clad in a fabric glove.

'It's a flimsy school, that,' she said, pointing her chin at the Fragonard; 'but I like your room. Harold Blade's pictures would look splendid here. Do you know his work?'

Fleur shook her head.

'Oh! I should have thought any –' The little lady stopped, as if she had seen a brink.

'Won't you sit down?' said Fleur. 'Have you still got your gallery off Cork Street?'

'That? Oh no! It was a hopeless place. I sold it for half what my father gave for it.'

'And what became of that Polo-American – Boris Strumo something – you were so interested in?'

'He! Oh! Gone to pieces utterly. Married, and does purely commercial work. He gets big prices for his things – no good at all. So Jon and his wife –' Again she stopped, and Fleur tried to see the edge from which she had saved her foot.

'Yes,' she said, looking steadily into June's eyes, which were moving from side to side, 'Jon seems to have abandoned America for good. I can't see his wife being happy over here.'

'Ah!' said June. 'Holly told me you went to America yourself. Did you see Jon over there?'

'Not quite.'

'Did you like America?'

'It's very stimulating.'

June sniffed.

'Do they buy pictures? I mean, do you think there'd be a chance for Harold Blade's work there?'

'Without knowing the work –'

'Of course, I forgot; it seems so impossible that you don't know it.'

She leaned towards Fleur and her eyes shone.

'I do so want you to sit to him, you know; he'd make such a wonderful picture of you. Your father simply must arrange that. With your position in Society, Fleur, especially after that case last year,' Fleur winced, if imperceptibly – 'it would be the making of poor Harold. He's such a genius,' June added, frowning; 'you *must* come and see his work.'

'I should like to,' said Fleur. 'Have you seen Jon yet?'

'No. They're coming on Friday. I hope I shall like her. As a rule, I like all foreigners except Americans and the French. I mean – with exceptions of course.'

'Naturally,' said Fleur. 'What time are you generally in?'

'Every afternoon between five and seven are Harold's hours for going out – he has my studio, you know. I can show you his work better without him; he's so touchy – all real geniuses are. I want him to paint Jon's wife, too. He's extraordinary with women.'

'In that case, I think you should let Jon see him and his work first.'

June's eyes stared up at her for a moment, and flew off to the Fragonard.

'When will your father come?' she asked.

'Perhaps it would be best for me to come first.'

'Soames naturally likes the wrong thing,' said June, thoughtfully; 'but if *you* tell him you want to be painted – he's sure to – he always spoils you –'

Fleur smiled.

'Well, I'll come. Perhaps not this week.' And, in thought, she added: 'And perhaps, yes — Friday.'

June rose. 'I like your house, and your husband. Where is he?'

'Michael? Slumming, probably; he's in the thick of a scheme for their conversion.'

'How splendid! Can I see your boy?'

'I'm afraid he's only just over measles.'

June sighed. 'It does seem long since I had measles. I remember Jon's measles so well; I got him his first adventure books.' Suddenly she looked up at Fleur: 'Do you like his wife? I think it's ridiculous his being married so young. I tell Harold he must never marry; it's the end of adventure.' Her eyes moved from side to side, as if she were adding: 'Or the beginning, and I've never had it.' And suddenly she held out both hands.

'I shall expect you. I don't know whether he'll like your hair!'

Fleur smiled.

'I'm afraid I can't grow it for him. Oh! Here's my father coming in!' She had seen Soames pass the window.

'I don't know that I want to see him unless it's necessary,' said June.

'I expect he'll feel exactly the same. If you just go out, he won't pay any attention.'

'Oh!' said June, and out she went.

Through the window Fleur watched her moving as if she had not time to touch the ground.

A moment later Soames came in.

'What's that woman want here?' he said. 'She's a stormy petrel.'

'Nothing much, dear; she has a new painter, whom she's trying to boost.'

'Another of her lame ducks! She's been famous for them all her life — ever since —' He stopped short of Bosinney's name. 'She'd never go anywhere without wanting something,' he added. 'Did she get it?'

'Not more than I did, dear!'

Soames was silent, feeling vaguely that he had been near the proverb, 'The kettle and the pot'. What was the use, indeed, of going anywhere unless you wanted something? It was one of the cardinal principles of life.

'I went to see that Morland,' he said; 'it's genuine enough. In fact, I bought it.' And he sank into a reverie. . . .

Acquainted by Michael with the fact that the Marquess of Shropshire had a Morland he wanted to sell, he had said at once: 'I don't know that I want to buy one.'

'I thought you did, sir, from what you were saying the other day. It's a white pony.'

'That, of course,' said Soames. 'What does he want for it?'

'The market price, I believe.'

'There isn't such a thing. Is it genuine?'

'It's never changed hands, he says.'

Soames brooded aloud. 'The Marquess of Shropshire – that's that red-haired baggage's grandfather, isn't it?'

'Yes, but perfectly docile. He'd like you to see it, he said.'

'I daresay,' said Soames, and no more at the moment. . . .

'Where's this Morland?' he asked a few days later.

'At Shropshire House – in Curzon Street, sir.'

'Oh! Ah! Well, I'll have a look at it.'

Having lunched at Green Street, where he was still staying, he walked round the necessary corners, and sent in his card, on which he had pencilled the words: 'My son-in-law, Michael Mont, says you would like me to see your Morland.'

The butler came back, and opening a door, said:

'In here, sir. The Morland is over the sideboard.'

In that big dining-room, where even large furniture looked small, the Morland looked smaller, between two still-lifes of a Dutch size and nature. It had a simple scheme – white pony in stable, pigeon picking up some grains, small boy on upturned basket eating apple. A glance told Soames that it was genuine, and had not even been restored – the chiaroscuro was considerable. He stood, back to the light, looking at it attentively. Morland was not so sought after as he used to be; on the other hand, his pictures were distinctive and of a handy size. If one had not much space left, and wanted that period represented, he was perhaps the most repaying after Constable – good Old Cromes being so infernally rare. A Morland was a Morland, as a Millet was a Millet; and would never be anything else. Like all collectors in an experimental epoch, Soames was continually being faced with the advisability of buying not only what was what, but what would remain what. Such modern painters as were painting modern stuff, would, in his opinion, be dead as doornails before he himself was; besides, however much he tried, he did not like the stuff. Such modern painters, like most of the academicians, as were painting ancient stuff, were careful fellows, no doubt, but who could say whether any of them would live? No! The only safe thing was to buy the dead, and only the dead who were going to live, at that. In this way – for Soames was not alone in his conclusions – the early decease of most living painters was ensured. They were already, indeed, saying that hardly one of them could sell a picture for love or money.

He was looking at the pony through his curved thumb and forefinger when he heard a slight sound; and, turning, saw a short old man in a tweed suit, apparently looking at him in precisely the same way.

Dropping his hand, and deciding not to say 'Your Grace', or whatever it ought to be, Soames muttered:

'I was looking at the tail – some good painting in that.'

The Marquess had also dropped his hand, and was consulting the card between his other thumb and forefinger.

'Mr Forsyte? Yes. My grandfather bought it from the painter. There's a note on the back. I don't want to part with it, but these are lean days. Would you like to see the back?'

'Yes,' said Soames; 'I always look at their backs.'

'Sometimes,' said the Marquess, detaching the Morland with difficulty, 'the best part of the picture.'

Soames smiled down the further side of his mouth; he did not wish the old fellow to receive a false impression that he was 'kow-towing', or anything of that sort.

'Something in the hereditary principle, Mr Forsyte,' the Marquess went on, with his head on one side, 'when it comes to the sale of heirlooms.'

'Oh! I can see it's genuine,' said Soames, 'without looking at the back.'

'Then, if you want to buy, we can have a simple transaction between gentlemen. You know all about values, I hear.'

Soames put his head to the other side, and looked at the back of the picture. The old fellow's words were so disarming, that for the life of him he could not tell whether or not to be disarmed.

' "George Morland to Lord George Ferrar," ' he heard, ' "for value received – £80. 1797." '

'He came into the title later,' said the Marquess. 'I'm glad Morland got his money – great rips, our grandfathers, Mr Forsyte; days of great rips, those.'

Subtly flattered by the thought that 'Superior Dosset' was a great rip, Soames expanded slightly.

'Great rip, Morland,' he said. 'But there were real painters then, people could buy with confidence – they can't now.'

'I'm not sure,' said the Marquess, 'I'm not sure. The electrification of art may be a necessary process. We're all in a movement, Mr Forsyte.'

'Yes,' said Soames, glumly; 'but we can't go on at this rate – it's not natural. We shall be standing-pat again before long.'

'I wonder. We must keep out minds open, mustn't we?'

'The pace doesn't matter so much,' said Soames, astonished at himself, 'so long as it leads somewhere.'

The Marquess resigned the picture to the sideboard, and putting his foot up on a chair, leaned his elbow on his knee.

'Did your son-in-law tell you for what I wanted the money? He has a scheme for electrifying slum kitchens. After all, we *are* cleaner and more humane than our grandfathers, Mr Forsyte. Now, what do you think would be a fair price?'

'Why not get Dumetrius's opinion?'

'The Haymarket man? Is his opinion better than yours?'

'That I can't say,' said Soames, honestly. 'But if you mentioned my name, he'd value the picture for five guineas, and might make you an offer himself.'

'I don't think I should care for it to be known that I was selling pictures.'

'Well,' said Soames. 'I don't want you to get less than perhaps you could. But if I told Dumetrius to buy me a Morland, five hundred would be my limit. Suppose I give you six.'

The Marquess tilted up his beard. 'That would be too generous, perhaps. Shall we say five-fifty?'

Soames shook his head.

'We won't haggle,' he said. 'Six. You can have the cheque now, and I'll take it away. It will hang in my gallery at Mapledurham.'

The Marquess took his foot down, and sighed.

'Really, I'm very much obliged to you. I'm delighted to think it will go to a good home.'

'If you care to come and see it at any time —' Soames checked himself. An old fellow with one foot in the House of Lords and one in the grave, and no difference between them, to speak of — as if he'd want to come !

'That would be delightful,' said the Marquess, with his eyes wandering, as Soames had suspected they would. 'Have you your own electric plant there?'

'Yes,' and Soames took out his cheque-book. 'May I have a taxi called? If you hang the still-lifes a little closer together, this won't be missed.'

With that doubtful phrase in their ears, they exchanged goods, and Soames, with the Morland, returned to Green Street in a cab. He wondered a little on the way whether or not the Marquess had done him, by talking about a transaction between gentlemen. Agreeable old chap in his way, but as quick as a bird, looking through his thumb and finger like that ! . . .

And now, in his daughter's 'parlour' he said :

'What's this about Michael electrifying slum kitchens?'

Fleur smiled, and Soames did not approve of its irony.

'Michael's over head and ears.'

'In debt?'

'Oh, no! Committed himself to a slum scheme, just as he did to Foggartism. I hardly see him.'

Soames made a sound within himself. Young Jon Forsyte lurked now behind all his thoughts of her. Did she really resent Michael's absorption in public life, or was it pretence – an excuse for having a private life of her own?

'The slums want attending to, no doubt,' he said. 'He must have something to do.'

Fleur shrugged.

'Michael's too good to live.'

'I don't know about that,' said Soames; 'but he's – er – rather trustful.'

'That's not your failing, is it, Dad? You don't trust *me* a bit.'

'Not trust you!' floundered Soames. 'Why not?'

'Exactly!'

Soames sought refuge in the Fragonard. Sharp! She had seen into him!

'I suppose June wants me to buy a picture,' he said.

'She wants you to have me painted.'

'Does she? What's the name of her lame duck?'

'Blade, I think.'

'Never heard of him!'

'Well, I expect you will.'

'Yes,' muttered Soames; 'she's like a limpet. It's in the blood.'

'The Forsyte blood? You and I, then, too, dear.'

Soames turned from the Fragonard and looked her straight in the eyes.

'Yes; you and I, too.'

'Isn't that nice?' said Fleur.

Chapter Eight

THE JOLLY ACCIDENT

◄◄►►

IN doubting Fleur's show of resentment at Michael's new 'stunt', Soames was near the mark. She did not resent it at all. It kept his attention off herself, it kept him from taking up birth control, for which she felt the country was not yet quite prepared, and it had a popular appeal denied to Foggartism. The slums were under one's nose, and what was under the nose could be brought to the attention even of party politics. Being a town proposition, slums would concern six-sevenths of the vote. Foggartism, based on the country life necessary to national stamina and the growth of food within and overseas, concerned the whole population, but only appealed to one-seventh of the vote. And Fleur, nothing if not a realist, had long grasped the fact that the main business of politicians was to be, and to remain, elected. The vote was a magnet of the first order, and unconsciously swayed every political judgement and aspiration; or, if not, it ought to, for was it not the touchstone of democracy? In the committee, too, which Michael was forming, she saw, incidentally, the best social step within her reach.

'If they want a meeting-place,' she had said, 'why not here?'

'Splendid!' answered Michael. 'Handy for the House and clubs. Thank you, old thing!'

Fleur had added honestly:

'Oh, I shall be quite glad. As soon as I take Kit to the sea, you can start. Norah Curfew's letting me her cottage at Loring for three weeks.' She did not add: 'And it's only five miles from Wansdon.'

On the Friday, after lunch, she telephoned to June:

'I'm going to the sea on Monday – *I could* come this afternoon, but I think you said Jon was coming. Is he? Because if so –'

'He's coming at four-thirty, but he's got to catch a train back at six-twenty.'

'His wife, too?'

'No. He's just coming to see Harold's work.'

'Oh! — well — I think I'd better come on Sunday, then.'

'Yes, Sunday will be all right; then Harold will see you. He never goes out on Sunday. He hates the look of it so.'

Putting down the receiver, Fleur took up the time-table. Yes, there was the train! What a coincidence if she happened to take it to make a preliminary inspection of Norah Curfew's cottage! Not even June, surely, would mention their talk on the phone.

At lunch she did not tell Michael she was going — he might want to come, too, or at least to see her off. She knew he would be at 'the House' in the afternoon, she would just leave a note to say that she had gone to make sure the cottage would be in order for Monday. And after lunch she bent over and kissed him between the eyes, without any sense of betrayal. A sight of Jon was due to her after these dreary weeks! Any sight of Jon was always due to her who had been defrauded of him. And, as the afternoon drew on, and she put her night things into her dressing-case, a red spot became fixed in each cheek, and she wandered swiftly, her hands restive, her spirit homeless. Having had tea, and left the note giving her address — an hotel at Nettlefold — she went early to Victoria Station. There, having tipped the guard to secure emptiness, she left her bag in a corner seat and took up her stand by the bookstall, where Jon must pass with his ticket. And while she stood there, examining the fiction of the day, all her faculties were busy with reality. Among the shows and shadows of existence, an hour and a half of real life lay before her. Who could blame her for filching it back from a filching Providence? And if anybody could, she didn't care! The hands of the station clock moved on, and Fleur gazed at this novel after that, all of them full of young women in awkward situations, and vaguely wondered whether they were more awkward than her own. Three minutes to the time! Wasn't he coming after all? Had that wretched June kept him for the night? At last in despair she caught up a tome called

Violin Obbligato, which at least would be modern, and paid for it. And then, as she was receiving her change, she saw him hastening. Turning, she passed through the wicket, walking quickly, knowing that he was walking more quickly. She let him see her first.

'Fleur!'

'Jon! Where are you going?'

'To Wansdon.'

'Oh! And I'm going to Nettlefold, to see a cottage at Loring for my baby. Here's my bag, in here – quick! We're off!'

The door was banged to, and she held out both her hands.

'Isn't this queer, and jolly?'

Jon held the hands, and dropped them rather suddenly.

'I've just been to see June. She's just the same – bless her!'

'Yes, she came round to me the other day; wants me to be painted by her present pet.'

'You might do worse. I said he should paint Anne.'

'Really? Is he good enough for *her?*'

And she was sorry; she hadn't meant to begin like that! Still – must begin somehow – must employ lips which might otherwise go lighting on his eyes, his hair, *his* lips! And she rushed into words: Kit's measles, Michael's committee, *Violin Obbligato,* and the Proustian School; Val's horses, Jon's poetry, the smell of England – so important to a poet – anything, everything, in a sort of madcap medley.

'You see, Jon, I must talk; I've been in prison for a month.' And all the time she felt that she was wasting minutes that might have been spent with lips silent and heart against his, if the heart, as they said, really extended to the centre of the body. And all the time, too, the proboscis of her spirit was scenting, searching for the honey and the saffron of his spirit. Was there any for her, or was it all kept for that wretched American girl he had left behind him, and to whom – alas! – he was returning? But Jon gave her no sign. Unlike the old impulsive Jon, he had learned secrecy. By a whim of memory, whose ways are so inscrutable, she remembered being taken, as a very little girl, to Timothy's on the Bayswater Road to her great-aunt Hester – an

old still figure, in black Victorian lace and jet and a Victorian
chair, saying in a stilly languid voice to her father: 'Oh, yes,
my dear : your Uncle Jolyon, before he married, was very much
in love with our great friend Alice Read; but she was consumptive, you know, and of course he felt he couldn't marry her – it
wouldn't have been prudent, he felt, because of children. And
then she died, and he married Edith Moor.' Funny how that had
stuck in her ten-year-old mind! And she stared at Jon. Old
Jolyon – as they called him in the family – had been his grandfather. She had seen his photograph in Holly's album – a
domed head, a white moustache, eyes deep-set under the brows,
like Jon's. 'It wouldn't have been prudent!' How Victorian!
Was Jon, too, Victorian? She felt as if she would never know
what Jon was. And she became suddenly cautious. A single
step too far, or too soon, and he might be gone from her again for
good! He was not – no, he was not modern! For all she knew,
there might be something absolute, not relative, in his 'make-
up', and to Fleur the absolute was strange, almost terrifying.
But she had not spent six years in social servitude without learning to adjust herself swiftly to the playing of a new part. She
spoke in a calmer tone, almost a drawl; her eyes became cool
and quizzical. What did Jon think about the education of boys
– before he knew where he was, of course, he would be having
one himself? It hurt her to say that, and, while saying it, she
searched his face; but it told her nothing.

'We've put Kit down for Winchester. Do you believe in the
Public Schools, Jon? Or do you think they're out of date?'

'Yes; and a good thing, too.'

'How?'

'I mean I should send him there.'

'I see,' said Fleur. 'Do you know, Jon, you really have
changed. You wouldn't have said that, I believe, six years ago.'

'Perhaps not. Being out of England makes you believe in
dams. Ideas can't be left to swop around in the blue. In England
they're not, and that's the beauty of it.'

'I don't care what happens to ideas,' said Fleur, 'but I don't
like stupidity. The Public Schools –'

'Oh, no; not really. Certain things get cut and dried there, of course, but then, they ought to.'

Fleur leaned forward, and with faint malice said: 'Have you become a moralist, my dear?'

Jon answered glumly:

'Why, no – no more than reason!'

'Do you remember our walk by the river?'

'I told you before – I remember everything.'

Fleur restrained her hand from a heart which had given a jump.

'We nearly quarrelled because I said I hated people for their stupid cruelties, and wanted them to stew in their own juice.'

'Yes; and I said I pitied them. Well?'

'Repression is stupid, you know, Jon.' And, by instinct, added: 'That's why I doubt the Public Schools. They teach it.'

'They're useful socially, Fleur,' and his eyes twinkled.

Fleur pursed her lips. She did not mind. But she would make him sorry for that; because his compunction would be a trump card in her hand.

'I know perfectly well,' she said, 'that I'm a snob – I was called so publicly.'

'What!'

'Oh, yes; there was a case about it.'

'Who dared?'

'Oh! my dear, that's ancient history. But of course you knew – Francis Wilmot must have –'

Jon made a horrified gesture.

'Fleur, you never thought I –'

'Oh, but of course! Why not?' A trump, indeed! Jon seized her hand.

'Fleur, say you knew I didn't –'

Fleur shrugged her shoulders. 'My dear, you have lived too long among the primitives. Over here we stab each other daily, and no harm is done.'

He dropped her hand, and she looked at him from beneath her lids.

'I was only teasing, Jon. It's good for primitives to have their

713

legs pulled. *Parlons d'autre chose.* Have you found your place, to grow things, yet?'

'Practically.'

'Where?'

'About four miles from Wansdon, on the south side of the downs – Green Hill Farm. Fruit – a lot of grass; and some arable.'

'Why, it must be close to where I'm going with Kit. That's on the sea and only five miles from Wansdon. No, Jon; don't be alarmed. We shall only be there three weeks at most.'

'Alarmed! It's very jolly. We shall see you there. Perhaps we shall meet at Goodwood anyway.'

'I've been thinking –' Fleur paused, and again she stole a look. 'We *can* be steady friends, Jon, can't we?'

Jon answered, without looking up. 'I hope so.'

If his face had cleared, and his voice had been hearty, how different – how much slower – would have been the beating of her heart!

'Then that's all right,' she murmured. 'I've been wanting to say that to you ever since Ascot. Here we are, and here we shall be – and anything else would be silly, wouldn't it? This is not the romantic age.'

'H'm!'

'What do you mean by that unpleasant noise?'

'I always think it's rot to talk about ages being this or that. Human feelings remain the same.'

'Do you really think they do? The sort of life we live affects them. Nothing's worth more than a tear or two, Jon. I found that out. But I forgot – you hate cynicism. Tell me about Anne. Is she still liking England?'

'Loving it. You see, she's pure Southern, and the South's old still, too, in a way – or some of it is. What she likes here is the grass, the birds, and the villages. She doesn't feel homesick. And, of course, she loves the riding.'

'I suppose she's picking up English fast?'

And to his stare she made her face quite candid.

'I should like you to like her,' he said, wistfully.

714

'Oh! of course I shall, when I know her.'

But a fierce little wave of contempt passed up from her heart. What did he think she was made of? Like her! A girl who lay in his arms, who would be the mother of his children. Like her! And she began to talk about the preservation of Box Hill. And all the rest of the way till Jon got out at Pulborough, she was more wary than a cat – casual and friendly, with clear candid eyes, and a little tremble up at him when she said:

'*Au revoir,* then, at Goodwood, if not before! This *has* been a jolly accident!'

But on the way to her hotel, driving in a station fly through air that smelled of oysters, she folded her lips between her teeth, and her eyes were damp beneath her frowning brows.

Chapter Nine

BUT – JON!

BUT Jon, who had over five miles to walk, started with the words of the Old English song beating a silent tattoo within him:

'How happy could I be with either,
Were t'other dear charmer away!'

To such confusion had he come, contrary to intention, but in accordance with the impulses of a loyal disposition. Fleur had been his first love, Anne his second. But Anne was his wife, and Fleur the wife of another. A man could not be in love with two women at once, so he was tempted to conclude that he was not in love with either. Why, then, the queer sensations of his circulatory system? Was popular belief in error? A French, or Old-English way of looking at his situation, did not occur to him. He had married Anne, he loved Anne – she was a darling! There it ended! Why, then, walking along a grassy strip beside the road, did he think almost exclusively of Fleur? However cynical, or casual, or just friendly she might seem, she no more deceived him than she at heart wished to. He knew she had her old feeling for him, just as he knew he had it, or some of it, for her. But then he had feeling for another, too. Jon was not more of a fool than other men, nor was he more self-deceiving. Like other men before him, he intended to face what was, and to do what he believed to be right; or, rather, not to do what he believed to be wrong. Nor had he any doubt as to what was wrong. His trouble was more simple. It consisted in not having control of his thoughts and feelings greater than that with which any man has hitherto been endowed. After all, it had not been his fault that he had once been wholly in love with Fleur, nor that she had been wholly in love with him; not his fault that he had met her again, nor that she was still in love with him. Nor again was it his fault that he was in love with his native land and tired of being out of it.

It was not his fault that he had fallen in love a second time or married the object of his affections. Nor, so far as he could see, was it his fault that the sight and the sound and the scent and the touch of Fleur had revived some of his former feelings. He was none the less disgusted at his double-heartedness; and he walked now fast, now slow, while the sun shifted over and struck on a neck always sensitive since his touch of the sun in Granada. Presently, he stopped and leaned over a gate. He had not been long enough back in England to have got over its beauty on a fine day. He was always stopping and leaning over gates, or in other ways, as Val called it, mooning!

Though it was already the first day of the Eton and Harrow Match, which his father had been wont to attend so religiously, hay harvest was barely over, and the scent of stacked hay still in the air. The downs lay before him to the south, lighted along their northern slopes. Red Sussex cattle were standing under some trees close to the gate, dribbling, and slowly swishing their tails. And away over there he could see others lingering along the hill-side. Peace lay thick on the land. The corn in that next field had an unearthly tinge, neither green nor gold, under the slanting sunlight. And in the restful beauty of the evening Jon could well perceive the destructiveness of love – an emotion so sweet, restless, and thrilling, that it drained Nature of its colour and peace, made those who suffered from it bores to their fellows and useless to the life of everyday. To work – and behold Nature in her moods! Why couldn't he get away to that, away from women? why – like Holly's story of the holiday slum girl, whose family came to see her off by train – why couldn't he just get away and say: 'Thank Gawd! I'm shut o' that lot!'

The midges were biting, and he walked on. Should he tell Anne that he had come down with Fleur? Not to tell her was to stress the importance of the incident; but to tell her was somehow disagreeable to him. And then he came on Anne herself, without a hat, sitting on a gate, her hands in the pockets of her jumper. Very lissome and straight she looked.

'Lift me down, Jon!'

He lifted her down in a prolonged manner. And, almost instantly, said:

'Whom do you think I travelled with? Fleur Mont. We ran up against each other at Victoria. She's taking her boy to Loring next week, to convalesce him.'

'Oh! I'm sorry.'

'Why?'

'Because I'm in love with you, Jon.' She tilted her chin, so that her straight and shapely nose looked a little more sudden.

'I don't see –' began Jon.

'You see, she's another. I saw that at Ascot. I reckon I'm old-fashioned, Jon.'

'That's all right, so am I.'

She turned her eyes on him, eyes not quite civilized, nor quite American, and put her arm round his waist.

'Rondavel's off his feed. Greenwater's very upset about it.'

' "Very", Anne.'

'Well, you can't pronounce "very" as I pronounce it, any more than I can as you do.'

'Sorry. But you told me to remind you. It's silly, though: why shouldn't you speak your own lingo?'

'Because I want to speak like you.'

'Want, then, not waunt.'

'Damn!'

'All right, darling. But isn't your lingo just as good?'

Anne disengaged her arm.

'No, you don't think that. You're awfully glad to be through with the American accent – you *are*, Jon.'

'It's natural to like one's own country's best.'

'Well, I do want – there! – to speak English. I'm English by law, now, and by descent, all but one French great-grandmother. If we have children, they'll be English, and we're going to live in England. Shall you take Green Hill Farm?'

'Yes. And I'm not going to play at things any more. I've played twice, and this time I'm going all out.'

'You weren't exactly playing in North Carolina.'

'Not exactly. But this is different. It didn't matter there. What are peaches anyway? It does here – it matters a lot. I mean to make it pay.'

'Bully!' said Anne: 'I mean – er – splendid. But I never believed you'd say that.'

'Paying's the only proof. I'm going in for tomatoes, onions, asparagus, and figs; and I mean to work the arable for all it's worth, and if I can get any more land, I will.'

'Jon! What energy!' And she caught hold of his chin.

'All right!' said Jon, grimly. 'You watch out, and see if I don't mean it.'

'And you'll leave the house to me? I'll make it just too lovely!'

'That's a bargain.'

'Kiss me, then.'

With her lips parted and her eyes looking into his, with just that suspicion of a squint which made them so enticing, Jon thought: 'It's quite simple. The other thing's absurd. Why, of course!' He kissed her forehead and lips, but, even while he did so, he seemed to see Fleur trembling up at him, and to hear her words: '*Au revoir!* It *was* a jolly accident!'

'Let's go and have a look at Rondavel,' he said.

In his box, when those two went in, the grey colt stood by the far wall, idly contemplating a carrot in the hand of Greenwater.

'Clean off!' said the latter over his shoulder: 'It's good-bye to Goodwood! The colt's sick.'

What had Fleur said: '*Au revoir* at Goodwood, if not before!'

'Perhaps it's just a megrim, Greenwater,' said Anne.

'No, ma'am; the horse has got a temperature. Well, we'll win the Middle Park Plate with him yet.'

Jon passed his hand over the colt's quarter: 'Poor old son! Funny! You can tell he's not fit by the feel of his coat!'

'You can that,' said Greenwater: 'But where's he got it from? There isn't a sick horse that I know of anywhere about. If there's anything in the world more perverse than horses –! We didn't train him for Ascot, and he goes and wins. We meant him for Goodwood, and he's gone amiss. Mr Dartie wants me to give him some South African stuff I never heard of.'

'They have a lot of horse sickness out there,' said Jon. 'See,' said the trainer, stretching his hand up to the colt's ears; 'no kick in him at all! Looks like blackberry sickness out of season. I'd give a good deal to know how he picked it up.'

The two young people left him standing by the colt's dejected head, his dark, hawk-like face thrust forward, as if trying to read the sensations within his favourite.

That night, Jon went up, bemused by Val's opinions on Communism, the Labour Party, the qualities inherent in the offspring of 'Sleeping Dove', with a dissertation on horse-sickness in South Africa. He entered a dim bedroom. A white figure was standing at the window. It turned when he came near and flung its arms round him.

'Jon, you mustn't stop loving me.'

'Why should I?'

'Because men do. Besides, it's not the fashion to be faithful.'

'Bosh!' said Jon gently; 'it's just as much the fashion as it ever was.'

'I'm glad we shan't be going to Goodwood. I'm afraid of her. She's so clever.'

'Fleur?'

'You *were* in love with her, Jon; I feel it in my bones. I wish you'd told me.'

Jon leaned beside her in the window.

'Why?' he said dully.

She did not answer. They stood side by side in the breathless warmth, moths passed their faces, a night-jar churred in the silence, and now and then, from the stables, came the stamp of a sleepless horse. Suddenly Anne stretched out her hand.

'Over there – somewhere – she's awake, and wanting you. I'm not happy, Jon.'

'Don't be morbid, darling!'

'But I'm *not* happy, Jon.'

Like a great child – slim within his arm, her cheek pressed to his, her dark earlock tickling his neck! And suddenly her lips came round to his, vehement.

'Love me!'

But when she was asleep, Jon lay wakeful. Moonlight had crept in and there was a ghost in the room – a ghost in a Goya dress, twirling, holding out its skirts, beckoning with its eyes, and with its lips seeming to whisper: 'Me, too! Me, too!'

And, raising himself on his elbow, he looked resolutely at the dark head beside him. No! There was – there should be – nothing but that in the room! Reality – reality!

Chapter Ten

THAT THING AND THIS THING

<<–>>

ON the following Monday at breakfast Val said to Holly:

'Listen to this!

DEAR DARTIE, –

I think I can do you a good turn. I have some information that concerns your 'Sleeping Dove' colt and your stable generally, worth a great deal more than the fifty pounds which I hope you may feel inclined to pay for it. Are you coming up to town this week-end? If so, can I see you at the Brummell? Or I could come to Green Street if you prefer it. It's really rather vital.

Sincerely yours,
AUBREY STAINFORD

'That fellow again!'

'Pay no attention, Val.'

'I don't know,' said Val glumly. 'Some gang or other are taking altogether too much interest in the colt. Greenwater's very uneasy. I'd better get to the bottom of it, if I can.'

'Consult your uncle, then, first. He's still at your mother's.'

Val made a wry face.

'Yes,' said Holly; 'but he'll know what you can do and what you can't. You really mustn't deal single-handed with people like that.'

'All right, then. There's hanky-panky in the wind, I'm sure. Somebody knew all about the colt at Ascot.'

He took the morning train and arrived at his mother's at lunch-time. She and Annette were lunching out, but Soames, who was lunching in, crossed a cold hand with his nephew's.

'Have you still got that young man and his wife staying with you?'

'Yes,' said Val.

'Isn't he ever going to do anything?'

On being told that Jon was about to do something, Soames grunted.

'Farm — in England? What's he want to do that for? He'll only throw his money away. Much better go back to America, or some other new country. Why doesn't he try South Africa? His half-brother died out there.'

'He won't leave England again, Uncle Soames — seems to have developed quite a feeling for the old country.'

Soames masticated.

'Amateurs,' he said, 'all the young Forsytes. How much has he got a year?'

'The same as Holly and her half-sister — only about two thousand, so long as his mother's alive.'

Soames looked into his wineglass and took from it an infinitesimal piece of cork. His mother! She was in Paris again, he was told. *She* must have three thousand a year, now, at least. He remembered when she had nothing but a beggarly fifty pounds a year, and that fifty pounds too much, putting the thought of independence into her head. In Paris again! The Bois de Boulogne, that Green Niobe — all drinking water, he remembered it still, and the scene between them there. . . .

'What have *you* come up for?' he said to Val.

'This, Uncle Soames.'

Soames fixed on his nose the glasses he had just begun to need for reading purposes, read the letter, and returned it to his nephew.

'I've known impudence in my time, but this chap — !'

'What do you recommend me to do?'

'Pitch it into the waste-paper basket?'

Val shook his head.

'Stainford dropped in on me one day at Wansdon. I told him nothing; but you remember we couldn't get more than fours at Ascot, and it was Rondavel's first outing. And now the colt's sick just before Goodwood; there's a screw loose somewhere.'

'What do you think of doing, then?'

'I thought I'd see him, and that perhaps you'd like to be present, to keep me from making a fool of myself.'

'There's something in that,' said Soames. 'This fellow's the coolest ruffian I ever came across.'

'He's pedigree stock, Uncle Soames. Blood will tell.'

'H'm!' muttered Soames. 'Well, have him here, if you must see him, but clear the room first and tell Smither to put away the umbrellas.'

Having seen Fleur and his grandson off to the sea that morning, he felt flat, especially as, since her departure, he had gathered from the map of Sussex that she would be quite near to Wansdon and the young man who was always now at the back of his thoughts. The notion of a return match with 'this ruffian' Stainford, was, therefore, in the nature of a distraction. And, as soon as the messenger was gone, he took a chair whence he could see the street. On second thoughts he had not spoken about the umbrellas – it was not quite dignified; but he had counted them. The day was warm and rainy, and, through the open window of that ground-floor dining-room, the air of Green Street came in, wetted and a little charged with the scent of servants' dinners.

'Here he is,' he said suddenly, 'languid beggar!'

Val crossed from the sideboard and stood behind his uncle's chair. Soames moved uneasily. This fellow and his nephew had been at college together, and had – goodness knew what other vices in common.

'By Jove!' he heard Val mutter. 'He does look ill.'

The 'languid beggar' wore the same dark suit and hat, and the same slow elegance that Soames had first noted on him; a raised eyebrow and the half-lidded eyes despised as ever the bitter crow's-footed exhaustion on his face. And that indefinable look of a damned soul, lost to all but its contempt for emotion, awakened within Soames, just as it had before, the queerest little quirk of sympathy.

'He'd better have a drink,' he said.

Val moved back to the sideboard.

They heard the bell, voices in the hall; then Smither appeared, red, breathless, deprecatory.

'Will you see that gentleman, sir, who took the you know what, sir?'

'Show him in, Smither.'

Val turned towards the door. Soames remained seated.

The 'languid beggar' entered, nodded to Val, and raised his eyebrows at Soames, who said:

'How d'you do, Mr Stainford?'

'Mr Forsyte, I think?'

'Whisky or brandy, Stainford?'

'Brandy, thanks.'

'Smoke, won't you? You wanted to see me. My uncle here is my solicitor.'

Soames saw Stainford smile. It was as if he had said: 'Really! How wonderful these people are!' He lighted the proffered cigar, and there was silence.

'Well?' said Val at last.

'I'm sorry your "Sleeping Dove" colt's gone amiss, Dartie.'

'How did you know that?'

'Exactly! But before I tell you, d'you mind giving me fifty pounds and your word that my name's not mentioned.'

Soames and his nephew stared in silence. At last Val said:

'What guarantee have I that your information's worth fifty pounds, or even five?'

'The fact that I knew your colt had gone amiss.'

However ignorant of the Turf, Soames could see that the fellow had scored.

'You mean you know where the leakage is?'

Stainford nodded.

'We were college pals,' said Val. 'What would you expect me to do if I knew that about a stable of yours?'

'My dear Dartie, there's no analogy. You're a man of means, I'm not.'

Trite expressions were knocking against Soames's plate. He swallowed them. What use in talking to a chap like this!

'Fifty pounds is a lot,' said Val. 'Is your information of real value?'

'Yes – on my word of honour.'

Soames sniffed audibly.

'If I buy this leakage from you,' said Val, 'can you guarantee that it won't break out in another direction?'

'Highly improbable that two pipes will leak in your stable.'

'I find it hard to believe there's one.'

'Well, there is.'

Soames saw his nephew move up to the table and begin counting over a roll of notes.

'Tell me what you know, first, and I'll give them to you if on the face of it your information's probable. I won't mention your name.'

Soames saw the languid eyebrows lift.

'I'm not so distrustful as you, Dartie. Get rid of a boy called Sinnet – that's where your stable leaks.'

'Sinnet?' said Val; 'my best boy? What proof have you?'

Stainford took out a dirty piece of writing-paper and held it up. Val read aloud:

'"The grey colt's amiss all right – he'll be no good for Good-wood." All right?' he repeated. 'Does that means he engineered it?'

Stainford shrugged his shoulders.

'Can I have this bit of paper?' said Val.

'If you'll promise not to show it to him.'

Val nodded, and took the paper.

'Do you know his writing?' asked Soames. 'All this is very fishy.'

'Not yet,' said Val, and to Soames's horror, put the notes into the outstretched hand. The little sigh the fellow gave was distinctly audible. Val said suddenly:

'Did you get at him the day you came down to see me?'

Stainford smiled faintly, shrugged his shoulders again and turned to the door. 'Good-bye, Dartie,' he said.

Soames mouth fell open. The return match was over! The fellow had gone!

'Here!' he said. 'Don't let him go like that. It's monstrous.'

'Dam' funny!' said Val suddenly, and began to laugh. 'Oh! dam' funny!'

'Funny!' muttered Soames. 'I don't know what the world's coming to.'

'Never mind, Uncle Soames. He's taken fifty of the best off me, but it was worth it. Sinnet, my best boy!'

Soames continued to mutter:

'To corrupt one of your men, and get you to pay him for it. It's the limit.'

'That's what tickles me, Uncle Soames. Well, I'll go back to Wansdon now, and get rid of that young blackguard.'

'I shouldn't have any scruple, if I were you, in telling him exactly how you got the knowledge.'

'Well, I don't know. Stainford's on his beam ends. I'm not a moralist, but I think I'll keep my word to him.'

For a moment Soames said nothing; then, with a sidelong glance at his nephew:

'Well, perhaps. But he ought to be locked up.'

With those words he walked into the hall and counted the umbrellas. Their number was undiminished, and taking one of them, he went out. He felt in need of air. With the exception of that Elderson affair, he had encountered little flagrant dishonesty in his time, and that only in connexion with the lower classes. One could forgive a poor devil of a tramp, or even a clerk or domestic servant. They had temptations, and no particular traditions to live up to. But what was coming to the world, if you couldn't rely on gentlemen in a simple matter like honesty! Every day one read cases, and for every one that came into Court one might be sure there were a dozen that didn't! And when you added all the hanky-panky in the City, all the dubious commissions, bribery of the police, sale of honours – though he believed that had been put a stop to – all the dicky-dealing over contracts; it was enough to make one's hair stand on end. They might sneer at the past, and no doubt there was more temptation in the present, but something simple and straightforward seemed to have perished out of life. By hook or by crook people had to get their ends, would no longer wait for their ends to come to them. Everybody was in such a hurry to make good, or rather bad! Get money at all costs – look at the quack remedies they sold and the books they published nowadays, without caring for truth or decency or anything. And the advertisements! Good Lord!

In the gloom of these reflections he had come to Westminster. He might as well call in at South Square and see if Fleur had telephoned her arrival at the sea! In the hall eight hats of differing shape and colour lay on the coat-sarcophagus. What the deuce was going on? A sound of voices came from the dining-room, then the peculiar drone of somebody making a speech. Some meeting or other of Michael's, and the measles only just out of the house!

'What's going on here?' he said to Coaker.

'Something to do with the slums, sir, I believe; they're converting of them, I heard Mr Mont say.'

'Don't put my hat with those,' said Soames; 'have you had any message from your mistress?'

'Yes, sir. They had a good journey. The little dog was sick, I believe. He will have his own way.'

'Well,' said Soames, 'I'll go up and wait in the study.'

On getting there, he noticed a water-colour drawing on the bureau: a tree with large dark green leaves and globular golden fruit, against a silvery sort of background — peculiar thing, amateurish, but somehow arresting. Underneath, he recognized his daughter's handwriting:

'The Golden Apple. F.M. 1926.'

Really he had no idea that she could use water-colour as well as that! She was a clever little thing! And he put the drawing up on end where he could see it better! Apple? Passion-fruit, he would have said, of an exaggerated size. Thoroughly uneatable – they had a glow like lanterns. Forbidden fruit! Eve might have given them to Adam. Was this thing symbolic? Did it fancifully reveal her thoughts? And in front of it he fell into sombre mood, which was broken by the opening of the door. Michael had entered.

'Hallo, sir!'

'Hallo!' replied Soames. 'What's this thing?'

Chapter Eleven

CONVERTING THE SLUMS

◄-►►

In an age governed almost exclusively by committees, Michael knew fairly well what committees were governed by. A committee must not meet too soon after food, for then the committee-men would sleep; nor too soon before food, because then the committee-men would be excitable. The committee-men should be allowed to say what they liked, without direction, until each was tired of hearing the others say it. But there must be someone present, preferably the chairman, who said little, thought more, and could be relied on to be awake when that moment was reached, whereupon a middle policy, voiced by him to exhausted receivers, would probably be adopted.

Having secured his bishop, and Sir Godfrey Bedwin, who specialized in chests, and failed with his Uncle Lionel Charwell, who had scented the work destined for Lady Alison his wife, Michael convened the first meeting for three o'clock in South Square on the day of Fleur's departure for the sea. Hilary was present, and a young woman, to take them down. Surprise came early. They all attended, and fell into conversation around the Spanish table. It was plain to Michael that the bishop and Sir Timothy Fanfield had expectations of the chair; and he kicked his father under the table, fearing that one of them might propose the other in the hope of the other proposing the one. Sir Lawrence then murmured:

'My dear, that's my shin.'

'I know,' muttered Michael; 'shall we get on with it?'

Dropping his eyeglass, Sir Lawrence said:

'Exactly! Gentlemen, I propose that the Squire takes the chair. Will you second that, Marquess?'

The Marquess nodded.

The blow was well received, and the Squire proceeded to the head of the table. He began as follows:

'I won't beat about the bush. You all know as much about it as I do, which is precious little. The whole thing is the idea of Mr Hilary Charwell here, so I'll ask him to explain it to us. The slums are C 3 breeders, and verminous into the bargain, and anything we can do to abate this nuisance, I, for one, should be happy to do. Will you give tongue, Mr Charwell?'

Hilary dropped at once into a warm, witty and thorough exposition of his views, dwelling particularly on the human character of a problem 'hitherto', he said, 'almost exclusively confined to Borough Councils, Bigotry and Blue Books'. That he had made an impression was instantly demonstrated by the

buzz of voices. The Squire, who was sitting with his head up
and his heels down, his knees apart and his elbows close to his
sides, muttered:

'Let it rip! Can we smoke, Mont?' And, refusing the cigars
and cigarettes proffered by Michael, he filled a pipe, and smoked
in silence for several minutes.

'Then we're all agreed,' he said, suddenly, 'that what we
want to do is to form this Fund.'

No one having as yet expressed any such opinion, this was the
more readily assented to.

'In that case, we'd better get down to it and draw up our
appeal.' And, pointing his pipe at Sir Lawrence, he added:

'You've got the gift of the gab with a pen, Mont; suppose you
and the bishop and Charwell here go into another room and
knock us out a draft. Pitch it strong, but no waterworks.'

When the designated three had withdrawn, conversation
broke out again. Michael could hear the Squire and Sir Godfrey
Bedwin talking of distemper, and the Marquess discussing with
Mr Montross the electrification of the latter's kitchen. Sir
Timothy Fanfield was staring at the Goya. He was a tall, lean
man of about seventy, with a thin, hooked nose, brown face,
and large white moustaches, who had been in the Household
Cavalry and come out of it.

A little afraid of his verdict on the Goya, Michael said
hastily:

'Well, Sir Timothy, the coal strike doesn't end.'

'No; they ought to be shot. I'm all for the working man; but
I'd shoot his leaders tomorrow.'

'What about the mine-owners?' queried Michael.

'I'd shoot their leaders, too. We shall never have industrial
peace till we shoot somebody. Fact is, we didn't shoot half
enough people during the war. Conshies and Communists and
profiteers – I'd have had 'em all against a wall.'

'I'm very glad you came on our committee, sir,' Michael
murmured; 'we want someone with strong views.'

'Ah!' said Sir Timothy, and pointing his chin towards the end
of the table, he lowered his voice. 'Between ourselves – bit too

moderate, the Squire. You want to take these scoundrels by the throat. I knew a chap that owned half a slum and had the face to ask me to subscribe to a Missionary Fund in China. I told the fellow he ought to be shot. Impudent beggar – he didn't like it.'

'No?' said Michael; and at this moment the young woman pulled his sleeve. Was she to take anything down?

Not at present – Michael thought.

Sir Timothy was again staring at the Goya.

'Family portrait?' he said.

'No,' said Michael; 'it's a Goya.'

'Deuce it is ! Goy is Jewish for Christian. Female Christian – what?'

'No, sir. Name of the Spanish painter.'

'No idea there were any except Murillo and Velasquez – never see anything like *them* nowadays. These modern painters, you know, ought to be tortured. I say,' and again he lowered his voice, 'bishop ! – what ! – they're always running some hare of their own – anti-birth-control, or missions of sorts. We want to cut this C 3 population off at the root. Stop 'em having babies by hook or crook; and then shoot a slum landlord or two – deal with both ends. But they'll jib at it, you'll see. D'you know anything about ants?'

'Only that they're busy,' said Michael.

'I've made a study of 'em. Come down to my place in Hampshire, and I'll show you my slides – most interestin' insects in the world.' He lowered his voice again :

'Who's that talkin' to the old Marquess? What ! The rubber man? Jew, isn't he? What axe is *he* grinding? The composition of this committee's wrong, Mr Mont. Old Shropshire's a charmin' old man, but –' Sir Timothy touched his forehead – 'mad as a March hare about electricity. You've got a doctor, too. They're too mealy-mouthed. What you want is a committee that'll go for those scoundrels. Tea? Never drink it. Chap who invented tea ought to have been strung up."

At this moment the sub-committee re-entering the room, Michael rose, not without relief.

'Hallo,' he heard the Squire say: 'you've been pretty slippy.'

The look of modest worth which passed over the faces of the sub-committee did not altogether deceive Michael, who knew that his Uncle had brought the draft appeal in his coat pocket. It was now handed up, and the Squire, putting on some horn-rimmed spectacles, began reading it aloud, as if it were an entry of hounds, or the rules of a race-meeting. Michael could not help feeling that what it lost it gained – the Squire and emphasis were somehow incompatible. When he had finished reading, the Squire said:

'We can discuss it now, clause by clause. But time's getting on, gentlemen. Personally, I think it about fills the bill. What do you say, Shropshire?'

The Marquess leaned forward and took his beard in his hand.

'An admirable draft, with one exception. Not sufficient stress is laid on electrification of the kitchens. Sir Godrey will bear me out. You can't expect these poor people to keep their houses clean unless you can get rid of the smoke and the smells and the flies.'

'Well, we can put in something more about that, if you'll give us the wording, Shropshire.'

The Marquess began to write. Michael saw Sir Timothy twirl his moustaches.

'*I'm* not satisfied,' he began, abruptly. 'I want something that'll make slum landlords sit up. We're here to twist their tails. The appeal's too mild.'

'M'm !' said the Squire; 'What do you suggest, Fanfield?'

Sir Timothy read from his shirt-cuff.

' "We record our conviction that anyone who owns slum property ought to be shot," These gentlemen –'

'*That* won't do,' said the Squire.

'Why not?'

'All sorts of respectable people own slum property – widows, syndicates, dukes, goodness-knows-who ! We can't go calling them gentlemen, and sayin' they ought to be shot. It won't *do*.'

The bishop leaned forward:

'Might we rather word it like this? "The signatories much

regret that those persons who own slum property are not more alive to their responsibilities to the community at large." '

'Good Lord!' burst from Sir Timothy.

'I think we might pitch it stronger than that, Bishop,' said Sir Lawrence: 'But we ought to have a lawyer here, to tell us exactly how far we can go.'

Michael turned to the chairman:

'I've got one in the house, sir. My father-in-law – I saw him come in just now. I daresay he'd advise us.'

'Old Forsyte!' said Sir Lawrence. 'The very man. We ought to have him on the committee, Squire. He's well up in the law of libel.'

'Ah!' said the Marquess: 'Mr Forsyte! By all means – a steady head.'

'Let's co-opt him, then,' said the Squire; 'a lawyer's always useful.'

Michael went out.

Having drawn the Fragonard blank, he went up to his study, and was greeted by Soames's 'What's this?'

'Pretty good, sir, don't you think? It's Fleur's – got feeling.'

'Yes,' muttered Soames; 'too much, I shouldn't wonder.'

'You saw the hats in the hall, no doubt. My Slum Conversion Committee are just drafting their appeal, and they'd be most frightfully obliged to you, sir, as a lawyer, if you'd come down and cast your eye over one or two of the allusions to slum land-lords. They want to go just far enough, you know. In fact, if it wouldn't bore you terribly, they'd like to co-opt you on the committee.'

'Would they?' said Soames: 'And who are *they*?'

Michael ran over the names.

Soames drew up a nostril. 'Lot of titles! Is this a wildcat thing?'

'Oh! no, sir. Our wish to have you on is a guarantee against that. Besides, our chairman, Wilfred Bentworth, has refused a title three times.'

'Well,' said Soames, 'I don't know. I'll come and have a look at them.'

'That's very good of you. I think you'll find them thoroughly respectable,' and he preceded Soames downstairs.

'This is quite out of my line,' said Soames on the threshold. He was greeted with a number of little silent bows and nods. It was his impression that they'd been having a scrap.

'Mr – Mr Forsyte,' said what he supposed was this Bentworth, 'we want you as a lawyer to come on this committee and keep us – er – straight – check our fire-eaters, like Fanfield there, if you know what I mean;' and he looked over his tortoiseshell spectacles at Sir Timothy. 'Just cast your eye over this, will you be so good?' He passed a sheet of paper to Soames, who had sat down on a chair slipped under him by the young woman. Soames began to read:

' "While we suppose that there may be circumstances which justify the possession of slum property, we nevertheless regret profoundly the apparent indifference of most slum owners to this great national evil. With the hearty cooperation of slum property owners, much might be done which at present cannot be done. We do not wish to hold them up to the execration of anyone, but we want them to realize that they must at least co-operate in getting rid of this blot on our civilization." '

He read it twice, holding the end of his nose between his thumb and finger: then said: ' "We don't wish to hold them up to the execration of anyone." If you don't you don't; then why say so? The word "execration"! H'm!'

'Exactly!' said the chairman: 'Most valuable to have you on the committee, Mr – Forsyte.'

'Not at all,' said Soames, staring round him: 'I don't know that I'm coming on.'

'Look here, sir!' And Soames saw a fellow who looked like a general in a story-book, leaning towards him: 'D'you mean to say we can't use a mild word like "execration", when we know they ought to be shot?'

Soames gave a pale smile: if there was a thing he couldn't stand, it was militarism.

'You can use it if you like,' he said, 'but not with me or any other man of judgement on the committee.'

At his words at least four members of the committee burst into speech. Had he said anything too strong?

'We'll pass that without those words, then,' said the chairman. 'Now for your clause about the kitchens, Shropshire. That's important.'

The Marquess began reading; Soames looked at him almost with benevolence. They had hit it off very well over the Morland. No one objected to the addition, and it was adopted.

'That's that, then. I don't think there's anything more. I want to get off.'

'A minute, Mr Chairman.' Soames saw that the words were issuing from behind a walrus-like moustache. 'I know more of these people than any of you here. I started life in the slums, and I want to tell you something. Suppose you get some money, suppose you convert some streets, will you convert those people? No, gentlemen; you won't.'

'Their children, Mr Montross, their children,' said a man whom Soames recognized as one of those who had married Michael to his daughter.

'I'm not against the appeal, Mr Charwell, but I'm a self-made man and a realist, and I know what we're up against. I'm going to put some money into this, gentlemen, but I want you to know that I do so with my eyes open.'

Soames saw the eyes, melancholy and brown, fixed on himself, and had a longing to say: 'You bet!' But, looking at Sir Lawrence, he saw that 'Old Mont' had the longing too, and closed his lips firmly.

'Capital!' said the chairman. 'Well, Mr Forsyte, are you joining us?'

Soames looked round the table.

'I'll go into the matter,' he said, 'and let you know.'

Almost instantly the committee broke towards their hats, and he was left opposite the Goya with the Marquess.

'A Goya, Mr Forsyte, I think, and a good one. Am I mistaken, or didn't it once belong to Burlingford?'

'Yes,' said Soames, astonished. 'I bought it when Lord Burlingford sold his pictures in 1910.'

'I thought so. Poor Burlingford! He got very rattled, I remember, over the House of Lords. But, you see, they've done nothing since. How English it all was!'

'They're a dilatory lot,' murmured Soames, whose political recollections were of the vaguest.

'Fortunately, perhaps,' said the Marquess; 'there is so much leisure for repentance.'

'I can show you another picture or two, here, if you care for them,' said Soames.

'Do,' said the Marquess; and Soames led him across the hall, now evacuated by the hats.

'Watteau, Fragonard, Pater, Chardin,' said Soames.

The Marquess was gazing from picture to picture with his head a little on one side.

'Delightful!' he said. 'What a pleasant, and what a worthless age that was! After all, the French are the only people that can make vice attractive, except perhaps the Japanese, before they were spoiled. Tell me, Mr. Forsyte, do you know any Englishman who has done it?'

Soames, who had never studied the question and was hampered by not knowing whether he wanted an Englishman to do it, was hesitating when the Marquess added:

'And yet no such domestic people as the French.'

"My wife's French,' said Soames, looking round his nose.

'Indeed!' said the Marquess; 'How pleasant!'

Soames was again about to answer, when the Marquess continued:

'To see them go out on Sundays – the whole family, with their bread and cheese, their sausage and wine! A truly remarkable people!'

'I prefer ourselves,' said Soames, bluntly. 'Less ornamental, perhaps, but –' he stopped short of his country's virtues.

'The first of my family, Mr Forsyte, was undoubtedly a Frenchman – not even a Norman Frenchman. There's a tradition that he was engaged to keep William Rufus's hair red, when it was on the turn. They gave him lands, so he must have been successful. We've had a red streak in the family ever since.

My granddaughter –' He regarded Soames with a bird-like eye
– 'But she and your daughter hardly got on, I remember.'

'No,' said Soames, grimly, 'they hardly got on.'

'I'm told they've made it up.'

'I don't think so,' said Soames; 'but that's ancient history.'

In the stress of his present uneasiness he could have wished it
were modern.

'Well, Mr Forsyte, I'm delighted to have seen these pictures.
Your son-in-law tells me he's going to electrify the kitchen here.
Believe me, there's nothing more conducive to a quiet stomach
than a cook who never gets heated. Do tell Mrs Forsyte that!'

'I will,' said Soames; 'but the French are conservative.'

'Lamentably so,' replied the Marquess, holding out his hand:
'Good-bye to you!'

'Good-bye!' said Soames, and remained at the window, gazing after the old man's short, quick figure in its grey-green
tweeds, with a feeling of having been slightly electrified.

Chapter Twelve

DELICIOUS NIGHT

◄◄→►►

FLEUR sat under a groyne at Loring. There were few things
with which she had less patience than the sea. It was not in her
blood. The sea, with its reputation for never being in the same
mood, blue, wet, unceasing, had for her a distressing sameness.
And, though she sat with her face to it, she turned to it the back
of her mind. She had been there a week without seeing Jon
again. They knew where she was, yet only Holly had been over;
and her quick instinct apprehended the cause – Anne must
have become aware of her. And now, as Holly had told her,
there was no longer even Goodwood to look forward to. Everywhere she was baulked and with all her heart resented it! She
was indeed in a wretched state of indecision. If she had known

precisely the end she wished to attain, she could have possessed her soul; but she knew it not. Even the care of Kit was no longer important. He was robust again, and employed all day, with spade and bucket.

'I can't stand it,' she thought; 'I shall go up to town. Michael will be glad of me.'

She went up after an early lunch, reading in the train a book of reminiscences which took away the reputations of various dead persons. Quite in the mode, it distracted her thoughts more than she had hoped from its title: and her spirits rose as the scent of oysters died out of the air. She had letters from her father and Michael in her bag, and got them out to read again.

DEAR HEART (ran Michael's – yes, she supposed she *was* still his dear heart) –

I hope this finds you and Kit as it leaves me 'at the present time of speaking'. But I miss you horribly as usual, and intend to descend on you before long, unless you descend on me first. I don't know if you saw our appeal in the papers on Monday. People are already beginning to take bonds. The committee weighed in well for a send-off. The walrus put down five thousand of the best, the Marquess sent your father's Morland cheque for six hundred, and your Dad and Bart each gave two-fifty. The Squire gave five hundred; Bedwin and Sir Timothy a hundred apiece, and the bishop gave us twenty and his blessing. So we opened with six thousand eight hundred and twenty from the committee alone – none so dusty. I believe the thing will go. The appeal has been reprinted, and is going out to everybody who ever gives to anything; and amongst other propaganda, we've got the Polytheum to promise to show a slum film if we can get one made. My Uncle Hilary is very bucked. It was funny to see your Dad – he was a long time making up his mind, and he actually went down to look at the Meads. He came back saying – he didn't know, it was a tumble-down neighbourhood, he didn't think it could be done for five hundred a house. I had my uncle to him that evening, and he knocked under to Hilary's charm. But next morning he was very grumpy – said his name would be in the papers as signing the appeal, and seemed to think it would do him harm. 'They'll think I've taken leave of my senses,' was his way of putting it. However, there he is, on the committee, and he'll get used to it in time. They're a rum team, and but for the bugs I don't think they'd hold together. We

737

had another meeting today. Old Blythe's nose is properly out of joint; he says I've gone back on him and Foggartism. I haven't, of course – but, dash it, one must have something real to do!

All my love to you and Kit.

MICHAEL

I've got your drawing framed and hung above my bureau, and very jolly it looks. Your Dad was quite struck. M.

Above his bureau – 'The golden apple!' How ironical! Poor Michael – if he knew –!

Her father's letter was short – she had never had a long one from him.

MY DEAR CHILD,

Your mother has gone back to 'The Shelter', but I am staying on at Green Street about this thing of Michael's. I don't know, I'm sure, whether there's anything in it; there's a lot of gammon talked about the slums; still, for a parson, I find his uncle Hilary an amiable fellow, and there are some goodish names on the committee. We shall see.

I had no idea you had kept up your water-colours. The drawing has considerable merit, though the subject is not clear to me. The fruit looks too soft and rich for apples. Still, I suppose you know what you were driving at. I am glad the news of Kit is so good, and that you are feeling the better for the sea air.

Ever your affectionate father,

S. F.

Knew what she was driving at! If only she did! And if only her father didn't! That was the doubt in her mind when she tore up the letter and scattered it on Surrey through the window. He watched her like a lynx – like a lover; and she did not want to be watched just now.

She had no luggage, and at Victoria took a cab for Chiswick. June would at least know something about those two; whether they were still at Wansdon, or where they were.

How well she remembered the little house from the one visit she had paid to it – in the days when she and Jon –!

June was in the hall, on the point of going out.

'Oh! it's you!' she said. 'You didn't come that Sunday!'

'No, I had too much to do before I went away.'

'Jon and Anne are staying here now. Harold is painting a

738

beautiful thing of her. It'll be quite unique. She's a nice little thing, I think,' (*she* was several inches taller than June, according to Fleur's recollection) 'and pretty. I'm just going out to get him something he specially wants, but I shan't be a quarter of an hour. If you'll wait in the meal-room till I come back, I'll take you up, and then he'll see you. He's the only man who's doing real work just now.'

'It's so nice that there's one,' said Fleur.

'Here's an album of reproductions of his pictures' – and June opened a large book on a small dining-table. 'Isn't that lovely? But all his work has such quality. You must look through it, and I'll come back.' And with a little squeeze of Fleur's shoulder, she fled.

Fleur did not look through the album, she looked through the window and round the room. How she remembered it, and that round, dim mirror of very old glass wherein she had seen herself while she waited for Jon. And the stormy little scene they had been through together in this room too small for storms, seven years ago! Jon staying here! Her heart beat, and she stared at herself again in that dim mirror. Surely she was no worse to look at than she had been then! Nay! She was better! Her face had a stamp on it now, line on the roundness of youth! Couldn't she let him know that she was here? Couldn't she see him somehow just for a minute alone! That little one-eyed fanatic – for so in her thoughts Fleur looked on June – would be back directly. And quick mind took quick decision. If Jon were in, she would find him! Touching her hair at the sides, the pearls round her neck, and flicking an almost powder-less puff over her nose, she went out into the hall and listened. No sound! And slowly she began mounting the stairs. In his bedroom he would be, or in the studio – there was no other covert. On the first landing, bedroom to right of her, bedroom to left of her, bathroom in front of her, the doors open. Blank! – and blank in her heart! The studio was all there was above. And there – as well as Jon, would be the painter and that girl, his wife. Was it worth it? She took two steps down, and then retraced them. Yes! It was. Slowly, very silently, she went. The studio door was open, for she could hear the quick, familiar shuffle of a painter to his canvas and away again. She closed her eyes a moment, and then again went up. On the landing, close to the open door, she stood still. No need to go farther. For, in the room directly opposite to her, was a long, broad mirror, and in it – unseen herself – she could see. Jon was sitting on the end of a low divan with an unsmoked pipe in his hand, staring straight before him. On the dais that girl was standing, dressed in white; her hands held a long-stemmed lily whose flower reached to within an inch of her chin. Oh! she was pretty – pretty and brown, with those dark eyes and that dark hair framing her face. But Jon's expression – deepset on the mark of his visage as the eyes in his head! She had seen lion cubs look like that, seeing nothing close to them, seeing – what? – in the distance. That girl's eyes, what was it Holly had called them? – 'best type of water-nymph's' – slid round and looked at him, and at once his eyes left the distance and smiled back. Fleur turned then, hurried down the stairs, and out of the house. Wait for June – hear her rhapsodize – be introduced to the painter – have to control her face in front of that girl? No! Mounting to the top of her bus, she saw June skimming round a corner, and thought with malicious pleasure of her disappointment – when one had been hurt, one wanted to hurt somebody. The bus carried her away down the King's Road, Hammersmith, sweating in the westering sunlight, away into the big town with its myriad lives and interests, untouchable, indifferent as Fate.

At Kensington Gardens she descended. If she could get her legs to ache, perhaps her heart would not. And she walked fast between the flowers and the nursemaids, the old ladies and the old gentlemen. But her legs were strong, and Hyde Park Corner came too soon for all but one old Gentleman who had tried to keep pace with her because, at his age, it did him good to be attracted. She crossed to the Green Park and held on. And she despised herself while she walked. She despised herself. She – to whom the heart was such *vieux jeu;* who had learned, as she thought, to control or outspeed emotions!

She reached home, and it was empty – Michael not in. She went upstairs, ordered herself some Turkish coffee, got into a hot bath, and lay there smoking cigarettes. She experienced some alleviation. Among her friends the recipe had long been recognised. When she could steep herself no more, she put on a wrapper and went to Michael's study. There was her *Golden Apple* – very nicely framed. The fruit looked to her extraordinarily uneatable at that moment. The smile in Jon's eyes, answering that girl's smile! Another woman's leavings! The fruit was not worth eating. Sour apples – sour apples! Even the white monkey would refuse fruit like that. And for some minutes she stood staring instead at the eyes of the ape in that Chinese painting – those almost human eyes that yet were not human because their owner had no sense of continuity. A modern painter could not have painted eyes like that. The Chinese artist of all those centuries ago had continuity and tradition in his blood; he had seen the creature's restlessness at a sharper angle than people could see it now, and stamped it there for ever.

And Fleur – charming in her jade-green wrapper – tucked a corner of her lip behind a tooth, and went back to her room to finish dressing. She put on her prettiest frock. If she could not have the wish of her heart – the wish that she felt would give her calm and continuity – let her at least have pleasure, speed, distraction, grasp it with both hands, eat it with full lips. And she sat down before her glass to make herself as perfect as she could. She manicured her hands, titivated her hair, scented her eyebrows, smoothed her lips, put on rouge, and the merest dusting of powder, save where the seaside sun had stained her neck.

Michael found her still seated there – a modern masterpiece – almost too perfect to touch.

'Fleur!' he said, and nothing more; but any more would have spoiled it.

'I thought I deserved a night out. Dress quickly, Michael, and let's dine somewhere amusing, and do a theatre and a club afterwards. You needn't go to the House this evening, need you?'

He had meant to go but there was in her voice what would have stopped him from affairs even more serious.

Inhaling her, he said:

'Delicious! I've been in the slums. Shan't be a jiff, darling!' and he fled.

During the jiffy she thought of him and how good he was; and while she thought, she saw the eyes and the hair and the smile of Jon.

The 'somewhere amusing' was a little restaurant full of theatrical folk. Fleur and Michael knew many of them, and they came up, as they passed out to their theatres, and said:

'How delightful to see you!' and looked as if they meant it – so strange! But then, theatre folk were like that! They looked things so easily. And they kept saying: 'Have you seen our show? Oh! You must. It's just too frightful!' or, 'It's a marvellous play!' And then, over the other shoulder they would see somebody else, and call out: 'Ha! How delightful to see you!' There was no boring continuity about them. Fleur drank a Cocktail and two glasses of champagne. She went out with her cheeks slightly flushed. 'Dat Lubly Lady' had been in progress over half an hour before they reached her; but this did not seem to matter, for what they saw conveyed to them no more than what they had not seen. The house was very full, and people were saying that the thing would 'run for years'. It had a tune which had taken the town by storm, a male dancer whose legs could form the most acute angles, and no continuity whatever. Michael and Fleur went out humming the tune, and took a taxi to the dancing club to which they belonged because it was the thing, rather than because they ever went there. It was a select club, and contained among its members a Cabinet Minister who had considered it his duty. They found a Charleston in progress, seven couples wobbling weak knees at each other in various corners of the room.

'Gawd!' said Michael. 'I do think it's the limit of vacuity! What's its attraction?'

'Vacuity, my dear, this is a vacuous age – didn't you know?'

'Is there no limit?'

'A limit,' said Fleur, 'is what you can't go beyond; one can always became more vacuous.'

The words were nothing, for, after all, cynicism was in fashion, but the tone made Michael shiver; he felt in it a personal ring. Did she, then, feel her life so vacuous; and, if so, why?

'They say,' said Fleur, 'there's another American dance coming, called "The White Beam", that's got even less in it.'

'Not possible,' muttered Michael; 'for congenial idiocy this'll never be surpassed. Look at those two!'

The two in question were wobbling towards them with their knees flexed as if their souls had slipped down into them; their eyes regarded Fleur and Michael with no more expression then could have been found in four first-class marbles. A strange earnestness radiated from them below the waist, but above that line they seemed to have passed away. The music stopped, and each of the seven couples stopped also and began to clap their hands, holding them low, as though afraid of disturbing the vacuity attained above.

'I refuse to believe it,' said Michael, suddenly.

'What?'

'That this represents our age – no beauty, no joy, no skill, not even devil – just look a fool and wobble your knees.'

'You can't do it, you see.'

'D'you mean you can?'

'Of course,' said Fleur; 'one must keep up with things.'

'Well, for the land's sake, don't let me see you.'

At this moment the seven couples stopped clapping their hands – the band had broken into a tune to which the knee could not be flexed. Michael and Fleur began to dance. They danced together, two foxtrots and a waltz, then left.

'After all,' said Fleur, in the taxi, 'dancing makes you forget yourself. That was the beauty of the canteen. Find me another job, Michael; I can bring Kit back in about a week.'

'How about joint secretaryship with me of our Slum Conversion Fund? You'd be invaluable to get up balls, bazaars, and *matinées*.'

'I wouldn't mind. I suppose they're worth converting.'

'Well, *I* think so. You don't know Hilary; I must get him and Aunt May to lunch; after that you can judge for yourself.'

He slipped his hand under her bare arm, and added: 'Fleur, you're not quite tired of me, are you?'

The tone of his voice, humble and a little anxious, touched her, and she pressed his hand with her arm.

'I should never be tired of you, Michael.'

'You mean you'd never have a feeling so definite towards me.'

It was easily what she had meant, and she hastened to deny it.

'No, dear boy; I mean I know a good thing, and even a good person, when I've got it.'

Michael sighed, and, taking up her hand, put it to his lips.

'I wish,' cried Fleur, 'one wasn't so complex. You're lucky to be so single-hearted. It's the greatest gift. Only, don't ever become serious, Michael. That'd be a misfortune.'

'No; after all, comedy's the real thing.'

'Let's hope so,' said Fleur, as the taxi stopped. 'Delicious night!'

And Michael, having paid the driver, looked at her lighted up in the open doorway. Delicious night! Yes – for him.

Chapter Thirteen

'ALWAYS!'

◄◄►►

THE announcement by Michael on the following Monday that Fleur would be bringing Kit home the next morning, caused Soames to say:

'I'd like to have a look at that part of the world. I'll take the car down this afternoon and drive them up tomorrow. Don't say anything to Fleur. I'll let her know when I get down to Nettlefold. There's an hotel there, I'm told.'

'Quite a good one,' said Michael. 'But it'll be full for Good-wood.'

'I'll telephone. They must find a room for me.'

He did, and they found for him a room which somebody else lost. He started about five – Riggs having informed him that it was a two-and-a-half hours' drive. The day had been somewhat English in character, but by the time he reached Dorking had become fine enough to enjoy. He had seen littl of the England that lay beyond the straight line between his river home and Westminster for many years; and this late afternoon, less pre-occupied than usual, he was able to give it a somewhat detached consideration. It was certainly a variegated and bumpy land, incorrigibly green and unlike India, Canada and Japan. They said it had been jungle, heath and marsh not fifteen hundred years ago. What would it be fifteen hundred years hence? Jungle, heath and marsh again, or one large suburb – who could say? He had read somewhere that people would live under-ground, and come up to take the air in their flying machines on Sundays. He thought it was unlikely. The English would still want their windows down and a thorough draught, and so far as he could see, it would always be stuffy to play with a ball underground and impossible to play with a ball up in the air. Those fellows who wrote prophetic articles and books were al-ways forgetting that people had passions. He would make a bet that the passions of the English in 3400 A.D. would still be: play-ing golf, cursing the weather, sitting in draughts, and revising the Prayer Book.

And that reminded him that old Gradman was getting very old; he must look out for somebody who could take his place. There was nothing to do in the family trusts now – the only essential was perfect honesty. And where was he going to find it? Even if there was some about, it could only be tested by prolonged experiment. Must be a youngish man, too, because he himself couldn't last very much longer. And, moving at forty miles an hour along the road to Billingshurst, he recalled being fetched by old Gradman at six miles an hour from Paddington Station to Park Lane in a growler with wet straw on the floor –

over sixty years ago – when old Gradman himself was only a boy of twenty, trying to grow side-whiskers and writing round-hand all day. 'Five Oaks' on a signpost; he couldn't see the oaks! What a pace that chap Riggs was going! One of these days he would bring the whole thing to grief, and be sorry for it. But it was somehow *infra dig.* to pull him up for speed when there wasn't a woman in the car; and Soames sat the stiller, with a slightly contemptuous expression as a kind of insurance against his own sensations. Through Pulborough, down a twisting hill, across a little bridge, a little river, into a different kind of country – something new to him – flat meadows all along, that would be marsh in the winter, he would wager, with large, dark red cattle, and black-and-white and strawberry roan cattle; and over away to the south, high rising downs of a singularly cool green, as if they were white inside. Chalk – outcropping here and there, and sheep up on those downs, no doubt – his father had always sworn by Southdown mutton. A very pretty light, a silvery look, a nice prospect altogether, that made you feel thinner at once and lighter in the head! So this was the sort of country his nephew had got hold of, and that young fellow Jon Forsyte. Well! It might have been worse – very individual; he didn't remember anything just like it. And a sort of grudging fairness, latent in Soames's nature, applauded slightly. How that chap Riggs was banging the car up this hill – the deuce of a hill, too, past chalk-pits and gravel-pits, and grassy down and dipping spurs of covert, past the lodge of a park, into a great beech-wood. Very pretty – very still – no life but trees, spreading trees, very cool, very green! Past a monstrous great church thing, now, and a lot of high walls and towers – Arundel Castle, he supposed; huge, great place; would look better, no doubt, the farther you got from it; then over another river and up another hill, banging along into this Nettlefold and the hotel, and the sea in front of you!

Soames got out.

'What time's dinner?'

'Dinner is on, sir.'

'Do they dress?'

'Yes, sir. There's a fancy dress dance, sir, this evening, before Goodwood.'

'What a thing to have! Get me a table; I'll be down directly.'

He had once read in a Victorian novel that the mark of a gentleman was being able to dress for dinner in ten minutes, tying his own tie. He had never forgotten it. He was down in twelve. Most people had nearly finished, but there was no one in fancy dress. Soames ate leisurely, contemplating a garden with the sea beyond. He had not, like Fleur, an objection to the sea – had he not once lived at Brighton for seven years, going up and down to his work in town? That was the epoch when he had been living down the disgrace of being deserted by his first wife. Curious how the injured party was always the one in disgrace! People admired immorality, however much they said they didn't. The deserted husband, the deserted wife, were looked on as poor things. Was it due to something still wild in human nature, or merely to reaction against the salaried morality of judges and parsons, and so forth? Morality you might respect, but salaried morality – no! He had seen it in people's eyes after his own trouble; he had seen it in the Marjorie Ferrar case. The fact was, people took the protection of the law and secretly disliked it because it was protective. The same thing with taxes – you couldn't do without them, but you avoided paying them when you could.

Having finished dinner, he sat with his cigar in a somewhat deserted lounge, turning over weekly papers full of ladies with children or dogs, ladies with clothes in striking attitudes, ladies with no clothes in still more striking attitudes; men with titles, men in aeroplanes, statesmen in trouble, race-horses; large houses prefaced with rows of people with the names printed clearly for each, and other evidences of the millennium. He supposed his fellow-guests were 'dolling up' (as young Michael would put it) for this ball – fancy dressing up at their age! But people *were* weak-minded – no question of that! Fleur would be surprised when he dropped in on her tomorrow early. Soon she would be coming down to him on the river – its best time of year – and perhaps he could take her for a motor trip into the west somewhere; it might divert her thoughts from this part of the country and that young man. He had often promised himself a visit to where the old Forsytes came from; only he didn't suppose she would care to look at anything so rustic as genuine farmland. The magazine dropped from his fingers, and he sat staring out of the large window at the flowers about to sleep, He hadn't so many more years before him now, he supposed. They said that people lived longer than they used to, but how he was going to outlive the old Forsytes, he didn't know – the ten of them had averaged eighty-seven years – a monstrous age! And yet he didn't feel it would be natural to die in another sixteen years, with the flowers growing like that out there, and his grandson coming along nicely. With age one suffered from the feeling that one might have enjoyed things more. Cows, for instance, and rooks, and good smells. Curious how the country grew on you as you got older! But he didn't know that it would ever grow on Fleur – she wanted people about her; still she might lose that when she found out once for all that there was so little in them. The light faded on the garden and his reverie. There were lots of people out on the sea front, and a band had begun to play. A band was playing behind him, too, in the hotel somewhere. They must be dancing! He might have a look at that before he went up. On his trip round the world with Fleur he had often put his nose out and watched the dancing on deck – funny business nowadays, shimmying, bunny-hugging, didn't they call it? – dreadful! – He remembered the academy of dancing where he had been instructed as a small boy in the polka, the mazurka, deportment and calisthenics. And a pale grin spread over his chaps – that little old Miss Shears, who had taught him and Winifred, what wouldn't she have died of if she had lived to see these modern-dances! People despised the old dances, and when he came to think of it, he had despised them himself, but compared with this modern walking about and shaking at the knees, they had been dances, after all. Look at the Highland schottische, where you spun round and howled, and the old gallop to the tune '*D'ye ken John Peel*' – some stingo in them; and you had to change your collar. No changing collars nowadays – they just dawdled. For an age that prided itself on enjoying life, they had a funny idea of it. He remembered once before his first marriage, going – by accident – to one of those old dancing clubs, the Athenians, and seeing George Forsyte and his cronies waltzing and swinging the girls round and round clean off their feet. The girls at those clubs, then, were all professional lights-o'-love. Very different now, he was told; but there it was – people posed nowadays, they posed as *viveurs*, and all the rest of it, but they didn't vive; they thought too much about how to.

The music – all jazz – died behind him and rose again, and he, too, rose. He would just have a squint and go to bed.

The ballroom was somewhat detached, and Soames went down a corridor. At its end he came on a twirl of sound and colour. They were hard at it, 'dolled up' to the nines – Mephistopheleses, ladies of Spain, Italian peasants, pierrots. His bewildered eyes with difficulty took in the strutting, wheeling mass; his bewildered ears decided that the tune was trying to be a waltz. He remembered that the waltz was in three-time, remembered the waltz of olden days – too well – that dance at Roger's, and Irene, his own wife, waltzing in the arms of young Bosinney; to this day remembered the look on her face, the rise and fall of her breast, the scent of the gardenias she was wearing, and that fellow's face when she raised to his her dark eyes – lost to all but themselves and their guilty enjoyment; remembered the balcony on which he had refuged from that sight, and the policeman down below him on the strip of red carpet from house to street.

'"Always !" – good tune !' said someone behind his ears.

Not bad, certainly – a sort of sweetness in it. His eyes, from behind the neck of a large lady who seemed trying to be a fairy, roved again among the dancers. What ! Over there ! Fleur ! Fleur in her Goya dress, grape-coloured – *La Vendimia* – the Vintage – floating out from her knees, with her face close to the face of a sheik, and his face close to hers. Fleur ! And that sheik, that Moor in a dress all white and flowing ! In Soames a groan was converted to a cough. *Those two !* So close – so – so

lost – it seemed to him! As Irene with Bosinney, so she with
that young Jon! They passed, not seeing him behind the fairy's
competent bulk. Soames's eyes tracked them through the shifting, yawing throng. Round again they came – her eyes so nearly
closed that he hardly knew them; and young Jon's over her
fichued shoulder, deep-set and staring. Where was the fellow's
wife? And just then Soames caught sight of her, dancing, too,
but looking back at them – a nymph all trailing green, the eyes
surprised and jealous. No wonder, since under her very gaze
was Fleur's swinging skirt, the rise and falling of her breast,
the languor in her eyes! 'Always!' Would they never stop
that cursed tune, stop those two, who with every bar seemed to
cling closer and closer! And, fearful lest he should be seen,
Soames turned away and mounted slowly to his room. He had
had his squint. It was enough!

The band had ceased to play on the sea front, people were
deserting, lights going out; by the sound out there, the tide
must be rising. Soames touched himself where he was sore,
beneath his starched shirt, and stood still. 'Always!' Incalculable consequences welled in on his consciousness, like the murmuring tide of that sea. Daughter exiled, grandson lost to him;
memories deflowered; hopes in the dust! 'Always!' Forsooth!
Not if he knew it – not for Joe! And all that grim power of
self-containment which but twice or three times in his life had
failed him, and always with disastrous consequence, again for a
moment failed him, so that to any living thing present in the
dim and austere hotel bedroom, he would have seemed like one
demented. The paroxysm passed. No use to rave! Worse than
no use – far; would only make him ill, and he would want his
strength. For what? For sitting still; for doing nothing; for
waiting to see! Venus! Touch not the goddess – the hot, the
jealous one with the lost dark eyes! He had touched her in the
past, and she had answered with a blow. Touch her not! Possess
his sore and anxious heart! Nothing to do but wait and see!

PART THREE

Chapter One

SOAMES GIVES ADVICE

◂◂◂►►►

O N her return to Nettlefold from her night in town, Fleur had continued to 'eat her heart out' by 'the sad sea wave'. For still neither Jon nor his wife came to see her. Clearly she was labelled 'poison'. Twice she had walked over to Green Hill Farm hoping for another 'jolly accident'. She had seen there an attractive old house with aged farm buildings flanked by a hill and a wide prospect towards the sea. Calm, broad, and home-like, the place roused hostility in her. It could never be *her* home, and so was inimical, part of the forces working against her. Loose ends in Jon's life were all in her favour. In exploita-tion of those calm acres he would be secured to that girl his wife, out of her reach again, this time for good – the twice-burnt child ! And yet, with all her heart-ache, she was still un-certain what, precisely, she wanted. Not having to grapple with actual decision, things seemed possible, which, in her bones, she knew might not be possible. Even to fling her 'cap over the windmill' did not seem like rank and staring madness. To re-trieve Spain with Jon ! Her hands clenched and her lips loosened at the thought of it – an Odyssey together, till in the shifting, tolerant, modern world, all was forgotten, if not forgiven ! Every form of companionship with him from decorous and platonic friendship to the world well lost; from guilty and secret liaison to orderly and above-board glimpses of him at not too long intervals. According to the tides in her blood, all seemed possible, if not exactly probable, so long as she did not lose him again altogether.

To these feverish veerings of her spirit, a letter from her Aunt Winifred supplied a point of anchorage:

'I hear from Val that they are not going to Goodwood after

751

all – their nice two-year-old is not in form. Such a bore. It's the most comfortable meeting of the year. They seem to be very busy settling about the farm that Jon Forsyte is going to take. It will be pleasant for Val and Holly to have them so close, though I'm afraid that American child will find it dull. Holly writes that they are going to an amusing little fancy dress affair at the hotel in Nettlefold. Anne is to go as a water-nymph – she will make quite a good one with her nice straight legs. Holly is to be Madame Vigée le Brun; and Val says he'll go as a tipster or not at all. I do hope he won't redden his nose. Young Jon Forsyte has an Arab dress he brought from Egypt.'

'And I,' thought Fleur, 'have the dress I wore the night I went to his room at Wansdon.' How she wished now that she had come out of that room his wife; after that nothing could have divided them. But they had been such innocents then!

For at once she had made up her mind to go to that dance herself. She was there first, and with malicious pleasure watched the faces of those two when she met them at the entrance of the room. Her grape-dress. She could see that Jon remembered it, and quickly she began to praise Anne's. A water-nymph to the life! As for Jon – another wife or two was all he needed to be perfect! She was discretion itself until that waltz; and even then she had tried to be discreet to all but Jon. For him she kept (or so she hoped) the closeness, the clinging and the languor of her eyes; but in those few minutes she let him know quite surely that love ran in her veins.

' "Always!",' was all she said when at last they stopped.

And, after that dance, she stole away home; having no heart to see him dance with his water-nymph. She crept up to her small bedroom trembling, and on her bed fell into a passion of silent weeping. And the water-nymph's browned face and eyes and legs flitted torturingly in the tangled glades of her vision. She quieted down at last. At least, for a few minutes, she had had him to herself, heart against heart. That was something.

She rose late, pale and composed again. At ten o'clock the startling appearance of her father's car completed the masking of her face. She greeted him with an emphatic gratitude quite unfelt.

'Dad! How lovely! Where have you sprung from?'

'Nettlefold. I spent the night there.'

'At the hotel?'

'Yes.'

'Why! I was there myself last night at a dance!'

'Oh!' said Soames, 'that fancy dress affair – they told me of it. Pleasant?'

'Not very; I left early. If I'd known you were there! Why didn't you tell me you were coming down to fetch us home?'

'It just came into my mind that it was better for the boy than the train.'

And Fleur could not tell what he had seen, or if, indeed, he had seen anything.

Fortunately, during the journey up, Kit had much to say, and Soames dozed, very tired after a night of anxiety, indecision, and little sleep. The aspect of the South Square house, choice and sophisticated, and the warmth of Michael's greeting, quite beautifully returned by Fleur, restored to him at least a measure of equanimity. Here, at all events, was no unhappy home; that counted much in the equation of a future into which he could no longer see.

After lunch he went up to Michael's study to discuss slum conversion. Confronted, while they were talking, with Fleur's water-colour, Soames rediscovered the truth that individuals are more interesting than the collection of them called the State. Not national welfare, but the painter of those passion fruits, possessed his mind. How prevent her from eating them?

'Yes, sir. That's really quite good, isn't it? I wish Fleur would take seriously to water-colour work.'

Soames started.

'I wish she'd take seriously to anything, and keep her mind occupied.'

Michael looked at him. 'Rather like a dog.' Soames thought, 'trying to understand.' Suddenly, he saw the young man wet his lips.

753

'You've got something to tell me, sir, I believe. I remember what you said to me some weeks ago. Is it anything to do with that?'

'Yes,' answered Soames, watching his eyes. 'Don't take it too much to heart, but I've reason to believe she's never properly got over the feeling she used to have. I don't know how much you've heard about that boy and girl affair.'

'Pretty well all, I think.' Again he saw Michael moisten his lips.

'Oh! From her?'

'No. Fleur's never said a word. From Miss June Forsyte.'

'That woman! *She's* sure to have plumped it all out. But Fleur's fond of you.'

'I belong.'

It seemed to Soames a queer way of putting it; pathetic somehow!

'Well,' he said, 'I've not made a sign. Perhaps you'd like to know how I formed my view.'

'No, sir.'

Soames glanced quickly at him and away again. This was a bitter moment, no doubt, for young Michael! Was one precipitating a crisis which one felt, deeply yet vaguely, had to be reached and passed? He himself knew how to wait, but did this modern young man, so feather-pated and scattery? Still, he was a gentleman. That at least had become a cardinal belief with Soames. And it was a comfort to him looking at the 'White Monkey' on the wall, who had so slender a claim to such a title.

'The only thing,' he muttered, 'is to wait —'

'Not "and see", sir; anything but that. I can wait and not see, or I can have the whole thing out.'

'No,' said Soames, with emphasis, 'don't have it out! I may be mistaken. There's everything against it; she knows which side her bread is buttered.'

'Don't!' cried Michael, and got up.

'Now, now,' murmured Soames; 'I've upset you. Everything depends on keeping your head.'

Michael emitted an unhappy little laugh.

'*You* can't go round the world again, sir. Perhaps *I'd* better, this time, and alone.'

Soames looked at him. 'This won't do,' he said. 'She's got a strong affection for you; it's just feverishness, if it's anything. Take it like a man, and keep quiet.' He was talking to the young man's back now, and found it easier. 'She was always a spoiled child, you know; spoiled children get things into their heads, but it doesn't amount to anything. Can't you get her interested in these slums?'

Michael turned round.

'How far has it gone?'

'There you go!' said Soames. 'Not any way so far as I know. I only happened to see her dancing with him last night at that hotel, and noticed her – her expression.'

The word 'eyes' had seemed somehow too extravagant.

'There's always his wife,' he added quickly, 'she's an attractive little thing; and he's going to farm down there – they tell me. That'll take him all his time. How would it be if I took Fleur to Scotland for August and September? With this strike on there'll be some places in the market still.'

'No, sir, that's only putting off the evil day. It must go to a finish, one way or the other.'

Soames did not answer for some time.

'It's never any good to meet trouble half-way,' he said at last. 'You young people are always in a hurry. One can do things, but one can't undo them. It's not,' he went on shyly, 'as if this were anything new – an unfortunate old business revived for the moment; it'll die away again as it did before, if it's properly left alone. Plenty of exercise, and keep her mind well occupied.'

The young man's expression was peculiar. 'And have you found that successful, sir, in your experience?' it seemed to say. That woman June had been blurting out his past, he shouldn't wonder!

'Promise me, anyway, to keep what I've said to yourself, and do nothing rash.'

Michael shook his head. 'I can't promise anything, it must depend; but I'll remember your advice, sir.'

And with this Soames had to be content.

Acting on that instinct, born of love, which guided him in his dealings with Fleur, he bade her an almost casual farewell, and next day returned to Mapledurham. He detailed to Annette everything that was not of importance, for to tell her what was would never do.

His home in these last days of July was pleasurable; and almost at once he went out fishing in the punt. There, in contemplation of his line and the gliding water, green with reflection, he felt rested. Bulrushes, water-lilies, dragon-flies, and the cows in his own fields, the incessant cooing of the wood-pigeons – with their precious 'Take *two* cows, David!' – the distant buzz of his gardener's lawn-mower, the splash of a water-rat, shadows lengthening out from the poplars and the willow trees, the scent of grass and of elder flowers bright along the banks, and the slow drift of the white river clouds – peaceful – very peaceful; and something of Nature's calm entered his soul, so that the disappearance of his float recalled him to reality with a jerk.

'It'll be uneatable,' he thought, winding at his line.

Chapter Two

OCCUPYING THE MIND

COMEDY the real thing! Was it? Michael wondered. In saying to Soames that he could not wait and see, he had expressed a very natural abhorrence. Watch, spy, calculate – impossible! To go to Fleur and ask for a frank exposure of her feelings was what he would have liked to do; but he could not help knowing the depth of his father-in-law's affection and concern, and the length of his head; and he had sufficient feeling to hesitate be-

fore imperilling what was as much 'old Forsyte's' happiness as
his own, the 'old boy' had behaved so decently in pulling up
his roots and going round the world with Fleur, that every
consideration was due to him. It remained, then, to wait without
attempting to see – hardest of all courses because least active.
'Keep her mind well occupied!' So easy! Recollecting his own
pre-nuptial feelings, he did not see how it was to be done. And
Fleur's was a particularly difficult mind to occupy with anything except that on which she had set her heart. The slums?
No! She possessed one of those eminently sane natures which
rejected social problems, as fruitless and incalculable. An immediate job, like the canteen, in which she could shine a little –
she would perform beautifully; but she would never work for a
remote object, without shining! He could see her clear eyes
looking at the slums as they had looked at Foggartism, and his
experiment with the out-of-works. He might take her to see
Hilary and Aunt May, but it would be futile in the end.

Night brought the first acute trouble. What were to be his
relations with her, if her feelings were really engaged elsewhere? To wait and not see meant continuation of the married
state. He suspected Soames of having wished to counsel that.
Whipped by longing, stung and half numbed by a jealousy he
must not show, and unwishful to wound her, he waited for a
sign, feeling as if she must know why he was waiting. He received it, and was glad, but it did not convince him. Still!

He woke much lighter in spirit.

At breakfast he asked her what she would like to do, now that
she was back and the season over. Did this slum scheme amuse
her at all, because if so, there was a lot to do in it; she would
find Hilary and May great sports.

'Rather! Anything really useful, Michael!'

He took her round to 'The Meads'. The result was better
than he had hoped.

For his uncle and aunt were human buildings the like of
which Fleur had not yet encountered – positively fashioned, concreted in tradition, but freely exposed to sun and air, tiled with
taste, and windowed with humour. Michael, with something

of their 'make-up', had neither their poise, nor active certainty. Fleur recognized at once that those two dwelt in unity unlike any that she knew, as if, in their twenty odd years together, they had welded a single instrument to carry out a new discovery – the unselfconscious day. They were not fools, yet cleverness in their presence seemed jejune, and as if unrelated to reality. They knew – especially Hilary – a vast deal about flowers, printing, architecture, mountains, drains, electricity, the price of living, Italian cities; they knew how to treat the ailments of dogs, play musical instruments, administer first and even second aid, amuse children, and cause the aged to laugh. They could discuss anything from religion to morality with fluency, and the tolerance that came from experience of the trials of others and forgetfulness of their own. With her natural intelligence Fleur admired them. They were good, but they were not dull – very odd! Admiring them, she could not help making up to them. Their attitude in life – she recognized – was superior to her own, and she was prepared to pay at least lip-service. But lip-service 'cut no ice' in 'The Meads'. Hand, foot, intellect and heart were the matter-of-course requirements. To occupy her mind, however, she took the jobs given her. Then trouble began. The jobs were not her own, and there was no career in them. Try as she would, she could not identify herself with Mrs Corrigan or the little Topmarshes. The girls, who served at Petter and Poplin's and kept their clothes in paper bags, bored her when they talked and when they didn't. Each new type amused her for a day, and then just seemed unlovely. She tried hard, however, for her own sake, and in order to deceive Michael. She had been at it more than a week before she had an idea.

'You know, Michael, I feel I should be ever so much more interested if I ran a place of my own in the country – a sort of rest-house that I could make attractive for girls who wanted air and that.'

To Michael, remembering the canteen, it seemed 'an idea' indeed. To Fleur it seemed more – a 'lease and release', as her father might have put it. Her scheming mind had seen the possibilities. She would be able to go there without let or cavil, and none would know what she did with her time. A base of operations with a fool-proof title was essential for a relationship, however innocent, with Jon. She began at once to learn to drive the car; for the 'rest-house' must not be so near him as to excite suspicion. She approached her father on the finance of the matter. At first doubtfully, and then almost cordially, Soames approved. If he would pay the rent and rates of the house, she would manage the rest out of her own pocket. She could not have bettered such a policy by way of convincing him that her interest was genuine; for he emphatically distrusted the interest of people in anything that did not cost them money. A careful study of the map suggested to her the neighbourhood of Dorking. Box Hill had a reputation for air and beauty, and was within an hour's fast drive of Wansdon. In the next three weeks she found and furnished a derelict house, rambling and cheap, close to the road on the London side of Box Hill, with a good garden and stables that could be converted easily. She completed her education with the car, and engaged a couple who could be left in charge with impunity. She consulted Michael and the Hilarys freely. In fact, like a mother cat, who carefully misleads the household as to where she is going to 'lay' her kittens, so Fleur, by the nature of her preparations, disguised her round-about design. 'The Meads Rest House', as it was called, was opened at the end of August.

All this time she possessed her soul with only the scantiest news of Jon. A letter from Holly told her that negotiations for Green Hill Farm were 'hanging fire' over the price, though Jon was more and more taken with it; and Anne daily becoming more rural and more English. Rondavel was in great form again, and expected to win at Doncaster. Val had already taken a long shot about him for the Derby next year.

Fleur replied in a letter so worded as to give the impression that she had no other interest in the world just then but her new scheme. They must all drive over to see whether her 'Rest House' didn't beat the canteen. The people were 'such dears' – it was all 'terribly amusing'. She wished to convey the feeling that she

had no fears of herself, no alarm in the thought of Jon; and
that her work in life was serious. Michael, never wholly deserted
by the naïveté of a good disposition, was more and more deceived. To him her mind seemed really occupied; and certainly
her body, for she ran up from Dorking almost daily and spent
the week-ends with him either at 'The Shelter', where Kit
was installed with his grandparents, or at Lippinghall, where
they always made a fuss of Fleur. Rowing her on the river in
bland weather, Michael recaptured a feeling of security. 'Old
Forsyte' must have let his imagination run away with him, the
old boy *was* rather like a hen where Fleur was concerned,
clucking and turning an inflamed eye on everything that came
near!

Parliament had risen, and slum conversion work was now all
that he was doing. These days on that river, which he ever
associated with his wooing, were the happiest he had spent since
the strike began – the strike that in narrowed form dragged
wearyingly on, so that people ceased to mention it, the weather
being warm.

And Soames? By his daughter's tranquil amiability, he, too,
was tranquillized. He would look at Michael and say nothing,
in accordance with the best English traditions, and his own
dignity. It was he who revived the idea of Fleur's getting painted
by June's 'lame duck'. He felt it would occupy her mind still
further. He would like, however, to see the fellow's work first,
though he supposed it would mean a visit to June's.

'If she were to be out,' he said to Fleur, 'I shouldn't mind
having a look round her studio.'

'Shall I arrange that, then, Dad?'

'Not too pointedly,' said Soames; 'or she'll get into a
fantod.'

Accordingly at the following week-end Fleur said to him:

'If you'll come up with me on Monday, dear, we'll go round.
The Rafaelite will be in, but June won't. She doesn't want to
see you any more than you want to see her.'

'H'm!' said Soames. 'She always spoke her mind.'

They went up in his car. After forming his opinion Soames

was to return, and Fleur to go on home. The Rafaelite met
them at the head of the stairs. To Soames he suggested a bull-
fighter (not that he had ever seen one in the flesh), with his
short whiskers and his broad, pale face which wore the expression: 'If you suppose yourself capable of appreciating my
work, you make a mistake.' Soames's face, on the other hand
wore the expression: 'If you suppose that I want to appreciate
your work, you make a greater.' And, leaving him to Fleur, he
began to look round. In truth he was not unfavourably impressed. The work had turned its back on modernity. The
surfaces were smooth, the drawing in perspective, and the
colouring full. He perceived a new note, or rather the definite
revival of an old one. The chap had undoubted talent; whether
it would go down in these days he did not know, but its texture
was more agreeable to live with than any he had seen for some
time. When he came to the portrait of June he stood for a
minute, with his head on one side, and then said, with a pale
smile:

'You've got her to the life.' It pleased him to think that June
had evidently not seen in it what he saw. But when his eyes
fell on the picture of Anne, his face fell, too, and he looked
quickly at Fleur, who said:

'Yes, Dad? What do you think of that?'

The thought had flashed through Soames's mind: 'Is it to
get in touch with *him* that she's ready to be painted?'

'Finished?' he asked.

The Rafaelite answered:

'Yes. Going down to them tomorrow.'

Soames's face rose again. That risk was over then!

'Quite clever!' he murmured. 'The lily's excellent.' And he
passed on to a sketch of the woman who had opened the door to
them.

'That's recognisable! Not at all bad.'

In these quiet ways he made it clear that, while he approved
on the whole, he was not going to pay any extravagant price.
He took an opportunity when Fleur was out of hearing, and
said:

'So you want to paint my daughter. What's your figure?'

'A hundred and fifty.'

'Rather tall for these days – you're a young man. However – so long as you make a good thing of it!'

The Rafaelite bowed ironically.

'Yes,' said Soames, 'I dare say; you think all your geese are swans – never met a painter who didn't. You won't keep her sitting long, I suppose – she's busy. That's agreed, then. Goodbye! Don't come down!'

As they went out he said to Fleur:

'I've fixed that. You can begin sitting when you like. His work's better than you'd think from the look of him. Forbidding chap, I call him.'

'A painter has to be forbidding, Dad; otherwise people would think he was cadging.'

'Something in that,' said Soames. 'I'll get back now, as you won't let me take you home. Good-bye! Take care of yourself, and don't overdo it.' And, receiving her kiss, he got into the car.

Fleur began to walk towards her eastward-bound bus as his car moved west, nor did he see her stop, give him some law, then retrace her steps to June's.

Chapter Three

POSSESSING THE SOUL

JUST as in a very old world to find things or people of pure descent is impossible, so with actions; and the psychologist who traces them to single motives is like Soames, who believed that his daughter wanted to be painted in order that she might see herself hanging on a wall. Everybody, he knew, had themselves hung sooner or later, and generally sooner. Yet Fleur, though certainly not averse to being hung, had motives that were hardly

so single as all that. In the service of this complexity, she went back to June's. That little lady, who had been lurking in her bedroom so as not to meet her kinsman, was in high feather.

'Of course the price is nominal,' she said. 'Harold ought really to be getting every bit as much for his portraits as Thorn or Lippen. Still, it's so important for him to be making something while he's waiting to take his real place. What have you come back for?'

'Partly for the pleasure of seeing you,' said Fleur, 'and partly because we forgot to arrange for the first sitting. I think my best time would be three o'clock.'

'Yes,' murmured June doubtfully, not so much from doubt as from not having suggested it herself. 'I think Harold could manage that. Isn't his work exquisite?'

'I particularly like the thing he's done of Anne. It's going down to them tomorrow, I hear.'

'Yes; Jon's coming to fetch it.'

Fleur looked hastily into the little dim mirror to see that she was keeping expression off her face.

'What do you think I ought to wear?'

June's gaze swept her from side to side.

'Oh! I expect he'll want an artificial scheme with you.'

'Exactly! But what colour? One must come in something.'

'We'll go up and ask him.'

The Rafaelite was standing before his picture of Anne. He turned and looked at them, without precisely saying: 'Good Lord! These women!' and nodded, gloomily, at the suggestion of three o'clock.

'What do you want her in?' asked June.

The Rafaelite stared at Fleur as if determining where her ribs left off and her hip-bones began.

'Gold and silver,' he said at last.

June clasped her hands.

'Now isn't that extraordinary? He's seen through you at once. Your gold and silver room. Harold, how *did* you?'

'I happen to have an old "Folly" dress,' said Fleur, 'silver and gold, with bells, that I haven't worn since I was married.'

'A "Folly"!' cried June. 'The very thing. If it's pretty. Some are hideous, of course.'

'Oh, it's pretty, and makes a charming sound.'

'He can't paint that,' said June. Then added dreamily: 'But you could suggest it, Harold – like Leonardo.'

'Leonardo!'

'Oh! Of course! I know, he wasn't –'

The Rafaelite interrupted.

'Don't make your face up,' he said to Fleur.

'No,' murmured Fleur. 'June, I do so like that of Anne. Has it struck you that she's sure to want Jon painted now?'

'Of course. I'll make him promise when he comes tomorrow.'

'He's going to begin farming, you know; he'll make that an excuse. Men hate being painted.'

'Oh, that's all nonsense,' said June. 'In old days they loved it. Anyway, Jon must sit before he begins. They'll make a splendid pair.'

Behind the Rafaelite's back Fleur bit her lip.

'He must wear a turn-down shirt. Blue, don't you think, Harold – to go with his hair?'

'Pink, with green spots,' muttered the Rafaelite.

'Then three o'clock tomorrow?' said Fleur hastily.

June nodded. 'Jon's coming to lunch, so he'll be gone before you come.'

'All right, then. Au revoir!'

She held her hand out to the Rafaelite, who seemed surprised at the gesture.

'Good-bye, June!'

June came suddenly close and kissed her on the chin. At that moment the little lady's face looked soft and pink, and her eyes soft; her lips were warm, too, as if she were warm all through.

Fleur went away thinking: 'Ought I to have asked her not to tell Jon I was going to be painted?' But surely June, the warm, the single-eyed, would never tell Jon anything that might stop him being useful to her Rafaelite. She stood, noting the geography around 'The Poplars'. The only approach to this backwater was by a road that dipped into it and came out again. Just here, she would not be seen from the house, and could see Jon leaving after lunch whichever way he went. But then he would have to take a taxi, for the picture. It struck her bitterly that she, who had been his first-adored, should have to scheme to see him. But if she didn't, she would never see him! Ah! what a ninny she had been at Wansdon in those old days when her room was next to his. One little act, and nothing could have kept him from her for all time, not his mother nor the old feud; not her father; nothing, and then there had been no vows of hers or his, no Michael, no Kit, no nymph-eyed girl in barrier between them; nothing but youth and innocence. And it seemed to her that youth and innocence were over-rated.

She lit on no plan by which she could see him without giving away the fact that she had schemed. She would have to possess her soul a little longer. Let him once get his head into the painter's noose, and there would be not one but many chances.

She arrived at three o'clock with her Folly's dress, and was taken into June's bedroom to put it on.

'It's just right,' said June; 'delightfully artificial. Harold will love it.'

'I wonder,' said Fleur. The Rafaelite's temperament had not yet struck her as very loving. They went up to the studio without having mentioned Jon.

The portrait of Anne was gone. And when June went to fetch 'the exact thing' to cover a bit of background, Fleur said at once:

'Well? Are you going to paint my cousin Jon?'

The Rafaelite nodded.

'He didn't want to be, but *she* made him.'

'When do you begin?'

'Tomorrow,' said the Rafaelite. 'He's coming every morning for a week. What's the good of a week?'

"If he's only got a week I should have thought he'd better stay here.'

'He won't without his wife, and his wife's got a cold.'

'Oh!' said Fleur, and she thought rapidly. 'Wouldn't it be

more convenient, then, for him to sit early in the afternoons? I could come in the mornings; in fact, I'd rather — one feels fresher. June could give him a trunk call.'

The Rafaelite uttered what she judged to be an approving sound. When she left, she said to June: 'I want to come at ten every morning, then I get my afternoons free for my "Rest House" down at Dorking. Couldn't you get Jon to come in the afternoons instead? It would suit him better. Only don't let him know I'm being painted — my picture won't be recognizable for a week, anyway.'

'Oh!' said June, 'you're quite wrong there. Harold always gets an unmistakable likeness at once; but of course he'll put it face to the wall, he always does while he's at work on a picture.'

'Good! He's made quite a nice start. Then if you'll telephone to Jon, I'll come tomorrow at ten.' And for yet another day she possessed her soul. On the day after, she nodded at a canvas whose face was to the wall, and asked:

'Do you find my cousin a good sitter?'

'No,' said the Rafaelite; 'he takes no interest. Got something on his mind, I should think.'

'He's a poet, you know,' said Fleur.

The Rafaelite gave her an epileptic stare. 'Poet! His head's the wrong shape — too much jaw — and the eyes too deep in.'

'But his hair! Don't you find him an attractive subject?'

'Attractive!' replied the Rafaelite — 'I paint anything, whether it's pretty or ugly as sin. Look at Rafael's Pope — did you ever see a better portrait, or an uglier man? Ugliness is not attractive, but it's there.'

'That's obvious,' said Fleur.

'I state the obvious. The only real novelties now are platitudes. That's why my work is important and seems new. People have got so far away from the obvious that the obvious startles them, and nothing else does. I advise you to think that over.'

'I'm sure there's a lot in it,' said Fleur.

'Of course,' said the Rafaelite, 'a platitude has to be stated with force and clarity. If you can't do that, you'd better go on slopping around and playing parlour tricks like the Ga-gaists.

They're a pathetic lot, trying to prove that cocktails are a better drink than old brandy. I met a man last night who told me he'd spent four years writing twenty-two lines of poetry that nobody can understand. How's that for pathos? But it'll make him quite a reputation, till somebody writes twenty-three lines in five years still more unintelligible. Hold your head up. . . . Your cousin's a silent beggar.'

'Silence is quite a quality,' said Fleur.

The Rafaelite grinned. 'I suppose you think I haven't got it. But you're wrong, madam. Not long ago I went a fortnight without opening my lips except to eat and say yes or no. *She* got quite worried.'

'I don't think you're very nice to her,' said Fleur.

'No, I'm not. She's after my soul. That's the worst of women – saving your presence – they're not content with their own.'

'Perhaps they haven't any,' said Fleur.

'The Mohammedan view – well, there's certainly something in it. A woman's always after the soul of a man, a child, or a dog. Men are content with wanting bodies.'

'I'm more interested in your platitudinal theory, Mr Blade.'

'Can't afford to be interested in the other? Eh! Strikes home? Turn your shoulder a bit, will you? No, to the left. ... Well, it's a platitude that a woman always wants some other soul – only people have forgotten it. Look at the Sistine Madonna! The baby has a soul of its own, and the Madonna's floating on the soul of the baby. That's what makes it a great picture, apart from the line and colour. It states a great platitude; but nobody sees it now. None of the cognoscenti, anyway – they're too far gone.'

'What platitude are you going to state in your picture of me?'

'Don't you worry,' said the Rafaelite. 'There'll be one all right when it's finished, though I shan't know what it is while I'm at it. Character will out, you know. Like a rest?'

'Enormously. What platitude did you express in the portrait of my cousin's wife?'

'Coo Lummy!' said the Rafaelite. 'Some catechism!'

'You surely didn't fail with that picture? Wasn't it plati-tudinous?'

'It got her all right. She's not a proper American.'

'How?'

'Throws back to something – Irish, perhaps, or Breton. There's nymph in her.'

'She was brought up in the backwoods, I believe,' said Fleur acidly.

The Rafaelite eyed her.

'You don't like the lady?'

'Certainly I do, but haven't you noticed that picturesque people are generally tame? And my cousin – what's his plati-tude to be?'

'Conscience,' said the Rafaelite; 'that young man will go far on the straight and narrow. He worries.'

A sharp movement shook all Fleur's silver bells.

'What a dreadful prophecy! Shall I stand again?'

Chapter Four

TALK IN A CAR

For yet one more day Fleur possessed her soul; then, at the morning's sitting, accidentally left her vanity bag behind her, in the studio. She called for it the same afternoon. Jon had not gone. Just out of the sitter's chair, he was stretching himself and yawning.

'Go on, Jon! Every morning I wish I had your mouth. Mr Blade, I left my bag; it's got my cheque-book in it, and I shall want it down at Dorking tonight. By the way, I shall be half an hour late for my sitting tomorrow, I'm afraid. Did you know I was your fellow victim, Jon? We've been playing "Box and Cox". How are you? I hear Anne's got a cold. Give her my sympathy. Is the picture going well? Might I have a peep, Mr Blade, and see how the platitude is coming out? Oh! It's going to be splendid! I can quite see the line.'

'Can you?' said the Rafaelite. 'I can't.'

'Here's my wretched bag! If you've finished, Jon, I could run you out as far as Dorking; you'd catch an earlier train. Do come and cheer me on my way. Haven't seen you for such ages!'

Threading over Hammersmith Bridge, Fleur regained the self-possession she had never seemed to lose. She spoke lightly of light matters, letting Jon grow accustomed to proximity.

'I go down every evening about this time, to see to my chores, and drive up in the morning early. So any afternoon you like I can take you as far as Dorking. Why shouldn't we see a little of each other in a friendly way, Jon?'

'When we do, it doesn't seem to make for happiness, Fleur.'

'My dear boy, what is happiness? Surely life should be as harmlessly full as it can be?'

'Harmlessly!'

'The Rafaelite says you have a terrible conscience, Jon.'

'The Rafaelite's a bounder.'

'Yes; but a clever one. You *have* changed, you usen't to have that line between your eyes, and your jaw's getting too strong. Look, Jon dear, be a friend to me – as they say, and we won't think of anything else. I always like Wimbledon Common – it hasn't been caught up yet. Have you bought that farm?'

'Not quite.'

'Let's go by way of Robin Hill, and look at it through the trees? It might inspire you to a poem.'

'I shall never write any more verse. It's quite gone.'

'Nonsense, Jon. You only want stirring up. Don't I drive well, considering I've only been at it five weeks?'

'You do everything well, Fleur.'

'You say that as if you disapproved. Do you know we'd never danced together before that night at Nettlefold? Shall we ever dance together again?'

'Probably not.'

'Optimistic Jon; That's right – smile! Look! Is that the church where you were baptized?'

'I wasn't.'

'Oh! No. That was the period, of course, when people were serious about those things. I believe I was done twice over – R.C. and Anglican. That's why I'm not so religious as you, Jon.'

'Religious? I'm not religious.'

'I fancy you *are*. You have moral backbone, anyway.'

'Really!'

'Jon, you remind me of American notices outside their properties – "Stop – look – take care – keep out!" I suppose you think me a frightful butterfly.'

'No, Fleur. Far from it. The butterfly has no knowledge of a straight line between two points.'

'Now what do you mean by that?'

'That you set your heart on things.'

'Did you get that from the Rafaelite?'

'No, but he confirmed it.'

'He did – did he? That young man talks too much. Has he expounded to you his theory that a woman must possess the soul of someone else, and that a man is content with bodies?'

'He has.'

'Is it true?'

'I hate to agree with him, but I think it is, in a way.'

'Well, I can tell you there are plenty of women about now who keep their own souls and are content with other people's bodies.'

'Are you one of them, Fleur?'

'Ask me another! There's Robin Hill!'

The fount of Forsyte song and story stood grey and imposing among its trees, with the sinking sun aslant on a front where green sun-blinds were still down.

Jon sighed. 'I had a lovely time there.'

'Till I came and spoiled it.'

'No; that's blasphemy.'

Fleur touched his arm.

'That's nice of you, dear Jon. You always were nice, and I shall always love you – in a harmless way. The coppice looks jolly. God had a brain-wave when He invented larches.'

'Yes. Holly says that the coppice was my grandfather's favourite spot.'

'Old Jolyon – who wouldn't marry his beloved, because she was consumptive?'

'I never heard that. But he was a great old fellow, my father and mother adored him.'

'I've seen his photographs – don't get a chin like his, Jon! The Forsytes all have such chins. June's frightens me.'

'June is one of the best people on earth.'

'Oh! Jon, you are horribly loyal.'

'Is that an offence?'

'It makes everything terribly earnest in a world that isn't worth it. No, don't quote Longfellow. When you get home, shall you tell Anne you've been driving with me?'

'Why not?'

'She's uneasy about me as it is, isn't she? You needn't answer, Jon. But I think it's unfair of her. I want so little, and you're so safe.'

'Safe?' It seemed to Fleur that he closed his teeth on the word, and for a moment she was happy.

'Now you've got your lion cub look. Do lion cubs have consciences? It's going to be rather interesting for the Rafaelite. I think your conscience might stop before telling Anne, though. It's a pity to worry her if she has a talent for uneasiness.' Then, by the silence at her side, she knew she had made a mistake.

'This is where I put in my clutch,' she said, 'as they say in the "bloods"!' And through Epsom and Leatherhead they travelled in silence.

'Do you love England as much as ever, Jon?'

'More.'

'It *is* a gorgeous country.'

'The last word I should have used – a great and lovely country.'

'Michael says its soul is grass.'

'Yes, and if I get my farm, I'll break some up, all right.'

'I can't see you as a real farmer.'

'You can't see me as a real anything – I suppose. Just an amateur.'

'Don't be horrid! I mean you're too sensitive to be a farmer.'

'No. I want to get down to the earth, and I will.'

'You must be a throw-back, Jon. The primeval Forsytes were farmers. My father wants to take me down and show me where they lived.'

'Have you jumped at it?'

'I'm not sentimental; haven't you realized that? I wonder if you've realized anything about me?' And drooping forward over her wheel, she murmured 'Oh! It's a pity we have to talk like this!'

'I said it wouldn't work!'

'No, you've got to let me see you sometimes, Jon. This is harmless enough. I must and will see you now and then. It's owed to me!'

Tears stood in her eyes, and rolled slowly down. She felt Jon touch her arm.

'Oh; Fleur, don't!'

'I'll put you out at North Dorking now, you'll just catch the five-forty-six. That's my house. Next time I must show you over it. I'm trying to be good, Jon; and you must help me. ... Well, here we are! Good-bye, dear Jon; and don't worry Anne about me, I beseech you!'

A hard hand-grip, and he was gone. Fleur turned from the station and drove slowly back along the road.

She put away the car, and entered her 'Rest House'. It was full, late holiday time still, and seven young women were resting limbs, tired out in the service of 'Petter, Poplin', and their like.

They were at supper, and a cheery buzz assailed Fleur's ears. These girls had nothing, and she had everything, except – the one thing that she chiefly wanted. For a moment she felt ashamed, listening to their talk and laughter. No! She would not change with them – and yet without that one thing she felt as if she could not live. And, while she went about the house, sifting the flowers, ordering for to-morrow, inspecting the bedrooms, laughter, cheery and uncontrolled, floated up and seemed to mock her.

Chapter Five

MORE TALK IN A CAR

‹‹—›—››

Jon had too little sense of his own importance to be simultaneously loved with comfort to himself by two pretty and attractive young women. He drove home from Pulborough, where now daily he parked Val's car, with a sore heart and a mind distraught. He had seen Fleur six times since his return to England, in a sort of painful crescendo. That dance with her had disclosed to him her state of heart, but still he did not suspect her of consciously pursuing him; and no amount of heart-searching seemed to make his own feelings clearer. Ought he to tell Anne about to-day's meeting? In many small and silent ways she had shown that she was afraid of Fleur. Why add to her fears without real cause? The portrait was not his own doing, and only for the next few days was he likely to be seeing Fleur. After that they would meet, perhaps, two or three times a year. 'Don't tell Anne – I beseech you!' Could he tell her after that? Surely he owed Fleur that much consideration. She had never consented to give him up; she had not fallen in love with Michael, as he with Anne. Still undecided, he reached Wansdon. His mother had once said to him: 'You must never tell a lie, Jon, your face will always give you away.' And so, though he did not tell Anne, her eyes following him about noted that he was keeping something from her. Her cold was in the bronchial stage, so that she was still upstairs, and tense from lack of occupation. Jon came up early again after dinner, and began to read to her. He read from *The Worst Journey in the World,* and on her side she lay with her face pillowed on her arm and watched him over it. The smoke of a wood fire, the scent of balsamic remedies, the drone of his own voice, retailing that epic of a penguin's egg, drowsed him till the book dropped from his hand.

'Have a snooze, Jon, you're tired.' Jon lay back, but he did not snooze. He thought instead. In this girl, his wife, he knew well that there was what her brother, Francis Wilmot, called 'sand'. She knew how to be silent when shoes pinched. He had watched her making up her mind that she was in danger; and now it seemed to him that she was biding her time. Anne always knew what she wanted. She had a singleness of purpose not confused like Fleur's by the currents of modernity, and she was resolute. Youth in her South Carolinian home had been simple and self-reliant; and unlike most American girls, she had not had too good a time. It had been a shock to her, he knew, that she was not his first love and that his first love was still in love with him. She had shown her uneasiness at once, but now, he felt, she had closed her guard. And Jon could not help knowing, too, that she was still deeply in love with him for all that they had been married two years. He had often heard that American girls seldom really knew the men they married; but it seemed to him sometimes that Anne knew him better than he knew himself. If so, what did she know? What was he? He wanted to do something useful with his life; he wanted to be loyal and kind. But was it all just wanting? Was he a fraud? Not what she thought him? It was all confused and heavy in his mind, like the air in the room. No use thinking! Better to snooze, as Anne said – better to snooze! He woke and said:

'Hallo! Was I snoring?'

'No. But you were twitching like a dog, Jon.'

Jon got up and went to the window.

'I was dreaming. It's a beautiful night. A fine September's the pick of the year.'

'Yes; I love the "fall". Is your mother coming over, soon?'

'Not until we're settled in. I believe she thinks we're better without her.'

'Your mother would always feel she was *de trop* before she was.'

'That's on the right side, anyway.'

'Yes, I wonder if I should.'

Jon turned. She was sitting up, staring in front of her, frowning. He went over and kissed her.

'Careful of your chest, darling!' and he pulled up the clothes.

She lay back, gazing up at him; and again he wondered what she saw. . . .

He was met next day by June's: 'So Fleur was here yesterday and gave you a lift! I told her what I thought this morning.'

'What *did* you think?' said Jon.

'That it mustn't begin again. She's a spoiled child not to be trusted.'

His eyes moved angrily.

'You'd better leave Fleur alone.'

'I always leave people alone,' said June; 'but this is my house, and I had to speak my mind.'

'I'd better stop sitting then.'

'Now, don't be silly, Jon. Of course you can't stop sitting — neither of you. Harold would be frightfully upset.'

'Damn Harold!'

June took hold of his lapel.

'That's not what I meant at all. The pictures are going to be splendid. I only meant that you mustn't meet here.'

'Did you tell Fleur that?'

'Yes.'

Jon laughed, and the sound of the laugh was hard.

'We're not children, June.'

'Have you told Anne?'

'No.'

'There, you see!'

'What?'

His face had become stubborn and angry.

'You're very like your father and grandfather, Jon — they couldn't bear to be told anything.'

'Can *you*?'

'Of course, when it's necessary.'

'Then please don't interfere.'

Pink rushed into June's cheeks, tears into her eyes; she winked them away, shook herself, and said coldly:

'I never interfere.'

'No?'

She went more pink, and suddenly stroked his sleeve. That touched Jon, and he smiled.

He 'sat' disturbed all that afternoon, while the Rafaelite painted, and June hovered, sometimes with a frown, and sometimes with yearning in her face. He wondered what he should do if Fleur called for him again. But Fleur did not call, and he went home alone. The next day was Sunday and he did not go up; but on Monday when he came out of 'The Poplars', after 'sitting' he saw Fleur's car standing by the kerb.

'I do want to show you my house to-day. I suppose June spoke to you, but I'm a reformed character, Jon. Get in!' And Jon got in.

The day was dull, neither lighted nor staged for emotion, and the 'reformed character' played her part to perfection. Not a word suggested that they were other than best friends. She talked of America, its language and books. Jon maintained that America was violent in its repressions and in its revolt against repressions.

'In a word,' said Fleur, 'young.'

'Yes; but so far as I can make out, it's getting younger every year.'

'I liked America.'

'Oh! I liked it all right. I made quite a profit, too, on my orchard when I sold.'

'I wonder you came back, Jon. The fact is — you're old-fashioned.'

'How?'

'Take sex – I couldn't discuss sex with you.'

'Can you with other people?'

'Oh! with nearly anyone. Don't frown like that! You'd be awfully out of it, my dear, in London, or New York, for that matter.'

'I hate fluffy talk about sex,' said Jon, gruffly. 'The French are the only people who understand sex. It isn't to be talked about as they do here and in America; it's much too real.'

Fleur stole another look.

'Then let us drop that hot potato. I'm not sure whether I could even discuss art with you.'

'Did you see that St Gaudens statue at Washington?'

'Yes; but that's *vieux jeu* nowadays.'

'Is it?' growled Jon. 'What do they want, then?'

'You know as well as I.'

'You mean it must be unintelligible?'

'Put it that way if you like. The point is that art now is just a subject for conversation; and anything that anybody can understand at first sight is not worth talking about and therefore not art.'

'I call that silly.'

'Perhaps. But more amusing.'

'If you see through it, how can you be amused?'

'Another hot potato. Let's try again! I bet you don't approve of women's dress, these days?'

'Why not? It's jolly sensible.'

'La, la! Are we coming together on that?'

'Naturally, you'd all look better without hats. You can wash your heads easily now, you know.'

'Oh! don't cut us off hats, Jon. All our stoicism would go. If we hadn't to find hats that suited us, life would be much too easy.'

'But they don't suit you.'

'I agree, my dear; but I know the feminine character better than you. One must always give babies something to cut their teeth on.'

777

'Fleur, you're too intelligent to live in London.'

'My dear boy, the modern young woman doesn't live any-where. She floats in an ether of her own.'

'She touches earth sometimes, I suppose.'

Fleur did not answer for a minute; then, looking at him:

'Yes; she touches earth sometimes, Jon.' And in that look she seemed to say again: 'Oh! what a pity we have to talk like this!'

She showed him the house in such a way that he might get the impression that she considered to some purpose the comfort of others. Even her momentary encounters with the denizens had that quality. Jon went away with a tingling in his palm, and the thought: 'She likes to make herself out a butterfly, but at heart – !' The memory of her clear eyes smiling at him, the half-comic quiver of her lips when she said: 'Good-bye, bless you!' blurred his vision of Sussex all the way home. And who shall say that she had not so intended?

Holly had come to meet him with a hired car.

'I'm sorry, Jon, Val's got the car. He won't be able to drive you up and down tomorrow as he said he would. He's had to go up to-day. And if he can get through his business in town, he'll go on to Newmarket on Wednesday. Something rather beastly's happened. His name's been forged on a cheque for a hundred pounds by an old college friend to whom he'd been particularly decent.'

'Very adequate reasons,' said Jon. 'What's Val going to do?'

'He doesn't know yet; but this is the third time he's played a dirty trick on Val.'

'Is it quite certain?'

'The bank described him unmistakably. He seems to think Val will stand anything; but it can't be allowed to go on.'

'I should say not.'

'Yes, dear boy; but what would you do? Prosecute an old college friend? Val has a queer feeling that it's only a sort of accident that he himself has kept straight.'

Jon started. *Was* it an accident that one kept straight?

'Was this fellow in the war?' he asked.

'I doubt it. He seems to be an absolute rotter. I saw his face once – bone slack and bone selfish.'

'Beastly for Val!' said Jon.

'He's going to consult his uncle, Fleur's father. By the way, have you seen Fleur lately?'

'Yes. I saw her to-day. She brought me as far as Dorking, and showed me her house there.'

The look on Holly's face, the reflective shadow between her eyes, were not lost on him.

'Is there any objection to my seeing her?' he said, abruptly.

'Only you can know that, dear boy.'

Jon did not answer, but the moment he saw Anne he told her. She showed him nothing by face or voice, just asked how Fleur was and how he liked the house. That night, after she seemed asleep, he lay awake, gnawed by uncertainty. *Was* it an accident that one kept straight – was it?

Chapter Six

SOAMES HAS BRAIN-WAVES

◄─►─►

THE first question Soames put to his nephew in Green Street, was: 'How did he get hold of the cheque form? Do you keep your cheque-books lying about?'

'I'm afraid I do, rather, in the country, Uncle Soames.'

'Um,' said Soames, 'then you deserve all you get. What about your signature?'

'He wrote from Brighton asking if he could see me.'

'You should have made your wife sign your answer.'

Val groaned. 'I didn't think he'd run to forgery.'

'They run to anything when they're as far gone as that. I suppose when you said "No", he came over from Brighton all the same?'

'Yes, he did; but I wasn't in.'

'Exactly; and he sneaked a form. Well, if you want to stop him, you'd better prosecute. He'll get three years.'

'That'd kill him,' said Val, 'to judge by his looks.'

Soames shook his head. 'Improve his health – very likely. Has he ever been in prison?'

'Not that I know of.'

'H'm!'

Silence followed this profound remark.

'I can't prosecute,' said Val, suddenly. 'College pal. There, but for the grace of God and all that, don't you know; one might have gone to the dogs oneself.'

Soames stared at him.

'Well,' he said, 'I suppose you might. Your father was always in some scrape or other.'

Val frowned. He had suddenly remembered an evening at the Pandemonium, when, in company with another college friend, he had seen his own father, drunk.

'But somehow,' he said, 'I've got to see that he doesn't do it again. If he didn't look such a "heart" subject, one could give him a hiding.'

Soames shook his head. 'Personal violence – besides, he's probably out of England by now.'

'No; I called at his club on the way here – he's in town all right.'

'You didn't see him?'

'No. I wanted to see you first.'

Flattered in spite of himself, Soames said sardonically:

'Perhaps he's got what they call a better nature?'

'By Jove, Uncle Soames, I believe that's a brain-wave!'

Soames shook his head. 'Not to judge by his face.'

'I don't know,' said Val. 'After all, he was born a gentleman.'

'That means nothing nowadays. And, apropos, before I forget it. Do you remember a young fellow called Butterfield, in the Elderson affair – no, you wouldn't. Well, I'm going to take him out of his publishing firm, and put him under old Gradman, to learn about your mother's and the other family Trusts. Old Gradman's on his last legs, and this young man can step into his shoes – it's a permanent job, and better pay than he's getting now. I can rely on him, and that's something in these days. I thought I'd tell you.'

'Another brain-wave, Uncle Soames. But about your first. Could you see Stainford, and follow that up?'

'Why should *I* see him?'

'You carry so much more weight than I do.'

'H'm! Seems to me I always have to do the unpleasant thing. However, I expect it's better than your seeing him.'

Val grinned. 'I shall feel much happier if you do it.'

'*I* shan't,' said Soames. 'That bank cashier hasn't made a mistake, I suppose?'

'Who could mistake Stainford?'

'Nobody,' said Soames. 'Well, if you won't prosecute, you'd better leave it to me.'

When Val was gone he remained in thought. Here he was, still keeping the family affairs straight; he wondered what they would do without him some day. That young Butterfield might be a brainwave, but who could tell – the fellow was attached to him, though, in a curious sort of way, with his eyes of a dog! He should put that in hand at once, before old Gradman dropped off. Must give old Gradman a bit of plate, too, with his name engraved, while he could still appreciate it. Most people only got them when they were dead or dotty. Young Butterfield knew Michael, too, and that would make him interested in Fleur's affairs. But as to this infernal Stainford? How was he going to set about it? He had better get the fellow here if possible, rather than go to his club. If he'd had the brass to stay in England after committing such a bare-faced forgery, he would have the brass to come here again and see what more he could get. And, smiling sourly, Soames went to the telephone.

'Mr Stainford in the club? Ask him if he'd be good enough to step over and see Mr Forsyte at Green Street.'

After a look round to see that there were no ornaments within reach, he seated himself in the dining-room and had Smither in.

'I'm expecting that Mr Stainford, Smither. If I ring, while he's here, pop out and get a policeman.'

At the expression on Smither's face he added:

'I don't anticipate it, but one never knows.'

'There's no danger, I hope, Mr Soames?'

'Nothing of the sort, Smither; I may want him arrested – that's all.'

'Do you expect him to take something again, sir?'

Soames smiled, and waved his hand at the lack of ornaments, 'Very likely he won't come, but if he does, show him in here.'

When she had gone, he settled down with the clock – a Dutch piece too heavy to take away; it had been 'picked up' by James, chimed everything, and had a moon and a lot of stars on its face. He did not feel so 'bobbish" before this third encounter with that fellow; the chap had scored twice, and so far as he could see, owing to Val's reluctance to prosecute, was going to score a third time. And yet there was a sort of fascination in dealing with what they called 'the limit', and a certain quality about the fellow which raised him almost to the level of romance. It was as if the idolised maxim of his own youth 'Show no emotion', and all the fashionableness that, under the ægis of his mother Emily, had clung about Park Lane, were revisiting him in the shape of this languid beggar. And probably the chap would come!

'Mr Stainford, sir.'

When Smither – very red – had withdrawn, Soames did not know how to begin, the fellow's face, like old parchment, was as if it had come from some grave or other. At last he said:

'I wanted to see you about a cheque. My nephew's name's been forged.'

The eyebrows rose, the eyelids dropped still further.

'Yes. Dartie won't prosecute.'

Soames's gorge rose.

'You seem very cocksure,' he said; 'my nephew has by no means made up his mind.'

'We were at college together, Mr Forsyte.'

'You trade on that, do you? There's a limit, Mr Stainford. That was a very clever forgery, for a first.'

There was just a flicker of the face; and Soames drew the forged cheque from his pocket. Inadequately protected, of course, not even automatically crossed! Val's cheques would have to have the words 'Not negotiable; Credit payee' stamped on them in future. But how could he give this fellow a thorough scare?

'I have a detective at hand,' he said, 'only waiting for me to ring. This sort of thing must stop. As you don't seem to understand that —'. and he took a step towards the bell.

A faint and bitter smile had come on those pale lips.

'You've never been down and out, I imagine, Mr Forsyte?'

'No,' answered Soames, with a certain disgust.

'I always am. It's very wearing.'

'In that case,' said Soames, 'you'll find prison a rest.' But even as he spoke them, the words seemed futile and a little brutal. The fellow wasn't a man at all – he was a shade, a languid bitter shade. It was as if one were bullying a ghost.

'Look here!' he said. 'As a gentleman by birth, give me your word not to try it on again with my nephew, or any of my family, and I won't ring.'

'Very well, you have my word – such as it is!'

'We'll leave it at that, then,' said Soames. 'But this is the last time. I shall keep the evidence of this.'

'One must live, Mr Forsyte.'

'I don't agree,' said Soames.

The 'shade' uttered a peculiar sound – presumably a laugh, and Soames was alone again. He went hastily to the door, and watched the fellow into the street. Live? Must one? Wouldn't a fellow like that be better dead? Wouldn't most people be better dead? And, astonished at so extravagant a thought, he went up to the drawing-room. Forty-five years since he had laid its foundations, and there it was, as full of marqueterie as ever. On the mantelpiece was a little old daguerreotype, slightly pinked in the cheeks, of his grandfather – 'Superior Dosset' set in a deep, enamelled frame. Soames contemplated it. The chin of the founder of the Forsyte clan was settled comfortably between the widely separated points of an old-fashioned collar. The eyes – with thick under-lids, were light and shrewd and rather japing; the side-whiskers grey; the mouth looked as if it could swallow a lot; the old-time tail-coat was of broadcloth; the hands those of a man of affairs. A stocky old boy, with a certain force, and a deal of character! Well-nigh a hundred years since that was taken of him. Refreshing to look at character, after that languid seedy specimen! He would like to see where that old chap had been born and bred before he emerged at the end of the eighteenth century and built the house of Forsyte. He would take Riggs, and go down, and if Fleur wouldn't come – perhaps all the better! Be dull for her! Roots were nothing to young people. Yes, he would go and look at his roots while the weather was still fine. But first to put old Gradman in order. It would do him good to see the old fellow after this experience – he never left the office till half-past five. And, replacing the daguerreotype, Soames took a taxi to the Poultry, reflecting as he went. How difficult it was to keep things secure, with chaps like Elderson and this fellow Stainford always on the look-out. There was the country too, no sooner was it out of one than it was into another mess; the coal strike would end when people began to feel the winter pinch, but something else would crop up, some war or disturbance or other. And then there was Fleur – she had plenty of money of her own. Had he been wrong to make her so independent? And yet – the idea of controlling her through money had always been repulsive to him. Whatever she did – she was his only child, one might say his only love. If she couldn't keep straight for love of her infant and himself, to say nothing of her husband – he couldn't do it for her by threat of cutting her off or anything like that! Anyway, things were looking better with her, and perhaps he had been wrong.

The City had just begun to disgorge its daily life. Its denizens were scurrying out like rabbits; they didn't scurry in like that, he would bet – work-shy, nowadays! Ten where it used to be nine; five where it used to be six. Still, with the telephone and one thing and another, they got through as much perhaps; and didn't drink all the beer and sherry and eat all the chops they used to — a skimpier breed altogether, compared with that old boy whose effigy he had just been gazing at, a shadowy, narrow-headed lot, with a nervy, anxious look, as if they'd invested in life and found it a dropping stock. And not a tailcoat or a silk hat to be seen. Settling his own more firmly on his head, he got out at the familiar backwater off the Poultry, and entered the offices of Cuthcott, Kingson and Forsyte.

Old Gradman was still there, his broad, bent back just divested of its workaday coat.

'Ah! Mr Soames, I was just going. Excuse me while I put on my coat.'

A frock-coat made in the year one, to judge by the cut of it!

'I go at half-past five now. There isn't much to do as a rule. I like to get a nap before supper. It's a pleasure to see you; you're quite a stranger.'

'Yes,' said Soames. 'I don't come in much, but I've been thinking. If anything should happen to either or both of us, things would soon be in Queer Street, Gradman.'

'Aow! We won't think about tha-at!'

'But we must; we're neither of us young men.'

'Well, I'm not a chicken, but you're *no* age, Mr Soames.'

'Seventy-one.'

'Dear, dear! It seems only the other day since I took you down to school at Slough. I remember what happened then better than I do what happened yesterday.'

'So do I, Gradman; and that's a sign of age. Do you recollect that young chap who came here and told me about Elderson?'

'Aow, yes! Nice young feller. Buttermilk or some such name.'

'Butterfield. Well, I'm going to put him under you here, and I want you to get him *au fait* with everything.'

The old fellow seemed standing very still; his face, in its surround of grey beard and hair, was quite expressionless. Soames hurried on:

'It's just precautionary. Some day you'll be wanting to retire.'

Gradman lifted his hand with a heavy gesture.

'I'll die in 'arness, I 'ope,' he said.

'That's as you like, Gradman. You'll remain as you always have been – in full charge; but you'll have someone to rely on if you don't feel well or want a holiday or what not.'

'I'd rather not, Mr Soames. To have a young man about the place –'

'A good young fellow, Gradman. And for some reason, grateful to me and to my son-in-law. He won't give you any trouble. We none of us live for ever, you know.'

The old chap's face had puckered queerly, his voice grated more than usual.

'It seems going to meet trouble. I'm quite up to the work, Mr Soames.'

'Oh! I know how you feel,' said Soames. 'I feel much the same myself but Time stands still for no man, and we must look to the future.'

A sigh escaped from its grizzled prison.

'Well, Mr Soames, if you've made up your mind, we'll say no more; but I don't like it.'

'Let me give you a lift to your station.'

'I'd rather walk, thank you; I like the air. I'll just lock up.'

Soames perceived that not only drawers but feelings required locking up, and went out.

Faithful old chap! One might go round to Polkingford's and see if one could pick up that bit of plate.

In that emporium, so lined with silver and gold, that a man wondered whether anything had ever been sold there, Soames stood considering. Must be something that a man could swear by – nothing arty or elegant. He supposed the old chap didn't drink punch – a chapel-goer! How about those camels in silver-gilt with two humps each and candles coming out of them? 'Joseph Gradman, in gratitude from the Forsyte family' engraved between the humps? Gradman lived somewhere near the Zoo. M'm! Camels? No! a bowl was better. If he didn't drink punch he could put rose-leaves or flowers into it.

'I want a bowl,' he said, 'a really good one.'

'Yes, sir, I think we have the very article.'

They always had the very article!

'How about this, sir – massive silver – a very chaste design.'

'Chaste!' said Soames. 'I wouldn't have it as a gift.'

'No, sir; it isn't perhaps *exactly* what you require. Now, this is a nice little bowl.'

'No, no; something plain and solid that would hold about a gallon.'

'Mr Bankwait – come here a minute. This gentleman wants an old-fashioned bowl.'

'Yes, sir; I think we have the very thing.'

Soames uttered an indistinguishable sound.

'There isn't much demand for the old-fashioned bowl; but we have a very fine second-hand, that used to be in the Rexborough family.'

'With arms on?' said Soames. 'That won't do. It must be new, or free from arms, anyway.'

'Ah! Then this will be what you want, sir.'

'My Lord!' said Soames; and raising his umbrella he pointed in the opposite direction. 'What's that thing?'

With a slightly chagrined air the shopman brought the article from its case.

Upon a swelling base, with a waist above, a silver bowl sprang generously forth. Soames flipped it with his finger.

'Pure silver, sir; and, as you see, very delicate edging; not too bacchanalian in design; the best gilt within. I should say the very thing you want.'

'It might do. What's the price?'

The shopman examined a cabalistic sign.

'Thirty-five pounds, sir.'

'Quite enough,' said Soames. Whether it would please old Gradman, he didn't know, but the thing was in good taste, and would not do the family discredit. 'I'll have that, then,' he said. 'Engrave these words on it,' and he wrote them down. 'Send it to that address, and the account to me; and don't be long about it.'

'Very good sir. You wouldn't like those goblets? – They're perfect in their way.'

'Nothing more!' said Soames. 'Good-evening!' And, handing the shopman his card, with a cold circular glance, he went out. That was off his mind!

September sun sprinkled him, threading his way west along Piccadilly into the Green Park. These gentle autumn days were very pleasant. He didn't get hot, and he didn't feel cold. And the plane trees looked their best, just making up their minds to turn; nice trees, shapely. And, crossing the grassy spaces, Soames felt almost mellow. A rather more rapid step behind impinged on his consciousness. A voice said:

'Ah! Forsyte! Bound for the meeting at Michael's? Might we go along together?'

Old Mont, perky and talkative as ever! There he went – off at once!

'What's your view of all these London changes, Forsyte? You remember the peg-top trouser, and the crinoline – Leech in his prime – Old Pam on his horse – September makes one reminiscent.'

'It's all on the surface,' said Soames.

'On the surface? I sometimes have that feeling. But there is a real change. It's the difference between the Austen and Trollope novels and these modern fellows. There are no parishes left. Classes? Yes, but divided by man, not by God, as in Trollope's day.'

Soames sniffed. The chap was always putting things in that sort of way!

'At the rate we're going, they'll soon not be divided at all,' he said.

'I think you're wrong there, Forsyte. I should never be surprised to see the horse come back.'

'The horse,' muttered Soames; 'what's he got to do with it?'

'What we must look for,' said Sir Lawrence, swinging his cane, 'is the millennium. Then we shall soon be developing individuality again. And the millennium's nearly here.'

'I don't in the least follow you,' said Soames.

'Education's free; women have the vote; even the workman

has or soon will have his car; the slums are doomed – thanks to you, Forsyte; amusement and news are in every home; the Liberal Party's up the spout; Free Trade's a movable feast; sport's cheap and plentiful; dogma's got the knock; so has the General Strike; Boy Scouts are increasing rapidly; dress is comfortable; and hair is short – it's all millennial.'

'What's all that got to do with the horse?'

'A symbol, my dear Forsyte. It's impossible to standardize or socialize the horse. We're beginning to react against uniformity. A little more millennium and we shall soon be cultivating our souls and driving tandem again.'

'What's that noise?' said Soames. 'Sounds like a person in distress.'

Sir Lawrence cocked his eyebrow.

'It's a vacuum cleaner, in Buckingham Palace. Very human things those.'

Soames grunted – the fellow couldn't be serious! Well! He might *have* to be before long. If Fleur –! But he would not contemplate that 'if'.

'What I admire about the Englishman,' said Sir Lawrence suddenly, 'is his evolutionary character. He flows and ebbs, and flows again. Foreigners may think him a stick-in-the-mud, but he's got continuity – a great quality, Forsyte. What are you going to do with your pictures when you take the ferry? Leave them to the nation?'

'Depends on how they treat me. If they're going to clap on any more death duties, I shall revoke the bequest.'

'The principle of our ancestors, eh? Voluntary service, or none. Great fellows, our ancestors.'

'I don't know about yours,' said Soames; 'mine were just yeomen. I'm going down to have a look at them tomorrow,' he added defiantly.

'Splendid! I hope you'll find them at home.'

'We're late,' said Soames, glancing in at the dining-room window, where the committee were glancing out. 'Half-past six! What a funny lot they look!'

'We always look a funny lot,' said Sir Lawrence, following

him into the house, 'except to ourselves. That's the first principle of existence, Forsyte.'

Chapter Seven

TOMORROW

►◄►►

FLEUR met them in the hall. After dropping Jon at Dorking she had exceeded the limit homewards, that she might appear to have nothing in her thoughts but the welfare of the slums. 'The Squire' being among his partridges, the bishop was in the chair. Fleur went to the sideboard, and, while Michael was reading the minutes, began pouring out the tea. The bishop, Sir Godfrey Bedwin, Mr Montross, her father-in-law, and herself drank China tea; Sir Timothy – whisky and soda; Michael nothing; the Marquess, Hilary, and her father Indian tea; and each maintained that the others were destroying their digestions. Her father, indeed, was always telling her that she only drank China tea because it was the fashion – she couldn't possibly like it. While she apportioned their beverages she wondered what they would think if they knew what, besides tea, was going on within her. Tomorrow was Jon's last sitting and she was going 'over the top l' All the careful possessing of her soul these two months since she had danced with him at Nettlefold would by this time tomorrow be ended. Tomorrow at this hour she would claim her own. The knowledge that there must be two parties to any contract did not trouble her. She had the faith of a pretty woman in love. What she willed would be accomplished, but none should know it l And, handing her cups, she smiled, pitying the ignorance of these wise old men. They should not know, nor anyone else, least of all the young man who last night had held her in his arms. And, thinking of one not yet so holding her, she sat down by the hearth, with her tea and her tablets, while her pulses throbbed and her half-closed eyes saw Jon's face turned round to her from the station door. Fulfilment! She, like Jacob, had served seven years – for the fulfilment of her love – seven long, long years! And – while she sat there listening to the edgeless booming of the bishop and Sir Godfrey, to the random ejaculations of Sir Timothy, to her father's close and cautious comments – that something clear, precise, unflinching, woven into her nature with French blood, silently perfected the machinery of the stolen life, that should begin tomorrow after they had eaten of forbidden fruit. A stolen life was a safe life if there were no chicken-hearted hesitation, no squeamishness, and no remorse! She might have experienced a dozen stolen lives already from the certainty she felt about that. She alone would arrange – Jon should be spared all. And no one should know!

'Fleur, would you take a note of that?'

'Yes.'

And she wrote down on her tablets: 'Ask Michael what I was to take a note of.'

'Mrs Mont!'

'Yes, Sir Timothy?'

'Could you get up one of those what d'you call 'ems for us?'

'Matinees?'

'No, no – jumble sales, don't they call 'em.'

'Certainly.'

The more she got up for them the more impeccable her reputation, the greater her freedom, and the more she would deserve, and ironically enjoy, her stolen life.

Hilary speaking now. What would *he* think if he knew?

'But I think we *ought* to have a matinee, Fleur. The public are so good, they'll always pay a guinea to go to what most of them would give a guinea any day not to go to. What do you say, Bishop?'

'A matinee – by all means!'

'Matinees – dreadful things!'

'Not if we got a pleasant play, Mr Forsyte – something a little old-fashioned – one of L.S.D.'s. It would advertise us, you know. What do you think, Lord Shropshire?'

'My granddaughter Marjorie would get one up for you. It would do her good.'

'H'm. if *she* gets it up, it won't be old-fashioned.' And Fleur saw her father's face turning towards her as he spoke. If only he knew how utterly she was beyond all that; how trivial to her seemed that heart-burning of the past.

'Mr Montross, have you a theatre in your pocket?'

'I can get you one, Mr Charwell.'

'First rate! Then, will you and Lord Shropshire and my nephew here take that under your wings. Fleur, tell us how your "Rest House" is doing?'

'Perfectly, Uncle Hilary. It's quite full. The girls are delightful.'

'Wild lot, I should think – aren't they?'

'Oh! no, Sir Timothy; they're quite model.'

If only the old gentleman could see over his moustache into the model lady who controlled them!

'Well then, that's that. If there's nothing more, Mr Chairman, will you excuse me? I've got to meet an American about ants. We aren't properly shaking up these landlords, in my opinion. Good night to you all!'

Motioning to Michael to stay behind, Fleur rose to see Sir Timothy out.

'Which umbrella is yours, Sir Timothy?'

'I don't know; that looks the best. If you get up a jumble sale, Mrs Mont, I wish you'd sell the bishop at it. I can't stand a fellow with a plum in his mouth, especially in the Chair.'

Fleur smiled, and the 'old boy' cocked his hat at her. They all cocked their hats at her, and that was pleasant! But would they if they knew! Dusk among the trees of the Square Garden, the lights just turned up – what luck to have such weather – dry and warm! She stood in the doorway, taking long breaths. By this time tomorrow she meant to be a dishonest wife! Well, not more than she had always been in secret aspiration.

'I'm glad Kit's down at "The Shelter",' she thought. *He* should never know, no one should! There would be no change –

no change in anything except in her and Jon. The Life Force would break bounds in a little secret river, which would flow — ah, where? Who cared?

'My dear Mont, honesty was never the best policy from a material point of view. The sentiment is purely Victorian. The Victorians were wonderful fellows for squaring circles.'

'I agree, Marquess, I agree; they could think what they wanted better than anybody. When times are fat, you can.'

Those two in the hall behind her — dried up and withered! Fleur turned to them with her smile.

'My dear young lady — the evening air! You won't take cold?'

'No, thank you, sir; I'm warm all through.'

'How nice that is!'

'May I give you a lift, my lord?'

'Thank you, Mr Montross. Wish I could afford a car myself. Are you coming our way, Mont? Do you know that song, Mr Montross: "We'll all go round to Alice's house"? It seems to have a fascination for my milk-boy. I often wonder who Alice is? I have a suspicion she may not be altogether proper. Good night to you, Mrs Mont. How charming your house is!'

'Good night, sir!'

His hand; 'the walrus's'; her father-in-law's.

'Kit all right, Fleur?'

'First rate.'

'Good night, my dear!'

His dear — the mother of his grandson! 'Tomorrow and tomorrow and tomorrow!'

The rug wrapped round the cargo of age, the door shut — what a smooth and silent car! Voices again:

'Will you have a taxi, Uncle Hilary?'

'No, thank you, Michael, the bishop and I will walk.'

'Then I'll come with you as far as the corner. Coming, Sir Godfrey? Bye-bye, darling. Your Dad's staying to dinner. I'll be back from old Blythe's about ten.'

The animals went out four by four!

'Don't stand there; you'll get cold!' Her father's voice! The one person whose eyes she feared. She must keep her mask on now.

'Well, Dad, what have you been doing today? Come into the "parlour" – we'll have dinner quite soon.'

'How's your picture? Is this fellow taking care not to exaggerate? I think I'd better have a look at it.'

'Not just yet, dear. He's a very touchy gentleman.'

'They're all that. I thought of going down West tomorrow to see where the Forsytes sprang from. I suppose you couldn't take a rest and come?'

Fleur heard, without giving a sign of her relief.

'How long will you be away, Dad?'

'Back on the third day. 'Tisn't two hundred miles.'

'I'm afraid it would put the gentleman out.'

'Well, I didn't think you'd care to. There's no kudos there. But I've meant to for a long time; and the weather's fine.'

'I'm sure it will be frightfully interesting, dear; you must tell me all about it. But what with the portrait and my "Rest House", I'm very tied just now.'

'Well, then, I'll look for you at the week-end. Your mother's gone to some friends – they do nothing but play bridge; she'll be away till Monday. I always want you, you know,' he added simply. And to avoid his eyes she got up.

'I'll just run up now, Dad, and change. Those Slum Committee meetings always make me feel grubby. I don't know why.'

'They're a waste of time,' said Soames. 'There'll always be slums. Still, it's something for you both to do.'

'Yes, Michael's quite happy about it.'

'That old fool, Sir Timothy!' And Soames went up to the Fragonard. 'I've hung that Morland. The Marquess is an amiable old chap. I suppose you know I'm leaving my pictures to the nation? You've no use for them. You'll have to live at that place Lippinghall some day. Pictures'd be no good there. Ancestors and stags' horns and horses – that sort of thing. M'ff!'

A secret life and Lippinghall! Long, long might that conjunction be deferred!

'Oh, Bart will live for ever, Dad!'

'M'yes! He's spry enough. Well, you run up!'

While she washed off her powder and put it on again Fleur thought: 'Dear Dad! Thank God! He'll be far away!'

Now that her mind was thoroughly made up, it was comparatively easy to bluff, and keep her freshly-powdered face, smiling and serene, above the Chelsea dinner service.

'Where are you going to hang your portrait, when it's done?' resumed Soames.

'Why! It'll be yours, dear.'

'Mine? Well, of course; but you'll hang it here; Michael'll want it.'

Michael – unknowing! *That* gave her a twinge.

Well, she would be as good to him after, as ever. No old-fashioned squeamishness!

'Thank you, dear. I expect he'll like it in the "parlour". The scheme *is* silver and gold – my "Folly" dress.'

'I remember it,' said Soames; 'a thing with bells.'

'I think all that part of the picture's very good.'

'What? Hasn't he got your face?'

'Perhaps – but I don't know that I approve of it frightfully.' After this morning's sitting, indeed, she had wondered. Something avid had come into the face as if the Rafaelite had sensed the hardening of resolve within her.

'If he doesn't do you justice I shan't take it,' said Soames.

Fleur smiled. The Rafaelite would have something to say to that.

'Oh! I expect it'll be all right. One never thinks one's own effigies are marvellous, I suppose.'

'Don't know,' said Soames, 'never was painted.'

'You ought to be, dear.'

'Waste of time! Has he sent away the picture of that young woman?'

Fleur's eyes did not flinch.

'Jon Forsyte's wife? Oh! Yes – long ago.'

She expected him to say: 'Seen anything of them?' But it did not come. And that disturbed her more than if it had come.

'I had your cousin Val to see me today.'

Fleur's heart stood still. Had they been talking?

'His name's been forged.'

Thank heaven!

'Some people have no moral sense at all,' continued Soames. Involuntarily her white shoulder rose; but he wasn't looking. 'Common honesty, I don't know where it is.'

'I heard Lord Shropshire say to-night that "Honesty's the best policy" was a mere Victorianism, Dad.'

'Well, he's ten years my senior, but I don't know where he got that from. Everything's twisted inside out, nowadays.'

'But if it's the best *policy*, there never was any particular virtue in it, was there?'

Soames took a sharp look at her smiling face.

'Why not?'

'Oh, I don't know. These are Lippinghall partridges, Dad.'

Soames sniffed. 'Not hung quite long enough. You ought to be able to swear by the leg of a partridge.'

'Yes, I've told cook, but she has her own views.'

'And the bread sauce should have a touch more onion in it. Victorianism, indeed! I suppose he'd call *me* a Victorian?'

'Well, aren't you, Dad? You had forty-six years of her.'

'I've had twenty-five without her, and hope to have a few more.'

'Many, many,' said Fleur softly.

'Can't expect that.'

'Oh yes! But I'm glad you don't consider yourself a Victorian; I don't like them. They wore too many clothes.'

'Don't you be too sure of that.'

'Well, to-morrow you'll be among Georgians, anyway.'

'Yes,' said Soames. 'There's a graveyard there, they say. And that reminds me – I've bought that corner bit in the churchyard down at home. It'll do for me as well as any other. Your mother will want to go to France to be buried, I expect.'

'Give Mr Forsyte some sherry, Coaker.'

Soames took a long sniff.

'This is some of your grandfather's. He lived to be ninety.'

If she and Jon lived to be ninety – would nobody still know? ... She left him at ten o'clock, brushing his nose with her lips.

'I'm tired, Dad; and you'll have a long day tomorrow. Good-night, dear!'

Thank God he would be among the Georgians tomorrow!

Chapter Eight

FORBIDDEN FRUIT

<---->>

HALTING the car suddenly in the by-road between Gage's farm and the Robin Hill coppice, Fleur said: 'Jon, dear, I've got a whim. Let's get out and go in there. The potentate's in Scotland.' He did not move and she added: 'I shan't see you again for a long time, now your picture's finished.'

Jon got out, then, and she unlatched the footpath gate. They stood a minute within, listening for sounds of anyone to interrupt their trespass. The fine September afternoon was dying fast. The last 'sitting' had been long, and it was late; and in the coppice of larch and birch the dusk was deepening. Fleur slid her hand within his arm.

'Listen! Still, isn't it? I feel as if we were back seven years, Jon. Do you wish we were? Babes in the wood once more?'

Gruffly he answered:

'No good looking back – things happen as they must.'

'The birds are going to bed. Used there to be owls?'

'Yes; we shall hear one soon, I expect.'

'How good it smells!'

'Trees and the cow-houses!'

'Vanilla and hay, as the poets have it. Are they close?'

'Yes.'

797

'Don't let's go farther, then.'

'Here's the old log,' said Jon. 'We might sit down, and listen for an owl.'

On the old log seat they sat down, side by side.

'No dew,' said Fleur. 'The weather will break soon, I expect. I love the scent of drought.'

'I love the smell of rain.'

'You and I never love the same thing, Jon. And yet — we've loved each other.' Against her arm it was as if he shivered.

'There goes the old clock! It's awfully late, Fleur! Listen! The owl!'

Startlingly close through the thin-branched trees the call came. Fleur rose. 'Let's see if we can find him.'

She moved back from the old log.

'Aren't you coming? Just a little wander, Jon.'

Jon got up and went along at her side among the larches.

'Up this way — wasn't it? How quickly it's got dark. Look! The birches are still white. I love birch trees.' She put her hand on a pale stem. 'The smoothness, Jon. It's like skin.' And, leaning forward, she laid her cheek against the trunk. 'There! feel my cheek, and then the bark. Could you tell the difference, except for warmth?'

Jon reached his hand up. She turned her lips and touched it.

'Jon — kiss me just once.'

'You know I couldn't kiss you "just once", Fleur.'

'Then kiss me for ever, Jon.'

'No, no! No, no!'

'Things happen as they must — you said so.'

'Fleur — don't! I can't stand it.'

She laughed — very low, softly.

'I don't want you to. I've waited seven years for this. No! Don't cover your face! Look at me! I take it all on myself. The woman tempted you. But, Jon, you were always mine. There! That's better. I can see your eyes. Poor Jon! Now kiss me!' In that long kiss her very spirit seemed to leave her; she could not even see whether his eyes were open or, like hers, closed. And again the owl hooted.

Jon tore his lips away. He stood there in her arms, trembling like a startled horse.

With her lips against his ear, she whispered:

'There's nothing, Jon; there's nothing.' She could hear him holding-in his breath, and her warm lips whispered on: 'Take me in your arms, Jon; take me!' The light had failed completely now; stars were out between the dark feathering of the trees, and low down, from where the coppice sloped up towards the east, a creeping brightness seemed trembling towards them through the wood from the moon rising. A faint rustle broke the silence, ceased, broke it again. Closer, closer – Fleur pressed against him.

'Not here, Fleur; not here. I can't – I won't –'

'Yes, Jon; here – now! I claim you.'

*

The moon was shining through the tree stems when they sat again side by side on the log seat.

Jon's hands were pressed to his forehead, and she could not see his eyes.

'No one shall ever know, Jon.'

He dropped his hands and faced her.

'I must tell her.'

'Jon!'

'I must!'

'You can't unless I let you, and I don't let you.'

'What have we done? Oh, Fleur, what *have* we done?'

'It was written. When shall I see you again, Jon?'

He started up.

'Never, unless she knows. Never, Fleur, – never! I can't go on in secret!'

As quickly, too, Fleur was on her feet. They stood with their hands on each other's arms, in a sort of struggle. Then Jon wrenched himself free, and, like one demented, rushed back into the coppice.

She stood trembling, not daring to call. Bewildered, she stood, waiting for him to come back to her, and he did not come.

Suddenly she moaned, and sank on her knees; and again she moaned. He must hear, and come back! He could not have left her at such a moment – he could not!

'Jon!' No sound. She rose from her knees and stood peering into the brightened dusk. The owl hooted; and, startled, she saw the moon caught among the tree-tops, like a presence watching her. A shivering sob choked in her throat, became a whimper, like a hurt child's. She stood, listening fearfully. No rustling; no footsteps; no hoot of owl – no sound save the distant whir of traffic on the London road! Had he gone to the car, or was he hiding from her in that coppice, all creepy now with shadows?

'Jon! Jon!' No answer! She ran towards the gate. There was the car – empty! She got into it and sat leaning forward over the driving-wheel with a numb feeling in her limbs. What did it mean? Was she beaten in the very hour of victory? He could not – no, he could not mean to leave her thus? Mechanically she turned on the car's lights. A couple on foot, a man on a bicycle, passed. And still Fleur sat there, numbed. This – fulfilment! The fulfilment she had dreamed of? A few moments of hasty and delirious passion – and this! And, to her chagrin, her consternation, were added humiliation that, after such a moment, he could thus have fled from her; and the fear that in winning him she had lost him!

At last she started the engine, and drove miserably on, watching the road, hoping against hope to come on him. Very slowly she drove, and only when she reached the Dorking road did she quite abandon hope. How she guided the car for the rest of the drive, she hardly knew. Life seemed suddenly to have gone out.

Chapter Nine

AFTERMATH

—‹‹·›·›—

JON, when he rushed back into the coppice, turned to the left, and, emerging past the pond, ran up through the field, towards the house, as if it were still his own. It stood above its terrace and lawns unlighted, ghostly in the spreading moonlight. Behind a clump of rhododendrons, where as a little boy he had played hide-and-seek, or pursued the staghorn beetle with his bow and arrow, he sank down as if his legs had turned to water, pressing his fists against his cheeks, both burning hot. He had known and he had not known, had dreamed and never dreamed of this! Overwhelming, sudden, relentless! 'It was written!' she had said. For her, every excuse, perhaps; but what excuse for him? Among those moonlit rhododendrons he could not find it. Yet the deed was done! Whose was he now? He stood up and looked at the house where he had been born, grown up, and played, as if asking for an answer. Whitened and lightless, it looked the ghost of a house, keeping secrets. 'And I don't let you tell! ... When shall I see you again?' That meant she claimed a secret lover. Impossible! The one thing utterly impossible. He would belong to one or to the other – not to both. Torn in every fibre of his being, he clung to the fixity of that. Behind the rhododendrons stretching along the far end of the lawn he walked, crouching, till he came to the wall of the grounds, the wall he had often scrambled over as a boy; and, pulling himself up, dropped into the top roadway. No one saw him, and he hurried on. He had a dumb and muddled craving to get back to Wansdon, though what he would do when he got there he could not tell. He turned towards Kingston.

All through that two hours' drive in a hired car Jon thought and thought. Whatever he did now, he must be disloyal to one or to the other. And with those passionate moments still rioting within him, he could get no grip on his position; and yet – he must!

He reached Wansdon at eleven, and, dismissing the car in the road, walked up to the house. Everyone had gone to bed, evidently assuming that he was staying the night at June's for a further sitting. There was a light in his and Anne's bedroom; and, at sight of it, the full shame of what he had done smote him. He could not bring himself to attract her attention, and he stole round the house seeking for some way of breaking in. At last he spied a spare-room window open at the top, and fetching a garden ladder, climbed it and got in. The burglarious act restored some self-possession. He went down into the hall, and out of the house, replaced the ladder, came in again and stole upstairs. But outside their door he halted. No light, now, came from under. She must be in bed. And, suddenly, he could not face going in. He would feel like Judas, kissing her. Taking off his boots and carrying them, he stole downstairs again to the dining-room. Having had nothing but a cup of tea since lunch, he got himself some biscuits and a drink. They altered his mood – no man could have resisted Fleur's kisses in that moonlit coppice – no man! Must he, then, hurt one or the other so terribly? Why not follow Fleur's wish? Why not secrecy? By continuing her lover in secret, he would not hurt Fleur; by not telling Anne, he would not hurt Anne! Like a leopard in a cage, he paced the room. And all that was honest in him refused, and all that was sage. As if one could remain the husband of two women, when one of them knew! As if Fleur would stand that long! And lies, subterfuge! And – Michael Mont! – a decent chap! He had done him enough harm as it was! No! A clean cut one way or the other! He stopped by the hearth, and leaned his arms on the stone mantelpiece. How still! Only that old clock which had belonged to his grandfather, ticking away time – time that cured everything, that made so little of commotions, ticking men and things to their appointed ends. Just in front of him on the mantelpiece was a photograph of his grandfather, old Jolyon, taken in his 'eighties – the last record of that old face, its broad brow, and white moustache, its sunken cheeks, deep, steady eyes, and strong jaw. Jon looked at it long! 'Take a course and stick to it!' the face, gazing back at him so deeply, seemed to say. He went to the bureau and sat down to write.

I am sorry I rushed away tonight, but it was better really. I had to think. I have thought. I'm only certain of one thing yet. To go on *in secret* is impossible. I shan't say a word about tonight, of course, until you let me. But, Fleur, unless I can tell everything, it must end. You wouldn't wish it otherwise, would you? Please answer to the Post Office, Nettlefold.

JON

He sealed this up, addressed it to her at Dorking, and, pulling on his boots, again stole out and posted it. When he got back he felt so tired, that, wrapped in an old coat, he fell asleep in an armchair. The moonlight played tricks through the half-drawn curtains, the old clock ticked, but Jon slept, dreamless.

He woke at daybreak, stole up to the bathroom, bathed and shaved noiselessly, and went out through a window, so as not to leave the front door unfastened. He walked up through the gap past the old chalk-pit, on to the Downs, by the path he had taken with Fleur seven years ago. Till he had heard from her he did not know what to do; and he dreaded Anne's eyes, while his mind was still distraught. He went towards Chanctonbury Ring. There was a heavy dew, and the short turf was all spun over with it. All was infinitely beautiful, remote and stilly in the level sunlight. The beauty tore at his heart. He had come to love the Downs – they had a special loveliness, like no other part of the world that he had seen. Did this mean that he must now leave them, leave England again – leave everything, and cleave to Fleur? If she claimed him, if she decided on declaring their act of union, he supposed it did. And Jon walked in confusion of heart, such as he had not thought possible to man. From the Ring he branched away, taking care to avoid the horses at their early exercise. And this first subterfuge brought him face to face with immediate decision. What should he do till he had heard from Fleur? Her answer could not reach Nettlefold till the evening or even next morning. He decided, painfully, to go back to breakfast, and tell them he had missed his train, and entered in the night burglariously so as not to disturb them.

That day, with its anxiety and its watchfulness of self, was one of the most wretched he had ever spent; and he could not free himself from the feeling that Anne was reading his thoughts. It was as if each passed the day looking at the other unobserved – almost unbearable! In the afternoon he asked for a horse to ride over to Green Hill Farm, and said he would be back late. He rode on into Nettlefold and went to the Post office. There was a telegram: 'Must see you. Will be at Green Hill Farm to-morrow at noon. Don't fail me.—F.'

Jon destroyed it, and rode homewards. Wretchedness and strain for another eighteen hours! Was there anything in the world worse than indecision? He rode slowly so as to have the less time at home, dreading the night. He stopped at a wayside inn to eat, and again went by way of Green Hill Farm to save at least the letter of his tale. It was nearly ten and full moonlight before he got back.

'It's a wonderful night,' he said, when he came into the drawing-room. 'The moonlight's simply marvellous.' It was Holly who answered; Anne, sitting by the fire, did not even look up. 'She knows,' thought Jon, 'she knows something.' Very soon after, she said she was sleepy, and went up. Jon stayed, talking to Holly. Val had gone on from town to Newmarket, and would not be back till Friday. They sat one on each side of the wood fire. And, looking at his sister's face, charming and pensive, Jon was tempted. She was so wise and sympathetic. It would be a relief to tell her everything. But Fleur's command held him back – it was not his secret.

'Well, Jon, is it all right about the farm?'

'I've got some new figures; I'm going into them to-night.'

'I do wish it were settled, and we knew you were going to be near for certain. I shall be awfully disappointed if you're not.'

'Yes; but I must make sure this time.'

'Anne's very set on it. She doesn't say much, but she really is. It's such a charming old place.'

'I don't want a better, but it must pay its way.'

'Is that your real reason, Jon?'

'Why not?'

'I thought perhaps you were secretly afraid of settling again. But you're the head of the family, Jon – you ought to settle.'

'Head of the family!'

'Yes, the only son of the only son of the eldest son right back to the primeval Jolyon.'

'Nice head!' said Jon bitterly.

'Yes – a nice head.' And, suddenly rising, Holly bent over and kissed the top of it.

'Bless you! Don't sit up too late. Anne's rather in the dumps.'

Jon turned out the lamp and stayed huddled in his chair before the fire. Head of the family! He had done them proud! And if – ! Ha! That would, indeed, be illustrious! What would the old fellow whose photograph he had been looking at last night think, if he knew? Ah, what a coil! For in his inmost heart he knew that Anne was more his mate, more her with whom he could live and work and have his being, than ever Fleur could be. Madness, momentary madness, coming on him from the past – the past, and the potency of her will to have and hold him! He got up, and drew aside the curtains. There, between two elm trees, the moon, mysterious and powerful, shone, and all was moving with its light up to the crest of the Downs. What beauty, what stillness! He threw the window up and stepped out; like some dark fluid spilled on the whitened grass, the ragged shadow of one elm tree reached almost to his feet. From their window above a light shone. He must go up and face it. He had not been alone with her since – ! If only he knew for certain what he was going to do! And he realized now that in obeying that impulse to rush away from Fleur he had been wrong; he ought to have stayed and threshed it out there and then. And yet, who could have behaved reasonably, sanely, feeling as he had felt? He stepped back to the window, and stopped with his heart in his mouth. There between firelight and moonlight stood Anne! Slender, in a light wrapper drawn close, she was gazing towards him. Jon closed the window and drew the curtain.

'Sorry, darling, you'll catch cold – the moonlight got me.' She moved to the far side of the hearth, and stood looking at him.

'Jon, I'm going to have a child.'

'You – !'

'Yes. I didn't tell you last month because I wanted to be sure.'

'Anne!'

She was holding up her hand.

'Wait a minute!'

Jon gripped the back of a chair, he knew what was coming.

'Something's happened between you and Fleur.'

Jon held his breath, staring at her eyes; dark, unflinching, startled, they stared back at him.

'Everything's happened, hasn't it?'

Jon bent his head.

'Yesterday? Don't explain, don't excuse yourself or her. Only – what does it mean?'

Without raising his head, Jon answered:

'That depends on you.'

'On me?'

'After what you've just told me. Oh! Anne, why didn't you tell me sooner?'

'Yes; I kept it too long!'

He understood what she meant – she had kept it as a weapon of defence. And, seeming to himself unforgivable, he said:

'Forgive me, Anne – forgive me!'

'Oh! Jon, I don't just know.'

'I swear that I will never see her again.'

He raised his eyes now, and saw that she had sunk on her knees by the fire, holding a hand out to it, as if cold. He dropped on his knees beside her.

'I think,' he said, 'love is the cruellest thing in the world.'

'Yes.'

She had covered her eyes with her hand; and it seemed hours

that he knelt there, waiting for a movement, a sign, a word. At last she dropped her hand.

'All right. It's over. But don't kiss me – yet.'

Chapter Ten

BITTER APPLE

L I F E revived in Fleur while she went about her business in the morning. Standing in sunshine before the hollyhocks and sun-flowers of the 'Rest House' garden, she reviewed past and future with feverish vigour. Of course Jon was upset! She had taken him by storm! He was old-fashioned, conscientious; he couldn't take things lightly. But since already he had betrayed his conscience, he would realize what had happened outweighed what more could happen. It was the first step that counted! They had always belonged to each other. She felt no remorse; then why should he – when his confusion was over? It was for the best, perhaps, that he had run away from her till he could see the inexorability of his position. Her design was quite un-shaken by the emotions she had been through. Jon was hers now, he could not betray their secret unless she gave him leave. He must and would conform to the one course possible – sec-recy. Infidelity had been achieved – one act or many, what did it matter? Ah! But she would make up to him the loss of self-respect with her love, and with her wisdom. She would make him a success. In spite of that American chit, he should succeed with his farming, become important to his county, to his country, perhaps. She would be circumspection itself – for his sake, for her own, for Michael's, Kit's, her father's.

With a great bunch of autumn flowers to which was clinging one bee, she went back into the house to put them in water. On the table in the hall were a number of little bags of bitter-apple prepared by her caretaker's wife against the moth, which were all over a house that had been derelict for a year. She busied herself with stowing them in drawers. The second post brought her Jon's letter.

She read it, and spots of burning colour became fixed in her cheeks. He had written this before he slept – it was all part of his confusion! But she must see him at once – at once! She got out the car, and, driving to a village where she was not known, sent a telegram to the post office at Nettlefold. Dreadful to have to wait over the night! But she knew it might be evening or even next morning before he could call for it.

Never did time go so slowly. For now she was shaken again. Was she over-estimating her power, relying too much on her sudden victory in a moment of passion, under-estimating Jon's strength after resolve taken? She remembered how in those old days she had failed to move him from renunciation. And, unable to keep still, she went up lonely on to Box Hill, and wandered among its yew trees and spindleberry bushes, till she was tired out and the sun was nearly down. With the sinking light the loneliness up there repelled her, for she was not a real nature-lover, and for an anxious heart Nature has little comfort. She was glad to be back, listening to the chatter of the supper-eating girls. It had no interest for her, but at least it was not melancholy like the space and shadows of the open. She suddenly remembered that she had missed her 'sitting' and had sent no word. The Rafaelite would gnash his teeth: perhaps he had set her 'Folly' dress up on a dummy, to paint the sound from its silver bells. Bells! Michael! Poor Michael! But was he to be pitied, who had owned her for years while at heart she belonged to another? She went up to bed early. If only she could sleep till it was time to start! This force that played with hearts, tore them open, left them quivering – made them wait and ache, and ache and wait! Had the Victorian Miss, whom they had taken to praising again, ever to go through what she had gone through since first she saw her fate in front of that grotesque Juno – or was it Venus? – in the gallery off Cork Street? The disciplined Victorian Miss? Admit – oh! freely – that she, Fleur Mont, was undisciplined; still, she hadn't worn her heart upon

her sleeve. She hadn't kicked and screamed. Surely she deserved
a spell of happiness! Not more than a spell – she wouldn't ask
for more than that! Things wore out, hearts wore out! But
to have the heart she wanted against her own, as last night,
and then to lose it straightaway? It could not be! And so at
last she slept, and the moon that had watched over her victory
came by, to look in through the curtain chinks, and make her
dream.

She woke and lay thinking with the preternatural intensity of
early morning thought. People would blame her if they knew;
and was there any real possibility that they would not come to
know? Suppose Jon remained immovably opposed to secrecy.
What then? Was she prepared to give up all and follow him?
It would mean more than in the ordinary case. It would mean
isolation. For always, in the background, was the old barrier of
the family feud; her father and his mother, and their abhorrence
of union between her and Jon. And all the worldly sense in
Fleur, brought to the edge of hard reality, shivered and recoiled.
Money! It was not that they would lack money. But position,
approval, appreciation, where in the world could they ever
regain all that? And Kit? He would be lost to her. The Monts
would claim him. She sat up in bed, seeing with utter clearness
in the dark a truth she had never before seen naked – that the
condition of conquest is sacrifice. Then she revolted. No! Jon
would be reasonable, Jon would come round! In secret they
would, they must, be happy, or if not happy, at least not starved.
She would have to share him, he to share her; but they would
each know that the other only pretended to belong elsewhere.
But would it be pretence with him? Was he at heart all hers?
Was he not, at least, as much his wife's? Horribly clear she
could see that girl's face, its dark, eager eyes, with the something strange and so attractive in their setting. No! She would
not think of her! It only weakened her power to win Jon over.
Dawn opened a sleepy eye. A bird cheeped, and daylight crept
in. She lay back resigned again to the dull ache of waiting. She
rose unrested. A fine morning, dry as ever – save for the dew
on the grass! At ten she would start! It would be easier to wait

in motion even if she had to drive slow. She gave her morning orders, got out the car, and left. She drove by the clock so as to arrive at noon. The leaves were turning already, it would be an early fall. Had she put on the right frock? Would he like this soft russet, the colour of gone-off apples? The red was prettier; but red caught the eye. And the eye must not be caught today. She drove the last mile at a foot's pace, and drew up in the wooded lane just where the garden of Green Hill Farm ended in orchard, and the fields began. Very earnestly she scrutinized her face in the small mirror of her vanity-bag. Where had she read that one always looked one's worst in a mirror? If so, it was a mercy. She remembered that Jon had once said he hated the look of lip salve; and, not touching her lips, she put away the mirror and got out. She walked slowly towards the entrance gate. From there a lane divided the house from the straw-yards and farm buildings sloping up behind it. In the fine autumn sunlight they ranged imposing, dry and deserted – no stock, not so much as a hen. Even Fleur's unlearned mind realized the stiff job before anyone who took this farm. Had she not often heard Michael say that farming was more of a man's job than any other in the England of today! She would let him take it, then that wretched conscience of his would be at rest on one score at least. She passed the gate and stood before the old house, gabled and red with Virginia creeper. Twelve had struck down in the village as she passed through. Surely he had not failed her! Five minutes she waited that seemed like five hours. Then, with her heart beating fast, she went up and rang the bell. It sounded far away in the empty house. Footsteps – a woman's!

'Yes, ma'am?'

'I was to meet Mr Forsyte here at noon about the farm.'

'Oh, yes, ma'am; Mr Forsyte came early. He was very sorry he had to go away. He left this note for you.'

'He's not coming back?'

'No, ma'am, he was very sorry, but he couldn't come back today.'

'Thank you.'

Fleur went back to the gate. She stood there, turning the note over and over. Suddenly she broke the seal and read:

Last night Anne told me of her own accord that she knew what had happened. She told me, too, that she is to have a child. I have promised her not to see you again. Forgive me and forget me, as I must forget you.

J O N

Slowly, as if not knowing, she tore the sheet of paper and the envelope into tiny fragments and buried them in the hedge. Then she walked slowly, as if not seeing, to her car, and got in. She sat there stonily, alongside the orchard with the sunlight on her neck and scent from wind-fallen rotting apples in her nostrils. For four months, since in the canteen she saw Jon's tired smile, he had been one long thought in her mind. And this was the end! Oh! Let her get away – away from here!

She started the car, and, once out of the lane, drove at a great pace. If she broke her neck, all the better! But Providence, which attends the drunk and desperate, was about her – spying out her ways; and she did not break her neck. For more than two hours she drove, hardly knowing where. At three in the afternoon she had her first impulse – a craving to smoke, a longing for tea. She got some at an inn, and turned her car towards Dorking. Driving more slowly now, she arrived between four and five. She had been at the wheel for nearly six hours. And the first thing she saw outside the 'Rest House' was her father's car. He! What had *he* come for? Why did people pester her? On the point of starting the engine again, she saw him come out of the front door, and stand looking up and down the road. Something groping in that look of his touched her, and, leaving the car, she walked towards him.

Chapter Eleven

'GREAT FORSYTE'

◄◄-►►

O N the morning after the Slum Conversion Committee meeting Soames had started early. It was his intention to spend the night somewhere 'down there', look at his roots the following morning, and motor part of the way home. On the day after, he would return to town and see if he couldn't carry Fleur back with him to Mapledurham for a long week-end. He reached a seaside hostel ten miles from his origin about six o'clock, ate a damp dinner, smoked his own cigar, and went to a bed in which, for insurance sake, he placed a camel's hair shawl.

He had thought things out, and was provided with an ordnance map on an inordinate scale. He meant to begin his investigation by seeing the church. For he had little to go by except a memory that his father James had once been down, and had returned speaking of a church by the sea, and supposing that there might be 'parish entries and that, but it was a long time back and he didn't know'.

After an early breakfast he directed Riggs towards the church. As James had said, it was close to the sea, and it was open. Soames went in. A little old grey church with funny pews and a damp smell. There wouldn't be any tablets to his name, he supposed. There were not, and he went out again, to wander among the gravestones, overcome by a sense of unreality – everything underground, and each gravestone, older than the last century, undecipherable. He was about to turn away when he stumbled. Looking down in disapproval at a flat stone, he saw on the worn and lichened surface a capital F. He stood for a minute, scrutinizing, then went down on his knees with a sort of thrill. Two names – the first had an undoubted capital *J*, a *y*, and an *n*; the second name began with that capital *F*, and had what looked like an *s* in the middle, and the remains of a tall

letter last but one! The date? By George – the date was legible!
1777. Scraping gingerly at the first name, he disinterred an *o*.
Four letters out of the six in Jolyon; three letters out of Forsyte.
There could hardly be a doubt that he had stumbled over his
great-great-grandfather! Supposing the old chap had lived to
the ordinary age of a Forsyte, his birth would be near the beginning of the eighteenth century! His eyes gimletted the stone
with a hard grey glance as though to pierce to the bones beneath
– clean as a whistle long since, no doubt! Then he rose from his
knees and dusted them. He had a date now. And, singularly
fortified, he emerged from the graveyard, and cast a suspicious
look at Riggs. Had he been seen on his knees? But the fellow
was seated, as usual, with his back to everything, smoking his
eternal cigarette. Soames got into the car.

'I want the vicarage now, or whatever it is.'

'Yes, sir.'

He was always saying 'Yes, sir', without having an idea of
where places were.

'You'd better ask,' he said, as the car moved up the rutted
lane. Sooner than ask, the fellow would go back to London! Not
that there was anyone to ask. Soames was impressed, indeed, by
the extreme emptiness of this parish where his roots lay. It
seemed terribly hilly, and full of space, with large fields, some
woods in the coombe to the left, and a soil that you couldn't
swear by – not red and not white and not brown exactly; the sea
was blue, however, and the cliffs, so far as he could judge, streaky.
The lane bent to the right, past a blacksmith's forge.

'Hi!' said Soames, 'pull up!' He himself got out to ask. That
fellow never made head or tail of what he was told.

The blacksmith was hammering at a wheel, and Soames
waited till his presence was observed.

'Where's the vicarage?'

'Up the lane, third 'ouse on the right.'

'Thank you,' said Soames, and, looking at the man suspi-
ciously, added:

'Is the name Forsyte known hereabouts nowadays?'

'What's that?'

'Have you ever heard the name Forsyte?'

'Farsyt? Noa.'

Soames heard him with a disappointed relief, and resumed his seat. What if he'd said: 'Yes, it's mine!'

A blacksmith's was a respectable occupation, but he felt that he could do without it in the family. The car moved on.

The vicarage was smothered in creeper. Probably the vicar would be, too! He rang a rusty bell and waited. The door was opened by a red-cheeked girl. It was all very rustic.

'I want the vicar,' said Soames. 'Is he in?'

'Yes, sir. What name?'

But at this moment a thin man in a thin suit and a thin beard came out from a doorway, saying:

'Am I wanted, Mary?'

'Yes,' said Soames; 'here's my card.'

There ought – he felt – to be a way of enquiring about one's origin that would be distinguished; but, not finding it, he added simply:

'My family came from hereabouts some generations back; I just wanted to have a look at the place, and ask you a question or two.'

'Forsyte?' said the vicar, glancing at the card: 'I don't know the name, but I daresay we shall find something.'

His clothes were extremely well worn, and Soames had the impression that his eyes would have been glad if they could. 'Smells a fee,' he thought; 'poor devil!'

'Will you come in?' said the vicar. 'I've got some records and an old tithe map. We might have a look at them. The registers go back to 1580. I could make a search for you.'

'I don't know if that's worth while,' said Soames, following him into a room that impressed him as dismal beyond words.

'Do sit down,' said the vicar. 'I'll get that map. Forsyte? I seem to remember the name now.'

The fellow was agreeable, and looked as if he could do with an honest penny!

'I've been up to the church,' said Soames; 'it seems very close to the sea.'

'Yes; they used to use the pulpit, I'm afraid, to hide their smuggled brandy.'

'I got a date in the graveyard — 1777; the stones are very much let down.'

'Yes,' said the vicar, who was groping in a cupboard: 'one's difficulty is the sea air. Here's the map I spoke of;' and, unrolling a large and dingy map, he laid it on the table, weighting down the corners with a tin of tobacco, an inkstand, a book of sermons, and a dog whip. The latter was not heavy enough, and the map curled slowly away from Soames.

'Sometimes,' said the vicar, restoring the corner, and looking round for something to secure it, 'we get very useful information from these old maps.'

'I'll keep it down,' said Soames, bending over the map. 'I suppose you get a lot of Americans, fishing for ancestors?'

'Not a lot,' said the vicar, with a sideway glance that Soames did not quite like. 'I can remember two. Ah! here,' and his finger came down on the map, 'I *thought* I remembered the name — it's unusual. Look! This field close to the sea is marked "Great Forsyte"!'

Again Soames felt a thrill.

'What size is that field?'

'Twenty-four acres. There was the ruin of an old house, I remember, just there; they took the stones away in the war to make our shooting range. "Great Forsyte" — isn't that interesting?'

'More interesting to me,' said Soames, 'if they'd left the stones.'

'The spot is still marked with an old cross — the cattle use it for a rubbing stone. It's close to the hedge on the right-hand side of the coombe.'

'Could I get to it with the car?'

'Oh, yes; by going round the head of the coombe. Would you like me to come?'

'No, thanks,' said Soames. The idea of being overlooked while inspecting his roots was unpleasant to him. 'But if you'd kindly make a search in the register while I'm gone, I could call back after lunch and see the result. My great-grandfather, Jolyon Forsyte, died at Studmouth. The stone I found was Jolyon Forsyte, buried in 1777 – he'd be my great-great-grandfather, no doubt. I daresay you could pick up his birth, and perhaps *his* father's – I fancy they were a long-lived lot. The name Jolyon seems to have been a weakness with them.'

'I could make a search at once. It would take some hours. What would you think reasonable?'

'Five guineas?' hazarded Soames.

'Oh! That would be generous. I'll make a very thorough search. Now, let me come and tell you how to get to it.' With a slight pang Soames followed him – a gentleman in trousers shiny behind.

'You go up this road to the fork, take the left-hand branch past the Post Office, and right on round the head of the coombe, always bearing to the left, till you pass a farm called "Uphays". Then on till the lane begins to drop; there's a gate on the right, and if you go through it you'll find yourself at the top of that field with the sea before you. I'm so pleased to have found something. Won't you have a little lunch with us when you come back?'

'Thank you,' said Soames, 'very good of you, but I've got my lunch with me,' and was instantly ashamed of his thought. 'Does he think I'm going to make off without paying?' Raising his hat slightly, he got into the car, with his umbrella in his hand, so as to poke Riggs in the back when the fellow took his wrong turnings.

He sat, contented, using the umbrella gingerly now and then. So! To get baptized and buried, they used to cross the coombe. Twenty-four acres was quite a field. 'Great Forsyte'; there must have been 'Little Forsytes', too.

The farm the vicar had spoken of appeared to be a rambling place of old buildings, pigs and poultry.

'Keep on,' he said to Riggs, 'until the lane drops, and go slow, I want a gate on the right.'

The fellow was rushing along as usual, and the lane already dropping downhill.

'Hold hard! There it is!' The car came to a standstill at a rather awkward bend.

'You've overshot it!' said Soames, and got out. 'Wait here! I may be some time.'

Taking off his overcoat and carrying it on his arm, he went back to the gate, and passed through into a field of grass. He walked downwards to the hedge on the left, followed it round, and presently came in view of the sea, bright, peaceful, hazy, with a trail of smoke in the distance. The air beat in from the sea, fresh air, strong and salt. Ancestral! Soames took some deep breaths, savouring it, as one might an old wine. Its freshness went a little to his head, so impregnated with ozone or iodine, or whatever it was nowadays. And then, below him, perhaps a hundred yards away, above a hollow near the hedge he saw the stone, and again felt that thrill. He looked back. Yes! He was out of sight of the lane, and had his feelings to himself! And, going up to the stone, he gazed down at the hollow between him and the hedge. Below it the field sloped to the beach, and what looked like the ghost of a lane ran up towards the hollow from the coombe. In that hollow then, the house had been; and there they'd lived, the old Forsytes, for generations, pickled in this air, without another house in sight – nothing but this expanse of grass in view and the sea beyond, and the gulls on that rock, and the waves beating over it. There they'd lived, tilling the land, and growing rheumatic, and crossing the coombe to church, and getting their brandy free, perhaps. He went up and examined the stone – upright, with another bit across the top – lintel of a barn, perhaps – nothing on it. Descending into the hollow, he poked about with his umbrella. During the war – the parson had said – they had removed the ruins. Only twelve years ago, but not a sign! Grassed over utterly, not even the shape visible. He explored up to the hedge. They'd made a clean sweep all right – nothing but grass now and a scrubble of fern and young gorse, such as would seize on a hollow for their growing. And, sitting on his overcoat with his back against the stone, Soames pondered. Had his forbears themselves built the house there in this lonely place – been the first to seat themselves on this bit of wind-swept soil? And something moved in him, as if the salty independence of that lonely spot were still in his bones. Old Jolyon and his own father and the rest of his uncles – no wonder they'd been independent, with this air and loneliness in their blood; and crabbed with the pickling of it – unable to give up, to let go, to die. For a moment he seemed to understand even himself. Southern spot, south aspect, not any of your northern roughness, but free, and salt, and solitary from sunrise to sunset, year in, year out, like that lonely rock with the gulls on it, for ever and for ever. And drawing the air deep into his lungs, he thought: 'I'm not surprised old Timothy lived to be a hundred!' A long time he sat there, nostalgically bemused, strangely unwilling to move. Never had he breathed anything quite like that air; or so, at least, it seemed to him. It had been the old England, when they lived down here – the England of pack-horses and very little smoke, of peat and wood fires, and wives who never left you, because they couldn't, probably. A static England, that dug and wove, where your parish was your world, and you were a churchwarden if you didn't take care. His own grandfather – begotten and born one hundred and fifty-six years ago, in the best bed, not two dozen paces from where he was sitting. What a change since then! For the better? Who could say? But here was this grass, and rock and sea, and the air and the gulls, and the old church over there beyond the coombe, precisely as they had been, only more so. If this field were in the market, he wouldn't mind buying it as a curiosity. Only, if he did, nobody would come and sit here! They'd want to play golf over it or something. And, uneasy at having verged on the sentimental, Soames put his hand down and felt the grass. But it wasn't damp, and he couldn't conscientiously feel that he was catching rheumatism; and still he sat there, with the sunlight warming his cheeks, and his eyes fixed on the sea. The ships went up and down, far out – steamers; no smugglers nowadays, and you paid the deuce of a price for brandy! In the old time here, without newspapers, with nothing from the outer world, you'd grow up without sense of the State or that sort of thing. There'd be the church and your Bible, he supposed, and the market some miles away, and you'd work and eat and sleep and breathe the air and drink your cider and embrace your wife and watch your children, from June to June; and a good thing, too! What more did you do now that brought you any satisfaction? 'Change, it's all on the surface,' thought Soames; 'the roots are the same. You can't get beyond them – try as you will!' Progress, civilization, what were they for? Unless – unless, indeed, to foster hobbies – collecting pictures, or what not? He didn't see how the old chaps down here could have had hobbies – except for bees, perhaps. Hobbies? Just for that – just to give people a chance to have hobbies? He'd had a lot of amusement out of his own; and but for progress would never have had it. No! He'd have been down here still, perhaps, shearing his sheep or following a plough, and his daughter would be a girl with sturdy ankles and one new hat. Perhaps it was just as well that you couldn't stop the clock! Ah! and it was time he was getting back to the lane before that chap came to look for him. And, getting up, Soames descended once more into the hollow. This time, close to the hedge, an object caught his eye, a very old boot – a boot so old that you could hardly swear by it. His lips became contorted in a faint smile. He seemed to hear his dead cousin George with his wry Forsytean humour cackling: 'The ancestral boot! What ho, my wild ones! Let the portcullis fall!' Yes! They would laugh at him in the family if they knew he'd been looking at their roots. He shouldn't say anything about it. And suddenly he went up to the boot, and, hooking the point of his umbrella under what was left of the toe-cap, flung it pettishly over the hedge. It defiled the loneliness – the feeling he had known, drinking-in that air. And very slowly he went back to the lane, so as not to get hot, and have to sit all damp in the car. But at the gate he stood, transfixed. What was all this? Two large, hairy horses were attached tandem to the back of his car with ropes, and beside them were three men, one of whom was Riggs, and two dogs, one of whom was lame. Soames perceived at once that it was all 'that fellow'! In trying to back up the hill, which he ought never to have gone down, he had jammed the car so that it couldn't move. He was always doing something! At this moment, however, 'the fellow' mounted the car and moved the wheel; while one of the men cracked a whip. 'Haup!' the hairy horses moved. Something in that slow, strong movement affected Soames. Progress! They had been obliged to fetch horses to drag Progress up the hill!

'That's a good horse!' he said, pointing to the biggest.

'Ah! We call 'im Lion – 'e can pull. Haup!'

The car passed on to the level ground, and the horses were detached. Soames went up to the man who had said 'Haup!'

'Are you from the farm back there?'

'Yes.'

'Do you own this field?'

'I farm it.'

'What do you call it?'

'Call it? The big field.'

'It's marked "Great Forsyte" on the tithe map. D'you know that name?'

'Farsyt? There's none of the name now. My grandmother was called Farsyt.'

'Was she?' said Soames, and again felt the thrill.

'Ah!' said the farmer.

Soames controlled himself.

'And what's *your* name, if I may ask?'

'Beer.'

Soames looked at him rather long, and took out his note-case.

'You must allow me,' he said, 'for your horses and your trouble.' And he offered a pound note. The farmer shook his head.

'That's naught,' he said; 'you're welcome. We're always haulin' cars off this 'ill.'

'I really can't take something for nothing,' said Soames. 'You'll oblige me!'

'Well,' said the farmer, 'I thank yeou,' and he took the note. 'Haup!'

The released horses moved forward and the men and the dogs

followed after them. Soames got into the car, and, opening his packet of sandwiches, began to eat.

'Drive back to the vicarage – slowly.' And, while he ate, he wondered why he had felt a thrill on discovering that some of his own blood ran in a hard-bitten looking chap called Beer – if, indeed, that *was* his name.

It was two o'clock when he reached the vicarage, and the vicar came to him with his mouth full.

'I find a great many entries, Mr Forsyte; the name goes back to the beginning of the register. I shall have to take my time to give you the complete list. That Jolyon seems to have been born in 1710, son of Jolyon and Mary; he didn't pay his tithes in 1757. There was another Jolyon born in 1680, evidently the father – he was churchwarden from 1715 on; described as 'Yeoman of Hays' – he married a Bere.'

Soames gazed at him, and took out his note-case. 'How do you spell it?' he said.

'B-e-r-e.'

'Oh! The farmer up there said that was his name, too. I thought he was gammoning me. It seems his grandmother was called Forsyte, and she was the last of them here. Perhaps you could send me the Bere entries, too, for an inclusive seven guineas?'

'Oh! Six will be ample.'

'No. We'll make it seven. You've got my card. I saw the stone. A healthy spot, right away from everything.' He laid the seven guineas on the table, and again had an impression, as of glad eyes. 'I must be getting back to London now. Good-bye!'

'Good-bye, Mr Forsyte. Anything I can find out I shall make a point of sending you.'

Soames shook his hand and went out to the car with the feeling that his roots would be conscientiously pulled up. After all, it was something to be dealing with a parson.

'Go on,' he said to Riggs; 'we'll get the best part of the way home.'

And, lying back in the car, thoroughly tired, he mused. Great Forsyte! Well! He was glad he had come down.

Chapter Twelve

DRIVING ON

◄◄‹•›►►

SOAMES spent the night at Winchester, a place he had often heard of but never seen. The Monts had been at school there, and that was why he didn't want Kit to go. He himself would prefer his own Marlborough, or Harrow, perhaps – some school that played at Lords – but not Eton, where young Jolyon had been. But then one wouldn't be alive to see Kit play; so perhaps it didn't matter.

The town seemed an old place. There was something in a cathedral, too; and after breakfast he went to it. The chancel was in activity – some choir practice or other. He entered noiselessly, for his boots were rubbered against damp, and sat down at the point of balance. With chin uplifted, he contemplated the arches and the glass. The place was rather dark, but very rich – like a Christmas pudding! These old buildings certainly gave one a feeling. He had always had it in St Paul's. One must admit at least a continuity of purpose somewhere. Up to a point – after that he wasn't sure. You had a great thing, like this, almost perfect; and then an earthquake or an air-raid, and down it went! Nothing permanent about anything, so far as he could see, not even about the best examples of ingenuity and beauty. The same with landscape! You had a perfect garden of a country, and then an ice-age came along. There was continuity, but it was always changing. That was why it seemed to him extremely unlikely that he would live after he was dead. He had read somewhere – though not in *The Times* – that life was just animated shape, and that when shape was broken it was no longer animated. Death broke your shape and there you were, he supposed. The fact was, people couldn't bear their own ends; they tried to dodge them with soft sawder. They were weak-minded. And Soames lowered his chin. They had lighted some candles up there in the chancel, insignificant in the daylight. Presently they would blow them out. There you were again, everything was blown out sooner or later. And it was no good pretending it wasn't. He had read the other day, again not in *The Times*, that the world was coming to an end in 1928, when the earth got between the moon and the sun – it had been predicted in the Pyramids – some such scientific humbug! Well, if it did, he, for one, wouldn't much mind. The thing had never been a great success, and if it were wiped out at one stroke there would be nothing left behind anyway; what was objectionable about death was leaving things that you were fond of behind. The moment, too, that the world came to an end, it would begin again in some other shape, anyway – that, no doubt, was why they called it 'world without end, Amen'. Ah! They were singing now. Sometimes he wished he had an ear. In spite of the lack, he could tell that this was good singing. Boys' voices! Psalms, too, and he knew the words. Funny! Fifty years since his church-going days, yet he remembered them as if it were yesterday! 'He sendeth the springs into the rivers; which run among the hills.' 'All beasts of the fields drink thereof; and the wild asses quench their thirst.' 'Beside them shall the fowls of the air have their habitation; and sing among the branches.' They were flinging the verses at each other across the aisle, like a ball. It was lively, and good, vigorous English, too. 'So is the great and wide sea also, wherein are things creeping innumerable, both small and great beasts.' 'There go the ships, and there is that Leviathan, whom Thou hast made to take his pastime therein.' Leviathan! That word used to please him. 'Man goeth forth to his work, and to his labour, until the evening.' He certainly went forth, but whether he did any work, any labour, was the question, nowadays. 'I will sing unto the Lord as long as I live; I will praise my God while I have my being.' Would he? He wondered. 'Praise thou the Lord, O my soul, praise the Lord.' The singing ceased, and Soames again lifted up his chin. He sat very still – not thinking now; lost, as it were, among the arches, and the twilight of the roof. He was experiencing a peculiar sensation, not unpleasant. To be in here was like being within a jewelled and somewhat scented box. The world might roar and stink and buzz outside, strident and vulgar, childish and sensational, cheap and nasty – all jazz and cockney accent, but here – not a trace of it heard or felt or seen. This great box – God-box the Americans would call it – had been made centuries before the world became industrialized; it didn't belong to the modern world at all. In here everyone spoke and sang the King's English; it smelt faintly of age and incense; and nothing was unbeautiful. He sat with a sense of escape.

A verger passed, glancing at him curiously, as if unaccustomed to a raised chin; halting just behind, he made a little noise with his keys. Soames sneezed; and, reaching for his hat, got up. He had no intention of being taken round by that chap, and shown everything he didn't want to see, for half-a-crown. And with a 'No, thank you; not to-day,' he passed the verger, and went out to the car.

'You ought to have gone in,' he said to Riggs; 'they used to crown the kings of England there. To London now.'

The opened car travelled fast under a bright sun, and not until he was in the new cut, leading to Chiswick, did Soames have the idea which caused him to say: 'Stop at that house, "The Poplars", where you took us the other day.'

It was not yet lunch time, and in all probability Fleur would still be 'sitting'; so why not pick her up and take her straight away with him for the week-end? She had clothes down at 'The Shelter'. It would save some hours of fresh air for her. The foreign woman, however, who opened the door, informed him that the lady had not been to 'sit' to-day or yesterday.

'Oh!' said Soames. 'How's that?'

'Nobody did know, sir. She 'ave not sent any message. Mr Blade is very decomposed.'

Soames chewed his thoughts a moment.

'Is your mistress in?'

'Yes, sir.'

'Then ask her if she'll see me, please. Mr Soames Forsyte.'

'Will you in the meal-room wait, sir.'

Soames waited uneasily in that very little room. Fleur had said she could not come with him because of her 'sittings'; and she had not 'sat'. Was she ill, then?

He was roused from disquiet contemplation of the poplar trees outside by the words:

'Oh! It's you. I'm not sorry you came.'

The cordiality of this greeting increased his uneasiness, and, stretching out his hand, he said:

'How are you, June? I called for Fleur. When did she come last?'

'Tuesday morning. I saw her late on Tuesday afternoon, too, in her car, outside —' Soames could see her eyes moving from side to side, and knew that she was about to say something unpleasant. It came. 'She picked up Jon.'

Feeling as if he had received a punch in his wind, Soames exclaimed:

'What! Your young brother? What was he doing here?'

' "Sitting"! of course.'

' "Sitting"! What business — I' and checking the words, 'had he to "sit", he stared at his cousin, who, flushing a deep pink, said:

'I told her she was not to see him here. I told Jon the same.'

'Then she'd done it before?'

'Yes, twice. She's so spoiled, you see.'

'Ah!' The reality of the danger had disarmed him. Antagonism seemed to him, thus faced with a sort of ruin, too luxurious.

'Where is she?'

'On Tuesday morning she said she was going down to Dorking.'

'And she picked him up?' repeated Soames.

June nodded. 'Yes, after his "sitting". His picture's finished. If you think that I want them to — any more than you —'

'No one in their sense could want them to —' said Soames, coldly. 'But why did you make him "sit", while she was coming here?'

June flushed a deeper pink.

'*You* don't know how hard it is for real artists. I *had* to think of Harold. If I hadn't got Jon before he began his farming –'

'Farming!' said Soames. 'For all we know they may –' but again he checked his words. 'I've been expecting something of this sort ever since I heard he was back. Well! I'd better get on to Dorking. D'you know where his mother is?'

'In Paris.'

Ah! But not this time would he have to beg that woman to let her son belong to his daughter! No! It would be to beg her to stop his belonging – if at all.

'Good-bye!' he said.

'Soames,' said June, suddenly, 'don't let Fleur – it's she who –'

'I'll hear nothing against her,' said Soames.

June pressed her clenched hands to her flat breast.

'I like you for that,' she said; 'and I'm sorry if –'

'That's all right,' muttered Soames.

'Good-bye!' said June. 'Shake hands!'

Soames put his hand in one which gave it a convulsive squeeze, then dropped it like a cold potato.

'Down to Dorking,' he said to Riggs, on regaining his car. The memory of Fleur's face that night at Nettlefold, so close to the young man's, so full of what he had never seen on her face before, haunted him the length of Hammersmith Bridge. Ah! what a wilful creature! Suppose – suppose she had flung her cap over the windmill! Suppose the worst? Good God! What should – what *could* he do, then? The calculating tenacity of her passion for this young man – the way she had kept it from him, from everyone, or tried to! Something deadly about it, and something that almost touched him, rousing the memory of his own pursuit of that boy's mother – memory of a passion that would not, could not let go; that had won its ends, and destroyed in winning. He had often thought she had no continuity, that, like all these 'fizz-gig' young moderns, she was just fluttering without basic purpose or direction. And it was the irony of this moment that he perceived how she – when she knew what she wanted – had as much tenacity of will as himself and his generation.

It didn't do, it seemed, to judge by appearances! Beneath the surface passions remained what they had been, and in the draughty corridors and spaces there was the old hot stillness when they woke and breathed. ...

That fellow was taking the Kingston road! Soon they would be passing Robin Hill. How all this part had changed since the day he went down with Bosinney to choose the site. Forty years – not more – but what a change! '*Plus ça change.*' Annette would say – '*plus c'est la même chose!*' Love and hate – no end to that, anyway! The beat of life went on beneath the wheels and whirr of traffic and the jazzy music of the band. Fate on its drum, or just the human heart? God knew! God? Convenient word. What did one mean by it? He didn't know, and never would! In the cathedral that morning he had thought – and then – that verger! There were the poplars, and the stable clock-tower, just visible, of the house he had built and never inhabited. If he could have foreseen a stream of cars like this passing day after day, not a quarter of a mile off, he would not have built it, and all that tragedy might never ... And yet – did it matter what you did? – some way, somehow life took you up and put you where it would. He leaned forward and touched his chauffeur's back.

'Which way are you going?'

'Through Esher, sir, and off to the left.'

'Well,' said Soames, 'it's all the same to me.'

It was past lunch-time, but he wasn't hungry. He wouldn't be hungry till he knew the worst. But that chap would be, he supposed.

'Better stop somewhere,' he said, 'and have a snack and a cigarette.'

'Yes, sir.'

He wasn't long in stopping. Soames sat on in the car, gazing idly at the sign – 'Red Lion'. Red Lions, Angels and White Horses – nothing killed them off. One of these days they'd try and bring in Prohibition, he shouldn't wonder; but that cock

wouldn't fight in England — too extravagant! Treating people
like children wasn't the way to make them grow up; as if they
weren't childish enough as it was. Look at this coal strike, that
went on and on — perfectly childish, hurting everybody and
doing good to none! Weak-minded! To reflect on the weak-
mindedness of his fellow-citizens was restful to Soames, faced
with a future that might prove disastrous. For, in view of her
infatuation, what could taking that young man about in her
car mean — except disaster? What a time Riggs was! He got out
and walked up and down. Not that there was anything he
could do — he supposed — when he did get there. No matter
how much you loved a person, how anxious you were about
her, you had no power — perhaps less power in proportion to
your love. But he must speak his mind at last, if he had the
chance. Couldn't let her go over the edge without putting out
a hand! The sun struck on his face, and he lifted it a little
blindly, as if grateful for the warmth. All humbug about the
world coming to an end, of course, but he'd be glad enough for
it to come before he was brought down in sorrow to the grave.
He saw with hideous clearness how complete disaster must be.
If Fleur ran off, there'd be nothing left to him that he really
cared about, for the Monts would take Kit. He'd be stranded
among his pictures and his cows, without heart for either, till
he died. 'I won't have it,' he thought. 'If it hasn't happened!'
I won't have it.' Yes! But how prevent it? And with the futility
of his own resolution staring him in the face, he went back to
the car. There was the fellow, at last, smoking his cigarette.

'Let's start!' he said. 'Push along!'

He arrived at three o'clock to hear that Fleur had gone out
with the car at ten. It was an immense relief to learn that at
least she had been there overnight. And at once he began to
make trunk calls. They renewed his anxiety. She was not at
home; nor at June's. Where, then, if not with that young man?
But at least she had taken no things with her — this he ascer-
tained, and it gave him strength to drink some tea and wait.
He had gone out into the road for the fourth time to peer up
and down when at last he saw her coming towards him.

The expression on her face – hungry and hard and feverish -
had the most peculiar effect on Soames; his heart ached, and
leaped with relief at the same time. That was not the face of
victorious passion! It was tragically unhappy, arid, wrenched.
Every feature seemed to have sharpened since he saw her last.
And, instinctively, he remained silent, poking his face forward
for a kiss. She gave it – hard and parched.

'So you're back,' she said.

'Yes; and when you've had your tea, I want you to come
straight on with me to "The Shelter" – Riggs'll put your car
away.'

She shrugged her shoulders and passed him into the house.
It seemed to him that she did not care what he saw in her, or
what he thought of her. And this was so strange in Fleur that
he was confounded. Had she tried and failed? Could it mean
anything so good? He searched his memory to recall how she
had looked when he brought her back the news of failure six
years ago. Yes! Only then she was so young, her face so round
– not like this hardened, sharpened, burnt-up face, that
frightened him. Get her away to Kit! Get her away, and
quickly! And with that saving instinct of his where Fleur only
was concerned, he summoned Riggs, told him to close the car
and bring it round.

She had gone up to her room. He sent up a message presently
that the car was ready. Soon she came down. She had coated
her face with powder and put salve on her lips; and again
Soames was shocked by that white mask with compressed red
line of mouth, and the live and tortured eyes. And again he
said nothing, and got out a map.

'That fellow will go wrong unless I sit beside him. It's cross-
country'; and he mounted the front of the car. He knew she
couldn't talk, and that he couldn't bear to see her face. So they
started. An immense time they travelled thus, it seemed to him.
Once or twice only he looked round to see her sitting like something dead, so white and motionless. And, within him, the two
feelings – relief and pity, continued to struggle. Surely it was
the end – she had played her hand and lost! How, where, when

– he felt would always be unknown to him; but she had lost!
Poor little thing! Not her fault that she had loved this boy, that
she couldn't get him out of her head – no more her fault than it
had been his own for loving that boy's mother! Only everyone's misfortune! It was as if that passion, born of an ill-starred
meeting in a Bournemouth drawing-room forty-six years before,
and transmitted with his blood into her being, were singing its
swan-song of death, through the silent crimsoned lips of that
white-faced girl behind him in the cushioned car. 'Praise thou
the Lord, O my soul! Praise the Lord!' Um! How could one!
They were crossing the river at Staines – from now on that
fellow knew his road. When they got home, how should he
bring some life into her face again? Thank goodness her mother
was away! Surely Kit would be some use! And her old dog,
perhaps. And yet, tired though he was after his three long days,
Soames dreaded the moment when the car should stop. To
drive on and on, perhaps, was the thing for her. Perhaps, for
all the world, now. To get away from something that couldn't
be got away from – ever since the war – driving on! When
you couldn't have what you wanted, and yet couldn't let go;
and drove, on and on, to dull the aching. Resignation – like
painting – was a lost art; or so it seemed to Soames, as they
passed the graveyard where he expected to be buried some day.

Close home now, and what was he going to say to her when
they got out? Words were so futile. He put his head out of the
window and took some deep breaths. It smelled better down
here by the river than elsewhere, he always thought – more
sap in the trees, more savour in the grass. Not the equal of
the air on 'Great Forsyte', but more of the earth, more cosy.
The gables and the poplars, the scent of a wood fire, the last
flight of the doves – here they were! And with a long sigh, he
got out.

'You've been doing too much,' he said, opening the door.
'Would you like to go straight up to bed when you've seen Kit?
I'll send up your dinner.'

'Thanks, Dad. Some soup is all I shall want. I've got a chill,
I think.'

Soames looked at her deeply for a moment and shook his head; then, touching her whitened cheek with a finger, he turned away.

He went round to the stables and released her old dog. It might want a run before being let into the house; and he took it down towards the river. A thin daylight lingered, though the sun had set some time, and while the dog freshened himself among the bushes, Soames stood looking at the water. The swans passed over to their islet while he gazed. The young ones were growing up – were almost white. Rather ghostly in the dusk, the flotilla passed – graceful things and silent. He had often thought of going in for a peacock or two, they put a finish on a garden, but they were noisy; he had never forgotten an early morning in Montpelier Square, hearing their cry, as of lost passion, from Hyde Park. No! The swan was better; just as graceful and didn't sing. That dog was ruining his dwarf arbutus.

'Come along to your mistress!' he said, and turned back toward the lighted house. He went up into the picture gallery. On the bureau were laid a number of letters and things to be attended to. For half an hour he laboured at them. He had never torn up things with greater satisfaction. Then the gong sounded, and he went down to be lonely, as he supposed.

Chapter Thirteen

FIRES

⧏⧏⧐⧐

Bᴜᴛ Fleur came down again. And there began for Soames the most confused evening he had ever spent. For in his heart were great gladness and great pity, and he must not show a sign of either. He wished now that he had stopped to look at Fleur's portrait; it would have given him something to talk of. He fell back feebly on her Dorking house.

'It seems a useful place,' he said; 'the girls –'

'I always feel they hate me. And why not? They have nothing, and I have everything.'

Her laugh cut Soames to the quick.

She was only pretending to eat, too. But he was afraid to ask if she had taken her temperature. She would only laugh again. He began, instead, an account of how he had found a field by the sea where the Forsytes came from, and how he had visited Winchester Cathedral; and, while he went on and on, he thought: 'She hasn't heard a word.'

The idea that she would go up to bed consumed by this smouldering fire at which he could not get, distressed and alarmed him greatly. She looked as if – as if she might do something to herself! She had no veronal, or anything of that sort, he hoped. And all the time he was wondering what had happened. If the issue were still doubtful – if she were still waiting, she might be restless, feverish, but surely she would not look like this! No! It was defeat. But how? And was it final, and he freed for ever from the carking anxiety of these last months? His eyes kept questioning her face, where her fevered mood had crept throught the coating of powder, so that she looked theatrical and unlike herself. Its expression, hard and hopeless, went to his heart. If only she would cry, and blurt everything out! But he recognized that in coming down at all, and facing

him, she was practically saying: *'Nothing* has happened!'
And he compressed his lips. A dumb thing, affection — one
couldn't put it into words! The more deeply he felt the more
dumb he had always been. Those glib people who poured themselves out and got rid of the feelings they had in their chests,
he didn't know how they could do it!

Dinner dragged to its end, with little bursts of talk from
Fleur, and more of that laughter which hurt him, and afterwards they went to the drawing-room.

'It's hot to-night,' she said, and opened the french window.
The moon was just rising, low and far behind the river bushes;
and a waft of light was already floating down the water.

'Yes, it's warm,' said Soames, 'but you oughtn't to be in the
air if you've got a chill.'

And, taking her arm, he led her within. He had a dread of
her wandering outside to-night, so near the water.

She went over to the piano.

'Do you mind if I strum, Dad?'

'Not at all. Your mother's got some French songs there.' He
didn't mind what she did, if only she could get that look off her
face. But music was emotional stuff, and French songs always
about love! It was to be hoped she wouldn't light on the one
Annette was for ever singing:

> *'Auprès de ma blonde, il fait bon — fait bon — fait bon,*
> *Auprès de ma blonde, il fait bon dormir.'*

The young man's hair! In the old days, beside his mother!
What hair *she'd* had! What bright hair and what dark eyes!
And for a moment it was as if, not Fleur, but Irene, sat there at
the piano. Music! Mysterious how it could mean to anyone
what it had meant to her. Yes! More than men and more than
money — music! A thing that had never moved him, that he
didn't understand! What a mischance! There she was, above
the piano, as he used to see her in the little drawing-room in
Montpelier Square; there, as he had seen her last in that
Washington hotel. There she would sit until she died, he supposed, beautiful, he shouldn't wonder, even then. Music!

He came to himself.

Fleur's thin, staccato voice tickled his ears, where he sat in the fume of his cigar. Painful! She was making a brave fight. He wanted her to break down, and he didn't want her to. For if she broke down he didn't know what he would do!

She stopped in the middle of a song and closed the piano. She looked almost old – so she would look, perhaps, when she was forty. Then she came and sat down on the other side of the hearth. She was in red, and he wished she wasn't – the colour increased his feeling that she was on fire beneath that mask of powder on her face and neck. She sat there very still, pretending to read. And he who had *The Times* in his hand, tried not to notice her. Was there nothing he could do to divert her attention? What about his pictures? Which – he asked – was her favourite? The Constable, the Stevens, the Corot, or the Daumier?

'I'm leaving the lot to the nation,' he said. 'But I shall want you to take your pick of four or so; and, of course, that copy of Goya's "Vendimia" belongs to you.' Then, remembering she had worn the 'Vendimia' dress at the dance in the Nettlefold hotel, he hurried on:

'With all this modern taste the nation mayn't want them; in that case I don't know. Dumetrius might take them off your hands; he's had a good deal out of most of them already. If you chose the right moment, clear of strikes and things, they ought to fetch money in a good sale. They stand me in at well over seventy thousand pounds – they ought to make a hundred thousand at least.'

She seemed to be listening, but he couldn't tell.

'In my belief,' he went on desperately, 'there'll be none of this modern painting in ten years' time – they can't go on for ever juggling in the air. They'll be sick of experiments by then, unless we have another war.'

'It wasn't the war.'

'How d'you mean – not the war? The war brought in ugliness, and put everyone into a hurry. You don't remember before the war.'

She shrugged her shoulders.

'I won't say,' continued Soames, 'that it hadn't begun before. I remember the first shows in London of those post-impressionists and early Cubist chaps. But they ran riot with the war, catching at things they couldn't get.'

He stopped. It was exactly what she – !

'I think I'll go to bed, Dad.'

'Ah!' said Soames. 'And take some aspirin. Don't you play about with a chill.'

A chill! If only it were! He himself went again to the open window and stood watching the moonlight. From the staff's quarters came the strain of a gramophone. How they loved to turn on that caterwauling, or the loud-speaker! He didn't know which he disliked most.

Moving to the edge of the veranda, he held out his palm. No dew! Dry as ever – remarkable weather! A dog began howling from over the river. Some people would take that for a banshee, he shouldn't wonder! The more he saw of people the more weak-minded they seemed; for ever looking for the sensational, or covering up their eyes and ears. The garden was looking pretty in the moonlight – pretty and unreal. That border of sunflowers and Michaelmas daisies and the late roses in the little round beds, and the low wall of very old brick – he'd had a lot of trouble to get that brick! – even the grass – the moonlight gave them all a stage-like quality. Only the poplars queered the dream-like values, dark and sharply outlined by the moon behind them. Soames moved out on to the lawn. The face of the house, white and creepered, with a light in her bedroom, looked unreal, too, and as if powdered. Thirty-two years he'd been here. One had got attached to the place, especially since he'd bought the land over the river, so that no one could ever build and overlook him. To be overlooked, body or soul – on on the whole he'd avoided that in life – at least, he hoped so.

He finished his cigar out there and threw the butt away. He would have liked to see her light go out before he went to bed – to feel that she was sleeping as when, a little thing, she went to bed with tooth-ache. But he was very tired. Motoring was hard on the liver. Well! He'd go in and shut up. After all, he couldn't do any good by staying down, couldn't do any good in any way. The old couldn't help the young – nobody could help anyone, if it came to that, at least where the heart was concerned. Queer arrangement – the heart! And to think that everybody had one. There ought to be some comfort in that, and yet there wasn't. No comfort to him, when he'd suffered, night in, day out, over that boy's mother, that she had suffered, too! No satisfaction to Fleur now, that the young man and his wife, too, very likely, were suffering as well! And, closing the window, Soames went up. He listened at her door, but could hear nothing; and, having undressed, took up Vasari's *Lives of the Painters*, and, propped against his pillows, began to read. Two pages of that book always sent him to sleep, and generally the same two, for he knew them so well that he never remembered where he had left off.

He was awakened presently by he couldn't tell what, and lay listening. It seemed that there was movement in the house. But if he got up to see he would certainly begin to worry again, and he didn't want to. Besides, in seeing to whether Fleur was asleep he might wake her up. Turning over, he dozed off, but again he woke, and lay drowsily thinking: 'I'm not sleeping well – I want exercise.' Moonlight was coming through the curtains not quite drawn. And, suddenly, his nostrils twitched. Surely a smell of burning! He sat up, sniffing. It *was*! Had there been a short circuit, or was the thatch of the pigeon-house on fire? Getting out of bed, he put on his dressing-gown and slippers, and went to the window.

A reddish, fitful light was coming from a window above. Great God! His picture gallery! He ran to the foot of the stairs that led up to it. A stealthy sound, a scent of burning much more emphatic, staggered him. He hurried up the stairs and pulled open the door. Heavens! The far end of the gallery, at the extreme left corner of the house, was on fire. Little red flames were licking round the woodwork; the curtains of the far window were already a blackened mass, and the waste-paper-basket, between them and his writing-bureau, was a charred wreck! On the parquet floor he saw some cigarette ash. Someone had been up here smoking! The flames crackled as he stood there aghast. He rushed downstairs and threw open the door of Fleur's room. She was lying on her bed asleep, but fully dressed! Fully dressed! Was it –? Had she –? She opened her eyes, staring up at him.

'Get up!' he said, 'there's a fire in the picture gallery. Get Kit and the servant out at once – at once! Send for Riggs! Telephone to Reading for the engines – quick! Get everyone out of the house!' Only waiting to see her on her feet, he ran back to the foot of the gallery stairs and seized a fire-extinguisher. He carried it up, a heavy great thing. He knew vaguely that you dashed the knob on the floor and sprayed the flames. Through the open doorway he could see that they had spread considerably. Good God! They were licking at his Fred Walker, and the two David Coxes. They had caught the beam, too, that ran round the gallery, dividing the upper from the lower tier of pictures; yes, and the upper beam was on fire also. The Constable! For a moment he hesitated. Should he rush at that and save it, anyway? The extinguisher mightn't work! He dropped it, and, running the length of the gallery, seized the Constable just as the flames reached the woodwork above it. The hot breath of them scorched his face as he wrenched the picture from the wall, and, running back, flung open the window opposite the door and placed it on the sill. Then, seizing the extinguisher again, he dashed it, violently, against the floor. A stream of stuff came out, and, picking the thing up, he directed that stream against the flames. The room was full of smoke now, and he felt rather giddy. The stuff was good, and he saw with relief that the flames didn't like it. He was making a distinct impression on them. But the Walker was ruined – ah! and the Coxes! He had beaten the fire back to the window-wall, when the stream ceased, and he saw that the beams had broken into flame beyond where he had started spraying. The writing-bureau, too, was on fire now – its papers had caught! Should he run down and get another of these things, all the way to

the hall! Where was that fellow Riggs? The 'Alfred Stevens'!
By heaven! He was not going to lose his 'Stevens' nor his
'Gauguins', nor his 'Corots'!

And a sort of demon entered into Soames. His taste, his
trouble, his money, and his pride – all consumed? By the Lord,
no! And through the smoke he dashed again up to the far wall.
Flame licked at his sleeve as he tore away the 'Stevens'; he could
smell the singed stuff when he propped the picture in the window beside the Constable.

A lick of flame crossed the Daubigny, and down came its
glass with a clatter – there was the picture exposed and fire
creeping and flaring over it! He rushed and grasped at a 'Gauguin' – a South Sea girl with nothing on. She wouldn't come
away from the wall; he caught hold of the wire, but dropped
it – red hot; seizing the frame he gave a great wrench. Away
it came, and over he went, backwards. But he'd got it, his
favourite Gauguin! He stacked that against the others, and ran
back to the Corot nearest the flames. The silvery, cool picture
was hot to his touch, but he got that, too! Now for the Monet!
The engines would be twenty minutes at least. If that fellow
Riggs didn't come soon –! They must spread a blanket down
there, and he would throw the pictures out. And then he uttered
a groan. The flames had got the other Corot! The poor thing!
Wrenching off the Monet, he ran to the head of the stairs. Two
frightened maids in coats over their nightgowns, and their
necks showing, were half-way up.

'Here!' he cried. 'Take this picture and keep your heads.
Miss Fleur and the boy out?'

'Yes, sir.'

'Have you telephoned?'

'Yes, sir.'

'Get me an extinguisher; and all of you hold a blanket spread
beneath the window down there to catch the pictures as I throw
them out. Don't be foolish – there's no danger! Where's Riggs?'

He went back into the gallery. Oh – h! There went his
precious little Degas! And with rage in his heart Soames ran
again at the wall and snatched at his other Gauguin. If ever he

had beaten Dumetrius, it was over that highly-coloured affair. As if grateful to him, the picture came away neatly in his scorched and trembling hands. He stacked it, and stood for a moment choked and breathless. So long as he could breathe up here in the draught between the opened door and window, he must go on getting them off the wall.

It wouldn't take long to throw them out. The Bonnington and the Turner – that fellow Turner wouldn't have been so fond of sunsets if he'd known what fire was like. Each time now that he went to the wall his lungs felt as if they couldn't stand another journey. But they must!

'Dad!'

Fleur with an extinguisher!

'Go down! Go out!' he cried. 'D'you hear! Go out of the house! Get that blanket spread, and make them hold it tight.'

'Dad! Let me! I must!'

'Go down!' cried Soames again, and pushed her to the stairs. He watched her to the bottom, then dashed the knob of the extinguisher on the floor and again sprayed the fire. He put out the bureau, and attacked the flames on the far wall. He could hardly hold the heavy thing, and when it dropped empty, he could barely see. But again he had gained on the fire. If only he could hold on!

And then he saw that his Harpignies was gone – such a beauty! That wanton loss gave him strength. And rushing up to the wall – the long wall now – he detached picture after picture. But the flames were creeping back again, persistent as hell itself. He couldn't reach the Sisley and the Picasso, high in the corner there, couldn't face the flames so close, for if he slipped against the wall he would be done. They must go! But he'd have the Daumier! His favourite – perhaps his very favourite. Safe! Gasping, and avidly drinking the fresher air, he could see from the window that they had the blanket down there now stretched between four maids, holding each a corner.

'Hold tight!' he cried; and tipped the Daumier out. He watched it falling. What a thing to do to a picture! The blanket dipped with the weight, but held.

'Hold it tighter!' he shouted. 'Look out!' And over went the Gauguin South Sea girl. Picture after picture he tipped from the sill; and picture after picture, they took them from the blanket, and laid them on the grass. When he had tipped them all, he turned to take the situation in. The flames had caught the floor now, in the corner, and were spreading fast along the beams.

The engines would be in time to save the right-hand wall. The left-hand wall was hopeless, but most of the pictures were beginning to get hold; he must go for that now. He ran as near to the corner as he dared, and seized the Morland. It was hot to his touch, but he got it – six hundred pounds' worth of white pony. He had promised it a good home! He tipped it from the window and saw it pitch headlong into the blanket.

'My word!'

Behind him, in the doorway, that fellow Riggs at last, in shirt and trousers, with two extinguishers and an open mouth!

'Shut your mouth!' he gasped, 'and spray that wall!'

He watched the stream and the flames recoiling from it. How he hated those inexorable red tongues. Ah! That was giving them pause!

'Now the other! Save the Courbet! Sharp!'

Again the stream spurted and the flames recoiled. Soames dashed for the Courbet. The glass had gone, but the picture was not harmed yet; he wrenched it away.

'That's the last of the bloomin' extinguishers, sir,' he heard Riggs mutter.

'Here, then!' he called. 'Pull the pictures off that wall and tip them out of the window one by one. Mind you hit the blanket. Stir your stumps!'

He, too, stirred his stumps, watching the discouraged flames regaining their lost ground. The two of them ran breathless to the wall, wrenched, ran back to the window, and back again – and the flames gained all the time.

'That top one,' said Soames; 'I must have that! Get on that chair. Quick! No, I'll do it. Lift me! – I can't reach!'

Uplifted in the grip of that fellow, Soames detached his James Maris, bought the very day the whole world broke into flames. 'Murder of the Archduke!' he could hear them at it now. A fine day; the sunlight coming in at the window of his cab, and he light-hearted, with that bargain on his knee. And there it went, pitching down! Ah! What a way to treat pictures!

'Come on!' he gasped.

'Better go down, sir! It's gettin' too thick now.'

'No!' said Soames. 'Come on!'

Three more pictures salved.

'If you don't go down, sir, I'll 'ave to carry you – you been up 'ere too long.'

'Nonsense!' gasped Soames. 'Come on!'

''Ooray! The engines!'

Soames stood still; besides the pumping of his heart and lungs he could hear another sound. Riggs seized his arm.

'Come along, sir; when they begin to play there'll be a proper smother.'

Soames pointed throught the smoke.

'I must have that one,' he gasped. 'Help me. It's heavy.'

The 'Vendimia' copy stood on an easel. Soames staggered up to it. Half carrying and half dragging, he bore that Spanish effigy of Fleur towards the window.

'Now lift!' They lifted till it balanced on the sill.

'Come away there!' called a voice from the doorway.

'Tip!' gasped Soames, but arms seized him, he was carried to the door, down the stairs, into the air half-conscious. He came to himself in a chair on the verandah. He could see the helmets of firemen and heard a hissing sound. His lungs hurt him, his eyes smarted terribly, and his hands were scorched, but he felt drugged and drowsy and triumphant in spite of his aches and smarting.

The grass, the trees, the cool river under the moon! What a nightmare it had been up there among his pictures – his poor pictures! But he had saved them! The cigarette ash! The waste-paper-basket! Fleur! No doubt about the cause! What on earth had induced him to put his pictures into her head that evening of all others, when she didn't know what she was doing? What awful luck! Mustn't let her know – unless – unless she did know? The shock – however! The shock might do her good! His Degas! The Harpignies! He closed his eyes to listen to the hissing of the water. Good! A good noise! They'd save the rest! It might have been worse! Something cold was thrust against his drooped hand. A dog's nose. They shouldn't have let him out. And, suddenly, it seemed to Soames that he must see to things again. They'd go the wrong way to work with all that water! He staggered-to his feet. He could see better now. Fleur? Ah! There she was, standing by herself – too near the house! And what a mess on the lawn – firemen – engines – maids, that fellow Riggs – the hose laid to the river – plenty of water, anyway! They mustn't hurt the pictures with that water! Fools! He knew it! Why! They were squirting the untouched wall. Squirting through both windows. There was no need of that! The right-hand window only – only! He stumbled up to the fireman.

'Not that wall! Not that! That wall's all right. You'll spoil my pictures! Shoot at the centre!' The fireman shifted the angle of his arm, and Soames saw the jet strike the right-hand corner of the sill. The Vendimia! There went its precious –! Dislodged by the stream of water, it was tilting forward! And Fleur! Good God! Standing right under, looking up. She must see it, and she wasn't moving! It flashed through Soames that she wanted to be killed.

'It's falling!' he cried. 'Look out! Look out!' And, just as if he had seen her about to throw herself under a car, he darted forward, pushed her with his outstretched arms, and fell.

The thing had struck him to the earth.

Chapter Fourteen

HUSH

→←←→→

OLD Gradman, off the Poultry, eating his daily chop, took up the early edition of the evening paper, brought to him with that collation:

FIRE IN A PICTURE GALLERY
WELL-KNOWN CONNOISSEUR SEVERELY INJURED

A fire, the cause of which is unknown, broke out last night in the picture gallery of Mr Soames Forsyte's house at Mapledurham. It was extinguished by fire-engines from Reading, and most of the valuable pictures were saved. Mr Forsyte, who was in residence, fought the fire before the firemen were on the spot, and, single-handed, rescued many of the pictures, throwing them out of the window of the gallery into a blanket which was held stretched out on the lawn below. Unfortunately, after the engines had arrived, he was struck on the head by the frame of a picture falling from the window of the gallery, which is on the second floor, and rendered unconscious. In view of his age and his exertions during the fire, very little hope is entertained of his recovery. Nobody else was injured, and no other part of the mansion was reached by the flames.

Laying down his fork, old Gradman took his napkin, and passed it over a brow which had grown damp. Replacing it on the table, he pushed away his chop, and took up the paper again. You never knew what to believe, nowadays, but the paragraph was uncommonly sober; and he dropped it with a gesture singularly like the wringing of hands.

'Mr Soames,' he thought. 'Mr Soames!' His two wives, his daughter, his grandson, the Forsyte family, himself! He stood up, grasping the table. An accidental thing like that! Mr Soames! Why – he was a young man, comparatively! But perhaps they'd got hold of the wrong stick! Mechanically he went to the telephone. He found the number with difficulty, his eyes being misty.

'Is that Mrs Dartie's – Gradman speaking. Is it true, ma-am? ... Not 'opeless, I do trust? Aow! Saving Miss Fleur's life? You don't say! You're goin' down? I think I'd better, too. Everything's in order, but he might want something, if he comes to. ... Dear, dear! ... Ah! I'm sure. ... Dreadful shock – dreadful!' He hung up the receiver, and stood quite still. Who would look after things now? There wasn't one of the family with any sense of business, compared with Mr Soames, not one who remembered the old days, and could handle house property as they used to, then. No, he couldn't relish any more chop – that was flat! Miss Fleur! Saving her life? Well, what a thing. She'd always been first with him. What must she be feelin'! He remembered her as a little girl; yes, and at her wedding. To think of it. She'd be a rich woman now. He took his hat. Must go home first and get some things – might have to wait there days! But for a full three minutes he still stood, as if stunned – a thick-set figure with a puggy face, in a round grey beard – confirming his uneasy grief. If the Bank of England had gone he couldn't have felt it more. That he couldn't.

When he reached 'The Shelter' in a station fly, with a bag full of night things and papers, it was getting on for six o'clock. He was met in the hall by that young man, Mr Michael Mont, whom he remembered as making jokes about serious things – it was to be hoped he wouldn't do it now!

'Ah! Mr Gradman; so good of you to come! No! They hardly expect him to recover consciousness; it was a terrible knock. But if he does, he's sure to want to see you, even if he can't speak. We've got your room ready. Will you have some tea?'

Yes, he could relish a cup of tea – he could indeed! 'Miss Fleur?'

The young man shook his head, his eyes looked distressed. 'He saved her life.'

Gradman nodded. 'So they say. Tt, tt! To think that he –!

His father lived to be ninety, and Mr Soames was always careful. Dear, dear!'

He had drunk a nice hot cup of tea when he saw a figure in the doorway – Miss Fleur herself. Why! What a face! She came forward and took his hand. And, almost unconsciously, old Gradman lifted her other hand and imprisoned hers between his two.

'My dear,' he said, 'I feel for you. I remember you as a little girl.'

She only answered: 'Yes, Mr Gradman.' and it seemed to him funny. She took him to his room, and left him there. He had never been in such a pleasant bedroom, with flowers and a nice smell, and a bathroom all to himself – really quite unnecessary. And to think that two doors off, Mr Soames was lying as good as gone!

'Just breathing,' she had said, passing the door. 'They daren't operate. My mother's there.'

What a face she had on her – so white, so hurt-looking – poor young thing! He stood at the open window, gazing out. It was warm – very warm for the end of September. A pleasant air – a smell of grass. It must be the river down there! Peaceful – and to think –! Moisture blurred the river out; he winked it away. Only the other day they'd been talking about something happening, and now it hadn't happened to him, but to Mr Soames himself. The ways of Providence! For Jesus Christ's sake – Our Lord! Dear, dear! To think of it! He would cut up a very warm man. Richer than his father. There were some birds out there on the water – geese or swans or something – ye-es! Swans! What a lot! In a row, floating along. He hadn't seen a swan since he took Mrs G. to Golder's Hill Park the year after the war. And they said – hopeless! A dreadful thing – sudden like that, with no time to say your prayers. Lucky the will was quite straightforward. Annuity to Mrs F., and the rest to his daughter for life, the remainder to her children in equal shares. Only one child at present, but there'd be others, no doubt, with all that money. Dear! What a sight of money there was in the family altogether, and yet, of the present generation,

Mr Soames was the only warm man. It was all divided up now, and none of the young ones seemed to make any. He would have to keep a tight hand on the estates, or they'd be wanting their capital out, and Mr Soames wouldn't approve of that! To think of outliving Mr Soames! And something incorruptibly faithful within that puggy face and thick figure, something that for two generations had served and never expected more than it had got, so moved old Gradman that he subsided on the window-seat with the words: 'I'm quite upset!'

He was still sitting there with his head on his hand, and darkness thickening outside, when, with a knock on the door, that young man said:

'Mr Gradman, will you come down for dinner, or would you like it up here?'

'Up here, if it's all the same to you. Cold beef and pickles or anything there is, and a glass of stout, if it's quite convenient.'

The young man drew nearer.

'You must feel it awfully, Mr Gradman, having known him so long. Not an easy man to know, but one felt –'

Something gave way in Gradman and he spoke:

'Ah! I knew him from a little boy – took him to his first school – taught him how to draw a lease – never knew him to do a shady thing; very reserved man, Mr Soames, but no better judge of an investment, except his uncle Nicholas. He had his troubles, but he never said anything of them; good son to his father – good brother to his sisters – good father to his child, as you know, young man.'

'Yes, indeed! And very good to me.'

'Not much of a church-goer, I'm afraid, but straight as a die. Never one to wear his 'eart on his sleeve; a little uncomfortable sometimes, maybe, but you could depend on him. I'm sorry for your young wife, young man – I am that! 'Ow did it 'appen?'

'She was standing below the window when the picture fell, and didn't seem to realize. He pushed her out of the way, and it hit him instead.'

'Why! What a thing!'

'Yes. She can't get over it.'

Gradman looked up at the young man's face in the twilight.

'You mustn't be down-'earted,' he said. 'She'll come round. Misfortunes will happen. The family's been told, I suppose. There's just one thing, Mr Michael – his first wife, Mrs Irene, that married Mr Jolyon after; she's still living, they say; she might like to send a message that byegones were byegones, in case he came round.'

'I don't know, Mr Gradman, I don't know.'

'Forgive us our trespasses, as we forgive them that trespass – 'e was greatly attached to 'er at one time.'

'So I believe, but there are things that – Still, Mrs Dartie knows her address, if you like to ask her. She's here, you know.'

'I'll turn it over. I remember Mrs Irene's wedding – very pale she was; a beautiful young woman, too.'

'I believe so.'

'The present one – being French, I suppose, she shows her feelings. However – if he's unconscious –' It seemed to him that the young man's face looked funny, and he added; 'I've never heard much of her. Not very happy with his wives, I'm afraid, he hasn't been.'

'Some men aren't, you know, Mr Gradman. It's being too near, I suppose.'

'Ah!' said Gradman: 'It's one thing or the other, and that's a fact. Mrs G. and I have never had a difference – not to speak of, in fifty-two years, and that's going back, as the saying is. Well, I mustn't keep you from Miss Fleur. She'll need cosseting. Just cold beef and a pickle. You'll let me know if I'm wanted – any time, day or night. And if Mrs Dartie'd like to see me I'm at her service.'

The talk had done him good. That young man was a nicer young fellow than he'd thought. He felt that he could almost relish a pickle. After he had done so a message came: Would he go to Mrs Dartie in the drawing-room?

'Wait for me, my dear,' he said to the maid: 'I'm strange here.'

Having washed his hands and passed a towel over his face, he followed her down the stairs of the hushed house. What a room to be sure! Rather empty, but in apple-pie order, with its cream-coloured panels, and its china, and its grand piano. Winifred Dartie was sitting on a sofa before a wood fire. She rose and took his hand.

'Such a comfort to see you, Gradman,' she said: 'You're the oldest friend we have.'

Her face looked strange, as if she wanted to cry and had forgotten how. He had known her as a child, as a fashionable young woman, had helped to draw her marriage settlement, and shaken his head over her husband many a time – the trouble he'd had in finding out exactly what that Gentleman owed, after he fell down the staircase in Paris and broke his neck! And every year still he prepared her income tax return.

'A good cry,' he said, 'would do you good, and I shouldn't blame you. But we mustn't say "die"; Mr Soames has a good constitution, and it's not as if he drank; perhaps he'll pull round after all.'

She shook her head. Her face had a square grim look that reminded him of her old aunt Ann. Underneath all her fashionableness she'd borne a lot – she had, when you came to think of it.

'It struck him here,' she said; 'a glancing blow on the right side of the head. I shall miss him terribly; he's the only –' Gradman patted her hand.

'Ye-es, ye-es! But we must look on the bright side. If he comes round, I shall be there.' What exact comfort he thought this was, he could not have made clear. 'I did wonder whether he would like Mrs Irene told. I don't like the idea of his going with a grudge on his mind. It's an old story, of course, but at the Judgement Day –'

A faint smile was lost in the square lines round Winifred's mouth.

'We needn't bother him with that, Gradman; it's out of fashion.'

Gradman emitted a sound, as though, within him, faith and respect for the family he had served for sixty years had bumped against each other.

'Well, you know best,' he said. 'I shouldn't like him to go with anything on his conscience.'

'On *her* conscience, Gradman.'

Gradman stared at a Dresden shepherdess.

'In a case of forgivin', you never know. I wanted to speak to him, too, about his steel shares; they're not all they might be. But we must just take our chance, I suppose. I'm glad your father was spared this, Mr James *would* have taken on. It won't be like the same world again, if Mr Soames —'

She had put her hand up to her mouth and turned away. Fashion had dropped from her thickened figure. Much affected, Gradman turned to the door.

'Shan't leave my clothes off, in case I'm wanted. I've got everything here. *Good*-night!'

He went upstairs again, tiptoeing past the door, and, entering his room, switched on the light. They had taken away the pickles; turned his bed down, laid his flannel nightgown out. They took a lot of trouble! And, sinking on his knees, he prayed in a muffled murmur, varying the usual words, and ending: 'And for Mr Soames, O Lord, I specially commend him body and soul. Forgive him his trespasses, and deliver him from all 'ardness of 'eart and impurities, before he goes 'ence, and make him as a little lamb again, that he may find favour in Thy sight. Thy faithful servant. Amen.' And, for some time after he had finished, he remained kneeling on the very soft carpet, breathing-in the familiar reek of flannel and old times. He rose easier in his mind. Removing his boots, laced and square-toed, and his old frock-coat, he put on his Jaeger gown, and shut the window, to keep out the night air. Then, taking the eiderdown, he placed a large handkerchief over his bald head, and, switching off the light, sat down in the armchair, with the eiderdown over his knees.

What an 'ush after London, to be sure, so quiet you could hear yourself think! For some reason he thought of Queen Victoria's first Jubilee, when he was a youngster of forty, and Mr James had give him and Mrs G. two seats. They had seen the whole thing — first chop! the Guards and the procession, the carriages, the horses, the Queen and the Royal Family. A beautiful summer day – a real summer that; not like the summers lately. And everything going on, as if it'd go on for ever, with three per cents at nearly par if he remembered, and all going to church regular. And only that same year, a bit later, Mr Soames had had his first upset. And another memory came. Queer he should remember that to-night, with Mr Soames lying there – must have been quite soon after the Jubilee, too! Going with a lease that wouldn't bear to wait to Mr Soames's private house, Montpelier Square, and being shown into the dining-room, and hearing someone singing and playing on the 'pianner'. He had opened the door to listen. Why – he could remember the words now! About 'laying on the grass', 'I die, I faint, I fail,' 'the champaign odours', something 'on your cheek' and something 'pale'. Fancy that! And suddenly, the door had opened and out she'd come – Mrs Irene – in a frock – ah!

'Are you waiting for Mr Forsyte? Won't you come in and have some tea?' And he'd gone in and had tea, sitting on the edge of a chair that didn't look too firm, all gilt and spindley. And she on the sofa in that frock, pouring it out, and saying:

'Are you fond of music, then, Mr Gradman?' Soft, a soft look, with her dark eyes and her hair – not red and not what you'd call gold – but like a turned leaf – Um? – a beautiful young woman, sad and sort of sympathetic in the face. He'd often thought of her – he could see her now! And then Mr Soames coming in, and her face all closing up like – like a book. Queer to remember that to-night! ... Dear me! ... How dark and quiet it was! That poor young daughter, that it was all about! It was to be 'oped she'd sleep! Ye-es! And what would Mrs G. say if she could see *him* sitting in a chair like this, with his teeth in, too. Ah! Well – she'd never seen Mr Soames, never seen the family – Maria hadn't! But what an 'ush! And slowly but surely old Gradman's mouth fell open, and he broke the hush.

Beyond the closed window the moon rode up, a full and brilliant moon, so that the stilly darkened country dissolved into shape and shadow, and the owls hooted, and, far off, a dog bayed; and flowers in the garden became each a little presence in a night-time carnival graven into stillness; and on the gleaming river every fallen leaf that drifted down carried a moonbeam; while, above, the trees stayed, quiet, measured and illumined, quiet as the very sky, for the wind stirred not.

Chapter Fifteen

SOAMES TAKES THE FERRY

＊＜＜＞＞＊

THERE was only just life in Soames. Two nights and two days they had waited, watching the unmoving bandaged head. Specialists had come, given their verdict: 'Nothing to be done by way of operation'; and gone again. The doctor who had presided over Fleur's birth was in charge. Though never quite forgiven by Soames for the anxiety he had caused on that occasion, 'the fellow' had hung on, attending the family. By his instructions they watched the patient's eyes; at any sign, they were to send for him at once.

Michael, from whom Fleur seemed inconsolably caught away, gave himself up to Kit, walking and talking and trying to keep the child unaware. He did not visit the still figure, not from indifference, but because he felt an intruder there. He had removed all the pictures left in the gallery, and, storing them with those which Soames had thrown from the window, had listed them carefully. The fire had destroyed eleven out of the eighty-four.

Annette had cried, and was feeling better. The thought of life without Soames was for her strange and – possible; precisely, in fact, like the thought of life with him. She wished him to recover, but if he didn't she would live in France.

Winifred, who shared the watches, lived much and sadly in the past. Soames had been her mainstay throughout thirty-four years chequered by Montague Dartie, had continued her mainstay in the thirteen unchequered years since. She did not see how things could ever be cosy again. She had a heart, and could not look at that still figure without trying to remember how to cry. Letters came to her from the family worded with a sort of anxious astonishment that Soames should have had such a thing happen to him.

Gradman, who had taken a bath, and changed his trousers to black, was deep in calculations and correspondence with the insurance firm. He walked too, in the kitchen garden, out of sight of the house; for he could not get over the fact that Mr James had lived to be ninety, and Mr Timothy a hundred, to say nothing of the others. And, stopping mournfully before the sea-kale or the Brussels sprouts, he would shake his head.

Smither had come down to be with Winifred, but was of little use, except to say: 'Poor Mr Soames! Poor dear Mr Soames! To think of it! And he so careful of himself, and everybody!'

For that was it! Ignorant of the long and stealthy march of passion, and of the state to which it had reduced Fleur; ignorant of how Soames had watched her, seen that beloved young part of his very self fail, reach the edge of things and stand there balancing; ignorant of Fleur's reckless desperation beneath that falling picture, and her father's knowledge thereof — ignorant of all this everybody felt aggrieved. It seemed to them that a mere bolt from the blue, rather than the inexorable secret culmination of an old, old story, had stricken one who of all men seemed the least liable to accident. How should they tell that it was not so accidental as all that!

But Fleur knew well enough that her desperate mood had destroyed her father, just as surely as if she had flung herself into the river and he had been drowned in saving her. Only too well she knew that on that night she had been capable of slipping down into the river, of standing before a rushing car, of anything not too deliberate and active, that would have put her out of her aching misery. She knew well enough that by her conduct she had invited his rush to the rescue. And now, sobered to the very marrow by the shock, she could not forgive herself.

With her mother, her aunt and the two trained nurses she divided the watches, so that there were never less than two, of whom she was nearly always one, in Annette's bedroom where Soames lay. She would sit hour after hour, almost as still as her father, with her eyes wistful and dark-circled, fixed on his face. Passion and fever had quite died out of her. It was as if, with his infallible instinct where she was concerned, Soames had taken the one step that could rid her of the fire which had been consuming her. Jon was remote from her in that room darkened by sun-blinds and her remorse.

Yes! She had meant to be killed by that picture. She had stood there under the window in a moment of passionate recklessness, watching the picture topple, wanting it all over and done with. Distraught that desperate night, she did not even now realize that she had caused the fire, by a cigarette flung down still lighted, not even perhaps that she had smoked up there. But only too well she realized that because she had wanted to die, had stood welcoming sudden extinction, her father was now lying there so nearly dead. How good he had always been to her! Incredible that he should die and take that goodness away, that she should never hear his flat-toned voice again, or feel the touch of his moustache on her cheeks or forehead. Incredible that he should never give her a chance to show that she really loved him – yes really, beneath all the fret and self-importance of her life. While watching him now, the little rather than the great things came back to her. How he would pitch a new doll down in the nursery and say: 'Well, I don't know if you'll care for this one; I just picked her up.' How once, after her mother had whipped her, he had come in, taken her hand and said: 'There, there. Let's go and see if there are some raspberries!' How he had stood on the stairs at Green Street after her wedding, watching, pale and unobtrusive, above the guests clustered in the hall, for a turn of her head and her last look back. Unobtrusive! That was the word – unobtrusive, always! Why, if he went, there would be no portrait – hardly

even a photograph, to remember him by! Just one of him as a
baby, in his mother's arms; one as a little boy, looking scep-
tically at his velvet knickers; one in '76 as a young man in a
full-tailed coat and short whiskers; and a snapshot or two taken
unawares. Had any man ever been less photographed? He had
never seemed to wish to be appreciated, or even remembered,
by anyone. To Fleur, so avid of appreciation, it seemed marvellously strange. What secret force within that spare form, lying there inert, had made him thus self-sufficing? He had been
brought up as luxuriously as herself, had never known want or
the real need of effort, but somehow had preserved a sort of
stoic independence of others, and what they thought of him.
And yet, as none knew better than herself, he had longed to be
loved. This hurt her most, watching him. He had longed for her
affection, and she had not shown it him enough. But she had felt
it – really felt it all the time. Something in him had repelled
feeling, dried up its manifestation. There had been no magnet in
his 'make-up'. And stealing to the bed – her mother's bed where
she herself had been conceived and born – she would stand beside that almost deserted body and drawn dun face, feeling so
hollow and miserable that she could hardly restrain herself.

So the days and nights passed. On the third day about three
o'clock, while she stood there beside him, she saw the eyes open
– a falling apart of the lids, indeed, rather than an opening, and
no speculation in the gaps; but her heart beat fast. The nurse,
summoned by her finger, came, looked, and went quickly to the
telephone. And Fleur stood there with her soul in her eyes, trying to summon his. It did not come, the lids drooped again. She
drew up a chair and sat down, not taking her eyes off his face.
The nurse came back to say that the doctor was on his rounds;
as soon as he came in he would be sent to them post-haste. As
her father would have said: 'Of course, "that fellow" wasn't in
when he was wanted!' But it would make no difference. They
knew what to do. It was nearly four when again the lids were
raised, and this time something looked forth. Fleur could not be
sure that he saw anything particular, recognized her or any
other object, but there was something there, some flickering

light, trying to focus. Slowly it strengthened, then went out again between the lids. They gave him stimulant. And again she sat down to watch. In half an hour his eyes re-opened. This time he *saw*! And for torturing minutes Fleur watched a being trying to *be,* a mind striving to obey the mandate of instinctive will power. Bending so that those eyes, which she now knew recognized her, should have the least possible effort, she waited with her lips trembling, as if in a kiss. The extraordinary tenacity of that struggle to come back terrified her. He *meant* to know and hear and speak. It was as if he must die from the sheer effort of it. She murmured to him. She put her hand under his cold hand, so that if he made the faintest pressure she would feel it. She watched his lips desperately. At last that struggle for coherence ceased, the half-blank, half-angry look yielded to something deeper, the lips moved. They said nothing, but they moved, and the faintest tremor passed from his finger into hers.

'You know me, darling?'

His eyes said: 'Yes.'

'You remember?'

Again his eyes said: 'Yes.'

His lips were twitching all the time, as if rehearsing for speech, and the look in his eyes deepening. She saw his brows frown faintly, as if her face were too close; drew back a little and the frown relaxed.

'Darling, you are going to be all right.'

His eyes said: 'No'; and his lips moved, but she could not distinguish the sound. For a moment she lost control, and said with a sob:

'Dad, forgive me!'

His eyes softened; and this time she caught what sounded like:

'Forgive? Nonsense!'

'I love you so.'

He seemed to abandon the effort to speak then, and centred all the life of him in his eyes. Deeper and deeper grew the colour and the form and the meaning in them, as if to compel something from her. And suddenly, like a little girl, she said:

'Yes, Dad; I will be good!'

A tremor from his finger passed into her palm; his lips seemed trying to smile, his head moved as if he had meant to nod, and always that look deepened in his eyes.

'Gradman is here, darling, and Mother, and Aunt Winifred, and Kit and Michael. Is there anyone you would like to see?'

His lips shaped: 'No – you!'

'I am here all the time.' Again she felt the tremor from his fingers, saw his lips whispering:

'That's all.'

And suddenly, his eyes went out. There was nothing there! For some time longer he breathed, but before 'that fellow' came, he had lost hold – was gone.

Chapter Sixteen

FULL CLOSE

⤙⤛⤜⤚

IN accordance with all that was implicit in Soames there was no fuss over his funeral. For a long time now, indeed, he had been the only one of the family at all interested in obsequies.

It was then, a very quiet affair, only men attending.

Sir Lawrence had come down, graver than Michael had ever known him.

'I respected old Forsyte,' he said to his son, while they returned on foot from the graveyard, where, in the corner selected by himself, Soames now lay, under a crab-apple tree. 'He dated, and he couldn't express himself; but there was no humbug about him – an honest man. How is Fleur bearing up?'

Michael shook his head. 'It's terrible for her to think that he –'

'My dear boy, there's no better death than dying to save the one you're fondest of. As soon as you can, let us have Fleur at Lippinghall – where her father and her family never were.

I'll get Hilary and his wife down for a holiday – she likes
them.'

'I'm very worried about her, Dad – something's broken.'

'That happens to most of us, before we're thirty. Some spring
or other goes; but presently we get our second winds. It's what
happened to the Age – something broke and it hasn't yet got its
second wind. But it's getting it, and so will she. What sort of a
stone are you going to put up?'

'A cross, I suppose.'

'I think he'd prefer a flat stone with that crab-apple at the
head and yew trees round, so that he's not overlooked. No "Beloved" or "Regretted". Has he got the freehold of that corner?
He'd like to belong to his descendants in perpetuity. We're all
more Chinese than you'd think, only with them it's the ancestors who do the owning. Who was the old chap who cried into
his hat?'

'Old Mr Gradman – sort of business nurse to his family.'

'Faithful old dog! Well! I certainly never thought Forsyte
would take the ferry before me. He looked permanent, but it's
an ironical world. Can I do anything for you and Fleur? Talk to
the nation about the pictures? The Marquess and I could fix that
for you. He had quite a weakness for old Forsyte, and his Morland's saved. By the way, that must have been a considerable
contest between him and the fire up there all alone. It's the sort
of thing one would never have suspected him of.'

'Yes,' said Michael: 'I've been talking to Riggs. He's full of it.'

'He saw it then?'

Michael nodded. 'Here he comes!'

They slackened their pace, and the chauffeur, touching his
hat, came alongside.

'Ah! Riggs,' said Sir Lawrence, 'you were up there at the fire,
I'm told.'

'Yes, Sir Lawrence. Mr Forsyte was a proper wonder – went
at it like a two-year-old, we fair had to carry him away. So particular as a rule about not getting his coat wet or sitting in a
draught, but the way he stuck it – at his age ... "Come on!"
He kept saying to me all through that smoke – a proper

champion! Never so surprised in all my life, Sir Lawrence – nervous gentleman like him. And what a bit o' luck! If he hadn't insisted on saving that last picture, it'd never have fallen and got 'im.'

'How did the fire begin?'

'Nobody knows, Sir Lawrence, unless Mr Forsyte did, and he never said nothing. Wish I'd got there sooner, but I was puttin' the petrol out of action. What that old gentleman did by 'imself up there; and after the day we'd had! Why! We came from Winchester that morning to London, on to Dorking, picked up Mrs Mont, and on here. And now he'll never tell me I've gone wrong again.'

A grimace passed over his thin face, seamed and shadowed by traffic and the insides of his car; and, touching his hat, he left them at the gate.

'"A proper champion,"' Sir Lawrence repeated softly. 'You might almost put that on the stone. Yes, it's an ironical world!'

In the hall they parted, for Sir Lawrence was going back to Town by car. He took Gradman with him, the provisions of the will having been quietly disclosed. Michael found Smither crying and drawing up the blinds, and in the library Winifred and Val, who had come, with Holly, for the funeral, dealing with condolences, such as they were. Annette was with Kit in the nursery. Michael went up to Fleur in the room she used to have as a little girl – a single room, so that he had been sleeping elsewhere.

She was lying on her bed, graceful, and as if without life.

The eyes she turned on Michael seemed to make of him no less, but no more, than they were making of the ceiling. It was not so much that the spirit behind them was away somewhere, as that there was nowhere for it to go. He went up to the bed and put his hand on hers.

'Dear Heart!'

Fleur turned her eyes on him again, but of the look in them he could make nothing.

'The moment you wish, darling, we'll take Kit home.'

'Any time, Michael.'

'I know exactly how you feel,' said Michael, knowing well that he did not. 'Riggs has been telling us how splendid your father was, up there with the fire.'

'Don't!'

There was that in her face which baffled him completely — something not natural, however much she might be mourning for her father. Suddenly she said:

'Give me time, Michael. Nothing matters, I suppose, in the long run. And don't worry about me — I'm not worth it.'

More conscious than he had ever been in his life that words were of no use, Michael put his lips to her forehead and left her lying there.

He went out and down to the river and stood watching it flow, tranquil and bright in this golden autumn weather, which had lasted so long. Soames's cows were feeding opposite. They would come under the hammer, now; all this that had belonged to him would come under the hammer, he supposed. Annette was going to her mother in France, and Fleur did not wish to keep it on. He looked back at the house, still marked and dishevelled by fire and water. And melancholy brooded in his heart, as if the dry grey spirit of its late owner were standing beside him looking at the passing away of his possessions, of all that on which he had lavished so much time and trouble. 'Change,' thought Michael, 'there's nothing but change. It's the one constant. Well! Who wouldn't have a river rather than a pond!' He went towards the flower border under the kitchen garden wall. The hollyhocks and sunflowers were in bloom there, and he turned to them as if for warmth. In the little summer-house at the corner he saw someone sitting. Mrs Val Dartie! Holly — a nice woman! And, suddenly, in Michael, out of the bafflement he had felt in Fleur's presence, the need to ask a question shaped itself timidly, ashamedly at first, then boldly, insistently. He went up to her. She had a book, but was not reading.

'How is Fleur?' she said.

Michael shook his head and sat down.

'I want to ask you a question. Don't answer if you don't want; but I feel I've got to ask. Can you — will you tell me: How are things between your young brother and her? I know what there was in the past. Is there anything in the present? I'm asking for her sake – not my own. Whatever you say shan't hurt her.'

She looked straight at him, and Michael searched her face. There was that in it from which he knew that whatever she did say, if indeed she said anything, would be the truth.

'Whatever there has been between them,' she said at last, 'and there *has* been something since he came back, is over for good. I know that for certain. It ended the day before the fire.'

'I see,' said Michael, very still. 'Why do you say it is over *for good*?'

'Because I know my young brother. He has given his wife his word never to see Fleur again. He must have blundered into something, I know there has been a crisis; but once Jon gives his word – nothing – *nothing* will make him go back on it. Whatever it was is over for good, and Fleur knows it.'

And again Michael said: 'I see.' And then, as if to himself: 'Whatever it was.'

She put out her hand and laid it on his.

'All right,' he said. 'I shall get my second wind in a minute. You needn't be afraid that I shall go back on my word, either. I know I've always played second fiddle. It shan't hurt her.'

The pressure on his hand increased; and, looking up, he saw tears in her eyes.

'Thank you very much,' he said; 'I understand now. It's when you don't understand that you feel such a dud. Thank you very much.'

He withdrew his hand gently and got up. Looking down at her still sitting there with tears in her eyes, he smiled.

'It's pretty hard sometimes to remember that it's all comedy; but one gets there, you know.'

'Good luck!' said Holly. And Michael answered: 'Good luck to all of us!'

That evening when the house was shuttered, he lit his pipe and stole out again. He had got his second wind. Whether he would have, but for Soames's death, he did not know. It was as if, by lying in that shadowy corner under a crab-apple tree, 'old

Forsyte' were still protecting his beloved. For her, Michael felt
nothing but compassion. The bird had been shot with both bar-
rels, and still lived; no one with any sporting instinct could hurt
it further. Nothing for it but to pick her up and mend the wings
as best he could. Something strong in Michael, so strong that he
hadn't known of its existence, had rallied to his aid. Sportsmanship – chivalry? No! It was nameless; it was an instinct, a feeling that there was something beyond self to be considered, even
when self was bruised and cast down. All his life he had detested
the ebullient egoism of the *crime passionnel*, the wronged spouse,
honour, vengeance, 'all that tommy-rot and naked savagery'. To
be excused from being a decent man! One was never excused
from that. Otherwise life was just where it was in the reindeer
age, the pure tragedy of the primeval hunters, before civilization
and comedy began.

Whatever had been between those two – and he felt it had
been all – it was over, and she, 'down and out'. He must stand
by her and keep his mouth shut. If he couldn't do that now, he
ought never to have married her, lukewarm as he had known
her to be. And, drawing deeply at his pipe, he went down the
dark garden to the river.

The sky was starry, and with the first touch of cold a slight
mist was rising, filming the black water so that it scarcely
seemed to move. Now and then in the stillness he could hear the
drone of a distant car, and somewhere a little beast squeaking.
Starlight, and the odour of bushes and the earth, the hoot of an
owl, bats flitting, and those tall poplar shapes, darker than the
darkness – what better setting for his mood just then!

An ironical world, his father had said! Yes, queerly ironical,
with shape melting into shape, mood into mood, sound into
sound, and nothing fixed anywhere, unless it were that starlight,
and the instinct within all living things which said: 'Go on!'

A drift of music came down the river. There would be a party
at some house. They were dancing probably, as he had seen the
gnats dancing that afternoon! And then something out of the
night semed to catch him by the throat. God! It was beautiful,
amazing! Breathing, in this darkness, as many billion shapes as

there were stars above, all living, and all different! What a
world! The Eternal Mood at work! And if you died, like that
old boy, and lay for ever beneath a crab-apple tree – well it was
the Mood resting a moment in your still shape – no! not even
resting, moving on in the mysterious rhythm that one called
Life. Who could arrest the moving Mood – who wanted to?
And if some pale possessor like that poor old chap, tried and
succeeded for a moment, the stars twinkled just a little more
when he was gone. To have and to hold! As though you could!

And Michael drew in his breath. A sound of singing came
down the water to him, trailing, distant, high and sweet. It was
as if a swan had sung!

FOR THE BEST IN PAPERBACKS, LOOK FOR THE 🐧

In every corner of the world, on every subject under the sun, Penguin represents quality and variety – the very best in publishing today.

For complete information about books available from Penguin – including Puffins, Penguin Classics and Arkana – and how to order them, write to us at the appropriate address below. Please note that for copyright reasons the selection of books varies from country to country.

In the United Kingdom: Please write to *Dept E.P., Penguin Books Ltd, Harmondsworth, Middlesex, UB7 0DA.*

If you have any difficulty in obtaining a title, please send your order with the correct money, plus ten per cent for postage and packaging, to *PO Box No 11, West Drayton, Middlesex*

In the United States: Please write to *Dept BA, Penguin, 299 Murray Hill Parkway, East Rutherford, New Jersey 07073*

In Canada: Please write to *Penguin Books Canada Ltd, 2801 John Street, Markham, Ontario L3R 1B4*

In Australia: Please write to the *Marketing Department, Penguin Books Australia Ltd, P.O. Box 257, Ringwood, Victoria 3134*

In New Zealand: Please write to the *Marketing Department, Penguin Books (NZ) Ltd, Private Bag, Takapuna, Auckland 9*

In India: Please write to *Penguin Overseas Ltd, 706 Eros Apartments, 56 Nehru Place, New Delhi, 110019*

In the Netherlands: Please write to *Penguin Books Netherlands B.V., Postbus 195, NL–1380AD Weesp*

In West Germany: Please write to *Penguin Books Ltd, Friedrichstrasse 10–12, D–6000 Frankfurt/Main 1*

In Spain: Please write to *Longman Penguin España, Calle San Nicolas 15, E–28013 Madrid*

In Italy: Please write to *Penguin Italia s.r.l., Via Como 4, I-20096 Pioltello (Milano)*

In France: Please write to *Penguin Books Ltd, 39 Rue de Montmorency, F-75003 Paris*

In Japan: Please write to *Longman Penguin Japan Co Ltd, Yamaguchi Building, 2–12–9 Kanda Jimbocho, Chiyoda-Ku, Tokyo 101*

CLASSICS OF THE TWENTIETH CENTURY

The Age of Reason Jean-Paul Sartre

The first part of Sartre's *Roads to Freedom* trilogy, set in the volatile Paris summer of 1938, is in itself 'a dynamic, deeply disturbing novel' (Elizabeth Bowen) which tackles some of the major issues of our time.

Death of a Salesman Arthur Miller

One of the great American plays of the century, this classic study of failure brings to life an unforgettable character, Willy Loman, the shifting and inarticulate hero who is none the less a unique individual.

The Echoing Grove Rosamond Lehmann

'No English writer has told of the pains of women in love more truly or more movingly than Rosamond Lehmann' – Marghanita Laski. 'This novel is one of the most absorbing I have read for years' – Simon Raven in the *Listener*

Three Lives Gertrude Stein

A turning point in American literature, these portraits of three women – thin, worn Anna, patient, gentle Lena and the complicated, intelligent Melanctha – represented in 1909 one of the pioneering examples of modernist writing.

In the American Grain William Carlos Williams

'It's as if no poet except Williams had really seen America or heard its language' – Robert Lowell. 'Mr Williams tries to bring into his consciousness America itself ... the great continent, its bitterness, its brackish quality, its vast glamour, its strange cruelty. Find this, Americans, and get it into your bones' – D. H. Lawrence

Man's Estate André Malraux

Man's Estate (*La Condition humaine*) emerged from Malraux's experience of witnessing the doomed Communist rising in Shanghai in 1927. Against a background of violence, betrayal and massacre, his characters are driven to try to transcend the 'human condition'.